ON THE DIAMOND

ABOUT THE EDITOR

MARTIN H. GREENBERG, who has been called "the king of the anthologists," now has some 145 of them to his credit. He is co-editor of *Detectives A to Z, 101 Mystery Stories, 101 Science Fiction Stories, A Treasury of American Horror Stories, Manhattan Mysteries*, and many others. He is professor of regional analysis and political science at the University of Wisconsin–Green Bay, where he also teaches a course in the history of science fiction.

ON THE DIAMOND

A TREASURY OF
BASEBALL STORIES

Edited and with an Introduction by
MARTIN H. GREENBERG

Bonanza Books
New York

Compilation copyright © 1987 by Martin H. Greenberg

First published in 1987 by Bonanza Books,
distributed by Crown Publishers, Inc.,
225 Park Avenue South, New York, New York 10003

Printed and Bound in the United States of America

Book design by Cynthia Dunne

LIBRARY OF CONGRESS CATALOGING-IN-PUBLICATION DATA

On the diamond.

1. Baseball stories.   2. Short stories, American.
3. American fiction—20th century.   I. Greenberg, Martin Harry.
PS648.B3705 1987   813′.01   86-26414
ISBN 0-517-62542-3

h g f e d c b

ACKNOWLEDGMENTS

Lardner—"One Hit, One Error, One Left," from *Lose with a Smile* by Ring Lardner, copyright 1933 by Charles Scribner's Sons and copyright renewed © 1961 by Ring Lardner, Jr. Reprinted with the permission of Charles Scribner's Sons.

Wolfe—Excerpt from "The Hidden Terror" from *You Can't Go Home Again*, copyright 1940 by Maxwell Perkins as Executor. Renewed © 1968 by Paul Gitlin, Administrator, C.T.A. Reprinted by permission of Harper & Row, Publishers, Inc.

Hano—"The Umpire Was a Rookie," first published in *The Saturday Evening Post*, copyright © 1956 by The Curtis Publishing Company. Used by permission of Arnold Hano.

Bradbury—"The Big Black and White Game" first published in *American Mercury*, copyright 1945; renewed © 1972 by Ray Bradbury. Reprinted by permission of Don Congdon Associates, Inc.

Temple—"A Most Unusual Season," first published in *Liberty Magazine*, copyright 1944 by Liberty Magazine Inc. Reprinted by permission of Harold Ober Associates Incorporated.

Serling—"The Mighty Casey," copyright © 1960 by Rod Serling. Reprinted by permission of International Creative Management, Inc.

Johnson—"The Humming Bird," reprinted by permission of the Literary Executor for the Estate of Owen Johnson.

Hoch—"The Theft of the Meager Beavers," first published in *Ellery Queen's Mystery Magazine*, copyright © 1969 by Edward D. Hoch. Reprinted by permission of the author.

Schramm—"My Kingdom for Jones," first published in *The Saturday Evening Post*, copyright 1944 by the Curtis Publishing Company. Reprinted by permission of Harold Ober Associates Incorporated.

Ritchie—"Popular Guy," copyright © 1956 by Columbia Publications. Reprinted by permission of Larry Sternig Literary Agency.

Malzberg and Pronzini—"On Account of Darkness," first published in *The Magazine of Fantasy and Science Fiction*, copyright © 1977 by Mercury Press, Inc. Reprinted by permission of the authors.

Lowry—"Little Baseball World," from *Happy New Year Kamerades!*, copyright 1954 by Robert James Collas Lowry. Reprinted by permission of the author.

Effinger—"Naked to the Invisible Eye," copyright © 1973 by Condé Nast Publications, Inc. Reprinted by permission.

CONTENTS

INTRODUCTION

People the world over love sports of all kinds. Sports represent a metaphor for life in all its complexity; for spectators, sports offer vicarious experience and a way to forget the troubles that always accompany life. In the United States, millions of people watch a wide variety of sports but, despite the popularity of football and basketball, baseball is still "America's game."

Baseball was first organized as a sport in 1845 and by 1866 it had come to be called the "national pastime." And although it traditionally was associated with rural America, baseball quickly became popular in towns and cities throughout the land. It attracted players from all over America and from among all the different immigrant groups that came to this country.

Baseball is also loved, played, and watched all over the world—in places as far apart as Mexico and Japan. In fact, the number of Latin American ballplayers who have come to the major leagues is such that a wonderful all-star team could easily be put together from players solely of Hispanic origin.

Baseball exemplifies to millions the athlete as hero, and, although most people are not conscious of it, the game provides a commentary on the maturation process, on growing old, on the joys of youth, on winning and losing.

Stories and novels about sports have become commonplace in American literature in both popular and "high" cultural outlets. During the heyday of the pulp magazines in the 1930s and 1940s an entire category of sports pulps that published nothing but fiction appeared, magazines with such titles as *Baseball Stories*, *Super Sports*, *Popular Sports*, and *Thrilling Sports*, to name only a few.

Similarly, the motion picture industry recognized the appeal of sports, and, with regard to baseball, numerous films have made their mark on the American cinema; a list would include such notable movies as *The Pride of the Yankees*, about the tragic life of the great Lou Gehrig; *The Stratton Story*; *The Winning Team*, with then-future president Ronald Reagan and Doris Day; the powerful *Fear Strikes Out* and *Bang the Drum Slowly*; musicals such as *Take Me Out to the Ballgame* and *Damn Yankees*; comedies such as *It Happens Every Spring*, *The Bingo Long*

Traveling All-Stars and Motor Kings, and *The Bad News Bears*; and simply wonderful examples of the filmmaker's art such as *The Natural*.

The number of distinguished or just plain good baseball novels is considerable. Mark Harris has produced four notable works: *The Southpaw* (1953), *Bang the Drum Slowly* (1956), *A Ticket for Seamstitch* (1957), and *It Looked Like Forever* (1979). Others include Eliot Asinof's *Man on Spikes* (1955); Zane Grey's *The Shortstop* (1909) and *The Young Pitcher* (1911); Owen Johnson's *The Hummingbird* (1910); Robert Coover's *The Universal Baseball Association, Inc., J. Henry Waugh, Prop.* (1968); Ring Lardner's *You Know Me Al* (1916); H. Allen Smith's *Rhubarb* (1946), about a cat that inherits a baseball team; and, of course, Bernard Malamud's *The Natural* (1952).

On the Diamond is the largest collection of baseball stories ever compiled and in its pages we are especially pleased to include, in its entirety, Jerome Charyn's wonderful novel, *The Seventh Babe*. You will also find stories by such renowned writers as Thomas Wolfe, Ray Bradbury, P. G. Wodehouse, Jay Neugeboren, and John O'Hara; science fiction and fantasy baseball stories by Rod Serling, Frederik Pohl, George Alec Effinger, Lloyd Biggle, and the team of Barry N. Malzberg and Bill Pronzini; stories by writers not traditionally known for their sports fiction such as John D. MacDonald, Edward D. Hoch, and Jack Ritchie; and of course, stories by writers who specialized in (among other things) sports fiction, men such as William R. Cox, Paul Gallico, and Ring Lardner.

And now...the pitcher looks down for the sign from the catcher.... Play ball! Let the reading begin.

February 1987   Martin H. Greenberg

ON THE DIAMOND

ONE HIT, ONE ERROR, ONE LEFT

Ring Lardner

Clearwater fla march 3

Dear Jessie well kid here it is the 3 of march and I am still in the big league but kidding on the square things is beggin to look pretty rosey as mgr Carey has now got Casey Stengel rooming with me and I guest I all ready told you about Stengel he is a kind of asst mgr and coach of the club and kind of took me in toe the 1st day we beggin to work out and now mgr Carey has got him rooming with me so it looks like there takeing a special interest in how I get a long as Stengel sets and talks to me by the hr about the fine points and gives me pointers about the fine points of the game that comes up durn practice.

I guest that sounds pretty good hay kid on account of the promise I give you the day I left home so you better get ready to pack up the old bag and all a board for Brooklyn or maybe you better wait a wile as maybe I will run a cross some kid I like better. No danger hay kid.

Stengels name aint Casey but that is just a nick name witch he says they call him that because he come from Kansas City but that dont make sense but some of the boys has got nick names like wear they come from like 1 of the pitchers Clyde Day but they call him Pea ridge Day because he come from a town name Pea ridge and he was the champion hog caller of Arkansaw and when he use to pitch in Brooklyn last yr he

1

use to give a hog call after every ball he throwed but the club
made him cut it out because the fans come down on the field
every time he give a call and the club had to hire the
champion of iowa to set up in the stand and call them back.
Then there is a infielder Tommy Thompson but some times
they call him Fresco and I thought it was because he come
from Frisco but Stengel says his hole name is Al Fresco and
his folks give him the name because he was born out doors
like restrants where they got tables under a tree and 1 of the
boys was asking if they call Wilson Hack because he was
born in a hack but Stengel says it was 2 of them and they had
to sell them to a junk dealer.

Wilson is the man who the Cubs had and 2 yrs ago he led
the both leagues in home runs but last yr he had a bad yr and
they trade it him to St Louis for Grimes but the St Louis club
found out that the Cubs had been paying him a salery so they
give him to Brooklyn as the St Louis players works on a
commission base and what ever amt you get out of the world
series the club leaves you keep it. Hack takes a good cut at
the ball and if he meets them square it is no wonder they go
for a ride as he ways as much as your piano but I can hit
them just as far and maybe farther as I got more strenth in
my rist but any ways we both hit right hand it and who plays
center field depends on witch is socking them the hardest tho
of course we will both be in there and maybe Frederick to if
any mgr is crazy enough to pitch a left hander. I says to
Stengel last night I says to Stengel if any mgr is crazy enough
· to pitch a left hander again this club they would put them in a
silium and Stengel says they are all ready there.

We was talking about nick names and Thompson says to
me wear do you come from Warner and I says Centralia and
Stengel says well we cant call him all that because he would
be back a sleep before you was half threw and we all ready
got a Jack Warner on the club so we better call this one
bench but that was the night before last and last night we was
out in front of the hotel and a couple of the boys beggin to
sing and I joined in kind of soft and ever since then they dont
call me nothing but Rudy on account of Rudy Valet and
Thompson says if I could groon like you I would not be plain
base ball and Stengel says he aint but any ways they all call
me Rudy and keep asking me wear did I lern to groon.

Will close for this time kid as am all tarred out as they had
me chason fly balls all day and not only that but mgr Carey

makes all the boys go threw a case of calsthenics and part of it is wear you lay on your back and push your ft up in the air like you are rideing a bycycle and I says to Stengel what is the idea of that kind of practice because when we get to Brooklyn I hope to live some wear wear I wont have to ride a bycycle to the ball pk and even if I did I wouldent never get there laying on my back and pushing my ft up in the air. Any ways am all tarred out but remember what I told you about get ready to pack up the old bag but dont breath nothing to nobody but just tell them you got a post card from me and am getting a long ok and the wether just like summer and here it is only the 3 of march.

Danny

Centralia, Ill. March 7

Dear Danny—You know what a poor hand I am at writing letters and I only wish I was a better letter writer. It is hard to imajine you having summer weather and here we have had more snow than usual and it has also rained some and snowed more than usual so it is hard to imajine you having summer weather.

I am a poor hand at writing letters and I only wish I could tell you how glad I am for your sake that all the managers are all taking so much interest in your work and of course there has never been no doubts in my mind about them keeping you, but as far as what you promised me is concerned I will not hold you to no promise and of course you know how I feel towards you and will never feel no different, but I know that the promise was just in fun, but any time you realy want me you know that I will be here, but will not hold you to no promise that was just in fun.

I can imajine how those other men must enjoy hearing you sing and I almost find myself wishing that you was going to drop in for a few minutes tonight and sing for me though I know I am a poor pianist and make too many mistakes.

Things have been very quite in the store and there is no news.

Was over to see Clara and Dave and their baby last Sunday, he is a cute baby and they both think there was never no other baby like him. I guess all parents feel the same way about their first baby, he is certainly cute all right.

Be sure and take good care of yourself and dont catch cold.

The weather gets cold even in Florida and if you will just keep your promise to write to me I will not hold you to no promise that was just made in fun, besides Mr. Carey may not want to have married men on his nine till they get older.

Yours,   Jessie

Clearwater fla march 12

Dear Jessie dont worry about me breaking no promises and as for mgr Carey he has got a wife and family himself and most of the men on the club has got a family and Babe Herman has got a wife and 2 kids and sells shirts and Lefty Odoul sells shoes in the winter and Jack Quinn is married and most of the other boys and mgr Carey has got a string of gas stations a round St Louis and minit rub witch is some kind of sauve that keeps the pitchers arms in shape and as for your piano plain you will do till some body better comes a long. mgr Carey calls me Rudy like the rest of the boys is calling me and he is a good singer himself but cant groon like I tho when he was in school he studed for the priest hood.

Well kid I told you to get the old bag packed and all as I ask is for you to keep your promise to not breath a word till I give you the word but between you and I it looks better then ever because last night some of the boys went to the picture and wanted I should go a long but I had all ready seen it twict and dident care nothing about seen it a 3d time so I come up in my room and who was there but mgr Carey and Stengel the both of them and I says I would go out for a walk and give them a chance to talk things over but Carey says no set down boy and maybe you will lern some thing as we got no secrets from you witch sound it like he all ready made up his mind to keep me hay kid and he says did you ever try hitting them left hand it and I says I guest I could hit them good enough 1 way and he says he was a turn a round hitter himself when he was plain base ball and it kept him in the league a long wile extra and if you could lern to hit left hand it and hit them long fly balls to right field like you hit them to left field it would not hurt you. So I says why dont you make Wilson hit left hand it and he says because Wilson can hit right hand it all the time and hit to 1 field as good as another and then Stengel says he himself was all so a turn a round hitter as he use to hit so good right hand it that the pitchers thretened to walk out unlest he would agree to hit left hand it all the time.

But he made a sucker out of them because he was even better left hand it then he had been right hand it and he says will I tell him how good I was Max and Carey says you proudly will and Stengel says well I was so good that they use to pass me on purpose in batting practice and 1 time I was in a world series again the Giants and the yankees and the empires called the game on account of darkness at 3pm with the sun shinning and judge Landis ast them to exclaim there decision and they said they thought it must be dark because Stengel only hit for 2 bases. So I menshuned about plain night base ball in Bloomington and Stengel says that exclaims it Max how the scouts sent that report in but mgr Carey says no that don't exclaim nothing because he seen a game in Bloomington himself and they had the field all lit up and it was bright as day.

Well this pm mgr Carey ast me to just try and hit a few left hand it and Jack Quinn was pitching and he aint got nothing on the ball only he dont throw it wear you can get a cut at it so I dident even foul 1 and then Clark throwed a few and he is a left hander and that made it all the worst and Wilson hit a couple out of the pk right hand it and I could of hit them twict as far only Carey made me keep trying left hand it and I told him I couldent do nothing that way and he says nobody can lern in 1 pm and when we got back to the hotel I complaint to Stengel and he says you ought to feel pretty good because if he dident take a interest in you he wouldent care if you hit them right hand it or left hand it or back words and I says maybe he is figureing on me to take Hermans place as Herman is still holeing out but Stengel says dont worry about Herman as all of these boys has to hole out till they can remember how they spell there name so you see kid I got reasons to remind you about your promise and be ready to pack up for Brooklyn as soon as I say the word.

We had 1 bad day a wk a go when the wind blowed 50 miles a hr. and I says it was a wonder we dident all get out heads blowed off and Stengel says it was a shame because that would improve the club and must close now and turn in as we play our 1st regular game tomorrow again Cincinnati at Tampa the capitol and the boys is all talking about a trade with there club witch would give us Joe Stripp or somebody and Stengel says you better not play as bad as you can or the reds will want you in the trade. I guest he ment as good.

Danny

Centralia, Ill. March 16

Dear Danny—Dave said he seen in the St. Louis paper that the Brooklyns had played Cincinnati and Newark, but it did not say who was the players on both sides, but I imajine you helped beat them, but did not know that Newark was in your league.

I am a poor hand at writing letters and there is so little news here, but the weather has been bad, rainy and snowing and it is hard to imajine you playing ball while we are having such nasty weather.

I told you in my last letter I would not hold you to no promise that was just made in fun and just forget all about that part of it, but I know the Brooklyns will keep you and give you a good position, though I cant understand Mr. Carey wanting you to bat with your left hand when the other way comes natural to you and I know I cant do anything with my left hand, not even write my name. I told Dave about Mr. Carey once studying to be a priest and Dave said he seen a world game in Pittsburgh one time when Mr. Carey was playing there and he bet Walter Johnson wished Mr. Carey had stayed in church. Probibly you will know to what he referred to.

Things have been very quite in the store and there is very little news. Things have been going on about as usual and I guess you know I am lonesome without me telling you and I wish things were busier at the store so I would not have so much time to get blue, but the worst time is the evenings. I cant play the piano good enough to even entertain myself and besides it seems to make me all the more lonesome and I try and read, but cant get interested in nothing only your letters, and I read them over and over, though I dont understand most of it, but I lov to read them just the same.

Yours,   Jessie

Clearwater fla march 23

Dear Jessie we been plain a game pretty near every day with some big league club ether here or some other place and I been in there pretty near every day but most of the time in right field or left field in place of Boone or Odoul and it looks like mgr Carey intend it to start the season with Wilson in center but it is a cinch they are going to keep me because they trade it Herman to Cincinnati. So remember what I told you about packing up the old bag as soon as I give you the word and it wont be more then a couple more days when I will know where I stand but after the way I been socking them it looks like I am all set. I got 4 in 4 again the As and I stared at bat again the cards. How is that again the 2 champions of the 2 big leagues but best of all is the way I been socking them to right field and when I had socked 2 over the right field wall again Newark mgr Carey quit trying to make me hit left hand it but he did make me change my stanch and Stengel says that is why I am hitting so good to right field.

Every time we go some place in a train or bus the boys start singing and next thing you know they are asking for Rudy to join in but as soon as I beggin to groon they all shet up and I wont have no voice left unlest they lay off me and night before last they was all after me to groon and I told them I was going to a picture and it happened I had promised the phone girl in the hotel to take her to a picture so I called her up and kept my promise. Her name is Vivian Duane and she was born in fla and talks with a funny drool but she calls me Rudy like the rest of the boys and she wants I should get her a job when I get up north. She is a good looker but I told her I would have to be sure of my own job before I promise to get her a job.

The other night a party of us went over to a place near here name Bellair wear they have got a caseno with a rulette wheel and 1 of the boys exclaimed on the way over there is 36 numbers and they roll a marble and half the numbers is black and half red and if you pick the right number they pay 35 to 1 and if you play red or black they pay you even money. So I seen that the way to beat it was play red 1 time and black the next time so I bought $10.00 worth of $.50 chips and wait it till they had roll the marble 1 time and it come red and then I bet $.50 on the black and sure enough it come black and then I win again on the red and I was counting how much was I a winner and forgot to bet and it come red witch was twict in a row. So I seen the game was queer so I says to the man cash me in and all the boys laughed but I was the 1 that had the laugh on the way home because I was the only 1 that win.

I guest I all ready told you about this Pea ridge Day the hog caller from Arkansaw. Well it seems that last spring he was down here and some of the boys bet him $10.00 he was scarred to jump in a fish pond with his close on and he took the bet and jumped in the pond and they had to pay him the $10.00 and the suit was too big for him when he got it and he

figured it might schrink to get it wet and it only cause him
$8.00 in the 1st place and he dried it out and had a man press
it for $1.00 and sure enough it schrink to just the right size.
So he had the laugh on them just like myself in the rulette
wheel.

This pm we got a game with a club called the House of
David witch aint in no league but they are members of a
religious sex in Michigan and Stengel says Jack Quinn will
pitch the hole game for our club because the other club all
wears beards and he says they have got 4 pitchers name
Mathews Mark and Luque and John and Mathews is a left
hander. Well I hope he pitchs and I will give some of them
outfielders a shave.

1 day last wk we was over to a place name Tarpon springs
wear they are all greeks and fish for sponges in a sail boat
and I bought 2 sponges and at 1st I was going to keep 1 of
them for myself and male you the other and then I happened
to think about your mother. So decide it to send the both of
them to you only 1 of them is for your mother but you wont
get them for a few days as I dident know how to rap them up
but happened to think about Vivian the phone girl and she is
going to rap them up and male them.

Stengel says I am doing the right thing because just 1 of
them wouldent do me no good but anyways you will know
who they come from even if it is her hand writeing.

Nobody calls me Danny no more only you. So I will sine
this letter Rudy.

Rudy

p.s. dont forget about packing the old bag when I give you the
word.

Rudy

Centralia, Ill., March 27

Dear Danny—You will never be nothing only Danny to
me. I dont care what other girls call you and I certainly will
not call you Rudy, as I would rather hear you sing than Rudy
Vallee 100 times.

Dave seen an article on the train the other day and was
going to bring it to me but forgot it, and it said Mr. Carey was
delighted in your improvement since he had changed your
stand up to bat and it looked like the Brooklyns were sure to
keep you as a pinch man. Well Danny I knew all along that
you would make good, but please dont talk about no promise
to me. You know how glad I am to have you make good, but

it is for your own sake and am not holding you to no silly promises. I only wish Brooklyn was not so far away, though of course you might as well be there as Bloomington as far as me seeing you is concerned.

For one thing I cant help from beleiving that Mr. Carey would not like you taking such a serious step like getting married so soon after giving you a position like pinch man and besides that there is the question about me leaving mamma and papa, though mamma has not felt as good in ten years as she feels this spring and papa dont need me in the store and says we would save money on coal bills if we closed up till business gets better, and you know how ignorant I am about things and do the player's wives travel around with them or all live together in some hotel or do they have summer homes on Coney Island or some place. I dont even know what clothes a person would have to have but I know I have not got nothing fit to wear only the dress I had last summer, and you would be ashamed of me and probibly the other player's wives would laugh when they seen my clothes.

I dont know why I am writing all this because as I told you, I am not going to hold you to no silly promise, but sometimes I get so lonesome and blue that I feel like I would go crazy, and I guess you think I am crazy writing a letter like this.

The sponges have not gotten here yet, but it was lovely of you to think of mamma and I with so much on your mind, but maybe your friend Miss Duane got jealous because you forgot to buy her a sponge and just did not send them. I am just joking Danny but maybe you will not see the joke and I guess I better close or you will think I have gone crazy.

Yours, Jessie

Clearwater fla march 24

Dear Jessie well kid I wrote you a letter yesterday am and here I am writeing to you again and how is that for keeping a promise but it is regards to another promise that I am writeing you this time and I mean the promise about I and you getting married if the Brooklyn club decide it to keep me.

Well kid mgr Carey told me last night that he was going to keep me and I need not worry about my job but I still got a few things to lern and he maybe will not play me regular for a wile but leave me warn the bench and use me for a pinch hitter and if I kept my eyes open and worked hard he will maybe give me a chance in place of 1 of the left hand it hitters against a left hander. So I better work out in both left and right field because he says center field is crowd it enough with just Wilson. So I thanked him and after words I and Stengel was in the room and I guest I was kind of nerves and Stengel says what is on your mind and I says I had made a promise that I would marry a little kid up home and I intend it to go threw with the promise even if it cause me my job and he says well it will cause you your job all right but if she is the right kind of a girl she will release you from your promise rather then see Max release you off of the ball club and you just tell her to do you a flavor and wait till fall or else you can check your trunk threw to Hartford.

Well kid it is all up to you and I will keep my promise if you say the word even if it cause me my job but when I made you the promise it was kind of a joke as I dident think I would make good so quick but Carey would be crazy to let me go the way I been socking them and yesterday I got 3 out of 4 off them beard it boys and 1 of there outfielders catched the other 1 in his wiskers and be sides Carey would have to get wafers and all as I am scarred of is the Reds or Phila or St Louis getting a hold of me and I would ether be with a 8 place club or put out to pasture some place all season but as I say I will go threw with my promise if you say the word but the boys is all puling for me to stay with this club so as they can lissen to me groon.

Stengel says wear does your girl live and I told him Centralia and he says you would be plain a fine trick on her makeing her leave her folks and her home town and move to a human zoo like Brooklyn and leave her there starveing to death half the time wile you travel a round the country and live in the best hotels and when your home she can come out to the ball pk and watch you in batting practice and maybe see you march up to the place onct a wk a mist a shower of boos. So I says how about the other boys that has got a wife and family and he says you can bet there getting more then $3000.00 a yr witch is $250.00 a mont and for 12 monts and I says how much would it cause me to live supose I was a lone and he says it wouldent cause you nothing because you eat so much on the road that you can lay off food durn the 80 days your in Brooklyn and the Brooklyn bench is pretty good place to sleep after you get use to the rore of the animals.

Well kid I guess that is enough on that subject and I will leave it to you to say yes or no and if you hold me to my

promise well in good I will go threw with my promise even if
it cause me my job.

1 of the Brooklyn papers has come out with a offer of
$1000.00 in cash to who ever can think of a new nick name
for the club as they been calling them the robins because
there mgr was Wm Robinson but Carey is the mgr now so
robins dont make no sense and all the boys has been trying to
think up some name and I wisht I could think up some name
hay kid and knock off that $1000.00 and why dont you try it
yourself kid and you might hit on some name that would be
as good as I could think up myself and I ast Vivian the phone
girl to try and she says why not call us the Brooks or the
Bridgers on account of Brooklyn bridge but when I repeat it
them to the boys they just laughed and speaking of Vivian
she says she is going to come up to Brooklyn and look for a
job when the season is over down here as it gets so hot durn
the summer and I was out to her house for a few minutes last
night and she has got a piano and can play like a street. So
they was nothing to do but I must groon a few dittys so I
hope she does come up to Brooklyn. That is if I have to be a
lone but speaking about a name for the club I ast Carey why
dident he give it a name himself and he says robins was ok
with him. So I says Yes but Robinson aint mgr no more and
Carey says I wisht he was and Stengel says if you got to get a
name that refers to the mgr why not call them the Max trux
but the way they been looking for the last few days we ought
to call them Cincinnati.

Well kid you will let me hear from you as soon as you
receive this and I know you will think I am trying to walk out
on my promise but I will go threw with it even if it cause me
my job and I am only telling you what Stengel thinks and
after all maybe you would be home sick and lone some a lone
so much of the time and with your mother not feeling so good
maybe you ought not to leave her a side from helping your
father in the store and it will be just the same this fall and I
can get some money saved up by that time. I wasent sure but
what Carey would object to a young man getting married
when I am just breaking in and I guest I better exclaim about
them other men on the club like Wilson who has got a wife
and kid but he gets a salery of $16500 witch is more than 5
times my salery and as for the boys that is all ready married
why Carey cant very well tell them to get rid of there wife or
he will trade them to Phila and of course in the case of a man

like Jack Quinn why he was married when Carey was lerning to talk.

It is different with a man like I wear I am just breaking in and all the time I was a way on the road I would be thinking about you all a lone there in Brooklyn and you couldent even go to a picture because the place is full of gunsters and maybe the very day we picked out to get married who ever we was plain again would pick that day to pitch a left hander and Carey would lay it all on you and I if the club lose a close game.

As I say kid if you say the word I will go threw with my promise but I only made it as a kind of a joke and I dont remember if I says right away or next fall and if you think we better wait I will keep on writeing you letters and write you a letter every day all season but be sure and let me know by return male.

Rudy

Centralia, Ill. March 28

Dear Danny—Your letter just came and I wrote you a letter yesterday, and I hope you wont pay no attention to some of the things I said in it as it was all just a joke, and please forget that crazy promise which I took as a joke, and I dont consider it a promise for now or next fall or any other time.

The sponges came yesterday and Miss Duane has got a pretty hand writing and I am glad she is going to Brooklyn and you will have some one that can realy play the piano for you to sing.

Mamma says thanks for the sponges and we are all glad that Mr. Carey is going to keep you, but I knew he would and now you must learn all you can from he and Mr. Stengel and take care of yourself and dont imajine for a minute that I would allow you to write to me every day as I am such a poor hand at writing letters and can give you nothing in return but if you ever have a little spare time you know how I will love to hear from you, and Dave says he will keep me posted on the Brooklyn nine as soon as the season opens in earnest, and I hope you beat everybody and all I ask is that if you ever do find time to write please dont sign Rudy but your own real name.

Jessie

NEBRASKA CRANE

Thomas Wolfe

A T THE FAR end of the car a man stood up and started back down the aisle toward the washroom. He walked with a slight limp and leaned upon a cane, and with his free hand he held onto the backs of the seats to brace himself against the lurching of the train. As he came abreast of George, who sat there gazing out the window, the man stopped abruptly. A strong, good-natured voice, warm, easy, bantering, unafraid, unchanged—exactly as it was when it was fourteen years of age—broke like a flood of living light upon his consciousness:

"Well I'll be dogged! Hi, there, Monkus! Where you goin'?"

At the sound of the old jesting nickname George looked up quickly. It was Nebraska Crane. The square, freckled, sunburned visage had the same humorous friendliness it had always had, and the tar-black Cherokee eyes looked out with the same straight, deadly fearlessness. The big brown paw came out and they clasped each other firmly. And, instantly, it was like coming home to a strong and friendly place. In another moment they were seated together, talking with the familiarity of people whom no gulf of years and distance could alter or separate.

George had seen Nebraska Crane only once in all the years since he himself had first left Libya Hill and gone away to college. But he had not lost sight of him. Nobody had lost sight of Nebraska Crane. That wiry, fearless little figure of the Cherokee boy who used to come down the hill on Locust Street with the bat slung

13

over his shoulder and the well-oiled fielder's mitt protruding from his hip pocket had been prophetic of a greater destiny, for Nebraska had become a professional baseball player, he had crashed into the big leagues, and his name had been emblazoned in the papers every day.

The newspapers had had a lot to do with his seeing Nebraska that other time. It was in August 1925, just after George had returned to New York from his first trip abroad. That very night, in fact, a little before midnight, as he was seated in a Childs Restaurant with smoking wheatcakes, coffee, and an ink-fresh copy of next morning's *Herald-Tribune* before him, the headline jumped out at him: "Crane Slams Another Homer." He read the account of the game eagerly, and felt a strong desire to see Nebraska again and get back in his blood once more the honest tang of America. Acting on a sudden impulse, he decided to call him up. Sure enough, his name was in the book, with an address way up in the Bronx. He gave the number and waited. A man's voice answered the phone, but at first he didn't recognize it.

"Hello! . . . Hello? . . . Is Mr. Crane there? . . . Is that you, Bras?"

"Hello." Nebraska's voice was hesitant, slow, a little hostile, touched with the caution and suspicion of mountain people when speaking to a stranger. "Who is that? . . . Who? . . . Is that *you, Monk?*"—suddenly and quickly, as he recognized who it was. "Well I'll be dogged!" he cried. His tone was delighted, astounded, warm with friendly greetings now, and had the somewhat high and faintly howling quality that mountain people's voices often have when they are talking to someone over the telephone: the tone was full, sonorous, countrified, and a little puzzled, as if he were yelling to someone on an adjoining mountain peak on a gusty day in autumn when the wind was thrashing through the trees. "Where'd you come from? How the hell are you, boy?" he yelled before George could answer. "Where you been all this time, anyway?"

"I've been in Europe. I just got back this morning."

"Well I'll be dogged!"—still astounded, delighted, full of howling friendliness. "When am I gonna see you? How about comin' to the game tomorrow? I'll fix you up. And say," he went on rapidly, "if you can stick aroun' after the game, I'll take you home to meet the wife and kid. How about it?"

So it was agreed. George went to the game and saw Nebraska knock another home run, but he remembered best what happened afterwards. When the player had had his shower and had dressed, the two friends left the ball park, and as they went out a crowd of young boys who had been waiting at the gate rushed upon them. They were those dark-faced, dark-eyed, dark-haired little urchins who spring up like dragon seed from the grim pavements of New York, but in whose tough little faces and raucous voices there still remains, curiously, the innocence and faith of children everywhere.

"It's Bras!" the children cried. "Hi, Bras! Hey, Bras!" In a moment they were pressing round him in a swarming horde, deafening the ears with their shrill cries, begging, shouting, tugging at his sleeves, doing everything they could to attract his attention, holding dirty little scraps of paper toward him, stubs of pencils, battered little notebooks, asking him to sign his autograph.

He behaved with the spontaneous warmth and kindliness of his character. He scrawled his name out rapidly on a dozen grimy bits of paper, skillfully working his way along through the yelling, pushing, jumping group, and all the time keeping up a rapid fire of banter, badinage, and good-natured reproof:

"All right—give it here, then! . . . Why don't you fellahs pick on somebody else once in a while? . . . Say, boy!" he said suddenly, turning to look down at one unfortunate child, and pointing an accusing finger at him—"what you doin' aroun' here again today? I signed my name fer you at least a dozen times!"

"No, sir, Misteh Crane!" the urchin earnestly replied. "Honest —not me!"

"Ain't that right?" Nebraska said, appealing to the other children. "Don't this boy keep comin' back here every day?"

They grinned, delighted at the chagrin of their fellow petitioner. "Dat's right, Misteh Crane! Dat guy's got a whole book wit' nuttin' but yoeh name in it!"

"Ah-h!" the victim cried, and turned upon his betrayers bitterly. "What youse guys tryin' to do—get wise or somep'n? Honest, Misteh Crane!—" he looked up earnestly again at Nebraska— "Don't believe 'em! I jest want yoeh ottygraph! Please, Misteh Crane, it'll only take a minute!"

For a moment more Nebraska stood looking down at the child with an expression of mock sternness; at last he took the outstretched notebook, rapidly scratched his name across a page, and handed it back. And as he did so, he put his big paw on the urchin's head and gave it a clumsy pat; then, gently and playfully, he shoved it from him and walked off down the street.

The apartment where Nebraska lived was like a hundred thousand others in the Bronx. The ugly yellow brick building had a false front, with meaningless little turrets at the corners of the roof, and a general air of spurious luxury about it. The rooms were rather small and cramped, and were made even more so by the heavy, overstuffed Grand Rapids furniture. The walls of the living room, painted a mottled, rusty cream, were bare except for a couple of sentimental colored prints, while the place of honor over the mantel was reserved for an enlarged and garishly tinted photograph of Nebraska's little son at the age of two, looking straight and solemnly out at all comers from a gilded oval frame.

Myrtle, Nebraska's wife, was small and plump and pretty in a doll-like way. Her corn-silk hair was frizzled in a halo about her face, and her chubby features were heavily accented by rouge and lipstick. But she was simple and natural in her talk and bearing, and George liked her at once. She welcomed him with a warm and friendly smile and said she had heard a lot about him.

They all sat down. The child, who was three or four years old by this time, and who had been shy, holding onto his mother's dress and peeping out from behind her, now ran across the room to his father and began climbing all over him. Nebraska and Myrtle asked George a lot of questions about himself, what he had been doing, where he had been, and especially what countries he had visited in Europe. They seemed to think of Europe as a place so far away that anyone who had actually been there was touched with an unbelievable aura of strangeness and romance.

"Whereall did you go over there, anyway?" asked Nebraska.

"Oh, everywhere, Bras," George said—"France, England, Holland, Germany, Denmark, Sweden, Italy—all over the place."

"Well I'll be dogged!"—in frank astonishment. "You sure do git aroun', don't you?"

"Not the way *you* do, Bras. You're traveling most of the time."

"Who—*me?* Oh, hell, I don't get anywhere—just the same ole places. Chicago, St. Looie, Philly—I seen 'em all so often I could find my way blindfolded!" He waved them aside with a gesture of his hand. Then, suddenly, he looked at George as though he were just seeing him for the first time, and he reached over and slapped him on the knee and exclaimed: "Well I'll be dogged! How you doin' anyway, Monkus?"

"Oh, can't complain. How about you? But I don't need to ask that. I've been reading all about you in the papers."

"Yes, Monkus," he said. "I been havin' a good year. But, boy!—" He shook his head suddenly and grinned—"do the ole dogs feel it!"

He was silent a moment, then he went on quietly:

"I been up here since 1919—that's seven years, and it's a long time in this game. Not many of 'em stay much longer. When you been shaggin' flies as long as that you may lose count, but you don't need to count—your legs'll tell you."

"But, good Lord, Bras, *you're* all right! Why, the way you got around out there today you looked like a colt!"

"Yeah," Nebraska said, "maybe I *looked* like a colt, but I felt like a plow horse." He fell silent again, then he tapped his friend gently on the knee with his brown hand and said abruptly, "No, Monkus. When you been in this business as long as I have, you know it."

"Oh, come on, Bras, quit your kidding!" said George, remembering that the player was only two years older than himself. "You're still a young man. Why, you're only twenty-seven!"

"Sure, sure," Nebraska answered quietly. "But it's like I say. You cain't stay in this business much longer than I have. Of course, Cobb an' Speaker an' a few like that—they was up here a long time. But eight years is about the average, an' I been here seven already. So if I can hang on a few years more, I won't have no kick to make. . . . Hell!" he said in a moment, with the old hearty ring in his voice, "I ain't got no kick to make, no way. If I got my release tomorrow, I'd still feel I done all right . . . Ain't that so, Buzz?" he cried genially to the child, who had settled down on his knee, at the same time seizing the boy and cradling him comfortably in his strong arm. "Ole Bras has done all right, ain't he?"

"That's the way me an' Bras feel about it," remarked Myrtle, who during this conversation had been rocking back and forth, placidly ruminating on a wad of gum. "Along there last year it looked once or twice as if Bras might git traded. He said to me one day before the game, 'Well, ole lady, if I don't get some hits today somethin' tells me you an' me is goin' to take a trip.' So I says, 'Trip where?' An' he says, 'I don't know, but they're goin' to sell me down the river if I don't git goin', an' somethin' tells me it's now or never!' So I just looks at him," continued Myrtle placidly, "an' I says, 'Well, what do you want me to do? Do you want me to come today or not?' You know, gener'ly, Bras won't let me come when he ain't hittin'—he says it's bad luck. But he just looks at me a minute, an' I can see him sort of studyin' it over, an' all of a sudden he makes up his mind an' says, 'Yes, come on if you want to; I couldn't have no more bad luck than I been havin', noway, an' maybe it's come time fer things to change, so you come on.' Well, I went—an' I don't know whether I brought him luck

or not, but somethin' did," said Myrtle, rocking in her chair com-
placently.

"Dogged if she didn't!" Nebraska chuckled. "I got three hits
out of four times up that day, an' two of 'em was home runs!"

"Yeah," Myrtle agreed, "an' that Philadelphia fastball thrower
was throwin' 'em, too."

"He sure was!" said Nebraska.

"I know," went on Myrtle, chewing placidly, "because I heard
some of the boys say later that it was like he was throwin' 'em up
there from out of the bleachers, with all them men in shirt-sleeves
right behind him, an' the boys said half the time they couldn't even
see the ball. But Bras must of saw it—or been lucky—because he
hit two home runs off of him, an' that pitcher didn't like it, either.
The second one Bras got, he went stompin' an' tearin' around out
there like a wild bull. He sure did look mad," said Myrtle in her
customary placid tone.

"Maddest man I ever seen!" Nebraska cried delightedly. "I
thought he was goin' to dig a hole plumb through to China. . . .
But that's the way it was. She's right about it. That was the day I
got goin'. I know one of the boys said to me later, 'Bras,' he says,
'we all thought you was goin' to take a ride, but you sure dug in,
didn't you?' That's the way it is in this game. I seen Babe Ruth go
fer weeks when he couldn't hit a balloon, an' all of a sudden he
lams into it. Seems like he just cain't miss from then on."

All this had happened four years ago. Now the two friends had
met again, and were seated side by side in the speeding train,
talking and catching up on one another. When George explained
the reason for his going home, Nebraska turned to him with open-
mouthed astonishment, genuine concern written in the frown upon
his brown and homely face.

"Well, what d'you know about that!" he said. "I sure am sorry,
Monk." He was silent while he thought about it, and embarrassed,
not knowing what to say. Then, after a moment: "Gee!—" he
shook his head—"your aunt was one swell cook! I never will fergit
it! Remember how she used to feed us kids—every danged one of
us in the whole neighborhood?" He paused, then grinned up shyly
at his friend: "I sure wish I had a fistful of them good ole cookies
of hers right this minute!"

Nebraska's right ankle was taped and bandaged; a heavy cane
rested between his knees. George asked him what had happened.

"I pulled a tendon," Nebraska said, "an' got laid off. So I
thought I might as well run down an' see the folks. Myrtle, she
couldn't come—the kid's got to git ready for school."

"How are they?" George asked.

"Oh, fine, fine. All wool an' a yard wide, both of 'em!" He was silent for a moment, then he looked at his friend with a tolerant Cherokee grin and said, "But I'm crackin' up, Monkus. Guess I cain't stan' the gaff much more."

Nebraska was only thirty-one now, and George was incredulous. Nebraska smiled good-naturedly again.

"That's an ole man in baseball, Monk. I went up when I was twenty-one. I been aroun' a long time."

The quiet resignation of the player touched his friend with sadness. It was hard and painful for him to face the fact that this strong and fearless creature, who had stood in his life always for courage and for victory, should now be speaking with such ready acceptance of defeat.

"But, Bras," he protested, "you've been hitting just as well this season as you ever did! I've read about you in the papers, and the reporters have all said the same thing."

"Oh, I can still hit 'em," Nebraska quietly agreed. "It ain't the hittin' that bothers me. That's the last thing you lose, anyway. Leastways, it's goin' to be that way with me, an' I talked to other fellahs who said it was that way with them." After a pause he went on in a low tone: "If this ole leg heals up in time, I'll go on back an' git in the game again an' finish out the season. An' if I'm lucky, maybe they'll keep me a couple more years, because they know I can still hit. But, hell," he added quietly, "they know I'm through. They already got me all tied up with string."

As Nebraska talked, George saw that the Cherokee in him was the same now as it had been when he was a boy. His cheerful fatalism had always been the source of his great strength and courage. That was why he had never been afraid of anything, not even death. But, seeing the look of regret on George's face, Nebraska smiled again and went on lightly:

"That's the way it is, Monk. You're good up there as long as you're good. After that they sell you down the river. Hell, I ain't kickin'. I been lucky. I had ten years of it already, an' that's more than most. An' I been in three World's Serious. If I can hold on fer another year or two—if they don't let me go or trade me—I think maybe we'll be in again. Me an' Myrtle has figgered it all out. I had to help her people some, an' I bought a farm fer Mama an' the Ole Man—that's where they always wanted to be. An' I got three hundred acres of my own in Zebulon—all paid fer, too!—an' if I git a good price this year fer my tobacco, I stan' to clear two thousand dollars. So if I can git two years more in the League an' one more good World's Serious, why—" he turned his square face

toward his friend and grinned his brown and freckled grin, just as
he used to as a boy—"we'll be all set."

"And—you mean you'll be satisfied?"

"Huh? Satisfied?" Nebraska turned to him with a puzzled look.
"How do you mean?"

"I mean after all you've seen and done, Bras—the big cities and
the crowds, and all the people shouting—and the newspapers, and
the headlines, and the World Series—and—and—the first of
March, and St. Petersburg, and meeting all the fellows again, and
spring training—"

Nebraska groaned.

"Why, what's the matter?"

"Spring trainin'."

"You mean you don't like it?"

"Like it! Them first three weeks is just plain hell. It ain't bad
when you're a kid. You don't put on much weight durin' the winter, an' when you come down in the spring it only takes a few days
to loosen up an' git the kinks out. In two weeks' time you're loose
as ashes. But wait till you been aroun' as long as I have!" He
laughed loudly and shook his head. "Boy! The first time you go
after a grounder you can hear your joints creak. After a while you
begin to limber up—you work into it an' git the soreness out
of your muscles. By the time the season starts, along in April,
you feel pretty good. By May you're goin' like a house afire, an'
you tell yourself you're good as you ever was. You're still goin'
strong along in June. An' when you hit July, an' you get them
double-headers in St. Looie! Boy, oh, boy!" Again he shook his
head and laughed, baring big square teeth. "Monkus," he said
quietly, turning to his companion, and now his face was serious
and he had his black Indian look—"you ever been in St. Looie in
July?"

"No."

"All right, then," he said very softly and scornfully. "An' you
ain't played *ball* there in July. You come up to bat with sweat
bustin' from your ears. You step up an' look out there to where
the pitcher ought to be, an' you see four of him. The crowd in the
bleachers is out there roastin' in their shirt-sleeves, an' when the
pitcher throws the ball it just comes from nowheres—it comes
right out of all them shirt-sleeves in the bleachers. It's on top of
you before you know it. Well, anyway, you dig in an' git a toe-
hold, take your cut, an' maybe you connect. You straighten out a
fast one. It's good for two bases if you hustle. In the old days you
could've made it standin' up. But now—boy!" He shook his head

slowly. "You cain't tell me nothin' about that ball park in St. Looie in July! They got it all growed out in grass in April, but after July first—" he gave a short laugh—"hell!—it's paved with concrete! An' when you git to first, them dogs is sayin', 'Boy, let's stay here!' But you gotta keep on goin'—you know the manager is watchin' you—you're gonna ketch hell if you don't take that extra base, it may mean the game. An' the boys up in the press box, they got their eyes glued on you, too—they've begun to say old Crane is playin' on a dime—an' you're thinkin' about next year an' maybe gittin' in another Serious—an' you hope to God you don't git traded to St. Looie. So you take it on the lam, you slide into second like the Twentieth Century comin' into the Chicago yards—an' when you git up an' feel yourself all over to see if any of your parts is missin', you gotta listen to one of that second baseman's wisecracks: 'What's the hurry, Bras? Afraid you'll be late fer the Veterans' Reunion?' "

"I begin to see what you mean, all right," said George.

"See what I mean? Why, say! One day this season I ast one of the boys what month it was, an' when he told me it was just the middle of July, I says to him: 'July, hell! If it ain't September I'll eat your hat!' 'Go ahead, then,' he says, 'an' eat it, because it ain't September, Bras—it's July.' 'Well,' I says, 'they must be havin' sixty days a month this year—it's the longest damn July *I* ever felt!' An' lemme tell you, I didn't miss it fer, either—I'll be dogged if I did! When you git old in this business, it may be only July, but you think it's September." He was silent for a moment. "But they'll keep you in there, gener'ly, as long as you can hit. If you can smack that ole apple, they'll send you out there if they've got to use glue to keep you from fallin' apart. So maybe I'll get in another year or two if I'm lucky. So long's I can hit 'em, maybe they'll keep sendin' me out there till all the other players has to grunt every time ole Bras goes after a ground ball!" He laughed. "I ain't that bad yet, but soon's I am, I'm through."

"You won't mind it, then, when you have to quit?"

He didn't answer at once. He sat there looking out the window at the factory-blighted landscape of New Jersey. Then he laughed a little wearily:

"Boy, this may be a ride on the train to you, but to *me*—say!— I covered this stretch so often that I can tell you what telephone post we're passin' without even lookin' out the window. Why, hell yes!—" he laughed loudly now, in the old infectious way—"I used to have 'em numbered—now I got 'em *named!*"

"And you think you can get used to spending all your time out on the farm in Zebulon?"

"Git used to it?" In Nebraska's voice there was now the same note of scornful protest that it had when he was a boy, and for a moment he turned and looked at his friend with an expression of astonished disgust. "Why, what are you talkin' about? That's the greatest life in the world!"

THE UMPIRE
WAS A ROOKIE

Arnold Hano

HIS NAME WAS Bill Needy, a man of up-and-down lines and high shoulders, not broad and tapering like the ballplayers who had trudged up the same iron stairway. So the fans clustered below did not ask him for autographs, even though he carried the same sort of black bag in his right hand.

He heard a hoarse voice say, "Must be a new trainer or somethin'," and then he was out of the chilly mid-April sunshine, moving quickly through the white-tile corridor to the door marked UMPIRES' DRESSING ROOM.

The three other men were already in their dark uniforms, and their eyes swung to him as he threw his bag onto a long wooden bench and began swiftly to undress.

The biggest of the three, a red-faced, white-haired man with a jaw that unhinged like a swinging lantern, put down the ball-and-strike indicator he was playing with, and walked over.

Needy knew him, of course. He was McQuinn, the senior umpire in the league. McQuinn, whom he had watched on his living-room screen during last year's World Series, a man with a bellowing voice and a quietly domineering manner.

"You Needy?" McQuinn said, and Needy was amused at how soft-spoken McQuinn really was, off the diamond.

Needy stood up. He was shirtless now, white-skinned compared with the others, thin and bony-chested. He sensed the difference between himself and them, and he hoped that it went no further than the tans they had acquired during spring training down South.

"Yes," he said, "I'm Needy." He was annoyed at the squeak in his voice. "You're Mr. McQuinn."

McQuinn laughed, and Needy heard the bellow, "You hear that? Mr. McQuinn. I hope you two bums learn something from that."

The tallest one, a turkey-necked, red-headed man, walked over, and even in those three steps, Needy saw the boy from the plow who had become one of the finest pitchers the league had seen in the last quarter century. He drawled, "I'm Carlson," and Needy wanted to say, "Yes, I've seen you pitch." Carlson had been with the Cubs for fourteen years until his fast ball deserted him. Five years ago he had returned to the major leagues as an umpire.

But Needy couldn't say that, because he had never seen Carlson pitch. He had never, in fact, been inside a major-league park before this day.

He nodded and took the tall man's hand and felt all the pressure that was at the same time warm and crushing.

The third man, short and thick through the waist, bowlegged and bald, waddled over to Needy. "If you mister me," he said, "I'll fall down dead. All I ever hear is insults. I'm Jankowicz."

"Needy," he said again, clearing his throat, and he stood there, wondering whether he would ever match up to them or even come close.

They eyed him with frank curiosity. He was the new man in the league, called up just yesterday to replace Jake Mandell, the umpire who had broken his leg getting off a plane at Idlewild, flying in from an exhibition in Cleveland. The doctors said Mandell would be staring up at the ceiling for nearly two months.

Wiley, the league president, had wired the three top minor-league heads for their recommendations. They all had different choices, but Needy's league president had called the commissioner of all baseball on his private phone and talked for a half hour. The commissioner spoke to Wiley. Wiley picked Needy.

So the three other umpires stood a few yards off and watched Needy. And Needy felt the perspiration trickle down his ribs.

McQuinn broke the silence finally. He said, "I suppose you've boned up on the ground rules?"

Needy nodded. "Your league has pretty much the same rules we had back in the Association. That makes it easier."

McQuinn nodded his great head. "It does," he said, "but this is a tough park."

Needy frowned. He had shown his new league badge to the park attendant earlier that day and walked all over Robin Field, studying the angles and the shadows, the high fence in right field where balls sometimes stuck in the chicken wire, the sharp corner in left where the play got out of sight unless the third-base umpire was swift in getting back. Needy was not to umpire at third, and he guessed that was why. He was to be at second base, where the plays were often tough and dusty and bruising, but where they fell into a pattern: double play, hit-and-run, steal, force-out, pick-off.

In a way, Needy was glad he was going to be at second. It might force a quick showdown. Tad Roush was the Robin manager. He also was the Robin shortstop. Needy knew Roush firsthand. The two had tangled in the Association five years ago.

Then Carlson broke in. "Not the playing field, son," he said, and Needy smiled thinly. They must have been within five years of the same age. "He means the park. The fans."

And Needy understood. The fans were different here, so Needy had heard, men and women who had become a legend, just as their borough on the wrong side of the muddy river had become a legend. They were fans who came early and started howling long before the first pitch—and Needy could hear them even now through the thick white-tile walls—fifty-two thousand of them, the most vociferous, partisan fans in the world.

Jankowicz said, "They're tough out here, all right." He shook his head and grinned. "I've had my share of beer in my day, but I hate to have it thrown at me."

"With soft tomatoes as a side dish," McQuinn added.

"I've been through it," Needy said quietly.

"Good," McQuinn said. "When you've been through it, you either go one way or the other. You must have gone the right way, boy, or you wouldn't be here today. They don't take chickens or lilies in this league. Now, the other league——" He snorted in contempt.

The other two laughed. Needy knew how each big league thought it was the only league. But Needy wasn't laughing. McQuinn didn't know the real trouble. Needy had seen fans litter the field with vile epithets and pulpy fruit. It had never bothered him much. The real trouble was himself and Roush. McQuinn didn't know about that. Needy doubted that anybody knew about it or remembered. Maybe Roush hadn't remembered. After all, it was an unimportant game, five years back, and Roush had gone a long way since then.

A bell rang softly in the dressing room and the three other men seemed to stiffen a bit, their smiles fading. "Come on," McQuinn said, taking Needy's arm; "let's go meet them." And the four umpires moved swiftly through the door and onto the gravel path, through the exit door next to the Robins' dugout.

They stepped to the plate while the fans called down their stereotyped insults, and Needy grinned. They weren't so tough. And then a raucous voice from the stands yelled, "All right, McQuinn, don't call 'em like you did when the Phils were in last time, you blind bum!" And a snicker filtered from the stands.

Needy stiffened. Lord, he thought, they remembered from one season to the next. They were riding McQuinn for a call he'd made no more recently than last September, at least seven months ago.

Needy stood at the plate, watching the opposing pitchers wheel in their last practice throws, while the ground crew motored its rollers over the moist, sweet-smelling infield dirt, and from the stands came a rising murmur as the new season rushed up.

And Roush came out of the Robin dugout, a prancing man with toed-in steps, head down, a sheet of paper in his hand. The fans saw him and began to roar, and Roush waved his free hand without looking up. From the Titan dugout came Chub Fowler, the line-up in his hand, too, and Needy heard Roush shoot a word at Fowler. The Titan manager's face flushed hot and angry. Roush, Needy knew then, hadn't changed.

Needy moved away from the cluster at the plate so that Roush would have to see him. He wanted that part over quickly. But Roush, head down, pushed by as though he knew he had the center of the stage. He was a showboat, Needy knew, and then, in his grudging heart, he added, *but a hell of a ballplayer*.

Roush stopped and nodded curtly to McQuinn and Carlson and Jankowicz. "Good afternoon, you blind bats," he said softly. Then he turned to Needy. He put his hands on his hips and said, "Hello, choke-up."

Needy felt his throat tighten and he knew the flush was rising to his temples.

McQuinn pushed past Jankowicz, coming chest to chest with Roush. "Cut it," he said quietly, but there was a bristling quality to his voice. "Cut it, I say. I won't stand for your language."

Roush didn't budge a half inch. His voice was as low as McQuinn's, but rasping and hard. "Listen," he said, "when you bums yell play ball, I'll watch my tongue. But right now you're just guests in this house, and my boss owns this house. Until that first pitch comes in, this game is in the hands of the club owners. Not you." He whirled on Needy again, and the venom lay in his throat. "Choke-up Needy, the yellowest umpire ever to call 'em wrong. Too chicken to call 'em as he sees 'em." Then he spun away and stalked off.

McQuinn roared this time. "Roush! Come here." And Roush turned, wide-eyed. "The ground rules," McQuinn said.

Roush waved his hands. "Whatever you say, Mac. We won't need any rules today." And he minced to the dugout.

McQuinn turned to Chub Fowler. He said, "I'm sorry, Chub. The smiling little skipper is off to his usual start."

Fowler growled and handed McQuinn his line-up. "Maybe we'll rub some of it off," he said, and he ambled to the visiting dugout.

Needy watched Fowler, and then he looked at McQuinn, and he froze. The big umpire was staring at him with icy blue eyes. "You're a major-league umpire, Needy," he said. "Act like one."

Needy nodded and tried to say something, but his voice failed him, and then McQuinn waved the three of them to their bases before he bent to the plate, whisk broom in his gnarled hand.

The field was empty except for the four umpires, and then the Robins poured from the dugout, Roush leading them, and the fifty-two thousand fans got up and roared. They stayed standing as the PA system crackled and the announcer said, "Ladies and gentlemen, our national anthem."

But Needy barely heard it. He turned to center field to watch the flag go up into the blue sky, and he remembered. . . .

It hadn't been an important game, though Needy knew now how important it really was. And, more than that, how important they all are, the 10–2 games between a first-place team and a cellar team, and a 2–1 affair between two clubs battling for the lead. To an umpire, they're all the same. Needy knew it now.

It was the end of September, and Roush's club had already clinched the Association flag. They were playing at home, three days before the season would end, most of the regulars resting, but Roush still in there. Roush's team was losing 6–1, though Roush had started one double play and pivoted like a flying ghost on two others, and now, in the bottom of the ninth, with two out, he had hit the ball to the center-field wall for a triple.

It was a hot day, Needy remembered, fearfully hot, and it had been a hot month, a hot summer. Needy was behind the plate, weighted down with mask and protector. Somebody had once said an umpire takes hell, but that the hours couldn't be beat. That was before night ball, Needy thought, and hot days like this.

So he leaned in behind the catcher, the ball-and-strike indicator telling him it was two out, one out away from the dressing room and a quick beer, and the pitcher missed twice with curve balls, as Roush pranced down the line from third base.

Nobody was watching very closely, most of the fans having gone home in the seventh inning when Roush's pitcher was hammered for four runs. Not that there had been many to begin with. Maybe twelve hundred, Needy thought. No more than five hundred still remained.

So, when Roush started down the line and seemed to stumble, Needy hoped he'd come in all the way, for he'd surely be out, and the game would be over. The pitcher hadn't started his motion, but Roush had had a bad start. Then the batter suddenly put his hand to his eyes and stepped out of the box. Four or five times that day, swirling spirals of dust had attacked home plate, and Needy had been forced to call "Time," each time a batter stepped out.

But somehow, as his hand went up and he started to say "Time," he saw Roush continue down the line, and he saw the pitcher quickly throw to the plate. The catcher took the toss, blocked off Roush and put the tag on the runner.

There was a feeble cheer from the stands, and five hundred people slowly began to walk across the field to the exit gates. Roush got up and looked at Needy. He jabbed the edge of his hand against his own throat. "You choke-up rat," he said, "why didn't you call time?"

Needy hadn't said anything, but he knew Roush was right. He had quit on his assignment. It wasn't important whether Roush stole home or not; it was only important that Needy call it as he saw it. And he had seen the batter step out before the pitcher went into action toward the plate. He knew it and Roush knew it, and maybe the batter knew it, but he hadn't seemed to care.

Roush cared. It was baseball, and baseball was life and blood to him. Needy knew he, too, should have cared. He should have called time even then, with the five hundred fans scattered all over the diamond, paper falling to the grass, the bags being ripped up by the ground-keepers. He should have waved his hands and roared until he had controlled them, and then resumed play.

But he hadn't. He had just walked past Roush, trying to reason that it hadn't mattered, that the ball game wouldn't have changed, that the team standings wouldn't have changed. He tried to forget. . . .

And standing here at second base in Robin Field, the flag flapping against the blue sky, he knew he had never forgotten it.

Nor had Roush. The ball came spinning out from behind the

plate, and Roush had it, tossing it to his second baseman, and then turning to Needy.

"Choke-up," he whispered to the umpire. "Chicken minor-leaguer."

Needy knew he didn't have to take it. The game was still not in the umpires' hands, but he was a human being being abused. There wasn't much he could do. But he could answer Roush, fire a hot word at the shortstop to let him know he was alive and fighting back.

Instead he moved behind the bag and slightly to the left of second base, as the first Titan moved in and McQuinn bellowed, "Play ball!" And just as quickly, Roush seemed to forget all about Needy, close to the bag. He bent slightly, his body swaying, his arms hanging, knees slightly hinged, and Needy watched his mouth move and a flow of words waft to the pitcher's mound. The game began.

Needy had heard it said that a major-league baseball game is unlike any minor-league game, no matter the quality of play. Now he believed it. A cloak hung over the field, a shimmering wave of electricity that coursed through the action, crackled in the air with every pitch, rose and fell with hits and outs. And behind the cloak was the booming that whooshed from the stands, like a heavy hand or the ocean rolling in. It was lightning and thunder, Needy thought, the sizzling atmosphere on the diamond and the roaring from the stands.

The Titans scored first. In the fourth inning, the Titan batter, a man named Jewell who batted left-handed and choked up on his stick three inches, pulled a line drive down the first-base line past Rogers, the Robin first baseman, and into the corner where the Robin bull-pen crew sat beneath a sun canopy.

The Robin right fielder raced to the line and into foul territory, took the rolling ball with his gloved hand, whirled and threw into second base. It was a fine throw, but Jewell hooked to the center of the diamond and grabbed off the inside edge of the bag. Needy bent to the play, head through the low cloud of dust, and he spread-eagled his hands.

Instantly Roush was at him, feet stamping, voice raised in indignant clamor, but Needy stood firm and when Roush wouldn't quit, he turned his back and walked away. It was not a serious beef, Needy knew, because Roush knew as well as he that Jewell had beaten the throw. So Roush growled and kicked dirt and went back to his position, and Needy grinned. Roush had played it four-square, fighting a close call against his team, but watching his tongue. Maybe, Needy thought, the Robin manager was going to let bygones be bygones.

The next hitter was Thomas, another left-hander, and though the Robin pitcher threw on the outside, Thomas still dragged his bunt down the first-base line, moving Jewell to third.

And Mayo, the Titans' No. 4 hitter, the league's home-run king and stolen-base leader, hit to the edge of the center-field wall, where Earl Rider had just enough room to make the catch. Jewell sauntered home and the Titans led 1–0.

It stayed that way into the seventh, a 1–0 game that was taking longer to play than any 1–0 game Needy had ever seen. The pitchers violated the twenty-second rule on nearly every pitch, and Needy knew how foolish the rule was.

When Mayo came up, there was always a short conference, and even after it ended, the Robin pitcher would lean in for a full thirty seconds, his eyes boring a path to the plate, trying to find the groove past Mayo's lunging bat. And Earl Rider had the Titan pitcher in the same grip, the long look, the signals shaken off again and again, catcher Festrun calling time and insisting on a pitch while the fans muttered and buzzed and called down their timeless hue.

In the seventh, Roush came up with one out. He slashed two bats at the grass, talking as he minced forward, and then he threw one behind him, and dug himself in.

The Titan pitcher threw, a quick white blur, and Roush was flat on his back. The mutter from the stands grew thick and ugly. But Roush was up, wiping himself off, snarling an obscenity that McQuinn behind the plate pretended he didn't hear. And Roush drilled the next pitch past the Titan pitcher's left ear and into center field.

At first base, Roush pointed his finger at the pitcher, and the Titan came down from the mound two steps to hurl a word at the Robin manager. McQuinn then hustled forward, waving his arms. And time dragged, while the sun faded, dipping to the lip of the stands over first base, lengthening the shadows.

Roush led off from first and taunted the pitcher with three quick steps down the line, drew a throw, and then started his lead again. On the second pitch, he went.

Festrun came out of his crouch with the ball in his clenched fist and he threw, true and swiftly, to the second baseman covering the bag. Needy drifted over, eyes searching, and Roush came in, one leg high. The tag was made and Needy started to go up with his right hand, but then the ball came squirting out of the glove, rolling toward the shortstop. Needy broke off his call and dropped his hands down low, yelling, "Safe, safe!"

The second baseman rolled to his feet and called "Time!" and held up his dripping red wrist.

The Titan doctor came out and cleaned the dirt from the spike wound, and then started to lead the infielder away. But the Titan insisted he could play, and the doctor shrugged, slapped on a piece of plaster and walked away, shaking his head.

Then the second baseman turned to Needy and said, "He kicked me, you know."

Needy nodded. "I guess he did, son. Nothing I can do about it. Kick him back next time," and Roush laughed out loud.

It was part of the game Needy didn't like, but there was nothing anybody ever did to remedy it. It was the way the game was played. There were rules about interference and roughness, but the line could seldom be drawn. So the umpire ignored the contact and watched the bases.

Now Roush led away, and the Titan pitcher threw four times to big Rogers, wasting one, and Rogers swung and missed three times.

The Titan pitcher then took off his glove and wiped his hand with a towel that he directed from the dugout, when Earl Rider took his bent-over stance, waving a big brown bat. And on the first pitch, Needy heard the pitcher groan with the delivery. It was what Casey Stengel liked to call a dead fish, a fast ball, down the pipe, waist high, thrown to Rider's strength.

The ball disappeared over the right-field wall, clearing it by about forty feet, and the Robins led, 2–1.

They stayed that way through the eighth, and Needy looked at his watch and saw that two and a half hours had gone by as they came into the ninth. The public-address announcer made his usual statement about fans' not being allowed on the playing field until all players had reached the dugouts, and the fans made a derisive sound.

It was then Needy realized that the game was nearly over, that Roush was not riding him any more than he was the other umpires. Needy felt suddenly that the problem had somehow resolved itself. He gave a short little laugh, and Roush, twelve feet away, looked at him cold-eyed, his mouth mocking and twisted. Needy felt the afternoon chill, and he knew he was wrong. It wasn't resolved. It wouldn't be until he and Roush had tangled again.

The first man in the ninth was a pinch hitter for the Titan pitcher, a red-faced man with a plug of tobacco in his cheek and the grinning self-confidence of a man who believed no pitcher on earth could get him out. He was Joads, who couldn't catch fly balls and couldn't throw, so he didn't play regularly, but who hit close to .350 in his two hundred at bats each season.

The Robin pitcher tried to curve Joads, but the ball hung on the inside corner, and Joads stroked it off the wall, where the right fielder made a swift recovery, and Joads lumbered into first, the grin still splitting his wide red face. Then he lumbered off again, for a pinch runner, and Roush spoke sharply with his pitcher.

Finally Roush called his catcher, a man named Camps, to the hill and they talked until McQuinn pushed his way to the mound.

Needy heard the big umpire say, "What's it to be, Roush? You sticking with him or you calling in the reliefer?"

Roush said, "I dunno. That's a real tough one."

McQuinn flushed and towered over Roush. "Don't con me," he said. "Make up your mind. I won't stand for any stalling."

Roush said, "Who's stalling? I'm trying to think. Get your beef off me, and I'll be able to figure it out."

McQuinn said quietly, "I'll give you fifteen seconds, Roush."

Roush stared at the sky and squinted, and Needy could see the Robin's manager's lips moving. Needy tried to hide his grin. Roush was actually counting off the seconds.

Then he stopped and said, "I got it. It's the reliefer." He waved to the bull pen with his right hand, and the right-handed knuckle-ball thrower strolled in, carrying his jacket, and began to warm up.

Needy watched from behind second, marveling that Camps could catch such a thing as the reliefer threw. Every one was a knuckler, writhing in mid-air like a drunken butterfly. Then Mc-Quinn held up his hand for the game to pick up where it had stopped, a Titan on first, nobody out, the ninth inning, and the Robins leading, 2–1.

The knuckler got Lark, the Titan lead-off hitter, to go for a chest-high floater, and the Titan hit it straight up in the air. The ball disappeared in Camps' mitt, and there was one out.

But Jewell, who hadn't been stopped all afternoon, singled to right field and the Titan runner fled past Needy into third.

The thunder was two-edged now, the Titan fans who had braved the river and crossed into enemy territory, and the Robins, upset and grumbling as the lead teetered.

Roush raised his hand and yelled "Time!" and turned to the bull pen. He wanted a left-hander to pitch to Thomas.

The sun fell over the edge of the stands, and the field lay in shadow, but lightning still hovered over the players' heads. Needy felt himself waiting with the fans now, impartial as ever concerning the game's outcome, yet intensely interested.

He watched the left-hander, a stocky hurky-jerky man named Lombardo, pitch curve balls to Thomas, but they were breaking too much and too soon, and on six pitches the bases were loaded.

Again Roush stopped the game, and a third time he signaled to the bull pen. The hitter was Mayo, the big, fleet Titan who could do everything so well. And when time was in again, Needy saw that Roush had his team playing halfway. Roush wanted to cut off the tying run at the plate, but he wasn't all the way in. The double play could still be made, though Needy knew that Mayo was as fast a man getting down the line as anybody in baseball.

The new pitcher eyed the bases, Thomas coming off first. The other Titan runners drifted away, and Roush kept darting toward second, feinting Jewell back to the bag. Roush's mouth was still moving, the words flowing to the mound, and Needy felt them hang like drones in the air.

"Come on, boy," Roush was saying. "Come on boy; nobody hits." Then the reliefer took a deep breath and threw hard to Mayo.

It was a fast ball, Needy thought, on the inside, and Mayo started to lunge. The pitch broke. It had not been a fast ball at all, but a curve, thrown hard and loose, fooling the big Titan.

But Mayo somehow got a piece of it, hitting it on a high bounce past the mound, headed for the hole between second base and Roush. Needy moved in toward the bag from behind, seeing Thomas hurtling down the line, Mayo bulleting his way toward first and Roush gliding over, surefooted, a swift ghost on the brown dirt.

The thought crossed Needy's mind that Thomas would be an easy force, once Roush came up with the ball, but the winging Mayo would be a different story. Then Needy banished the thought; his problem lay at second, not first.

Roush reached to his left with his gloved hand while on the dead run eight feet from second base, and then he plucked the ball out with his right hand, leveled his arm back and threw like a rifle to first, a split second before his foot hit second base, kicking dust high into the air.

It was then that Needy's ankle buckled under him and he fell, sprawling heavily while the picture of Roush making his throw before he touched second became frozen-fixed in his mind. Needy never knew that big Rogers, at first, stretched into the diamond while Mayo leaped for the bag. Nor did Needy hear the ball spank into the first baseman's glove, umpire Carlson booming, "He's out!" All Needy heard was the thunder pounding out from the stands as he rolled to his feet to make his call.

But nobody was watching him, the players fleeing to the dugouts, and fifty-two thousand people starting to pour onto the field. Even Roush was gone. Only Thomas was near, sitting on second base, staring up at Needy, openmouthed.

For Needy stood stock-still, arms spread-eagled, yelling, "Safe, safe, safe!" He knew why Thomas couldn't believe the call. Roush had him beaten by five full steps. But Roush had taken the chance that Needy wouldn't have the guts to make the insane call he was now making. Roush had thrown the ball before his foot touched second, and the force play had never been made.

Needy knew it, and he knew why it had happened. He'd have bet his life on it. Roush had seen what he had seen. The shortstop knew that Mayo, moving like a whippet down the first-base line, would beat the throw unless he got rid of the ball right away. The tying run was thundering homeward.

It was McQuinn who finally noticed Needy, still standing at second, arms held out and low, the time-honored sign of a man being called safe.

The big ump charged to second base and said, "What's the matter, man? Are you crazy?"

Needy looked at his chief. The park cops were in a tight cordon at the foul lines, keeping the fans from trampling the young infield grass, but they couldn't keep them from roaming all over the outfield. It was a swirling, still roaring throng, most of them happy, all of them knowing they had seen a fine game, and glad to be on their way home.

"I'm sorry, Mac, but the man is safe."

McQuinn looked at him peculiarly and said, "Roush touched the bag. I saw the dust rise up."

Needy shook his head stubbornly. He thought, *What am I getting into?* The field was strewn with debris. It was like that day five years ago, except a thousand times worse. He said, "He touched the bag after he got rid of the ball. Thomas is safe."

McQuinn started to rub his jaw and then he began to grin, and finally he started to laugh out loud, a bellowing laugh that brought tears to his eyes. "I swear," he said, "if you weren't standing here, I wouldn't believe it. Now what do we do?"

Needy said, "We get the game going again."

McQuinn turned and yelled, "Carl, Janko, come here! This

crazy pup's starting a rhubarb and we'll have to back him up!''
The two umpires raced to second and scratched their heads as
McQuinn filled them in.

Thomas suddenly got up from his perch on second base and said,
"Excuse me, but if I'm safe, is time still in?" He was ready to
keep running.

McQuinn roared. "Hell, no! I call time right now!"

Thomas began to yell to the near-empty Titan dugout. "Hey,
I'm safe, I'm safe!"

Needy said, "And your club is leading three–two."

McQuinn howled, "Now, what the devil does that mean?"

Carlson grinned. "I get him, chief. He means the men on second
and third. They both scored. As a matter of fact," he said, winking
at McQuinn, "I noticed Jewell touch home plate in case you
didn't. The lad's right. The Titans are ahead, three–two."

"And probably piling out of their uniforms this minute," Jankowicz said. "What happens now?"

Needy said, "You boys wouldn't want me to change my decision, would you? Because," he said, "I won't, you know."

A handful of Titans began to drift onto the field. The word began
to spread through the filing throng and Needy heard the first ominous mutter.

Somebody said. "Whaddya mean, the game's not over? Sure it
is."

"No," somebody else said, fifteen feet from second. "That new
jerk of an umpire says Thomas ain't out. They ought to mobilize
the bum."

McQuinn turned to Needy. "All right, bum, take it from here."

Needy said, "It's very simple. The rules don't cover it, but
you're in charge. Make an announcement over the PA that the
game isn't over, that you'll give everybody—fans and players—a
half hour to get back in their seats and to their positions, and that
the game will continue."

Carlson said, "We could have 'em play it off some other time."

Jankowicz grinned. "No," he said. "That's too easy. I like the
lad's idea. . . . Go on, Mac, make the announcement."

"Not me," McQuinn said. "Don't pass the buck to me. Let the
lad do it."

Jankowicz said, "Go to it, boy. I must say you've got guts. Are
they going to love you here!"

Needy shook his head. He knew it didn't matter. Love him or
hate him, it didn't matter. Respect him. That was all. He started to
walk to the Robin dugout to ask where the PA mike was. It would

have been very easy to make the out call, he knew. But he had never even thought of it.

And thirty minutes later, before a crowd gone blood-mad as it heaped abuse on Needy, Tad Roush led his ball club back onto the field.

The shortstop took his post, raised two fingers in the air and called, "Two out, men, two out! We'll get it back!"

Then Roush turned, before his pitcher threw, and said to Needy, "Welcome to the big league, you blind bat." He was grinning. Needy ignored him, to watch the ball game.

THE BIG BLACK
AND WHITE GAME

Ray Bradbury

THE PEOPLE FILLED the stands behind the wire screen, waiting. Us kids, dripping from the lake, ran between the white cottages, past the resort hotel, screaming, and sat on the bleachers, making wet bottom marks. The hot sun beat down through the tall oak trees around the baseball diamond. Our fathers and mothers, in golf pants and light summer dresses, scolded us and made us sit still.

We looked toward the hotel and the back door of the vast kitchen, expectantly. A few colored women began walking across the shade-freckled area between, and in ten minutes the far left section of the bleachers was mellow with the color of their fresh-washed faces and arms. After all these years, whenever I think back on it, I can still hear the sounds they made. The sound on the warm air was like a soft moving of dove voices each time they talked among themselves.

Everybody quickened into amusement, laughter rose right up into the clear blue Wisconsin sky, as the kitchen door flung wide and out ran the big and little, the dark and high-yellar uniformed Negro waiters, janitors, bus boys, boatmen, cooks, bottle washers, soda jerks, gardeners, and golf-link tenders. They came capering, showing their fine white teeth, proud of their new red-striped uniforms, their shiny shoes rising and coming down on the green grass as they skirted the bleachers and drifted with lazy speed out on the field, calling to everybody and everything.

37

Us kids squealed. There was Long Johnson, the lawn-cutting man, and Cavanaugh, the soda-fountain man, and Shorty Smith and Pete Brown and Jiff Miller!

And *there* was Big Poe! Us kids shouted, applauded!

Big Poe was the one who stood so tall by the popcorn machine every night in the million-dollar dance pavilion farther down beyond the hotel on the lake rim. Every night I bought popcorn from Big Poe and he poured lots of butter all over it for me.

I stomped and yelled, "Big Poe! Big Poe!"

And he looked over at me and stretched his lips to bring out his teeth, waved, and shouted a laugh.

And Mama looked to the right, to the left, and back of us with worried eyes and nudged my elbow. "Hush," she said. "Hush."

"Land, land," said the lady next to my mother, fanning herself with a folded paper. "This is quite a day for the colored servants, ain't it? Only time of year they break loose. They look forward all summer to the big Black and White game. But this ain't nothing. You seen their Cake-walk Jamboree?"

"We got tickets for it," said Mother. "For tonight at the pavilion. Cost us a dollar each. That's pretty expensive, I'd say."

"But I always figure," said the woman, "once a year you got to spend. And it's really something to watch them dance. They just naturally got . . ."

"Rhythm," said Mother.

"That's the word," said the lady. "Rhythm. That's what they got. Land, you should see the colored maids up at the hotel. They been buying satin yardage in at the big store in Madison for a month now. And every spare minute they sit sewing and laughing. And I seen some of the feathers they bought for their hats. Mustard and wine ones and blue ones and violet ones. Oh, it'll be a sight!"

"They been airing out their tuxedos," I said. "I saw them hanging on lines behind the hotel all last week!"

"Look at them prance," said Mother. "You'd think they thought they were going to win the game from our men."

The colored men ran back and forth and yelled with their high, fluting voices and their low, lazy, interminable voices. Way out in center field you could see the flash of teeth, their upraised naked black arms swinging and beating their sides as they hopped up and down and ran like rabbits, exuberantly.

Big Poe took a double fistful of bats, bundled them on his huge bull shoulder, and strutted along the first-base line, head back, mouth smiling wide open, his tongue moving, singing:

"—gonna dance out both of my shoes,
When they play them Jelly Roll Blues;
Tomorrow night at the Dark Town Strutters' Ball!"

Up went his knees and down and out, swinging the bats like musical batons. A burst of applause and soft laughter came from the left-hand grandstands, where all the young, ripply colored girls with shiny brown eyes sat eager and easy. They made quick motions that were graceful and mellow because, maybe, of their rich coloring. Their laughter was like shy birds; they waved at Big Poe, and one of them with a high voice cried, "Oh, Big Poe! Oh, Big Poe!"

The white section joined politely in the applause as Big Poe finished his cakewalk. "Hey, Poe!" I yelled again.

"Stop that, Douglas!" said Mother, straight at me.

Now the white men came running between the trees with their uniforms on. There was a great thunder and shouting and rising up in our grandstand. The white men ran across the green diamond, flashing white.

"Oh, there's Uncle George!" said Mother. "My, doesn't he look nice?" And there was my uncle George toddling along in his outfit which didn't quite fit because Uncle has a potbelly, and jowls that sit out over any collar he puts on. He was hurrying along, trying to breathe and smile at the same time, lifting up his pudgy little legs. "My, they look *so* nice," enthused Mother.

I sat there, watching their movements. Mother sat beside me, and I think she was comparing and thinking, too, and what she saw amazed and disconcerted her. How easily the dark people had come running first, like those slow-motion deer and buck antelopes in those African moving pictures, like things in dreams. They came like beautiful brown, shiny animals that didn't know they were alive, but lived. And when they ran and put their easy, lazy, timeless legs out and followed them with their big, sprawling arms and loose fingers and smiled in the blowing wind, their expressions didn't say, "Look at *me* run, look at *me* run!" No, not at all. Their faces dreamily said, "Lord, but it's sure nice to run. See the ground swell soft under me? Gosh, I feel good. My muscles are moving like oil on my bones and it's the best pleasure in the world to run." And they ran. There was no purpose to their running but exhilaration and living.

The white men worked at their running as they worked at everything. You felt embarrassed for them because they were alive too much in the wrong way. Always looking from the corners of their eyes to see if you were watching. The Negroes didn't care if you watched or not; they went on living, moving. They were so sure of playing that they didn't have to think about it any more.

"My, but our men look so nice," said my mother, repeating herself rather flatly. She had seen, compared the teams. Inside, she realized how laxly the colored men hung swaying in their uniforms, and how tensely, nervously, the white men were crammed, shoved, and belted into *their* outfits.

I guess the tenseness began then.

I guess everybody saw what was happening. They saw how the white men looked like senators in sun suits. And they admired the graceful unawareness of the colored men. And, as is always the case, that admiration turned to envy, to jealousy, to irritation. It turned to conversation like:

"That's my husband, Tom, on third base. Why doesn't he pick up his feet? He just *stands* there."

"Never you mind, never you mind. He'll pick 'em up when the time comes!"

"That's what *I* say! Now, take my Henry, for instance. Henry mightn't be active all the time, but when there's a crisis—just you *watch* him. Uh—I do wish he'd wave or something, though. Oh, *there!* Hello, Henry!"

"Look at that Jimmie Cosner playing around out there!"

I looked. A medium-sized white man with a freckled face and red hair was clowning on the diamond. He was balancing a bat on his forehead. There was laughter from the white grandstand. But it sounded like the kind of laughter you laugh when you're embarrassed for someone.

"Play ball!" said the umpire.

A coin was flipped. The colored men batted first.

"Darn it," said my mother.

The colored men ran in from the field happily.

Big Poe was first to bat. I cheered. He picked up the bat in one hand like a toothpick and idled over to the plate and laid the bat on his thick shoulder, smiling along its polished surface toward the stands where the colored women sat with their fresh flowery cream dresses stirring over their legs, which hung down between the seat intervals like crisp new sticks of ginger; their hair was all fancily spun and hung over their ears. Big Poe looked in particular at the little, dainty-as-a-chicken-bone shape of his girl friend Katherine. She was the one who made the beds at the hotel and cottages every morning, who tapped on your door like a bird and politely asked if you was done dreaming, 'cause if you was she'd clean away all them old nightmares and bring in a fresh batch—please use them *one* at a time, thank yoah. Big Poe shook his head, looking at her, as if he couldn't believe she was there. Then he turned, one hand balancing the bat, his left hand dangling free at his side, to await the trial pitches. They hissed past, spatted into the open mouth of the catcher's mitt, were hurled back. The umpire grunted. The next pitch was the starter.

Big Poe let the first ball go by him.

"Stee-rike!" announced the umpire. Big Poe winked good-naturedly at the white folks. Bang! "Stee-rike two!" cried the umpire.

The ball came for the third time.

Big Poe was suddenly a greased machine pivoting; the dangling hand swept up to the butt end of the bat, the bat swiveled, connected with the ball—*Whack!* The ball shot up into the sky, away down toward the wavering line of oak trees, down toward the lake, where a white sailboat slid silently by. The crowd yelled, me loudest! There went Uncle George, running on his stubby, wool-stockinged legs, getting smaller with distance.

Big Poe stood for a moment watching the ball go. Then he began to run. He went around the bases, loping, and on the way home from third base he waved to the colored girls naturally and happily and they waved back, standing on their seats and shrilling.

Ten minutes later, with the bases loaded and run after run being driven in, and Big Poe coming to bat again, my mother turned to me. "They're the most inconsiderate people," she said.

"But that's the game," I said. "They've only got two outs."

"But the score's seven to nothing," my mother protested.

"Well, just you wait until *our* men come to bat," said the lady next to my mother, waving away a fly with a pale blue-veined hand. "Those Negroes are too big for their britches."

"Stee-rike two!" said the umpire as Big Poe swung.

"All the past week at the hotel," said the woman next to my mother, staring out at Big Poe steadily, "the hotel service has been simply terrible. Those maids don't talk about a thing save the Cakewalk Jamboree, and whenever you want ice water it takes them half an hour to fetch it, they're so busy sewing."

"Ball one!" said the umpire.

The woman fussed. "I'll be glad when this week's over, that's what I got to say," she said.

"Ball two!" said the umpire to Big Poe.

"Are they going to *walk* him?" asked my mother of me. "Are they crazy?" To the woman next to her: "That's right. They been acting funny all week. Last night I had to tell Big Poe twice to put extra butter on my popcorn. I guess he was trying to save money or something.''

''Ball three!'' said the umpire.

The lady next to my mother cried out suddenly and fanned herself furiously with her newspaper. ''Land, I just *thought*. Wouldn't it be awful if they *won* the game? They *might,* you know. They might do it.''

My mother looked at the lake, at the trees, at her hands. ''I don't know why Uncle George had to play. Make a fool of himself. Douglas, you run tell him to quit right now. It's bad on his heart.''

''You're out!'' cried the umpire to Big Poe.

''Ah,'' sighed the grandstand.

The side was retired. Big Poe laid down his bat gently and walked along the base line. The white men pattered in from the field looking red and irritable, with big islands of sweat under their armpits. Big Poe looked over at me. I winked at him. He winked back. Then I knew he wasn't so dumb.

He'd struck out on purpose.

Long Johnson was going to pitch for the colored team.

He ambled out to the rubber, worked his fingers around in his fists to limber them up.

First white man to bat was a man named Kodimer, who sold suits in Chicago all year round.

Long Johnson fed them over the plate with tired, unassuming, controlled accuracy.

Mr. Kodimer chopped. Mr. Kodimer swatted. Finally Mr. Kodimer bunted the ball down the third-base line.

''Out at first base,'' said the umpire, an Irishman named Mahoney.

Second man up was a young Swede named Moberg. He hit a high fly to center field which was taken by a little plump Negro who didn't look fat because he moved around like a smooth, round glob of mercury.

Third man up was a Milwaukee truck driver. He whammed a line drive to center field. It was good. Except that he tried to stretch it into a two-bagger. When he pulled up at second base, there was Emancipated Smith with a white pellet in his dark, dark hand, waiting.

My mother sank back in her seat, exhaling. ''Well, I *never!*''

''It's getting hotter,'' said the lady elbow-next. ''Think I'll go for a stroll by the lake soon. It's too hot to sit and watch a silly game today. Mightn't you come along with me, missus?'' she asked Mother.

It went on that way for five innings.

It was eleven to nothing and Big Poe had struck out three times on purpose, and in the last half of the fifth was when Jimmie Cosner came to bat for our side again. He'd been trying all afternoon, clowning, giving directions, telling everybody just where he was going to blast that pill once he got hold of it. He swaggered up toward the plate now, confident and bugle-voiced. He swung six bats in his thin hands, eyeing them critically with his shiny green little eyes. He chose one, dropped the others, ran to the plate, chopping out little islands of green fresh lawn with his cleated heels. He pushed his cap back on his dusty red hair. "Watch this!" he called out loud to the ladies. "You watch me show these dark boys! Ya-hah!"

Long Johnson on the mound did a slow serpentine windup. It was like a snake on a limb of a tree, uncoiling, suddenly darting at you. Instantly Johnson's hand was in front of him, open, like black fangs, empty. And the white pill slashed across the plate with a sound like a razor.

"Stee-rike!"

Jimmie Cosner put his bat down and stood glaring at the umpire. He said nothing for a long time. Then he spat deliberately near the catcher's foot, took up the yellow maple bat again, and swung it so the sun glinted the rim of it in a nervous halo. He twitched and sidled it on his thin-boned shoulder, and his mouth opened and shut over his long nicotined teeth.

Clap! went the catcher's mitt.

Cosner turned, stared.

The catcher, like a black magician, his white teeth gleaming, opened up his oily glove. There, like a white flower growing, was the baseball.

"Stee-rike two!" said the umpire, far away in the heat.

Jimmie Cosner laid his bat across the plate and hunched his freckled hands on his hips. "You mean to tell me that was a strike?"

"That's what I said," said the umpire. "Pick up the bat."

"To hit you on the head with," said Cosner sharply.

"Play ball or hit the showers!"

Jimmie Cosner worked his mouth to collect enough saliva to spit, then angrily swallowed it, swore a bitter oath instead. Reaching down, he raised the bat, poised it like a musket on his shoulder.

And here came the ball! It started out small and wound up big in front of him. Powie! An explosion off the yellow bat. The ball spiraled up and up. Jimmie lit out for first base. The ball paused, as if thinking about gravity up there in the sky. A wave came in on the shore of the lake and fell down. The crowd yelled. Jimmie ran. The ball made its decision, came down. A lithe high-yellar was under it, fumbled it. The ball spilled to the turf, was plucked up, hurled to first base.

Jimmie saw he was going to be out. So he jumped feet-first at the base.

Everyone saw his cleats go into Big Poe's ankle. Everybody saw the red blood. Everybody heard the shout, the shriek, saw the heavy clouds of dust rising.

"I'm safe!" protested Jimmie two minutes later.

Big Poe sat on the ground. The entire dark team stood around him. The doctor bent down, probed Big Poe's ankle, saying, "Mmmm," and "Pretty bad. Here." And he swabbed medicine on it and put a white bandage on it.

The umpire gave Cosner the cold-water eye. "Hit the showers!"

"Like hell!" said Cosner. And he stood on that first base, blowing his cheeks out and in, his freckled hands swaying at his sides. "I'm safe. I'm stayin' right here, by God! No nigger put *me* out!"

"No," said the umpire. "A white man did. *Me. Get!*"

"He dropped the ball! Look up the rules! I'm safe!"

The umpire and Cosner stood glaring at each other.

Big Poe looked up from having his swollen ankle tended. His voice was thick and gentle and his eyes examined Jimmie Cosner gently.

"Yes, he's safe, Mr. Umpire. Leave him stay. He's safe."

I was standing right there. I heard the whole thing. Me and some other kids had run out on the field to see. My mother kept calling me to come back to the stands.

"Yes, he's safe," said Big Poe again.

All the colored men let out a yell.

"What'sa matter with you, black boy? You get hit in the head?"

"You heard me," replied Big Poe quietly. He looked at the doctor bandaging him. "He's safe. Leave him stay."

The umpire swore.

"Okay, okay. So he's safe!"

The umpire stalked off, his back stiff, his neck red.

Big Poe was helped up. "Better not walk on that," cautioned the doctor.

"I can walk," whispered Big Poe carefully.

"Better not play."

"I can play," said Big Poe gently, certainly, shaking his head, wet streaks drying under his white eyes. "I'll play *good*." He looked no place at all. "I'll play plenty good."

"Oh," said the second-base colored man. It was a funny sound.

All the colored men looked at each other, at Big Poe, then at Jimmie Cosner, at the sky, at the lake, the crowd. They walked off quietly to take their places. Big Poe stood with his bad foot hardly touching the ground, balanced. The doctor argued. But Big Poe waved him away.

"Batter up!" cried the umpire.

We got settled in the stands again. My mother pinched my leg and asked me why I couldn't sit still. It got warmer. Three or four more waves fell on the shore line. Behind the wire screen the ladies fanned their wet faces and the men inched their rumps forward on the wooden planks, held papers over their scowling brows to see Big Poe standing like a redwood tree out there on first base, Jimmie Cosner standing in the immense shade of that dark tree.

Young Moberg came up to bat for our side.

"Come on, Swede, come on, Swede!" was the cry, a lonely cry, like a dry bird, from out on the blazing green turf. It was Jimmie Cosner calling. The grandstand stared at him. The dark heads turned on their moist pivots in the outfield; the black faces came in his direction, looking him over, seeing his thin, nervously arched back. He was the center of the universe.

"Come on, Swede! Let's show these black boys!" laughed Cosner.

He trailed off. There was complete silence. Only the wind came through the high, glittering trees.

"Come on, Swede, hang one on that old pill. . . . "

Long Johnson, on the pitcher's mound, cocked his head. Slowly, deliberately, he eyed Cosner. A look passed between him and Big Poe, and Jimmie Cosner saw the look and shut up and swallowed, hard.

Long Johnson took his time with his windup.

Cosner took a lead off base.

Long Johnson stopped loading his pitch.

Cosner skipped back to the bag, kissed his hand, and patted the kiss dead center on the bag. Then he looked up and smiled around.

Again the pitcher coiled up his long, hinged arm, curled loving dark fingers on the leather pellet, drew it back and—Cosner danced off first base. Cosner jumped up and down like a monkey. The pitcher did not look at him. The pitcher's eyes watched secretively, slyly, amusedly, sidewise. Then, snapping his head, the pitcher scared Cosner back to the bag. Cosner stood and jeered.

The third time Long Johnson made as if to pitch, Cosner was far off the bag and running toward second.

Snap went the pitcher's hand. Boom went the ball in Big Poe's glove at first base.

Everything was sort of frozen. Just for a second.

There was the sun in the sky, the lake and the boats on it, the grandstands, the pitcher on his mound standing with his hand out and down after tossing the ball; there was Big Poe with the ball in his mighty black hand; there was the infield staring, crouching in at the scene, and there was Jimmie Cosner running, kicking up dirt, the only moving thing in the entire summer world.

Big Poe leaned forward, sighted toward second base, drew back his mighty right hand, and hurled that white baseball straight down along the line until it reached Jimmie Cosner's head.

Next instant, the spell was broken.

Jimmie Cosner lay flat on the burning grass. People boiled out of the grandstands. There was swearing, and women screaming, a clattering of wood as the men rushed down the wooden boards of the bleachers. The colored team ran in from the field. Jimmie Cosner lay there. Big Poe, no expression on his face, limped off the field, pushing white men away from him like clothespins when they tried stopping him. He just picked them up and threw them away.

"Come on, Douglas!" shrieked Mother, grabbing me. "Let's get home! They might have razors! Oh!"

That night, after the near riot of the afternoon, my folks stayed home reading magazines. All the cottages around us were lighted. Everybody was home. Distantly I heard music. I slipped out the back door into the ripe summernight darkness and ran toward the dance pavilion. All the lights were on, and music played.

But there were no white people at the tables. Nobody had come to the Jamboree.

There were only colored folks. Women in bright red and blue satin gowns and net stockings and soft gloves, with wine-plume hats, and men in glossy tuxedos. The music crashed out, up, down, and around the floor. And laughing and stepping high, flinging their polished shoes out and up in the cakewalk, were Long Johnson and Cavanaugh and Jiff Miller and Pete Brown, and—limping— Big Poe and Katherine, his girl, and all the other lawn-cutters and boatmen and janitors and chambermaids, all on the floor at one time.

It was so dark all around the pavilion; the stars shone in the black sky, and I stood outside, my nose against the window, looking in for a long, long time, silently.

I went to bed without telling anyone what I'd seen.

I just lay in the dark smelling the ripe apples in the dimness and hearing the lake at night and listening to that distant, faint and wonderful music. Just before I slept I heard those last strains again:

> "—gonna dance out both of my shoes,
> When they play those Jelly Roll Blues;
> Tomorrow night at the Dark Town Strutters' Ball!"

A MOST
UNUSUAL SEASON

Willard H. Temple

O NE THING ABOUT the war, it gives a baseball manager the best alibi in the world. When Sam Hartman, the owner, asks me what we got this year, I tell him it's a dream team and naturally I mean nightmare. We start out last winter with twenty-three players and five of them are down on the farm, and they get billets-doux from the draft board telling them to stay down on the farm or else.

Slip Hennessey, our first baseman, is drafted, and likewise Pete Wilmot and Louis Ferrazi, and Jumbo Rourke is in a shipyard, and when we come up to the line we got a collection of old men and Four-Fs, and when on opening day they march out to the flagpole for ceremonies, I just hope nobody collapses on the way from the exertion.

But we manage to nab Moose Cullen. They don't want the Moose in the Army, and this is largely on account of his feet, because they are the flattest feet in captivity as well as the biggest, and when he takes his physical, the doc asks him will he consider leaving his feet to medical science when he gets thumbed out for the last time. This irritates the Moose very much, because he is not only sensitive about his dogs, but also raring to get in the Army, and in fact the doc is lucky the Moose does not tramp all over him.

But we keep him, and while the Moose is not a guy who could catch an apple in a washtub, he is a great guy with that stick, and on opening day he gets two singles and a double which would have been an inside-the-park home run even for Ernie Lombardi. And while he lets in three runs by waving at balls that go by first, he drives in four, and I figure we are off for the first division at that.

And everything is swell for us until one night when the Moose goes to one of those dance halls where they have hostesses. The Moose is a great lover of dancing, but is somewhat handicapped by the fact that no girls will dance with him, which I got to admit is a problem, because a guy cannot go around dancing by himself without people making remarks about him. It is not that the girls find the Moose objectionable, because he is quite handsome, and not a yes-and-no guy like a lot of ballplayers, but has a pretty fair line of chatter and, they tell me, even read a book one time when he was rained out five days running in Little Rock.

But it seems that the girls in the dance halls are afraid of being stepped on by the Moose's big feet, and they figure it is too much of an occupational hazard to dance with the Moose, because if he ever plants one of his fourteen-and-a-half-D shoes on her foot, the hostess will have to make a living the rest of her life sitting down or maybe dancing on one foot, which is frowned upon in the higher-class dance halls which the Moose frequents, being a guy who insists on everything Grade A.

So when the Moose asks a hostess to dance they all suggest he sit this one out, and it goes to show the Moose is different, because the average ballplayer can sit like the Sphinx, but the Moose loves to dance, particularly the rumba, and is very discouraged when the girls ask him to sit down. And so, of course, he is very delighted when he runs across a girl who is willing to dance with him.

The girl's name is Mabel Sussman and she even seems to enjoy dancing with the Moose, and she tells me one time that it makes dancing more exciting when you know if you make a wrong move it costs you a foot.

And in fact Mabel is not only fast on her feet on a dance floor, but she is the same Mabel Sussman who is once a professional track star and golfer, and who has to retire because after cleaning up on all the women no men will take her on. And before I meet Mabel I figure she will look about as feminine as a General Grant tank, but she is only about five feet three in her nylons and a neat little trick, if you like them wiry and are not particular about curves.

So it is very natural that the Moose should fall in love with Mabel, and she seems to like him too, but she tells him she couldn't consider marriage until after the war. The reason for this is that

Mabel is very patriotic. She figures it is her duty to be nice to soldiers in town on leave, and it seems she has been doing this ever since Pearl Harbor, and comes pretty close to being the sweetheart of the Army, Navy, and Marines, as well as Coast Guard.

"It never happened to anybody else," says the Moose to me. "I got to compete with maybe five million guys or more."

"She ain't in love with any of them," I say. "She's just being patriotic."

"If I had on a uniform instead of this monkey suit," he says, "she'd be Mrs. Moose Cullen. Suppose she does marry me after the war, it ain't like she's marrying a serviceman; it's just like she cheated all those guys. Most likely she'd get to brooding on it."

And it's at this time that my troubles commence. Because the dance hall don't open until night, and every afternoon Mabel is out being patriotic to some serviceman on leave, and what does she do but bring them out to the ball park and sit back of first base in a box. And the first time she does this my worries begin.

In the first inning the Moose hits one off the wall in right, and by hard running manages to get to first ahead of the relay. He steps off the bag and looks toward the stands and sees Mabel in the box with a major and just when he looks the major is holding Mabel's hand and the pitcher lobs the ball and the Moose is caught off by ten feet and don't even hear the coach screaming at him to get back.

The Moose says to me, "If that guy was a civilian I would make him hard to catch, but I can't go around popping no guys in uniform. When you come right down to it," says the Moose, "that guy is fighting so a lug like me can keep on playing ball."

And the very next day Mabel is in the park with a lieutenant and it is a tight game, and in the ninth we got a one-run lead with the other side up. They get two on and two out, and the batter hits a pop fly over by the stands. It's so high that even the Moose can get under it in time.

He plants himself there and Mabel and the lieutenant are in front of him, and I think the game is over, and then wonder if the Moose is crazy, because he just stands there and the ball comes down and hits him on the noggin and bounces fifty feet in the stands. This gives the batter a life and he hits the next pitch over the roof and we lose the game, and in the dressing room I give the Moose fits.

"The guy had lipstick on his ear," says the Moose.

Well, I call up Mabel and tell her the least she can do is be a little more subtle, and she says indignantly that it wasn't lipstick on the lieutenant's ear but blood where he cut himself shaving, but by then the damage is done, and two days later she comes in with a bomber crew and the Moose hits into four double plays.

"Y'know," he says to me, "I ain't never going to marry Mabel. She's had seven hunnert and sixty-three proposals. Now those guys know they can't all win, and they don't mind too much losing, but think how they'll feel if they lost to a civilian Four-F. And because I think a lot of those service guys myself, I wouldn't propose to Mabel until the war is over and those guys get another chance to propose."

"If she loves you," I say, "she'll wait."

The Moose shakes his head. "She loves me," he said, "but she's awful patriotic."

I hope it will be better when we hit the road. But Chicago is the first stop and the manager of the Chicago team is Eddie Sykes and the league's worst barber. In our half of the first inning Clayton walks, is sacrificed to second, and after Finney pops to left, the Moose is up. And I know he can hit this Chicago cousin with his eyes closed. But just as he gets set for the first pitch, Eddie Sykes sticks his head out of the dugout and yells, "Where's Mabel?" and the Moose turns around and don't even see the fast pitch that cuts the plate for a strike.

The Moose finally gets set again and the Chicago pitcher tells him where Mabel is, and the Moose throws his bat at him and comes within a quarter of an inch of making the Chicago pitcher a permanent Four-F. And the umpire gives the Moose the old heave-ho.

I look along the bench and old Slag Carter is sitting there with his hands across his stomach, and Slag was a pretty fair pitcher twenty years ago and figured that this year he might as well sleep in a dugout and get paid for it. So I say, "Did you ever play first?" and Slag opens his eyes and looks at me in horror and says he don't feel good and it was probably something he et on the train last night, but he plays first anyway. I don't really mean he plays first, but he goes down to the bag and puts on the glove and stands there the rest of the game anyway.

When we go in the locker room after the game the Moose is on the long-distance telephone and Mabel ain't in, and the Moose puts in a call every twenty minutes, but he can't find Mabel. And everywhere we go on the road, the other teams ask him where is Mabel, and not only that, but they tell him, and the Moose goes twenty-three times without a hit, and Sam Hartman comes out to see me.

"You told me his hitting would make up for his fielding," says Sam. "You know what he's hitting?"

"I know," I say, "but I wouldn't repeat it out loud."

"It'll be better when we get back home," I say, but I don't even believe this myself, and when we get back, it is the same story, with the Moose keeping half an eye on the ball game, and the other eye and a half on Mabel and the armed forces.

We give him all sorts of fight talks and tell him how there are boys across the water listening to him stink by short wave and he is letting them down as well as the ball club and is practically acting like a Jappo toward our loyal rooters in the armed services, and it don't do any good.

But what finally drives me crazy is when the Moose starts waking me up every night. Now, in these days we do not have many training rules because they are apt to irk a ballplayer and these days we do not want to irk any guy that can climb into a uniform, although what I am going to do to some of these monkeys after the war is nobody's business. But anyway, the training rules are relaxed, and if a player wants to stay out a little late, so long as he stays awake on the ball field, I don't jump him.

But when the Moose wakes me up four nights running at 2:30 A. M., it is the last straw. The Moose wakes me up each night by dropping his shoes, and the first night I think we have finally been bombed and am halfway under the bed before I realize the Moose rooms just above me.

And after he has done this to me four nights, the next day, after he blows another ball game, I corner him in the office, and find out that he is dancing every night and don't get in until two thirty.

"Bawl me out later," he says. "I'm in a rush. I gotta go see Mabel."

"You can't dance from now until two thirty," I say. "It ain't humanly possible, although, I admit you didn't get no exercise at first this afternoon."

"It ain't a dance," he says. "It's a softball game. Mabel's playing in it. It's a benefit, a couple of girls' softball teams. Why don't you come along?"

Well, I go along because I figure I can stand a laugh, and it is funny, at that, but Mabel does all right out on third. I mean she throws like a man and don't let nothing get by her and makes four straight hits. It don't mean anything to me at the time, but when I wake up at two thirty the next night when the Moose drops his shoes, the idea pops right into my noggin.

I tell myself I am nuts, but fate steps in. We have had three third basemen this year and none of them acts like they ever met up with the bag before, and the next afternoon my current ingénu hits a ball past the infield and is so surprised he trips over first base, not being familiar with it, and breaks his ankle.

So Sam Hartman comes into my office after the game and chews a couple aspirin and says, "There ain't a third baseman in the country between the ages of sixteen and sixty-five."

"I got a prospect," I say.

"Huh?" he gasps. "What's his name?"

"The name," I say, "is Mabel Sussman."

"No," he says, shaking his head. "No guy with a girl's front name could play ball in this league." Then he stares at me. "Mabel Sussman," he says, "is a girl. Moose Cullen's girl. The trouble with you is you been standing out in the hot sun too long." And he starts backing slowly away from me. "Don't take it to heart," he says, "they can cure most anything these days. Don't act violent. I'm your friend, Sam Hartman, and I'll take care of you."

"There's nobody else," I say. "And there's no law against it. Look it up. Besides, even if she can't play, it'll help the Moose."

Well, he ain't got any other solution and finally we go see Mabel and put it up to her, thinking maybe she will send for a squad car. "Why, listen," she says. "You haven't had a third sacker yet who could go to his left. Why, in high school," she says, "I was the best player they had, but the boys wouldn't let me on the team."

So we sign her up, but although there's no rule against women, we decide to play it safe and let the news out that we come across a promising seventeen-year-old ballplayer named Babe Hurst—this last being her middle name—and we get her a boy's haircut. And after a few days' practice she is ready to make her debut. I got to admit that some of the boys object a little, and there is a little locker-room problem, but we solve this by giving Mabel my office as a dressing room and keep Slag Carter at the door acting as guard.

We got our fingers crossed when we put her in a game, but in a baseball suit she don't look like anything but a sawed-off rookie, and her being built straight up and down helps, and the baseball cap completes the illusion.

The team we are playing naturally start to give her the business like they do any rookie, and Terry Plant leads off and dumps a bunt toward third.

The ball goes bouncing across the grass, and then I see a streak of white and Mabel snags it in one hand, and *pouf!* A bullet hits the Moose's glove three steps ahead of Plant. In his box, Sam Hartman grins and stops chewing his straw hat, and on first the Moose grins a yard wide.

Well, finally we win a game. And while Mabel don't get any hits she handles third base like she seen it before, and what makes me happy is that the Moose finally snaps out of it, and in the seventh with the bags loaded, he pokes one four hundred feet over the right field wall.

So on we go and I think my problems are solved. Mabel will never become much of a hitter, but she has a good eye and is so small she is hard to pitch to and gets walked now and again, and I don't care about the hitting because the Moose goes on a rampage and lambastes everything that comes within reach of his big bat. In fact we win nine straight games and are on top of the world when the Sox come to town.

The Sox go down in order to start the opener, and in our half of the first we get a man on and the Moose steps in. Eddie Sykes sticks his head out of the dugout and bawls, "Hey, Moose, what happened to Mabel? She ain't in the stands today. The fleet must be in. You know them sailors, Moose."

And the Moose grins lazy like and hits a fast curve in the middle of the break and knocks it clean out past the flagpole.

"Well," says Eddie Sykes, loud enough for me to hear, "the dope must have fallen out of love. That gag won't work any more."

But Eddie is not a guy to keep quiet, and between innings when he walks out to third he begins to ride Mabel, just giving it to a rookie like they do. And the first thing he does is put his hand on Mabel's cheek and say, "When you going to start shaving, sonny boy? You got a skin like a peach. You're a cute little thing. Pretty soon you'll be able to blow your own nose."

Now, we have instructed Mabel never to open her yap on the ball field, because the first time she talks it will be a dead give-away, so she don't say anything, although I can see she has a terrible struggle.

She is up the next inning, the eighth, and when she steps in the box, Eddie Sykes leans out of the dugout.

"Hey, ladder legs," he says, "ain't your mommy learned you to talk yet?"

"Who's he calling ladder legs?" growls the Moose, reaching for a bat. "I'll teach that blubbermouth some manners. I'll ladder-legs him—"

"Don't let that lug worry you," I say, hauling him back into the dugout.

"He's insulting a lady, the bum," roars the Moose.

"He don't know she's a lady. Siddown," I say.

Mabel strikes out and comes back to the bench with fire in her eye. "I'm liable to forget myself and get my hands in that bird's hair," she says.

"He ain't got any hair left," I say. "Forget him."

"I'll pertect you, Mabel," says the Moose.

And sitting there I get a feeling like this thing is too big for me, like a guy in a tar-paper shack must feel when he sees a twister coming across the plains. There ain't nothing left but the power of prayer.

And in addition to Sykes some fat-faced guy in a box leans out and with a foghorn voice begins hollering at Mabel.

"You ain't good enough to play in the Bloomer Girls' League!" he yells and he don't know how wrong he is.

But this is the first time the wolves in the stands start riding Mabel, and when she goes out to third Eddie Sykes gives it to her. I can't hear what he's saying, but I can see her blush, and pretty soon an easy ground ball goes right through her mitts.

They bunt her on the next play and she throws the ball ten feet over the Moose's head. Then the foghorn fat face in the stands turns on the heat and the Moose bawls at him to shut up.

"Now listen to that," says Eddie Sykes loud enough for Moose to hear. "Ain't that nice? Are you the nursemaid for this innocent child, Moose? I bet you even tuck the Babe in bed each night."

"That's enough out of you," roars the Moose, turning purple and charging across the infield.

I intercept the Moose just past the pitcher's·mound and calm him down a little and protest to the umpire that I thought this was a gentleman's game, and ask him what he's getting paid for.

But of course I get no sympathy from the ump. "Nobody has insulted me yet," he says. "Play ball."

The Sox got the rally going and on the next play the Moose manages to get in front of a fast hopper and he makes the peg to third to cut off the runner. Well, the ball gets there in time, but something Eddie Sykes says makes Mabel forget about it. In fact she don't even try to catch it, but opens up her mouth on the field for the first and last time.

"That's no way to address a lady," she says.

And I am wrong when I say Eddie Sykes has no hair left, because he has a fringe, and it is long enough for Mabel to get one hand in it and hang on, while she is slapping him silly with the other. The Moose rushes over and is halfway there when the foghorn guy in the stands yells, "Kill the bum, Eddie!"

The Moose hesitates, then charges into the stands, looking as big as a Flying Fortress and, for all his flat feet, going almost as fast. And the last I see of the Moose is his back going out of the gates with the fat guy beating him to the exit by a short neck.

And the Moose is out of the ball game of course, and Mabel is out, and Eddie Sykes and three or four other guys who start punching each other just to get into the spirit of the thing.

So we go on and manage to win the game anyway, and a couple hours later the Moose comes in our hotel grinning from ear to ear. "I caught him," he says, disappearing into the elevator.

Right away Sam Hartman decides to keep Mabel out for a few days, because nobody has caught on yet, so we give her a couple days' rest, and Eddie Sykes goes around looking very thoughtful and saying nothing, which is most unusual for him.

Then the last day of the series the Moose doesn't show up for the game, and I don't see him until seven that night, when he comes in the hotel with Mabel.

"Congratulate us," he says. "We got married."

So I say, "Well, Mabel, I hope you'll be very happy, although I am surprised you married a civilian."

"She didn't," says the Moose. "You remember that guy I chased out of the stands? Well, he's on my draft board, and whether he did it for spite, or whether it come natural, I'll never know, but I got called back for a re-examination. And I passed. I'm in the Army."

"His feet are much better," says Mabel. "The doctor said it might have been all that dancing that strengthened his arches."

"I owe it all to the little woman," says the Moose. "I'm sorry about leaving the ball club, but I got to go help my country; and I'm also sorry, but I can't let Mabel play with you no more. Ladies' softball teams are O. K., but the majors are not refined enough for my wife, especially without me there."

So there goes half my infield. And that night I give a short interview to the press saying that baseball will carry on under all obstacles, and when they ask what happens to Babe, I say the Babe went home to the family and retired, which is not out of line either.

And that night I am musing in a lobby chair when Eddie Sykes comes along, and he looks pretty good now, with most of the scratches healed.

"Too bad you had to let that little third baseman go," he says.

"Wasn't it?" I say.

"Nicknamed Babe," he says very casual. "What did you say the first name was?"

"I didn't say," I tell him, looking him straight in the eye.

"Oh, well," he says, "It's a most unusual season, like they say in California."

So I don't know if he knows or not. But I got suspicious. Because he sends them a very fancy cut-glass candy dish for a wedding present and on the card he writes, "To Moose and Mabel, from Eddie Sykes, your old pal, first, third and always."

THE MIGHTY CASEY

Rod Serling

T HERE IS A LARGE, extremely decrepit stadium overgrown by weeds and high grass that is called, whenever it is referred to (which is seldom nowadays), Tebbet's Field, and it lies in a borough of New York known as Brooklyn. Many years ago it was a baseball stadium housing a ball club known as the Brooklyn Dodgers, a major league baseball team then a part of the National League. Tebbet's Field today, as we've already mentioned, houses nothing but memories, a few ghosts and tier after tier of decaying wooden seats and cracked concrete floors. In its vast, gaunt emptiness nothing stirs except the high grass of what once was an infield and an outfield, in addition to a wind that whistles through the screen behind home plate and howls up to the rafters of the overhang of the grandstand.

This was one helluva place in its day, and in its day, the Brooklyn Dodgers was one rip-roaring ball club. In the last several years of its existence, however, it was referred to by most of the ticket-buying, turnstile-passers of Flatbush Avenue as "the shlumpfs!" This arose from the fact that for five years running the Brooklyn Dodgers were something less than spectacular. In their last year as members of the National League, they won exactly forty-nine ball games. And by mid-August of that campaign a "crowd" at Tebbet's Field was considered to be any ticket-buying group of more than eighty-six customers.

After the campaign of that year, the team dropped out of the league. It was an unlamented, unheralded event, pointing up the fact that baseball fans have a penchant for winners and a short memory for losers. The paying customers proved more willing to travel uptown to the Polo Grounds to see the Giants, or crosstown to Yankee Stadium to see the Yankees, or downtown to any movie theater or bowling alley than to watch the Brooklyn Dodgers stumble around in the basement of the league season after season. This is also commentative on the forgetfulness of baseball enthusiasts, since there are probably only a handful who recollect that for a wondrous month and a half, the Brooklyn Dodgers were a most unusual ball club that last season. They didn't start out as an unusual ball club. They started out as shlumpfs, as any Dodger fan can articulately and colorfully tell you. But for one month and one-half they were one helluva club. Principally because of a certain person on the team roster.

It all began this way. Once upon a time a most unusual event happened on the way over to the ball park. This unusual event was a left-hander named Casey!

It was tryout day for the Brooklyn Dodgers, and Mouth Mc-Garry, the manager of the club, stood in the dugout, one foot on the parapet, both hands shoved deep into his hip pockets, his jaw hanging several inches below his upper lip. "Tryout days" depressed Mouth McGarry more than the standing of his ball club, which was depressing enough as it stood, or lay—which would be more apt, since they were now in last place, just thirty-one games out of first. Behind him, sitting on a bench, was Bertram Beasley, the general manager of the ball club. Beasley was a little man whose face looked like an X ray of an ulcer. His eyes were sunk deep into his little head, and his little head was sunk deep in between two narrow shoulder blades. Each time he looked up to survey McGarry, and beyond him, several gentlemen in baseball uniforms, he heaved a deep sigh and saw to it that his head sank just a few inches deeper into his shoulder blades. The sigh Bertram Beasley heaved was the only respectable heave going on within a radius of three hundred feet of home plate. The three pitchers that scout Maxwell Jenkins had sent over turned out to be pitchers in name only. One of them, as a matter of fact, had looked so familiar that McGarry swore he'd seen him pitch in the 1911 World Series. As it turned out, McGarry had been mistaken. It was not he who had pitched in the 1911 World Series but his nephew.

Out on the field McGarry watched the current crop of tryouts and kept massaging his heart. Reading left to right they were a tall, skinny kid with three-inch-thick glasses; a seventeen-year-old fat boy who weighed about two hundred and eighty pounds and stood five feet two; a giant, hulking farm boy who had taken off his spike shoes; and the aforementioned "pitcher," who obviously had dyed his hair black, but it was not a fast color and the hot summer sun was sending black liquid down both sides of his face. The four men were in the process of doing calisthenics. They were all out of step except the aging pitcher, who was no longer doing calisthenics. He had simply sat down and was fanning himself with his mitt.

Beasley rose from the bench in the dugout and walked over to McGarry. Mouth turned to look at him.

"Grand-looking boys!"

"Who were you expecting?" Beasley said, sticking a cigar in his mouth. "The All-Stars? You stick out a tryout sign for a last division club"—he pointed to the group doing the calisthenics—"and this is the material you usually round up." He felt a surge of anger as he stared into the broken-nosed face of Mouth McGarry. "Maybe if you were any kind of manager, McGarry, you'd be able to whip stuff like this into shape."

McGarry stared at him like a scientist looking through a microscope at a bug. "I couldn't whip stuff like that into shape," he said, "if they were eggs and I was an electric mixer. You're the general manager of the club. Why don't you give me some ballplayers?"

"You'd know what to do with them?" Beasley asked. "Twenty games out of fourth place and the only big average we've got is a manager with the widest mouth in either league. Maybe you'd better get reminded that when the Brooklyn Dodgers win one game we gotta call it a streak! Buddy boy," he said menacingly, "when contract time comes around, *you* don't have to." His cigar went out and he took out a match and lit it. Then he looked up toward home plate, where a pitcher was warming up. "How's Fletcher doing?" he asked.

"Are you kidding?" Mouth spat thirty-seven feet off to the left. "Last week he pitched four innings and allowed only six runs. That makes him our most valuable player of the month!"

The dugout phone rang and Beasley went over to pick it up. "Dugout," he said into the receiver. "What? Who?" He cupped his hand over the phone and looked over at Mouth. "You wanta look at a pitcher?" he asked.

"Are you kidding?" Mouth answered.

Beasley talked back into the phone. "Send him down," he said. He hung up the receiver and walked back over to Mouth. "He's a lefty," he announced.

"Lefty, Shmefty," Mouth said. "If he's got more than one arm and less than four—he's for us!" He cupped his hands over his mouth and yelled out toward the field. "Hey, Monk!"

The catcher behind home plate rose from his squat and looked back over toward the dugout. "Yeah?"

"Fletcher can quit now," Mouth called to him. "I've got a new boy coming down. Catch him for a while."

"Check," the catcher said. Then he turned toward the pitcher. "Okay, Fletch. Go shower up."

Beasley walked back over to sit on the bench in the dugout. "You got the lineup for tonight?" he asked the manager.

"Working on it," Mouth said.

"Who starts?"

"You mean pitcher? I just feel them one by one. Whoever's warm goes to the mound." He spat again and put his foot back up on the parapet, staring out at the field. Once again he yelled out toward his ballplayers. "Chavez, stop already with the calisthenics."

He watched disgustedly as the three men stopped jumping up and down and the old man sitting on the ground looked relieved. Chavez thumbed them off the field and turned back toward the bench and shrugged a what-the-hell-can-I-do-with-things-like-this kind of shrug.

Mouth took out a handkerchief and wiped his face. He walked up the steps of the dugout and saw the sign sticking in the ground which read: "Brooklyn Dodgers—tryouts today." He pulled back his right foot and followed through with a vicious kick, which sent the sign skittering along the ground. Then he went over to the third-base line, picked up a piece of grass, and chewed it thoughtfully. Beasley left the dugout to join McGarry. He kneeled down alongside of him and picked up another piece of grass and began to chew. They knelt and lunched together until McGarry spit out his piece of grass and glared at Beasley.

"You know something, Beasley?" he inquired. "We are so deep in the cellar that our roster now includes an infield, an outfield and a furnace! And you know whose fault that is?"

Beasley spit out his own piece of grass and said, "You tell me!"

"It ain't mine," McGarry said defensively. "It just happens to be my luck to wind up with a baseball organization whose farm system consists of two silos and a McCormick reaper. The only thing I get sent up to me each spring is a wheat crop."

"McGarry," Beasley stated definitely, "if you had material, would you really know what to do with it? You ain't no Joe McCarthy. You ain't one half Joe McCarthy."

"Go die, will you," McGarry said. He turned back to stare down the third-base line at nothing in particular. He was unaware of the cherubic little white-haired man who had just entered the dugout. Beasley *did* see him and stared wide-eyed. The little old man came up behind Mouth and cleared his throat.

"Mr. McGarry?" he said. "I am Dr. Stillman. I called about your trying out a pitcher."

McGarry turned slowly to look at him, screwed up his face in distaste. "All right! What's the gag? What about it, Grandpa? Did this muttonhead put you up to it?" He turned to Beasley. "This is the pitcher, huh? Big joke. Yak, yak, yak. Big joke."

Dr. Stillman smiled benignly. "Oh, I'm not a pitcher," he said, "though I've thrown baseballs in my time. Of course, that was before the war."

"Yeah," Mouth interjected. "Which war? The Civil War? You don't look old enough to have spent the winter at Valley Forge." Then he glared at him intently. "Come to think of it—was it really as cold as they say?"

Stillman laughed gently. "You really have a sense of humor, Mr. McGarry." Then he turned and pointed toward the dugout. "Here's Casey now," he said.

Mouth turned to look expectantly over the little old man's shoulder. Casey was coming out of the dugout. From cleats to the button on top of his makeshift baseball cap there was a frame roughly six feet, six inches high. The hands at his sides were the dimensions of two good-sized cantaloupes. His shoulders, McGarry thought to himself, made Primo Carnero look like the "before" in a Charles Atlas ad. In short, Casey was long. He was also broad. And in addition, he was one of the most powerful men either McGarry or Beasley had ever seen. He carried himself with the kind of agile grace that bespeaks an athlete, and the only jarring note in the whole picture was a face that should have been handsome, but wasn't, simply because it had no spark, no emotion, no expression of any sort at all. It was just a face. Nice teeth, thin lips, good straight nose, deep-set blue eyes, a shock of sandy hair that hung out from under his baseball cap. But it was a face, McGarry thought, that looked as if it had been painted on.

"You're the lefty, huh?" McGarry said. "All right." He pointed toward the home plate. "You see that guy with the great big mitt on? He's what's known as a catcher. His name is Monk. Throw a few into him."

"Thanks very much, Mr. McGarry," Casey said dully.

He went toward home plate. Even the voice, McGarry thought.

Even the voice. Dead. Spiritless. McGarry picked up another long piece of grass and headed back to the dugout followed by Beasley and the little old man, who looked like something out of Charles Dickens. In the dugout, McGarry assumed his familiar pose of one foot on the parapet, both fists in his hip pockets. Beasley left the dugout to return to his office, which was his custom on days the team didn't play. He would lock himself in his room and add up attendance figures, then look through the want ads of *The New York Times*. Just Stillman and Mouth McGarry stood in the dugout now, and the elderly little man watched everything with wide, fluttering eyes, like a kid on a tour through a fireworks factory. McGarry turned to him.

"You his father?"

"Casey's?" Stillman asked. "Oh, no. He has no father. I guess you'd call me his—well, kind of his creator."

Dr. Stillman's words went past McGarry the way the super-chief goes by a water tank. "That a fact?" he asked rhetorically. "How old is he?"

"How old is he?" Stillman repeated. He thought for a moment. "Well, that's a little difficult to say."

Mouth looked over toward the empty bench with a see-the-kind-of-idiocy-I-have-to-put-up-with kind of look. "That's a little difficult to say," he mimicked fiercely.

Stillman hurriedly tried to explain. "What I mean is," he said, "it's hard to be chronological when discussing Casey's age. Because he's only been in existence for three weeks. What I mean is —he has the physique and mind of roughly a twenty-two year old, but in terms of how long he's been here—the answer to that would be about three weeks."

The words had poured out of Dr. Stillman's mouth, and McGarry had blinked through the whole speech.

"Would you mind going over that again?" he asked.

"Not at all," Dr. Stillman said kindly. "It's really not too difficult. You see, I made Casey. I built him." He smiled a big, beatific smile. "Casey's a robot," he said. The old man took a folded and creased document from his vest pocket and held it out to Mouth. "These are the blueprints I worked from," he said.

Mouth swatted the papers out of the old man's hand and dug his gnarled knuckles into the sides of his head. That goddamn Beasley. There were no depths to which that son of a bitch wouldn't go to make his life miserable. He had to gulp several times before he could bring himself to speak to the old man, and when finally words came, the voice didn't sound like his at all.

"Old friend." His voice came out in a wheeze. "Kind, sweet old man. Gentle grandfather, with kind eyes, I am very happy that he's a robot. Of course, that's what he is." He patted Stillman's cheek. "That's just what he is, a nice robot." Then there was a sob in his voice as he glared up at the roof of the dugout. "Beasley, you crummy son of a bitch!" A robot yet. This fruity old man and that miserable ball club and the world all tumbling down and it just never ended and it never got any better. A robot!

Dr. Stillman scurried after Mouth, who had walked up the steps of the dugout and out onto the field. He paused along the third-base line and began to chew grass again. Over his shoulder Casey was throwing pitches into the catcher at home plate, but Mouth didn't even notice him.

"I dunno," he said to nobody in particular. "I don't even know what I'm *doing* in baseball."

He looked uninterested as Casey threw a curve ball that broke sharply just a foot out in front of home plate and then shrieked into the catcher's mitt like a small, circular, white express train.

"That Beasley," Mouth said to the ground. "That guy's got as much right in the front office as I've got in the Alabama State Senate. This guy is nothing, that's all. Simply a nothing. He was born a nothing. He's a nothing now!"

On the mound Casey wound up again and threw a hook that screamed in toward home plate, swerved briefly to the left, shot back to the right, and then landed in the catcher's mitt exactly where it had been placed as a target. Monk stared at the ball wide-eyed and then toward the young pitcher on the mound. He examined the ball, shook his head, then threw it back to him, shaking his head slowly from side to side.

Meanwhile Mouth continued his daily analysis of the situation to a smiling Dr. Stillman and an empty grandstand. "I've had bum teams before," he way saying. "Real bad outfits. But this one!" He spat out the piece of grass. "These guys make Abner Double-day a criminal! You know where I got my last pitcher? He was mowing the infield and I discovered that he was the only guy on the club who could reach home plate from the pitcher's mound on less than two bounces. He is now ensconced as my number two starter. That's exactly where he's ensconced!"

He looked out again at Casey to see him throw a straight fast ball that landed in Monk's glove and sent smoke rising from home plate. Monk whipped off the glove and held his hand agonizedly. When the pain subsided he stared at the young pitcher disbeliev-ingly. It was then and only then that picture and sound began to register in Mouth McGarry's mind. He suddenly thought about the last two pitches that he'd seen and his eyebrows shot up like elevators. Monk approached him, holding his injured hand.

"You see him?" Monk asked in an incredulous voice. "That kid? He picks up where Feller left off, I swear to God! He's got a curve, hook, knuckler, slider, and a fast ball that almost went through my palm! He's got control like he uses radar. This is the best pitcher I ever caught in my life, Mouth!"

Mouth McGarry stood there as if mesmerized, staring at Casey, who was walking slowly away from the mound. Monk tucked his catcher's mitt under his arm and started toward the dugout.

"I swear," he said as he walked, "I never seen anything like it. Fantastic. He pitches *like nothing human!*"

Mouth McGarry and Dr. Stillman looked at one another. Dr. Stillman's quiet blue eyes looked knowing, and Mouth McGarry chewed furiously down the length of a piece of grass, his last bite taking in a quarter inch of his forefinger. He blew on it, waved it in the air and stuck it in his mouth as he turned toward Stillman, his voice shaking with excitement.

"Look, Grandpa," Mouth said, "I want that boy! Understand? I'll have a contract drawn up inside of fifteen minutes. And don't give me no tough talk either! You brought him here on a tryout and that gives us first option."

"He's a robot, you know," Stillman began quietly.

Mouth grabbed him and spoke through clenched teeth. "Grampa," he said in a quiet fury, "don't ever say that to nobody! We'll just keep that in the family here." Then suddenly remembering, he looked around wildly for the blueprint, picked it up from the ground and shoved it in his shirt pocket. He saw Stillman looking at him.

"Would that be honest?" Stillman said, rubbing his jaw.

Mouth pinched his cheek and said, "You sweet old guy, you're looking at a desperate man. And if the baseball commissioner ever found out I was using a machine—I'd be dead. D-E-D! Dead, you know?" Mouth's face brightened into a grimace that vaguely brought to mind a smile when he saw Casey approaching. "I like your stuff, kid," Mouth said to him. "Now you go into the locker room and change your clothes." He turned to Stillman. "He wears clothes, don't he?"

"Oh, by all means," Stillman answered.

"Good," Mouth said, satisfied. "Then we'll go up to Beasley's office and sign the contract." He looked at the tall pitcher standing there and shook his head. "If you could pitch once a week like I

just seen you pitch, the only thing that stands between us and a
pennant is if your battery goes dead or you rust in the rain! As of
right now, Mr. Casey—you're the number-one pitcher of the
Brooklyn Dodgers!''

Stillman smiled happily and Casey just looked impassive, no
expression, no emotion, neither satisfied nor dissatisfied. He just
stood there. Mouth hurried back to the dugout, took the steps
three at a time and grabbed the phone.

"General Manager's office," he screamed into it. "Yeah!" In a
moment he heard Beasley's voice. "Beasley?" he said. "Listen,
Beasley, I want you to draw up a contract. It's for that left-hander.
His name is Casey. That's right. Not just good, Beasley. Fantastic.
Now you draw up that contract in a hurry." There was an angry
murmur at the other end of the line. "Who do you think I'm giving
orders to?" Mouth demanded. He slammed the phone down, then
turned to look out toward the field.

Stillman and Casey were heading toward the dugout. Mouth
rubbed his jaw pensively. Robot-shmobot, he said to himself. He's
got a curve, knuckler, fast ball, slider, change of pace and—hallelujah—he's got two arms!

He picked up one of Bertram Beasley's cigars off the ground,
smoothed out the pleats and shoved it into his mouth happily. For
the first time in many long and bleak months Mouth McGarry had
visions of a National League pennant fluttering across his mind.
So must John McGraw have felt when he got his first look at
Walter Johnson, or Muller Higgins when George Herman Ruth
came to him from the Boston Red Socks. And McGarry's palpita-
tions were surely not unlike those of Marse Joseph McCarthy
when a skinny Italian kid named DiMaggio ambled out into center
field for the first time. Such was the bonfire of hope that was
kindled in Mouth McGarry's chest as he looked at the blankfaced,
giant left-hander walking toward him, carrying on his massive
shoulders, albeit invisibly, the fortunes of the Brooklyn Dodgers
and Mrs. McGarry's son, Mouth!

It was a night game against St. Louis forty-eight hours later. The
dressing room of the Brooklyn Dodgers was full of noise, clattering
cleats, slammed locker doors, the plaintive protests of Bertram
Beasley, who was accusing the trainer of using too much liniment
(at seventy-nine cents a bottle), and the deep, bullfrog profanity of
Mouth McGarry, who was all over the room, on every bench, in
every corner, and in every head of hair.

"You sure he's got the signals down, Monk?" he asked his
catcher for the fourteenth time.

Monk's eyes went up toward the ceiling and he said tiredly, "Yes, boss. He knows them."

Mouth walked over to the pitcher, who was just tying up his shoes. "Casey," he said urgently, wiping the sweat from his forehead, "if you forget them signals—you call time and bring Monk out to you, you understand? I don't want no cross-ups." He took a large handkerchief and mopped his brow, then he pulled out a pill from his side pocket and plopped it into his mouth. "And above all," he cautioned his young pitcher, "—don't be nervous!"

Casey looked up at him puzzled. "Nervous?" he asked.

Stillman, who had just entered the room, walked over to them smiling. "Nervous, Casey," he explained, "ill at ease. As if one of your electrodes were—"

Mouth drowned him out loudly, "You know 'nervous,' Casey! Like as if there's two outs in the ninth, you're one up, and you're pitchin' against DiMaggio and he comes up to the plate lookin' intent!"

Casey stared at him deadpan. "That wouldn't make me nervous. I don't know anyone named DiMaggio."

"He don't know anyone named DiMaggio," Monk explained seriously to Mouth McGarry.

"I heard 'im," Mouth screamed at him. "I heard 'im!" He turned to the rest of the players, looked at his watch, then bellowed out, "All right, you guys, let's get going!"

Monk took Casey's arm and pulled him off the bench and then out the door. The room resounded with the clattering cleats on concrete floor as the players left the room for the dugout above. Mouth McGarry stood alone in the middle of the room and felt a dampness settle all over him. He pulled out a sopping wet handkerchief and wiped his head again.

"This humidity," he said plaintively to Dr. Stillman, who sat on the bench surveying him, "is killing me. I've never felt such dampness—I swear to God!"

Stillman looked down at Mouth's feet. McGarry was standing with one foot in a bucket of water.

"Mr. McGarry." He pointed to the bucket.

Mouth lifted up his foot sheepishly and shook it. Then he took out his bottle of pills again, popped two of them in his mouth, gulped them down, and pointed apologetically to his stomach. "Nerves," he said. "Terrible nerves. I don't sleep at night. I keep seeing pennants before my eyes. Great big, red-white-and-blue pennants. All I can think about is knocking off the Giants and then taking four straight from the Yanks in the World Series." He sighed deeply. "But for that matter," he continued, "I'd like to knock off the Phillies and the Cards, too. Or the Braves or Cincinnati." A forlorn note crept into his voice now. "Or anybody, when you come down to it!"

Dr. Stillman smiled at him. "I think Casey will come through for you, Mr. McGarry."

Mouth looked at the small white-haired man. "What have you got riding on this?" he asked. "What's your percentage?"

"You mean with Casey?" Stillman said. "Just scientific, that's all. Purely experimental. I think that Casey is a superman of a sort and I'd like that proved. Once I built a home economist. Marvelous cook. I gained forty-six pounds before I had to dismantle her. Now with Casey's skills, his strength and his accuracy, I realized he'd be a baseball pitcher. But in order to prove my point I had to have him pitch in competition. Also, as an acid test, I had to have him pitch with absolutely the worst ball team I could find."

"That's very nice of you, Dr. Stillman," Mouth said. "I appreciate it."

"Don't mention it. Now shall we go out on the field?"

Mouth opened the door for him. "After you," he said.

Dr. Stillman went out and Mouth was about to follow him when he stopped dead, one eyebrow raised. "Wait a minute, dammit," he shouted. "The worst?" He started out after the old man. "You should have seen the Phillies in 1903!" he yelled after him.

An umpire screamed, "Play ball!" and the third baseman took a throw from the catcher, then, rubbing up the ball, he carried it over to Casey on the mound, noticing in a subconscious section of his mind that this kid with the long arms and the vast shoulders had about as much spirit as a lady of questionable virtue on a Sunday morning after a long Saturday night. A few moments later, the third baseman cared very little about the lack of animation on Casey's features. This feeling was shared by some fourteen thousand fans, who watched the left-hander look dully in for a sign, then throw a sidearm fast ball that left them gasping and sent the entire dugout of the St. Louis Cardinals to their feet in amazement.

There are fast balls and fast balls, but nothing remotely resembling the white streak that shot out of Casey's left hand, almost invisibly, toward the plate, had ever been witnessed. A similar thought ran through the mind of the St. Louis batter as he blinked at the sound of the ball hitting the catcher's mitt and took a moment to realize that the pitch had been made and he had never laid eyes on it.

This particular St. Louis batter was the first of twenty-nine men to face Casey that evening. Eighteen of them struck out and only two of them managed to get to first base, one on a fluke single that was misjudged over first base. By the sixth inning most of the people in the stadium were on their feet, aware that they were seeing something special in the tall left-hander on the mound. And by the ninth inning, when Brooklyn had won its first game in three weeks by a score of two to nothing, the stadium was in a frenzy.

There was also a frenzy of a sort in the Brooklyn dugout. The corners of Mouth McGarry's mouth tilted slightly upward in a grimace that the old team trainer explained later to a couple of mystified players was a "smile." Mouth hadn't been seen to smile in the past six years.

Bertram Beasley celebrated the event by passing out three brand-new cigars and one slightly used one (to McGarry). But the notable thing about the Brooklyn dugout and later the locker room was that the ball team suddenly looked different. In the space of about two and a half hours, it had changed from some slogging, lead-footed, aging second-raters to a snappy, heads-up confident-looking crew of ballplayers who had a preoccupation with winning. The locker room resounded with laughter and horseplay, excited shouting drifted out from the showers. All this in a room that for the past three years had been as loud and comical as a funeral parlor.

While wet towels sailed across the room and cleated shoes banged against locker doors, one man remained silent. This was the pitcher named Casey. He surveyed the commotion around him with a mild interest, but was principally concerned with unlacing his shoes. The only emotion he displayed was when Doc Barstow, the team trainer, started to massage his arm. He jumped up abruptly and yanked the arm away, leaving Barstow puzzled. Later on Barstow confided to Mouth McGarry that the kid's arm felt like a piece of tube steel. McGarry gulped, smiled nervously and asked Doc how his wife had been feeling. All this happened on the night of July 1.

Three weeks later the Brooklyn Dodgers had moved from the cellar to fifth place in the National League. They had won twenty-three games in a row, seven of them delivered on a platter by one left-handed pitcher named Casey. Two of his ball games were no-hitters, and his earned-run average was by far the lowest not only in either League, but in the history of baseball. His name was on every tongue in the nation, his picture on every sports page, and contracts had already been signed so that he would be appearing on cereal boxes before the month was out. And as in life itself, winning begot winning. Even without Casey, the Dodgers were becoming a feared and formidable ball club. Weak and ineffectual bat-slappers, who had never hit more than .200 in their lives, were becoming Babe Ruths. Other pitchers who had either been too green or too decrepit were beginning to win ball games along with Casey. And there was a spirit now—an aggressiveness, a drive, that separated the boys from the pennant-winners and the Brooklyn Dodgers were potentially the latter. They looked it and they played it.

Mouth McGarry was now described as "that master strategist" and "a top field general" and, frequently, "the winningest manager of the year" in sports columns that had previously referred to him as "that cement-headed oaf who handles a ball club like a bull would handle a shrimp cocktail." The team was drawing more customers in single games than they'd garnered in months at a time during previous seasons. And the most delightful thing to contemplate was the fact that Casey, who had begun it all, looked absolutely invulnerable to fatigue, impervious to harm, and totally beyond the normal hazards of pitchers. He had no stiff arms, no sore elbows, no lapses of control, no nothing. He pitched like a machine and while it was mildly disconcerting, it was really no great concern that he also walked, talked, and acted like a machine. There was no question about it. The Dodgers would have been in first place by mid-August at the very latest, if a shortstop on the Philadelphia Phillies had not hit a line ball directly at Casey on the mound, which caught him just a few inches above his left eye.

The dull, sickening thud was the shot heard all around the borough, and if anyone had clocked Mouth McGarry's run from the dugout to the mound, where his ace left-hander was now sprawled face downward, two guys named Landy and Bannister would have been left in eclipse. Bertram Beasley, in his box seat in the grandstand, simply chewed off one quarter of his cigar and swallowed it, then fell off his seat in a dead faint.

The players grouped around Casey, and Doc Barstow motioned for a stretcher. McGarry grabbed his arm and whispered at him as if already they were in the presence of the dead.

"Will he pull through, Doc? Will he make it?"

The team doctor looked grim. "I think we'd better get him to a hospital. Let's see what they say about him there."

Half the team provided an escort for the stretcher at it moved slowly off the field. It looked like a funeral cortège behind a recently deceased head of state, with Mouth McGarry as the principal mourner. It was only then that he remembered to motion into the bull pen for a new pitcher, an eager young towhead out of the Southern Association League who had just been called up.

The kid ambled toward the mound. It was obvious that at this moment he wished he were back in Memphis, Tennessee, sorting black-eyed peas. He took the ball from the second baseman, rubbed it up, then reached down for the rosin bag. He rubbed his hands with the bag, then rubbed the ball, then rubbed the bag, then put down the ball, wound up and threw the rosin bag. As it turned out, that was his best pitch of the evening. Shortly thereafter he walked six men in a row and hit one man in the head. Luckily, it was a hot-dog vendor in the bleachers, so that no harm was done in terms of moving any of the men on base. This was taken care of by his next pitch to the number-four batter on the Philadelphia Phillies squad, who swung with leisurely grace at what the kid from Memphis referred to as his fast ball, and sent it on a seven-hundred-foot trip over the center-field fence, which took care of the men on the bases. The final score was thirteen to nothing in favor of the Phillies, but Mouth McGarry didn't even wait until the last out. With two outs in the ninth, he and Beasley ran out of the park and grabbed a cab. Beasley handed the driver a quarter and said, "Never mind the cops. Get to the hospital."

The hackie looked at the quarter, then back toward Beasley and said, "This better be a rare mint, or I'll see to it that you have your baby in the cab!"

They arrived at the hospital twelve minutes later and pushed their way through a lobby full of reporters to get to an elevator and up to the floor where Casey had been taken for observation. They arrived in his room during the last stages of the examination. A nurse shushed them as they barged into the room.

"Boobie," McGarry gushed, racing toward the bed.

The doctor took off his stethoscope and hung it around his neck. "You the father?" he asked Mouth.

"The father," McGarry chortled. "I'm closer than any father."

He noticed now for the first time that Dr. Stillman was sitting quietly in the corner of the room, looking like a kindly old owl full of wisdom hidden under his feathers.

"Well, gentlemen, there's no fracture that I can see," the doctor announced professionally. "No concussion. Reflexes seem normal—"

Beasley exhaled, sounding like a strong north wind. "I can breathe again," he told everyone.

"All I could think of," Mouth said, "was there goes Casey!

There goes the pennant! There goes the Series!'' He shook his head forlornly, ''And there goes my career.''

The doctor picked up Casey's wrist and began to feel for the pulse. ''Yes, Mr. Casey,'' he smiled benevolently down into the expressionless face and unblinking eyes, ''I think you're in good shape. I'll tell you, though, when I heard how the ball hit you in the temple I wondered to myself how—''

The doctor stopped talking. His fingers compulsively moved around the wrist. His eyes went wide. After a moment he opened up Casey's pajamas and sent now shaking fingers running over the chest area. After a moment he stood up, took out a handkerchief and wiped his face.

''What's the matter?'' Mouth asked nervously. ''What's wrong?''

The doctor sat down in a chair. ''There's nothing wrong,'' he said softly. ''Not a thing wrong. Everything's fine. It's just that—''

''Just that what?'' Beasley asked.

The doctor pointed a finger toward the bed. ''It is just that this man doesn't have any pulse. No heartbeat.'' Then he looked up toward the ceiling. ''This man,'' he said in a strained voice, ''this man isn't alive.''

There was absolute silence in the room, marred only by the slump of Beasley's body as he slid quietly to the floor. No one paid any attention to him. It was Dr. Stillman who finally spoke.

''Mr. McGarry,'' he said in a quiet, firm voice, ''I do believe it'll have to come out now.''

Beasley opened his eyes. ''All right, you son of a bitch, McGarry. What are you trying to pull off?''

Mouth looked around the room as if searching for an extra bed. He looked ill. ''Beasley,'' he said plaintively, ''you ain't gonna like this. But it was Casey or it was nothing. God, what a pitcher! And he was the only baseball player I ever managed who didn't eat nothing.''

Stillman cleared his throat and spoke to the doctor. ''I think you should know before you go any further that Casey has no pulse or heartbeat . . . because he hasn't any heart. He's a robot.''

There was the sound of another slump as Bertram Beasley fell back unconscious. This time he didn't move.

''A *what?*'' the doctor asked incredulously.

''That's right,'' Stillman said. ''A robot.''

The doctor stared at Casey on the bed, who stared right back at him. ''Are you sure?'' the doctor asked in a hushed voice.

"Oh, by all means. I built him."

The doctor slowly removed his coat and then took off his tie. He marched toward the bed with his eyes strangely wide and bright. "Casey," he announced, "get up and strip. Hear me? Get up and strip."

Casey got up and stripped and twenty minutes later the doctor had opened the window and was leaning out breathing in the evening air. Then he turned, removed the stethoscope from around his neck, and put it in his black bag. He took the blood pressure equipment from the nightstand and added it to the bag. He made a mental note to check the X rays as soon as they came out, but knew this would be gratuitous because it was all very, very evident. The man on the bed wasn't a man at all. He was one helluva speciman, but a man he wasn't! The doctor lit a cigarette and looked across the room.

"Under the circumstances," he said, "I'm afraid I must notify the baseball commissioner. That's the only ethical procedure."

"What do you have to be ethical about it for?" McGarry challenged him. "What the hell are you—a Giant fan?"

The doctor didn't answer. He took the twenty or thirty sheets of paper that he'd been making notes on and rammed them in his pocket. He mentally ran down the list of medical societies and organizations that would have to be informed of this. He also devised the opening three or four paragraphs to a monumental paper he'd write for a medical journal on the first mechanical man. He was in for a busy time. He carried his black bag to the door, smiled, and went out, wondering just how the American Medical Association would react to this one. The only sound left in the room was Beasley's groaning, until McGarry walked over to Casey on the bed.

"Casey," he said forlornly, "would you move over?"

The Daily Mirror had it first because one of the interns in the maternity ward was really a leg man for them. But the two wire services picked it up twenty minutes later, and by six the following morning the whole world knew about Casey—the mechanical man. Several scientists were en route from Europe, and Dr. Stillman and Casey were beleaguered in a New York hotel room by an army of photographers and reporters. Three missile men at Cape Canaveral sent up a fabulous rocket that hit the moon deadeye, only to discover that the feat made page twelve of the afternoon editions because the first eleven pages were devoted exclusively to a meeting to be held by the commissioner of baseball, who had announced he would make a decision on the Casey case by suppertime.

At four thirty that afternoon the commissioner sat behind his desk, drumming on it with the end of a pencil. A secretary brought him in a folder filled with papers, and in the brief moment of the office door opening, he could see the mob of reporters out in the corridor.

"What about the reporters?" the secretary asked him.

Mouth McGarry, sitting in a chair close to the desk, made a suggestion at this point as to what might be done to the reporters or, more specifically, what they could do to themselves. The secretary looked shocked and left the room. The commissioner leaned back in his chair.

"You understand, McGarry," he said, "that I'm going to have to put this out for publication. Casey must definitely be suspended."

Bertram Beasley, sitting on a couch across the room, made a little sound deep in his throat, but stayed conscious.

"Why?" Mouth demanded noisily.

The commissioner pounded a fist on the desk top. "Because he's a robot, goddamn it," he said for the twelfth time that hour.

Mouth spread out his palms. "So he's a robot," he said simply.

Once again the commissioner picked up a large manual. "Article six, Section two, the Baseball Code," he said pontifically. "I quote: 'A team should consist of nine men,' end of quote. Men, understand, McGarry? Nine *men*. Not robots."

Beasley's voice was a thin little noise from the couch. "Commissioner," he said weakly. "To all intents and purposes—he *is* human." Then he looked across the room at the tall pitcher, who stood in the shadows practically unnoticed. "Casey, talk to him. Tell him about yourself."

Casey swallowed. "What—what should I say," he asked hesitantly.

"See," Mouth shouted. "He talks as good as me. And he's a helluva lot smarter than most of the muttonheads I got on my ball team!"

The commissioner's fist pounded on the desk. *"He is not human!"*

Again the weak voice of desperation from the couch. "How human do you want him?" the general manager asked. "He's got arms, legs, a face. He talks—"

"And no heart," the commissioner shouted. "He doesn't even own a heart. How could he be human without a heart?"

McGarry's voice absolutely dripped with unassailable logic and fundamental truth. "Beasley don't have a heart neither," he said, "and he owns forty per cent of the club."

The commissioner pushed the papers away from him and put the flat of his hands down on the desk. This was a gesture of finality, and it fitted perfectly the judicial tone of his voice. "That's it, gentlemen," he announced. "He doesn't have a heart. That means he isn't human, and that's a clear violation of the baseball code. Therefore, he doesn't play."

The door opened and Dr. Stillman walked quietly into the room in time to hear the last words of this proclamation. He waved at Casey, who waved back. Then he turned to the commissioner.

"Mr. Commissioner," he said.

The commissioner stopped halfway to his feet and looked at the old man. "Now what?" he asked tiredly.

Stillman walked over to the desk. "Supposing," he asked, "we gave him a heart? If that essentially is the only thing that makes him different from the norm, I believe I could operate and supply him with a mechanical heart."

"That's thinking!" McGarry shrieked into the room.

Beasley inched forward on the couch and took out a cigar. The commissioner sat back and looked very, very thoughtful. "This is irregular. This is highly irregular." Then he picked up the telephone and asked to speak to the examining physician who had sent in the report in the first place. "Doctor," he asked, "relative to the Casey matter, if he were to be given a mechanical heart— would you classify him as—what I mean is—would you call him a—" Then he held the phone close to his face, nodding into it. "Thank you very much, Doctor."

The commissioner looked across the room at Casey. He drummed on the desk top with the pencil, puckered up his lips, and made smacking sounds inside his mouth. McGarry took out his bottle of pills and plopped three of them into his mouth.

"All right," the commissioner announced. *"With* a heart, I'll give him a temporary okay, until the League meeting in November. Then we'll have to take it up again. The other clubs are gonna scream bloody murder!"

Beasley struggled to his feet. The look of massive relief on his face shone like a beacon. "It's all settled then," he said. "Casey here needs an accreditation as being human, and this requires a simple—" He stopped, looking over toward Stillman. "Simple?" he asked.

"Relatively," Stillman answered.

Beasley nodded. "A simple operation having to do with a mechanical heart." He walked across the room to the door and opened it. The reporters, milling around, stopped talking instantly. "Gentlemen," Beasley called out to them, "you may quote me."

The reporters made a beeline for the door and within a moment had filled up the room.

"You may quote me, gentlemen," Beasley repeated when the room was quiet once again. "The mighty Casey will be back in the lineup within forty-eight hours." He threw another questioning look at Stillman. "Forty-eight hours?"

"About," Stillman answered quietly.

Questions shot around the room like bolts of lightning, and for the next few moments McGarry, Beasley, and Casey were innundated by notebooks and cigarette smoke. Then the room started to empty. Mouth McGarry took a position close to the desk, stuck a cigar in his mouth, lit it, took a deep drag and held it out away from his body, gently flicking ashes on the floor.

"Gentlemen," he announced, "as manager of the Brooklyn Dodgers, I want to tell you, and since I was the man who discovered Casey—"

The reporters rapidly left the room, followed by the commissioner and his secretary, followed by Casey and Stillman.

"It behooves me to tell you, gentlemen," Mouth continued, wetting his lips over the word "behooves" and wondering to himself where he got the word. "It behooves me to make mention of the fact that the Brooklyn Dodgers are the team to beat. We've got the speed, the stamina," he recollected now the Pat O'Brien speech in the Knute Rockne picture—"the vim, the vigor, the vitality—"

He was unaware of the door slamming shut and unaware that Bertram Beasley was the only other man in the room. "And with this kind of stuff," he continued, in the Knute Rockne voice, "the National League pennant and the World Series and—"

"McGarry," Beasley yelled at him.

Mouth started as if suddenly waking from a dream.

Beasley rose from the couch. "Why don't you drop dead?" He walked out of the room, leaving Mouth all by himself, wondering how Pat O'Brien wound up that speech in the locker room during the halftime of that vital Army–Notre Dame game.

How either McGarry or Bertram Beasley got through the next twenty-odd hours was a point of conjecture with both of them. Mouth emptied his bottle of nerve pills and spent a sleepless night pacing his hotel-room floor. Beasley could recall only brief moments of consciousness between swoons that occurred every time the phone rang.

The following night the team was dressing in the locker room. They were playing the first of a five-game series against the New York Giants, and McGarry had already devised nine different batteries, then torn them all up. He now sat on a bench surveying his absolutely silent ballplayers. There was not a sound. At intervals each pair of eyes would turn toward the phone on the wall. Beasley had already phoned Dr. Stillman's residence seven times that evening and received no answer. He was on the phone now, talking to the long-distance operator in New Jersey.

"Yeah," Beasley said into the phone. "Yeah, well, thank you very much, operator."

Mouth and the rest of the players waited expectantly.

"Well?" Mouth asked. "How is he?"

Beasley shook his head. "I don't know. The operator still can't get an answer."

Monk, the big catcher, rose from the bench. "Maybe he's right in the middle of the operation," he suggested.

Mouth whirled around at him, glaring. "So he's in the middle of the operation! Whatsa matter, he can't use one hand to pick up a phone?" He looked up at the clock on the wall, then jutted his jaw fiercely, his eyes scanning the bench. "We can't wait no longer," he announced. "I got to turn in a battery. Corrigan," he said, pointing toward one of the players, "you'll pitch tonight. And now the rest of you guys!" He stuck his hands in his back pockets and paced back and forth in front of them in a rather stylized imitation of Pat O'Brien.

"All right, you guys," he said grimly. "All right, you guys!" He stopped pacing and pointed toward the door. "That's the enemy out there," he said, his voice quivering a little. "That's the New York Giants." He spoke the words as if they were synonymous with a social disease. "And while we're out there playing tonight" —again his voice quivered—"there's a big fellah named Casey lying on a table, struggling to stay alive."

Tears shone in Monk's eyes as the big catcher got a mental picture of a courageous kid lying on a hospital table. Gippy Resnick, the third baseman, sniffed and then honked into a handkerchief as a little knot of sentiment tightened up his throat. Bertram Beasley let out a sob as he thought about what the attendance record was, six weeks B.C.—before Casey—and did some more projecting on what it would be without Casey. Mouth McGarry walked back and forth before the line of players.

"I know," he said, his voice tight and strained. "I know that his last words before the knife went into his chest were—'Go up there, Dodgers, and win one for the big guy!' "

The last words of this speech were choked by the tears that rolled down McGarry's face and the sob that caught in his own chest.

The street door to the locker room opened and Dr. Stillman came in, followed by Casey. But all the players were watching Mouth McGarry, who had now moved into his big finale scene.

"I want to tell you something, guys! From now on"—he sniffed loudly—"from now on there's gonna be a ghost in the dugout. Every time you pick up a bat, look over to where Casey used to sit—because he's gonna be there in spirit rooting for us, cheering for us, yellin', 'Go Dodgers, go!' "—McGarry turned and looked at Casey, who was smiling at him. Mouth nodded perfunctorily. "Hello there, Casey," he said and turned back to the team. "Now I'm gonna tell you something else about that big guy. This fellah has a heart. Not a real heart, maybe, but this fellah that's lyin' there with a hole in his chest—"

Mouth's lower jaw dropped seven inches, as he turned very slowly to look at Casey. He had no chance to say anything, however, because the team had pushed him aside as they rushed toward the hero, shaking his hand, pounding him on the back, pulling, grabbing, shouting at him. Mouth spent a moment recovering and then screamed, "All right, knock it off! Let's have quiet! Quiet! QUIET!" He pulled players away from Casey and finally stood in front of the big pitcher. "Well?" he asked.

Stillman smiled. "Go ahead, Casey. Tell him."

It was then that everyone in the room noticed Casey's face. He was smiling. It was a big smile. A broad smile. An enveloping smile. It went across his face and up and down. It shone in his eyes. "Listen, Mr. McGarry," he said proudly. He pointed a thumb at his chest and Mouth put his ear there. He could hear the steady tick, tick, tick.

Mouth stepped back and shouted excitedly. "You got a heart!"

There was a chorus of delighted exclamation and comment from all the players and Beasley, poised for a faint, decided against it.

"And look at that smile," Stillman said over the shouting. "That's the one thing I couldn't get him to do before—smile!"

Casey threw his arm around the old man. "It's wonderful. It's just wonderful. Now I feel—I feel—like—togetherness!"

The team roared their approval and Bertram Beasley mounted a rubbing-table, cupping his hands like a megaphone, and shouted,

"All right, Dodgers, out on the field. Let's go, team. Casey starts tonight. The new Casey!"

The team thundered out onto the field, pushing Mouth McGarry out of the way and blotting out the first part of the speech which had begun, "All right, you guys, with vim, vigor and vital—" He never got to finish the speech because Monk, Resnick, and a utility infielder had carried him with their momentum out the door and up to the dugout.

When Casey's name was announced as the starter for the Dodgers that night the crowd let out a roar that dwarfed any thunder ever heard in or around the environs of New York City. And when Casey stepped out on the field and headed toward the mound, fifty-seven thousand eight hundred and thirty-three people stood up and applauded as one, and it was only the second baseman who, as he carried the ball over to the pitcher, noticed that there were tears in Casey's eyes and an expression on his face that made him pause. True, he'd never seen any expression on Casey's face before, but this one made him stop and look over his shoulder as he went back to his base.

The umpire shouted, "Play ball," and the Dodgers began the running stream of chatter that always prefaced the first pitch. Monk, behind the plate, made a signal and then held up his glove as a target. Start with a fast ball, he thought. Let them know what they're up against, jar them a little bit. Confuse them. Unnerve them. That was the way Monk planned his strategy behind the plate. Not that much strategy was needed when Casey was on the mound, but it was always good to show the big guns first. Casey nodded, went into his windup and threw. Twelve seconds later a woman in a third-floor apartment three blocks away had her bedroom window smashed by a baseball that had traveled in the neighborhood of seven hundred feet out of Tebbet's Field.

Meanwhile, back at the field, the crowd just sat there silently as the lead-off batter of the New York Giants ambled around the base path heading home to the outstretched hands of several fellow Giants greeting him after his lead-off home run.

Mouth McGarry at this moment felt that he would never again suffer a stab of depression such as the one that now intruded into his head. He would recall later that his premonition was quite erroneous. He would feel stabs of depressions in innings number two, three and four that would make that first stab of depression seem like the aftereffect of a Miltown tablet. That's how bad it got forty-five minutes later, when Casey had allowed nine hits, had walked six men, had thrown two wild pitches, and had muffed a pop fly to the mound, which, McGarry roared to the bench around him, "could have been caught by a palsied Civil War veteran who lost an arm at Gettysburg."

In the seventh inning Mouth McGarry took his fifth walk over to the mound and this time didn't return to the bench till he'd motioned to the bullpen for Casey's relief—a very eager kid, albeit a nervous one, who chewed tobacco going to the mound and got violently sick as he crossed the third-base line because he'd swallowed a piece. Coughing hard, he arrived at the mound and took the ball from Mouth McGarry. Casey solemnly shoved his mitt into his hip pocket and took the long walk back toward the showers.

At ten minutes to midnight the locker room had been emptied. All the players save Casey had gone back to the hotel. Bertram Beasley had left earlier—on a stretcher in the sixth inning. In the locker room were a baseball manager who produced odd grunts from deep within his throat and kept shaking his head back and forth—and a kindly white-haired old man who built robots. Casey came out of the shower, wrapped in a towel. He smiled gently at Mouth and then went over to his locker, where he proceeded to dress.

"Well?" Mouth shouted at him. "Well? One minute he's three Lefty Groves, the next minute he's the cousin to every New York Giant who ever lived. He's a tanker. He's a nothing. All right—you wanna tell me, Casey? You wanna explain? You might start by telling me how one man can throw nine pitched balls and give up four singles, two doubles, a triple and two home runs!"

The question remained unanswered. Stillman looked toward Casey and said very softly, "Shall I tell him?"

Casey nodded apologetically.

Stillman turned toward McGarry. "Casey has a heart," he said quietly.

Mouth fumed. "So? Casey has a heart! So I know he's gotta heart! So this ain't news, Prof! Tell me something that is!"

"The thing is," Casey said in his first speech over three sentences since McGarry had met him. "The thing is, Mr. McGarry, I just couldn't strike out those poor fellahs. I didn't have it in me to do that—to hurt their feelings. I felt—I felt compassion!" He looked toward Stillman as if for confirmation.

Stillman nodded. "That's what he's got, Mr. McGarry. Compassion. See how he smiles?"

Casey grinned obediently and most happily, and Stillman returned his smile. "You see, Mr. McGarry," Stillman continued.

"You give a person a heart—particularly someone like Casey, who hasn't been around long enough to understand things like competitiveness or drive or ego. Well"—he shrugged—"that's what happens."

Mouth sat down on the bench, unscrewed the bottle of pills and found it was empty. He threw the bottle over his shoulder. "That's what happens to *him*," he said. "Shall I tell you what happens to me? I go back to being a manager of nine gleeps so old that I gotta rub them down with formaldehyde and revive them in between innings." He suddenly had a thought and looked up at Casey. "Casey," he asked, "don't you feel any of that compassion for the Brooklyn Dodgers?"

Casey smiled back at him. "I'm sorry, Mr. McGarry," he said. "It's just that I can't strike out fellahs. I can't bring myself to hurt their careers. Dr. Stillman thinks I should go into social work now. I'd like to help people. Right, Dr. Stillman?"

"That's right, Casey," Stillman answered.

"Are you going?" Casey asked McGarry as he saw the manager head for the door.

Mouth nodded.

"Well good-bye, Mr. McGarry," Casey said. "And thank you for everything."

Mouth turned to him. The grin on his face was that of dying humanity all over the world. "Don't mention it," he said.

He sighed deeply and walked out to the warm August evening that awaited him and the black headlines on a newspaper stand just outside the stadium that said "I told you so" at him, even though the lettering spelled out, "Casey Shelled from Mound." A reporter stood on the corner, a guy McGarry knew slightly.

"What about it, McGarry?" the reporter asked. "What do you do for pitchers now?"

Mouth looked at him dully. "I dunno," he sighed. "I just feel them one by one and whoever's warm—"

He walked past the reporter and disappeared into the night, a broken-nosed man with sagging shoulders who thought he heard the rustle of pennants in the night air, and then realized it was three shirts on a clothesline that stretched across two of the adjoining buildings.

THE HUMMING BIRD

Owen Johnson

I: FINNEGAN IN THE GLUMS

Young Brian de Boru Finnegan Chronicles Baseball

THEY LAY INCONGRUOUSLY entwined, reveling on the greensward, making disparaging remarks on the candidates for the Kennedy baseball nine, who flung themselves to and fro in lumbering, unprofessional attempts to capture the cannonade of grounders and liners that Captain Glendenning delivered to them from homeplate.

The three on the coaching line were P. Lentz, the King of the Kennedy, whose two hundred and fifty-six pounds, though it had served the varsity football team in many a grueling battle, was somewhat unfitted by nature to gambol on the diamond; Rosebud Mason, whose hands were too delicate, and Dennis de Brian de Boru Finnegan, aged twelve, who, despite his complete and amazing theoretical knowledge of the game, was too small to be distinguished back of second base. And of the three only Finnegan grieved at the deprivation.

Now, the Kennedy aggregation was not one to be proud of, and on this particular afternoon they were not even living up to their own discouraged opinion of themselves. In consequence, Glendenning at the bat, the Gutter Pup at second, and P. Lentz and Finnegan in the observation row, were voluble in their comments. Only

Rosebud, who did not wish to discourage Fatty Harris at third—for whom he substituted—remained discreetly silent.

"One out, man on third," announced Glendenning.

The ball went ripping and twisting toward third, where Fatty Harris valorously stopped it with his chest, dove clumsily for it, and after a moment's wild juggling seized it and threw to second. The rest sat down and roared.

"What's the matter?" said Fatty Harris, rubbing his chest and looking foolish.

"Great brain," said Glendenning. "Magnificent! Wonderful!"

"Pretty quick thinking, that," said the Gutter Pup seriously.

"Splendid!" said P. Lentz.

"You see," continued the Gutter Pup mercilessly, "Fatty calculated that the man on third, the moment he fumbled the ball, would run back to second!"

The Kennedy House cheered and hooted.

"You said 'man on first,' " said Harris stubbornly.

" 'Third.' "

"I heard you say 'first,' " Harris insisted.

"Too bad. I beg your pardon. Pray excuse me. I probably do not speak distinctly. Try again. Man on third and first; one out. Where is the man, *Mr.* Harris?"

"On third and first."

"I congratulate you. How many out?"

"One."

"Wonderful! Are you quite ready, Mr. Harris?"

"Hang it, go on!" said Harris miserably.

But instead of knocking the ball to Harris, Glendenning sent it sizzling to short, where Lovely Mead, who had settled down to enjoy the further confusion of Harris, caught unawares, stood helplessly, ball in hand, trying to remember the directions.

The four guardians of the sacks sat down and pretended to weep. Glendenning, deeming it about time to orate, shouted:

"Come on, come on! Do something with it. Don't stand there fondling it. Throw it away from you—it ain't good to eat. Throw it to right field or over the backstop—anywhere. But throw it, throw it!"

The ball came bounding home.

"Great work! Fine! Bright boy, Lovely. You stop the man at first from scoring. Say, this team is a wonder. This is the finest bunch of vaudeville jugglers ever gotten together. What are you—a lot of truck gardeners? Are we playing button, button, who's got the button?—or what?"

The silence was respectful.

"Say, if this goes on, I tell you what I'm going to do. I'm going to disband this bunch and organize the Kennedy croquet champions. Then we might beat someone. Now, once more. Repeat the play, and please, *please* remember there is such a thing as second base!"

Finnegan, pillowed on P. Lentz's leviathan back, was silent in disgust—which indeed was the only time silence descended on him.

"What do you think of it, Irish?" said P. Lentz with a grunt.

Finnegan refused to answer.

King Lentz looked at him and saw he was actually suffering.

"Suppose, young Irish, you think you ought to be there?"

Finnegan's fists closed spasmodically.

"Lord! Firecrackers," sang out King Lentz, "that bunch of yours is so rank even our gab factory here can't express himself."

The Tennessee Shad, who had once pitched an outcurve to the Gutter Pup in practice, came up with Jock Hasbrouck, the catcher, and fell languidly over the receptive King Lentz, who remarked sarcastically:

"How about that ancient outcurve they tell about?"

"I think I pitched another today," said the Shad, grinning.

King Lentz affected an immense surprise and looked at Jock Hasbrouck for confirmation.

"Straight ball," said Hasbrouck.

"Why, Jock," said the Tennessee Shad sorrowfully, "it did curve."

"Down."

"Hush," said the Shad, laughing. "Think of the Woodhull. We must carefully spread the impression, sort of let it percolate, that I've got everything—outsweeps and inshoots and fancy drops, etcetera, etceteray. Am I right, young Irish?"

Finnegan still refused to comment.

"What's the matter with our rapid-fire talker?" said Jock Hasbrouck in surprise.

"He's taken it to heart," said King Lentz, stopping to gaze mournfully at the spectacle of the Waladoo Bird on first muffing a pop fly that was only trying to steal into his pocket. "Irish doesn't appreciate the humor of it."

"You're all right, Irish," said big Jock Hasbrouck, pulling his ear affectionately. "That's the proper fighting spirit. Still, Bub, we can't win every house championship. The Dickenson has it pinched."

"And the Woodhull?" said Finnegan abruptly.

At this mention of their appointed and malignant enemy a mournful silence fell.

"The Woodhull's bum enough," said the Rosebud feebly.

"As bum as that?" said Finnegan with a contemptuous jerk of his thumb.

There was no protest.

"After what happened last fall," said Finnegan tearfully, "we've got to beat the Woodhull; we've just got to."

"Well, young sporting authority," said P. Lentz, somewhat irritated, "what chunk of pearly wisdom have you to offer?"

Dennis de Brian de Boru Finnegan drew himself up to his full four-feet-ten and gazed at them with scorn.

"Give *me* a chance at this nurserymaids' union," he said, and turned on his heel.

II: THE CAUSE OF ALL THE TROUBLE

Now, when Irish had referred to the Woodhull he had touched them on the raw. In the system of the school it naturally follows that certain houses become traditional rivals, but with the Kennedy and the Woodhull it was more serious. It had all begun with the annual football game in November. The consequent misunderstanding was slightly increased when the Woodhull, in a revengeful spirit, diverted a flock of geese into the Kennedy, and it was not at all alleviated when, in reciprocity, some martyr from the Kennedy caged a skunk and padlocked it to the exit of the Woodhull. A few minor occurrences helped to fan the feud to vendetta heat by the opening of the baseball season; but at the bottom the original difference of opinion went back to the now famous disputed game of football which is posted on the Kennedy records as: Kennedy 6, Woodhull 0; and on the Woodhull records: Woodhull 6, Kennedy 0 (forfeited). Several versions of the myth are now extant (the true story will some day be related), but all agree that the Tennessee Shad, quarterback on the Kennedy, was the originator of the trick. Two questions are still in debate: who won the game, and who smashed the ball? The Woodhull version lays the last to the Tennessee Shad and a sharpened nail; the other eleven variations allow proper credit to the Shad, but give to King Lentz and his two hundred and fifty-six pounds the glory of the unparalleled achievement. However that may be, the facts are these: At the beginning of the first half the Woodhull center fumbled the ball, P.

Lentz hurled his two hundred and fifty-six pounds on the coveted pigskin, there was a report like a dynamite explosion, the Tennessee Shad wriggled into the melee, seized the flattened leather, concealed it under his jersey and innocently ambled across the goal line, while the entire Woodhull eleven were frantically grubbing for the ball.

Here the game ended and the theoretical discussion began. Jack Rabbit Lawson, the referee, when face to face with the awful dilemma which he was expected to decide, wisely scudded for the Upper after exclaiming: "I resign!"

The Woodhull claim, tersely put, was that a ball is "dead" when it becomes a dead ball. The Kennedys asserted that the play had not been stopped, that the rules make no mention of the case, and that, anyway, the Woodhulls would have done the same thing if they had had the chance—which last argument in the logic of boyhood is recognized as a clincher.

At any rate, the question has never been decided, Jack Rabbit Lawson having absolutely refused to commit himself. Each house posted a victory on its records, swore its freshmen on the altar of eternal hatred, and began at once to prepare for the contest in baseball.

III: THE LANDING OF FINNEGAN

Finnegan knew baseball—he knew its theory and he knew its history. There prevails a popular error that boys do not study at boarding school. Nothing could be more unjust. Finnegan studied the sporting almanacs, and his knowledge was thorough and minute. He knew the records of the major leagues from the days of the Baltimore Orioles and Pop Anson, and though he was a little weak on the Southern and Pacific Coast circuits it was not due to any negligence on his part, but to the present deplorable insufficiency of data.

At this period, when Snorky Green covertly aspired to the Presidency, Doc Macnooder to the control of Standard Oil, while the Tennessee Shad believed that the mantle of the late P. T. Barnum might not be misplaced on his shoulders, and the Gutter Pup—fed on certain popular novels—dreamed of donning a mask and boxing the holder of the heavyweight championship of the world, Irish's ambition was to play third base on the Pittsburghs.

It is true that, witnessing an extravaganza at an early age, he was first tempted to be an Amazon and wheel and march in the gorgeous, stage-lit parades. But after things were explained to him he stifled this indiscretion and buried the secret in his heart, as one of the bitter delusions of youth.

Now, Finnegan was a character whom the school esteemed because it had been unable to tame him, for a school, unlike a college, respects individuality.

To go no further back than the beginning, on the opening of the school year, as the veterans of the Kennedy were sprawled magnificently on the side lawn, inspecting the new arrivals with caustic, terrifying comments, a buggy deposited on the roadside an immense bag and a small specimen of skin and bones. The new arrival was still in knickerbockers, his necktie had crept up under one ear, his visored cap was slanted over the other, underneath were two very bright eyes, an immense mouth and a nose that pointed to the north star.

"He's under six inches!" said the Gutter Pup. "Someone throw him back in the pond."

"He'll do to black shoes," said the Tennessee Shad, who had the languid Southern point of view.

Now, there are two moments in the life of a prep-school boy which are distinguished from all others: One is when as a senior he feels older, wiser, bigger than all the rest of the world, and the moment when he feels smaller, more foolish and more ridiculous than at any other time of his existence—that other moment when the carriage that has brought him deserts him, and he has to pass the gauntlet of thirty-odd older boys expressly gathered to make his arrival as uncomfortable as possible. Most newcomers hesitate a long moment and then go stumbling up the path with their eyes on their boots until halted by an imperious volley of questions:

"Stop there! What's your name?"

"Hi there, freshman! Take off your hat!"

"Give your name and what's your excuse for living!"

On the present occasion the diminutive new arrival only gave a tug or two at the telescope bag, straightened up with comical pertness, knocked farther back the visored cap, surveyed the terrifying group of veterans and exclaimed in Gatling-gun fashion:

"Hi there, one of you lazy, long-legged, spindle-shanked, knock-kneed, bowlegged, good-for-nothing roustabouts, jump up there now and give me a hand with me luggage. Lively now, lively!"

The Gutter Pup looked at the Waladoo Bird, who looked at Firecrackers Glendenning, who looked at Lovely Mead, whose jaw dropped as he looked sorrowfully at the Tennessee Shad.

Then, with one accord they gazed in perplexity at the impertinent little urchin standing at perfect ease at the end of the walk. The situation was absolutely novel. There was no precedent to govern the case. Had the newcomer been full-sized the probabilities are that his feet would not have touched the ground before he found himself on the third floor back, on his own appointed bed, underneath a heaping pile of his solicitous housemates reaching to the ceiling in what is known as a "pie" formation. But he wasn't full-sized; he was plainly, as the Gutter Pup expressed it, "under six inches," of the class which ought to arrive tearful and homesick. So the receiving committee frowned horribly and sat in stony perplexity.

"Hi there!" said the youngster, unabashed. "What's the matter with you? Is this a deaf and dumb asylum, or am I in Lawrenceville, John C. Green Foundation? Will someone kindly answer? Eh, what?"

"Come here," said the Waladoo Bird, as severe as the Roman himself.

"Come here yourself."

"Come here, you sawed-off, loudmouthed freshman!" the Waladoo Bird replied in a concise roar.

"Coming, sir, coming at once," said the youngster, who arrived with a handspring, saluted, and said roguishly: "Ah there, you sports!"

"Young suckling," said P. Lentz, "you're fresh."

"Why not? I'm young and tender."

"What's your name?"

"What's yours?"

"Freshman, *what's your name?*"

"Are we telling our names?"

"What!"

"Oh, very well. I'll begin," said the youngster pleasantly. And before they could recover from their amazement he had executed a rapid double-shuffle, ending with a slap to either boot, and begun in singsong:

> *"Wow, wow, wow; wow wow!*
> *Oh, me father's name was Finnegan,*
>   *Me mother's name was Kate.*
> *Me ninety-nine relations*
>   *To you I'll now relate.*

> *"Wow, wow, wow; wow wow!*
> *There was Dan the son of Michael's son,*

> *And O'Toole the son of Mat.*
> *And every son had sixteen sons*
> *Except the son of Pat.*

> *"Wow, wow, wow; wow wow!*
> *Oh, every son had sixteen sons,*
> *But some of them were girls.*
> *And Maggie married Hoolehan,*
> *And Peg refused three earls."*

"Stop!" shouted King Lentz fiercely, in order to maintain his gravity.

The urchin stopped.

"What's wrong?"

"Did you hear me ask your name? Did you?"

"That's the next verse," said the unabashed, and immediately started up again:

> *"Wow, wow, wow; wow wow!*
> *Now Dannie's sons were Flaherties*
> *And Michael's sons were Flynns,*
> *But Patrick's son was a son of a gun,*
> *And that's where I come in."*

"Stop, you wild Irishman!" cried the King again. "Your name's Finnegan?"

"Cute little boy," said Finnegan, smiling.

"Is it?"

"On again, off again, back again, Finnegan."

"What's the rest of it?"

"Dennis de Brian de Boru."

King Lentz looked at Finnegan like a judge of the Inquisition, but the urchin's face remained seraphic.

"Well, Dennis de Brian de Boru Finnegan," said the Gutter Pup, coming to the aid of imperiled tradition, "we won't do a thing to you—oh, no! You're going to be put on an allowance right now, quick!"

"Me no savvy," said the irrepressible.

"We'll give you just fifty words a day and then we're going to hermetically seal you up."

"You are?" said Finnegan defiantly. "You think you can bluff me, do you?—you candy dude, you hog-backed, pipe-legged, squint-eyed, stub-nosed, flop-eared——"

"Grab him," said the Gutter Pup.

Finnegan left the ground with a jerk and landed in P. Lentz's lap.

"Gag him," continued the Gutter Pup.

Five minutes later Dennis de Brian de Boru Finnegan, gagged and manacled, was carefully leaned against the brick wall while the Gutter Pup sternly addressed him:

"Young Irish, you've got a lot to learn, a lot, but don't let that worry you. Oh dear no! That's what we're here for. You are about the freshest green tomato that ever came down the pike, but we like 'em fresh; it gives us exercise, keeps our muscles in good condition. Now, you mark what I say to you: fifty words a day is your limit and then the gag for you. We'll see if this house is going to be turned into an echo parlor for you or any other sassy little squib from Squedunk."

The freckled features of Finnegan contracted violently, while the muscles of his jaw seemed to twitch over the inserted gag.

"Why, even the gag won't stop him," said the Tennessee Shad in admiration. "He's still talking."

IV: FINNEGAN AND DESTINY

For a week the regime was rigidly enforced without seeming in the least to check the inexhaustible flow of language. Finally, the allowance was increased to five thousand, and when it seemed that that liberal limit had been exceeded King Lentz would raise one finger, after the manner of the London police, and say:

"P. Lentz would like a little silence from you, young Irish, or, . . ."

And as Finnegan had learned that royalty's decrees are a command he at once subsided, waiting martyrlike for permission to break out again into double adjectives.

Gradually the urchin's absolute good humor and friendly offers won their way. He became a privileged character, and the Kennedy claimed him as a celebrity.

In the early days of spring the real Finnegan blossomed with the violets. He brought out a cap which had once been worn by a member of the Baltimore Orioles, he encased his left hand in a fielder's glove (not an effeminate mitt) and went daily to the baseball cage to advise Cap Keifer with the baseball candidates.

When the diamond hardened and the pitchers could try their skill in the open, Dennis de Brian de Boru Finnegan took up his position behind the box and made critical comments undeterred by ribald jesting.

With the opening of the baseball season, having become an active member of the staff of the *Lawrence,* he was naturally assigned to cover the first game. He came back to the Kennedy all in a flutter.

"Why, young Irishman," said the Tennessee Shad, who observed him in surprise, "you seem dreadfully excited, all up on your toes, what can be the matter?"

"I've got my chance," said Dennis de Brian de Boru, glowing and yet with a certain solemnity.

"Explanations."

"I'm to write up the game."

"Oh, is that all?"

"All!" said Dennis de Brian de Boru Finnegan, with a pitying smile. "Wait—just wait!"

Now Finnegan in his revolutionary, irreverent, little soul had a definite idea of the way such contests should be clothed in literary raiment. All that afternoon and evening he shut himself up in his room and, prone on the floor, chin in hands, he roved through his voluminous collection of picturesque accounts of famous contests on the diamond. The more he read the more the prosy, narrow English of the classroom receded before the unbridled images and tropical eloquence, and the conviction grew that here was the only, the long-awaited, the genuine American Epic. Thus fired with poetic fervor he awaited the day that should enroll him among the great creative forces of English prose.

The game itself was an unusually commonplace one—6 to 1 in favor of the home team against a scrub nine from Princeton.

Dennis de Brian de Boru Finnegan, with a notebook that seemed as large as a blackboard, camped down near first base and sharpened a pencil with complete disdain of the jibes and witticisms that instantly saluted him from the banked school behind. They were creatures of the minute—his duty was to posterity.

When the game was over he gravely interviewed both captains, with special reference as to the effect of the foul-strike rule on amateur batting, thanked them, shook hands and went straight to his room. After supper he took a brisk three turns of the Circle, peremptorily refusing all company and, ascending to his room again, sported the oak.

The next evening the future sporting editor of the *New York Sun,* still dissatisfied—as genius should be—with the inadequacy of his efforts, reluctantly trudged to the Upper and laid his copy before his chief—Socrates Smith.

Dennis de Brian de Boru Finnegan, boy, would have scorned to show either reverence or fear, Dennis de Brian de Boru Finnegan, artist, humble and aspiring to perfection, waited with sinking hopes.

"Please, Socrates," he said, at last alarmed by the protracted silence, "what do you think of it?"

Smith swayed back, cracked his chair, kicked it aside and went to another without his gaze leaving the copy.

"I say, how does it read?"

"I say, is it any good at all?"

"I say—I might do it over."

Smith finished the reading, looked up and noticed the apprehensive Finnegan for the first time.

"Well?" said Dennis all in a breath.

"I suppose you know Bingham's away, our beloved censor," said Smith dreamily.

"Yes—but——"

"They may expel me for publishing it," said Socrates solemnly, gazing at the manuscript. "They probably will expel me. But, by the great Horned Spoon, this goes in!"

As luck would have it Mr. Bingham, the senior English master, to whom devolved the duty of a general supervision of the *Lawrence* and the *Lit.*, was called away to make an address in New York, and that issue of the school paper went to publication unsuspected and unmolested.

V: FINNEGAN AND THE GREAT AMERICAN EPIC

The *Lawrence* usually is languidly circulated on a Saturday. On the present occasion twenty minutes after it was put on sale the faculty telephones were buzzing with excited inquiries, while Bingham, standing at his receiver, gazed in horror at a copy of the *Lawrence* and sought in a dazed way to explain to each rapidly succeeding inquirer just how it had happened. Meanwhile a crowd of delirious nonsubscribers was storming the *Lawrence* editor and offering twenty-five cents each for the remaining copies of the following picturesque account, which Bingham still gazed at in classic horror:

SPINKED!
LAWRENCEVILLE SPANKS THE PIPPIN ON THE NOSE!
LAWRENCEVILLE, 6; PRINCETON, 1

Barrett, the peerless one, the nifty ten-thousand-dollar beauty from Walla Walla, was in form—that's all. His delivery would have kept a cryptograph specialist figuring through the night. His outdrop had the Princeton scrub carving arabesques on the ozone in mad, frantic, muscle-racking lunges for the elusive horsehide. He had 'em digging trenches with his drops and climbing for cherries with his high ones. He had 'em reaching for the wide ones, like July tomcats sitting on the edge of a fountain and striking for goldfish.

Ross, the scrub pitcher, was very much appreciated by our favorite sons. They bumped him for five ordinaries, soaked a couple of repeats, spanked a three-sacker and smeared the bun for one smoking, sizzling homer.

SCORE BY INNINGS

Smith, the first to lift the locust for the Jungle Puppies, pushed a hoist to Walader, who swallowed it without blinking. Hanson frisked the daisytops with a whistler that Hicks gobbled up and posted to Stevens. Branch stung a boiler that DeSoto stonewalled and wafted to first.

For Lawrenceville, Charlie DeSoto lounged until he drew four misfits, burglared the second story, and whisked to third when Hickey spilled a Texas leaguer to right. Walader jolted a fast bounder to second, which Hanson congealed in time to slaughter Hickey at the midway, DeSoto sneaking up the home boulevard with the first brass ring. Butcher Stevens pushed a blue-domer to center. Hastings slapped a screamer over first and, when the foot race was over, Walader was carving his initials on the door mat and our Bill was dusting third. Billy Barnes held up two strikes and three balls to draw for fours, but got three of a kind instead. Hard luck, Bill!

SECOND INNING

Oberfield miscued twice and then shot a safe one over second pocket. Maguire was out in a floater to Hickey. Ross died in his tracks with three fractures, and Hickson chopped a playful one to DeSoto, who jabbed it into Oberfield, making the third demise.

Flash Condit worked out a pass. Cap Keefer, our cerise specialist, could do no better than a gentle winger to center, Barrett nicked one to the chicken coop, which Maguire annexed, while DeSoto raised a steeplechaser which scratched the nebulae.

THIRD INNING

Our peerless one's assorted strikes continued as deceptive as the green spectacles the farmer put on the cow who wouldn't eat straw.

Wright was sent up for three murderous assaults, Rogers diverted one to the poultry yard, Cap Keefer hugged it, and Smith popped up to Walader.

Hickey refused to bite on a wild one and splashed a rippler over third. Walader expired to send him to Second Avenue with a slow chugger to third; Butcher Stevens caught a sweeper on the solar plexus and hammered it where the nightingale warbles its plaintive lays. Hickey ambled home, and Butcher Stevens roosted on third. Billy Barnes went after a fadeaway and died on a zephyr to the curve box. Flash Condit received the courtesy of the house and toddled, but Keefer was slaughtered on a twister that beat him to first by the Ross-Smith route.

FOURTH INNING

Things looked as squally as an actors' boardinghouse when the invited guest takes two charlotte russes on the first pass. Hanson reached the initial hassock on a butterfinger specialty of Walader's, Branch dropped a hot one in left field, Maguire poached another on the same order, Hanson dusting the pan. Ross showed himself a cute little waiter and strolled as a deadhead, filling the bases. Hickson smote a broncho-bucker to Hickey, who massacred it and nailed Branch to the rubber; Hickson bit the dust on Keefer's quick flip to first. Wright ended the suspense by boosting a ladybird to short.

At this point Mr. Bingham's self-possession completely deserted him. He fell into an easy chair, ran his lank fingers wildly through his hair and stared at the *Lawrence* in awe, amazement and consternation.

At this moment who should come in smiling but Dennis de Brian de Boru Finnegan in the flesh. A smile of perfect content was on the young revolutionist, while his right hand held proudly secure his next installment.

"Finnegan," said Bingham, waving the *Lawrence* toward him. "Did you—? Is this your work?"

"Why, yes, sir," said Finnegan brightly. "How did you like it?"

Mr. Bingham slowly collected his wits, and his feelings turned from awe to admiration. What he wanted to say was: "Good heavens, you extraordinary youngster, how did you ever concoct it?" But it is not always wise for a master to say what he thinks. There was the English of Spenser and Addison to be protected. So he simply stared.

"It was a bit rough, sir," said Finnegan apologetically, "but I've done better with this. I think it will please you."

"You have done another, Finnegan?"

"Why, yes, sir—yesterday's game. Would you like to hear it, sir?"

The expounder of the Elizabethan line drew his hand across his forehead, steadied himself and said: "You may begin, Finnegan."

Finnegan curled up on the sofa, flattened his manuscript over his knee, gazed at it fondly a moment and began as preface:

"I thought I'd tell the story by innings, sir. It makes it more dramatic, I think, than to give a résumé first."

"Is that a criticism on modern journalism, Finnegan?"

"Well, sir," said Finnegan with unusual modesty, "I think this is an improvement. It holds you in suspense—gives you the feeling of being there, you know."

"Go on, Finnegan."

" 'Lawrenceville, 5; Pennington, 4,' " said Finnegan. " 'In the breakaway Tyrell, the first to dust the rubber for the Chaperons——' "

"Chaperons?" said Bingham, puzzled.

"It's coed, you know, sir. 'Chaperons' gives rather a touch of humor, don't you think?"

"I see."

" 'In the breakaway Tyrell, the first to dust the rubber for the Chaperons, selected a hole in the circumambient and poked a buzzer over short . . .' "

"Go slow, Finnegan."

"Yes, sir—'Minds soaked a clover-kisser to the far station, which Walader kittened to and whipped to first. . . .' "

"I don't get that, Finnegan."

"What is it, sir?"

"Well, the whole episode is a trifle hazy. What is a clover-kisser?"

"Why, a daisy scorcher, sir."

"You mean a grounder?"

"A certain kind of grounder, sir, very low—one that doesn't rise from the grass. Quite different from a bronchobuster or a dewdrop, sir."

"I'm afraid I have specialized too much in medieval English; what is this thing you call 'a bronchobuster'?"

"A bronchobuster is a grounder, a rather tabasco grounder, that bucks and kicks."

"Very lucid, Finnegan, and a 'dewdrop'?"

"Why, that's a weakling—a toddler—all luck, you know."

"Ah, yes. Now let me think, Walader stopped the daisy scorcher——"

"Clover-kisser, sir"

"Exactly. So Walader stopped it and retired the man at first?"

"Why, yes, sir."

"Proceed, Finnegan, proceed."

" 'Tyrell, who had purloined the second perch, started to ramble to Waladersburg when Jackson stung the planet DeSoto-wise for a safety, but our iridescent little body snatcher lassoed it and slaughtered the rally with a staccato lunge to the midway that completed the double demise.' "

"Ah yes, that is simpler," said the Master gravely. "Now for Lawrenceville."

" 'DeSoto streaked the empyrean blue with a white winger that was strangled in center.' "

"A fly, Finnegan?"

"Yes, sir."

"Just an ordinary fly?"

"Oh no, sir, a rather high one."

"Continue."

" 'Hickey ticked off a slow freight to the pretzel counter and cannon-balled to first just ahead of Tyrell's slap.' "

"Let us go back."

"Why, what's wrong, sir?"

"Ticked off a slow freight?"

"Bunted a slow one."

"Naturally—but pretzel counter?"

"The curve box—the pitcher."

"Of course!"

" 'Stevens frisked the lozenge once to the backwoods and then unmuzzled a humming bird to the prairies which nested in Jackson's twigs—' "

"Repeat that."

" 'Stevens unmuzzled a humming bird which—' "

"I don't like unmuzzled."

"I could say uncorked, sir."

"No, I don't fancy uncorked, either."

"Unhitched, then."

"Never unhitched. The fact is, the use of the words humming bird in this connection does not seem to me appropriate at all."

Finnegan looked very solemn and said with difficulty: "Please, sir, I would like to keep that expression, sir. I'm rather proud of that. A humming bird is a liner, you know, that hums. Please, sir, I hope you'll let me leave that in?"

"Finnegan," said Mr. Bingham with difficult gravity, "you may as well know the truth now. We have decided to adhere to the English of our fathers."

"I beg pardon."

"I mean that I shall have to edit your copy in future down to the comprehension of the most ignorant college graduate."

"Isn't the grammar right, sir?"

"The grammar is irreproachable."

"What are you going to do, sir?"

"I'm going to translate, Finnegan."

"Translate!"

"And you're going to help me, Finnegan," said Bingham, taking up paper and pencil. "From what I gather the first inning should begin like this: 'Tyrell singled, Minds was out on a grounder to Walader, Tyrell, who had started for third, was caught off second on DeSoto's brilliant catch of Jackson's liner.' "

Finnegan sat silent, staring at his thumbs.

"Is that the way it's got to be done?" he said at last.

"I'm afraid so, Finnegan."

"You're not going to leave in the humming bird, sir?"

"I'm afraid not, Finnegan. 'Unmuzzled' or 'uncorked' or 'unchained' a 'humming bird' is daring, enthusiastic and undoubtedly expressive, but at the present moment the English Department of the Lawrenceville School does not feel strong enough to offer it to the nation."

"What are you going to do with it?" said Finnegan abruptly.

"We'll say: 'Stevens' sizzling liner went straight into the mitt of—' "

"I won't sign it," said Finnegan hoarsely.

"No, Finnegan, you shall not be subjected to that humiliation."

"You won't let it stand, sir?" said Finnegan, with a last hope.

"No, Finnegan."

"Then I *resign!*" said Finnegan, walking out of the room with trembling lips.

The shock was terrific. Nobody could console him, not even the Tennessee Shad, who told him for his consolation how Keats and Shelley, English poets, had been cut off in the flower of youth by just such savage critics. For two whole days Irish remained dumb, to the great alarm of the entire house.

Then suddenly, as though nothing had happened, he turned up as voluble as ever. But if outwardly he seemed to have forgotten, inwardly he cherished a mighty scheme of revenge. The Woodhull must taste the bitter dregs of defeat—Bingham was the master of the Woodhull.

VI: THE APOTHEOSIS OF FINNEGAN

When finally the Woodhull and the Kennedy gathered for the fray there was but one plan of campaign in both camps—to rattle the enemy! Both teams had been outclassed in the house series, and no one cared particularly about the outcome—no one except the Woodhull and the Kennedy.

Each nine arrived in gang formation. The Woodhull camped down directly behind third base in combative attitudes, and the Kennedy occupied strong ground opposite, as close to first as the law allows. The Woodhull's fish-horn double octet was led by Toots Cortell and his celebrated Confederate bugle. The Kennedys, more ambitious, had organized a symphony orchestra composed of two drums, several cowbells, a harmonica, one lonely flute and supporting horns.

As Fusser McCarty (cousin of Tough McCarty), pitcher for the Woodhull, stepped into the box and prepared to wind himself up for his famous gyroscope delivery, he was greeted by the following chant from the Kennedy minstrels, led by the vindictive Finnegan:

> "Oh McCarty is a pretty boy.
>   (So they say.)
> And all the girls think Mac's just too sweet for words.
>   (I wonder why?)
> 'Cause he parts his hair in the middle and he has a lily cheek.
>   (Oh, is that all?)
> Well, his ways are soft and pretty and he has a coaxing smile.
>   (Yes, but can he pitch?)

CHORUS:

"Look at the part in his hair,
Look at the rose in his cheek,
Look at his arm, his soft, white arm,
BUT watch for the yellow streak!"

Under these favorable circumstances McCarty, with an appearance of extreme insouciance, hurled the ball over the backstop.

Finnegan sprang up solemnly.

"Don't cheer, boys," he cried; "he's rattled!"

McCarty shrugged his shoulders, deliberately calculated the height of the backstop and carefully pitched a drop that struck ten feet in front of home plate.

Whereupon Legs Brocket, who hated a pitched ball worse than a yellow jacket, contemptuously reversed his bat, crossed his feet and assumed a bored, Apollo Belvedere, waiting attitude.

The Glee Club sang:

"Good-by, McCarty, we're going to lose you now.
Good-by, McCarty, you couldn't fan a cow.
Good-by, McCarty, you certainly are a pie.
So, good-by, McCarty, good-by!"

When the inning ended McCarty had given three bases on balls and allowed two hits, which had produced two runs.

The Tennessee Shad—who had once pitched an outcurve—stepped confidently into the box. Snorky Green's bat, in trying to dodge a wild one, met the ball accidentally and knocked a grounder to Fatty Harris. It was an easy ball, what Finnegan called a foozled dewdrop, and under ordinary circumstances even Harris, who loathed the game, would have covered himself with glory. But right alongside the impressionable third baseman were camped the busy Woodhull rooters, and from the moment he had taken his position Harris had listened to the following:

"Don't cross your feet, Fat."

"Look out, you're going to trip."

"You're playing too close."

"You'll get it in the smeller."

"Fat, you'll get hurt!"

"It's awful rough ground."

"There's a bump just behind you."

"Don't listen to us."

"Keep your mind on the game!"

At this moment the ball from little Snorky's bat came gently bounding toward him. The chorus rose to a shriek:

"Run back!"

"Fall down!"

"Fumble it!"

"Juggle it!"

And Fat, in a buck fever, juggled it.

"Throw high!"

"Throw low!"

"Throw it wild!"

"Wild!"

"Hold it!"

Snorky Green, likewise frightened to death, reached first like a runaway rabbit, to find himself a hero. Instantly he turned, shifted his chewing gum to the other cheek, and spat on his hands.

"Aw, he's a cinch, Crazy," he cried contemptuously to the next batter. "Soak out another beauty."

When the inning ended Finnegan was in glum despair. On five errors and no hits the Woodhull had duplicated the Kennedy's total.

In the second inning, due to the annoying delay in the appearance of the Tennessee Shad's famous outcurve, the score stood Woodhull 5, Kennedy 3. By the middle of the eighth inning it stood Woodhull 9, Kennedy 5.

The Tennessee Shad flung himself down beside Finnegan.

"It looks bad, Irish, doesn't it?" he said.

"It looks awful, awful," said Finnegan brokenly.

"There's not enough moisture in the air," said the Tennessee Shad by way of explanation. "I think that's the trouble with that outcurve of mine."

"The game's being thrown away," said Irish, devastating the turf in front of him. "You're all right; they only made ten hits off you."

The Tennessee Shad looked at him from under his eyelids.

"Sure, Shad, we're hitting McCarty just as hard. It's Fatty Harris at third is the trouble."

"You see yourself there, do you?"

"Fat has made six errors."

"You can't bat, Irish."

"I can work 'em for a base on balls; but that ain't it. Oh, Shad, just give me a chance on the coaching line—just one inning, Shad!"

"Why, what would you do?"

"I'd have the whole blooming Woodhull bunch so woozy that they'd have to stop the game every five minutes to unsnarl their fingers."

"You know, Irish, that's a rather swift idea of yours," said the Tennessee Shad, impressed.

"Oh, Shad, will you ask Glendenning, will you? And, Shad, I've got even a better idea."

"Produce it."

"It's a shift formation."

"Say, do you think this is a game of feet ball?"

"No. Listen to me, Shad. What's the matter with us? It's second base, third and short, isn't it?"

"Well?"

"Our outfield is O. K., but it's the infield that loses the game. Now, we want to shift."

"Yes, and have every fly go for a home run."

"Not at all. There are only four fellows on the Woodhull can knock the ball out of the diamond, and they're bunched at the head of the list, aren't they?"

"Sure!"

"Use two formations, Shad. Keep your outfield where it is for the good ones, and shift it for the dubs."

"My wonder, boy!" said the Tennessee Shad in admiration. "That idea will revolutionize house championships. You come with me."

And seizing Finnegan by the collar he swung him to his feet and carried him over to Glendenning.

Ten minutes later the sun burst into a new glory, for Finnegan, encased in a martial mitt, strode out magnificently to left field, rounded a hold in his glove with his fist, cocked his visored cap and proclaimed aloud:

"Hi, Shad—strike out these fuzzy carpetbeaters."

The new formation worked wonders with the astonished Woodhulls; for the first time in the game they ended their inning blanked.

"Now, Irish, you young dictionary," said the Tennessee Shad as the Kennedy frolicked in to bat, "we are all looking at you. We need four runs; go up to the coaching line and make good!"

Finnegan disdained to boast. He marched like a gladiator to the coaching box, stuck his arms and legs akimbo, cocked his freckled, star-pointed little nose, and began shrilly:

"Here I am, McCarty, here I am. Over here, right over here. That's it, this way!"

McCarty, surprised, committed the indiscretion of looking over.

"All right, Mac, it's me. It's Finnegan—Dennis de Brian de Boru Finnegan. He's right here, talking to you. But don't look! Keep your eyes on the plate! Don't look over! Don't look, don't. Hi yi, yi yi yi! Ball one! Don't mind me, Mac; don't listen to me. Try and keep your mind on the game. Hi! wild pitch! I'm not going to rattle you, Mac; no, siree; oh no! Whoopee! Up and down the Orinoco River, Timbuctoo and North and South Rome Centers. Hi yi, yi yi! Wow! Ball three! Good waiting, Fat; he's scared of you. Watch his eyes now! Watch his rolling eye. Base on balls as good as a hit. What, a strike? Never mind, Fat; I'm here. Finnegan's here. The next is a wide one. Look out now! look out, it's coming! It's—Whoopee! Kibosh! Walla Walla! Wow! Come right up to first, Fat. Thank you, Mister McCarty. I hope my little jocularity doesn't annoy you, Mac. Does it? 'Cause if it does, will I stop it? Ask me. Say, McCarty, do I disturb you? Another ball? Why, Mac, I didn't say anything. Did I? Man on first, Mac. Don't forget that. Throw over now! Throw quick and wild! No? Too bad. Another ball? How sad! Always take Mother's advice. Now, all together, on your toes! Spank the good ones, Lovely. On your toes! Here it comes. Ball three! Is it possible? Say, McCarty, I'm here; right over here. Don't forget me, Mac—Finnegan. You know Finnegan, don't you?

> *"Wow, wow, wow; wow, wow, wow!*
> *Oh, me father's name was Finnegan,*
> *Me mother's name was Kate.*
> *Me ninety-nine relations*
> *To you I'll now relate."*

While the embattled McCarty, abjured by every one of his mates to keep cool, to hold his nerve, to steady down, strove to banish from his mind the pest on the coaching line, Finnegan, with arms extended in whirling-dervish fashion, continued to rotate to the slogan of the Finnegans, while the assembled Kennedys periodically broke into the wolfish chorus:

"Wow, wow; wow, wow, wow!"

Now, there is something peculiarly irritating in the last interjection, irritating and insultingly exultant. McCarty was not conscious of being rattled, and yet he had passed two men on balls and was in a fair way to pass a third. He was a little distracted, that was all, by the shrill insect that kept piping:

"Here I am, McCarty! Right over here! Finnegan. It's Finnegan. Just over here. This way."

McCarty tried getting angry, frowning horribly, gripping the ball and hurling it with vindictive energy. Then he tried to appear amused and succeeded worse. Finally, with a run in and the bases full, a consultation was held at the insistence of the entire Wood-hull team. Instantly, the Kennedy Glee Club struck up:

> *"Look at the part in his hair,*
> *Look at the rose on his cheek,*
> *Look at his arm, his lily-white arm,*
> *BUT watch for the yellow streak.*

> *"Watch for the yellow streak, boys,*
> *McCarty never owned a curve.*
> *Watch for the yellow streak, boys!*
> *Watch for the dub who's lost his nerve.*

> *"He may be the ladies' darling, boys,*
> *They like 'em soft and sleek;*
> *But we'll get him in any old inning, boys,*
> *FOR McCarty has a yellow streak."*

Now, McCarty happened to be captain of the Woodhull nine and so could not be ousted violently. He had, in fact, decided to retire in favor of some less impressionable member; but this song was too much for him. He angrily quelled the revolt and strolled back into the box. Besides, Dennis de Brian de Boru was at the bat, and he couldn't resist the opportunity to crush his tormentor.

When Finnegan took up a professional position in the batter's box the space permitted McCarty for strikes was exceedingly small. Likewise, Finnegan materially diminished the slender opportunity. In the first place, he pulled his trousers above the knees and anxiously drew the umpire's attention to their exact location. Then, with heels neatly together and his bat tucked under one ear in the fashion of the perennial Willie Keeler, he selected the frontier edge of the batter's box and impudently declared:

"Give me a nice inshoot, you yellow man, and I'll soak her out."

But McCarty had evolved a crafty scheme for the humiliation of Finnegan. He stood still and with gentle underhand motion tossed the ball over the plate.

"Strike one!" cried Turkey Reiter, umpire.

"Aw, give me man's size!" said Finnegan angrily.

"Baby ones for baby boys," said McCarty, grinning.

He tossed a second strike amid the jeers of his supporters. But he tried it once too often. On the next ball the enraged Finnegan struck blindly, and to the amazement of all sent a safe hit over third, who was playing in. Two men scored, and Finnegan, triumphant, danced a breakdown on second, cakewalked to third and came home turning cart wheels. Meanwhile, the bases on balls succeeded one another like cigars doled out at a political picnic. And Finnegan, back on the coaching line, piped forth:

"Back again, on the job again, here we are again, Finnegan. Keep it up, McCarty, keep it up! No favoritism, every man a base on balls!

" *'As we go round the mulberry bush,*
The mulberry bush, the mulberry bush.'

"Ball three! Thank you, Mr. Umpire. Wonderful control, Fusser, wonderful control—he hasn't let a ball go over the plate, not a ball!

" *'Mother, may I go out to pitch?*
Yes, my darling Fusser,
Chuck the ball around the lot
But don't go near the batter.'

"Four balls, well, well! Come right on up, Mr. Mead, you won't have any trouble finding the way home; don't run, we've got to do a lot of walking this evening. Hi! yi! Ypsylanti! Sockarooger! Walla walla, Wow!!! All right, McCarty, that's me, Finnegan. Does it annoy you, does it? Never mind, I'll stop. I'm going to stop right now, Fusser, right now. If you'll ask me. But ask me *po*-litely! I'm so sensitive! Tonawanda! Put 'em over!! Yi, yi, Whoopee, Hot Tamale, Kibosh, Ke, Zow, Zow!!!

"Another ball, you don't say so. Never mind, think of the record you are making, McCarty, think of that! Don't forget. I'll stop any time you ask me, any time, McCarty! Any time you ask me *po*-litely. What was that? I'm glad I don't annoy you, oh, I'm so glad! Are you getting ready to pitch again? Wait a moment. Just one moment, Squedunk, Raritan, Pocono, San José and Sacramento! All hands around! Swing your partners. Look out! Look out! Yi, yi, yi, yi, yi! Thank you. Ball two, take a chair, Shad, take a couch, take a nap. I'll wake you when it's time to come up. I say, Fusser, I say! This way! You're all right, aren't you? Perfectly cool? Good boy! Glee Club, a little burst of melody. Are you ready? Go!

" *'Gee! it's nice to be a fusser,*
And to fuss the darling girls!

It's a cinch to be a fusser
And have them smooth your curls!
  BUT—
Oh me! Oh my!
Ain't it awful when the fusser,
One, two, three! Um, di, doodle, di!
GETS FUSSED!!!' "

Whereupon McCarty retired and the Glee Club, in mournful accents, sang his demise:

"Will someone tell his mother
  How poor McCarty died.
Will someone write his brother
  Who stood there by his side.

"He weakened in the second,
  In the third he gasped for breath.
But the truth about McCarty is
  He was simply scared to death!"

The Woodhull sent in four pitchers to face the Kennedy batters and Dennis de Brian de Boru Finnegan, and each fell before the torrent of words. When the inning ended ten runs had gone to the credit of the Kennedy and the victory was won.

A quarter of an hour later, as Finnegan and the Tennessee Shad returned exultingly through the village, they met Mr. Bingham of the Woodhull.

"Ah, Finnegan," said the master pleasantly, "game over?"

"Yes, sir.'

"Good game?"

"Pretty good, sir."

"Close?"

"Not very close, sir."

"Who won?" said the master, forced at last to the demand direct.

And Finnegan answered proudly:

"I did."

Finnegan likewise wrote a classic account of the contest for private distribution. It began:

"The game was tucked away when Dennis unmuzzled a humming bird . . ."

THE THEFT OF
THE MEAGER BEAVERS

Edward D. Hoch

T HE MAN WAS slim and dark and Latin, and his name was
Jorge Asignar. He sat across the table from Nick Velvet,
studying him through narrow, uncertain eyes.

"I understand that you steal things," he said, speaking with a
pronounced accent.

"Some things," Nick admitted. "Unusual things." He'd been
at home with Gloria, relaxing with a cold beer, when the call had
come from Asignar. He disliked the man immediately, but personal
feelings never entered into his professional activities. "What do
you want stolen?"

Jorge Asignar smiled, showing a line of gold-capped teeth. "A
baseball team."

"A baseball team?" In his business nothing ever surprised Nick
Velvet. "Any special one?"

The Latin shrugged. "I leave the choice to you. Your fee, I
believe, is $20,000?"

"That's correct, under ordinary circumstances. But for especially difficult or dangerous assignments I charge thirty thousand.
With something this size I believe the larger fee would be justified."

Asignar waved an indifferent hand. "Agreeable. Half the money
now and the balance on delivery."

"Fine."

"Then the choice of a team and all other arrangements are

106

yours. It must be a major league professional team, and it must be delivered intact to my country within the next two weeks.''

Nick glanced at the calendar in his wallet. Two weeks would give him till August 16th. ''And what is your country?''

''The island Republic of Jabali. Not far beyond Cuba, in the Caribbean.''

''I see,'' Nick said slowly. ''And might I ask what the Republic of Jabali wants with an American baseball team?''

Asignar curled his lips in a sort of smile, showing again the gold-capped teeth. ''Our president, General Tras, is a great baseball fan. In past years your teams occasionally played exhibition games in Jabali, but there have been none in several years. General Tras has personally trained and equipped a Jabali national team, but they have no one to play.''

''Let me get this straight,'' Nick said. ''You want me to steal an entire baseball team and transport it to Jabali just so your president can have competition for his private team?''

Asignar bristled a bit. ''You are well paid to perform a service, Mr. Velvet. I had understood from some satisfied customers that you never questioned the peculiarity of an assignment.''

''And I don't. But do you realize what this theft might do to relations between Jabali and the United States? There was a time when it would have brought a boatload of Marines to your shore. Even now you could hardly escape without denouncement in Congress and possibly some sort of economic sanctions.''

''As soon as the team is in our hands we plan to issue a statement that the theft is merely temporary. We will return the team safely after one game with our Jabali team. We could hardly expect to hold the American players indefinitely.''

''You're still in for a lot of trouble from Washington,'' Nick warned. But then, having said it, he accepted Asignar's half fee— in cash.

''What are you doing, Nick?'' Gloria asked later that evening. They were sitting in the back-yard patio, after dinner, as he pondered the evening paper.

''Checking the baseball standings.''

''I never knew you were interested, except at World Series time.''

''I'll be away on another trip,'' he told her. ''Just wanted to see what games I'll miss.''

Nick had already decided that the theft of the baseball team must not be allowed to interfere with the pennant races in the two leagues. But this early in August most of the teams were still in contention. He did some quick figuring and found that only one team was definitely out of it—the hapless Beavers. Though Nick followed the sport only occasionally he was—like nearly everyone else in the country—well aware of the Beavers' plight. They had replaced the old Brooklyn Dodgers and then the New York Mets as the butt of comedians' jokes, and after losing 14 straight games earlier in the season the sports sections had dubbed them the "Meager Beavers."

All right, Nick decided. Since the choice was his to make, it would be the Beavers. Perhaps with the Beavers to play against, General Tras might even be victorious with his own team, and that would certainly please him.

Next Nick checked the schedules of the Beavers at home and on the road for the next two weeks. They flew to New York for a weekend series with the Mets on Thursday. Then, on Monday, they flew on to Atlanta to play the Braves before returning home. Nick checked the standings again and confirmed that the Braves were also far down in the National League. A postponed or canceled game would not affect their standing, either.

Then that's what it would be—the Beavers on next Monday—a full week ahead of Asignar's deadline.

Pop Hastin had been manager of the Beavers for as long as anyone—even the sportswriters—could remember. He'd come up with the team from Triple-A baseball when the National League expanded, and it was only a high personal regard for Pop that had kept the Beavers from ridicule this long.

He was a gray, bristly man in his early sixties, and his reputation for eating umpires alive had got him thrown out of many ball games. The fans and the sportswriters loved it, of course, as they loved everything Pop did. They'd turned against his Meager Beavers only with the greatest reluctance.

"You're a writer?" Pop asked, eyeing Nick with open suspicion. They'd met in the dressing room at Shea Stadium, just after the Mets defeated the Beavers by a score of 9 to 1.

"That's right," Nick confirmed, passing over a card. "With *Sports Weekly*. We want to do an article on your team."

Pop Hastin grunted, rolling the plug of chewing tobacco to his other cheek. "More Meager Beaver stuff?"

"Nothing like that. My editors want an in-depth article with a sympathetic slant, to balance some of the other stuff."

"How long will it take? We're flying to Atlanta in the morning."

Nick hesitated, then said, "I was going to suggest that I might fly down with you. That way we could talk at leisure and I'd get to meet some of your key players."

Hastin snorted. "This year the Beavers got no key players. We haven't gotten more than four runs in any game all summer."

"Still, there's Karowitz at first base—"

"Yeah, he's pretty good."

"And that rookie shortstop, Nesbitt."

"The kid, yeah." Pop Hastin shifted the tobacco again. "Well, I guess you could fly down with us. There's plenty of room these days. Not many of your sportswriters come along any more."

Nick Velvet smiled. "I'll meet you at the airport in the morning, then."

The chartered jet which flew the Beavers between cities on the National League circuit was piloted by a young man named Farnsworth. He stood by the ramp with a pretty, long-legged stewardess welcoming the players aboard, smiling and joking with them about the previous day's game.

Nick Velvet, walking beside Pop Hastin, boarded the plane with a friendly nod toward the pilot and stewardess. It was a clear August morning, perfect for flying, and the players seemed in a good mood considering their recent losses. There were nineteen of them making the trip, plus Pop and the coaches. A publicity man —a slight harried individual named Roswell—was also along, as were the trainer, batboy, and a few others.

"Sometimes we have a planeload," Hastin explained, settling comfortably into his seat and strapping himself down. "But this isn't much of a trip and a few of the regulars aren't making it. We have a couple of injured players back home, and some of the front-office people stayed in New York for a league meeting."

Roswell, the publicity man, dropped into the seat across the aisle, eyeing Nick with open suspicion. It had not been an easy season for him. "What sort of an article did you say you were writing?" he asked.

Pop Hastin interrupted, trying to avoid trouble. "All the equipment on board, Ros?"

"Sure it is. That's not my job, anyway." He turned his attention back to Nick. "We've had a pretty bad press the last few months —all this Meager Beaver stuff. If you're going to write something like that, forget it."

"No, nothing like that," Nick reassured them. "I'm planning something that will put the Beavers on the front pages of every paper in the country and make people forget you're in last place in the National League.''

The jet had risen smoothly from the runway and was climbing into the clear blue sky. Pop Hastin relaxed. ''We're on our way,'' he said. ''Now just how do you propose to give us all this publicity? Through *Sports Weekly?*''

''Partly,'' Nick answered vaguely. ''Suppose you introduce me to a few of the players.''

They went forward in the plane and Pop spoke to the team's muscular first baseman. ''Stan Karowitz, this is Mr. Nicholas, a writer with *Sports Weekly*. He's going to give us a good article.''

Nick dropped into the seat next to Karowitz and started asking the Beavers' star some routine questions, taking notes as he talked. ''Do you think the Beavers are coming out of their slump, Stan?''

''It's a little late in the year now,'' Karowitz replied, ''but we think our rookies might make a strong foundation for next season.''

Nick had been watching the stewardess walk past them to the cockpit and unlock the door with a key that dangled from her waist. She was carrying a tray with two steaming cups of coffee. ''Pardon me,'' he interrupted Karowitz.

He moved quickly down the aisle behind the girl, catching the door before she could close it. The flight was still young, but he might not get another chance this good. He pushed past her, shoved the copilot aside, and pointed a pistol at the pilot's head.

Farnsworth, the pilot, turned as the stewardess gasped. He started to rise, then thought better of it. ''Where to?'' he asked in a resigned tone. ''Havana?''

''No,'' Nick told him. ''The island of Jabali.''

''We may not have enough fuel for that.''

Nick kept the pistol steady. ''Well, let's give it a try anyway, shall we?''

Hours later, as the jet settled down on the runway at Jabali Airport, Nick Velvet breathed a sigh of relief. The fuel had indeed been low, and he wondered what he would have done if they'd run dry over the Caribbean. Or if the pilot and copilot had put up a fight. He'd never killed an innocent person during any of his assignments, and he wouldn't have started now. More likely he would have knocked them out and tried to bring the big plane in himself—though he'd never piloted anything larger than army transports during a brief period of the Korean war.

When he stepped out of the cockpit he faced Pop Hastin, the manager's face flushed with fury. "Why did you bring us here?" Hastin demanded.

"Calm down," Nick told him. "You're in no danger." He motioned with his gun for Pop and the players to leave the plane.

Roswell pushed his way through the crush. "You had no intention of writing an article! It was all a lie to hijack this plane!"

"It wasn't entirely a lie," Nick pointed out. "You'll get plenty of publicity out of this."

"Publicity?" Pop Hastin looked out the window at the welcome signs. "You mean somebody wanted to kidnap the Beavers?"

Nick Velvet smiled. "That's right. Welcome to Jabali."

The President of Jabali, General Tras, was waiting to greet them with his eight cabinet ministers. He was an imposing man in his full military uniform, smiling broadly yet giving an unmistakable picture of power. There were armed bodyguards on both sides of him, and his gloved fists were clenched with expectation.

"We had your radio message, Señor Velvet. You have truly fulfilled your mission! Let us proceed to the National Hall, where I can more formally greet my guests."

Jorge Asignar stepped forward, wearing the purple sash of a cabinet minister. "I have the balance of your money," he told Nick. "The President is very pleased."

"What are you? Secretary of Kidnaping?"

"Minister of Information," Asignar replied with a thin smile. Then, motioning toward the plane, he questioned, "Who are all these people?"

"Baseball teams aren't just nine men and a rack of bats. Not these days. They need a trainer, batboy, and press agent. They need pitching and batting coaches. They need—"

Stan Karowitz came barreling over, looking for a fight. "What is this, anyway? Are we prisoners here?"

Nick tried to calm him. "Their president likes baseball. You'll be home in a few days."

"A few days!"

But already the armed guards were moving in, steering everyone toward a big waiting bus. There was no opportunity for argument. Nick rode to the National Hall in the black limousine of General Tras, sitting in the back seat between the President and Asignar. On the front fenders fluttered the flag of Jabali—a field of red with a wild boar's head in the center, enclosed by a black triangle with three seashells along each of the triangle's sides.

"Jabali," Nick observed. "The wild boar?"

"At one time they overran our little island," General Tras remarked. "Now they are confined to the zoos and a few game preserves back in the hills."

Here and there along the highway were people to cheer and wave as the big presidential car went by. When the marble-faced auditorium came into view, the crowds grew thicker.

"This was really Jorge's idea," the President said, patting Asignar approvingly on the knee. "I had been training our own team for some years as a hobby, but it all meant nothing without real competition."

"I hope you're prepared to risk the wrath of my government," Nick commented dryly.

Tras dismissed it with a wave of his hand. "The Beavers will be safely returned after a single game with the Jabali team. No one will go to war over it."

The auditorium was about half full when they entered. Asignar motioned Nick to a seat on the side, saying, "General Tras and the cabinet ministers always sit in row J. You can follow the proceedings from here."

"Fine," Nick agreed. He'd been sitting only a few moments when a strikingly beautiful girl with long black hair slipped into place next to him.

"You're Nick Velvet?" she asked quietly.

Her English was perfect, which was his first surprise. And she knew his name. "That's right. And you are—?"

"Maria Tras."

"The President's—"

She laughed lightly at his hesitation. "Daughter."

"Are you a baseball fan too?" Up on the stage Asignar was beginning to speak. Nick's slight knowledge of Spanish indicated he was introducing the President.

"Not like my father," the girl was saying in answer to his question. "In fact, I was against this whole scheme. I was at Columbia for four years and I know how seriously you Americans take your baseball."

"That's what I tried to tell Asignar."

"That man!" She made a face.

"What does your father want? Just a game?"

"That's all. It was wise of you to steal the Beavers. At least it'll be something of an even match."

General Tras mounted the stage and held up his hand for silence. Surprisingly, Pop Hastin was at his side. Tras spoke a few words in Spanish and then switched quickly to English. "I want now to welcome a fine and famous American baseball manager, the pride of the National League—our guest, Pop Hastin of the Beavers!"

Even Pop seemed taken aback by the applause with which the introduction was greeted. If he'd planned to denounce the kidnaping from the stage he must have had second thoughts. He cleared his throat, grinned weakly, and said, "I can't approve of being brought here against our will, but I am pleased at the reception we've received. We look forward to meeting the Jabali team on the field."

The audience cheered and General Tras smiled. Off to one side of the stage the shortstop Mike Nesbitt and some other players seemed far from pleased at the turn of events, but there was little they could do. General Tras resumed his speech. The big game would take place in two days' time, on Wednesday. The teams would have Tuesday to practice.

"I can't wait to see it," Maria Tras told Nick as they left the building.

"I'm surprised that Pop Hastin gave in so easily."

"Now that it's done, the game should be an exciting one." She glanced sideways at Nick. "Will you be staying for it?"

"I have no reason to. Asignar paid me the rest of my fee. But it might be wise to stay down here for a few days. Even though my true identity isn't known I'm sure the authorities back in the States will be watching for me."

"I wish you would stay."

"Thanks."

"And I hope you can dine with us at the presidential palace tonight. My father is inviting Pop Hastin and all the others."

"I don't know if I dare face him," Nick told her. But there was something odd about the whole business, something that bothered him. He knew he'd be there.

The presidential palace was as regal as Nick had expected—a great white building that must have dated from the early years of the century. In certain rooms there had been obvious attempts to copy the decor of the White House in Washington, but the venture had been ruined by a tasteless plushness more in keeping with kings than presidents.

"Our country was founded in 1899 by the great revolutionary leader Palidez," General Tras explained as he led them on a brief tour. "He wrote our constitution and built this house. *Nueve—*

that was the word he lived by. This is called the *Casa Nueve,* a fitting name.''

Nick nodded. ''The New House,'' he translated, ''for a new country.''

Maria shot him an odd glance and started to say something, but then Asignar joined them with Pop Hastin and Roswell, the publicity man. ''Shall we go in to dinner?'' the Minister of Information suggested.

Roswell was seated next to Nick, and as they sat down the publicity man said, ''We might make something out of this yet, no thanks to you.''

''Oh?''

''Pop thinks it's a great publicity break for the team, and he's right, of course. Every magazine in the country will want our story when we get back.''

Later, after a meal of wild boar more fitted to a medieval monarch than a Caribbean president, Nick had an opportunity for a private word with Pop Hastin. ''I'm glad you realize the publicity value in all this,'' he said.

Pop reached for some chewing tobacco. ''I was upset at first, but now I'm beginning to like the idea. All season long I've listened to sports commentators chuckle about the Meager Beavers, and at my age that wasn't easy to take. But now we've been kidnaped by you and brought down here to play the Jabali team. You didn't kidnap the Yankees or Cards or Pirates—you kidnaped the Beavers!''

''Well, yes,'' Nick admitted. He wasn't about to mention that he'd picked the Beavers simply because they were last in the league standing.

''Coming out to the practice tomorrow?'' Pop asked.

''I'll be there.''

By morning the news of the stolen Beavers had made headlines around the world. The storm was particularly heavy in Washington, as Nick had feared, but Pop's statement to the American Ambassador that they were well-treated and anxious to play the game had done much to cool the tense situation.

At the stadium for the practice session Pop Hastin had a further statement for reporters. ''We are here as guests of the President and we consider it an honor to be so chosen. We'll be returning home after the exhibition game tomorrow.'' In answer to persistent questions he added, ''We are not being held against our wills or mistreated in any way.''

Nick breathed a sigh of relief as he settled onto a bench to watch the practice. At least Pop's statement should take some of the pressure off him. He glanced up to see Tras and his daughter coming over to join him. The President was obviously excited, like a small boy on a Sunday afternoon at Yankee Stadium. The General watched intently as Stan Karowitz took batting practice and actually cheered when the tall first baseman hit a line drive to the farthest corner of left field.

"Do you think your team can take them?" Nick asked.

"The Beavers are very good. It will be a real event for my people and I do not really care which team is victorious. But of course I will be cheering for Jabali." He watched the pitchers for a time and then added, "Jorge has suggested a patriotic pageant before the game tomorrow. Our independence day is in a few weeks—on September 9th—and he thinks an early celebration is in order. He's to speak to both teams about taking part."

Nick grunted and lit a cigarette. A few minutes later, when General Tras went down on the field to speak with his own brightly uniformed team, Maria moved next to Nick. "Something's troubling you," she observed.

"I'm running low on American cigarettes."

"Something besides that. I've known you only a day, but I can see the worried look in your eyes."

"It's just this whole setup," he admitted. "I could understand one man, an absolute ruler, getting the crazy idea to steal a baseball team and bring it here, overriding the objections of his advisers. But this is different. Your father told me it was Asignar's idea. And yet Asignar apparently isn't even a baseball fan. At least he's nowhere in sight today."

"You worry needlessly," she assured him. "After all, the Beavers are happy with their new fame. My father is happy. You should be happy with the money you were paid. Why look for trouble?"

"Because I brought them here. If anything happens, I'll feel responsible."

That night Nick dined with Maria at Jabali's most expensive restaurant. On the way home he noticed an anti-Tras slogan chalked in Spanish on the side of a building. Maria seemed to miss seeing it, and he did not call it to her attention.

Nick had arranged to escort Maria to the baseball game the following day, since her father would be busy on the field during the opening ceremonies of the pageant. When he called for her at the presidential palace just after noon, he still carried the pistol he'd used to hijack the plane. He wondered why he hadn't left it in his room, yet knew somehow that it belonged with him, even at a baseball game.

"There's already a lot of traffic," he told Maria. "I didn't know there were so many people on the island."

"It is a great day for them."

"Few foreigners, though."

"My father does not encourage them. He has the airport watched. Even the number of newsmen is limited."

"So I noticed." They were walking through the downstairs rooms toward the door when Nick paused to examine the large oil painting over a massive stone fireplace. It was of a handsome bearded man in military uniform. "Who's this?" he asked.

"Palidez, our liberator. Father mentioned him at dinner the other night. Founder of our country, author of our constitution, builder of this house—"

Nick studied the painting more closely. "He's missing a finger."

"Lost in the Revolution. It became a sort of symbol. He died in 1920, rich and famous—and loved by his people."

One of the servants had turned on the radio and they could hear the sounds of the stadium ceremonies. "They're starting without us," Nick said. "We'd better hurry."

"I'm ready."

He led her out to the official car, where a dark-skinned driver waited by the open door. "Too bad all your servants can't come."

"Most of them went, but the house requires so much work— you can imagine, with nine rooms on each floor."

Nick froze with his hand on the car door. "My Spanish is rusty," he said, hardly breathing. "Your father said this place is called the *Casa Nueve*—"

Maria chuckled. "I started to correct you the other night. New House would be *Casa Nuevo*. The presidential palace is called *Casa Nueve*, which means—"

"Nine House! Nine rooms on each floor! And nine was the word Palidez lived by!" From the car radio came the sounds of the pageant ceremonies, the rolling of drums, the blowing of bugles. "Come on! We've got to get there fast!"

"But why?"

"Don't ask questions. What I need are answers and you can give them to me." The car pulled away from the palace grounds and headed toward the stadium. "Jorge Asignar is up to something and it's no good."

"Asignar? I don't understand."

Nick Velvet leaned back in his seat, eyes closed, trying to see it all. "The thing was Asignar's idea from the start. At the airport Monday he was surprised to see nineteen players with manager and coaches and all. He didn't need them. He only needed nine men—a baseball team. Nine men who could enter the country without attracting your father's suspicions, without being noticed by his airport guards."

"Nine men—"

"Don't you see, Maria? This whole country is built on the mystical number nine. There are nines everywhere—the President and eight cabinet ministers—nine in all. Nine seashells on your national flag. And the cabinet always sits in row J at the auditorium —the ninth row, since theaters hardly ever have a row I. The country was liberated in 1899, on September 9—the ninth day of the ninth month. And nine-fingered Palidez did it all. He wrote the constitution and built the palace, Nine House, with its nine rooms on each floor."

"I know all that," she said.

"Then tell me what else there is. Something in the constitution that Palidez wrote. Something that Jorge Asignar needs nine men for."

"Nine men—" And suddenly her hand flew to her mouth. "My God, the firing squad!"

It was then that the driver pulled over to the curb and turned to face them with a pistol in his hand.

Nick Velvet fired a single shot through the back of the seat, hoping his aim was good. It was—the driver crumpled sideways without a sound.

"Help shove him over," Nick told Maria. "I'll drive."

"He's one of Asignar's people," she gasped.

"He was. I'm glad I still had the gun with me. Which way should I go?"

"Straight ahead—you can see it from here, over on the left." As he drove she kept talking. "Palidez's constitution states that the President of Jabali can be removed from office and sentenced to death by a secret panel of judges in a time of national crisis. But the actual execution of a President can only be carried out by a nine-man firing squad. To insure that the firing squad itself is impartial, none of the men can be citizens of Jabali."

"So Asignar brought the Beavers in to be public executioners. He's planning to take over the country, but he wants it all nice and legal. He doesn't want the citizens upset."

"But how can he get the Beavers to shoot my father?"

"However it is, I've got to stop it. I agreed to steal a baseball team, not to provide a firing squad. Asignar suggested the pre-game pageant. He must be planning it for then."

The voice on the radio droned on in Spanish. Nick missed many words, but he got the general idea. Both teams were lined up on the field, facing the President who was standing on a raised plat-form. The teams carried rifles, symbolic of Jabali's revolution, but they would soon exchange them for bats, symbolic of today's peaceful life.

"Faster!" Maria urged. "They have guns, and father is now down on the field."

Nick swung into the stadium driveway, saw a policeman signal-ing him away, and brushed the man aside like a fly. Then he headed the car toward the metal gates that blocked the entrance to the field. "Keep your head down," he warned Maria.

The car hit the gates with a force that cracked the windshield and crushed in the radiator, but they were through. The Beavers, nine of them, were facing General Tras, aiming their rifles in the air in some sort of salute. Nick drove the crippled car forward in a final burst of speed that almost bowled the players over.

"Don't shoot!" he yelled to Nesbitt, the shortstop. "It's a trick!"

There was shouting from the stands, and Nick saw soldiers run-ning onto the field. "They're only blanks," Karowitz protested. "Asignar told us to fire over the President's head as part of the pageant."

Nick grabbed one of the rifles and ejected a blank cartridge. "Then he's somewhere with a high-powered rifle. He couldn't expect you fellows to really execute the President, but he wanted it to look that way."

General Tras was running over now, his face ashen. "What is it? What's happening?"

"Asignar is planning to kill you and make it look like an execu-tion. Once you're dead no one would know the difference. The judges who condemned you in secret must be part of Asignar's plot."

There was the crack of a rifle, from far off, and Tras stumbled to the ground. The bullet had hit the fleshy part of his thigh. "He's on the roof, over there!" Nick shouted. He grabbed one of the rifles and then remembered they held blanks. A soldier had reached them, his rifle pointed, and Nick grabbed the soldier's rifle as a second shot sounded from the roof.

"Everybody down!" he shouted. The second shot, fired in

haste, had missed. Now Jorge Asignar was up and running along the edge of the roof. Nick fired two quick shots, then took an extra few seconds to squeeze off the third round at the running figure.

Asignar went off the edge of the roof, falling without a sound, and hit the top of the Beavers' third-base dugout.

"There are men faithful to me," General Tras said as they bandaged his leg. "We will round up the rest of the plotters."

"With Asignar dead they'll be off and running," Nick told him. They were still in the center of the field, surrounded by players and soldiers.

"How can I thank you?" Maria Tras asked Nick.

"There must be a way."

From the dugout Pop Hastin had finally fought his way through the mob. "What is all this shooting?" he demanded. "Let's get that body out of here and play ball!"

MY KINGDOM
FOR JONES

Wilbur Schramm

THE FIRST DAY Jones played third base for Brooklyn was like the day Galileo turned his telescope on the planets or Columbus sailed back to Spain. First, people said it couldn't be true; then they said things will never be the same.

Timothy McGuire, of the Brooklyn Eagle, told me how he felt the first time he saw Jones. He said that if a bird had stepped out of a cuckoo clock that day and asked him what time it was, he wouldn't have been surprised enough to blink an Irish eye. And still he knew that the whole future of baseball hung that day by a cotton thread.

Don't ask Judge Kenesaw Mountain Landis about this. He has never yet admitted publicly that Jones ever played for Brooklyn. He has good reason not to. But ask an old-time sports writer. Ask Tim McGuire.

It happened so long ago that it was even before Mr. Roosevelt became President. It was a lazy Georgia-spring afternoon, the first time McGuire and I saw Jones. There was a light-footed little breeze and just enough haze to keep the sun from burning. The air was full of fresh-cut grass and wistaria and fruit blossoms and the ping of baseballs on well-oiled mitts. Everyone in Georgia knows that the only sensible thing to do on an afternoon like that is sleep. If you can't do that, if you are a baseball writer down from New York to cover Brooklyn's spring-training camp, you can stretch out on the grass and raise yourself every now and then on one elbow to steal a glance at fielding practice. That was what we were doing—meanwhile amusing ourselves halfheartedly with a game involving small cubes and numbers—when we first saw Jones.

The Times wasn't there. Even in those days they were keeping their sports staff at home to study for Information Please. But four of us were down from the New York papers—the World, the Herald, Tim and I. I can even remember what we were talking about.

I was asking the World, "How do they look to you?"

"Pitchers and no punch," the World said. "No big bats. No great fielders. No Honus Wagner. No Hal Chase. No Ty Cobb."

"No Tinker to Evers to Chance," said the Herald. "Seven come to Susy," he added soothingly, blowing on his hands.

"What's your angle today?" the World asked Tim.

Tim doesn't remember exactly how he answered that. To the best of my knowledge, he merely said, "Ulk." It occurred to me that the Brooklyn Eagle was usually more eloquent than that, but the Southern weather must have slowed up my reaction.

The World said, "What?"

"There's a sorsh," Tim said in a weak, strangled sort of voice —"a horse . . . on third . . . base."

"Why don't they chase it off?" said the Herald impatiently. "Your dice."

"They don't . . . want to," Tim said in that funny voice.

I glanced up at Tim then. Now Tim, as you probably remember, was built from the same blueprints as a truck, with a magnificent red nose for a headlight. But when I looked at him, all the color was draining out of that nose slowly, from top to bottom, like turning off a gas mantle. I should estimate Tim was, at the moment, the whitest McGuire in four generations.

Then I looked over my shoulder to see where Tim was staring. He was the only one of us facing the ball diamond. I looked for some time. Then I tapped the World on the back.

"Pardon me," I asked politely, "do you notice anything unusual?"

"If you refer to my luck," said the World, "it's the same pitiful kind I've had since Christmas."

"Look at the infield," I suggested.

"Hey," said the Herald, "if you don't want the dice, give them to me."

"I know this can't be true," mused the World, "but I could swear I see a horse on third base."

The Herald climbed to his feet with some effort. He was built in the days when there was no shortage of materials.

"If the only way to get you guys to put your minds on this game is to chase that horse off the field," he said testily, "I'll do it myself."

He stared toward the infield, rubbed his eyes and fainted dead away.

"I had the queerest dream," he said, when we revived him. "I dreamed there was a horse playing third base. My God!" he shouted, glancing toward the diamond. "I'm still asleep!"

That is, word for word, what happened the first day Jones played third base for Brooklyn. Ask McGuire.

When we felt able, we hunted up the Brooklyn manager, who was a chunky, red-haired individual with a whisper like a foghorn. A foghorn with a Brooklyn accent. His name was Pop O'Donnell.

"I see you've noticed," Pop boomed defensively.

"What do you mean," the Herald said severely, "by not notifying us you had a horse playing third base?"

"I didn't guess you'd believe it," Pop said.

Pop was still a little bewildered himself. He said the horse had wandered on the field that morning during practice. Someone tried to chase it off by hitting a baseball toward it. The horse calmly opened its mouth and caught the ball. Nothing could be neater.

While they were still marveling over that, the horse galloped thirty yards and took a ball almost out of the hands of an outfielder who was poised for the catch. They said Willie Keeler couldn't have done it better. So they spent an hour hitting fungo flies—or, as some wit called them, horse flies—to the horse. Short ones, long ones, high ones, grass cutters, line drives—it made no difference; the animal covered Dixie like the dew.

They tried the horse at second and short, but he was a little slow on the pivot when compared with men like Napoleon Lajoie. Then they tried him at third base, and knew that was the right, the inevitable place. He was a great wall of China. He was a flash of brown lightning. In fact, he covered half the shortstop's territory and two thirds of left field, and even came behind the plate to help the catcher with foul tips. The catcher got pretty sore about it. He said that anybody who was going to steal his put-outs would have to wear an umpire's uniform like the other thieves.

"Can he hit?" asked the World.

"See for yourself," Pop O'Donnell invited.

The Superbas—they hadn't begun calling them the Dodgers yet —were just starting batting practice. Nap Rucker was tossing them in with that beautiful smooth motion of his, and the horse was at bat. He met the first ball on the nose and smashed it into left field. He laid down a bunt that waddled like a turtle along the base line. He sizzled a liner over second like a clothesline.

"What a story!" said the World.

"I wonder," said the Herald—"I wonder how good it is."

We stared at him.

"I wouldn't say it is quite as good as the sinking of the Maine, if you mean that," said Tim.

"I wonder how many people are going to believe it," said the Herald.

"I'll race you to the phone," Tim said.

Tim won. He admits he had a long start. Twenty minutes later he came back, walking slowly.

"I wish to announce," he said, "that I have been insulted by my editor and am no longer connected with the Brooklyn Eagle. If I can prove that I am sober tomorrow, they may hire me back," he added.

"You see what I mean," said the Herald.

We all filed telegraph stories about the horse. We swore that every word was true. We said it was a turning point in baseball. Two of us mentioned Columbus; and one, Galileo. In return, we got advice.

THESE TROUBLED TIMES, NEWSPAPERS NO SPACE FOR FICTION EXPENSE ACCOUNT NO PROVISION DRUNKEN LEVITY, the Herald's wire read. The World read, ACCURACY, ACCURACY, ACCURACY, followed by three exclamation points, and signed "Joseph Pulitzer." CHARGING YOUR TELEGRAM RE BROOKLYN HORSE TO YOUR SALARY, my wire said. THAT'S A HORSE ON YOU!

Have you ever thought what you would do with a purple cow if you had one? I know. You would paint it over. We had a horse that could play third base, and all we could do was sit in the middle of Georgia and cuss our editors. I blame the editors. It is their fault that for the last thirty years you have had to go to smoking rooms or Pullman cars to hear about Jones.

But I don't entirely blame them either. My first question would have been: How on earth can a horse possibly bat and throw? That's what the editors wondered. It's hard to explain. It's something you have to see to believe—like dogfish and political conventions.

And I've got to admit that the next morning we sat around and asked one another whether we really had seen a horse playing third base. Pop O'Donnell confessed that when he woke up he said to himself, *It must be shrimp that makes me dream about horses.*

Then all of us went down to the park, not really knowing whether we would see a horse there or not.

We asked Pop was he going to use the horse in games.

"I don't know," he thundered musingly. "I wonder. There are many angles. I don't know." he said, pulling at his chin.

That afternoon the Cubs, the world champs, came for an exhibition game. A chap from Pennsylvania—I forget his name—played third base for Brooklyn, and the horse grazed quietly beside the dugout. Going into the eighth, the Cubs were ahead, 2–0, and Three-Finger Brown was tying Brooklyn in knots. A curve would come over, then a fast one inside, and then the drop, and the Superbas would beat the air or hit puny little rollers to the infield which Tinker or Evers would grab up and toss like a beanbag to Frank Chance. It was sickening. But in the eighth, Maloney got on base on an error, and Jordan walked. Then Lumley went down swinging, and Lewis watched three perfect ones sail past him. The horse still was grazing over by the Brooklyn dugout.

"Put in the horse!" Frank Chance yelled. The Cubs laughed themselves sick.

Pop O'Donnell looked at Chance, and then at the horse, and back at Chance, as though he had made up his mind about something. "Go in there, son, and get a hit," he said. "Watch out for the curve." "Coive," Pop said.

The horse picked up a bat and cantered out to the plate.

"Pinch-hitting for Batch," announced the umpire dreamily, "this horse." A second later he shook himself violently. "What am I saying?" he shouted.

On the Cubs' bench, every jaw had dropped somewhere around the owner's waist. Chance jumped to his feet, his face muscles worked like a coffee grinder, but nothing came out. It was the only time in baseball history, so far as I can find out, that Frank Chance was ever without words.

When he finally pulled himself together he argued, with a good deal of punctuation, that there was no rule saying you could play a horse in the big leaguer. Pop roared quietly that there was no rule saying you couldn't, either. They stood there nose to nose, Pop firing methodically like a cannon, and Chance crackling like a machine gun. Chance gave up too easily. He was probably a little stunned. He said that he was used to seeing queer things in Brooklyn, anyway. Pop O'Donnell just smiled grimly.

Well, that was Jones' first game for Brooklyn. It could have been a reel out of a movie. There was that great infield—Steinfeldt, Tinker, Evers and Chance—so precise, so much a machine, that any ball hit on the ground was like an apple into a sorter. The infield was so famous that not many people remembered Sheckard and Slagle and Schulte in the outfield, but the teams of that day knew them. Behind the plate was Johnny Kling, who could rifle a ball to second like an 88-mm. cannon. And on the mound stood Three-Finger Brown, whose drop faded away as though someone were pulling it back with a string.

Brown took a long time getting ready. His hand shook a little, and the first one he threw was ten feet over Kling's head into the grandstand. Maloney and Jordan advanced to second and third. Brown threw the next one in the dirt. Then he calmed down, grooved one, and whistled a curve in around the withers.

"The glue works for you, Dobbin!" yelled Chance, feeling more like himself. Pop O'Donnell was mopping his forehead.

The next pitch came in fast, over the outside corner. The horse was waiting. He leaned into it. The ball whined all the way to the fence. Ted Williams was the only player I ever saw hit one like it. When Slagle finally got to the ball, the two runners had scored and the horse was on third. Brown's next pitch got away from Kling a few yards, and the horse stole home in a cloud of dust, all four feet flying. He got up, dusted himself off, looked at Chance and gave a horselaugh.

If this sounds queer, remember that queerer things happen in Brooklyn every day.

"How do we write this one up?" asked the Herald. "We can't put just 'a horse' in the box score."

That was when the horse got his name. We named him Jones, after Jones, the caretaker who had left the gate open so he could wander onto the field. We wrote about "Horse" Jones.

Next day we all chuckled at a banner headline in one of the metropolitan papers. It read: JONES PUTS NEW KICK IN BROOK-LYN.

Look in the old box scores. Jones got two hits off Rube Waddell, of Philadelphia, and three off Cy Young, of Boston. He pounded Eddie Plank and Iron Man McGinnity and Wild Bill Donovan. He robbed Honus Wagner of a hit that would have been a double against any other third baseman in the league. On the base paths he was a bullet.

Our papers began to wire us, WHERE DOES JONES COME FROM? SEND BACK-GROUND, HUMAN INTEREST, INTERVIEW. That was a harder assignment than New York knew. We decided by a gentle-men's agreement that Jones must have come from Kentucky and

got his first experience in a Blue Grass league. That sounded reasonable enough. We said he was long-faced, long-legged, dark, a
vegetarian and a nonsmoker. That was true. We said he was a
horse for work, and ate like a horse. That was self-evident. Interviewing was a little harder.

Poor Pop O'Donnell for ten years had wanted a third baseman
who could hit hard enough to dent a cream puff. Now that he had
one he wasn't quite sure what to do with it. Purple-cow trouble.
"Poiple," Pop would have said.

One of his first worries was paying for Jones. A stropping big
farmer appeared at the clubhouse, saying he wanted either his
horse or fifty thousand dollars.

Pop excused himself, checked the team's bank balance, then
came back.

"What color is your horse?" he asked.

The farmer thought a minute. "Dapple gray," he said.

"Good afternoon, my man," Pop boomed unctuously, holding
open the door. "That's a horse of another color." Jones was
brown.

There were some audience incidents too. Jonathan Daniels, of
Raleigh, North Carolina, told me that as a small boy that season
he saw a whole row of elderly ladies bustle into their box seats,
take one look toward third base, look questioningly at one another,
twitter about the sun being hot, and walk out. Georgia police records show that at least five citizens, cold sober, came to the ball
park and were afraid to drive their own cars home. The American
medical journals of that year discovered a new psychoneurosis
which they said was doubtless caused by a feeling of insecurity
resulting from the replacement of the horse by the horseless carriage. It usually took the form of hallucination—the sensation of
seeing a horse sitting on a baseball players' bench. Perhaps that
was the reason a famous pitcher, who shall here go nameless, came
to town with his team, took one incredulous look at Brooklyn
fielding practice, and went to his manager, offering to pay a fine.

But the real trouble was over whether horses should be allowed
to play baseball. After the first shock, teams were generally
amused at the idea of playing against a horse. But after Jones had
batted their star pitchers out of the box, they said the Humane
Society ought to protect the poor Brooklyn horse.

The storm that brewed in the South that spring was like nothing
except the storm that gathered in 1860. Every hotel that housed
baseball players housed a potential civil war. The better orators
argued that the right to play baseball should not be separated from

the right to vote or the responsibility of fighting for one's country. The more practical ones said a few more horses like Jones and they wouldn't have any jobs left. Still others said that this was probably just another bureaucratic trick on the part of the Administration.

Even the Brooklyn players protested. A committee of them came to see old Pop O'Donnell. They said wasn't baseball a game for human beings? Pop said he had always had doubts as to whether some major-league players were human or not. They said touché, and this is all right so long as it is a one-horse business, so to speak. But if it goes on, before long won't a man have to grow two more legs and a tail before he can get in? They asked Pop how he would like to manage the Brooklyn Percherons, instead of the Brooklyn Superbas? They said, what would happen to baseball if it became a game for animals—say giraffes on one team, trained seals on a second and monkeys on a third? They pointed out that monkeys had already got a foot in the door by being used to dodge baseballs in carnivals. How would Pop like to manage a team of monkeys called the Brooklyn Dodgers, they asked.

Pop said heaven help anyone who has to manage a team called the Brooklyn Dodgers. Then he pointed out that Brooklyn Dodgers hadn't lost an exhibition game, and that the horse was leading the league in batting with a solid .516. He asked whether they would rather have a world series or a two-legged third baseman. They went on muttering.

But his chief worry was Jones himself.

"That horse hasn't got his mind on the game," he told us one night on the hotel veranda.

"Ah, Pop, it's just horseplay," said the World, winking.

"Nope, he hasn't got his heart in it," said Pop, his voice echoing lightly off the distant mountains. "He comes just in time for practice and runs the minute it's over. There's something on that horse's mind."

We laughed, but had to admit that Jones was about the saddest horse we had ever seen. His eyes were great brown pools of liquid sorrow. His ears drooped. And still he hit well over .500 and covered third base like a rug.

One day he missed the game entirely. It was the day the Giants were in town, and fifteen thousand people were there to watch Jones bat against the great Matty. Brooklyn lost the game, and Pop O'Donnell almost lost his hair at the hands of the disappointed crowd.

"Who would have thought," Pop mused, in the clubhouse after the game, "that that (here some words are omitted) horse would turn out to be a prima donna? It's all right for a major-league ball player to act like a horse, but that horse is trying to act like a major-league ball player.''

It was almost by accident that Tim and I found out what was really bothering Jones. We followed him one day when he left the ball park. We followed him nearly two miles to a race track.

Jones stood beside the fence a long time, turning his head to watch the Thoroughbreds gallop by on exercise runs and time trials. Then a little stable boy opened the gate for him.

"Po' ol' hoss," the boy said. "Yo' wants a little runnin'?''

"Happens every day," a groom explained to us. "This horse wanders up here from God knows where, and acts like he wants to run, and some boy rides him a while, bareback, pretending he's a race horse.''

Jones was like a different horse out there on the track; not drooping any more—ears up, eyes bright, tail like a plume. It was pitiful how much he wanted to look like a race horse.

"That horse," Tim asked the groom, "is he any good for racing?''

"Not here, anyway," the groom said. "Might win a county-fair race or two.''

He asked us whether we had any idea who owned the horse.

"Sir," said Tim, like Edwin M. Stanton, "that horse belongs to the ages.''

"Well, mister," said the groom, "the ages had better get some different shoes on that horse. Why, you could hold a baseball in those shoes he has there.''

"It's very clear," I said as we walked back, "what we have here is a badly frustrated horse.''

"It's clear as beer," Tim said sadly.

That afternoon Jones hit a home run and absent-mindedly trotted around the bases. As soon as the game was over, he disappeared in the direction of the race track. Tim looked at me and shook his head. Pop O'Donnell held his chin in his hands.

"I'll be boiled in oil," he said. "Berled in erl," he said.

Nothing cheered up poor Pop until someone came in with a story about the absentee owner of a big-league baseball club who had inherited the club along with the family fortune. This individual had just fired the manager of his baseball farm system, because the farms had not turned out horses like Jones. "What are farms for if they don't raise horses?" the absentee owner had asked indignantly.

Jones was becoming a national problem second only to the Panama Canal and considerably more important than whether Mr. Taft got to be President.

There were rumors that the Highlanders—people were just beginning to call them the Yankees—would withdraw and form a new league if Jones was allowed to play. It was reported that a team of kangaroos from Australia was on its way to play a series of exhibition games in America, and Pres. Ban Johnson, of the American League, was quoted as saying that he would never have kangaroos in the American League because they were too likely to jump their contracts. There was talk of a constitutional amendment concerning horses in baseball.

The thing that impressed me, down there in the South, was that all this was putting the cart before the horse, so to speak. Jones simply didn't want to play baseball. He wanted to be a race horse. I don't know why life is that way.

Jones made an unassisted triple play, and Ty Cobb accused Brooklyn of furnishing fire ladders to its infielders. He said that no third baseman could have caught the drive that started the play. At the end of the training season, Jones was batting .538, and fielding .997, had stolen twenty bases and hit seven home runs. He was the greatest third baseman in the history of baseball, and didn't want to be!

Joseph Pulitzer, William Randolph Hearst, Arthur Brisbane and the rest of the big shots got together and decided that if anyone didn't know by this time that Jones was a horse, the newspapers wouldn't tell him. He could find it out.

Folks seemed to find it out. People began gathering from all parts of the country to see Brooklyn open against the Giants—Matty against Jones. Even a tribe of Sioux Indians camped beside the Gowanus and had war dances on Flatbush Avenue, waiting for the park to open. And Pop O'Donnell kept his squad in the South as long as he could, laying plans to arrive in Brooklyn only on the morning of the opening game.

The wire said that night that 200,000 people had come to Brooklyn for the game, and 190,000 of them were in an ugly mood over the report that the league might not let Jones play. The governor of New York sent two regiments of the national guard. The Giants were said to be caucusing to decide whether they would play against Jones.

By game time, people were packed for six blocks, fighting to get into the park. The Sioux sent a young buck after their tomahawks, just in case. Telephone poles a quarter of a mile from the field were

selling for a hundred dollars. Every baseball writer in the country
was in the Brooklyn press box; the other teams played before cub
reporters and society editors. Just before game time I managed to
push into Pop O'Donnell's little office with the presidents of the
two major leagues, the mayor of New York, a half dozen other
reporters, and a delegation from the Giants.

"There's just one thing we want to know," the spokesman for
the Giants was asking Pop. "Are you going to play Jones?"

"Gentlemen," said Pop in that soft-spoken, firm way of his that
rattled the window blinds, "our duty is to give the public what it
wants. And the public wants Jones."

Like an echo, a chant began to rise from the bleachers, "We
want Jones!"

"There is one other little thing," said Pop. "Jones has disappeared."

There were about ten seconds of the awful silence that comes
when your nerves are paralyzed, but your mind keeps on thrashing.

"He got out of his boxcar somewhere between Georgia and
Brooklyn," Pop said. "We don't know where. We're looking."

A Western Union boy dashed in. "Hold on!" said Pop. "This
may be news!"

He tore the envelope with a shaky hand. The message was from
Norfolk, Virginia. HAVE FOUND ELEPHANT THAT CAN BALANCE
MEDICINE BALL ON TRUNK, it read. WILL HE DO? If Pop had said
what he said then into a telephone, it would have burned out all
the insulators in New York.

Down at the field, the President of the United States himself was
poised to throw out the first ball. "Is this Jones?" he asked. He
was a little nearsighted.

"This is the mayor of New York," Pop said patiently. "Jones is
gone. Run away."

The President's biographers disagree as to whether he said at
that moment, "Oh, well, who would stay in Brooklyn if he could
run?" or "I sympathize with you for having to change horses in
mid-stream."

That was the saddest game ever covered by the entire press
corps of the nation. Brooklyn was all thumbs in the field, all wind-
mills at bat. There was no Jones to whistle hits into the outfield
and make sensational stops at third. By the sixth inning, when they
had to call the game with the score 18–1, the field was ankle-deep
in pop bottles and the Sioux were waving their tomahawks and
singing the scalp song.

You know the rest of the story. Brooklyn didn't win a game until the third week of the season, and no team ever tried a horse again, except a few dark horses every season. Pittsburgh, I believe, tried trained seals in the outfield. They were deadly at catching the ball, but couldn't cover enough ground. San Francisco has an entire team of Seals, but I have never seen them play. Boston tried an octopus at second base, but had to give him up. What happened to two rookies who disappeared trying to steal second base against Boston that spring is another subject baseball doesn't talk about.

There has been considerable speculation as to what happened to Jones. Most of us believed the report that the Brooklyn players had unfastened the latch on the door of his boxcar, until Pop O'Donnell's Confidential Memoirs came out, admitting that he himself had taken the hinges off the door because he couldn't face the blame for making baseball a game for horses. But I have been a little confused since Tim McGuire came to me once and said he might as well confess. He couldn't stand to think of that horse standing wistfully beside the track, waiting for someone to let him pretend he was a race horse. That haunted Tim. When he went down to the boxcar he found the door unlatched and the hinges off, so he gave the door a little push outward. He judged it was the will of the majority.

And that is why baseball is played by men today instead of by horses. But don't think that the shadow of Jones doesn't still lie heavy on the game. Have you ever noticed how retiring and silent and hang-door major-league ball players are, how they cringe before the umpire? They never know when another Jones may break away from a beer wagon or a circus or a plow, wander through an unlocked gate, and begin batting .538 to their .290. The worry is terrible. You can see it in the crowds too. That is why Brooklyn fans are so aloof and disinterested, why they never raise their voices above a whisper at Ebbets Field. They know perfectly well that this is only minor-league ball they are seeing, that horses could play it twice as well if they had a chance.

That is the secret we sports writers have kept all these years; that is why we have never written about Jones. And the Brooklyn fans still try to keep it secret, but every once in a while the sorrow eats like lye into one of them until he can hold it back no longer, and then he sobs quietly and says, "Dem bums, if dey only had a little horse sense!"

POPULAR GUY

Jack Ritchie

CHAD HAWLEY looked into the locker room mirror and adjusted the knot of his tie. He noticed the angry red on his cheekbones and clamped his mouth tight on the words that were forming. "McGuire."

McGuire of the *Journal* leaned against the wall and watched him. "So you came in fourth in the poll. Considering that there are seven other regular second basemen in the league, you didn't do so bad, did you, Chad?"

Sprague, the florid-faced manager of the Falcons, came over. "Lay off him, McGuire."

"All I'm doing is talking," McGuire said. "How about it, Chad? Can I get some quotes on what you think of the All-Star Poll?"

The locker room was quiet as the rest of the Falcons waited expectantly.

"He thinks they're great," Sprague said. "A true expression of democracy. He thinks that O'Brien deserved the honor and he's happy for him."

"That right, Chad?" McGuire asked, grinning.

"You heard him," Chad said.

"Let's see," McGuire said, making a big process of racking his memory for the statistics. "You led the league in fielding your position for three straight years. And in the last two of them your batting average topped .290. O'Brien never did more than .275, and that was six years ago."

Chad Hawley put on his sport jacket and buttoned it. He could feel the blood hot in his veins.

Sprague put a hand on his shoulder. "Take it easy, kid."

"Sure," McGuire said. "Run some cold water over your wrists. How about a word of thanks to the fans who did vote for you? Something to the effect that you appreciate their support."

"Why the hell should I?" Hawley snapped.

Sprague pushed him toward the door. "Better take off now, Chad."

McGuire followed them. "Or a few words about the fans who didn't vote for you. Especially the hometown ones? Or something about how it feels to be a loner on the team, with even your teammates not particularly thrilled by your personality?"

Chad stopped at the door and turned. "All right; you're needling for a blow-off, and here it is." He shrugged aside Sprague's hand. "If the fans who come to this park had to pass an intelligence test to get in, the stands would be empty; they don't know baseball from a Bull Durham sign. Even in his good days, O'Brien was nothing to rave about. But he's a holler guy, on the field and off; and if there's anything that impresses the morons who come to a ball park, it's a lot of wind and noise."

Chad's teammates were silently busy and they avoided his eyes. He looked them over. "What the rest of the team thinks of me doesn't make me lose sleep. I'm in this game because it pays me good money and for no other reason; if that bothers them, I'm not going to cry about it."

Sprague sat down on a bench and sighed. "You satisfied now, McGuire?"

Chad left through the players' exit and passed a mob of kids shoving slips of paper at Morris, the Falcon's slugging right fielder. The boys glanced at him disinterestedly and continued to shove for autographs.

Chad got into the players' bus and took a seat in the rear. In fifteen minutes the bus filled and Charley Alpin, the Falcon first sacker, took the only remaining seat next to Chad.

Alpin smiled thinly as he noticed Chad stiffen. "Relax," he said. "I got nothing to say." But after a few moments he spoke. "Popping off is the sucker's way. It'll take a long while for people to forget about being called morons—maybe never."

Chad turned on him. "I thought you had nothing to say."

After breakfast the next morning, Chad went to the hotel newsstand and bought himself a paper. He turned to the sports pages and read about himself. "Chad Hawley Bitter at Poll Results. Calls Fans Morons. O'Brien Loudmouth."

The afternoon game was the rubber of a three-game series with the visiting fourth-place Bruins. The Falcons, in first by two and a half, had tucked away the first game in a walk-away 8 to 2, and dropped the second, 3 to 1.

The fans started on Chad as soon as he stepped onto the field for the pre-game practice and they didn't let up. Chad kept his eyes from the stands and ignored the catcalls.

The Bruins went down in order in the top half and the Falcons trotted in. Heald, the shortstop and lead-off man, fouled off a couple and then managed to sweat out a free trip to first.

When Chad stepped into the batter's box, he thought he was ready for the reception the fans would give him; but the chorus of boos and foot stamping brought a flush to his cheeks.

He squared off for the expected bunt on the first pitch and rapped it too hard. The Bruin third sacker, halfway to the plate, gloved the pop-up and rifled to first to double up Heald.

Hawley shouldered his way through the derisive shouts of the paying customers and stepped down into the dugout. Pomfret flied out to center to end the inning.

In the second, the first Bruin batter poked one down the right-field line to the corner, and by the time the relay came in, he had a stand-up triple.

The next Bruin batter tried too hard for the long sacrifice fly and went down swinging.

Hagg, the Falcon pitcher, missed the corner on a three-two count and Neyhardt, the Bruin third baseman, trotted down to first.

With men on first and third and one out, Hagg kept the pitches low to Bowman, a weak hitter, hoping for the double play rap. Bowman cooperated by stroking one toward second.

Chad Hawley scooped it up, stepped on second, and poured the ball to Alpin on first. The throw was wide. Alpin managed to tip it with his glove, but it got by and rolled into the visitors' dugout. The unearned run scored from third and Bowman scurried to second.

There was a long groan of pain from the fans at Chad's error. He turned his back on them and studied the scoreboard until Hagg was ready to pitch again. The next Bruin was retired without any more damage.

The pitching kept tight and the score held at 1 to 0. Chad struck out twice with men in scoring position; in the last of the seventh he grounded out, third to first.

The Falcons started the last of the ninth the right way when

Kirkwood, the catcher, singled to left. Avril, batting for Hagg, pushed him to second on a sacrifice. The Bruin center fielder made a shoe string catch of Heald's liner, and Kirkwood had to hustle back to second.

When Chad Hawley came up for his turn the fans groaned, and some of them set up a chant for a pinch-hitter.

Chad pounded the dirt out of his spikes and dug in. The first pitch was a chin-high duster and Hawley sat down hard and fast to get out of the way. He heard the roar of laughter from the crowd.

Chad fingered the rosin sack and stepped back in, his lips set in a tight line.

The Bruin hurler made the mistake of serving up a fat one, shoulder high. Chad's wrists snapped as he laced into the pitch.

The left fielder saw what was coming and turned his back as he raced for the wall. After eight or nine steps, he looked over his shoulder and slowed down to a stop. He stood with his hands on his hips as he watched the ball clear the fence, fair by about ten feet.

Sprague was there between home and third to pat his shoulder as Chad trotted in with the winning run, but he was the only one.

There was a strange silence from the fans. They wanted their Falcons to win, but they didn't want Hawley to be the one to do it for them. A murmur finally broke the silence. There were no boos for Chad, but neither was there any applause.

When Chad was through showering, Sprague met him with a telegram in his hand. "The Commissioner wants to see you," he said.

Hawley slipped into his shirt. "He's six hundred miles away; I'd miss a couple of games."

"You'd miss them even if you don't go; you're suspended." Sprague studied Chad's expressionless face. "It's not my doing. I know you were needled into this. But the Commissioner would like to know the facts firsthand."

Chad shrugged. "If he wants talk, I'll give him some."

"You got a good record, Chad. You never shot off your mouth before. All that's likely to happen is that you get to stand in front of a loudspeaker and make an apology to the fans."

"Would you like to bet?"

Sprague's eyes met Chad's. "On your train ride, take time to think things over. If you're stubborn about this, it may finish you in baseball."

When Chad Hawley reported to the Commissioner's offices, he was met in the anteroom by a dozen newspapermen. They crowded around him.

"I understand Ted Williams is getting jealous because you irritate the fans more than he does. You got anything to say about that?'' one of them asked, grinning.

A spectacled reporter edged his voice in. ''Is it true that you wear the largest size cap in the major leagues?''

Commissioner Walker came out of the inner offices and shouldered his way to Hawley's side. ''We'll issue a statement later,'' he said. ''Now be good scribblers and clear the way.''

The newsmen pressed for words from Chad, but he kept his mouth shut as he preceded Walker into his office and the door closed behind them.

''Take a chair,'' Walker said. He took a cigar out of a humidor and lit it. Walker was a big heavy man with graying hair and a touch of humor in his eyes. He sat down and his eyes went over Hawley. ''I suppose you were misquoted?''

''Not enough for it to make much difference.''

''Well, good; at least we got that settled. You don't know how refreshing it is to hear somebody admit something like that.'' Walker opened the manila folder on his desk and leafed through a few of the loose sheets. ''Would you care to explain your reasons for saying what you did?''

''It's what I thought and still think.''

Walker nodded absently and kept his eyes on the papers. ''Did you think the same things before the results of the All-Star Poll came out?''

Chad flushed and said nothing.

Walker closed the folder and looked up. ''Maybe you think you're the best second baseman in the league, and maybe you're right; but All-Stars get picked for a lot of reasons. Some because they play for big-city teams, and big cities can rout out more votes for their players than small cities can. Some because they make a lot of noise and get noticed. And some because of what they have contributed to the game.''

The Commissioner glanced down at the papers for a moment before he continued. ''Nowadays they have figures on everything in the game. I wouldn't be surprised if they count the hangnails a first baseman gets in the course of a season. But even with all the statisticians cluttering up the place, there are some things they'll never get down on paper.''

Walker tapped off some cigar ash. ''Things like what one RBI means when it wins a game, and how little three or four of them mean when your team is ahead 8 to 0. Things like how you get along with the rest of the team. Things like trying hard, even if it means bruising your delicate skin.''

Walker's eyes met Chad's. "Am I making myself clear?"

"I heard you," Chad said. "In other words I got to learn to smile, and be a good fellow, and die for the dear old Falcons. If I do that I might win a popularity contest too."

Walker looked out of the window for a while. "You're going to have to make a public apology, you know."

"I'll think about it."

Ice came into Walker's voice. "Do that; you're on vacation until you make up your mind." He shifted in his chair and dismissed Chad by picking up a newspaper. "If you don't want to meet the reporters, you can go out the back way. Or maybe you've got something more to say to them?"

Chad Hawley got up and took the back way out.

The Senior Leaguers won the All-Star game the next afternoon and O'Brien did his bit with fancy fielding. He had three for five at the plate and drove in two runs.

When Chad reported back to the Falcons, Sprague took him aside. "I hate to say it, Chad, but you'd better make up your mind about that apology pretty soon. I can't have you sitting out a dozen games while you're being stubborn; you know we're weak in utility men. I'm trying out this kid Michalak in your position, but I have my doubts. I may have to call up Runyon from Triple A; that will mean I have to make room for him. I hope you get the hint."

The second-place Lions came into town riding a five-game winning streak. At game time, Chad came into the dugout wearing civvies and took a seat beside Sprague.

"Technically, I don't suppose I should be allowed to sit here while I'm suspended. Want to kick me out?"

"Not particularly," Sprague said. He looked out on the field. "I'm worried about Michalak. He'll be good some day, but he's green now."

There wasn't any scoring in the first half for the Lions, and during the home try Michalak swung at two bad pitches and then watched a third good one go by. He came back into the dugout and avoided Sprague's eyes.

Chad looked at his hands for a while and then he cleared his throat. "Don't let it get you, kid. The first day I put on a big-league uniform, I struck out three times out of four trips."

Sprague waited until the top of the second when the team was on the field before he turned to Chad. "If I remember right, you got four for four that day."

"I keep forgetting," Hawley said.

As he watched the men on the diamond, a strange feeling came to the pit of his stomach. He'd always been more or less a loner, but this was different. Here he was sitting on the bench, a complete outsider. It gave him a feeling of more complete loneliness than he had ever experienced before.

Michalak had no business come his way until the third. Then he made a beautiful backhanded stop of a hard smash. He whirled and fired to Alpin at first. Alpin made a desperate leap, but the ball was over his glove and the runner went to second before he could run down the ball.

Reinhold, who was on the mound for the Falcons, let the poor support rattle him and made the next pitch too good. Toliver, the Lion's left fielder, met the pitch with the fat of his bat and poled it 390 feet into the bleachers, making the score 2 to 0.

Reinhold settled down after that and retired the side.

When Michalak returned to the dugout, he sat with his eyes studying the cement floor between his knees. "Nice stop," Chad said.

Michalak glanced at him. "What have you got to say about the throw?"

"I've made plenty of them, too; don't let the crowd make you nervous."

"I don't," Michalak said. "I know they're just people. They make mistakes, too."

Chad looked startled for a moment and he eyed the stands as though trying to confirm the statement.

In the fourth, Michalak made another nice stop and this time made the throw to first good. He got a round of applause for the play.

Chad remembered the applause he used to get. Nothing sensational like that which followed when Morris blasted out another four bagger, but good substantial applause to show that the fans appreciated a particularly good play.

He remembered, too, the boos he had received the last time he'd appeared on the field. Chad kicked at the steps of the dugout.

The Lions added to their lead in the fifth and sixth and the Falcons never caught up. The final score was five to three. Michalak handled two more chances without a miscue and got a scratch single in the eighth.

The visitors repeated the next day with a 5 to 0 whitewash and narrowed the Falcon lead to one half game. Michalak handled himself flawlessly in the field, but he failed to do anything at the plate.

Chad was sitting alone in the lobby of the hotel when Sprague lowered himself into the easy chair beside him. "We got just this game tomorrow night," he said, "and then the road-trip. Tonight's your last chance to apologize to the home fans. Tell me, should I send for Runyon?"

Chad sighed. He rose to his feet. "I'm going up to my room and write that damn apology."

Sprague grinned with relief. "Keep it short; you're not running for office."

The next evening, fifteen minutes before game time, Chad stood in the public address system booth, clutching a sheet of paper while the announcer introduced him.

The chorus of Bronx cheers and cat-calls welled up like a gigantic wave and Chad nervously fingered the paper while he waited for it to subside.

He stepped up to the microphone. "I would like to apologize to the people in this ball park and to all the other fans of the Falcons for the words I used in reference to them last Monday."

Chad was somewhat surprised at the way his voice boomed through the park. He cleared his throat and continued. "I sincerely regret having said the things I did, and I would like to apologize also to Ed O'Brien of the Lions for what I may have said about him. O'Brien is one of the finest players in the league."

He debated for a second whether he should read the last paragraph and then decided he would. "And at this time, I would like to thank all of you who voted for me in the recent All-Star Poll. I will try to live up to the confidence you have shown in me, and in the future I will try to be a credit to a great game."

As he stepped away from the microphone, the crowd made it known that it had not been appeased. But here and there were small islands of applause.

Down on the field, Chad took a deep breath and went over to the Lions' dugout. The eyes of the Lions players were cold as they waited for what he had to say. O'Brien's face was impassive as Chad stood before him.

"I'm sorry, Ed," Chad said. "I lost my temper, and the words turned out bad; I didn't really mean them." He held out his hand.

O'Brien looked at it for half a minute. Then he made the handshake short and turned his back on Chad.

When the infield crews finished with their rakes, Chad trotted out to his position.

O'Brien, leadoff man for the Lions, crouched his way to first on a walk. He danced off the bag, tantalizing Curtis, the Falcon pitcher, to waste energy on a couple of pegs to first.

Curtis finally completed his abbreviated wind-up, and O'Brien was off with the pitch on a hit and run.

The batter pulled too much and Chad webbed the grounder neatly. He stepped on second just as O'Brien made the slide.

Chad's legs went out from under him and the ball dribbled a couple of feet out of reach. When Chad recovered the ball, it was too late for a play at first.

O'Brien stood on the bag, grinning. "You got to learn to hold on to the ball if you want to be an All-Star."

Chad returned the grin and went back to his position without comment. The fans rumbled in a confused way.

The runners were sacrificed to second and third. Curtis gave an intentional pass to the next batter to fill the bases, hoping for a double play or a play at the plate. But the runner on third scored on a long fly. The next man up fouled out to the catcher to end the first half with the Lions ahead, 1 to 0.

In the Falcon half, Heald grounded out to short. Chad followed with a liner that the right fielder had to chase down.

Chad made the turn and took off for second. The throw came in late and as Chad lay in the dirt with his toe hooked safe on the bag, O'Brien brought the ball down hard and viciously to his side.

The crowd got to its feet, expectant. Chad looked toward his dugout, but he saw that no one appeared interested. Only Sprague came strolling out of the coaching box to get in a few words.

Chad waited for the burn on his side to ebb and then he motioned for Sprague to forget it. He smiled at O'Brien. "I figure we're even now. Play your position, but don't get cute."

Pomfret rapped out a single that brought Chad home to knot the score and the next two Falcons went down without changing it.

In the fifth, Oberg, the Lions' clean-up hitter, put his muscle into a waist-high pitch and sent it over the scoreboard to bring in a runner ahead of him and put the Lions on the long end of the 3 to 1 score.

Going into the last of the sixth, with two out, Chad had to bob under a high fast one inside. The next pitch was just as far inside, but lower. Chad couldn't manage to get out of the way of that one and took it on the fleshy part of his arm.

As he massaged it, he looked down at the pitcher and then at his own bench. Only Michalak was on the lip of the dugout.

Chad trotted down to first.

Chad had a long lead as the catcher called for a pitchout. He dived headlong back to first. The backstop's throw was low and it got by the first baseman.

Chad leaped to his feet and steamed for second. The first baseman tracked down the short roll and pegged to second. The ball caught Chad between the shoulder blades. He pulled up at second as O'Brien recovered the ball and blinked away the redness that flashed before his eyes.

When he recovered, Sprague and Michalak were on the diamond heading for second. Sprague's face was beet-red and he seemed about to explode; but instead he restrained Michalak and took Chad aside. "They're laying for you," he said. "I'm taking you out before you get killed."

Chad listened to the ominous rumbling coming from the grandstands with a slight smile on his face. "I'll stay," he said. Then his eyes went to the Falcon dugout where his teammates sat without moving.

Sprague's glance followed his and then he shrugged and walked off the diamond.

The umpires got the game going again. O'Brien, close to the bag for a possible pickoff, spoke sardonically. "You're a real popular guy with your teammates. I notice how much support they give you."

The next Falcon batter lifted a high fly to center for the third out.

The score held until the last of the ninth, when Ames, batting for the Falcon pitcher, and Heald put doubles back to back to change it to 3 to 2.

Chad tossed away the leaded bat and stepped into the box. He got the bunt sign and squared off as the pitch came in. It was hard and high, straight for his head. Chad dropped fast to get out of the way. There were shouts of indignation from the fans.

Chad turned to the catcher. "You'd better go out there and tell your boy that I'm tired of going up and down like a yo-yo. If the next one comes even close, I'm going to visit him with a bat in one hand."

The ump decided to take over and called time. He walked out to the mound. The Lions' pitcher grinned while the umpire gave him the warning.

The next two pitches were low, but good, and Chad laid down bunts that dribbled over the foul line.

With the count one and two, Chad took his full cut on the next one. He poled a long one between center and right and it rolled into the far corner. Heald dashed across home to tie the score.

Racing into third, Chad got the go-ahead from Sprague. He lost a fraction of a second when he slipped on the turn, but he righted himself and headed for home.

O'Brien, on the edge of the outfield grass, took the peg from center and snapped the ball toward home plate. The toss came in to the third-base side of home plate and caught Chad on the side of the jaw just as he was beginning his slide.

Hot pain shot through the side of his face, but he pulled himself together enough to touch home plate for the winning run before the catcher could pounce on the ball.

Chad lay there in the dirt with his eyes closed, listening to the roar of the fans. When he opened his eyes, he found Falcons streaming on the field, some of them to see how much he was hurt and the others making a beeline for second base. Michalak got to O'Brien first and began trading punches. The cops and ushers were having a hard time keeping the angry fans off the field.

The rhubarb lasted for more than ten minutes before order was restored by the umps and some of the more cool-headed players.

After an examination by the trainer, Chad indicated that he felt well enough to walk, but he needed help to get to the club house.

The club doctor spent several minutes examining the jaw. "We'll take X-rays right away, of course," he said. "I don't think anything is broken, but I'm afraid you'll be out for a while."

Chad looked at his teammates gathered around him and he saw in their eyes what he thought he'd never missed before; he was one of them now. Chad found it painful to grin, but he did it anyway. "You'll have to take over my position, Slugger," he said to Michalak. "But don't get too good; I want to be missed."

McGuire edged his way through the players. "Got anything I can print to say about O'Brien?"

Chad kept grinning. "He's a fine player. A real gentleman, and I'd trust him with my sixteen-year-old sister."

"That last throw that caught you on the jaw. You figure that was an accident?"

Chad found it was just as painful to stop grinning, but he became serious for a moment. "A good throw would have had me at the plate. O'Brien's too much of a team man to throw away a game for any reason."

The locker room attendant pushed his way through. "There's a bunch of people outside who want to know how you are and they want your autograph if you're not hurt too bad. Should I tell them you can't make it?"

"Hell, no!" Chad said. "Somebody hand me a ballpoint; I'll be right out."

ON ACCOUNT
OF DARKNESS

Barry N. Malzberg
and Bill Pronzini

S O I TOOK the Holographic Magnifier and the stick figures over to the Agency, talked myself past three secretaries, paid my one hour of humiliation waiting in the outside offices, and finally got into Evers' office. "I've got some terrific stuff here," I said, pulling it out of the case and laying it in front of him. "Jackie Robinson, the Duke, the Babe, the Splendid Splinter, a hundred more. A veritable Cooperstown of the mind."

"What's a Cooperstown?" he said.

"It was a famous museum where the uniforms and memorabilia of the greats were kept," I said. "Not that it matters. What matters is this: I can let you have the holographic stuff at a very reasonable price. Very reasonable."

"Football," Evers said. "There's no market for football anymore."

"This isn't football, it's baseball. Football was a contact sport of the twentieth century; baseball, purely of American origin, was played with a small round ball and a long thin piece of timber called a bat—"

"I'm not interested," Evers said. "Nothing personal, it's just that we have lots of problems here. The whole question of entertainment. . . ." He shrugged.

"Well, I can appreciate the range of your problems," I said.

"But what I've got here is really something special. Suppose I just give you a little demonstration?"

Evers yawned.

"Oh, come on," I said. "You let me in here, you let me get this far, you know you're a little interested already." I gave him an ingratiating smile. "Did you know there was a baseball player called Evers who was very famous in the early part of the twentieth century? A second baseman for the Chicago Cubs. Tinkers to Evers to Chance—that was this legendary double-play combination—"

"What's a Chicago Cub?" Evers said.

The trouble with the people at the Agency is that they are efficient but they have little historical sense. Historicity? Historicalness? They are extremely good on details, and they certainly know what will sell along the range of available techniques, but their grasp of specifics is limited. Not that I hold this against them, of course. They're only trying to do a job.

I began to set up the Magnifier, working with it until it hummed and glowed and vibrated on Evers' desk. He looked at it in a bored way and didn't look at me at all. So I said, "For that matter, there was a Hoot Evers who played for the Detroit Tigers, an outfielder in the 1950's. Hoot wasn't his real name, but that was what they called him. I think his real name was Charles."

"What's a Detroit?" Evers asked.

I concealed a sigh, setting up certain figures which I had preselected. Then I set the Magnifier for one-tenth life-size and hit the button, and the room was suddenly filled with heat and light and those strange smells that are supposed to be grass and peanuts and hot dogs. The ballplayers in their uniforms were darting all over the office, like energetic little animals.

"Look at this," I said. "National League All-Stars of the middle twentieth century versus the greatest single team in baseball history, the 1927 New York Yankees. Yankees are the home team, so they're in the field first. The pitcher is Herb Pennock, Lou Gehrig is on first, Tony Lazzeri is at second . . ."

I went on to give him the lineups. He didn't seem to be listening, but he had one eye cocked on Jackie Robinson striding up to the plate to lead off the game. "What's the object of all this, anyway?" he said.

"Well, the batter has to use the stick in his hands to hit the ball out of range of the fielders. If he does that, or if the pitcher misses that plate-shaped target, the batter is allowed to take one or more bases. Four bases constitute a run, and the team with the most runs at the end of the game—"

Evers raised a hand. "That's enough," he said, but he still had the one eye cocked on Robinson.

So I launched into a play-by-play, a technique which I have developed in the classic sense. Robinson hit Pennock's third pitch and grounded out to Koenig at short, and then Bobby Thompson took a called third strike. The next batter was Ted Kluzewski.

"This is pretty clever stuff," Evers said in a grudging way. He had both eyes on the game now. "I've got to admit that."

"Oh, it's very clever," I said. "You can really get absorbed in it, you know. One thing you should keep in mind is that this is only a one-tenth magnification here; you can imagine what the game is like when you lay it out in a conventionally sized stadium."

"I suppose so. But I still don't see the point of it all."

"Entertainment," I said. "Abstraction. Hundreds of years ago people used to obtain amusement watching these baseball games."

"But *why?*"

"Aesthetics," I said vaguely.

"How come you're so familiar with the subject?"

"I have a background. My great-great-grandfather worked for the last commissioner's office, and all of this was passed down through the family. A kind of heritage. And a hobby too."

"A strange hobby."

"Each to his own."

"Mmm," Evers said.

Kluzewski hit a ground ball between first and second for a single; Ruth tossed the ball back in to Lazzeri. "Next batter is Stan Musial," I said. "He might have been the best batter in his division during his time. Note the very unusual position he takes; that's the famous Musial Crouch. He's virtually batting on his knees, as you can see."

Evers didn't say anything.

Musial, a first-ball hitter if ever there was one, sent a towering fly ball to right center that Earle Combs couldn't quite reach. The translucent ball bounced off the wall, rolled back to the infield; Lazzeri scooped it up and fired it to the catcher, Benny Bengough, holding Kluzewski at third and Musial at second.

"That was a typical Musial double," I said.

Evers said, "I think I'm losing interest. This may be clever stuff, but it doesn't entertain or amuse me at all."

"You haven't seen enough of it yet," I said as Willie Mays came up and popped the first pitch up to Koenig at short. "Now the teams switch places and the Yankees come to bat—"

"I'm just not interested," Evers said. "Turn it off."

I hesitated, but I could see that it was hopeless; sometimes you can press the point and sometimes you dare not. So much in this business is a matter of timing. I turned off the Magnifier, began to gather it and the stick figures together.

"The thing is," Evers said, "there's no real audience for it. I can see the elements of diversion, of course, but there just aren't enough of them."

I said nothing. There is a time to talk and then there is a time not to talk, and off this great balance wheel are conducted all relationships and dealings.

"I suppose," Evers said, "that we might be able to do a little something with it in the Outlying Districts. But then again, it would hardly repay our investment. Visuals are a tricky commodity, you know."

A certain feeling of revulsion and pain began to work in me then. I had held it well down throughout this meeting, but it comes at odd moments, in little layers and surges of feeling. I seemed to see myself in ten other offices like Evers', past and present, at the mercy of people like him, who understood very little and yet, somehow, controlled everything; I seemed to see myself getting older, beginning to die in stages, while the batteries in the Holographic Magnifier lost power and the figures of the great baseball players lost definition and finally faded altogether. . . .

I had to say something then. So I said, "All right, I'll be going now; if you don't understand, I can't make you understand. You'll just never know, that's all, what a beautiful game it was." I turned and started for the door.

"Wait a minute now," Evers said.

I pivoted back toward him. "What?"

Evers cleared his throat. "I said there was very little in it, but, still and all, there might be *something* worthwhile. We might be able to convert it into an amusement for the juveniles, for example. Or there's the possibility of an exhibit over in the Central District of minor artifacts that we're planning to open." He fixed me with shrewd, veiled eyes. "We might be able to make a small bid, after all."

"How small?"

"Fifteen," he said.

"That's ridiculous. This is baseball, all of *baseball.*"

"Nobody knows what baseball is. I didn't; I still don't."

"It's something beautiful, something irreplaceable. . . ."

"Seventeen," Evers said. "That's my final offer."

"I've got to have twenty-five."

"Not from us."

"Twenty-two then. I have expenses to cover."

"Eighteen—but that's it. Yes or no? I'll have to put it on the Terminals right away."

"Eighteen," I said. "Listen, you're talking about an entire way of life for hundreds of thousands of people—"

"Good-bye," Evers said.

"Now wait—"

"Eighteen, or good-bye."

The pain and revulsion deepened within me, but I said, "All right. But I'm giving you my whole life here; I'm giving you hundreds of thousands of lives."

"We'll program the eighteen in," he said. "You can get a Verificatory from my secretary." He stood up. "It's been a pleasure having you and your quaint little pastime here, but now, if you don't mind . . ."

He didn't offer his hand; he just looked away, dismissing me. So I took one last look at the Magnifier and the stick figures, and then I went out of there and took a railcab to my cubicle. Outside, the sky was just beginning to darken; night was coming on.

And the game is over, I thought. But then, if you wanted to look at it another way, they'd have called it anyway in the old days. On account of darkness. Called on account of darkness.

Then, still filled with pain, I sat down and went through my materials and tried to figure out the best places to unload hockey, basketball, and horse racing.

LITTLE
BASEBALL WORLD

Robert Lowry

ELEN TURNED IT on very low so that nobody else in the house would know she was listening (she'd sworn before them all never to listen again, because they had kidded her about it), and then as soon as she'd heard the score she turned it off and sat staring at the back yard.

The score was five to two in favor of the Cubs and it was only the last half of the third inning with the Reds at bat—who was batting? Lombardi? Lombardi was a good hitter, you couldn't tell what they were going to do now . . . of course the Reds would lose, they always lost, they did so many completely stupid things just when they got you all excited about how good they were that you wanted to throw the radio out of the window. Who was batting anyhow? She turned on the radio again, very softly, and listened, leaning forward in her rocker.

"Lombardi on second, Harry Craft at bat with one ball and two strikes—" Lombardi on second! She leaned forward to listen.

"All right," said the announcer, "Bill Lee is ready—" and the black-eyed buxom girl rocked back and forth in the rocker before the radio. She was ready too, it was evident, she was waiting for whatever was sure to come. She just had no faith at all in the Reds any more, they lost yesterday and they'd lose today, they weren't going to be leading the League for much longer. . . . Like what happened yesterday, they were winning until the first of the ninth, then that Johnny Vander Meer let the bases get full by walking so many, and Hartnett came in to pinch-hit and made a home run, and that was the end of your old ball game. That was the way they always did—got you all worked up then betrayed you.

". . . hits a long fly ball into right field—and he's *out!*"

"Oh my God," Helen said, and snapped the radio off.

She went to the kitchen, got herself a glass of water, then came back into the dining-room. She sat stiffly in her rocker, staring out at the back yard. She wouldn't turn it on for ten minutes, then she'd see what happened. Not that she expected anything good to happen.

But all the radios up and down Hutton Street were blaring forth the game, and before three minutes were up she couldn't resist, she switched it on.

"—and the Reds are out in front again! Now let me turn you over to Dick Bray who has a few words to say about the Breakfast of Champions . . . "

She'd missed the best part—the score and everything. There was that Dick Bray talking away in his tenor voice about Wheaties, the Breakfast of Champions—he wouldn't tell it.

"Shut up about your Wheaties and tell us the score," she said out loud. "We know all about your Wheaties, just shut up and tell us something we want to know."

But no, he just wouldn't. Finally Red Barber came on to announce the first half of the fourth, and she found out the Reds were leading six to five.

Well, that was better than nothing—she rocked away in her rocker. They'd lose it anyhow, though. They always did something good then went ahead and lost it anyhow. They didn't care how hard you rooted.

She'd certainly done her part—been here by her radio since the opening game in spring, shouting at the announcer, getting angry when the Reds fumbled, furious when the Giants or Cards or Phillies made a run. Anyhow the Reds were leading the League, even if they wouldn't win the pennant. It was the last of July, everybody else on that street was sure they were going to be champions and play in the World Series, but she laughed at that, you never could depend on them just when you thought they were so good. That was when they always lost.

"Well, the Reds are out in front now with that one-run margin," Red Barber said, "but we still have six-long-innings to go and—"

"Six long innings is true," Helen said right back. "And don't kid yourself that plenty can't happen between now and then."

She sure did know, this was her second year listening and they sure made plenty of mistakes. Of course she *wanted* them to win —tuned in even on Sunday when the club officials wouldn't let the game be broadcast in detail because it hurt attendance. She read the papers in front of the radio then and waited for the pause in the recorded music when Red Barber gave the runs, hits and errors.

Seven days out of the week she was here, but she didn't care. People could just leave her alone to sit here, they could mind their own business. Her mother never told her to go out and get a job or anything, but she knew that was what they were all thinking and she didn't care. Her brother Tom would make some remark to her, and she'd tell him off. Just let me alone, just go away and never speak to me.

She didn't care if she *never* went out of the house again. She almost never did either, except to go downtown to the library. She hated clothes, she hated getting all dressed up. She felt so conspic-uous on the streetcar. Wearing those silly gloves.

They didn't understand, nobody else had anything wrong with them. They didn't have to wear silly gloves when they went out. Tom thought he was smart and could do anything he wanted, go anywhere he wanted. He was a boy seventeen, a year younger than she was—she'd wanted a sister anyhow.

Well, yesterday she'd told off her mother all right. Her mother had said, "Why don't you ever go out any more? Why don't you and some of your girl friends go to the movies?" She'd told her mother then. "Because of my hand, that's why. Because I'm crip-pled," she'd said right out. Her mother had begun crying and Helen hadn't even felt sorry. "Now you know, so just stop crying. I'm not ever going anywhere again, so just don't bother me. I'm not ever going to go out and get all dressed up and wear those silly gloves again."

They could all just leave her alone, she was happy. She was glad she was all through with high school—glad she had no friends— glad she didn't have anything to do but listen to the baseball game —glad she was crippled. If anybody didn't like it they could just not look at her, that was all. She knew she was ugly and they could just all stay away.

Baseball was more interesting anyhow. She'd never seen a game but that didn't matter, she didn't want to. She knew all the players, she read the papers and listened to all the sports broadcasts and she liked the players better than any people she knew. Paul Derrin-ger was the best of them—he was tall and slender and always going out to the night clubs so sometimes he couldn't play the next day. She liked little Eddie Joost too—he was like a grade-school boy, never failing to do something crazy like fumbling the ball when it was an easy play. Ernie Lombardi supported a lot of his relatives out in California and she felt he played awfully serious—not like Frank McCormick who was good-looking and so sure of himself.

Her mother asked once how could she know what a ball game looked like if she'd never seen one, and she'd got mad and told her mother she didn't *want* to know. But she knew all right—she could picture Harry Craft "shifting his chaw of tobacco from the left side of his mouth to the right and stepping up to the plate" or Whitey Moore "pounding his fist in the palm of his glove and glancing over at first." Red Barber was a really good announcer, he could say funny things about the players and make it all humorous. Of course he made a lot of mistakes too, sometimes got so excited he forgot what he was saying, and you had to wait till he calmed down to find out if it was a hit or an out.

Well, here we go into the first of the ninth, she thought. Cubs at bat. The Reds better watch out with their old one-run lead—they always were leading up to the last inning just to throw the game away by making errors. Who was batting anyhow?

"Quit talking about last inning and tell us who's batting," she said to Red Barber, and he answered by saying: "Wham-bo! It's a *hard* bouncing ball down to Joost at third—and Joost *fumbles!* He makes the throw to first—but too late!—and Wilson is tucked away there safely with——"

"Did you do those dishes?"

She turned scarlet and whirled around on her mother standing in the doorway. "Let me alone!" Helen shouted. "Can't you see I'm listening?"

"If you don't do them I'll do them," her mother said. "They've been around here all afternoon and I'm sick of seeing them."

Her face was toward her mother but her plump body was bent eagerly toward the radio.

"Just tell me," her mother began again, but Helen really turned on her then: "Now you made me miss who was next at bat! Don't bother me! I'll do them! Just let me alone!"

It was a long fly ball—Craft would never catch it—going back, back, the sun in his eyes—oh, he caught it! She looked around then, and her mother was gone.

The rest of the inning was nothing, a ground ball and a strike-out so the Reds won and they were lucky they did. She turned the radio off and rocked away. She had to admit that she *wanted* them to win even if she didn't really believe in them—days they won she felt so good.

Her brother came into the room from outside. "What'd they do today, lose?"

She felt her hand clench. "Well, they almost did but they didn't," she said. "It was a crazy game—the Cubs got five runs in the third inning, then the Reds got three more runs and it was six to five. So the Cubs couldn't do anything till the first of the ninth and Wilson got on first—that crazy Eddie Joost had a ground ball and he fumbled it. The next batter up hit a long fly and I thought Craft would never catch it—he had to go all the way back to the stands. So they won all right—but I bet they're still shaking in their boots!"

"That's all right," Tom said, "just so they won. It won't be long till they have the pennant clinched, if they just keep winning."

"Well, they better do better than they're doing if they're going to beat out St. Louis," Helen said. "All the fumbles they've been making. Wait'll the series next week when they meet the Cards. Johnny Mize made two home runs yesterday."

"That don't mean anything," Tom said. "How about Lombardi yesterday? He made a home run and a double."

"Yes, he has to hit a home run or not get anything, he's so slow! Red Barber said that double yesterday would have been a triple if Bill Werber or Craft had hit it. The other team makes fumbles and everything and they still get old Lombardi out."

"How about Goodman?" Tom asked. "He made a triple yester-day."

"Goodman!" she shouted. "Don't talk to me about Goodman! Today when he came up to the plate in the first the crowd was clapping and everything because of that triple and all he did was stand there, while Bill Lee whizzed three of them over and he went back to sit down. The crowd was so stunned it didn't know what to say. All Red Barber said was, 'Well, that's the way it goes'— Red Barber says such dumb things sometimes."

She was feeling all warmed up, the way she always did whenever she talked about baseball. Her brother was the only one in the family who really knew anything about it. He'd played on the Turkey Bottoms Blues when he'd been in grade school, so she always liked to hear what he had to say. Sometimes she would even flatter him by asking his opinion on something.

"I feel like going sometime," Tom said. "I haven't seen them play all this season."

"It costs too much," Helen said. "It costs a dollar and ten cents just for regular seats."

She felt him looking at her intently, but she wouldn't look back at him. She never did know what he was thinking. "Let's get tickets and go to the World Series if the Reds win," he said.

Helen's hand clenched up tight and the color all drained out of her face. She couldn't answer, maybe he was making fun of her because she just sat here all day, she looked at one of the Gruber fox terriers smelling at something in the back yard.

"I think Cokie Myers' father can get me tickets, he works at the park," Tom said. "Should we go if I can get them?"

"You can't get them," she said loudly. "So just don't bother me!"

"I can get them."

"Just don't bother me!" she said. "You can't get them so just don't even talk to me about it!"

"I tell you I can get them!" he said, getting mad too. "Will you go if I get them?"

She jumped up from the chair, her face white, her hair all mussed. "Just leave me alone!" she shouted at him. "Just quit making fun of me and leave me alone!" And she went out into the kitchen and turned on the hot water for the dishes.

At the supper table that night she got so mad, her mother and her brother were so optimistic about the Reds and they didn't know anything about it. When they said some of the things they did, she just couldn't help but shout at them. They always thought the Reds were going to win.

"They're not going to win tomorrow," she shouted. "They always lose on Friday. Joe Aston in the sports page yesterday analyzed how many times they lost on Friday, and it turned out to be eight or ten times."

"That doesn't mean anything," Tom said, breaking a piece of white bread and mopping up gravy with it. "They're in a winning streak now and they're going to keep on going. I bet you they win tomorrow."

She just got furious, she waved her hand and could hardly speak he made her so mad. "Why? Why?" she demanded, leaning forward, her black eyes jumping out of her head, her hair flying all over. "How can you say they're going to win tomorrow?"

"Because of Derringer, that's why."

"Yeah, yeah, Derringer!" Helen stopped eating altogether and sat back in her chair. "Look what he did in his last game—got knocked out of the box in the second inning by the Boston Bees! Derringer! Don't talk to me about Derringer!"

"Well, Derringer *is* good," her mother put in innocently. "He's a good pitcher," she added.

Helen turned on her mother with a fixed expression of horror, her left hand clenched in close to her and her right thrown out as if to defend herself. "Good pitcher! Yes! Good pitcher! He pitches good when he wants to, but that's only about twice a month! I know him!"

For five minutes there was silence while her mother and brother ate, but she could hardly eat anything, they made her so mad. Then she turned on Tom suddenly when he was just about to put a forkful of peas into his mouth and said: "You should have heard the booing the crowd gave Joost today when he dropped that bunt! Boy!"

She liked to sit in the dark like this—the kitchen light was on but it didn't shine on her rocker by the radio at all. The *Round the Town* program had been a disappointment—Dick Bray and Red Barber hadn't had time to do anything but give their opinions on the Reds' pennant chances, and she always knew what their opinions were, they were so optimistic.

There was just dance music now and she didn't feel like dialing around. She was tired, she'd been so keyed up all day. She was glad her mother was upstairs lying down and her brother was out to Ray's Place. Sometimes she just didn't want to be with anybody at all, she just wanted to be alone. She only felt natural when she was alone, and they didn't like her anyhow. She didn't care, they could just leave her alone if they didn't like her.

Well, her father would be down soon—she heard her mother up now, waking him. "Come on, William, get up—it's ten o'clock."

She went out to the kitchen and poured herself a glass of milk. She began to feel better, thinking about the day's game—wait till her father heard what almost happened in the ninth inning!

"Hello, Helen," he said—he was still sleep-dazed, she hardly felt he saw her out of his eyes. It was funny, when he got up in the evening he seemed about a foot smaller than when he came home from work in the morning. He was dressed in his blue work shirt buttoned at the collar and his brown whipcord pants. He was a small man with a potbelly and arms too thin and long for his body. She always felt strange with him, maybe because he looked so different—his face was altogether different from hers, he had a strong nose with a little bend in it and small gray eyes under gray eyebrows. A kind of bony face. She looked like her mother— round like her mother, with large dark eyes and full lips.

"Old Bucky Walters thought he was so good today!" she said as he went to the icebox and brought out a large plate of sliced tomatoes and cucumbers and a bottle of beer. "He had to go and let the Cubs get three hits in the first inning, and everybody thought the Reds were sunk.''

He poured salt and pepper over the salad and opened the beer. ''Yeah?'' he said, sitting at the table.

''Then they got two more runs in the second, and we got two runs. That made it five to two. You should have heard the crowd booing the umpire when he called Frey out at third in the fourth inning! That was when Werber singled and it looked like we were going to get some runs. The umpire was the only guy who believed old Frey was out. Roger Baker said it was the worst booing he'd heard in years.''

He drank the beer and wiped the foam off his mouth. He was always so quiet when he was sleepy—he only really talked a lot when he came home tanked up from Ray's Place in the afternoon.

''Well, who won?'' he asked finally.

''Oh, we won,'' Helen said, hating to tell him the end of the game first. ''But it's a wonder. Roger Baker almost threw a fit when Joost fumbled in the ninth inning and the Cubs had Wilson on first. We were only leading by one run—six to five. But then Goodman did something good for a change—he made a one-handed catch all the way back to the stands with the sun in his eyes and, boy, the crowd really cheered then, I thought the radio was coming apart. Then there was a ground ball and a strike-out and that was all. Oh I forgot to tell you, they put in Gene Thompson to pitch in the eighth inning.''

''Gene Thompson?'' he said. ''I didn't know he was playing with the Reds any more.''

''Sure he is. They always talk about trading him but they never do. He did pretty good too, except for that last inning. If Goodman hadn't been awake for a change Thompson would just have another loss on his record.''

She followed him out in the hall, where he put on his blue work coat. ''Tomorrow the Giants come to town, then we'll see! Carl Hubbell is supposed to pitch—and after what he did to the Reds last time they better be lying awake tonight thinking about it.''

She followed him back into the kitchen—he stuffed lots of kitchen matches into his pockets for his stogies. She watched him, trying to think of something else to say, as he took out his gold pocket watch and noted the time. She always felt desperate when he was leaving in the evening, she hadn't told him half of what happened.

''Ten forty,'' he said. ''Got to get down there.''

She followed him to the front door. ''Everybody's so sure

they're going to win the pennant," she said, "but I'm not so sure. If they can take two games out of three from the Giants they'll be all right."

"Oh, they'll win," he said. "Good night."

She watched him through the window, lighting a stogie on the front porch, and then she turned and went upstairs. She didn't feel tired now, she felt all excited again. But she thought she might as well go to bed anyhow, there was nothing else to do.

She went right on through August with them, never missing a game, and she never gave them the benefit of the doubt but they kept winning anyhow, she didn't know how because they did so many things wrong. She still wouldn't believe they were going to be champions even when they were within two games of clinching it. They'll do something, she kept thinking, they always do. And besides Johnny Vander Meer has a sore arm and can't pitch.

But then they took a game from Philadelphia and they were only one game away from the pennant and she was so nervous the next day because they didn't play, they were on their way back to Cincinnati to meet St. Louis, and that was the hardest team of all —St. Louis had all the batters, Johnny Mize, Enos Slaughter, all of them.

She didn't talk back to Red Barber very much during that St. Louis game, she just sat there, her heart high in her chest, both her hands clenched, listening to every play.

It was the last half of the ninth and Frey was on second, the score was still nothing to nothing and she wasn't making a sound. Jimmy Ripple was coming up to the plate and Red Barber gave a long description of everything he did—dusted his hands with dirt, picked up the bat, stepped over to the plate. She was leaning forward, her head almost touching the radio, her teeth tight together, when suddenly the scream of the crowd hit her full in the face—

"It's a smashing line drive into left field and Frey is rounding third—"

He was scoring, he was scoring! She couldn't sit down, she jumped up and walked around the room, her mouth open, her eyes blazing, her hand clutched in tight against her breast.

"—and the Cincinnati Reds are now—"

All of Hutton Street was screaming, Mrs. Must next door was screaming to her husband Allen who was out in the back yard: "Allen, Allen, they did it—"

She stood very still in the middle of the room, no longer hearing the radio, her body full and free, all her doubts gone. Should I go up and wake him? she thought, but instead she ran out on the front porch where her mother and Tom were sitting in the swing.

"They—" she said, but they already knew, they were both standing up shouting something to Mr. Keager across the street and here came Mrs. Gruber over from next door.

"What's the matter?" Mrs. Gruber asked.

"The Reds just won the pennant," Tom said.

"My God, I thought war was declared or something."

Helen's mother was beaming. "Tom's going to get tickets and take you," she said.

"What?" Helen asked, looking from Tom to her mother.

"Tom's getting tickets from Mr. Myers to one of the World Series games and he's going to take you."

She felt like crying—she hated them, they were always making fun of her. "You leave me alone," she said, the tears popping into her eyes. She began to scream: "All of you just leave me alone, I'm happy the way I am so just leave me alone!" She ran off the porch around to the back yard.

"I don't care!" she said. "I'm not going!"

Tom had the tickets in his hand. "You want me to tear them up?" he asked. "Just say tear them up and I'll do it right now."

She didn't know what to say—she knew why he'd gone and got them, just because she didn't want him to. He was always making fun of her, she listened to the game all the time and he thought she was silly. That's why he'd got the tickets, just to show her up.

"You can go by yourself!" she shouted and ran out on the front porch. She just wanted to get away, she hated them.

But they were at her day and night, they acted as if they couldn't understand why she wouldn't go. As if she wanted to get all dressed up and wear those silly gloves!

Her mother kept pounding away at her till she thought she'd go crazy. "It would be so nice for the two of you to go out together once in a while," her mother said, and that almost made her burst a blood vessel.

"Nice!" she said. "Nice! Do you think I want to go out with *him?* He doesn't like me and I know it! He can just go out by himself whenever he wants to."

"Why don't you go with Tom?" her father said one evening while he was eating his snack. "He got those tickets and now you won't go with him."

Somehow she never really got angry with her father, he didn't talk at her like her mother did. But now she felt so emotional she couldn't answer him, and she left the room. They were all the same —none of them understood. None of them would leave her be. They all had to keep picking on her.

The day before the game she found her mother pressing her blue dress.

"You can do all that you want," Helen said, "but I'm not going!"

Her mother didn't answer her—just went on pressing. And Helen sat down and watched her mother working, wishing she'd argue. "Tom doesn't want to take me anyhow—he just did it because you made him." But still her mother didn't answer and Helen got up and left the kitchen.

The sun wasn't even up—she looked at the alarm clock beside her bed. Five twenty. And then she remembered, this was the day! Today we'll see, she thought. Today we'll know whether they're any good or not. Derringer was going to pitch—she wished it were Bucky Walters. Derringer was more brilliant sometimes, but Bucky could really be depended on more.

She wondered if Tom would try to make her go—well, she wasn't going, he could put that in his pipe and smoke it. All of them could try to make her go but she wouldn't.

She couldn't stay in bed, she was too excited, she'd never been so excited about anything in her life before. She got up and dressed and went downstairs. There were some peaches in the icebox so she ate them and drank a glass of milk. Then she went out on the front porch and Hutton Street looked so strange, the air smelled good and the street was quiet, deserted. Just Mr. Timpkins' car parked down the street and none of the kids who were always around. Wait a minute—here came Mr. Kobble up the street. She dashed back into the house, she didn't want him to see her.

At eleven she was sitting on the front porch reading the *Ladies' Home Journal* but not really getting anything out of the story because she was so excited, when Tom came out. She wouldn't look up at him but he came over to her anyhow.

"You better get dressed," he said.

She still didn't look at him, there was a strange feeling in her chest. She surprised herself when she jumped up. "All right then, I will." And she went into the house and up the stairs.

When she was all dressed she stared at herself in the mirror. I don't look so fat when I'm fixed up, she thought. She wore her blue dress with the little white collar, and on her head was the hat she'd got last spring—a white hat that sat back from her face and had a black bow on it. She hadn't been out for three months, she'd almost forgotten how neat and clean it felt to be all dressed up with her girdle on and everything.

"You can wear your new gloves," her mother said when she arrived down in the kitchen. And she didn't get mad, she just took the gloves from her mother and started working the left one on. She had a hard time, the hand always persisted in clenching up hard whenever she wanted to do anything with it, but finally she got it and then worked the right one on by using the edge of the kitchen table. Tom and her mother did not watch her. Tom was looking out of the back door and her mother was washing a skillet at the sink.

She wished her mother wouldn't come out on the porch with them, but she didn't say anything. She felt so strange all dressed up, she just knew that people were staring out of their windows at her as she came down off the porch steps behind Tom—for a moment she almost decided to dash back into the house but then they were on their way, going past Mrs. Must's. Tom turned once at the top of the street and waved to his mother, but she didn't want to even look at that house, besides it was silly.

They climbed the footbridge over the railroad tracks and then they were standing side by side at the car stop on Eastern Avenue. She couldn't resist glancing at Tom as they stood there—he did look handsome in his brown suit and his tie. She got car tickets out of her handbag. "Here, drop these," she said, as the trolley came swaying toward them from the end of the line. And then they were on the car, bumping against each other as they sat on the straw seat.

Part of a swarm, she moved forward toward the high wall that was the ball park, Tom somewhere behind her, but she didn't look around. She felt that life had caught her and was dragging her along toward something she must know . . . something so inevitable she could not escape now even if she struggled. She was carried in through a doorway cut in the green wall, Tom was handing the tickets, then they were free again, going up the ramp into the grandstand. And suddenly she thought: is this the day I've been waiting for for two years? The struggle she had put up against coming certainly did seem ridiculous now that she was here— nobody noticed her, they all just rushed along, nobody stopped and laughed at her and stared at her gloved hands.

They were following an usher down to their seats and she was so busy watching her step she didn't get a good look at the field till she sat down—and then she looked, and she could not believe it. It was little! It was a dozen times smaller than she'd expected—she looked at the center field wall over which Lombardi had hit so many home runs and it did not seem any distance at all. She looked at the diamond itself—the distance between the bases was so short. And she had not known about the signs out there surrounding the outfield—signs advertising insurance, loans, suits of clothes, ham. They made everything so commercial.

Tom bought two bottles of Coke. "Did they really charge you fifteen cents each for these?" she asked. Everywhere were men in white suits selling things to the crowd—popcorn, Cracker Jacks, score cards, souvenir pins. Red Barber had never mentioned all of this.

But the players didn't have anything to do with it, she thought. These were just a lot of people trying to make . . . Well, it wouldn't be long now, the groundkeepers were smoothing out the infield. She watched them, trying to feel the excitement she always had at home just before the game, but she couldn't—two men on her left were discussing Florida and in front of her a Spanish-looking fellow was pressing kisses on the cheek of a little blonde. Wasn't anybody interested in the game?

"Where's the broadcasting booth?" she asked Tom.

"It's up above us, you can't see it," he said. "But look down there, there's Dick Bray interviewing people."

"Fans in the Stands," she said—but Dick Bray was lost in a knot of people, she couldn't see him.

Then the band was playing—*The Star-Spangled Banner*—and everyone was standing. Why did she always feel so silly standing —feeling everyone would look at her? "There's the Reds!" Tom said, nudging her.

She started, she strained toward them, even bending forward a little. They came stringing out on the field from their dugout, tiny loping men, each one like the other way down there—and she didn't know them!

She didn't know a single one of them. Had she been foolish enough to think they would be bigger than life, that she could actually see and know each one? They were all alike in their white suits with the big numbers on the back—just miniature men, who seemed to have nothing to do with her or the rest of the crowd. And here came Derringer out to the mound—but it was not really Derringer at all, Derringer was taller than Gary Cooper, Derringer was nonchalant, masterful, and this was just a tiny man in a white suit.

The game was starting—Derringer threw to Wilson. But she couldn't see the ball. She realized, as the first inning progressed and Detroit had men on base, that the game itself was just like the park—it was all in miniature, it wasn't like the game she'd imagined at all. They were just a lot of little men down there standing around, and she didn't know any of them. Even when the ball was hit nobody seemed to do very much—one man out in the field ran around a little and then there was someone on first or second, Derringer had the ball again and was throwing to the plate.

Detroit was making runs but she didn't care—she didn't know any of those men, she didn't care what they did. The crowd was screaming because Detroit was scoring again but she felt disgusted —she felt unclean. It isn't mine at all, she thought, it belongs to everybody and it isn't anything.

It was the second inning but she wasn't even watching any longer, she wasn't even trying to identify the players . . . she could not even look at them, she studied the ads on her score card. Her stomach was swimming in her, she felt she would drown if she had to stay the whole game, her head was bursting. Just to get out of here, to run away from here she didn't care where. . . . "Tom," she said, but he didn't hear her, he was shouting something down at the players.

She stood up and someone behind her pushed her shoulder and said, "Sit down!" but she kept on going, stumbling over people, rushing to the aisle.

When she got to the exit Tom was beside her. "You going?" he asked. She didn't answer, she walked on. "You can't leave now—"

She saw the sign LADIES REST ROOM, and she rushed toward it, not even looking around at him. Nobody inside at all, that was good. She slumped down in an armchair, it was over. The crowd was screaming out there but she didn't care—she didn't care whether the Reds won or lost.

And suddenly she saw herself as she had been—in that sloppy house dress, sitting by the radio for two years. It was a dream, she thought, it wasn't real. I made it all up myself. There is no such person as Paul Derringer, Bucky Walters and Lonnie Frey and Bill Werber—they are all just people I made up. No one has ever seen them but me.

I have just told lies, that's all, she thought. I lied to myself every day of the week. It's all really a silly game, with nothing important happening in it, but I made it the most important thing in the world. I acted as if they were playing just for me, and here they were playing for everybody. They would not know me if they saw me, and I did not know them. Really it was just a silly dream.

Thinking this she began to feel better. She'd been sick, that was it. And after you'd been sick for two years you wanted to wash yourself clean and never be sick again.

These silly gloves, she said to herself, working off the left-hand one, these silly gloves that I've been wearing all my life. She had to use her mouth to pull off the other. Then she pushed up her sleeves and began. She washed her crippled hand last and most thoroughly.

Finished, she dried with a paper towel. So it was all over. It wasn't real and I don't want it. Now I will just have to change, that's all. I will have to be someone different.

She picked up her handbag and started to reach for the gloves, then turned quickly and hurried to the door.

NAKED TO
THE INVISIBLE EYE

George Alec Effinger

HERE WERE FEWER than a thousand spectators in the little
ballpark, their chatter nearly inaudible compared to the
heartening roar of the major league crowds. The fans sat
uneasily, as if they had wandered into the wake of a legendary
hero. No longer was baseball the national pastime. Even the big
league teams, roving from franchise to franchise in search of yesterday's loyal bleacher fanatics, resorted to promotional gimmicks
to stave off bankruptcy. Here the Bears were in third place, with
an unlikely shot at second. The Tigers had clinched the pennant
early, now leading the second-place Kings by nine games and the
Bears by an even more discouraging number. There was no real
tension in this game—oh, with a bad slump the Bears might fall
down among the cellar teams, but so what? For all intents and
purposes, the season had ended a month ago.

There was no real tension, no pennant race any longer, just an
inexpensive evening out for the South Carolina fans. The sweat on
the batter's hands was the fault of his own nervous reaction; the
knots in his stomach were shared by no one. He went to the on-
deck circle for the pine-tar rag while he waited for the new pitcher
to toss his warm-ups.

The Bear shortstop was batting eighth, reflecting his lame .219
average. Like a great smoothed rock this fact sat in the torrent of
his thinking, submerged at times but often breaking through the
racing surface. With his unsteady fielding it looked as if he would

be out of a job the next spring. To the players and to the spectators the game was insignificant; to him it was the first of his last few chances. With two runs in already in the eighth, one out and a man on first, he went to the plate.

He looked out toward the kid on the mound before settling himself in the batter's box. The pitcher's name was Rudy Ramirez, he was only nineteen and from somewhere in Venezuela. That was all anyone knew about him; this was his first appearance in a professional ball game. The Bear shortstop took a deep breath and stepped in.

This kid Ramirez looked pretty fast during his warm-ups, he thought. The shortstop damned the fate that made him the focus of attention against a complete unknown. The waters surged; his thoughts shuffled and died.

The Venezuelan kid looked in for his sign. The shortstop looked down to the third base coach, who flashed the *take* signal; that was all right with him. *I'm only batting two-nineteen, I want to see this kid throw one before . . .*

Ramirez went into his stretch, glanced at the runner on first . . .

With that kid Barger coming off the disabled list I might not be able to . . .

Ramirez' right leg kicked, his left arm flung back . . .

The shortstop's shrieking flood of thought stilled, his mind was as quiet as the surface of a pond stagnating. The umpire called the pitch a ball.

Along the coaching lines at third Sorenson was relaying the *hit-and-run* sign from the dugout. *All right,* thought the shortstop, *just make contact, get a good ground ball, maybe a hit, move the man into scoring position . . .*

Ramirez nodded to his catcher, stretched, checked the runner . . .

My luck, I'll hit an easy double-play ball to the right side . . .

. . . kicked, snapped, pitched . . .

The shortstop's mind was silent, ice-cold, dead, watching the runner vainly flying toward second, the catcher's throw beating him there by fifteen feet. Two out. One ball and one strike.

Sorenson called time. He met the shortstop halfway down the line.

"You damn brainless idiot!" said the coach. "You saw the sign, you *acknowledged* the sign, you stood there with your thumb in your ear looking at a perfect strike! You got an awful short memory?"

"Look, I don't know—"

"I'll tell you what I *do* know," said Sorenson. "I'll bet that'll cost you twenty dollars. Maybe your spot in the lineup."

The shortstop walked to the on-deck circle, wiped his bat again with the pine tar. His head was filled with anger and frustration. Back in the batter's box he stared toward the pitcher in desperation.

. On the rubber Ramirez worked out of a full windup with the bases empty. His high kick hid his delivery until the last moment. The ball floated toward the plate, a fat balloon belt-high, a curve that didn't break . . .

The hitter's mind was like a desert, his mind was like an empty glass, a blank sheet of paper, his mind was totally at rest . . .

The ball nicked the outside corner for a called strike two. The Tiger catcher chuckled. "Them people in the seats have to pay to get in," he said. "They're doin' more'n you!"

"Shut up." The Bear shortstop choked up another couple of inches on the handle. *He'll feed me another curve, and then the fast ball . . .*

Ramirez took the sign and went into his motion.

Lousy kid. I'm gonna rap it one down his lousy Cuban throat . . .

The wrist flicked, the ball spun, broke . . .

The shortstop watched, unawed, very still, like a hollow thing, as the curve broke sharply, down the heart of the plate, strike three, side retired.

The Tigers managed to score an insurance run in the top half of the ninth, and Rudy Ramirez went back to the mound with a 5–3 lead to protect. The first batter that he was scheduled to face was the Bear pitcher, who was replaced in the order by pinch hitter Frank Asterino.

A sense of determination, confidence made Asterino's mind orderly. It was a brightly lit mind, with none of the shifting doubts of the other. Rudy felt the will, he weighed the desire, he discovered the man's dedication and respected it. He stood off the rubber, rubbing the shine from the new ball. He reached for the rosin bag, then dropped it. He peered in at Johnston, his catcher. The sign: the fast ball.

Asterino guarded the plate closely. Johnston's mitt was targeted on the inside—start off with the high hard one, loosen the batter up. Rudy rocked back, kicked the leg high, and threw. The ball did not go for the catcher's mark, sailing out just a little. A not overpowering pitch right down the pipe—a perfect gopher ball.

Rudy thought as the ball left his hand. He found Asterino's will, and he held it gently back. *Be still. Do not move; yes, be still,* and Asterino watched the strike intently as it passed.

Asterino watched two more, both curves that hung tantalizing but untouched. Ramirez grasped the batter's desire with his own, and blotted up all the fierce resolution there was in him. Asterino returned to the bench, disappointed but unbewildered, amid the boos of the fans. He had struck out but, after all, that was not so unusual.

The top of the batting order was up, and Rudy touched the minds of the first and second hitters. He hid their judgment behind the glare of his own will, and they struck out; the first batter needed five pitches and the second four. They observed balls with as much passive interest as strikes, and their bats never left their shoulders. No runs, no hits, no errors, nothing across for the Bears in the ninth. The ball game was over; Rudy earned a save for striking out the four batters he faced in his first pro assignment.

Afterward, local reporters were met by the angry manager of the Bears. When asked for his impression of the young Tiger relief pitcher, he said, "I didn't think he looked that sharp. I mean, Queen Elizabeth would look good pitching to the bunch of zombies I've got on this team. How you supposed to win?" In the visitors' clubhouse the Tiger manager was in a more expansive mood.

"Where did Ramirez come from?" asked one reporter.

"I don't really know," he said. "Charlie Cardona checks out Detroit's prospects down there. All I know is the telegram said that he was signed, and then here he is. Charlie's dug up some good kids for us."

"Did he impress you tonight?"

Marenholtz settled his wire-rim glasses on his long nose and nodded. "He looked real cool for his first game. I'm going to start him in the series with the Reds this weekend. We'll have a better idea then, of course, but I have a feeling he won't be playing Class B baseball very long."

After the game with the Bears, the Tigers showered quickly and boarded their bus. They had a game the next night against the Selene Comets. It was a home game for the Tigers, and they were all glad to be returning to Cordele, but the bus ride from the Bears' stadium would be four or five hours. They would get in just before dawn, sleep until noon, have time for a couple of unpleasant hamburgers, and get out to the park in time for practice.

The Tigers won that game, and the game the next night also. The

Comets left town and were replaced by the Rockhill Reds, in for a Saturday afternoon game and a Sunday doubleheader. This late in the summer the pitching staffs were nearly exhausted. Manager Marenholtz of the Tigers kept his promise to the newspapermen; after the Saturday loss to the Reds he went to Chico Guerra, his first-string catcher, and told him to get Rudy Ramirez ready for the second game the next day.

Ramirez was eager, of course, and confident. Marenholtz was sitting in his office when Rudy came into the locker room before the Sunday doubleheader, a full half hour before practice began. Marenholtz smiled, remembering his own first game. He had been an outfielder; in the seventh inning he had run into the left field wall chasing a long fly. He dropped the ball, cracked his head, and spent the next three weeks listening to the games on the radio. Marenholtz wished Ramirez better luck.

The Tigers' second-string catcher, Maurie Johnston, played the first game, and Guerra sat next to Ramirez in the dugout, pointing out the strengths and weaknesses of the opposing batters. Ramirez said little, just nodding and smiling. Marenholtz walked by them near the end of the first game. "Chico," he said, "ask him if he's nervous."

The catcher translated the question into Spanish. Ramirez grinned and answered. "He say no," said Guerra. "He jus' wan' show you what he can do."

The manager grunted a reply and went back to his seat, thinking about cocky rookies. The Tigers lost the first game, making two in a row dropped to the last-place Reds. The fans didn't seem to mind; there were only twenty games left until the end of the season, and there was no way possible for the Tigers to fall from first place short of losing all of them. It was obvious that Marenholtz was trying out new kids, resting his regulars for the Hanson Cup playoffs. The fans would let him get away with a lot, as long as he won the cup.

Between games there was a high school band marching in the outfield, and the local Kiwanis club presented a plaque to the Tigers' center fielder, who was leading the league with forty-two home runs. Ramirez loosened up his arm during all this; he stood along the right field foul line and tossed some easy pitches to Guerra. After a while the managers brought out their lineup cards to the umpires and the grounds crew finished grooming the infield. Ramirez and Guerra took their positions on the field, and the rest of the team joined them, to the cheers of the Tigers' fans.

Skip Stackpole, the Reds' shortstop and leadoff batter, was settling himself in the batter's box. Rudy bent over and stared toward Guerra for the sign. An inside curve. Rudy nodded.

As he started into his windup he explored Stackpole's mind. It was a relaxed mind, concentrating only because Stackpole enjoyed playing baseball; for him, and for the last-place Reds, the game was without urgency. Rudy would have little difficulty.

Wait, thought Rudy, forcing his will directly into Stackpole's intellect. *Not this one. Wait.* And Stackpole waited. The ball broke sharply, over the heart of the plate, for the first strike. There was a ripple of applause from the Tiger fans.

Guerra wanted a fast ball. Rudy nodded, kicked high, and threw. *Quiet,* he thought, *do not move.* Right down the pipe, strike two.

This much ahead of the hitter, Guerra should have called for a couple of pitches on the outside, to tease the batter into swinging at a bad pitch. But the catcher thought that Stackpole was off balance. The Reds had never seen Ramirez pitch before. Guerra called for another fast ball. Rudy nodded and went into his windup. He kept Stackpole from swinging. The Reds' first hitter was called out on strikes; the Tiger fans cheered loudly as Guerra stood and threw the ball down to third base. Ramirez could hear his infielders chattering and encouraging him in a language that he didn't understand. He got the ball back and looked at the Reds' second man.

The new batter would be more of a challenge. He was hitting .312, battling with two others for the last place in the league's top ten. He was more determined than anyone Ramirez had yet faced. When Rudy pitched the ball, he needed more mental effort to keep the man from swinging at it. The pitch was too high. Ramirez leaned forward; Guerra wanted a low curve. The pitch broke just above the hitter's knees, over the outside corner of the plate. One ball, one strike. The next pitch was a fast ball, high and inside. Ball two. Another fast ball, over the plate. *Wait,* thought Rudy, *wait.* The batter waited, and the count was two and two. Rudy tried another curve, and forced the batter to watch it helplessly. Strike three, two out.

Ramirez felt good now. The stadium full of noisy people didn't make him nervous. The experienced athletes on the other team posed no threat at all. Rudy knew that he could win today; he knew that there wasn't a batter in the world that could beat him. The third hitter was no problem for Rudy's unusual talent. He struck out on four pitches. Rudy received a loud cheer from the fans as he walked back to the dugout. He smiled and waved, and took a seat next to the water cooler with Guerra.

The Tigers scored no runs in their part of the first inning, and

Rudy went back to the mound and threw his allotment of warm-ups. He stood rubbing up the ball while the Reds' cleanup hitter settled himself at the plate. Rudy disposed of the Reds' best power hitter with three pitches, insolently tossing three fast balls straight down the heart of the plate. Rudy got the other two outs just as quickly. The fans gave him another cheer as he walked from the mound.

The Tigers got a hit but no runs in the second, and Ramirez struck out the side again in the top of the third. In the bottom of the third Doug Davies, the Tiger second baseman, led off with a sharp single down the left field line. Rudy was scheduled to bat next; he took off his jacket and chose a light bat. He had never faced an opposing pitcher under game conditions before. He had never even taken batting practice in the time he had been with the Tigers. He walked to the plate and took his place awkwardly.

He swung at two and watched two before he connected. He hit the ball weakly, on the handle of the bat, and it dribbled slowly down the first base line. He passed it on his way to first base, and he saw the Reds' pitcher running over to field it. Rudy knew that he'd be an easy out. *Wait,* he thought at the pitcher, *stop. Don't throw it.* The pitcher held the ball, staring ahead dazedly. It looked to the fans as if the pitcher couldn't decide whether to throw to first or try for the lead runner going into second. Both runners were safe before Rudy released him.

Rudy took a short lead toward second base. He watched the coaches for signs. On the next pitch Davies broke for third. Rudy ran for second base. The Reds' catcher got the pitch and jumped up. *Quiet,* thought Rudy. *Be still.* The catcher watched both Davies and Rudy slide in safely.

Eventually the Tigers' leadoff man struck out. The next batter popped up in the infield. The third batter in the lineup, Chico Guerra, hit a long fly to right field, an easy enough chance for the fielder. But Rudy found the man's judgment and blocked it with his will. *Not yet,* he thought, *wait.* The outfielder hesitated, seeming as if he had lost the ball in the setting sun. By the time he ran after it, it was too late. The ball fell in and rolled to the wall. Two runs scored and Guerra huffed into third base. "Now we win!" yelled Rudy in Spanish. Guerra grinned and yelled back.

The inning ended with the Tigers ahead, three to nothing. Rudy was joking with Guerra as he walked back on the field. His manner was easy and supremely confident. He directed loud comments to the umpire and the opposing batters, but his Spanish went uninterpreted by his catcher. The top of the Reds' batting order was up again in the fourth inning, and Rudy treated them with total disregard, shaking off all of Guerra's signs except for the fast ball, straight down the middle. Stackpole, the leadoff batter, struck out again on four pitches. The second batter needed only three, and the third hitter used four. No one yet had swung at a pitch. Perhaps the fans were beginning to notice, because the cheering was more subdued as the Tigers came back to the bench. The Reds' manager was standing up in the dugout, angrily condemning his players, who went out to their positions with perplexed expressions.

The game proceeded, with the fans growing quieter and quieter in the stands, the Reds' manager getting louder in his damnations, the Tiger players becoming increasingly uneasy about the Reds' lack of interest. Rudy didn't care; he kept pitching them in to Guerra, and the Rockhill batters kept walking back to their dugout, shrugging their shoulders and saying nothing. Not a single Rockhill Red had reached first base. The ninth inning began in total silence. Rudy faced three pinch hitters and, of course, struck them out in order. He had not only pitched a no-hit game, not only pitched a *perfect* game, but he had struck out twenty-seven consecutive batters. Not once during the entire game did a Rockhill player even swing at one of his pitches.

A perfect game is one of the rarest of baseball phenomena. Perhaps only the unassisted triple play occurs less frequently. There should have been a massive crowd pouring out to congratulate Rudy. Players and fans should have mobbed him, carried him off the field, into the clubhouse. Beer should have been spilled over his head. Pictures should have been taken with Fred Marenholtz' arm around Rudy's neck. Instead, the infielders ran off the field as quickly as they could. They patted Rudy's back as they passed him on the way to the dugout. The fans got up and went home, not even applauding the Tiger victory. Marenholtz was waiting in the dugout. "Take a shower and see me in my office," he said, indicating both Guerra and Ramirez. Then the manager shook his head and went down the tunnel to the dressing room.

Marenholtz was a tall, thin man with sharp, birdlike features. He was sitting at his desk, smoking a cigar. He smoked cigars only when he was very angry, very worried, or very happy. Tonight, while he waited for Guerra and the new kid, he was very worried. Baseball, aged and crippled, didn't need this kind of notoriety.

There were half a dozen local newsmen trying to force their way into the dressing room. He had given orders that there would be no interviews until he had a chance to talk to Ramirez himself. He had phone calls from sportswriters, scouts, fans, gamblers, politicians, and relatives. There was a stack of congratulatory telegrams. There was a very worried telegram from the team's general manager, and a very worried telegram from the front office of the Tigers' major league affiliate.

There was a soft knock on the door. "Guerra?" Marenholtz called out.

"*Si*."

"Come on in, but don't let anybody else in with you except Ramirez."

Guerra opened the door and the two men entered. Behind them was a noisy, confused crowd of Tiger players. Marenholtz sighed; he would have to find out what happened, and then deal with his team. Then he had to come up with an explanation for the public.

Ramirez was grinning, evidently not sharing Marenholtz' and Guerra's apprehension. He said something to Guerra. The catcher frowned and translated for Marenholtz. "He say, don' he do a good job?"

"That's what *I* want to know!" said Marenholtz. "What *did* he do? You know, it looks a little strange that not a single guy on that team took swing number one."

Guerra looked very uncomfortable. "*Si*, maybe he just *good*."

Marenholtz grunted. "Chico, did he look *that* good?"

Guerra shook his head. Ramirez was still smiling. Marenholtz stood up and paced behind his desk. "I don't *mind* him pitching a perfect game," he said. "It's a memorable achievement. But I think his effort would be better appreciated if one of those batters had tried *hitting*. At least *one*. I want you to tell me why they didn't. If you can't, I want you to ask *him*."

Guerra shrugged and turned to Ramirez. They conversed for a few seconds, and then the catcher spoke to Marenholtz. "He say he don' wan' them to."

Marenholtz slammed his fist on his desk. "That's going to make a great headline in *The Sporting News*. Look, if somehow he paid off the Reds to throw the game, even *they* wouldn't be so stupid as to do it that way." He paused, catching his breath, trying to control his exasperation. "All right, I'll give him a chance. Maybe he *is* the greatest pitcher the world has ever known. Though I doubt it." He reached for his phone and dialed a number. "Hello, Thompson? Look, I need a favor from you. Have you turned off the field lights yet? Okay, leave 'em on for a while, all right? I don't care. I'll talk to Mr. Kaemmer in the morning. And hang around for another half hour, okay? Well, screw the union. We're having a little crisis here. Yeah, Ramirez. Understand? Thanks, Jack.'' Marenholtz hung up and nodded to Guerra. "You and your battery mate here are going to get some extra practice. Tell him I want to hit some off him, right now. Don't bother getting dressed again. Just put on your mask and get out on the field." Guerra nodded unhappily and led Rudy away.

The stadium was deserted. Marenholtz walked through the dugout and onto the field. He felt strangely alone, cold and worried; the lights made odd, vague shadows that had never bothered him before. He went to the batter's box. The white lines had been all but erased during the course of the game. He leaned on the bat that he had brought with him and waited for the two men.

Guerra came out first, wearing his chest protector and carrying his mask and mitt. Behind him walked Ramirez silently, without his usual grin. He was dressed in street clothes, with his baseball spikes instead of dress shoes. Rudy took his place on the mound. He tossed a ball from his hand to his glove. Guerra positioned himself and Marenholtz waved to Rudy. No one had said a word.

Rudy wound up and pitched, a medium fast ball down the middle. Marenholtz swung and hit a low line drive down the right field line that bounced once and went into the stands. Rudy threw another and Marenholtz hit it far into right center field. The next three pitches he sent to distant, shadowed parts of the ball park. Marenholtz stepped back for a moment. "He was throwing harder during the game, wasn't he?" he asked.

"I think so," said Guerra.

"Tell him to pitch me as hard as he did then. And throw some good curves, too." Guerra translated, and Ramirez nodded. He leaned back and pitched. Marenholtz swung, connected, and watched the ball sail in a huge arc, to land in the seats three hundred and fifty feet away in right field.

Rudy turned to watch the ball. He said nothing. Marenholtz tossed him another from a box on the ground. "I want a curve now," he said.

The pitch came, breaking lazily on the outside part of the plate. Marenholtz timed it well and sent it on a clothesline into center field, not two feet over Ramirez' head. "All right," said the manager, "tell him to come here." Guerra waved, and Rudy trotted to join them. "One thing," said Marenholtz sourly. "I want him to explain why the Reds didn't hit him like that."

"I wanna know, too," said Guerra. He spoke with Ramirez, at last turning back to Marenholtz with a bewildered expression. "He say he don' wan' *them* to hit. He say you wan' hit, he *let* you hit."

"Oh, hell," said Marenholtz."I'm not stupid."

Rudy looked confused. He said something to Guerra. "He say he don' know why you wan' hit *now*, but he do what you say."

The manager turned away in anger. He spat toward the dugout, thinking. He turned back to Guerra. "We got a couple of balls left," he said. "I want him to pitch me just like he did to the Reds, understand? I don't want him to *let* me hit. Have him try to weave his magic spell on me, too."

Rudy took a ball and went back to the mound. Marenholtz stood up to the plate, waving the bat over his shoulder in a slow circle. Ramirez wound up, kicked, and threw. His fastest pitch, cutting the heart of the plate.

Quiet, thought Rudy, working to restrain his manager's furious mind. *Easy now. Don't swing. Quiet.*

Marenholtz' mind was suddenly peaceful, composed, thought-less. The pitch cracked into Guerra's mitt. The manager hadn't swung at it.

Rudy threw ten more pitches, and Marenholtz didn't offer at any of them. Finally he raised his hand. Rudy left the mound again. Marenholtz stood waiting, shaking his head. "Why didn't I swing? Those pitches weren't any harder than the others." Guerra asked Rudy.

"He jus' say he don't wan' you to swing. In his head he tell you. Then you don' swing. He say it's easy."

"I don't believe it," said the manager nervously. "Yeah, okay, he can do it. He *did* do it. I don't like it." Guerra shook his head. The three stood on the empty field for several seconds in uneasy silence. "Can he do that with anybody?" asked Marenholtz.

"He say, *si.*"

"Can he do it any time? *Every* time?"

"He say, *si.*"

"We're in trouble, Chico." Guerra looked into Marenholtz' frightened face and nodded slowly. "I don't mean just us. I mean *baseball*. This kid can throw a perfect game, every time. What do you think'll happen if he makes it to the majors? The game'll be dead. Poor kid. He scares me. Those people in the stands aren't going to like it any better."

"What you gonna do, Mr. Marenhol'?" asked Guerra.

"I don't know, Chico. It's going to be hard keeping a bunch of perfect games secret. Especially when none of the hitters ever takes the bat off his shoulder."

The following Thursday the Tigers had a night game at home against the Kings. Rudy came prepared to be the starting pitcher, after three days' rest. But when Marenholtz announced the starting lineup, he had the Tigers' long relief man on the mound. Rudy was disappointed, and complained to Guerra. The catcher told him that Marenholtz was probably saving him for the next night, when the Kings' ace left-hander was scheduled to pitch.

On Friday Ramirez was passed over again. He sat in the dugout, sweating in his warm-up jacket, irritated at the manager. Guerra told him to have patience. Rudy couldn't understand why Marenholtz wouldn't pitch him, after the great game Ramirez had thrown in his first start. Guerra just shrugged and told Rudy to study the hitters.

Rudy didn't play Saturday, or in either of the Sunday double-header's games. He didn't know that the newspapermen were as mystified as he. Marenholtz made up excuses, saying that Rudy had pulled a back muscle in practice. The manager refused to make any comments about Ramirez' strange perfect game, and as the days passed the clamor died down.

The next week Rudy spent on the bench, becoming angrier and more frustrated. He confronted Marenholtz several times, with Guerra as unwilling interpreter, and each time the manager just said that he didn't feel that Ramirez was "ready." The season was coming to its close, with only six games left, and Rudy was determined to play. As the games came and went, however, it became obvious that he wasn't going to get the chance.

On the day of the last game, Marenholtz announced that Irv Tappan, his number two right-hander, would start. Rudy stormed into the clubhouse in a rage. He went to his locker and started to change clothes. Marenholtz signaled to Guerra, and they followed Ramirez.

"All right, Ramirez, what're you doing?" asked the manager.

"He say he goin' home," said Guerra, translating Rudy's shouted reply.

"If he leaves before the game is over, he's liable to be fined. Does he know that?"

"He say he don' care."

"Tell him he's acting like a kid," said Marenholtz, feeling relieved inside.

"He say go to hell."

Marenholtz took a deep breath. "Okay, Chico. Tell him we've enjoyed knowing him, and respect his talent, and would like to invite him to try out for the team again next spring."

"He say go to hell."

"He's going home?" asked Marenholtz.

"He say you 'mericanos jealous, and waste his time. He say he can do other things."

"Well, tell him we're sorry, and wish him luck."

"He say go to hell. He say you don' know your *ano* from a hole in the groun'."

Marenholtz smiled coldly. "Chico, I want you to do me a favor. Do yourself a favor, too; there's enough here for the two of us. You let him finish clearing out of here, and you go with him. I don't know where he's going this time of day. Probably back to the hotel where he stays. Keep with him. Talk to him. Don't let him get away, don't let him get drunk, don't let him talk to anybody else, okay?"

Guerra looked puzzled, but nodded. Ramirez was turning to leave the clubhouse. Marenholtz grabbed Guerra's arm and pushed him toward the furious boy. "Go on," said the manager, "keep him in sight. I'll call the hotel in about three or four hours. We got a good thing here, Chico, my boy." The catcher frowned and hurried after Rudy. Marenholtz sighed; he walked across the dressing room, stopping by his office. He opened the door and stared into the darkened room for a few seconds. He wanted desperately to sit at his desk and write the letters and make the phone calls, but he still had a game to play. The job seemed so empty to him now. He *knew* this would be the last regular game he'd see in the minor leagues. Next spring he and Ramirez would be shocking them all at the Florida training camps. Next summer he and Ramirez would own the world of major league baseball.

First, though, there was still the game with the Bears. Marenholtz closed the door to the office and locked it. Then he went up the tunnel to the field. All that he could think of was going back to the Big Time.

After the game, Fred Marenholtz hurried to his office. The other players grabbed at him, swatting at his back to congratulate him on the end of the season. The Tigers were celebrating in the clubhouse. Cans of beer were popping open, and sandwiches had been supplied by the front office. The manager ignored them all. He locked the door to the office behind him. He called Ramirez' hotel and asked for his room.

Guerra answered, and reported that Ramirez was there, taking a nap. The catcher was intstructed to tell Rudy that together they were all going to win their way to the major leagues. Guerra was doubtful, but Marenholtz wouldn't listen to the catcher's puzzled questions. The manager hung up. He pulled out a battered address book from his desk drawer, and found the telephone number of an old friend, a contract lawyer in St. Louis. He called the number, tapping a pencil nervously on the desk top while the phone rang.

"Hello, Marty?" he said when the call was finally answered.

"Yes. Who's this calling, please?"

"Hi. You won't remember me, but this is Fred Marenholtz."

"Freddie! How are you? Lord, it's been fifteen years. Are you in town?"

Marenholtz smiled. Things were going to be all right. They chatted for a few minutes, and then Marenholtz told his old friend that he was calling on business.

"Sure, Freddie," said the lawyer. "For Frantic Fred Marenholtz, anything. Is it legal?" Marenholtz laughed.

The photographs on the office wall looked painfully old to Marenholtz. They were of an era too long dead, filled with people who themselves had long since passed away. Baseball itself had withered, had lost the lifeblood of interest that had infused the millions of fans each spring. It had been too many years since Fred Marenholtz had claimed his share of glory. He had never been treated to his part of the financial rewards of baseball, and after his brief major league career he felt it was time to make his bid.

Marenholtz instructed the lawyer in detail. Old contracts were to be broken, new ones drawn up. The lawyer wrote himself in for five percent as payment. The manager hung up the phone again. He slammed his desk drawer closed in sheer exuberance. Then he got up and left his office. He had to thank his players for their cooperation during the past season.

"Tell him he's not going to get anything but investigated if he doesn't put in with us." It was late now, past midnight. Ramirez' tiny hotel room was stifling. Rudy rested on the bed. Guerra sat in a chair by the single window. Marenholtz paced around, his coat thrown on the bed, his shirt soaked with perspiration.

"He say he don' like the way you run the club. He don' think you run him better," said Guerra wearily.

"All right. Explain to him that we're not going to cost him anything. The only way *we* can make any money is by making sure *he* does okay. We'll take a percentage of what he makes. That's his insurance."

"He wan' know why you wan' him now, you wouldn't play him before."

"Because he's a damn fool, is why! Doesn't he know what would happen if he pitched his kind of game, week after week?"

"He think he make a lot of money."

Marenholtz stopped pacing and stared. "Stupid Spanish bastard!" he said. Guerra, from a farming village in Panama, glared resentfully. "I'm sorry, Chico. Explain it to him." The catcher went to the edge of the bed and sat down. He talked with Rudy for a long while, then turned back to the manager.

"Okay, Mr. Marenhol'. He didn't think anybody noticed that."

"Fine," said Marenholtz, taking Guerra's vacated chair. "Now let's talk. Chico, what were you planning to do this winter?"

Guerra looked puzzled again. "I don't know. Go home."

Marenholtz smiled briefly and shook his head. "No. You're coming with me. We're taking young Mr. Ramirez here and turn him into a pitcher. If not that, at least into an educated thrower. We got a job, my friend."

They had six months, and they could have used more. They worked hard, giving Rudy little time to relax. He spent weeks just throwing baseballs through a circle of wire on a stand. Guerra and Marenholtz helped him learn the most efficient way to pitch, so that he wouldn't tire after half a game; he studied tapes of his motions, to see where they might be improved, to fool the hitters and conserve his own energy. Guerra coached him on all the fundamentals: fielding his position, developing a deceptive throw to first base, making certain that his windup was the same for every different pitch.

After a couple of months Ramirez' control was sharp enough to put a ball into Guerra's mitt wherever the catcher might ask. Marenholtz watched with growing excitement—they were going to bring it off. Rudy was as good as any mediocre pitcher in the majors. Marenholtz was teaching him to save his special talent for the tight situations, the emergencies where less attention would be focused on the pitcher. Rudy was made to realize that he had eight skilled teammates behind him; if he threw the ball where the catcher wanted it, the danger of long hits was minimized. A succession of pop-ups and weak grounders would look infinitely better than twenty-seven passive strikeouts.

Before the spring training session began, Rudy had developed a much better curve that he could throw with reasonable control, a passable change-up, a poor slider, and a slightly off-speed fast ball. He relied on Guerra and Marenholtz for instructions, and they schooled him in all the possible situations until he was sick of the whole scheme.

"Freddie Marenholtz! Damn, you look like you could still get out there and play nine hard ones yourself. Got that phenom of yours?"

"Yeah, you want him to get dressed?" Marenholtz stood by a

batting cage in the training camp of the Nashville Cats, a team
welcomed into the American League during the expansion draft
three years previously. The Florida sun was already fierce enough
in March to make Marenholtz uncomfortable, and he shielded his
eyes with one hand as he talked to Jim Billy Westfahl, the Cats'
manager.

"All right," said Westfahl. "You said you brought this kid Ramirez and a catcher, right? What's his name?"

"Guerra. Only guy Ramirez ever pitched to."

"Yeah, well, you know we got two good catchers in Portobenez
and Staefler. If Guerra's going to stick, he's going to have to beat
them out."

Marenholtz frowned. Guerra was *not* going to beat them out of
their jobs. But he had to keep the man around, both because he
could soothe Ramirez' irrational temper and because Guerra presented a danger to the plan. But the aging catcher might have to
get used to watching the games from the boxes. He collected three
and a half percent of Rudy's income, and Marenholtz couldn't see
that Guerra had reason to complain.

Rudy came out of the locker room and walked to the batting
cage. Guerra followed, looking uneasy among the major league
talents on the field. Ramirez turned to Westfahl and said something
in Spanish. Guerra translated. "He say he wan' show you what he
can do."

"Okay. I'm game. *Somebody's* going to have to replace Mc-
Anion. It may as well be your kid. Let's see what he looks like."

Rudy pitched to Guerra, and Westfahl made a few noncommittal
remarks. Later in the day Rudy faced some of the Cats' regulars,
and the B squad of rookies. He held some of them back, pitched
to some of them, and looked no less sharp than any of the other
regular pitchers after a winter's inactivity. In the next two weeks
Marenholtz and Guerra guided Rudy carefully, letting him use his
invisible talent sparingly, without attracting undue notice, and Ramirez seemed sure to go north with the team when the season
began. Guerra didn't have the same luck. A week before spring
training came to an end he was optioned to the Cats' AA farm
club. Guerra pretended to be upset, and refused to report.

By this time Marenholtz had promoted a large amount of money.
The newly appointed president of *RR Star Enterprises* had spent
the spring signing contracts while his protégé worked to impress
the public. Permission and royalty fees were deposited from trading card companies, clothing manufacturers, fruit juice advertisements, sporting goods dealers, and grooming product

endorsements—Rudy was hired to look into a camera and say, "I like it. It makes my hair neat without looking greasy." He was finally coached to say, "I like it," and the rest of the line was given to a sexy female model.

The regular season began at home for the Cats. Rudy Ramirez was scheduled to pitch the third game. Rudy felt little excitement before his game; what he did was in no way different in kind or quantity from his nervousness before his first appearance with the Cordele Tigers. The slightly hostile major league crowd didn't awe him: he was prepared to awe the four thousand spectators who had come to watch the unknown rookie.

Fred Marenholtz had briefed Rudy thoroughly; before the game they had decided that an impressive but nonetheless credible effort would be a four- or five-hit shutout. For an added touch of realism, Rudy might get tired in the eighth inning, and leave for a relief pitcher. Marenholtz and Guerra sat in field boxes along the first base side, near the dugout. Ramirez could hear their shouts from the mound. He waved to them as he took his place before the "National Anthem" was sung.

Rudy's pitches were not particularly overpowering. His fast ball was eminently hitable; only the experience of the Cats' catcher prevented pitches from sailing time after time over the short left field fence. Ramirez' weeks of practice saved him: his pitches crossed the plate just above the batters' knees, or handcuffed them close around the fists, or nicked the outside edge of the plate. Rudy's curve was just good enough to keep the hitters guessing. The first batter hit a sharp ground ball to short, fielded easily for the first out. The second batter lofted a fly to right field for the second out. Rudy threw three pitches to the third batter, and then threw his first mistake, a fast ball belt high, down the middle. Rudy knew what would happen—a healthy swing, and then a quick one-run lead for the White Sox. Urgently, desperately he sought the batter's will and grasped it in time. The man stood stupidly, staring at the most perfect pitch he would see in a long while. It went by for a called strike three, and Rudy had his first official major league strikeout.

Marenholtz stood and applauded when Rudy trotted back to the dugout. Guerra shouted something in Spanish. Ramirez' team-mates slapped his back, and he smiled and nodded and took his place on the bench. He allowed a double down the line in the second inning, set the White Sox down in order in the third and fourth, gave up a single and a walk in the fifth, a single in the sixth, no hits in the seventh and eighth, and two singles to the first two batters in the ninth. Rudy had pitched wisely, combining his infe-rior skill with judicious use of his mental talent. Sometimes he held back a batter for just a fraction of a second, so that the hitter would swing late. Other times he would prevent a batter from running for an instant, to insure his being thrown out at first. He caused the opposition's defense to commit errors so that the Cats could score the runs to guarantee victory.

The manager of the Cats came out to the mound to talk with Ramirez in the ninth. Carmen Velillo, the Cats' third baseman, joined the conference to translate for Rudy. Ramirez insisted that he was strong enough to finish, but the manager brought in a relief pitcher. Rudy received a loud cheer from the fans as he went off the field. He didn't watch the rest of the game, but went straight to the showers. The Cats' new man put down the rally, and Rami-rez had a shutout victory. After Rudy and Velillo had answered the endless questions of the newsmen, Marenholtz and Guerra met him for a celebration.

Marenholtz held interviews with reporters from national maga-zines or local weeklies. Coverage of Ramirez' remarkable suc-cesses grew more detailed; as the season progressed Rudy saw his picture on the front of such varied periodicals as *Sports Illustrated* and *People Magazine*. By June Rudy had won eleven games and lost none. His picture appeared on the cover of *Time* after he won his fifteenth in a row. An article in the New York *Post* announced that he was the greatest natural talent since Grover Cleveland Alexander. He appeared briefly on late-night television programs. He was hired to attend shopping center openings in the Nashville area. He loved winning ball games, and Marenholtz, too, gloried in returning a success to the major leagues that had treated him so shabbily in his youth.

The evening before Ramirez was to start his sixteenth ball game, he was having dinner with Marenholtz and Guerra. The older man was talking about his own short playing career, and how baseball had deteriorated since then. Guerra nodded and said little. Ramirez stared quietly at his plate, toying with his food and not eating. Suddenly he spoke up, interrupting Marenholtz' flow of memories. He spoke in rapid Spanish; Marenholtz gaped in surprise. "What's he saying?" he asked.

Guerra coughed nervously. "He wan' know why he need us," he said. "He say he do pretty good by himself."

Marenholtz put his cigar down and stared angrily at Ramirez. "I was wondering how long it would take him to think he could cut us out. You can tell him that if it hadn't been for us he'd either be

in trouble or in Venezuela. You can tell him that if it hadn't been
for us he wouldn't have that solid bank account and his poor gray
mama wouldn't have the only color television in her banana won-
derland. And if that doesn't work, tell him maybe he *doesn't* need
us, but he signed the contracts."

Guerra said a few words, and Rudy answered. "What's he say
now?" asked Marenholtz.

"Nothing," said Guerra, staring down at his own plate. "He
jus' say he thank you, but he wan' do it by himself."

"Oh, hell. Tell him to forget that and pitch a good game tomorrow. I'll do the worrying. That's what I'm for."

"He say he do that. He say he pitch you a good game."

"Well, thank you, Tom, and good afternoon, baseball fans
everywhere. In just a few moments we'll bring you live coverage
of the third contest of this weekend series, a game between the
Nashville Cats, leaders in the American League Midlands Division, and the Denver Athletics. It looks to be a pitchers' duel
today, with young Rudy Ramirez, Nashville's astonishing rookie,
going against the A's veteran right-hander, Morgan Stepitz."

"Right, Chuck, and I think a lot of the spectators in the park
today have come to see if Ramirez can keep his amazing streak
alive. He's won fifteen now and he hasn't been beaten so far in his
entire professional career. Each game must be more of an ordeal
than the last for the youngster. The strain will be starting to take
its toll."

"Nevertheless, Tom, I have to admit that it's been a very long
time since I've seen anyone with the poise of that young man. The
interesting thing is that he hasn't let his success make him overcon-
fident, which is possibly the greatest danger to him now. I'm sure
that defeat, when it comes, will be a hard blow, but I'm just as
certain that Rudy Ramirez will recover and go on to have a truly
remarkable season."

"A lot of fans have written in to ask what the record is for most
consecutive games won. Well, Ramirez has quite a start on that,
but he has a little way to go. The major league record is nineteen,
set in 1912 by Rube Marquard. But even if Ramirez doesn't go on
to break that one, he's still got the makings of a spectacular year.
He's leading both leagues with an earned run average of 1.54, and
it looks like he has an excellent shot at thirty wins—"

"All right, let's go down to the field, where it's time for the
singing of 'The Star-Spangled Banner.' "

After the spectators cheered and settled back into their seats, after the Cats' catcher whipped the ball down to second base, and after the infielders tossed it around and, finally, back to the pitcher, Rudy looked around the stadium. The Nashville park was new, built five years ago in hopes of attracting a major league franchise. It was huge, well-designed, and generally filled with noisy fans. The sudden success of the usually hapless Cats was easily traced: Rudy Ramirez. He was to pitch again today, and his enthusiastic rooters crowded the spacious park. Bedsheet banners hung over railings, wishing him luck and proclaiming Ramirez to be the best-loved individual on the continent. Rudy, still innocent of English, did not know what they said.

He could see Marenholtz and Guerra sitting behind the dugout. They saw him glance in their direction and stood, waving their arms. Rudy touched the visor of his cap in salute. Then he turned to face the first of the Athletics' hitters.

"Okay, the first batter for the A's is the second baseman, number twelve, Jerry Kleiner. Kleiner's batting .262 this season. He's a switch-hitter, and he's batting right-handed against the southpaw, Ramirez.

"Ramirez takes his sign from Staefler, winds, and delivers. Kleiner takes the pitch for a called strike one. Ramirez has faced the A's only once before this season, shutting them out on four hits.

"Kleiner steps out to glance down at the third base coach for the signal. He steps back in. Ramirez goes into his motion. Kleiner lets it go by again. No balls and two strikes."

"Ramirez is really piping them in today, Tom."

"That's right, Chuck. I noticed during his warm-ups that his fast ball seemed to be moving exceptionally well. Today it will tend to tail in toward a right-handed hitter. Here comes the pitch—strike three! Kleiner goes down looking."

"Before the game we talked with Cats' catcher Bo Staefler, who told us that Ramirez' slider is improving as the season gets older. You know that can only be bad news for the hitters in the American League. It may be a while before they can solve his style."

"Stepping in now is the A's right fielder, number twenty-four, Ricky Gonzalvo. Gonzalvo's having trouble with his old knee injury this year, and his average is down to .244. He crowds the plate a little on Ramirez. The first pitch is inside, knocking Gonzalvo down. Ball one.

"Ramirez gets the ball back, leans forward for his sign. And the pitch—in there for a called strike. The count is even at one and one."

"He seems to have excellent control today, wouldn't you say, Tom?"

"Exactly. Manager Jim Westfahl of the Cats suggested last week that the pinpoint accuracy of his control is sometimes enough to intimidate a batter into becoming an easy out."

"There must be *some* explanation, even if it's magic."

"Ramirez deals another breaking pitch, in there for a called strike two. I wouldn't say it's all magic, Chuck. It looked to me as though Gonzalvo was crossed up on that one, probably expecting the fast ball again."

"Staefler gives him the sign. Ramirez nods, and throws. Fast ball, caught Gonzalvo napping. Called strike three. Two away now in the top of the first.

"Batting in the number three position is the big first baseman, Howie Bass. Bass' brother, Eddie, who plays for the Orioles, has the only home run hit off Ramirez this season. Here comes Ramirez' pitch—Bass takes it for strike one."

"It seems to me that the batters are starting out behind Ramirez, a little overcautious. That's the effect that a winning streak like his can have. Ramirez has the benefit of a psychological edge working for him, as well as his great pitching."

"Right, Tom. That pitch while you were talking was a called strike two, a good slider that seemed to have Bass completely baffled."

"Staefler gives the sign, but Ramirez shakes his head. Ramirez shakes off another sign. Now he nods, goes into his windup, and throws. A fast ball, straight down the middle, strike three. Bass turns to argue with the umpire, but that'll do him no good. Three up and three down for the A's, no runs, no hits, nothing across."

The Cats' fans jumped to their feet, but Fred Marenholtz listened angrily to their applause. He caught Rudy's eye just as the pitcher was about to enter the dugout. Before Marenholtz could say anything, Rudy grinned and disappeared inside. Marenholtz was worried that the sophisticated major league audience would be even less likely to accept the spectacle of batter after batter going down without swinging at Ramirez' pitches. The older man turned to Guerra. "What's he trying to do?" he asked.

Guerra shook his head. "I don' know. Maybe he wan' strike out some."

"Maybe," said Marenholtz dubiously, "but I didn't think he'd be that dumb."

The Cats got a runner to second base in their part of the first inning, but he died there when the cleanup hitter sent a line drive

over the head of the A's first baseman, who leaped high to save
the run. Rudy walked out to the mound confidently, and threw his
warm-ups.

"All right," said Marenholtz, "let's see him stop that nonsense
now. This game's being televised all over the country." He
watched Ramirez go into his motion. The first pitch was a curve
that apparently didn't break; a slow pitch coming toward the plate
as fat as a basketball. The A's batter watched it for a called strike.
Marenholtz swore softly.

Rudy threw two more pitches, each of them over the plate for
strikes. The hitter never moved his bat. Marenholtz' face was turning red with controlled fury. Rudy struck out the next batter on
three pitches. Guerra coughed nervously and said something in
Spanish. Already the fans around them were remarking on how
strange it was to see the A's being called out on strikes without
making an effort to guard the plate. The A's sixth batter took his
place in the batter's box, and three pitches later he, too, walked
back to the bench, a bewildered expression on his face.

Marenholtz stood and hollered to Ramirez. "What the hell you
doing?" he said, forgetting that the pitcher couldn't understand
him. Rudy walked nonchalantly to the dugout, taking no notice of
Marenholtz.

Guerra rose and edged past Marenholtz to the aisle. "You going
for a couple of beers?" asked Marenholtz.

"No," said Guerra. "I think I jus' *goin'*."

"Well, Tom, it's the top of the third, score tied at nothing to
nothing. I want to say that we're getting that pitchers' battle we
promised. We're witnessing one heck of a good ballgame so far.
The Cats have had only one hit, and rookie Rudy Ramirez hasn't
let an Athletic reach first base."

"There's an old baseball superstition about jinxing a pitcher in a
situation like this, but I might mention that Ramirez has struck out
the first six men to face him. The record for consecutive
strikeouts is eleven, held by Cannon Shen of the old Cleveland
Indians. If I remember correctly, that mark was set the last
year the Indians played in Cleveland, before their move to New
Orleans."

"This sort of game isn't a new thing for Ramirez, either, Tom.
His bio in the Cats' pressbook mentions that in his one start in the
minor leagues, he threw a perfect game and set a Triangle League
record for most strikeouts in a nine-inning game."

"Okay, Chuck. Ramirez has finished his warm-ups here in the

top of the third. He'll face the bottom of the A's order. Batting in
the seventh position is the catcher, number sixteen, Tolly Knecht.
Knecht's been in a long slump, but he's always been something of
a spoiler. He'd love to break out of it with a hit against Ramirez
here. Here's the pitch—Knecht was taking all the way, a called
strike one.''

"Maybe the folks at home would like to see Ramirez' form here
on the slow-motion replay. You can see how the extra-high kick
tends to hide the ball from the batter until the very last moment.
He's getting the full force of his body behind the pitch, throwing
from the shoulder with a last powerful snap of the wrist. He ends
up here perfectly balanced, ready for any kind of defensive move.
From the plate the white ball must be disguised by the uniform,
appearing suddenly out of nowhere. A marvelous athlete and a
terrific competitor.''

"Thanks, Chuck. That last pitch was a good breaking ball;
Knecht watched it for strike two. I think one of the reasons the
hitters seem to be so confused is the excellent arsenal of pitches
that Ramirez has. He throws his fast ball intelligently, saving it for
the tight spots. He throws an overhand curve and a sidearm curve,
each at two different speeds. His slider is showing up more and
more as his confidence increases.''

"Ramirez nods to Staefler, the catcher. He winds up and
throws. Strike three! That's seven now. Knecht throws his bat
away in frustration. The fans aren't too happy, either. Even the
Cats' loyal crowd is beginning to boo. I don't think I've ever seen
a team as completely stymied as the A's are today.''

"I tell you, I almost wish I could go down there myself. Some
of Ramirez' pitches look just too good. It makes me want to grab
a bat and take a poke at one. His slow curves seem to hang there,
inviting a good healthy cut. But, of course, from our vantage point
we can't see what the batters are seeing. Ramirez must have tremendous stuff today. Not one Athletic hitter has taken a swing at
his pitches.''

When the eighth Athletic batter struck out, the fans stood and
jeered. Marenholtz felt his stomach tightening. His mouth was dry
and his ears buzzed. After the ninth batter fanned, staring uninter-
estedly at a mild pitch belt high, the stadium was filled with shouts
and catcalls. Marenholtz couldn't be sure that they were all directed at the unlucky hitters.

Maybe I ought to hurry after Guerra, thought Marenholtz.
Maybe it's time to talk about that bowling alley deal again. This

*game is rotten at its roots already. It's not like when I was out
there. We cared. The fans cared. Now they got guys like Grobert
playing, they're nearly gangsters. Sometimes the games look like
they're produced from a script. And Ramirez is going to topple it
all. The kid's special, but that won't save us. Good God, I feel
sorry for him. He can't see it coming. He won't see it coming.
He's out there having a ball. And he's going to make the loudest
boom when it all falls down. Then what's he going to do? What's
he going to do?*

Rudy walked jauntily off the field. The spectators around Marenholtz screamed at the pitcher. Rudy only smiled. He waved to
Marenholtz and pointed to Guerra's empty seat. Marenholtz
shrugged. Ramirez ducked into the dugout, leaving Marenholtz to
fret in the stands.

After the Cats were retired in the third, Rudy went out to pitch
his half of the fourth. A policeman called his name, and Rudy
turned. The officer stood in the boxes, at the edge of the dugout,
stationed to prevent overeager fans from storming the playing
field. He held his hand out to Rudy and spoke to him in English.
Rudy shook his head, not understanding. He took the papers from
the policeman and studied them for a moment. They were contracts that he had signed with Marenholtz. They were torn in half.
Ramirez grinned; he looked up toward Marenholtz' seat behind the
dugout. The man had followed Guerra, had left the stadium before
he could be implicated in the tarnished proceedings.

For the first time since he had come to the United States, Rudy
Ramirez felt free. He handed the contracts back to the mystified
police officer and walked to the mound. He took a few warm-ups
and waited for Kleiner, the A's lead-off batter. Ramirez took his
sign and pitched. Kleiner swung and hit a shot past the mound.
Rudy entered Kleiner's mind and kept him motionless beside the
plate for a part of a second. The Cats' shortstop went far to his
left, grabbed the ball and threw on the dead run; Kleiner was out
by a full step. There were mixed groans and cheers from the spectators, but Rudy didn't hear. He was watching Gonzalvo take his
place in the batter's box. Maybe Rudy would let him get a hit.

NINE LADIES
VS. FATE

Lynn Montross

T HE PRESIDENT of the Olympic Athletic Goods Co. was in a wide and amiable mood attuned to the May afternoon which smiled back at him from the open windows of his office. He nodded indulgently at Youth across the desk while the languid reporter explained, "And so the *Evening Argus* would like a photo, Mr. Howe, and a personal sketch for the series about state business leaders—how you got started, to what you attribute your success and all that, you know."

Behind octagonal spectacles, Harrison C. Howe's plump face was smooth and youthful, only a slight contour below the chest hinting that he was in his middle forties. He answered dreamily, absent-mindedly, as the reporter jotted down bored and inept notes:

"Born 1889, Teheran, Wis.—pop. 900. Grad. high school. Job groc. store 3 yrs. before came city. Attribs. early suc. to home & mother & hard work, etc., same old bull. Started Olymp. Co. with borrowed $—spread on thick about early struggles, etc. Wife, 3 kids. Belongs all best clubs (be sure look up). Hobby, baseball. Pres. of Twilight b. b. League, etc. *Nuts* about b. b.—"

"Did you ever," said Harrison C. Howe, and his eyes cherished a fondly reminiscent glow, "happen to hear of the Bloomer girls in baseball?"

The cub hadn't, but he nodded. His blank features lighted up with a creditable assumption of interest as he accepted a cigar and settled back in a comfortable armchair.

It was too soon to return to the city room and he listened drowsily until the mention of legs aroused his attention . . .

Two blondes (Howe was saying with a mellow air as if talking to himself) led the rest of the Bloomer club on the way up Main Street from the depot. They wore peekaboo waists and slit skirts which showed more silk stocking and green satin petticoat than we were used to seeing in Teheran those days. I was carrying a bag of flour from the store to a buggy outside, but probably I stopped to stare like everybody else. The loafers in front of the pool hall began whistling so the blondes would have to keep step, I remember, and somebody yelled, "Oh, you beautiful doll!"

It was my first summer on the town baseball nine and I felt pretty bashful about playing that afternoon. None of the various traveling ladies' baseball outfits had ever played in Teheran before and we young fellows on the team took a lot of spoofing when the announcements were put in the store windows.

The wooden grandstand was filled before the game was called, and people sat in buggies or cars behind the base lines. There must have been a crowd of two hundred or so. It was always late when I got off work and changed into uniform; the Bloomers were already in the field practicing, and it sounded funny to hear their shrill voices.

They wore baseball caps pinned on high mounds of hair and their bloomers were cut full and baggy, with blouses to match in gray and red.

Snip Barton, the barber, our catcher and captain, called me to the bench first thing. "Lookit," he said with a grin, "you got to play with the Bloomers. One of their girls quit—took the noon train—and I promised to lend 'em somebody."

My ears felt hot as I crossed over to the Bloomer side, the way I got kidded. "You tell 'em, Harry, I stutter!" "If you can't be good, be careful!" . . . Things like that.

A slim, dark-haired kid, looking about eighteen, smiled at me and I sat down beside her. "Poor Gus!" she said, pointing out the catcher who was one of the two men on their team. "Gee, he'll have to get another girl right away to take Emma's place, and he's had the most frightful luck with his players, and we've been losing money ever since we started out, and—"

She was still chattering away when the game was called. They put me in at third, a new position for me, and the little, dark-eyed girl started as pitcher. It was a couple of innings before I came to bat for the ladies and there were two on. But I'd played catch with Tommy Leach ever since we were knee-high, and I knew an inshoot was coming when he stuck out his tongue that way. I got set and put my weight behind it: the ball sailed over the creek in left for a round trip. "Gee, you're good!" said the little southpaw when I trotted back to the bench. She was so excited that I was afraid she'd hug me, right in front of everybody. "Hell," she said. "I wish't Gus would keep you."

She must have spoken to him about it, because he was waiting for me after the next inning. "Listen," he said, "how'd you like to fill in for us till I can hire a couple more girls? A week or two, say?"

"Gosh, I couldn't!" I said, feeling scared at the idea. "I'd lose my job and—"

"Huh!" said Gus, looking disgusted. He was a big fellow with hard, blue eyes and a sort of battered face.

By the sixth I was well enough acquainted with the left-handed pitcher to call her Lucy. There was something so young and fresh about her, like sweet peas early in the morning, that I got over my gawky bashfulness. Her brown eyes were wide and serious as she kept on teasing me to play with the Bloomers; and it kept on getting harder for me to refuse. "I don't know what we'll *do!*" she said. "Last week Thelma got sick and left us without a sub. Then, Emma quitting cold today, it might take Gus a week to hire another girl and—and won't you please and pretty please?"

"All right!" I gulped. I don't know what made me do it—some such reason as the freckles around her snub nose, maybe. But after committing myself I wasn't going to back out. Not for a girl, I wasn't.

The decision left me so weak that I muffed an easy foul and struck out my last time up, but I promised Gus to join the Bloomers that night at the 11:21 train.

Mother was helping out at the Ladies' Aid baked bean supper, so Dad and I ate leftovers in the kitchen. He looked scared, too, when I finally got up nerve enough to tell him. A hard day at the shoe store had left him more tired and stooped than usual; he kept on shaking his head and muttering, "Harry, I don't know what *she'll* say to this!" He sighed. "Far's I'm concerned, I don't mind. I know you'll act like a gentleman, and I remember I always wanted to travel and see a little of the world before I got married and settled down."

After packing my baseball uniform and new suit I left a note in the dining room where Mother would find it in the morning.

At the grocery store where I worked, Mr. Sipps took a fresh chew of snuff and eyed my suitcase. "H'm," he said. "What you up to now?"

He was a pinched-up little man and I made myself stare at the wart on the side of his nose that I'd always hated. I spoke up, too loudly, "Well, I haven't had a day off in three years and I'd like a two-week vacation—Oscar can take my place."

He thought it over, narrowing his small watery eyes with the pale lashes.

"Well," he said, "just so's you don't expect no pay and get back on time, I'm willing."

That left only Vera Snyder yet to tell, and I had a date with her. She and I had been going steady ever since high school and it was sort of understood we'd be married someday. She looked almost noble under a street lamp that evening—the kind of sweet, sensible girl who'd make a young fellow want to settle down—and I wondered if Lester Crane, the new manual training teacher, would beat my time while I was gone. It was like pulling teeth to break the news.

"Why, Harry Howe!" she said, starting to cry. "Those women are nothing but *strumpets*."

Somehow, coming from Vera, the words sounded worse than anything I'd ever heard in the barber shop. I had to beg a long while before she dried her eyes; and I can still remember that wooden sidewalk and the big dark leaves of the catalpas against the sky.

"Oh, all right," she said at last. "I suppose if you must, you must." That was as near as she came to approval, and I felt guilty when I parted from her.

At train time I dodged up a back street to the depot, and waited at the end of the cinder platform, climbing aboard the last coach. Gus scowled at me. He was in a bad temper because Ed, the big pitcher who took Lucy's place in the box after a few innings had got drunk that night and now lay sprawled over two seats, like a bag of meal. "It's a shame, too," said Lucy solemnly. "He'd be up in the big leagues if he didn't booze so bad."

The local stopped for every milk can, and it was turning gray in the east when we got off at Ozone City. But it gave me a big thrill to straggle along with the sleepy troupe to a rooming house across the depot.

The bashful ordeal of meeting the ladies again at breakfast had me awake and dressing before six. My peg-tops ballooned at the hips and tapered down to three-inch cuffs; the coat came half-way to the knees with a stylish outward flare, and the pockets had pointed flaps which buttoned. With a narrow brimmed hat, lofty collar, bumpty-toed shoes and fire opal stick pin, I felt as nobby as any traveling man. But even new clothes couldn't save me from embarrassment in the dining room and I was glad when Lucy asked me to take her for a walk.

She had the trusting, confiding air of a puppy. As she trotted along beside me in her tight hobble-skirt, she told me that she had been raised on an Indiana farm, the tomboy of a large family, and had run away to join a tent show when she was sixteen.

The two gilt blondes were the "Davere sisters," Sadie and Flo, keeping the alluring name after a brief vaudeville tour. During the winter they were in cheap burlesque, which made them feel more sophisticated than the rest of the girls. They laced heroically and were very proud of their fashionable hour-glass figures; when Main Street loafers ogled them they were always ready with, "Twenty-three for you!" or "Buy a drum and beat it!" . . . After firing one girl for an all-night date with a traveling man, Gus watched Flo and Sadie suspiciously.

But Mrs. Bensinger, who shared the outfield with them, was a motherly soul. Thirty-six seemed aged to me then, and I was amazed at the nimble way she could beat out a bunt to first. A Dakota farm wife, she'd learned the game with her three sons; she saved her earnings all summer, doing the club mending for extra pay, and went back to the lonely homestead when the season ended.

The tall, statuesque Miss Simmons, who held down first base as well as any man, was nicknamed "Lady Macbeth." She had played a few such heavy roles in obscure stock companies and never quite recovered. She was a melancholy ash blonde, at least thirty, and used an affected stage voice in speaking of the most ordinary things.

Our best lady player was Bea Swanson at shortstop. I'll always remember her in the hotel parlor threading a pink ribbon through an enormous camisole . . . how she'd blush and hide the garment. She was huge, elephantine, grotesque as anything in a comic strip; and in defense she had become a suffragette. "Ay ban batter man than any man on earth!" she would boast; but her childish eyes were pitiful, pleading, and I understood why Gus had once punched a fellow for mocking her. Yet on the diamond she was amazingly fast, even graceful, and after Gus the best sticker on the team.

Six ladies and three men, without a substitute, we were small pumpkins compared with the other Bloomer teams touring the country. We took what they left, often without a guarantee on a risky percentage. It was Gus's first shaky venture as a promoter on his own hook, and he'd been licked from the start. It rained most of my beginning week with the club and we collected on only three games. A big Sunday date which Gus counted on for pay-day was stopped by the preachers at the last minute, and the ghost limped in with five dollars apiece.

My second week was no better. At Lark, Illinois, we played to about forty people and the next day it had to rain again. The big Fourth of July game at Acropolis, down in the coal mine country, was our last hope. We hit town with less than ten dollars in the treasury and Gus called us all in the hotel parlor for a conference. He stared at the wire racks of picture post cards and began:

"I guess you know we're busted. All season you nine ladies—"

"Only six," pointed out Sadie Devere.

Gus scowled. "You're a ladies' nine, aren't you? Well! What I started to say was that after all this hard luck—"

"*Fate!*" interrupted Lady Macbeth in a rich, dramatic whisper.

"All right, call it fate if you want to, but we've been versus lots of bad breaks and we're through for the season unless we win tomorrow. These miners are hot sports and I made a deal to play 'em for the gate, winner take all, see? That's our last chance. They got a hired pitcher but if Ed gets going good and Bea hits we got a show for the money."

"I'll pitch league ball," Ed promised. His weak chin and sad, alcoholic eyes meant what he said, too, but he always tumbled off the wagon right when he was needed most. Just one little snort for a bracer, then he was lost.

So it wasn't any surprise when he turned up missing after supper, the night before the game at Acropolis, and Gus sent us out looking for him. Lucy and I went together around the carnival grounds and finally stopped at the outdoor dance pavilion. The band was playing "Everybody's Doing It" and the dancers were swaying to the bear or turkey trot. Suddenly I glanced at Lucy and she was crying! She hurried away from the crowd and I followed.

"That music's so pretty!" she said when she could talk. "And —and I'm so daffy about Gus, I can't bear it if we bust up tomorrow and I lose him!"

I hadn't realized. It was a jolt to me, because I had quite a crush on Lucy myself, but I tried to comfort her with awkward thumps on the shoulder.

Ed was carried up to his room by several miners about four in the morning—probably they'd got him soused on purpose. By game time he was still so bleary and unsteady that the best he could do was play right field without being propped up.

Lucy was our only pitcher and she'd never been strong enough for more than three or four innings. We were first to bat, of course, and Gus was mad enough to sock his own mother when he stepped over to the plate. He slammed the very first pitched ball over the right fielder's head for a three-bagger!

That took some of the confidence out of the hired Acropolis hurler, and the crowd was so silent you could hear it. There must have been twelve or fourteen hundred, the biggest mob I'd ever seen at a ball game then, and they looked tough enough to lynch us if they lost.

Ed was next to bat. Probably he never saw the ball but by some miracle he managed to poke a Texas leaguer over second, fetching Gus home. The girls on the bench were screaming for a hit when I walked up to the platter, and I remember praying myself. The first pitch, a fast one with a wicked hop, showed me that the big semi-pro had the stuff all right; but my line drive went between short and third for a stinging single.

Big Bea was our "cleanup man." Her little blue eyes danced with rage and I don't think that even Ed Walsh could have fanned her that time. She had a strike and two balls on her—then at the crack of the bat I started running and didn't stop until I slid into home. Bea wound up at second, still muttering at the pitcher.

Mrs. Bensinger laid down a bunt and beat it to first while Bea was held on second. Lady Macbeth let four wide ones go past and filled the bases. . . . But this was too good to last, so near the end of our batting order. One Devere sister struck out, the other fouled to first. Lucy, our weakest hitter, fanned.

The boost to our spirits was worth more than the three runs. We took the field with new pep, not as a team beaten before it started. Gus sent Lucy into the box with an encouraging whack. "Slow-ball 'em to death, kid! These hicks aren't used to southpaw throw-ing, see?"

She gulped and nodded. Her slow round-house curves and the new knuckle ball that Ed had taught her had the mine boys falling all over themselves trying to kill it. They went down in a row on pop flies or soft infield assists.

The next two innings were goose-eggs for both sides, even when Acropolis shoved a man as far as third. But in the fourth the miners began to time Lucy better; they connected for two earned runs and with two out filled the bases.

"Steady, girl! Take it easy, honey!" Gus called from behind the plate. Her freckled face, already white with strain, lighted up ea-gerly.

The batter got under a teaser and arched a high fly to right that any schoolboy could have nabbed. But Ed's bloodshot eyes mis-judged the ball and two more scores trickled in.

Acropolis 4, Bloomers 3—with five innings yet to play.

In the last of the fifth they tallied again by smacking Lucy for three straight singles, and we were lucky to get off that easy. It was the same old story in the sixth when another run put them three ahead. Both sessions we went down in a row, eating out of the pitcher's hand.

Somehow Lucy managed to hold them scoreless in the seventh, although she was so tired that the plate must have seemed a mile away. I came up to bat in our half of the eighth and made first on an infield error. Bea stopped glaring at the pitcher long enough to rap out a single, but I was stopped at second until Mrs. Bensinger's weak grounder forced me out at third. Lady Macbeth, looking haughty as ever in spite of the yells from the crowd, lifted one over third to load the bags with only one out.

The hired pitcher bore down and Sadie Devere whiffed. Then with two out and two strikes on Flo, another miracle saved our necks—the Acropolis shortstop muffed her easy pop-up and threw wild, handing us our fourth score on a silver tray.

Lord, Lord! Two out and three on, with Lucy at bat! It was tough that the big chance had to bring up our poorest hitter, and the head of the batting list just around the corner.

Her shoulders sagging, Lucy let the first one streak past for a called strike. A ball was next. Another ball. And then while I held my breath the pitcher wound up, there was the white flash of his fast one and the sickening impact of hard leather against soft flesh. Lucy dropped her bat, writhing as she clutched her left arm.

It was so perfect that I wasn't sure myself whether it was an accident or not. Anyhow, that umpire had intestines. He motioned Lucy to first and half a dozen constables pushed the bellowing crowd out of the diamond. Bea was forced home for another run while Lucy held up her wrist with a white, sick grin.

Now we were only one behind and Gus would have connected with a cannon ball to drive home those gate receipts! His scream-ing double put us one run to the good, and with the count seven to six in our favor we were too excited to care when Ed fanned.

But Lucy didn't go back to the mound when she took the field in the last of the eighth. She and Gus went into a huddle at the plate which ended with a call for me. "You got to pitch," he told me. "Lucy's hurt bad and Ed's too shaky—you got to stop 'em two innings or I'll cut your heart out and eat it!"

It was no good protesting . . . I pitched. How I don't know, because all I had was a glove and a prayer. But what a prayer, what a prayer! I prayed that they wouldn't hit or if they did that it wouldn't go to Lucy on second base with her fractured throwing arm. She was doing a good job of pretending but Acropolis knew they had us in a hole.

That inning took years. We retired them at last, after two hits against me, but I was sure my hair was turning gray. We were easy marks at bat in our half of the ninth and it was up to me again. "Them gate receipts, remember!" Gus croaked hoarsely as he shoved me toward the box.

The first man singled. But I knew there was a Santa Claus when the next batter hit into an easy double play. Bea covering second. With two out, just like that, it must have gone to my head—I turned with a sick feeling in the solar plexus and watched my next pitch sail over Mrs. Bensinger's head for a triple. Only her quick relay saved us from a homer and a tied game.

While the runner danced off third, the man at the plate swung a club that looked to me like a wagon tongue. He took a mighty swipe and missed. Gus made me kill time till I felt better, and I put everything I had into my one roundhouse curve. The batter straightened it out into a sizzling grounder between first and second. I tumbled in my wild dive for the ball but Lucy was waiting and took it on the bounce with her gloved hand.

With the man on third tearing for home she hesitated—only a ghastly fraction of a second—before she ran toward first, her left arm hanging limp, to beat the runner to the bag. When she saw it was too late she made a last desperate lunge for momentum and pushed rather than threw with her gloved hand. The ball dropped halfway and rolled to one side, but Lady MacBeth somehow picked it out of the dirt in time.

After it was all over Lucy collapsed in a heap, just where she stood. Gus charged across the diamond without taking off his mask and carried her to the bench.

"How damn dumb of me," she said when she opened her eyes, "not to get hit some other place!"

At the hotel the mining company doctor treated her for a slight green-stick fracture. And when the Acropolis miners heard that Lucy and Gus were to be married, nothing would do but a public ceremony, on the fair grounds next day after the airplane flight. Of course I had to stay for the wedding even if it did mean getting home a day late for my job.

Gus had 'phoned a Chicago agency for three new lady players but he invited me with the team as long as I liked. "O. K.," he said when I made my excuses. "But any time you want to try your luck in the city, let me know. I got a pal in the athletic goods graft, see?"

The train that hauled me back to Teheran didn't realize how I felt or it would have started backing up. On the depot platform Snip Barton spotted me first thing. "Hi, Harry!" he yelled so all the loafers could hear. "The new manual training teacher has went and beat your time with Vera!"

He didn't muff it. After Mother had lectured me and gone to bed with one of her sick headaches, I found a package addressed in Vera's round, regular hand. She'd sent back my letters and the lavaliere I gave her. . . . And when I reported at the store in the morning, Mr. Sipps fired me in less time than it takes to tell it. Oscar Nelson had my job—in fact, he still has it to this day.

With my girl, my job and my reputation lost, there was only one thing left to do: I wired Gus for help and started for the city. And here I am.

The sudden silence in the office was long enough to bridge the gap of years between Teheran, Wis. and the *Olympic Athletic Goods Co.* The *Argus* reporter still leaned forward, a dead cigar in his clutch. . . . But all at once an annoyed frown crossed the plump features of Harrison C. Howe, as if he felt that he had been doddering. The old brisk decision came back as he glanced at the electric grandfather clock. "Naturally," he said, "these trifling reminiscences are not for publication, and I shall expect to see the proofs. . . . Home training, country environment, early discipline, sticking to the job—I believe I've already sufficiently emphasized those qualities which make for business success. That's all!"

THE REDHEADED OUTFIELD

Zane Grey

THERE WAS DELANEY'S red-haired trio—Red Gilbat, left fielder; Reddy Clammer, right fielder, and Reddie Ray, center fielder, composing the most remarkable outfield ever developed in minor league baseball. It was Delaney's pride, as it was also his trouble.

Red Gilbat was nutty—and his batting average was .371. Any student of baseball could weigh these two facts against each other and understand something of Delaney's trouble. It was not possible to camp on Red Gilbat's trail. The man was a jack-o'-lantern, a will-o'-the-wisp, a weird, long-legged, long-armed, red-haired illusive phantom. When the gong rang at the ball grounds there were ten chances to one that Red would not be present. He had been discovered with small boys peeping through knotholes at the vacant left field he was supposed to inhabit during play.

Of course what Red did off the ball grounds was not so important as what he did on. And there was absolutely no telling what under the sun he might do then except once out of every three times at bat he could be counted on to knock the cover off the ball.

Reddy Clammer was a grand-stand player—the kind all managers hated—and he was hitting .305. He made circus catches, circus stops, circus throws, circus steals—but particularly circus catches. That is to say, he made easy plays appear difficult. He was always strutting, posing, talking, arguing, quarreling—when he was not engaged in making a grand-stand play. Reddy Clammer

197

used every possible incident and artifice to bring himself into the limelight.

Reddie Ray had been the intercollegiate champion in the sprints and a famous college ball player. After a few months of professional ball he was hitting over .400 and leading the league both at bat and on the bases. It was a beautiful and a thrilling sight to see him run. He was so quick to start, so marvelously swift, so keen of judgment, that neither Delaney nor any player could ever tell the hit that he was not going to get. That was why Reddie Ray was a whole game in himself.

Delaney's Rochester Stars and the Providence Grays were tied for first place. Of the present series each team had won a game. Rivalry had always been keen, and as the teams were about to enter the long homestretch for the pennant there was battle in the New England air.

The September day was perfect. The stands were half full and the bleachers packed with a white-sleeved mass. And the field was beautifully level and green. The Grays were practicing and the Stars were on their bench.

"We're up against it," Delaney was saying. "This new umpire, Fuller, hasn't got it in for us. Oh, no, not at all! Believe me, he's a robber. But Scott is pitchin' well, Won his last three games. He'll bother 'em. And the three Reds have broken loose. They're on the rampage. They'll burn up this place today."

Somebody noted the absence of Gilbat.

Delaney gave a sudden start. "Why, Gil was here," he said slowly. "Lord!—he's about due for a nutty stunt."

Whereupon Delaney sent boys and players scurrying about to find Gilbat, and Delaney went himself to ask the Providence manager to hold back the gong for a few minutes.

Presently somebody brought Delaney a telephone message that Red Gilbat was playing ball with some boys in a lot four blocks down the street. When at length a couple of players marched up to the bench with Red in tow Delaney uttered an immense sigh of relief and then, after a close scrutiny of Red's face, he whispered, "Lock the gates!"

Then the gong rang. The Grays trooped in. The Stars ran out, except Gilbat, who ambled like a giraffe. The hum of conversation in the grand stand quickened for a moment with the scraping of chairs, and then grew quiet. The bleachers sent up the rollicking cry of expectancy. The umpire threw out a white ball with his stentorian "Play!" and Blake of the Grays strode to the plate.

Hitting safely, he started the game with a rush. With Dorr up, the Star infield played for a bunt. Like clockwork Dorr dumped the first ball as Blake got his flying start for second base. Morrissey tore in for the ball, got it on the run and snapped it underhand to Healy, beating the runner by an inch. The fast Blake, with a long slide, made third base. The stands stamped. The bleachers howled. White, next man up, batted a high fly to left field. This was a sun field and the hardest to play in the league. Red Gilbat was the only man who ever played it well. He judged the fly, waited under it, took a step back, then forward, and deliberately caught the ball in his gloved hand. A throw-in to catch the runner scoring from third base would have been futile, but it was not like Red Gilbat to fail to try. He tossed the ball to O'Brien. And Blake scored amid applause.

"What do you know about that?" ejaculated Delaney, wiping his moist face. "I never before saw our nutty Redhead pull off a play like that."

Some of the players yelled at Red, "This is a two-handed league, you bat!"

The first five players on the list for the Grays were left-handed batters, and against a right-handed pitcher whose most effective ball for them was a high fast one over the outer corner they would naturally hit toward left field. It was no surprise to see Hanley bat a skyscraper out to left. Red had to run to get under it. He braced himself rather unusually for a fielder. He tried to catch the ball in his bare right hand and muffed it. Hanley got to second on the play while the audience roared. When they got through there was some roaring among the Rochester players. Scott and Captain Healy roared at Red, and Red roared back at them.

"It's all off. Red never did that before," cried Delaney in despair. "He's gone clean bughouse now."

Babcock was the next man up and he likewise hit to left. It was a low, twisting ball—half fly, half liner—and a difficult one to field. Gilbat ran with great bounds, and though he might have got two hands on the ball he did not try, but this time caught it in his right, retiring the side.

The Stars trotted in, Scott and Healy and Kane, all veterans, looking like thunderclouds. Red ambled in the last and he seemed very nonchalant.

"By Gosh, I'd 'a' ketched that one I muffed if I'd had time to change hands," he said with a grin, and he exposed a handful of peanuts. He had refused to drop the peanuts to make the catch with two hands. That explained the mystery. It was funny, yet nobody laughed. There was that run chalked up against the Stars, and this game had to be won.

"Red, I—I want to take the team home in the lead," said Delaney, and it was plain that he suppressed strong feeling. "You didn't play the game, you know."

Red appeared mightily ashamed.

"Del, I'll git that run back," he said.

Then he strode to the plate, swinging his wagon-tongue bat. For all his awkward position in the box he looked what he was—a formidable hitter. He seemed to tower over the pitcher—Red was six feet one—and he scowled and shook his bat at Wehying and called, "Put one over—you wienerwurst!" Wehying was anything but red-headed, and he wasted so many balls on Red that it looked as if he might pass him. He would have passed him, too, if Red had not stepped over on the fourth ball and swung on it. White at second base leaped high for the stinging hit, and failed to reach it. The ball struck and bounded for the fence. When Babcock fielded it in, Red was standing on third base, and the bleachers groaned.

Whereupon Chesty Reddy Clammer proceeded to draw attention to himself, and incidentally delay the game, by assorting the bats as if the audience and the game might gladly wait years to see him make a choice.

"Git in the game!" yelled Delaney.

"Aw, take my bat, Duke of the Abrubsky!" sarcastically said Dump Kane. When the grouchy Kane offered to lend his bat matters were critical in the Star camp.

Other retorts followed, which Reddy Clammer deigned not to notice. At last he got a bat that suited him—and then, importantly, dramatically, with his cap jauntily riding his red locks, he marched to the plate.

Some wag in the bleachers yelled into the silence, "Oh, Maggie, your lover has come!"

Not improbably Clammer was thinking first of his presence before the multitude, secondly of his batting average and thirdly of the run to be scored. In this instance he waited and feinted at balls and fouled strikes at length to work his base. When he got to first base suddenly he bolted for second, and in the surprise of the unlooked-for play he made it by a spread-eagle slide. It was a circus steal.

Delaney snorted. Then the look of profound disgust vanished in a flash of light. His huge face beamed.

Reddie Ray was striding to the plate.

There was something about Reddie Ray that pleased all the senses. His lithe form seemed instinct with life; any sudden movement was suggestive of stored lightning. His position at the plate was on the left side, and he stood perfectly motionless, with just a

hint of tense waiting alertness. Dorr, Blake and Babcock, the outfielders for the Grays, trotted round to the right of their usual
position. Delaney smiled derisively, as if he knew how futile it was
to tell what field Reddie Ray might hit into. Wehying, the old fox,
warily eyed the youngster, and threw him a high curve, close in. It
grazed Reddie's shirt, but he never moved a hair. Then Wehying,
after the manner of many veteran pitchers when trying out a new
and menacing batter, drove a straight fast ball at Reddie's head.
Reddie ducked, neither too slow nor too quick, just right to show
what an eye he had, how hard it was to pitch to. The next was a
strike. And on the next he appeared to step and swing in one
action. There was a ringing rap, and the ball shot toward right,
curving down, a vicious, headed hit. Mallory, at first base,
snatched at it and found only the air. Babcock had only time to
take a few sharp steps, and then he plunged down, blocked the hit
and fought the twisting ball. Reddie turned first base, flitted on
toward second, went headlong in the dust, and shot to the base
before White got the throw-in from Babcock. Then, as White
wheeled and lined the ball home to catch the scoring Clammer,
Reddie Ray leaped up, got his sprinter's start and, like a rocket,
was off for third. This time he dove behind the base, sliding in a
half circle, and as Hanley caught Strickland's perfect throw and
whirled with the ball, Reddie's hand slid to the bag.

Reddie got to his feet amid a rather breathless silence. Even the
coachers were quiet. There was a moment of relaxation,
then Wehying received the ball from Hanley and faced the batter.

This was Dump Kane. There was a sign of some kind, almost
imperceptible, between Kane and Reddie. As Wehying half turned
in his swing to pitch, Reddie Ray bounded homeward. It was not
so much the boldness of his action as the amazing swiftness of it
that held the audience spellbound. Like a thunderbolt Reddie came
down the line, almost beating Wehying's pitch to the plate. But
Kane's bat intercepted the ball, laying it down, and Reddie scored
without sliding. Dorr, by sharp work, just managed to throw Kane
out.

Three runs so quick it was hard to tell how they had come. Not
in the major league could there have been faster work. And the
ball had been fielded perfectly and thrown perfectly.

"There you are," said Delaney, hoarsely. "Can you beat it? If
you've been wonderin' how the cripped Stars won so many games
just put what you've seen in your pipe and smoke it. Red Gilbat
gets on—Reddy Clammer gets on—and then Reddie Ray drives
them home or chases them home."

The game went on, and though it did not exactly drag it slowed down considerably. Morrissey and Healy were retired on infield plays. And the sides changed. For the Grays, O'Brien made a scratch hit, went to second on Strickland's sacrifice, stole third and scored on Mallory's infield out. Wehying missed three strikes. In the Stars' turn the three end players on the batting list were easily disposed of. In the third inning the clever Blake, aided by a base on balls and a hit following, tied the score, and once more struck fire and brimstone from the impatient bleachers. Providence was a town that had to have its team win.

"Git at 'em, Reds!" said Delaney gruffly.

"Batter up!" called Umpire Fuller, sharply.

"Where's Red? Where's the bug? Where's the nut? Delaney, did you lock the gates? Look under the bench!" These and other remarks, not exactly elegant, attested to the mental processes of some of the Stars. Red Gilbat did not appear to be forthcoming. There was an anxious delay. Capt. Healy searched for the missing player. Delaney did not say any more.

Suddenly a door under the grand stand opened and Red Gilbat appeared. He hurried for his bat and then up to the plate. And he never offered to hit one of the balls Wehying shot over. When Fuller had called the third strike Red hurried back to the door and disappeared.

"Somethin' doin'," whispered Delaney.

Lord Chesterfield Clammer paraded to the batter's box and, after gradually surveying the field, as if picking out the exact place he meant to drive the ball, he stepped to the plate. Then a roar from the bleachers surprised him.

"Well, I'll be dog-goned!" exclaimed Delaney. "Red stole that sure as shootin'."

Red Gilbat was pushing a brand-new baby carriage toward the batter's box. There was a tittering in the grand stand; another roar from the bleachers. Clammer's face turned as red as his hair. Gilbat shoved the baby carriage upon the plate, spread wide his long arms, made a short presentation speech and an elaborate bow, then backed away.

All eyes were centered on Clammer. If he had taken it right the incident might have passed without undue hilarity. But Clammer became absolutely wild with rage. It was well known that he was unmarried. Equally well was it seen that Gilbat had executed one of his famous tricks. Ball players were inclined to be dignified about the presentation of gifts upon the field, and Clammer, the dude, the swell, the lady's man, the favorite of the baseball gods

—in his own estimation—so far lost control of himself that he threw his bat at his retreating tormentor. Red jumped high and the bat skipped along the ground toward the bench. The players side-stepped and leaped and, of course, the bat cracked one of Delaney's big shins. His eyes popped with pain, but he could not stop laughing. One by one the players lay down and rolled over and yelled. The superior Clammer was not overliked by his co-players.

From the grand stand floated the laughter of ladies and gentlemen. And from the bleachers—that throne of the biting, ironic, scornful fans—pealed up a howl of delight. It lasted for a full minute. Then, as quiet ensued, some boy blew a blast of one of those infernal little instruments of pipe and rubber balloon, and over the field wailed out a shrill, high-keyed cry, an excellent imitation of a baby. Whereupon the whole audience roared, and in discomfiture Reddy Clammer went in search of his bat.

To make his chagrin all the worse he ingloriously struck out. And then he strode away under the lea of the grand-stand wall toward right field.

Reddie Ray went to bat and, with the infield playing deep and the outfield swung still farther round to the right, he bunted a little teasing ball down the third-base line. Like a flash of light he had crossed first base before Hanley got his hands on the ball. Then Kane hit into second base, forcing Reddie out.

Again the game assumed less spectacular and more ordinary play. Both Scott and Wehying held the batters safely and allowed no runs. But in the fifth inning, with the Stars at bat and two out, Red Gilbat again electrified the field. He sprang up from somewhere and walked to the plate, his long shape enfolded in a full-length linen duster. The color and style of this garment might not have been especially striking, but upon Red it had a weird and wonderful effect. Evidently Red intended to bat while arrayed in his long coat, for he stepped into the box and faced the pitcher. Capt. Healy yelled for him to take the duster off. Likewise did the Grays yell.

The bleachers shrieked their disapproval. To say the least, Red Gilbat's crazy assurance was dampening to the ardor of the most blindly confident fans. At length Umpire Fuller waved his hand, enjoining silence and calling time.

"Take it off or I'll fine you."

From his lofty height Gilbat gazed down upon the little umpire, and it was plain what he thought.

"What do I care for money!" replied Red.

"That costs you twenty-five," said Fuller.

"Cigarette change!" yelled Red.

"Costs you fifty."

"Bah! Go to an eye doctor," roared Red.

"Seventy-five," added Fuller, imperturbably.

"Make it a hundred!"

"It's two hundred."

"Rob-b-ber!" bawled Red.

Fuller showed willingness to overlook Red's back talk as well as costume, and he called, "Play!"

There was a mounting sensation of prophetic certainty. Old fox Wehying appeared nervous. He wasted two balls on Red; then he put one over the plate, and then he wasted another. Three balls and one strike! That was a bad place for a pitcher, and with Red Gilbat up it was worse. Wehying swung longer and harder to get all his left behind the throw and let drive. Red lunged and cracked the ball. It went up and up and kept going up and farther out, and as the murmuring audience was slowly transfixed into late realization the ball soared to its height and dropped beyond the left-field fence. A home run!

Ray Gilbat gathered up the tails of his duster, after the manner of a neat woman crossing a muddy street, and ambled down to first base and on to second, making prodigious jumps upon the bags, and round third, to come down the homestretch wagging his red head. Then he stood on the plate, and, as if to exact revenge from the audience for the fun they made of him, he threw back his shoulders and bellowed: *"Haw! Haw! Haw!"*

Not a handclap greeted him, but some mindless, exceedingly adventurous fan yelled: "Redhead! Redhead! Redhead!"

That was the one thing calculated to rouse Red Gilbat. He seemed to flare, to bristle, and he paced for the bleachers.

Delaney looked as if he might have a stroke. "Grab him! Soak him with a bat! Somebody grab him!"

But none of the Stars was risking so much, and Gilbat, to the howling derision of the gleeful fans, reached the bleachers. He stretched his long arms up to the fence and prepared to vault over. "Where's the guy who called me redhead?" he yelled.

That was heaping fuel on the fire. From all over the bleachers, from everywhere, came the obnoxious word. Red heaved himself over the fence and piled into the fans. Then followed the roar of many voices, the tramping of many feet, the pressing forward of line after line of shirt-sleeved men and boys. That bleacher stand suddenly assumed the maelstrom appearance of a surging mob round an agitated center. In a moment all the players rushed down the field, and confusion reigned.

However, the game had to go on. Delaney, no doubt, felt all was over. Nevertheless there were games occasionally that seemed an unending series of unprecedented events. This one had begun admirably to break a record. And the Providence fans, like all other fans, had cultivated an appetite as the game proceeded. They were wild to put the other redheads out of the field or at least out for the inning, wild to tie the score, wild to win and wilder than all for more excitement. Clammer hit safely. But when Reddie Ray lined to the second baseman, Clammer, having taken a lead, was doubled up in the play.

Of course, the sixth inning opened with the Stars playing only eight men. There was another delay. Probably everybody except Delaney and perhaps Healy had forgotten the Stars were short a man. Fuller called time. The impatient bleachers barked for action.

Capt. White came over to Delaney and courteously offered to lend a player for the remaining innings. Then a pompous individual came out of the door leading from the press boxes—he was a director Delaney disliked.

"Guess you'd better let Fuller call the game," he said brusquely.

"If you want to—as the score stands now in our favor," replied Delaney.

"Not on your life! It'll be ours or else we'll play it out and beat you to death."

He departed in high dudgeon.

"Tell Reddie to swing over a little toward left," was Delaney's order to Healy. Fire gleamed in the manager's eye.

Fuller called play then, with Reddy Clammer and Reddie Ray composing the Star outfield. And the Grays evidently prepared to do great execution through the wide lanes thus opened up. At that stage it would not have been like matured ball players to try to crop hits down into the infield.

White sent a long fly back of Clammer. Reddy had no time to loaf on this hit. It was all he could do to reach it and he made a splendid catch, for which the crowd roundly applauded him. That applause was wine to Reddy Clammer. He began to prance on his toes and sing out to Scott: "Make 'em hit to me, old man! Make 'em hit to me!" Whether Scott desired that or not was scarcely possible to say; at any rate, Hanley pounded a hit through the infield. And Clammer, prancing high in the air like a check-reined horse, ran to intercept the ball. He could have received it in his hands, but that would never have served Reddy Clammer. He timed the hit to a nicety, went down with his old grand-stand play and blocked the ball with his anatomy. Delaney swore. And the bleachers, now warm toward the gallant outfielder, lustily cheered him. Babcock hit down the right-field foul line, giving Clammer a long run. Hanley was scoring and Babcock was sprinting for third base when Reddy got the ball. He had a fine arm and he made a hard and accurate throw, catching his man in a close play.

Perhaps even Delaney could not have found any fault with that play. But the aftermath spoiled the thing. Clammer now rode the air; he soared; he was in the clouds; it was his inning and he had utterly forgotten his team mates, except inasmuch as they were performing mere little automatic movements to direct the great machinery in his direction for his sole achievement and glory.

There is fate in baseball as well as in other walks of life. O'Brien was a strapping fellow and he lifted another ball into Clammer's wide territory. The hit was of the high and far-away variety. Clammer started to run with it, not like a grim outfielder, but like one thinking of himself, his style, his opportunity, his inevitable success. Certain it was that in thinking of himself the outfielder forgot his surroundings. He ran across the foul line, head up, hair flying, unheeding the warning cry from Healy. And, reaching up to make his crowning circus play, he smashed face forward into the bleachers fence. Then, limp as a rag, he dropped. The audience sent forth a long groan of sympathy.

"That wasn't one of his stage falls," said Delaney. "I'll bet he's dead. . . . Poor Reddy! And I want him to bust his face!"

Clammer was carried off the field into the dressing room and a physician was summoned out of the audience.

"Cap., what'd it—do to him?" asked Delaney.

"Aw, spoiled his pretty mug, that's all," replied Healy, scornfully. "Mebee he'll listen to me now."

Delaney's change was characteristic of the man. "Well, if it didn't kill him I'm blamed glad he got it. . . . Cap, we can trim 'em yet. Reddie Ray'll play the whole outfield. Give Reddie a chance to run! Tell the boy to cut loose. And all of you git in the game. Win or lose, I won't forget it. I've a hunch. Once in a while I can tell what's comin' off. Some queer game this! And we're goin' to win. Gilbat lost the game; Clammer throwed it away again, and now Reddie Ray's due to win it. . . . I'm all in, but I wouldn't miss the finish to save my life."

Delaney's deep presaging sense of baseball events was never put to a greater test. And the seven Stars, with the score tied, exhibited the temper and timber of a championship team in the last ditch. It was so splendid that almost instantly it caught the antagonistic bleachers.

Wherever the tired Scott found renewed strength and speed was a mystery. But he struck out the hard-hitting Providence catcher and that made the third out. The Stars could not score in their half of the inning. Likewise the seventh inning passed without a run for either side; only the infield work of the Stars was something superb. When the eighth inning ended, without a tally for either team, the excitement grew tense. There was Reddie Ray playing outfield alone, and the Grays with all their desperate endeavors had not lifted the ball out of the infield.

But in the ninth, Blake, the first man up, lined low toward right center. The hit was safe and looked good for three bases. No one looking, however, had calculated on Reddie Ray's fleetness. He covered ground and dove for the bounding ball and knocked it down. Blake did not get beyond first base. The crowd cheered the play equally with the prospect of a run. Dorr bunted and beat the throw. White hit one of the high balls Scott was serving and sent it close to the left-field foul line. The running Reddie Ray made on that play held White at second base. But two runs had scored with no one out.

Hanley, the fourth left-handed hitter, came up and Scott pitched to him as he had to the others—high fast balls over the inside corner of the plate. Reddy Ray's position was some fifty yards behind deep short, and a little toward center field. He stood sideways, facing two-thirds of that vacant outfield. In spite of Scott's skill, Hanley swung the ball far round into right field, but he hit it high, and almost before he actually hit it the great sprinter was speeding across the green.

The suspense grew almost unbearable as the ball soared in its parabolic flight and the red-haired runner streaked dark across the green. The ball seemed never to be coming down. And when it began to descend and reached a point perhaps fifty feet above the ground there appeared more distance between where it would alight and where Reddie was than anything human could cover. It dropped and dropped, and then dropped into Reddie Ray's outstretched hands. He had made the catch look easy. But the fact that White scored from second base on the play showed what the catch really was.

There was no movement or restlessness of the audience such as usually indicated the beginning of the exodus. Scott struck Babcock out. The game still had fire. The Grays never let up a moment on their coaching. And the hoarse voices of the Stars were grimmer than ever. Reddie Ray was the only one of the seven who kept silent. And he crouched like a tiger.

The teams changed sides with the Grays three runs in the lead.

Morrissey, for the Stars, opened with a clean drive to right. Then Healy slashed a ground ball to Hanley and nearly knocked him down. When old Burns, by a hard rap to short, advanced the runners a base and made a desperate, though unsuccessful, effort to reach first the Providence crowd awoke to a strange and inspiring appreciation. They began that most rare feature in baseball audiences—a strong and trenchant call for the visiting team to win.

The play had gone fast and furious. Wehying, sweaty and disheveled, worked violently. All the Grays were on uneasy tiptoes. And the Stars were seven Indians on the warpath. Halloran fouled down the right-field line; then he fouled over the left-field fence. Wehying tried to make him too anxious, but it was in vain. Halloran was implacable. With two strikes and three balls he hit straight down to white, and was out. The ball had been so sharp that neither runner on base had a chance to advance.

Two men out, two on base, Stars wanting three runs to tie, Scott, a weak batter, at the plate! The situation was disheartening. Yet there sat Delaney, shot through and through with some vital compelling force. He saw only victory. And when the very first ball pitched to Scott hit him on the leg, giving him his base, Delaney got to his feet, unsteady and hoarse.

Bases full, Reddie Ray up, three runs to tie!

Delaney looked at Reddie. And Reddie looked at Delaney. The manager's face was pale, intent, with a little smile. The player had eyes of fire, a lean, bulging jaw and the hands he reached for his bat clutched like talons.

"Reddie, I knew it was waitin' for you," said Delaney, his voice ringing. "Break up the game!"

After all this was only a baseball game, and perhaps from the fans' viewpoint a poor game at that. But the moment when that lithe, redhaired athlete toed the plate was a beautiful one. The long crash from the bleachers, the steady cheer from the grand stand, proved that it was not so much the game that mattered.

Wehying had shot his bolt; he was tired. Yet he made ready for a final effort. It seemed that passing Reddie Ray on balls would have been a wise play at that juncture. But no pitcher, probably, would have done it with the bases crowded and chances, of course, against the batter.

Clean and swift, Reddie leaped at the first pitched ball. Ping! For a second no one saw the hit. Then it gleamed, a terrific drive, low along the ground, like a bounding bullet, straight at Babcock in right field. It struck his hands and glanced viciously away to roll toward the fence.

Thunder broke loose from the stands. Reddie Ray was turning first base. Beyond first base he got into his wonderful stride. Some runners run with a consistent speed, the best they can make for a given distance. But this trained sprinter gathered speed as he ran. He was no short-stepping runner. His strides were long. They gave an impression of strength combined with fleetness. He had the speed of a race horse, but the trimness, the raciness, the delicate legs were not characteristic of him. Like the wind he turned second, so powerful that his turn was short. All at once there came a difference in his running. It was no longer beautiful. The grace was gone. It was now fierce, violent. His momentum was running him off his legs. He whirled around third base and came hurtling down the homestretch. His face was convulsed, his eyes were wild. His arms and legs worked in a marvelous muscular velocity. He seemed a demon—a flying streak. He overtook and ran down the laboring Scott, who had almost reached the plate.

The park seemed full of shrill, piercing strife. It swelled, reached a highest pitch, sustained that for a long moment, and then declined.

"My Gawd!" exclaimed Delaney, as he fell back. "Wasn't that a finish? Didn't I tell you to watch them redheads?"

WHO'S ON FIRST?

Lloyd Biggle, Jr.

PRIORITY RATING: Routine.
FROM: Jard Killil, Minister of Juvenile Affairs.
TO: All Planetary Police Organizations,
     All Interplanetary Patrol Units.
SUBJECT: Juvenile detention escape Muko Zilo.
ENCLOSURES: Character analysis, film strips, retinal patterns.

All law enforcement agencies are hereby informed of the escape of Muko Zilo from the Juvenile Rehabilitation Center on Philoy, Raff III, Sector 1311. Escapee is presumed to have fled the planet in a stolen space yacht, Stellar Class II, range unlimited. His probable destination is unknown.

Escapee is not considered dangerous. He possesses low-grade intelligence and has no psi ability higher than Class F.

Kindly notify Philoy JRC immediately upon detention.

The major league baseball season of 1998 was only two weeks old, and Manager Pops Poppinger wished it were over and done with. Since opening day his Pirates had managed to lose fourteen games while winning none, and Pops had only the Baseball Managers' Tenure Act of 1993 to thank for the fact that he was still gainfully employed. As a matter of fact, he had that same Act to thank for his regular paychecks during the 1996 and 1997 seasons.

"But it can't last," he muttered. "Congress will repeal the thing and cite me as the reason."

He strode through the locker room without a glance at his loung-
ing ballplayers, entered his private office, and slammed the door.
He did not want to talk to anyone, especially if that anyone happened to be wearing a Pirate uniform. He dropped an armful of
newspapers onto his desk, tilted back in his chair until he could get
his size-thirteen feet in a comfortable position, and opened the top
paper to the sports pages. The headline made him wince. "When
Is a Pirate?" it demanded. Pop stuck a cigar in his mouth as he
read and forgot to light it.

"In the venerable days of yore," the article said, "when professional athletic organizations found it necessary to attach themselves to some unfortunate city in the mistaken belief that civic
loyalty would induce the population to attend games in person and
pay for the privilege, the fair city of Pittsburgh spawned two notable gangs of thieves, the baseball Pirates and the football Steelers.
Both organizations had their days of glory. The record book says,
if you care to believe it, that back in the seventies the Pirates won
five consecutive world championships and the Steelers four.

"Those days of myth and fable are far behind us. If the Steelers
stole anything during the football season just concluded, it escaped
this writer's attention. The 1998 Pirates are so far removed from
thievery that they will not take a game as a gift. They emphatically
demonstrated their moral uprightness yesterday, when their opposition was stricken with that most tragic of baseball diseases,
paralytic generosity. The Dodgers committed six errors and presented the Pirates with nine unearned runs. The Dodgers won, 27
to 9."

Pops carefully folded the paper and tossed it over his shoulder.
"Bah!" he said, "Let 'em rave. It's for sure I ain't got any ballplayers, but I got lots of tenure."

The telephone rang, and he picked it up and growled a response.

"Who's pitching today, Pops?" a cheerful voice asked.

"I dunno," Pops said. "If you find some guy up there in the
press box that ain't got a sore arm, send him down."

He slammed down the phone and reached for another paper.
"Pirates Still in Reverse," a headline said. Pops tossed that one
aside without reading it.

A knock rattled the door, and it opened wide enough to admit
the large, grinning face of Dipsey Marlow, the Pirates' third-base
coach.

"Scram!" Pops snapped.

"Some kid here to see you, Pops."

"Tell him I got a bat boy. I got a whole team of bat boys."

"He's older than that—I think. He's got a letter for you."

Pop straightened up and grinned. "From Congress?"

"It's from Pete Holloway."

"Send him in."

The kid shuffled in awkwardly. His dimensions looked to be about five feet five inches—in both directions. Oddly enough, he was not fat—in fact, there was an unhealthy thinness about his freckled face, and his overly large ears gave his features a whimsical grotesqueness—but he was shaped like a box, and he moved like one. He dragged to a stop in front of Pops's desk, fumbled through four pockets, and came up with a letter.

"Mr. Poppinger?"

The high, squeaky voice made Pops's ears ring. "I'm ashamed to admit it," Pops said, "but that's my name."

"Mr. Holloway told me to give this to you."

"The last I heard of Pete Holloway, he was lost in the woods up in Maine."

"He still is, sir. I mean, he's still in Maine."

"You came clear out here to California just to give me this?"

"Yes, sir."

Pops took the envelope and ripped it open.

"Dear Pops," he read. "This here kid Zilo is the most gawdawful ballplayer I ever see on two legs. He is also the luckiest man south of the North Pole. Put him in center with a rocking chair and a bottle of beer and every ball hit to the outfield will drop in his lap. He'll even catch some of them. Sign him, and you'll win the pennant. Yours, Pete. P.S. He is also lucky with the bat."

Pops scratched his head and squinted unbelievingly at Zilo. "What d'ya play?"

"Outfield," Zilo said. He quickly corrected himself. "Outfield, sir."

"Where in the outfield?"

"Anywhere, sir. Just so it's the outfield, sir."

Pops wasn't certain whether he should throw him out or go along with the gag. "I got three outfielders that get by. How about second or short? Between first and third I got nothing but grass."

"Oh, no, sir. Mr. Holloway had me play short, and I made nine errors in one inning. Then he moved me to the outfield."

"I'm surprised he didn't kill you," Pops said. "But you played ball for Pete?"

"Yes, sir. Last summer, sir. I went to see him a week ago to find out when I could start playing again, and he said he thought you could use me because your season started before his did."

What'd you bat?''

"Six forty, sir.''

Pops winced. "What'd you field?''

"A thousand, sir. In the outfield. It was—zero, in the infield.''

Pops got up slowly. "Son, Pete Holloway is an old friend of mine, and he never gave me a bad tip yet. I'll give you a tryout.''

"That's very kind of you, sir.''

"The name is Pops. And it ain't kind of me after what happened yesterday.''

Pops was standing in the corner of the dugout with Ed Schwartz, the club secretary, when the new Pirate walked out onto the field. Pops took one look, clapped his hand to his forehead, and gasped, "My God!''

"I told you I'd find him a uniform,'' Ed said. "I didn't guarantee to find him one that fit. He just isn't made the way our uniforms are made, and if I were you I'd make sure I wanted to keep him before I called the tailor. Otherwise, if you release him we'll have a set of uniforms on our hands that won't fit anyone or anything except maybe that oversized water cooler in the league offices.''

Pops walked over to the third-base coaching box, where Dipsey Marlow was standing to watch batting practice. The Dodger dugout had just got its first incredulous look at Zilo, and Pops waited until the uproar subsided somewhat before he spoke.

"Think Pete is pulling my leg?'' he asked.

"It wouldn't be like Pete, but it's possible.''

"The way things is going, he ought to know better. I'll look him up when the season is over and shoot him.''

Dipsey grinned happily. He was rather pleased with himself in spite of yesterday's loss. As third-base coach he'd been the loneliest man in the Western Hemisphere for seven straight days while the Pirates were being shut out without a man reaching third. Even if his team was losing, he liked to have some traffic to direct.

"You got nothing to lose but ball games,'' he said.

Zilo had taken his place in the batter's box. He cut on the first pitch, and the ball dribbled weakly out toward the pitcher's mound.

"He's a fly swatter,'' Dipsey said disgustedly.

Zilo poked two more lazy ground balls back at the pitcher and lifted a pop fly to the third baseman. Apparently satisfied, he borrowed a glove and wandered out to left field. He dropped a couple of balls that were hit right at him and stumbled over his own feet trying to reach one a few steps to his left.

"It's a joke," Pops said. "Pete must have seen him catch one. That's what he means by him being lucky."

Dipsey walked out to left field to talk with Zilo. He came back looking foolish. "The kid says it's all right—he's just testing the atmosphere, or something like that. It'll be different when the game starts."

"He says he hit six forty," Pops said dreamily.

"You going to use him?"

"Sure I'll use him. If I'm gonna shoot Pete, I gotta have a reason that'll stand up in court. As soon as we get ten runs behind, in he goes."

Pops headed back toward the dugout, and the tourists in the grandstand lifted a lusty chorus of boos. Pops scowled and ducked into the dugout out of sight. The dratted tourists were ruining the game. There had been a time when a manager could concentrate on what he was doing, but now he had to operate with a mob of howling spectators literally hanging over his shoulder and shouting advice and criticism into his ears. It got on the players' nerves, too. There was the Giants' Red Cowan, who'd been a good pitcher until they opened the game to tourists. The noise so rattled him that he had to retire.

"Why can't they stay home and see it on TV, like everybody else?" Pops growled.

"Because they pay money, that's why," Ed Schwartz said. "There's a novelty or something in seeing a ball game in the flesh, and it's getting so some of these tourists are planning their vacations so they can take in a few games. Bill Willard—you know, the L.A. *Times* man—he was saying that the National League is now California's number-one tourist attraction. The American League is doing the same thing for Arizona."

"I don't mind their watching," Pops said, "if only they'd keep their mouths shut. When I started managing there wasn't anyone around during a game except the TV men, and they were too busy to be giving me advice. Even the sportswriters watched on TV. Now they camp here the whole season, and you can't go out after the morning paper without finding one waiting for an interview."

"The tourists are here to stay, so you might as well get used to them. There's even some talk about putting up hotels for them, so they won't have to commute from Fresno to see the games."

Pops sat down and borrowed Ed's pen to make out his lineup. Ed looked over his shoulder and asked, "How come you're not using that new guy?"

"I'm saving him," Pops said, "until we get far enough behind."

"You mean until the second inning?" Ed said, and ducked as Pops fired a catcher's mask.

"That's the trouble with these tenure laws," Pops said. "They had to go and include the club secretaries."

The game started off in a way sadly familiar to Pops. The Dodgers scored three runs in the first inning and threatened to blast the Pirates right out of the league. Then, with the bases loaded and one out, the Pirate third baseman managed to hang on to a sizzling line drive and turn it into a double play. Pop's breathing spell lasted only until the next inning. Lefty Effinger, the Pirate pitcher, spent a long afternoon falling out of one hole into another. In nine innings he gave up a total of seventeen hits, but a miraculous sequence of picked-off runners, overrun bases and double plays kept the Dodgers shut out after those first three runs.

In the meantime, Dodger pitcher Rube Ruster was having one of his great days. He gave up a scratch single in the second and a walk in the fourth, and by the ninth inning he had fanned twelve, to the gratification of the hooting, jeering tourists.

The last of the ninth opened with Ruster striking out the first two Pirates on six pitches, and the Pirates in the dugout started sneaking off to the dressing room. Then first baseman Sam Lyle ducked away from an inside pitch that hit his bat and blooped over the infield for a single. Pops called for the hit-and-run, and the next batter bounced the ball at the Dodger shortstop. The shortstop threw it into right field, and the runners reached second and third. Ruster, pacing angrily about the mound, walked the next batter on four pitches.

Pops jumped from the dugout and called time. "Hit six forty, did he?" he muttered, and yelled, "Zilo!"

The beaming Zilo jumped up from the far end of the bench. "Yes, sir?"

"Get out there and hit!"

"Yes, sir!"

He shuffled toward the plate, and the uproar sent up by the tourists rocked the grandstand. Dipsey Marlow called time again and hurried over to the dugout.

"You off your rocker? We got a chance to win this one."

"I know," Pops said.

"Then get that thing out of there and use a left-hander."

"Look," Pops said, "you know derned well the way Ruster is pitching we're lucky to get a loud foul off of him. That hit was luck, and the error was luck, and the base on balls happened only because Ruster got mad. He'll cool off now, and the only thing that keeps this going is luck. Pete says the kid's lucky, and I want some of it.''

Marlow turned on his heel and stalked back to the coaching box.

Ruster coiled up and shot a bullet at home plate. Zilo swatted at it awkwardly—and popped it up.

The second baseman backed up three steps, waved the rest of the infield away, and got ready to end the game. The Pirate base runners, running furiously with two out, came down the stretch from third in a mournful procession. Zilo loped along the base path watching the Dodger second baseman and the ball.

The ball reached the top of its arc and suddenly seemed to carry. The second baseman backed confidently into position, changed his mind, and backed up again. Suddenly he whirled and raced toward center field with his eyes on the misbehaving ball. The center fielder was jogging toward the infield, and he picked up speed and came at a rush. The second baseman leaped for the ball. The center fielder dived for it. Neither man touched it, and they went down in a heap as the ball frolicked away.

The lumbering Zilo crossed home plate before the startled right fielder could retrieve the ball. The Pirates had won, four to three, and they hoisted Zilo to their shoulders and bore him off to the dressing room. The Dodgers quitted the field to an enthusiastic chorus of boos.

Pops went to the Dodger dugout to claim the ball. When he returned he found Dipsey Marlow still standing in his third-base coaching box staring vacantly toward the outfield.

"Luck," Pops said and gently led him away.

Rodney Wilks, the Pirates' brisk little president, flew over from L.A. that evening and threw a victory celebration in the ultramodern building that housed the National League offices. All of the players were there, and those who had families brought them. Women and children congregated in one room and the men in another. Champagne and milk flowed freely in both rooms.

National League President Edgar Rysdale looked in on the party briefly but approvingly. A team in a slump was bad for all the teams—bad for the league. When the race was a good one, fans frequently paid a double TV fee, watching two games at once or, if they had only one set, switching back and forth. If one team was floundering, National League fans would watch only one game. They might even patronize the American League. So the victory pleased the league president and also the other owners, who stopped by to sample the champagne and talk shop with Wilks.

Even Fred Carter, the Dodger manager, did not seem mournful, though Zilo's freak pop fly had ruined a nine-game winning streak for him. He backed Pops into a corner and said with a grin, "I been watching pop flies for thirty-five years, and I never saw one act like that. Did the kid magnetize his bat, or something?"

Pops shrugged. "I been watching baseball forty-five years, and I see something new seven times a week."

"Just the same, the next time that kid comes up I pass out the butterfly nets. He don't look like much of a hitter. Where'd you get him?"

"Pete Holloway sent him out."

Carter arched his eyebrows. "He must have something then."

"Pete says he ain't got a thing except luck."

"Isn't that enough? Think I'll go over and watch the Reds and Giants. Want to come?"

"Nope. Now that I finally won one, I'm gonna get some sleep tonight."

Pops saw Ed Schwartz talking to Zilo, and he went over to see what line the club secretary might be handing out. Ed was talking about the old days, and Zilo was listening intently, his dark eyes sparkling.

"Each team had its own city," Ed said, "and its own ball park. Think of the waste involved. There were twenty-four teams in each league, forty-eight parks, and even during the playing season they were in use only half the time, when the teams were playing at home. And the season lasted only six months. And there was all that traveling. We froze one day in Montreal and baked the next in New Orleans. Our hotel bill for the season used to look like the national debt, not to mention the plane fares. It was rough on the players in other ways. They only saw their families when they were playing at home, and just as they got settled somewhere they'd be traded and maybe have to move clear across the country—only to be traded again the next season or even next week. Putting the entire league in one place solved everything. The climate is wonderful, and we almost never have a game postponed because of bad weather. We're down to eight teams in a league, which anyway is as many as the fans can keep track of. We have two fields, and they're used twice a day, for two afternoon and two night games. Each team has its own little community. Baseball, Cal., is growing, boy, and lots of players are settling here permanently and buying their own homes. You'll want to, too. It's a wonderful place."

"It's a soft place for club secretaries," Pops growled. "Ed used to have to worry about baggage, plane schedules, hotel reservations and a million and one other things. Now all he has to do is get the equipment moved a couple of hundred yards from one park to the other, now and then, and he gripes about it. Has he stopped talking long enough to get you settled?"

"Oh, yes, sir," Zilo said. "I'm rooming with Jerry Fargo."

"All right. Come out early tomorrow. You gotta learn to catch a fly ball without getting hit on the head."

Dipsey Marlow nudged Pops's arm and pulled him aside. "Going to play him tomorrow?"

"Might. We could use a little luck every day."

"I been listening to the big boys. Know what they're going to do? Put up a flock of temporary stands at World Series time. They think they might get fifteen thousand people out here for every game."

"That's their business," Pops said.

"Just tell me why anyone wants to take a trip and pay a stiff price to see a ball game when he can sit at home in his easy chair and see it for fifty cents?"

"People are funny," Pops said. "Sometimes they're almost as funny as ballplayers."

President Wilks came over and placed a full glass in Pops's hand. Pops sipped the champagne and grimaced. "It's all right, I guess, but it'll never take the place of beer."

"Finish in first division," Wilks said, "and I'll buy you enough beer to take you through the off season."

Pops grinned. "How about putting that in my contract?"

"I will," Wilks promised. "Do you want it in bottles or kegs?"

"Both."

"I'll take care of it first thing in the morning." He grinned and prodded Pops in the ribs, but behind the grin his expression was anxious. "Do you think we have a chance?"

"Too early to say. Sure, we only won one out of fifteen, but we're only ten games out of first. We been looking like a bunch of school kids, and if we keep that up we finish last. If we snap out of it—well, the season's got a long way to go."

"I hope you snap out of it," Wilks said. "Managers have tenure, but presidents haven't."

Pops found a bottle of beer to kill the taste of the champagne, and he made a quiet exit after instructing Marlow to get the players home to bed at a reasonable hour. The National League's two playing fields were a blaze of light, and the shouts of the two

crowds intermingled. There seemed to be a lot of tourists in attendance—and tourists at night games made even less sense than
tourists at afternoon games. It'd be nine or ten o'clock before some
of them got back to their hotels. Pops walked slowly back to Pi-
rateville, grumbling to himself. The large mansion designed for the
manager Pops had turned over to Dipsey Marlow, who needed
space for his eight kids. Pops lived in a small house a short distance
down the street. His middle-aged daughter Marge kept house for
him, and she was already in bed. She didn't like baseball.

PRIORITY RATING: Routine.
FROM: Jard Killil, Minister of Juvenile Affairs.
TO: All Planetary Police Organizations, Sectors 1247, 2162,
889, 1719,
All Interplanetary Patrol Units, Sectors 1247, 2162, 889,
1719.
SUBJECT: Juvenile Detention Escapee Muko Zilo.
REFERENCE: Previous memorandum of 13B927D8 and enclosures.
Information from several sources indicates that an uniden-
tified ship, possibly that of Escapee Zilo, traveled on a course
roughly parallel to Trade Route 79B, which would take it into
or through your sectors. Because of the time elapsed since his
escape, it is assumed that Zilo has found an effective planetary
hiding place. Immediate investigation requested. Escapee is
not—repeat: not—dangerous.
Kindly notify Philoy JRC immediately upon detention.

Pops opened a three-game series against the Cubs with Zilo in
left field. He figured the youngster would do the least damage
there, since he was pitching Simp Simpson, his best right-hander,
and the Cubs had seven left-handed batters in their lineup. At least
that much of his strategy worked. In the first six innings only two
balls were hit to left. One was a line drive single that Zilo bobbled
for an error as the runner reached second. The other was a foul fly
on which Zilo seemed about to make a miraculous catch until his
feet got tangled and spilled him. At the plate he waved his bat
futilely and struck out twice while the Cubs were taking a five-run
lead.

In the last of the sixth the Pirates got men on first and second,
and it was Zilo's turn to bat. Dipsey Marlow called time, and as
the tourists hooted impatiently he strode back to the dugout.
"Take him out," he said.

"Why?" Pops asked. "He's still batting .333. That's better than anyone else on this team."

"You gotta understand this luck thing. Yesterday it was luck to put him in. Today it's luck to take him out. I found a spider in my locker today, and that means . . ."

"Hit and run on the first pitch," Pops said.

Zilo fanned the air lustily and dribbled a grounder toward the first baseman. Suddenly it took an unaccountable eight-foot bounce over his head and rolled into the outfield, picking up speed. Zilo pulled up at first, breathing heavily, and two runners scored.

Sam Lyle followed with a lazy fly ball to right. Zilo moved off first base and halted to watch the progress of the ball. The right fielder seemed to be having difficulties. He wandered about shading his eyes, backed up, finally lost the ball in the sun. The center fielder had come over fast, and he shouted the right fielder away, backed up slowly, and finally turned in disgust to watch the ball drop over the fence. Lyle trailed the floundering Zilo around the bases, and the score was 5 to 4.

Three fast outs later, Dipsey Marlow returned to the dugout and squeezed in beside Pops. "I take it all back," he said. "I won't argue with you again the rest of the season. But this spider of mine . . ."

Pops cupped his hands and shouted, "Let's HOLD 'em now. Let's WIN this one!"

" . . . this spider of mine was in my sweat shirt, and my old mother always used to say spider in your clothes means money. Will the players get a cut of what those fifteen thousand tourists pay to watch a series game?"

"We got two hundred and twenty-four games to go," Pops said. "After this one. Get to work and pick us off a sign or two."

In the eighth inning Zilo got a rally started with a pop fly that three infielders chased futilely. He moved to second on a ground ball that took a bad hop and scored on a soft line drive that curved sharply and landed between the outfielders. The Pirates pushed over two more runs on hits that were equally implausible and took a two-run lead into the ninth.

The Cubs came back with a vengeance. The first two batters lashed out sizzling singles. Pops prodded his bullpen into action and went out to talk with Simpson. They stood looking down at the next Cub batter, the burly catcher Bugs Rice.

"Don't let him pull one," Pops said.

"He won't pull one," Simp said determinedly through clenched teeth.

Rice did not pull one. He didn't have to. He unloaded on the first pitch and drove it far, far away into left field, the opposite field. Pops sat down with the crack of the bat and covered his face with his hands.

"Now we gotta come from behind again," he moaned. "And we won't. I know we ain't *that* lucky."

Suddenly the men on the bench broke into excited cheers and a scattering of applause came from the tourists. Pops looked up, saw runners on second and third, saw the scoreboard registering one out.

"What happened?" he yelped.

"Zilo caught it," Dipsey Marlow said. "Didn't think he had it in him, but he backed up to the fence and made a clean catch. Took so much time getting the ball back to the infield that the runners had time to touch up and advance, but he caught it."

"He didn't. I know a homer when I see one, and that ball was gone. I can tell by the way it sounds and I can tell by the way it leaves the bat. I heard that one, and I saw it go. It should have cleared the fence by twenty feet."

"Your eyes aren't as young as they used to be. Zilo caught it against the fence."

Pops shook his head. He huddled down in a corner of the dugout while Simpson fanned one batter and got another on a tap to the infield and the Pirates had won two in a row.

That was the beginning. The Pirates pushed their winning streak to twelve, lost one, won eight more. They were twenty and fifteen and in fourth place. Zilo became something of a national sensation. Lucky Zilo Fan Clubs sprang up across the country, and he kept his batting average around the .450 mark and even got another home run when a solid fly ball to the outfield took crazy bounces in nineteen directions while Zilo lumbered around the bases. The rest of the team took courage and started playing baseball.

But not even a Lucky Zilo could lift the Pirates above fourth place. Pops's pitching staff was a haphazard assortment of aching, overage veterans and unpredictable, inexperienced youths. One day they would be unhittable, the next day they'd be massacred; and Pops found to his sorrow that luck was no answer to a nine-teen-run deficit. Still, the season drifted along with the Pirates holding desperately to fourth, and Pops began to think they might even stay there.

Then Zilo sprained his ankle. The trainer outfitted him with crutches and applied every known remedy and a few unknown ones that Zilo suggested himself, but the ankle failed to respond.

"It beats me," the trainer said to Pops. "Things that should make it better seem to make it worse."

"How long will he be out?" Pops asked gloomily.

"I won't even guess. The way its reacting, it could last him a lifetime."

Pops breathed a profane farewell to first division.

Zilo hobbled to every game on his crutches and watched with silent concentration from a box behind the dugout. Oddly enough, for a time the team's luck continued. Ground balls took freakish bounces, fly balls responded to unlikely air currents, and on some days opposition pitchers suffered such a loss of control that they would occasionally wander in and stare at home plate as though to assure themselves that it was still there. Ollie Richards, the Reds' ace and one of the best control pitchers in either league, walked seventeen men in three innings and left the game on the short end of a 6–3 score without having given up a hit.

Zilo's broad, good-natured face took on an unhealthy pallor. Wrinkles furrowed his brow, and his eyes held a tense, haunted look. As the team's luck began to fade, he grew increasingly irritable and despondent. On the day they slipped to fifth place, he met Pops after the game and asked, "Could I speak with you, sir?"

"Sure," Pops said. "Come along."

Pops held the door as Zilo swung through on his crutches. He got the youngster seated and settled back with his own feet propped up on his desk. "Ankle any better?"

"I'm afraid not, sir."

"Takes time, sometimes."

"Sir," Zilo said. "I know I'm not a good ballplayer. Like they say, I'm just lucky. Maybe this will be the only season I'll play."

"I wouldn't say that," Pops said. "You're young. Luck has took a lot of men a long way in baseball."

"Anyway, sir, I like to play, even if I'm not good. And I'd like to have us win the pennant and play in the World Series."

"Wouldn't mind having another winner myself before I retire."

"What I'd like to do, sir, is go home for a while. I think I could get my ankle fixed up there, and I'd like to bring back some friends who could help us."

Pops was amused. "Ballplayers?"

"I think they'd be better than I am, sir. Or luckier, maybe. Do you—would you give them a trial?"

"I'd give anyone a trial," Pops said seriously. "Mostly short-stops and second basemen and pitchers, but I'd have a look at anybody."

Zilo pushed himself erect on his crutches. "I'll get back as soon as I can."

"All right. But leave a little of that luck here, will you?"

Zilo turned and looked at Pops strangely. "I wish I could, sir. I really wish I could."

Ed Schwartz took Zilo to L.A. and put him on a plane for the East. For Maine. And at Baseball, Cal., the Pirates won two more games and went into a cataclysmic slump. They lost ten straight and slipped to sixth place. Pops put through a phone call to the Maine address Zilo had given him and was informed that there was no such place. Then he called Pete Holloway.

"I wondered what was happening to you," Pete said. "I haven't seen the kid. He dropped out of nowhere last summer and played a little sandlot ball for me. He never told me where he came from, but I don't think it was Maine. If he shows up again, I'll get in touch with you."

"Thanks," Pops said. He hung up slowly.

Ed Schwartz said thoughtfully, "I suppose I better get a detective on it."

"Detectives," Pops said and wearily headed for the field and another Pirate beating.

Two more weeks went by. The detectives traced Zilo to Maine, where he seemed to have vanished from the ken of mortal man. The Pirates were tottering on the brink of last place.

Then Pops received an airmail letter from Zilo—from Brazil.

"I got lost," he wrote plaintively. "We crashed in the jungle and they won't let us leave the country."

Pops called President Wilks into conference, and Wilks got on the phone to Washington. He knew enough of the right people to make the necessary arrangements and keep the matter out of the papers. Zilo was flown back on a chartered plane, and he brought four friends with him.

Ed Schwartz met them in L.A. and rushed them out to Baseball in President Wilks's own plane. They arrived during the fourth inning of another Pirate beating.

"How's the ankle?" Pops demanded.

Zilo beamed. "Just fine, sir."

"Get in there, then."

Zilo got his friends seated in the president's box and went out to loft a long fly ball over the fence for a home run. The Pirates came to life. Everyone hit, and a 10-to-0 drubbing was transformed like magic into a 25-to-12 victory.

After the game Zilo introduced his friends—as John Smith, Sam

Jones, Robert White, and William Anderson. Smith and Jones, Zilo said, were infielders. White and Anderson were pitchers.

Ed Schwartz took in their proportions with a groan and went to work on the uniform problem. Their builds were that of Zilo on a more lavish scale. They towered over Pops, answered his questions politely, and showed a childlike interest in all that went on about them.

Pops called one of his catchers over and introduced him to White and Anderson. "See what they got," he said.

He took Smith and Jones out for a little infield practice and watched goggle-eyed as they covered ground like jet-propelled gazelles and made breathtaking leaps to pull down line drives.

The catcher returned, drew Pops aside, and said awesomely, "They got curves that break three feet. They got sliders that do a little loop-the-loop and cross the plate twice. They got fast balls that I'm scared to catch. They got pitches that change speed four times between the mound and the plate. If you're figuring on pitching those guys, you can get yourself another catcher."

Pops turned the ceremony of signing them over to Ed Schwartz, handed releases to four players who weren't worth the space they were taking up on the bench, and went home to his first good night's sleep in more than a month.

> PRIORITY RATING: Urgent.
> FROM: Jard Killil, Minister of Juvenile Affairs.
> TO: All Planetary Police Organizations,
>   All Interplanetary Patrol Units.
> SUBJECT: Juvenile detention escapees.
> ENCLOSURES: Character analyses, film strips, retinal patterns.
>   All law-enforcement agencies are hereby informed of the escape of four inmates of the Juvenile Rehabilitation Center on Philoy, Raff III, Sector 1311. Escapees have high psi ratings and may use them dangerously. Kindly give this matter top priority attention and notify Philoy JRC immediately upon detention.

The next day Pops started Anderson against the Braves. The Pirates bounced forty hits over and through and around the infield and scored thirty-five runs. Anderson pitched a no-hit game and struck out twenty-seven. White duplicated the performance the following day. Thereafter Pops pitched them in his regular rotation. He wasn't sure whether they hypnotized everyone on the field or just the ball, but as Dipsey Marlow put it, they made the ball do everything but stop and back up.

Pops's other pitchers suddenly began to look like champions with Smith and Jones playing behind them. In spite of their boxlike builds, they ranged about the infield with all the agility of jackrabbits. No one ever measured how high they went up after line drives, but one sportswriter claimed they were a hazard to air traffic and should be licensed as aircraft. They sped far into the outfield after fly balls. Jones made more catches in right field than the right fielder, and it was not an unusual sight to see Jones and Smith far out in center contesting the right to a descending ball while the center fielder beat a hasty retreat. And both men swung murderous bats.

The Pirates had won fifty-seven games in a row and rewritten the record book when Zilo timidly knocked on the door of Pops's office. He was carrying a newspaper, and he looked disturbed.

"Sir," he said anxiously, "it says here that we're ruining baseball."

Pops chuckled. "They always say that when one team starts to pull away."

"But—is it true?"

"Well, now. If we kept on winning the way we are now, we wouldn't do the game any good. People like to see a close race, and if one team wins too much, or loses too much, a lot of people stop watching the games. And that ain't good. But don't let it worry you—we'll do our best to go on winning, but we'll drop a few, one of these days, and things will go back to normal. Your friends been playing over their heads and we've been luckier than usual. That can't last forever."

"I see," Zilo said thoughtfully.

That evening Pops ruefully wished he'd kept his big mouth shut. Talking about a slump when you're winning . . .

Anderson got knocked out in the first inning and lost his first game. White failed the next day, and the Pirates dropped five straight. Then they got off on another winning streak, but the talk about their ruining the game had quieted down. Pops never bothered to remind Zilo how right he'd been. He wasn't going to jinx the team again.

"Those baseball players of yours," his daughter said to him one evening. "You know—the funny-looking ones."

"Sure, I know," Pops said. "What about 'em?"

"They're supposed to be pretty good, aren't they?"

Pops grinned wickedly. "Pretty fair." It would have been a waste of time referring Marge to the record book—or what was left of it now.

"I was over at the bowling alley with Ruth Wavel, and they were there bowling. They had everybody excited."

"How'd they do?"

"I guess they must be pretty good at that, too. They knocked all the pins over."

Pops grinned again. Marge's idea of a sport was crossword puzzles, and she could go through an entire season without seeing a single game. "Nothing unusual about that," he said. "Happens all the time."

She seemed surprised. "Does it? The people there thought it was something special."

"Someone was pulling your leg. How many strikes did they get?"

"How many what?"

"How many times did they knock all the pins down?"

"I didn't count them. They knocked all of them down every time. All evening. It was the first time they'd ever bowled, too."

"Natural athletic ability," Pops muttered. He was thinking that they'd never played baseball before, either, except that Zilo told him he'd been coaching them. The more he thought about it, the odder it seemed, but he was not one to argue with no-hit games and home runs and sensational fielding plays. No manager would argue with those.

TO ALL SHIPS OF THE SPACE NAVY SECTORS 2161, 2162, 2163. GENERAL ALERT: Five escapees Juvenile Rehabilitation Center Philoy Raff III, piloting stolen space yacht Stellar Class II, range unlimited, have been traced through Sector 2162. Destination unsurveyed quadrant C97. Contact base headquarters Sector 2162 for patrol assignments. Acknowledge. Zan, First Admiral.

The season leveled into a five-team race for first place. The Pirates stayed in first or second, playing either with unbelievable brilliance or with incredible ineptitude. Pops took the race stoically and shrugged off the tourist hysteria that enveloped Baseball, Cal. He was doing so much better than he had thought possible in his wildest moments of pre-season optimism that it really didn't matter where he finished. He was a cinch to be Manager of the Year. He might add a pennant and a World Series, or he might not. It didn't matter.

Another season might see him in last place again, and a smart manager quit when he was ahead—especially when he was well along in his sixties. Pops called a news conference and announced his retirement at the end of the season.

"Before or after the World Series?" a reporter asked.

"No comment," Pops said.

The club owners erected their World Series stands early and the tourists jammed them—fifteen thousand for every game. Pops wondered where they came from. National League President Rysdale wandered about smiling fondly over the daily television receipts, and President Wilks sent Pops a load of beer that filled his basement.

Over in Baseball, Arizona, the American League officials were glum. The Yankees, who were mainly distinguished for having finished last more frequently than any other team in major league history, had suddenly and inexplicably opened up a twenty-game lead, and nobody cared any longer what happened in the American League.

"Three weeks to go," Pops told his team. "What d'ya say we wrap this thing up?"

"Right!" Zilo said happily.

"Right!" Smith, Jones, Anderson and White chorused.

The Pirates started on another winning streak.

TO ALL SHIPS OF THE SPACE NAVY PATROLLING UNSURVEYED QUADRANT C97: Prepare landing parties for planetary search. This message your authorization to investigate any planet with civilization at level 10 or below. Contact with civilizations higher than level 10 forbidden. Space intelligence agents will be furnished each ship to handle high-civilization planets. Acknowledge. Zan, First Admiral.

The last week of the season opened with the Pirates in first place, five games ahead of the Dodgers. A provident schedule put the Dodgers and Pirates in a three-game series. The league hastily erected more stands, and with twenty-two thousand howling tourists in attendance and half of Earth's population watching on TV, White and Anderson put together no-hit games and the Pirate batters demolished the Dodger pitching staff. The Pirates took all three games.

Pops felt enormously tired, and relieved that it was finished. He had won his pennant and he didn't see how he could lose the World Series. But he had never felt so old.

President Wilks threw another champagne party, and the sportswriters backed Pops into a corner and fired questions.

"How about retirement, Pops? Still going through with it?"

"I've gone through with it."

"Is it true that Dipsey Marlow will take your place?"

"That's up to the front office. They ain't asked my opinion."

"What if they did ask your opinion?"

"I'd faint."

"Who'll start the Series? Anderson or White?"

"I'll flip a coin," Pops said. "It don't matter. Either of them could pitch all thirteen games and not feel it."

"Does that mean you'll go all the way with just Anderson and White?"

"I'll use four starters, like I have most of the season."

"Going to give the Yankees a sporting chance, eh?"

"No comment," Pops said.

President Wilks and League President Rysdale rescued him from the reporters and took him to Rysdale's private office.

"We have a proposal from the American League," Rysdale said. "We'd like to know what you think of it, and what you think the players would think of it. They want to split up the Series and play part of the games here and part of them in Arizona. They think it would stir up more local interest."

"I wouldn't like it," Pops said. "What's wrong with the way it is now? Here one year, there the next year, it's fair to both sides. What do they want to do—travel back and forth between games?"

"We'd start out with four games here, and then play five in Arizona and the last four back here. Next year we'd start out with four in Arizona. It used to be done that way years ago."

"I know," Pops said. "But I like it better the way it is. One ball park is just like another, so why change around?"

"They think we would draw more tourists that way. As far as we're concerned, we're drawing capacity crowds now. It might make a difference in Arizona, because there are fewer population centers there."

"They just thought of it because it's in California this year," Pops said. "Next year they'd want to change it back."

"That's a thought," Rysdale said. "I think I'll tell them it's too late to change, but we might consider it for next year. That'll give us time to figure all the angles."

"Good," Pops said. "Next year you can play in Brazil, for all I care."

In the hallway Pops encountered half a dozen of his players crowding around infielder Jones. "What's up?" he asked Dipsey Marlow.

"Just some horsing around. They were practicing high jumps, and Jones cleared nine feet."

"So?"

"That's a world record by six inches. I looked it up."

> TO JARD KILLIL, MINISTER OF JUVENILE AFFAIRS: Spaceship presumed that of JRC escapees found down in jungle unsurveyed quadrant C97. Planet has type 17D civilization. Intelligence agents call situation critical. Am taking no action pending receipt of further instructions. Requesting Ministry take charge and assume responsibility. Zan, First Admiral.

Pops retired early the night before the Series opened, having ordered his players to do the same. Marge was out somewhere, but Pops left the night light on and went to bed. He didn't sleep, but he was relaxing comfortably when she came in an hour later.

She marched straight through the house and into his bedroom. "Those ballplayers of yours—the funny-looking ones—they were at the bowling alley."

Pops took a deep breath. "They were?"

"They'd been drinking!"

Pops sat up and reached for his shoes. "You don't say."

"And they were bowling, only—they weren't bowling. They'd pretend to throw the ball but they wouldn't throw it, and the pins would fall down anyway. The manager was mad."

"No doubt," Pops said, pulling on his trousers.

"They wouldn't tell anyone how they did it, but every time they waved the ball all the pins would fall down. They'd been drinking."

"Maybe that's how they did it," Pops said, slipping into his shirt.

"How?"

"By drinking."

He headed for the bowling alley on a dead run. The place was crowded with players from other teams, American and National leagues, and quite a few sportswriters were around. The writers headed for Pops, and he shoved them aside and found the manager. "Who was it?" he demanded.

"Those four squares of yours. Jones, Smith, Anderson, White."

"Zilo?"

"No. Zilo wasn't here."

"Did they make trouble?"

"Not the way you mean. They didn't get rough, though I had a time getting them away from the alleys. They left maybe ten minutes ago.''

"Thanks," Pops said.

"When you find them, ask them how they pulled that gag with the pins. They were too drunk to tell me.''

"I got some other things to ask them," Pops said.

He pushed through to a phone booth and called Ed Schwartz.

"I'll take care of it," Ed said. "Don't worry about a thing."

"Sure. I won't worry about a thing."

"They may be back at their rooms by now, but we won't take any chances. I'll handle it.''

"I'll meet you there," Pops said.

He slipped out a side door and headed for Bachelor's Paradise, the house where unmarried Pirates lived with a couple of solicitous houseboys to look after them. All the players were in bed—except Smith, Jones, Anderson, White and Zilo. The others knew nothing except that Zilo had been concerned about his friends' absence and had gone looking for them.

"You go home," Ed said. "I'll find them."

Pops paced grimly back and forth, taking an occasional kick at the furniture. "You find them," he said, "and I'll fine them.''

He went home to bed, but he did not sleep. Twice during the night he called Ed Schwartz, and Ed was out. Pops finally reached him at breakfast time, and Ed said, trying to be cheerful, "No news is supposed to be good news, and that's what I have. No news. I couldn't find a trace of them.''

The reporters had picked up the story, of course, and their headlines mocked Pops over his coffee: PIRATE STARS MISSING!

Ed Schwartz had notified both President Wilks and President Rysdale, and the league president had called in the FBI. By ten o'clock police in every city in the country and a number of cities in other countries were keeping their eyes open for missing Pirates. And they remained missing.

When Pops reached the field for a late-morning workout there was still no word. He banned newsmen from the field and dressing room, told Lefty Effinger he might have to start, and went around trying to cheer up his players. The players remembered only too well their fourteen-game losing streak at the beginning of the season and the collapse that followed Zilo's departure. The gloom hung so thickly in the dugout that if Pops could have thought of a market for it he'd have bottled and sold it.

An hour before game time, Pops was called to the telephone. It was Ed Schwartz, calling from L.A. "I found them," he said. "They're on their way back. They'll be there in plenty of time."

"Good," Pops said.

"Bad. They're still pretty high—all except Zilo. I don't know if you can use them, but that's your problem."

Pops slammed down the phone.

"Did they find 'em?" Dipsey Marlow asked.

"Found 'em dead drunk."

Marlow rubbed his hands together. "Just let me at 'em. Ten minutes, and I'll have 'em dead sober. I've had experience."

"I dunno," Pops said. "These guys may not react like you'd expect."

The delinquent players were delivered with time to spare, and Marlow went to work enthusiastically. He started by shoving them into a cold shower, fully dressed. Zilo stood looking on anxiously.

"I'm sorry," he said to Pops. "I'd have stopped them, but they went off without me. And they never had any of that alcohol before and they didn't know what it would do to them."

"That's all right," Pops said. "It wasn't your fault."

Zilo had tears in his eyes. "Do you think they can play?"

"Leave 'em to me," Marlow said. "I'm just getting started." But when he emerged later he looked both confused and frustrated. "I just don't know," he said. "They tell me they're all right, and they look all right, but I think they're still drunk."

"Can they play?" Pops asked anxiously.

"They can walk a straight line. I won't say how long a straight line. I suppose you got nothing to lose by playing them."

"There ain't much else I can do," Pops said. "I could start Effinger, but what would I use for infielders?"

There is something about a World Series. Even Pops, who had seen every one for forty-five years as player, manager, or spectator, felt a momentary thrill and a clutching emptiness in his stomach as he moved to the top step of the dugout and looked out across the sunlit field. Along both foul lines the temporary stands were jammed with tourists. Beyond them areas were roped off for standees, and the "Standing Room Only" signs had been taken down hours before. There was no space left of any kind.

Ed Schwartz stood at Pop's elbow looking at the crowd. "What is it that's different about a hot dog when you buy it at a ball park?" he asked.

"Ptomaine," Pops growled.

Clutching his lineup, he strode toward home plate to meet the umpires and Yankee manager Bert Basom.

Basom grinned maliciously. "Your men well rested? I hear they keep late hours."

"They're rested well enough," Pops said.

A few minutes later, with the national anthem played and the flag raised, Pops watched critically as Anderson took his last warm-up pitches. He threw lazily, as he always did, and if he was feeling any aftereffects it wasn't evident to Pops.

But Anderson got off to a shaky start. The Yankees' lead-off man clouted a tremendous drive to left, but Zilo made one of his sensational lumbering catches. The second batter drove one through the box. Jones started after it, got his feet tangled, and fell headlong. Smith flashed over with unbelievable speed, gloved the ball, and threw to first—too late. Anderson settled down then and struck out the next two batters.

Zilo opened the Pirates' half of the first with one of his lucky hits, and Smith followed him with a lazy fly ball that cleared the fence. The Pirates led, 2–0.

The first pitch to Jones was a called strike. Jones whirled on the umpire, his big face livid with rage. His voice carried over the noise of the crowd. "You wouldn't know a strike zone if I measured it out for you!"

Pops started for home plate, and Jones saw him coming and meekly took his place in the box. Pops called time and went over to talk to Dipsey Marlow.

"Darned if I don't think he's still tight. Think I should lift him?"

"Let him bat," Marlow said. "Maybe he'll connect."

The pitcher wasted one and followed it with a curve that cut the outside corner. "Strike two!" the umpire called.

Jones's outraged bellow rattled the center-field fence. "What?" he shrieked. He stepped around the catcher and stood towering over the umpire. "Where's the strike zone? Where was the pitch?"

The umpire gestured patiently to show where the ball had crossed the plate. Pops started out of the dugout again. The umpire said brusquely, "Play ball!"

Still fuming, Jones moved back to the batter's box. His high-pitched voice carried clearly. "You don't even know where the strike zone is!"

The pitcher wound up again, and as the ball sped plateward Jones suddenly leaped into the air—and stayed there. He hovered six feet above the ground. The ball crossed the plate far below his dangling legs, was missed completely by the startled catcher, and bounced to the screen.

The umpire did not call the pitch. He took two steps forward and stood looking at Jones. The crowd came to its feet and players from both teams edged from their dugouts. A sudden paralyzed hush gripped the field.

"Come down here," the umpire called weakly.

"What'd you call that pitch? Strike, I suppose. Over the plate between my knees and armpits, wasn't it?"

"Come down here!"

"You can't make me!"

"Come down here!"

"You show me where it says in the rules that I have to bat with both feet on the ground."

The umpire moved down the third-base line and summoned his colleagues for a conference. Pops walked out to home plate, and Zilo followed him.

"Jones," Zilo said pleadingly.

"Go to hell," Jones said. "I know I'm right. I'm still in the batter's box."

"Please," Zilo pleaded. "You'll spoil everything. You've already spoiled everything."

"So what? It's about time we showed them how this game should be played."

"I'm taking you out, Jones," Pops said. "I'm putting in a pinch hitter. Get back to the dugout."

Jones shot up another four feet. "You can't make me."

The umpire returned. "I'm putting you out of the game," he said. "Leave the field immediately."

"I've already left the field."

Pops, Zilo and the umpire stood glaring up at Jones, who glared down at them. At that critical moment Smith took charge. He walked slowly to home plate, soared over the heads of those on the ground, and clouted Jones on the jaw. Jones descended heavily. Smith landed nearby, calmly drying his hands on his trousers.

Effective as his performance was, nobody noticed it. All eyes were on the sky, where a glistening tower of metal was dropping slowly toward the outfield. It came ponderously to rest on the outfield grass while the outfielders fled in panic. The crowd remained silent.

A port opened in the side of the looming tower, and a landing ramp came down. The solitary figure that emerged did not use the ramp. He stepped out into midair and drifted slowly toward the congregation at home plate. There he landed, a tremendous figure, square like Zilo and his friends but a startling eight feet tall, trimly uniformed in a lustrous brown with ribbons and braid in abundance.

Zilo, Jones, and Smith stood with downcast eyes while the others stared. Anderson and White moved from the dugout and moved forward haltingly. The stranger spoke one crisp sentence that nobody understood—nobody, that is, except Zilo, Jones, Smith, Anderson, and White.

Smith and Jones lifted slowly and floated out to the ship, where they disappeared through the port. Anderson and White turned obediently and trudged to the outfield to mount the ramp. Only Zilo lingered.

A few policemen moved nervously from the stands and surrounded the ship. The hush continued as the tourists stared and half of Earth's population watched on TV.

Pops looked from the ship to the lofty stranger to Zilo. Tears streaked Zilo's face.

"I'm sorry, Pops," Zilo said. "I hoped we could finish it off for you. I really wanted to win this World Series. But I'm afraid we'll have to go."

"Go where?" Pops asked absently.

"Where we came from. It's another world."

"I see. Then—then that's how come you guys played so well."

Zilo wiped his eyes and blubbered miserably. His big, good-natured face was in the throes of torment. "The others did," he sobbed. "I'm only a Class F telekinetic myself, and that isn't much where I come from. I guess you'd call me a moron. I did the best I could, but it was a terrible strain keeping the balls I hit away from the fielders and stopping balls from going over the fence and holding balls up until I could catch them. When I hurt my ankle I tried to help out from the bench, and it worked for a while. Sometimes I could even control the ball enough to spoil a pitcher's control, but usually when the ball was thrown fast or hit hard I couldn't do anything with it unless I was in the outfield and it had a long way to go. So I went back where I could get my ankle fixed, and I brought back the others. They're really good—all of them Class A. Anderson and White—those are just names I had them use—they could control the ball so well they made it look like they were pitching. And no matter how hard the ball was hit they could control it, even when they were sitting on the bench."

Pops scratched his head and said dazedly, "Made it *look* like they were pitching?"

"They just pretended to throw, and then they controlled the ball —well, mentally. Any good telekinetic could do it. They could have pitched just as well sitting on the bench as they did on the pitcher's mound, and they could help out when one of our other pitchers was pitching. And Smith and Jones are levitators. They could cover the ground real fast and go up as high as they wanted to. I had a terrible time keeping them from going too high and spoiling everything. I was going to bring a telepath, too, to steal signs and things, but the four were the only ones who'd come. But we did pretty good anyway. When we hit the ball Anderson and White could make it go anywhere they wanted, and they could control the balls the other team hit, and nothing could get past Smith and Jones unless we wanted it to. We could have won every game, but the papers said we were spoiling baseball, so we talked it over and decided to lose part of the time. We did the best we could. We won the pennant, and I hoped we would win this World Series, but they had to go and drink some of that alcohol, and I guess Jones would have spoiled everything even if we hadn't been caught.''

The stranger spoke another crisp sentence, and Zilo wiped the tears from his face and shook Pops's hand. "Good-bye, Pops," he said. "It was lots of fun. I really like this baseball."

He walked slowly out to the ship, passing the police without a glance, and climbed the ramp.

Reporters were edging out onto the field, and the stranger waved them back and spoke English in a booming voice. "You shall have a complete explanation at the proper time. It is now my most unpleasant duty to call upon your President to deliver the apologies of my government. Muko Zilo says he did the best he could. He did entirely too much."

He floated back to the ship. The ramp lifted, and the police scattered as the ship swished upward. The umpire-in-chief shrugged his shoulders and gestured with his mask. "Play ball!"

Pops beckoned to a pinch hitter, got a pitcher warming up to replace Anderson, and strode back to the dugout. "They been calling me a genius," he muttered to himself. "Manager of the Year they been calling me. And how could I lose?"

A sportswriter leaned down from the stands. "How about a statement, Pops?"

Pops spoke firmly. "You can say that the best decision I made this year was to resign."

An official statement was handed out in Washington before the game was over. That the Yankees won the game, 23–2, was irrelevant. No one cared, least of all the ballplayers.

PRIORITY RATING: Routine.
FROM: Jard Killil, Minister of Juvenile Affairs.

TO: Milz Woon, Minister of Justice.

SUBJECT: Escapees from the Juvenile Rehabilitation Center, Philoy, Raff III, Sector 1311.

A full report on the activity of these escapees has no doubt reached your desk. The consequences of their offense are so serious they have not yet been fully evaluated. Not only have these escapees forced us into premature contact with a Type 17D civilization for which neither we nor they were prepared, but our best estimate is that the escapees have destroyed a notable cultural institution of that civilization. I believe that their ages should not be used to mitigate their punishment. They are all juveniles, but they are nevertheless old enough to know right from wrong, and their only motive seems to be that they were enjoying themselves. I favor a maximum penalty.

Baseball, as students of the game never tired of pointing out, was essentially a game of records and statistics. The records were there for all to see—incredible records, with Jones and Smith tied with 142 home runs and batting above .500, with Anderson and White each hurling two dozen no-hit games, and with the strikeouts, and the extra base hits, and the double plays, and the games won, and the total bases, and the runs batted in, and the multitudinous individual and team records that the Pirates had marked up during the season. The record book was permanently maimed.

It was not the beginning of the end. It was the end.

Who had done all this? Four kids, four rather naughty kids, who, according to the strange man from outer space, were not especially bright. Four kids from another world, who had entered into a game requiring the ultimate in skill and intelligence and training and practice, entered into it without ever playing it before, and made the best adult ballplayers the planet Earth could offer look like a bunch of inept Little Leaguers.

The records could be thrown out, but they could not be forgotten. And it could not be forgotten that the four kids had made those records when they weren't half trying—because they didn't want to make Earth's ballplayers look too bad.

Supposing—just supposing—the people from outer space were to send a team made up of intelligent adults? No one cared to contemplate that possiblity.

So it was the end. The Yankees took the World Series in seven straight games, and no one cared. The stands were empty, and so few people paid to see the games on TV that the series ended as a financial catastrophe. A committee met to decide what to do about the aliens' records and reached no decision. Again, no one cared. The various awards for the most valuable players and managers of the year and the various individual championships were never made. The oversight was not protested. People had other things on their minds.

And when a dozen TV comedy teams simultaneously resurrected an ancient, half-legendary, half-forgotten comedy sketch, they got no laughs whatsoever. The sketch was called "Who's on First?"

THE
THIRD STRIKE

William R. Cox

W HEN THE MAN who called himself Arny Benedick came to Coleville, he knew it was close to an ending of some sort. He was unshaven, parched and ragged. At 32, his skin was slack upon sinews once cushioned in muscle. His possessions comprised one scuffed leather bag containing almost nothing.

Coleville was lost in the backwater, a valley town among rippling hills which wore October browns. It was a neat, pleasant town, the center of a truck-farming district, modestly prosperous.

Benedick paused before an establishment which bore a sign: COLE GRAIN AND FEED CO.—ICE, COAL AND WOOD. Then hesitantly he entered. Behind a high old-fashioned desk was a young woman in a white blouse. She had brown eyes and chestnut hair brushed back from her brow, and a coolly impersonal manner. "I'm afraid you won't do. We need a man to drive a coal truck."

He said, "I heard this was a baseball town. I can drive a truck and play a little ball."

From an inner office a voice roared, "Baseball? Who said baseball? Send him in, Mamie."

Benedick went into a room where a stout, bald, graying, burly-shouldered man looked him over and said, "On the bum, huh?"

"Sort of." Benedick gazed at the framed pictures on the walls, all autographed shots of ballplayers. "I've been sick."

"I'm Samuel Cole. I run the ball club. We got a franchise in the Inter-County League for next spring. Where'd you play last?"

Benedick made a gesture. "Out West. California." Ten years ago, he failed to add.

"You a hitter?"

"Yeah. I play first." He had learned to play first pretty well and he had always been a fair stickman.

Samuel Cole eyed him carefully. Then he said, "You got some age on you. I need experience. Tell you what. If you can drive my coal truck and last until spring, you got a deal."

"Thanks."

The stout man fumbled, handed over a ten-dollar bill. "Get a room, straighten yourself up. Take a drink. You need one. But don't show up here drunk or even near drunk."

Benedick took the money. A bottle and bus fare, he thought. He could head south and duck the winter. It was a break, better than he had expected. He went out of Cole's office and the girl was looking at him. He stared defiantly.

Then he read the bitterest of all messages and dropped his gaze. The girl pitied him.

She said, "Mrs. Donner serves good meals at her boarding house. We'll give you some help on the truck until you break in."

He nodded and went slinking onto the street. There was a diner nearby and he went in for coffee and something to line his stomach against the booze he would buy next. He looked out of the window while he was eating and wondered how many towns he had been in that were just like Coleville. He was running out of towns.

He paid the counterman and on impulse asked Mrs. Donner's address. He walked down the street to a liquor store and bought a half pint of bourbon. He found the boarding house and to his own amazement he gave the woman a five-dollar advance and took a room.

It was a clean, comfortable room with a soft bed. He uncorked the bottle and took a big drink. He sat on the bed and through his window he could see an oak tree, bent with age, its sere leaves dropping gently in a slight west wind.

For the first time in years he slipped gently off to sleep, the remainder of the liquor untouched. The next morning he looked at the little bottle for a moment. Then he turned quickly, got out his toothbrush and went down the hall. He showered, and toweled himself hard. He came back, put the booze in his bag and went to the coal yard.

They gave him a three-ton hoist truck, a map of the town and its surroundings, and a boy named Calvin to show him the ropes. He drove under the chutes, loaded up with chestnut coal, and received instructions in a few details by Bottsy Dorgan, a husky young man who acted as straw boss around the place. Mamie gave him delivery tickets—one ton was C.O.D. He drove out of the yard.

It was simple enough to arrange the truck chutes to the window and let the coal slide into a bin. But the third delivery was a "carry job." The iron baskets each held 100 pounds of anthracite, and it was necessary to tote them on his back for 50 yards before dumping them. Twenty trips—he barely made it.

Gasping, rubber-legged, he wondered why he bothered. He could take the C.O.D. money, stall the kid named Cal, and get out of town inside an hour.

He drove back to the yard. He turned in his tickets and Mamie —her last name was also Cole, she was Samuel's niece—took one look at him and said, "Bottsy's got some chores around the storeroom. These other deliveries can go tomorrow."

Benedick said, "I'm all right. I can rest while I'm driving."

He made three more loads, somehow got back to his room, and collapsed exhausted on the bed.

The weather turned cold inside a week and the work was so hard he could think of nothing else. He became so impregnated with coal dust that when he wasn't slaving he was bathing. He ached from head to foot all the time through Thanksgiving.

Then one day he realized he felt no pain in his muscles. And when Samuel Cole whistled him into the back office at the conclusion of work and offered him a drink of good whiskey, Benedick said, as if amazed at himself, "I haven't had a drink in four weeks. And I don't even *want* a drink."

"You must be crazy," said the stout man mildly. "Call Bottsy and we'll talk some more about the cut-off play."

In previous bull sessions about the game he had discovered that Cole was strong on statistics, while Bottsy was merely a sounding board. Benedick had been led into lectures, beginning with the fundamentals of strategy, until finally the two would be an audience, rapt and pleased. Sometimes Mamie came to the door and listened—and when he caught her eye the pity was gone, replaced by thoughtful respect.

He had long ago noted the sad air about this pretty girl. Bottsy explained that her fiancé had been killed in an auto accident. A one-man girl, Bottsy observed, shaking his head. She was still unwilling to look around at willing and husky suitors—such as a yard foreman. . . .

Changing the subject, Bottsy said: "The old man's gonna put

you in charge of the team. Midburg got its franchise last year, y'know. We got to beat Midburg.''

"There's no coal business in the summertime," said Benedick.

"He's takin' on a gas-and-oil contract. Just to keep us busy.''

"Is everybody in Coleville as baseball nutty as he is?''

"Everybody better be. We ain't gonna have Midburg lordin' it over us, not now or never.'' Bottsy's voice roughened and his ears grew pink.

With the first thaw he started playing catch with Bottsy in the coal yard. His arm was rusty, but he knew it was still sound. He found Bottsy to be a strong boy with more eagerness than skill and began coaching him. He got a fungo bat and began knocking flies.

In nothing flat he had an army of recruits. They came from everywhere and cluttered up the yard, chasing baseballs until their eyes bulged. When work became impeded, Bottsy would yell and a dozen pairs of hands would fall to until everything was shipshape again. . . .

The day the ball park was pronounced fit for practice, Benedick led his motley crew to a skinned diamond bordered by a clipped outfield which would have done credit to the leagues. Small boys had mowed the grass, aided by a flock of sheep loaned for the purpose. There was a small bleacher-grandstand and room for hundreds of cars to park within viewing distance.

It was the spirit of the thing that moved him, though. It was like his college days at little Corbin U., where every student was active.

He was able to weed out his best men and from the culls pick a Yannigan squad to which he diplomatically promised future action on the "varsity." Between his baseball activities and new duties at the yard, he had no time to think of danger, of the future. The days sped by and he grew tanned and eager, looking forward to each day as he had not in ten long years.

Samuel Cole had a final conference with him just before the opener against Midburg. "Never expected to put such a good team on the field. But Midburg has brought in ringers. My spies tell me they're onto us and are good and ready.''

"In baseball nobody wins them all," Benedick cautioned him.

"Coleville wins them all against Midburg," said his boss stoutly. "What's our weakness, Arny?''

Benedick fingered the mustache he'd grown. "Pitching. Hob Evarts is all right. But we've only got Bottsy behind him.''

"Bottsy can throw, but he's wild.''

"The others won't do. I'm working with young Cal, but he won't be ready for weeks. Maybe not then."

Samuel Cole said, "Never did see a man take holt like you have. Must have had a lot of experience."

"I've had some." It was not the first time the kindly merchant had hinted that he was open for confidences. Benedick's lips were stiff with effort. "Nothing to talk about."

"Well. . . . Going to the dance tonight?"

Benedick said, "Guess I'll have to show." It was a big pre-game affair, again reminding him of college days.

The older man hesitated, then said awkwardly, "Mebbe you could take Mamie?"

"Why—sure, Uncle Sam. I could ask her." He was startled, but the idea pleased him.

But all the way into the office he knew it was a mistake. He had gone far enough, possibly too far. One more crack-up would finish him. He had felt the beginning of the end when he arrived in Coleville. Despite everything good that had happened, he could clearly remember how close he had been to disintegration in October.

Yet he went directly to her and asked, "How about the dance tonight, Mamie?"

She half-raised a hand, then put it back down on the desk. "Yes. I'd love to go with you."

"I know about George." The fiancé's name had been George Geary. "You can't grieve forever. At least I don't think you can."

She nodded. "You've been through it?"

"A long time ago." Ten years ago. She had walked out with no regrets. Not that he blamed her; he blamed himself for everything. But she had been so cool about it.

Wearing his new dark gray suit he felt born anew, escorting a girl. She wore a white dress, simple but smart. There were a hundred people in the hall and every one of them knew his name, spoke cheerily to him, prophesying dire events on the morrow for the Midburg invaders.

He found Mamie an adept dancing partner. Once she said, "You're professional in everything you do, aren't you?" and he slowed down. He wanted none of that old nickname, "The Dancing Kid." It was one of the things that had started it all.

He walked her home. The hills lay softly beneath a lambent moon, the crickets had begun their seasonal hymn, the soft scent of new blossoms perfumed the night. He asked, "New beginnings are all right, aren't they?"

"I'm trying to manage one." She was always direct. Moonlight softened her hair; when she was relaxed there was a lovely serenity which overlay her, conveying promise.

"I'm trying to imagine one," he said softly.

She nodded. "You've had your share of trouble, haven't you?"

"I made it for myself." He choked it off. No good to talk about it, not ever, not to anyone. He had never been able to alibi it to himself.

"George drank too much," she said. "I knew it. But I loved him. I couldn't help loving him. He was drunk the night he ran into that pole, you know. But with all his drinking . . . well, it just didn't make any difference."

"Yes," he said. "Sometimes right or wrong doesn't count." He hadn't thought anyone else ever figured that way. They paused at Samuel Cole's garden gate.

"But it must," she said. "There must be a set of rules. Like baseball. Rules to be obeyed. That's what I'm trying to learn."

His enthusiasm died. "Sure. I know you're right. Well—good-night, Mamie. Thanks for going with me."

He walked away, hands thrust deep in his pockets.

He knew the rules, all right—he'd always known and understood them. Then how long, he asked himself, must he pay?

And he answered himself: All the years of your life.

The day of the game was bright enough and clear enough for even Midburg's wildly cheering citizenry, a crew of leather-lungs arriving in buses and immediately challenging every Coleville fan with green money openly displayed. Benedick watched from the bench and asked Samuel Cole, "What is this, Las Vegas?"

"It's the bounden duty of everyone to bet on his team," said the fat man, grinning. "I got a thousand on you."

"A thousand bucks? Are you crazy, Uncle Sam? You can't afford to bet that much on a baseball game."

"Reckon it wouldn't be so much fun if I could afford it."

"Boys will be boys, I suppose," said Mamie, beside him on the bench. She smiled, and then arose and made her way to her seat in the stands.

The Midburg manager was approaching with the line-up. With him was a slouching tall fellow in uniform, a tobacco-chewing man with abnormally long arms. Samuel Cole met him grimly, no nonsense, all business.

Benedick sat stock still. For a million dollars he could not have arisen from the planks of the bench.

"This is Jack Donovan. We got him registered just under the deadline," said the Midburg man defiantly. "I brought an affadavit, knowin' you'd beef."

Samuel Cole examined the document with utmost care, then eyed Donovan. "A pitcher, huh?"

"He ain't a bean-bag player!"

"Okay. Pitch him, then. Now, about fly balls into the crowd. . . . " The two moved off.

Donovan remained a moment, staring at Benedick. He said, "Hiya. Where you been?"

Benedick said, "Around." His voice was a hoarse whisper.

"The mustache almost fooled me." Donovan moved close. There were deep, malicious lines around his hard mouth. "Geez, it's been nine, ten years."

Benedick said, "Maybe you've got me wrong. I'm Arny Benedick."

"Sure. And I'm Jack Donovan."

He was Chick Bartlett. He had been a great pitcher with the Sox until they caught up with him. Betting on games, they said when they barred him. But there had been other things, too. A woman, a fight in which a man was killed, and a horse-race fix had also figured in the secret hearings.

So now Chick Bartlett was Jack Donovan. Benedick said, "Let's let it go at that."

"How much you got ridin'?"

"Not a dime," said Benedick.

"Okay. I got plenty on it. So we win."

"No dice," said Benedick.

Donovan cocked an eyebrow. "You kiddin', pal? If you ain't got a bet up, you got some stake. You better see we win."

Benedick said, "Lay off me, Donovan. I'm not with it. Do you understand?"

"Like that, huh?" Donovan spat tobacco juice, wiped his chin. "Look, pal, after this one I'm lammin'. You blow the whistle on me, I'm long gone. What about you?"

"Nothing," said Benedick harshly. "I said no dice."

The two managers were returning. Donovan said quickly, "What the heck. We're neither of us hay-shakers. Maybe we can get together later and do some good. I'll leave it lay, kid. But I can't let you beat us today. I can't, understand?"

He shambled away, his huge hands swinging low. He was on the booze, Benedick thought. He was no longer great, and if Hob

Evarts could hold the Midburgs . . . Coleville's kids could hit and run and they had acquired a lot of baseball knowledge in the past weeks.

Samuel Cole was saying to him, "You know the big lug?"

"He's a ringer, all right," said Benedick evasively.

"How good is he?"

"Maybe not good enough." He was regaining his composure now. He could think again. He went on the field for the workout. He kept an eye on Donovan, knew the old leaguer was watching him. He conferred briefly with Evarts, managed to shake his head once or twice as though debating. Then he donned the first-baseman's mitt and walked to his position. He chanced a glance at Donovan, received a wave of the hand in return.

He was all right. Because Donovan had never known him as a first baseman he was safe. Donovan had known him as a pitcher. He only needed not to hit in a timely spot and Donovan would believe he was going along with it. He could be safe as a dollar. One man could only do so much to throw a ball game.

The umpire bawled the time-honored, "Play ball!" and Evarts toed the mound. Mechanically the infield talked it up. "Get the leadin' man in there, Hob, ol' boy, get him outa there. Let him hit it, ol' boy, everybody hits, we got him, ol' boy . . . " Senseless, mechanical, unvarying chatter—and it meant everything.

Evarts was sharp. He was trying with everything he had. He struck out two and got one on a pop and Benedick walked off the field with him, warning, "Don't bear down too hard. You've got nine innings to go, remember."

He fastened his attention on Donovan, pushing the specters back into their lairs. He found himself admiring the easy motion of the former great pitcher. The fast one still seemed to have zip. And the Midburg catcher, another rugged veteran, seemed to be working in a rocking chair.

He spoke to his youngsters. "This man Donovan is tough. Wait him out. Make him throw."

His nerves were like violin strings. He was batting fifth and he found himself wishing no one would get on, so that he could bat with no pressure on him. He needn't have worried. Nobody on Coleville was hitting Donovan in the early innings.

He trotted out to first base again. Evarts could not relax. Every throw had his all in it. Benedick began to identify himself with his pitcher's problem, talking to him, advising him. It eased his own travail.

He went off the field, knowing he was on deck. He knelt in the box, seeing everything with great clarity. He could weasel out of it, he knew. Bottsy Dorgan swung valiantly and fouled to the catcher.

Donovan grinned at him from the mound. He stood easily at the plate, relaxed. He looked over a couple of curves and then the swift one came in. He blinked at it. He could never have got a piece of it, not on his best day. Relief surged through him. Even if he tried he could not hit Donovan's stuff.

Then he did try—and went down swinging.

As the game went on without a score the rivalry between the teams waxed, until the heat generated fire. Gilroy, the tough Midburg shortstop, slid hard into second and a fight began. Benedick was in it before he remembered, then aided in making peace. The tension mounted as the final inning approached.

Samuel Cole was sweating it out with the team. The stands were poised for the slightest manifestation of a rally by either club. In the beginning of the eighth Benedick sensed impending trouble.

Bottsy was up with two out. Donovan wound up, threw. Benedick came to his feet with the motion. Donovan's fast ball was coming in without the necessary stuff. Bottsy swung and the sound of wood on leather left no doubt in anyone's mind. Bottsy went into second standing up.

Benedick's hands were wet. He walked slowly to the plate. Donovan shoved back his cap, stalled a moment. Then he eyed Benedick, ball in hand.

Both knew the truth. Donovan had lost his speed. He had some control, a curve perhaps. But the big one was gone.

The big pitcher nodded as though accepting the catcher's sign. Benedick knew better. This was the pay-off. Donovan meant business now. It was on the table, plain to see: Strike out or listen later, while Donovan blows his whistle.

Benedick made no gesture for anyone to see. He was remembering another time when he had made a choice. He held the bat high, with slightly open stance, watching the ball in Donovan's hand.

The curve came in for a ball.

Then another curve missed the plate.

Donovan would have to get it over. He dared not walk Benedick and open the gates for young, eager boys to learn that he had weakened.

Benedick waited. He saw the pitch, fat and straight as a string, coming waist-high. He brought the bat around, pulling for right field, behind the runner. He smacked the fat of the bat into the ball and began running.

He might just as well run out of the park, he thought. He saw the ball bounce, the right fielder make a grab, turned to see Bottsy chasing home. He slid into second, came to his feet and looked across at Donovan.

The pitcher's face was grim and foreboding. He turned and threw to the next hitter, who obligingly swung too late and fouled out. Then he walked slowly across the field so that Benedick would have to cross his path. He said, "You asked for it and you're gonna get it."

Evarts took the mound and proceeded to come apart. He walked two men. Benedick went to him again and Evarts was white-faced, scared.

"We got'em licked, Arny. But I can't finish. My arm—it's dead. Can Bottsy do it?

Bottsy couldn't and Benedick knew it. Now Donovan was rising from the bench, shading his eyes with a hand, gesturing. Benedick understood that gesture well enough. Donovan didn't want a beef. He wanted the ball game.

Throw Bottsy in cold. Let him take his lumps. Donovan would keep his mouth shut, even now, if Benedick would only cooperate.

Samuel Cole was on the field. "What we gonna do, Arny?"

Just put Bottsy in there, thought Benedick. Let the strong boy take the beating. Nothing to it. Nobody will ever know. You can be home free. You already felt what it is like to buck Donovan when you got that hit. You're through if you don't get wise to yourself. You know you can't run any more. You've known that since last October.

His mind raced. Again he thought that this was the beginning of it, the cradle of it. A decision made here was like a stone in a still pond, sending its ripples to the big leagues, to the Series.

Finally he knew what counted and it was not himself. He asked Evarts, "Can you play first?"

Uncle Samuel Cole said nothing. Evarts was startled. "But what about Bottsy?"

"Give me the ball," said Benedick. He looked at Samuel Cole. The stout man was already walking to the bench.

He was alone on the mound and nobody had ever been such a stark target. He molded the new ball in his hands and looked for Donovan. The pitcher was already talking into the ear of the Midburg manager, gesticulating, pointing toward Benedick.

He shrugged, motioning to Popper Poole, the Coleville catcher.

He threw easy pitches even as the Midburg manager moved to the Coleville bench to protest to Samuel Cole. A hitter came up.

He found his old motion like a man easing into an old coat. He brought back his arm and showed them that famed follow-through which had made big-leaguers blink those days ten years ago.

He used only his speed and a change-up. When he pulled the string the ball hung there before dipping beneath swinging bat, and one man had struck out.

On the bench Samuel Cole was jabbing a thick index finger at the Midburg mentor. Benedick shrugged. He pitched.

He swung side-arm, still not using the curve. He had the man completely off-balance when he served it inside, on the corner, handcuffing him. The ball rolled off the handle back to the box. Benedick picked it up and rifled it to second. Two out. A man on third, a man on first.

He took his time. The hitter was a big, strong boy. He set Strong Boy up with a duster, then curved at last. Popper almost muffed it despite warning. The boy missed a mile.

There was an argument at the bench. Donovan had gone over to get into it. Benedick smiled, coldness in him, ready to finish it all, wanting only to get to Donovan.

Because, if this was the cradle of the game, Donovan was the snake manacing the infant. Spreading his evil counsel, his deception and treachery, he could do incalculable harm among the less than brainy athletes who aspired to the big time. This was enough, Benedick thought, for making the ending he had known was inevitable.

He unleashed his fast one. The strong boy shuddered away from the plate to take the second strike. Then he threw a nasty little hook that came in where no bush-leaguer could expect it to. The boy struck out and the game ended.

Benedick went into the melee about the bench. Bottsy was making the long run from right field and the stands were emptying. Benedick said, "Break it off or there'll be murder. Beat it, Donovan."

Donovan and the Midburg manager seemed, miraculously, already daunted. They were retreating. The fight was over. Mamie had come to stand by her uncle. Benedick set his jaw.

In low tones he said, "He's right. I'm—I mean, I *was* Kid Carney. But he was Chick Bartlett, so they haven't got a beef."

Samuel Cole said, "Shut up and let's get out of here before we're mobbed."

With some difficulty they escaped the cheering citizenry. Benedick rode to the coal yard without changing and in Samuel Cole's office Mamie and her uncle were quiet, looking at him.

"Ten years ago I threw a game," said Benedick. "I got into a jam and I was sore at the manager and I still haven't got an excuse."

"Yep," said Samuel Cole. "I know."

"How could you know anything about it? Ten years. . . . "

"You might recollect I follow baseball pretty close. You was the Dancin' Kid and your wife was a show gal and you was twenty-two. You did wrong."

Benedick looked at Mamie. "Now maybe you understand—things."

She said, "Uncle Sam told me, long ago."

There didn't seem anything he could say, then. He started for the door.

Samuel Cole asked, "Where you goin'?"

"I can't play ball for you any more."

"Just a minute. You gonna quit?"

"You mean I'm not fired?" He put one hand on the door jamb, looking across the cluttered office at them.

"You could have got out of it—three times today. You think I don't know that?"

Mamie said, "Uncle Sam bought that oil business for you and Bottsy to run summers."

Uncle Samuel said, "Only thing I see against you is takin' that fool name to torture yourself. Arny Benedick! Benedict Arnold! That's plumb stupid."

"You made a mistake," said Mamie. "Who hasn't?"

"Nobody's gonna stop you from coachin' my ballplayers," said Uncle Sam. "Who knows the wrong things better?"

Mamie said, "You've learned the rules now. Where better can you go to live by them?"

Uncle Sam said, "You served ten years. That's a long sentence. Don't be a danged fool."

Benedick couldn't say anything. He held tight to the door frame until his eyes cleared and he could see them again.

You got two strikes on you, he thought. But it takes three. Maybe you got the big one left.

THE PITCHER
AND THE PLUTOCRAT

P. G. Wodehouse

THE MAIN DIFFICULTY in writing a story is to convey to the reader clearly yet tersely the natures and dispositions of one's leading characters. Brevity, brevity—that is the cry. Perhaps, after all, the playbill style is the best. In this drama of love, baseball, frenzied finance, and tainted millions, then, the principals are as follows, in their order of entry:

Isabel Rackstraw (a peach).

Clarence Van Puyster (a Greek god).

Old Man Van Puyster (a proud old aristocrat).

Old Man Rackstraw (a tainted millionaire).

More about Clarence later. For the moment let him go as a Greek god. There were other sides, too, to Old Man Rackstraw's character; but for the moment let him go as a Tainted Millionaire. Not that it is satisfactory. It is too mild. He was *the* Tainted Millionaire. The Tainted Millions of other Tainted Millionaires were as attar of roses compared with the Tainted Millions of Tainted Millionaire Rackstraw. He preferred his millions tainted. His attitude toward an untainted million was that of the sportsman toward the sitting bird. These things are purely a matter of taste. Some people like Limburger cheese.

It was at a charity bazaar that Isabel and Clarence first met. Isabel was presiding over the Billiken, Teddy Bear, and Fancy Goods stall. There she stood, that slim, radiant girl, buncoing the Younger Set out of its father's hard-earned with a smile that alone was nearly worth the money, when she observed, approaching, the handsomest man she had ever seen. It was—this is not one of those mystery stories—it was Clarence Van Puyster. Over the heads of the bevy of gilded youths who clustered round the stall their eyes met. A thrill ran through Isabel. She dropped her eyes. The next moment Clarence had bucked center; the Younger Set had shredded away like a mist; and he was leaning toward her, opening negotiations for the purchase of a yellow Teddy Bear at sixteen times its face value.

He returned at intervals during the afternoon. Over the second Teddy Bear they became friendly; over the third, intimate. He proposed as she was wrapping up the fourth Golliwog, and she gave him her heart and the parcel simultaneously. At six o'clock, carrying four Teddy Bears, seven photograph frames, five Golliwogs, and a Billiken, Clarence went home to tell the news to his father.

Clarence, when not at college, lived with his only surviving parent in an old red-brick house at the north end of Washington Square. The original Van Puyster had come over in Governor Stuyvesant's time in one of the then fashionable ninety-four-day boats. Those were the stirring days when they were giving away chunks of Manhattan Island in exchange for trading-stamps; for the bright brain which conceived the idea that the city might possibly at some remote date extend above Liberty Street had not come into existence. The original Van Puyster had acquired a square mile or so in the heart of things for ten dollars cash and a quarter interest in a peddler's outfit. The *Columbus Echo and Vespucci Intelligencer* gave him a column and a half under the heading: "Reckless Speculator. Prominent Citizen's Gamble in Land." On the proceeds of that deal his descendants had led quiet, peaceful lives ever since. If any of them ever did a day's work, the family records are silent on the point. Blood was their long suit, not Energy. They were plain, homely folk, with a refined distaste for wealth and vulgar hustle. They lived simply, without envy of their richer fellow citizens, on their three hundred thousand dollars a year. They asked no more. It enabled them to entertain on a modest scale; the boys could go to college, the girls buy an occasional new frock. They were satisfied.

Having dressed for dinner, Clarence proceeded to the library, where he found his father slowly pacing the room. Silver-haired old Vansuyther Van Puyster seemed wrapped in thought. And this was unusual, for he was not given to thinking. To be absolutely frank, the old man had just about enough brain to make a jay-bird fly crooked, and no more.

"Ah, my boy," he said, looking up as Clarence entered. "Let

us go in to dinner. I have been awaiting you for some little time now. I was about to inquire as to your whereabouts. Let us be going.''

Mr. Van Puyster always spoke like that. This was due to Blood.

Until the servants had left them to their coffee and cigarettes, the conversation was desultory and commonplace. But when the door had closed, Mr. Van Puyster leaned forward.

"My boy," he said quietly, "we are ruined."

Clarence looked at him inquiringly.

"Ruined much?" he asked.

"Paupers," said his father. "I doubt if when all is over, I shall have much more than a bare fifty or sixty thousand dollars a year."

A lesser man would have betrayed agitation, but Clarence was a Van Puyster. He lit a cigarette.

"Ah," he said calmly. "How's that?"

Mr. Van Puyster toyed with his coffee spoon.

"I was induced to speculate—rashly, I fear—on the advice of a man I chanced to meet at a public dinner, in the shares of a certain mine. I did not thoroughly understand the matter, but my acquaintance appeared to be well versed in such operations, so I allowed him to—and, well, in fact, to cut a long story short, I am ruined."

"Who was the fellow?"

"A man of the name of Rackstraw. Daniel Rackstraw."

"Daniel Rackstraw!"

Not even Clarence's training and traditions could prevent a slight start as he heard the name.

"Daniel Rackstraw," repeated his father. "A man, I fear, not entirely honest. In fact, it seems that he has made a very large fortune by similar transactions. Friends of mine, acquainted with these matters, tell me his behavior toward me amounted practically to theft. However, for myself I care little. We can rough it, we of the old Van Puyster stock. If there is but fifty thousand a year left, well—I must make it serve. It is for your sake that I am troubled, my poor boy. I shall be compelled to stop your allowance. I fear you will be obliged to adopt some profession." He hesitated for a moment. "In fact, work," he added.

Clarence drew at his cigarette.

"Work?" he echoed thoughtfully. "Well, of course, mind you, fellows *do* work. I met a man at the club only yesterday who knew a fellow who had met a man whose cousin worked."

He reflected for a while.

"I shall pitch," he said suddenly.

"Pitch, my boy?"

"Sign on as a professional ballplayer."

His father's fine old eyebrows rose a little.

"But, my boy, er—the—ah—family name. Our—shall I say *noblesse oblige?* Can a Van Puyster pitch and not be defiled?"

"I shall take a new name," said Clarence. "I will call myself Brown." He lit another cigarette. "I can get signed on in a minute. McGraw will jump at me."

This was no idle boast. Clarence had had a good college education, and was now an exceedingly fine pitcher. It was a pleasing sight to see him, poised on one foot in the attitude of a Salome dancer, with one eye on the batter, the other gazing coldly at the man who was trying to steal third, uncurl abruptly like the mainspring of a watch and sneak over a swift one. Under Clarence's guidance a ball could do practically everything except talk. It could fly like a shot from a gun, hesitate, take the first turning to the left, go up two blocks, take the second to the right, bound in mid-air like a jack rabbit, and end by dropping as the gentle dew from heaven upon the plate beneath. Briefly, there was class to Clarence. He was the goods.

Scarcely had he uttered these momentous words when the butler entered with the announcement that he was wanted by a lady at the telephone.

It was Isabel.

Isabel was disturbed.

"Oh, Clarence," she cried, "my precious angel wonder-child, I don't know how to begin."

"Begin just like that," said Clarence approvingly. "It's fine. You can't beat it."

"Clarence, a terrible thing has happened. I told Papa of our engagement, and he wouldn't hear of it. He was furious. He c-called you a b-b-b—"

"A what?"

"A p-p-p—"

"That's a new one on me," said Clarence, wondering.

"A b-beggarly p-pauper. I knew you weren't well off, but I thought you had two or three millions. I told him so. But he said no, your father had lost all his money."

"It is too true, dearest," said Clarence. "I am a pauper. But I'm going to work. Something tells me I shall be rather good at work. I am going to work with all the accumulated energy of generations of ancestors who have never done a hand's turn. And some day when I—"

"Goodbye," said Isabel hastily, "I hear Papa coming."

The season during which Clarence Van Puyster pitched for the
Giants is destined to live long in the memory of followers of baseball. Probably never in the history of the game has there been such
persistent and widespread mortality among the more distant relatives of office-boys and junior clerks. Statisticians have estimated
that if all the grandmothers alone who perished between the
months of April and October that year could have been placed end
to end they would have reached considerably further than Minne-
apolis. And it was Clarence who was responsible for this holo-
caust. Previous to the opening of the season skeptics had shaken
their heads over the Giants' chances for the pennant. It had been
assumed that as little new blood would be forthcoming as in other
years, and that the fate of Our City would rest, as usual, on the
shoulders of the white-haired veterans who were boys with Lafay-
ette.

And then, like a meteor, Clarence Van Puyster had flashed upon
the world of fans, bugs, chewing gum, and nuts (pea and human).
In the opening game he had done horrid things to nine men from
Boston; and from then onward, except for an occasional check,
the Giants had never looked back.

Among the spectators who thronged the bleachers to watch
Clarence perform there appeared week after week a little, gray,
dried-up man, insignificant except for a certain happy choice of
language in moments of emotion and an enthusiasm far surpassing
that of the ordinary spectator. To the trained eye there is a subtle
but well marked difference between the fan, the bug, and—the last
phase—the nut of the baseball world. This man was an undoubted
nut. It was writ clear across his brow.

Fate had made Daniel Rackstraw—for it was he—a Tainted Millionaire, but at heart he was a baseball spectator. He never missed
a game. His library of baseball literature was the finest in the
country. His baseball museum had but one equal, that of Mr. Jacob
Dodson of Detroit. Between them the two had cornered, at enormous expense, the curio market of the game. It was Rackstraw
who had secured the glove worn by Neal Ball, the Cleveland shortstop, when he made the only unassisted triple play in the history
of the game; but it was Dodson who possessed the bat which Hans
Wagner used as a boy. The two men were friends, as far as rival
connoisseurs can be friends; and Mr. Dodson, when at leisure,
would frequently pay a visit to Mr. Rackstraw's country home,
where he would spend hours gazing wistfully at the Neal Ball glove
buoyed up only by the thought of the Wagner bat at home.

Isabel saw little of Clarence during the summer months, except from a distance. She contented herself with clipping photographs of him from the evening papers. Each was a little more unlike him than the last, and this lent variety to the collection. Her father marked her new-born enthusiasm for the national game with approval. It had been secretly a great grief to the old buccaneer that his only child did not know the difference between a bunt and a swat, and, more, did not seem to care to know. He felt himself drawn closer to her. An understanding, as pleasant as it was new and strange, began to spring up between parent and child.

As for Clarence, how easy it would be to cut loose to practically an unlimited extent on the subject of his emotions at this time. One can figure him, after the game is over and the gay throng has dispersed, creeping moodily—but what's the use? Brevity. That is the cry. Brevity. Let us on.

The months sped by. August came and went, and September; and soon it was plain to even the casual follower of the game that, unless something untoward should happen, the Giants must secure the National League pennant. Those were delirious days for Daniel Rackstraw. Long before the beginning of October his voice had dwindled to a husky whisper. Deep lines appeared on his forehead; for it is an awful thing for a baseball nut to be compelled to root, in the very crisis of the season, purely by means of facial expression. In this time of affliction he found Isabel an ever-increasing comfort to him. Side by side they would sit at the Polo Grounds, and the old man's face would lose its drawn look, and light up, as her clear young soprano pealed out above the din, urging this player to slide for second, that to knock the stitching off the ball; or describing the umpire in no uncertain voice as a reincarnation of the late Mr. Jesse James.

Meanwhile, in the American League, Detroit had been heading the list with equal pertinacity; and in far-off Michigan Mr. Jacob Dodson's enthusiasm had been every whit as great as Mr. Rackstraw's in New York. It was universally admitted that when the championship series came to be played, there would certainly be something doing.

But, alas! How truly does Epictetus observe: "We know not what awaiteth us around the corner, and the hand that counteth its chickens ere they be hatched ofttimes graspeth but a lemon." The prophets who anticipated a struggle closer than any on record were destined to be proved false.

It was not that their judgment of form was at fault. By every law of averages the Giants and the Tigers should have been the two most evenly matched nines in the history of the game. In fielding there was nothing to choose between them. At hitting the Tigers held a slight superiority; but this was balanced by the inspired pitching of Clarence Van Puyster. Even the keenest supporters of either side were not confident. They argued at length, figuring out the odds with the aid of stubs of pencils and the backs of envelopes, but they were not confident. Out of all those frenzied millions two men alone had no doubts. Mr. Daniel Rackstraw said that he did not desire to be unfair to Detroit. He wished it to be clearly understood that in their own class the Tigers might quite possibly show to considerable advantage. In some rural league down South, for instance, he did not deny that they might sweep all before them. But when it came to competing with the Giants— here words failed Mr. Rackstraw, and he had to rush to Wall Street and collect several tainted millions before he could recover his composure.

Mr. Jacob Dodson, interviewed by the Detroit *Weekly Rooter,* stated that his decision, arrived at after a close and careful study of the work of both teams, was that the Giants had rather less chance in the forthcoming tourney than a lone gumdrop at an Eskimo tea-party. It was his carefully considered opinion that in a contest with the Avenue B Juniors the Giants might, with an effort, scrape home. But when it was a question of meeting a live team like Detroit—here Mr. Dodson, shrugging his shoulders despairingly, sank back in his chair, and watchful secretaries brought him round with oxygen.

Throughout the whole country nothing but the approaching series was discussed. Wherever civilization reigned, and in Jersey City, one question alone was on every lip: Who would win? Octogenarians mumbled it. Infants lisped it. Tired businessmen, trampled underfoot in the rush for the West Farms express, asked it of the ambulance attendants who carried them to hospital.

And then, one bright, clear morning, when all Nature seemed to smile, Clarence Van Puyster developed mumps.

New York was in a ferment. I could have wished to go into details, to describe in crisp, burning sentences the panic that swept like a tornado through a million homes. A little encouragement, the slightest softening of the editorial austerity, and the thing would have been done. But no. Brevity. That was the cry. Brevity. Let us on.

The Tigers met the Giants at the Polo Grounds, and for five days the sweat of agony trickled unceasingly down the corrugated foreheads of the patriots who sat on the bleachers. The men from Detroit, freed from the fear of Clarence, smiled grim smiles and proceeded to knock holes through the fence. It was in vain that the home fielders skimmed like swallows around the diamond. They could not keep the score down. From start to finish the Giants were a beaten side.

Broadway during that black week was a desert. Gloom gripped Lobster Square. In distant Harlem red-eyed wives faced silently scowling husbands at the evening meal, and the children were sent early to bed. Newsboys called the extras in a whisper.

Few took the tragedy more nearly to heart than Daniel Rackstraw. Each afternoon found him more deeply plunged in sorrow. On the last day, leaving the ground with the air of a father mourning over some prodigal son, he encountered Mr. Jacob Dodson of Detroit.

Now, Mr. Dodson was perhaps the slightest bit shy on the finer feelings. He should have respected the grief of a fallen foe. He should have abstained from exulting. But he was in too exhilarated a condition to be magnanimous. Sighting Mr. Rackstraw, he addressed himself joyously to the task of rubbing the thing in. Mr. Rackstraw listened in silent anguish.

"If we had had Brown—" he said at length.

"That's what they all say," whooped Mr. Dodson. "Brown! Who's Brown?"

"If we had had Brown, we should have—" He paused. An idea had flashed upon his overwrought mind. "Dodson," he said, "listen here. Wait till Brown is well again, and let us play this thing off again for anything you like a side in my private park."

Mr. Dodson reflected.

"You're on," he said. "What side bet? A million? Two million? Three?"

Mr. Rackstraw shook his head scornfully.

"A million? Who wants a million? I'll put up my Neal Ball glove against your Hans Wagner bat. The best of three games. Does that go?"

"I should say it did," said Mr. Dodson joyfully. "I've been wanting that glove for years. It's like finding it in one's Christmas stocking."

"Very well," said Mr. Rackstraw. "Then let's get it fixed up."

Honestly, it is but a dog's life, that of the short-story writer. I particularly wished at this point to introduce a description of Mr. Rackstraw's country home and estate, featuring the private ball park with its fringe of noble trees. It would have served a double purpose, not only charming the lover of nature, but acting as a fine stimulus to the youth of the country, showing them the sort of home they would be able to buy some day if they worked hard and saved their money. But no. You shall have three guesses as to what was the cry. You give it up? It was "Brevity! Brevity!" Let us on.

The two teams arrived at the Rackstraw house in time for lunch. Clarence, his features once more reduced to their customary finely chiseled proportions, alighted from the automobile with a swelling heart. He could see nothing of Isabel, but that did not disturb him. Letters had passed between the two. Clarence had warned her not to embrace him in public, as McGraw would not like it; and Isabel accordingly had arranged a tryst among the noble trees which fringed the ball park.

I will pass lightly over the meeting of the two lovers. I will not describe the dewy softness of their eyes, the catching of their breath, their murmured endearments. I could, mind you. It is at just such descriptions that I am particularly happy. But I have grown discouraged. My spirit is broken. It is enough to say that Clarence had reached a level of emotional eloquence rarely met with among pitchers of the National League, when Isabel broke from him with a startled exclamation, and vanished behind a tree; and, looking over his shoulder, Clarence observed Mr. Daniel Rackstraw moving toward him.

It was evident from the millionaire's demeanor that he had seen nothing. The look on his face was anxious, but not wrathful. He sighted Clarence, and hurried up to him.

"Say, Brown," he said, "I've been looking for you. I want a word with you."

"A thousand, if you wish it," said Clarence courteously.

"Now, see here," said Mr. Rackstraw. "I want to explain to you just what this ball game means to me. Don't run away with the idea I've had you fellows down to play an exhibition game just to keep me merry and bright. If the Giants win today, it means that I shall be able to hold up my head again and look my fellow man in the face, instead of crawling around on my stomach feeling like thirty cents. Do you get that?"

"I am hep," replied Clarence with simple dignity.

"And not only that," went on the millionaire. "There's more to it. I have put up my Neal Ball glove against Mr. Dodson's Wagner bat as a side bet. You understand what that means? It means that either you win or my life is soured for keeps. See?"

"I have got you," said Clarence.

"Good. Then what I wanted to say was this. Today is your day for pitching as you've never pitched before. Everything depends on whether you make good or not. With you pitching like mother used to make it, the Giants are some nine. Otherwise they are Nature's citrons. It's one thing or the other. It's all up to you. Win, and there's twenty thousand dollars waiting for you above what you share with the others.''

Clarence waved his hand deprecatingly.

''Mr. Rackstraw,'' he said, ''keep your dough. I care nothing for money.''

''You don't?'' cried the millionaire. ''Then you ought to exhibit yourself in a dime museum.''

''All I ask of you,'' proceeded Clarence, ''is your consent to my engagement to your daughter.''

Mr. Rackstraw looked sharply at him.

''Repeat that,'' he said. ''I don't think I quite got it.''

''All I ask is your consent to my engagement to your daughter.''

''Young man,'' said Mr. Rackstraw, not without a touch of admiration, ''you have gall.''

''My friends have sometimes said so,'' said Clarence.

''And I admire gall. But there is a limit. That limit you have passed so far that you'd need to look for it with a telescope.''

''You refuse your consent.''

''I never said you weren't a clever guesser.''

''Why?''

Mr. Rackstraw laughed. One of those nasty, sharp, metallic laughs that hit you like a bullet.

''How would you support my daughter?''

''I was thinking that you would help to some extent.''

''You were, were you?''

''I was.''

''Oh?''

Mr. Rackstraw emitted another of those laughs.

''Well,'' he said, ''it's off. You can take that as coming from an authoritative source. No wedding bells for you.''

Clarence drew himself up, fire flashing from his eyes and a bitter smile curving his expressive lips.

''And no Wagner bat for you!'' he cried.

Mr. Rackstraw started as if some strong hand had plunged an auger into him.

''What!'' he shouted.

Clarence shrugged his superbly modeled shoulders in silence.

''Say,'' said Mr. Rackstraw, ''you wouldn't let a little private difference like that influence you any in a really important thing like this ball game, would you?''

"I would."

"You would hold up the father of the girl you love?"

"Every time."

"Her white-haired old father?"

"The color of his hair would not affect me."

"Nothing would move you?"

"Nothing."

"Then, by George, you're just the son-in-law I want. You shall marry Isabel; and I'll take you into partnership this very day. I've been looking for a good, husky bandit like you for years. You make Dick Turpin look like a preliminary three-round bout. My boy, we'll be the greatest team, you and I, that ever hit Wall Street."

"Papa!" cried Isabel, bounding happily from behind her tree.

Mr. Rackstraw joined their hands, deeply moved, and spoke in low, vibrant tones:

"Play ball!"

Little remains to be said, but I am going to say it, if it snows. I am at my best in these tender scenes of idyllic domesticity.

Four years have passed. Once more we are in the Rackstraw home. A lady is coming down the stairs, leading by the hand her little son. It is Isabel. The years have dealt lightly with her. She is still the same stately, beautiful creature whom I would have described in detail long ago if I had been given half a chance. At the foot of the stairs the child stops and points at a small, wooden object in a glass case.

"Wah?" he says.

"That?" says Isabel. "That is the bat Mr. Wagner used to use when he was a little boy."

She looks at a door on the left of the hall, and puts a finger to her lip.

"Hush!" she says. "We must be quiet. Daddy and Grandpa are busy in there cornering wheat."

And softly mother and child go out into the sunlit garden.

PINCH PITCHER

William R. Cox

WILLY GAYE THREW his hat into the room. He waited a moment, then projected his grin around the corner of the jamb.

The big, graying man sat behind a desk and stared long and stonily at his new pitcher.

Willy stared back at him. "I hear you're the toughest manager in baseball, Mr. Knight. Bark for me!"

He was a medium-sized man, this Willy Gaye, no longer young, but with youthfulness riding him like a floating cloak. His snub nose, his wide smile, his short haircut were the appurtenances of youth, his gliding step was springy, his blue eyes wide and ingenuous.

Eddie Knight said, "You heard right. You should be scared, but not of me. You should be scared that this is your last stop."

Willy perched on a straight chair, his abnormally large hands folded in his lap. He said meekly, "Yes, sir."

Eddie Knight refused to respond in kind. He said, "Gaye, we've known each other for years. You've beaten my team as often as any pitcher. You've had your own way with the Bears, on and off the field. Now the Bears can't take you any more."

Willy Gaye said, "Mainly because I was beginning to lose games for them, Eddie, ol' kid."

"Mainly because you've played away the years," said Eddie. "You drink too much beer. You sing in too many night spots. And you just don't give a damn."

"Could be," grinned Willy Gaye.

"I got you in a trade. I didn't ask for you. I could get rid of you right away."

Willy said, "It might be better for both of us if you did."

"The Colts haven't got much chance this year," said Eddie Knight. "We're building with youth. We've got fighting kids. Next year . . . Well, Gaye, I need a bull-pen pitcher."

Willy Gaye's grin did not fade, but something happened to his eyes. They seemed bluer than before. He said, "You mean I'm no longer a starter? Even with the Colts? Come on, Eddie! You're kiddin'."

The manager of the Colts said, "Your arm isn't what it was. If we were going places I'd get rid of you. As we're not, I can use you—in the bull pen."

Willy stood up.

"A relief man with the Colts," he mused. "How far can you sink?"

"Out of baseball," snapped Knight. "Think it over. Good-bye, Willy."

The slim man turned. At the door he paused. The grin was wider than ever. He said, "You sure look silly sittin' there, yakking at me. Remember the time after the Bears won the World Series? The year you were our coach? Before they made you a manager? We got stiff as boards and you insisted on imitating Judge Landis, standin' on a table in Tony's place? Your hair was on end and you wore a lady's hat you'd picked up somewheres."

"Get out of here," roared Eddie Knight. "Go and start thinking up ways of making trouble, and I'll have you out of the game in a month!"

"Yes, sir," said Willy meekly. He chuckled and disappeared.

The square face of baseball's toughest manager relaxed. He sighed. He wondered how Willy could grin and make jokes. The Bears had thrown him into the deal which brought four rookies to their farm system. The Colts had taken Gaye and Tom Gordon, another fading veteran. Gordon would steady the kid outfield, though. Willy Gaye—Willy was just another gamble, and not much of one at that. He had won only nine and lost ten for the Bears, pennant winners of last season. He had begun to lose even behind good hitting.

Yet Eddie Knight could remember other days, a laughing, rubber-armed, careless youth with speed far beyond his seeming muscular development and heft. There is no sentiment in baseball, Eddie Knight ruminated—except underneath where it doesn't show.

It was mid-season. The Bears were coming to town. The Colts gathered in the clubhouse for a morning meeting. Eddie Knight stood and surveyed them. His eyes kindled.

He said in his hard, dry voice, "I'm proud. They picked you to finish low in the second division. You're in second place. You've got a chance to club those Bears and get the lead."

They were a fine bunch of clean-cut boys. There were no roisterers on the team. Tom Gordon had indeed held the outfield together. The kids who patrolled the infield, George Dunn at first, Pat Carney at second, Matty Pelota at third and Jack Stahl at short had proved themselves overnight phenoms. The pitchers had done heroic work and big Hub Egan had caught every game, including double-headers.

It was the pitching staff which worried Eddie. Slim Crane, Augie Hall, Doc Collins and Cat Bellowe had done all the heavy work. They had worked their hearts out for a club which was not a hitting success.

Willy Gaye perched on the rubbing table. His grin was bright. He said, "We can beat the Bears."

They paid him scant heed. He had been in there often enough. He had thrown his nothing ball at pinch hitters. He had saved a few games. But he was not one with the Colts, those serious young men.

The Colts were mostly college boys. They were industrious young workmen. They behaved themselves, always, on and off the field. They had fight enough, but it didn't show in their behavior. Willy Gaye was from another era, a throwback to the days of McGraw and Fletcher and Dooling. He was not for them.

Eddie Knight threw Willy a glance. He said calmly, "Gaye was with the Bears for years, as we all know. Tell them, Gaye."

"You've played them before. But they weren't gunning for you. They didn't take you serious," said Willy, swinging his legs. "When they go after you, when they really fight, look out! They ain't bully boys. They're real fighters. Down to the ruddy bricks. And they hit. In the clutches, pals, they hit."

Eddie Knight said, "We'll go over the hitters."

Willy recited, "Torrey . . . Likes high balls. Feed him inside low. Acton . . . Curves, he murders. Speed inside to him. Jones . . . Hits anything, but likes slow stuff. Cal Roble"—he paused and his grin flashed at them—"Chuck it and duck. Cal's got ice in his veins; no weakness."

It was a long tale. Willy told it without pausing. Then he arose from the table, and said casually, "I'm thirsty. Take over, Eddie. I'll be around when you need me."

That afternoon the Colts took the field, tanned, eager—and a bit anxious. Slim Crane was to pitch the opener against the Bears. The elongated left-hander warmed up. Crane was laying it in there and Eddie warned him about wasting his arm.

Out in the bull pen Willy Gaye was sitting on the bench, his legs stretched out before him. His blue eyes never left the field. While the Bears worked out, he watched them.

For years he had toiled for them. Guy Lott, the pugnacious manager, had never liked Willy, but he had used him. Willy had the speed, then.

And then the arm had begun to go. Willy had not realized it at first. He fingered his right elbow. It hurt.

The Bears were as polished as ever afield. They were out to crush the upstart Colts in four straight and clinch the pennant by breaking their spirit. Willy knew all about Bear strategy. Fingers Day would be the pitcher. Fingers could sneak in a duster which should scare weak hitters to death.

Willy sighed and re-crossed his legs. The ball game began.

Torrey led off for the Bears. He lined the second pitch into right field for a single. Up from the Bears' bench came a mighty roar. Bats rattled. Imprecations swept out to envelop the Colts. It was a stunning attack.

Acton doubled to left. Torrey came home. Rad Jones, swinging three bats, screamed at Crane, threw two of the sticks to the bench and strode to the plate. Behind him the huge and redoubtable Cal Roble was ready.

Willy languidly picked up his glove and motioned to Butch Hogue, the bull-pen catcher. Butch said, "He won't use you so soon."

"I know. But I'm cold," said Willy. "We'll take it easy." He threw gently, watching the game. Eddie made Crane walk Cal Roble. Eddie was okay. The pitch went in to Austin Graham. The Bears' center-fielder rapped smartly and the ball raced down to Jack Stahl at short. Jack gobbled it, chucked it to Pat Carney. The little second-sacker made a beautiful cross-body throw. Dunn stretched and the double play was perfect, with Acton going to third.

Crane steadied down. He struck out Tex Houston, the tough third baseman. Willy sat on the bench again.

Fingers Day had his stuff. He mowed the Colts down with contempt. Willy shook his head. Not enough power, he thought. The kids were good enough, but they lacked that hitting strength.

Guy Lott, strutting, met his men coming off the field and abjured them.

Crane had regained his form. He pitched along, rating himself, feeding the Bears the right stuff. It was one to nothing in the eighth. Crane threw with all his heart.

Fats Tillou, burly Bears catcher, led off. Crane worked two strikes over. Fats let the waste ball go. Crane missed the corners twice, then, and was in the hole. He wiped sweat from his brow, took his time. He threw a curve for the outside corner. It missed.

Lott put a runner in for Tillou, sent Jap Paley up to bat for Fingers Day.

Willy threw to Butch, working a little harder. It had been a long, tough haul for Crane. The slim pitcher was walking around the mound, cursing himself for walking the Bears catcher. He threw to Paley, a jumping-jack hitter. Paley grimaced and jittered. Crane walked him, too.

Eddie Knight went out from the bench. Willy threw four hard ones. Eddie turned and the buzzer sounded. It was three rings. Willy nodded to Butch. The catcher said, "Well, anyway, it's your game if you win it."

"Hell of a thing," nodded Willy. "Can't lose, can I?"

He knew what he could lose. With the Bears ahead, the game would not count against Willy's record, if the Colts lost. But Willy wasn't being paid on won and lost records. Relief pitchers never are . . .

The Colts infield gathered around, wide-eyed, watching him take his warm-up throws. Willy picked up the resin bag and addressed the Colts. "All right, kids. Now you're in a real ball game. Watch the pitches."

They went back to position. Behind third Guy Lott was putting on a show. He was waving a fist, howling, "Here's that sore-arm Happy Charlie guy. He's our meat. You know his stuff!"

Willy glanced over. He said, "Aw, shut up, Big Mouth. You want me to—"

The umpire growled, "Play ball, Gaye."

Hub Egan was behind the plate, giving the sign. Jed Torrey was waving his stick. Willy looked at the base runners. He wheeled and suddenly pitched.

It sailed inside, low. Torrey let it go.

"Stuh-rike one!"

Torrey dropped back, protesting. Willy held the ball. He feinted for the bag behind him, then threw before Torrey had time to set. Again it was low and inside. Torrey swung.

The ball came down to Willy on a big hop. He leaped, grabbed it. He swung to third. The runner was out a mile. Houston slammed the ball at second. Carney took it and slapped the bag with his spikes.

"Simple, ain't it?" Willy called over to Lott. "Two out already. You're all gettin' old!"

Lott howled insults. Willy laughed.

Bull Acton was up. The husky first baseman was really dangerous. Willy had known him well, had roomed with him for a year, before Bull's marriage. Willy called, "How's Mary, pal?"

Bull growled, "Throw it in here, sore-arm."

"You don't have to be so rough," said Willy mildly. "I always liked you. I even like Mary, if she is sorta ugly."

Before Bull could catch his breath, Willy threw one straight as a string over the center of the plate.

He laughed. He threw again, straight stuff, with no special speed. Bull seemed hypnotized, watching the corner sliced by the pitch. When Willy threw the third one, low and outside, he swung with all his might.

The ball plopped up into the air and down into the eager hands of Pat Carney behind second. The inning was over. The Bears still led by a single run, with Hub Egan coming up to begin the Colts' last raps.

Bull Acton was struggling with Lott and another Bear. "He said my wife was ugly! I'll kill him!"

Willy paused. He said, "Oh, come off, Bull. She's not very ugly!" He sauntered to the bench, laughing.

Eddie Knight said sternly, "We don't go for those personal insults, Gaye. Now you've got them fighting mad."

Willy selected a bat. There would be no pinch hitter. Willy batted over .300 every year he was in baseball. He said, "You got to fight those bozos."

"I don't stand for brawling," Eddie warned him.

"You stand for winning baseball?" asked Willy mildly. He walked to the on-deck box. Hub Egan popped to left field for the first out. People began filing out of the stands.

Willy went to bat. Immediately the Bears were howling, begging Haley, the relief hurler, to dust him off, to knock out his brains.

Willy laughed. The pitcher, who did not know him, threw a curve.

Willy belted into the ball. He gave it all he had, snapping his wrists. The ball started straight at the pitcher, then rose sharply. It curved down into left center and skidded. Willy went down to first, still laughing.

Bull almost punched him. Willy stuck out his tongue, took a

lead, danced back when the throw came. Bull slammed the ball into him.

It was like a knockout punch. It hurt, all the way through Willy's body. He got up, dusted himself and said, "That all you got, Bull? You are gettin' old, ain't you?"

The first baseman said, "I'll kill you, yuh dirty bum!"

Haley was ready to pitch. Willy streaked off the bag. He went down to second like a flash of light. The throw was in. He kicked with both spikes as he slid over the sack. He kicked Marble clear into center field. He saw the ball roll free and was on his feet. He ran like a madman, threw himself in the dirt again.

Tex Houston stared down at him. He drawled, "You gone nuts, Willy?"

"I'm just a happy kid," said Willy. "Can I help it if you old men can't hold me?"

Eddie Knight's face was a picture. He had given no signal to steal, of course. Yet here was his cast-off pitcher on third with the tying run. He signed for the hit and run.

Pat Carney tapped the ball, pulling it into right field. Willy walked home, laughing all the way. Carney beat the throw and took a lead.

Joe Zazzali, the lanky center fielder, stood calm as a rock. Haley tried to burn it through. Zazzali banged it right into the left-field stands. The ball game was over and the Colts had upset the fighting, ferocious Bears.

Bull Acton started across the field, fists doubled, face red and angry. His intent was obvious. The Colts hesitated, then stepped aside for him. He ran up to Willy and swung.

Willy ducked and danced away. As Bull rushed again Willy hit him with a left hook, and Bull sat down.

Willy said, "I wouldn't hit you with my pitchin' hand. If I did, you'd be dead, you bum. Remember how I gave you boxin' lessons, you clumsy dope? G'wan—tell the rest of those old codgers I'll be ready for 'em any time."

He turned and went into the dugout and up through the ramp. Eddie Knight said, "I just won't stand for fighting, Willy! Dammit, we don't play the game that way."

Willy said plaintively, "Can I help it if those nasty men attack me?"

George Dunn, the first baseman from Yale, burst into laughter. Joe Zazzali joined in. Slim Crane said, "They sure jumped the wrong guy!"

Eddie Knight decided to drop it. He listened to the Colts holler-

ing in the dressing room and scrambling with wet towels in the
showers. He saw Willy undressing in a corner, examining a large
black-and-blue spot on his body where Bull had given it to him.
He went into his office and thought about the next day—and the
doubleheader on Sunday.

Augie Hall decided to have a day. He shut out the Bears for
eight innings. Then he weakened. The three rings sounded in the
bull pen. Butch said, "This one is on you, either way."

"Ain't we got fun?" Willy grinned. He went in. He pitched to
Acton. The first baseman was too angry to hit. He pitched to
Jones. The right fielder grounded out to first. He threw one low
ball to Roble. The grounder almost tore off his legs, but Willy
fielded it and threw out the left fielder.

He strolled in, past the cat-calling, blasphemous Bears bench.
He doffed his cap to them. "Old men," he called. "Tired old
men!"

Pat Carney led off. He singled. Zazzali teed off and knocked the
first pitch for a triple and the game was again in the sack for the
Colts.

It was unbelievable. The newspaper sports pages screamed with
it. The kid team had turned the tables on the veterans who had
been expected to break them apart and end their hopes for a pennant. Now, unless the Bears won both ends of Sunday's doubleheader they would be in second place.

One writer said, "Willy Gaye, Bears cast-off, seems to be the
touchstone. When he comes in the game, boom go the Bears."

It gave them a slogan. The Colts, cocky and cheerful, repeated
it. "Boom go the Bears!" It sounded swell in the clubhouse before
the first game of the Sunday pair.

Eddie Knight came out of his office and looked around. He said,
"Where is Gaye?"

"Why—I dunno," said George Dunn, who acted as captain of
the team.

Nobody had seen Willy. Eddie looked at his watch. His heart
skipped a beat. No one knew better than he what Gaye had meant
in this series.

Doc Collins, a careful worker but not robust, was to start the
game. The trouble was that Eddie had no one in reserve. If Doc
failed to go the route, there was only Slim Crane again, or one of
the rookie strong-arms who were all right against the tail-end teams
but not the men for this spot. And Slim would not be ready; he
needed his full rest.

Eddie went back into the office and called the hotel. Willy Gaye had left in plenty of time to make the park. Eddie chewed his cigar. If Gaye had gone on a party . . .

Game time came. There was no sign of Gaye. The Colts took the field.

It was a game to age a manager beyond endurance. Doc started shakily, giving up a run in the first, then steadied down. The Colts could do nothing with Manny Levine. The game rocked along, full of incidents which grayed Eddie's hair by the hour.

The Bears were back in the driver's seat again. All day they had been arguing about decisions, tagging the runners with slamming blows, sliding into the infielders with flying spikes. Now at the end of the eighth, with five runs to the Colts' one, they were strutting, shouting.

Eddie said, on the bench, "Can't you win without Gaye? Are you going to lay down because that bum didn't show up? What kind of ballplayers are you guys? Get after that Levine!"

Zazzali, hitless that day, led off. He went up and hit one into left for a double. Gordon, the veteran, waited for a fat one, picked on it and laced a homer into the stands.

From third base, Eddie trumpeted his hands and bellowed, "Boom go the Bears! Everybody hits!"

Haley came in for the Bears. Buck Jelliff, right fielder of the Colts, snaked one down the third-base line and took first. George Dunn walked. Matty Pelota beat out an infield hopper and everyone was safe. Jack Stahl struck out and Hub Egan came up.

With the Bears howling and the fans breathless, Hub socked the ball. It soared and lazily turned over, dropped, took a bit more life. It sank into the left-field stands.

The amazing Colts, without Willy Gaye, had pulled another game out of the fire.

Eddie Knight went into the dressing room. From the corner of the room a voice said calmly, "That was a nice finish. I caught it from the stands."

"Gaye! Where the hell you been?"

His spikes under his arm, Willy strolled forward. He was dressed and ready. He said, "I was kinda busy . . ."

"I smell whiskey! Damn you, you've been drinking!" Eddie was beside himself. "You're fined five hundred, Gaye. I'll run you out of baseball for this!"

Willy Gaye regarded the manager. He said, "Who's going to pitch this game for you?"

Eddie Knight said, "Never mind who's going to pitch."

Willy held out a hand. It was steady as a rock. He said, "I'm goin' to pitch this game, Eddie."

"You sot! You no-good playboy! You quit the team when I need you and then you try to come back and—"

"You won the game," Willy said mildly. "I was busy."

"You'll never pitch another game for me! You can't start. You won't last."

Willy said, "I'm pitchin' this one. It may be my last, but I'm startin'. You can yell and holler, but you know what'll happen if you throw a strongarm kid in there. Or a tired pitcher. I ain't tired. I know those Bears. You better think fast and hard, Eddie. This game is the pay-off."

Eddie Knight was a great manager. He held tight to his temper. He said quietly, "All right, Gaye. You start. And when you get knocked out just keep on going, because you'll be through!"

"Sure," Willy nodded. "That's all right." He walked out, his spikes under his arm. He was certainly not drunk, Eddie knew. He might have had a couple, but he was steady and sure. Eddie wiped his sweating brow.

It was the sixth inning. There had been no score. The slim, laughing figure of Willy Gaye had dominated the game. Lefty Smart had pitched well for the Bears, but the attention of the baseball world was focused, inning after inning, on the cast-off veteran who seemed so young and carefree, whose control was perfect.

Jack Stahl came in to take the harmless grounder as irate Bull Acton grimly raced for first. Stahl reached cupped hands. The ball hit an obstruction. It bounced. It went over Jack's shoulder. He chased it. Tom Gordon had raced in from left to back up. Acton was safe on first. There was none out.

Stahl was red-faced, his eyes hurt. He stammered, "Gee, Willy—"

"It shouldn't happen to a dog," said Willy gravely.

Guy Lott was bawling, "There goes the balloon. Now his luck is gone. Get after the sore-arm bum."

Stahl said, "Gee, Willy, your arm. Is it all right?"

Willy said, "Get two, kid, get two. G'wan, it wasn't your fault."

His elbow—it was a funny thing—it hurt a little, but didn't interfere with his pitching, as it had last year. He surveyed Red Jones. He cuddled the ball. He made his deceptive motion which kept the clumsy Bull tight to first. He threw for the inside corner. The ball zipped into Egan's mitt. The ump called it a strike.

Willy did not even hear Guy Lott and the Bears as they cursed him. He wrapped his large hand around the white alley. He reared back and came down and through another hard one. Red Jones whacked at it.

It was a liner straight into the hands of Pelota, down at third. The attempt to double Bull was unsuccessful. Bull began to holler for a hit.

Willy said, "That's more'n you got, you big bum."

Bull said, "I'll kill you yet, yuh . . ."

Willy threw the ball to first. Pain shot through him. Bull got back safe. Willy took the toss from George Dunn and bit his lip. Then he grinned and threw to Cal Roble.

Roble laced one. It was a towering fly and for a moment it seemed it would go into the right-field stands. Then Jeliff climbed an invisible rope and trapped the sphere in his glove. Willy laughed, looking over at Guy Lott.

"Did you think you could luck me out of the game?" He made a derisive motion with his hand. He threw to Graham, the doughty center fielder and long-ball hitter of the Bears. Graham cut viciously and the ball banged down to short. Jack Stahl went to his left, almost fell, fielded the ball, recovered balance. He got it down to second to force Acton. The side was out.

Willy went to the dugout. He sat gingerly on the bench, grinning. Stahl was selecting his bat. Willy said to him, "It wasn't an error, kid. It was a hit. A lucky hit, but a hit."

The Colts seemed to sigh in unison. Jack said in a brittle voice, "Look, nobody ever says nothing about it. I see the hit signal went up. I know it goes for a hit. And we all know I spoiled a no-hitter for you, Willy."

Willy said, "That's all right, kid."

Jack said, "If I'd waited for it . . ."

Willy said, "Get one, kid. We want the ball game." He watched the kid go to the plate. Stahl was a sweet kid. Nobody knew better than Willy that he had been pitching no-hit ball. But Stahl was okay. Nobody could have fielded the bad bounce on that ball.

Stahl crouched, waving his bat. He was no hitter, he was seventh in the batting order. He was a slick fielder, a hustle guy, but no batter.

Lefty Smart threw one of his crookarm hooks. Stahl leaped and hammered. The ball shot between first and second for a clean single. Willy came off the bench hollering like a Comanche. He reached for a bat.

Hub Egan took a sturdy stance. Willy paused in the on-deck

box, howling for Hub to cream one, but all the time thinking, thinking hard.

Smart got himself into a hole and had to groove one. He got it in there too nice. Hub Egan lined it into right and Stahl tore around and slid safely into third while the catcher took first.

Guy Lott was out haranguing his southpaw star. Lefty Smart jawed right back at the manager. Acton was roaring that they had easy men coming up, to bear down, to dust off this dirty so-and-so at bat. That was Willy, with a slender stick, grinning at them.

Lott retired and Smart prepared to pitch. Now the Colts were whooping it up. Willy heard Hub's bass voice, down at first, telling Acton that if it was a fight he wanted Hub Egan would personally see to it that Bull got a fight. Furthermore, if Bull touched Willy Gaye, Hub added, there would be dark deeds. He mentioned some of the things that would happen to Bull, and Willy Gaye grinned.

Smart bore down with one inside and around the letters. Willy never liked that pitch. But he knew it was in and he shortened his cut and knocked at it with all his forearm and wrist strength.

The ball slithered down the third-base line. Tex Houston made a valiant dive for it. He missed. Stahl romped home. Hub Egan went to third.

Lefty Smart clammed up. He gritted his teeth and pitched. He struck out Pat Carney. Joe Zazzali rapped one down to second and the double play was on. Willy ran and jumped into the air to break it up, but Torrey reached out and threw past him to Acton and the inning was over.

Willy got his glove and went slowly into the box. He took his warm-up throws, easing the ball in there to Hub. He watched the catcher peg to second and it was a little harder to grin, now.

But he got Houston, Marble and Tillou in order. They all hit, but he made them hit in the dirt with his low stuff. He did not throw a fast ball that inning. He went in and sat on the bench, grinning and yelling at the Colts. They could do nothing, either, and the score remained one to nothing in their favor as the eighth began.

Eddie Knight stopped Willy on his way to the box. He said, "Dammit, you ought to be dead beat."

Willy winked. "I'm tough, remember?" He picked up the resin bag and roughened his long, strong fingers. He struck out Lefty Smart, he got Torrey on a grounder and Bull Acton, the angry, ferocious fighter, on a long fly.

He went in once more. Three more men, he thought. Just three more. He held his arms tight against his body and grinned at the

Colts. It was funny, the way they hovered near him now. They even seemed to want to touch him, his uniform, his shoulder, before they went to bat. It did not do them any good. Smart got them out and it was the last of the ninth.

Willy went out and toed the slab. There was Red Jones. He could hit anything, but he liked slow stuff.

Willy took his time. He used his full wind-up. He came over and through, until his pitching hand dragged in the dirt after the throw. Jones stood, staring in disbelief. The ball tore across the outside corner. Hub Egan's jaw sagged.

The umpire strangled, "Stuh-rike one." His eyes bulged, too. The ump hadn't seen Willy throw his fast one for a couple of seasons now.

Willy grinned. The corners of his mouth strained, but he managed to mock them. He kept thinking. The strange part of it was that his elbow did not hurt any more after the hard pitch than it had before.

On the bench Eddie Knight leaned forward, chin cupped in hands. This was weird. This did not make sense. Willy Gaye was not an ordinary character, but this was different again, Eddie Knight thought. . . .

Willy was winding up. His foot jerked high, came down. Again there was that sweeping, graceful follow-through of the lean body. Jones swung at this one. It was in Hub's glove when he swung. Jones fell out of the box, glowering at Willy.

Willy laughed out loud. He said, "Swift one too much for you, Red, ole boy? Try this."

Jones took his stance. Willy went through the same motion. The knuckler, spinning and ducking, slid in close. It was a ball Jones would ordinarily kill. But Jones was unsettled by the speed of the previous pitches. He swung weakly, struck out.

The ball went around the Colts' infield like a rifle bullet. Stahl was yapping, "You got the leadin' lady. Now let's get this tramp!"

Roble was no tramp. Cal Roble could break up any ball game. The giant home-run hitter was calm as a rock. Willy sighed behind the grin which was not a mask.

He threw to Roble. He threw twisting, tantalizing curves which nicked the corners of the plate—or just missed. Roble looked them over calmly. The count became three and two.

Hub Egan held his glove, giving the sign. It was for the hardest of all clutch balls, the high, hard one, across the letters, the pitch that takes a rubber arm, a great heart and the skill of a magician. It is the pitch which must be perfect to fool a great hitter.

Willy's grin faded as he reared back. He felt the pain, now. It was not in his arm, but it was not good either.

He made the fast throw again. It came in, letter-high. Roble knew it was coming. The great bat swung round. There was a hollow sound. The sound was made by the ball striking, not wood, but the leather of Hub's mitt. The mighty Roble had struck out.

Guy Lott was yelling, but the tone was different, Willy knew. Graham was up. Graham was a long hitter, all right, but he was Graham, not Roble. Willy threw him the mixed soft stuff.

The count was two and two. Willy threw the high, hard one, sneaking it in. Graham swung. The ball came off his bat like a rifle. Willy Gaye swung, turned his back to the plate and flipped his left hand above his head. The liner struck leather, stayed in the pocket of the old, limp mitt. Willy dropped back to earth.

He staggered a moment. Then he stared at the ball, wrapped his hands about it as all hell broke loose in the park. George Dunn and Stahl ran to grab him, hug him. Laughingly he broke away and ran toward the dugout. Bull Acton blocked his way.

Hub Egan shed mask and protector and came racing. He yelled, "If you touch him . . ."

Bull said, "Hell. He was my roomie. Mary is his pal. I just wanted to shake hands. It was baseball, that's all. Baseball. Pal, you were great."

He made the dressing room. He leaned against his locker and his face was older now. Stahl said, "Lemme see. There's something wrong here." He was plucking at Willy's shirt.

George Dunn, with amazingly tender hands, helped strip the lean veteran. Around his torso was a swathe of bandages.

Willy said, recovering himself slightly, "Now, don't get dumb and excited. It was nothin'. I had to get over to Jersey, see? And then it was okay."

Eddie Knight broke in. His voice was shaky. He said, "Old Doc Borden. He's the only one who could ever bandage a broken rib . . . Bull broke your rib. When he put the ball on you!"

"I didn't know it right away," Willy apologized. His grin had returned. "Doc made me take a drink when he bandaged me. He's old school, like me. So I took a couple—three or four. You want to make that fine stick, Eddie?"

The manager said, "The fine doesn't go. And you stay with the club. And you're no relief pitcher. You couldn't take your regular turn. Not at your age. But you're something else, from now, Willy. You're my pinch pitcher!"

Slim Crane said, "That's it! Better than a relief! A guy for the pinches, the important spots. That's you, Willy."

"A one-hitter!" said George Dunn. "If the blinkety-blanked scorers had done right, a no-hitter! In the pinch!"

Eddie Knight went quietly into his office. He had a pennant. He would not be surprised if he had a World Series. He said aloud, to no one but himself, "All right. I made a mistake. I forgot. I forgot there were guys with baseballs for hearts!"

BREAD ALONE

John O'Hara

T WAS THE eighth inning, and the Yankees had what the sportswriters call a comfortable lead. It was comfortable for them, all right. Unless a miracle happened, they had the ball game locked up and put away. They would not be coming to bat again, and Mr. Hart didn't like that any more than he was liking his thoughts, the thoughts he had been thinking ever since the fifth inning, when the Yanks had made their five runs. From the fifth inning on, Mr. Hart had been troubled with his conscience.

Mr. Hart was a car-washer, and what colored help at the Elbee Garage got paid was not much. It had to house, feed, and clothe all the Harts, which meant Mr. Hart himself; his wife, Lolly Hart; his son, Booker Hart; and his three daughters, Carrie, Linda, and the infant, Brenda Hart. The day before, Mr. Ginsburg, the book-keeper who ran the shop pool, had come to him and said, "Well, Willie, you win the sawbuck."

"Yes sir, Mr. Ginsburg, I sure do. I was watchin' them newspapers all week," said Mr. Hart. He dried his hands with the chamois and extended the right.

"One, two, three, four, five, six, seven, eight, nine, anduh tenner. Ten bucks, Willie," said Mr. Ginsburg.

"Well, what are you gonna do with all that dough? I'll bet you don't tell your wife about it."

"Well, I don't know, Mr. Ginsburg. She don't follow the scores, so she don't know I win. I don't know what to do," said Mr. Hart. "But say, ain't I suppose to give you your cut? I understand it right, I oughta buy you a drink or a cigar or something."

"That's the custom, Willie, but thinking it over, you weren't winners all year."

"No sir, that's right," said Mr. Hart.

"So I tell you, if you win another pool, you buy me *two* drinks or *two* cigars. Are you going in this week's pool?"

"Sure am. It don't seem fair, though. Ain't much of the season left and maybe I won't win again. Sure you don't want a drink or a cigar or something?"

"That's all right, Willie," said Mr. Ginsburg.

On the way home, Mr. Hart was a troubled man. That money belonged in the sugar bowl. A lot could come out of that money: a steak, stockings, a lot of stuff. But a man was entitled to a little pleasure in this life, the only life he ever had. Mr. Hart had not been to a ball game since about fifteen or twenty years ago, and the dime with which he bought his ticket in the pool every week was his own money, carfare money. He made it up by getting rides home, or pretty near home, when a truck-driver or private chauffeur friend was going Harlem-ward; and if he got a free ride, or two free rides, to somewhere near home every week, then he certainly was entitled to use the dime for the pool. And this was the first time he had won. Then there was the other matter of who won it for him: the Yankees. He had had the Yankees and the Browns in the pool, the first time all season he had picked the Yanks, and it was they who made the runs that had made him the winner of the ten dollars. If it wasn't for those Yankees, he wouldn't have won. He owed it to them to go and buy tickets and show his gratitude. By the time he got home his mind was made up. He had the next afternoon off, and, by God, he was going to see the Yankees play.

There was, of course, only one person to take; that was Booker, the strange boy of thirteen who was Mr. Hart's only son. Booker was a quiet boy, good in school, and took after his mother, who was quite a little lighter complected than Mr. Hart. And so that night after supper he simply announced, "Tomorrow me and Booker's going over to see the New York Yankees play. A friend of mine happened to give me a choice pair of seats, so me and Booker's taking in the game." There had been a lot of talk, and naturally Booker was the most surprised of all—so surprised that Mr. Hart was not sure his son was even pleased. Booker was a very hard one to understand. Fortunately, Lolly believed right away that someone had really given Mr. Hart the tickets to the game; he had handed over his pay as usual, nothing missing, and that made her believe his story.

But that did not keep Mr. Hart from having an increasingly bad time from the fifth inning on. And Booker didn't help him to forget. Booker leaned forward and he followed the game all right but never said anything much. He seemed to know the game and to recognize the players, but never *talked*. He got up and yelled in the fifth inning when the Yanks were making their runs, but so did everybody else. Mr. Hart wished the game was over.

DiMaggio came to bat. Ball one. Strike one, called. Ball two. Mr. Hart wasn't watching with his heart in it. He had his eyes on DiMaggio, but it was the crack of the bat that made Mr. Hart realize that DiMaggio had taken a poke at one, and the ball was in the air, high in the air. Everybody around Mr. Hart stood up and tried to watch the ball. Mr. Hart stood up too. Booker sort of got up off the seat, watching the ball but not standing up. The ball hung in the air and then began to drop. Mr. Hart was judging it and could tell it was going to hit about four rows behind him. Then it did hit, falling the last few yards as though it had been thrown down from the sky, and smacko! It hit the seats four rows behind the Harts, bounced high but sort of crooked, and dropped again to the row directly behind Mr. Hart and Booker.

There was a scramble of men and kids, men hitting kids and kids darting and shoving men out of the way, trying to get the ball. Mr. Hart drew away, not wanting any trouble, and then he remembered Booker. He turned to look at Booker, and Booker was sitting hunched up, holding his arms so's to protect his head and face.

"Where the hell's the ball? Where's the ball?" Men and kids were yelling and cursing, pushing and kicking each other, but nobody could find the ball. Two boys began to fight because one accused the other of pushing him when he almost had his hand on the ball. The fuss lasted until the end of the inning. Mr. Hart was nervous. He didn't want any trouble, so he concentrated on the game again. Booker had the right idea. He was concentrating on the game. They both concentrated like hell. All they could hear was a mystified murmur among the men and kids. "Well, somebody must of got the goddam thing." In two minutes the Yanks retired the side and the ball game was over.

"Let's wait till the crowd gets started going, Pop," said Booker.

"O.K.," said Mr. Hart. He was in no hurry to get home, with the things he had on his mind and how sore Lolly would be. He'd give her what was left of the ten bucks, but she'd be sore anyhow. He lit a cigarette and let it hang on his lip. He didn't feel so good sitting there with his elbow on his knee, his chin on his fist.

"Hey, Pop," said Booker.

"Huh?"

"Here," said Booker.

"What?" said Mr. Hart. He looked at his son. His son reached inside his shirt, looked back of him, and then from the inside of the shirt he brought out the ball. "Present for you," said Booker.

Mr. Hart looked down at it. "Lemme see that!" he said. He did not reach for it. Booker handed it to him.

"Go ahead, take it. It's a present for you," said Booker.

Suddenly Mr. Hart threw back his head and laughed. "I'll be a goddam holy son of a bitch. You got it? The ball?"

"Sure. It's for you," said Booker.

Mr. Hart threw back his head again and slapped his knees. "I'll be damn—boy, some Booker!" He put his arm around his son's shoulders and hugged him. "Boy, some Booker, huh? You givin' it to me? Some Booker!"

A YOUNG MAN'S GAME

John D. MacDonald

H E CAME AWAKE in the first gray of morning, and saw the palm tops above the mist, coming toward the car and sliding by the window on his side. He rubbed a hand across his face and massaged the back of his neck with big fingers, shifting in the seat and feeling the tingle of circulation along a half-numbed leg. Madge sat small and alert on her cushion, hands tight on the wheel, chin uplifted, as she watched the road ahead where the car lights yellowed the mist.

"Good sleep, honey?" she asked, not taking her eyes from the road ahead.

"I don't know yet. How far we get?"

"Into Florida. We ought to be there in time for lunch."

He stretched in a massive way, hearing the muscles of his right shoulder pop, yawned wide, growled as he yawned. With his left arm still outstretched, he knuckled the back of her fair head lightly.

"Hey!" she said.

"Lots of years, kid. Lots of trips. Lots of blubber to work off every spring."

"Not so much this year, Wally," she said defensively. "Gosh, not like last year."

"About twelve pounds will do it," he agreed.

She gave him a quick glance. "Don't try to do it too fast."

"Want me to drive now?"

"Wait until you're all waked up. I'm not really tired yet."

Usually they managed better, bringing the car down, but this year there had been a hitch in turning the reins of the business over to Thomasson. The accountants wanted to install a new system and Wally Prows wanted to wait and see how it worked out. He hadn't wanted to show up late. Every year, it was just that much harder to get into shape—without complicating matters by losing the first few days. He told Madge he could fly down and then she could bring the car on down, taking her time, but he saw the sharp disappointment in her eyes even as she agreed. So they worked it out, figuring that if they took turns driving, they could make it—just make it. He hoped it would be warm. Heat would make it easier to melt off the winter fat.

Once the sun cut the mist, they began to make better time. He took the wheel and Madge sat beside him, legs pulled up under her. Her head sagged against his shoulder and she slept.

At eleven-thirty, when they were a few miles out of town, he awakened her gently. She patted her hair and fixed her lipstick. He went out of his way to drive by the field. He saw that the stands had been enlarged and repainted. The turf on the field looked new and good. Three men in heavy gray sweat suits were jogging across the outfield grass. The staff would have been in town for a week, getting things lined up, sorting equipment, making up training schedules. The trainer would have the whirlpools set up and the tables and hot lamps. As he drove slowly by it seemed to him that he could detect the familiar locker room smell—socks and sweat and liniments and astringents and oiled leather.

It was a good town, a good place to train. He drove on out to the beach. Old Man Giffert was in the rental office. Mrs. Giffert came trotting in moments later.

"By golly," Giffert said. "By golly—Wally Prews. And how you, Miz Prews? It's sure fine to see you folks again. Now the baseball's started for sure. We got you in the same cabaña again. Number seven. Anything you need, just anything at all, you just holler. By golly, Wally, you sure got a-holt of one in that last Cleveland game. By golly, you put it out of the park. Pinch-hit home run. Bet it felt real fine."

"It felt fine, Dan. We'll go get settled in. It's good to be back."

He unloaded the car, and while Madge unpacked, he called Lew at the hotel.

"Lew? This is Wally. Yeah, just got in. What do you mean, shape? I'm a fat old man. Look, we got to get some lunch. Is Alice down yet? Fine. Suppose we stop around later. See you."

He hung up, aware of Madge standing motionless by the dresser, some of his shirts in her hand, watching him.

"All right," he said, too harshly. "He sounded okay. What's he supposed to do? Run over here and kiss me?"

"Please, Wally."

"I'm sorry," he said.

He walked out onto the beach. There had been some erosion. The beach wasn't as large as before. But the sand was clean and white. He snapped his cigarette away. When she came out and said she was ready, they went and ate at the beach restaurant they liked.

"I didn't mean to snap at you," he told her gently.

"I guess he just scares me, honey. He didn't used to. But you know how he is. Oh, he's nice enough, I guess—but people mean absolutely nothing to him."

"It has to be that way. He's an old man. Suppose he gets sentimental. Then he starts fielding teams full of crocks like me and every game is old-timer's day. He'd give me his shirt, his car and his bank account if he thought I needed it. But he sees me dogging it and he yanks me out like he never saw me before. But I'm okay this year. He's got too many kids. He needs balance. I'm okay this year."

"Of course, you are, dear."

And something about the way she said it brought back some of the dull anger. He forced it away and smiled at her. "You going to eat this place clean out of shrimp again this year?"

"Mmmm," she said. "Bushels and tons."

He watched her as she scanned the menu. The booth light touched the gray streak over her ear. Eighteen years in organized ball. Seventeen years married. A long time. So that the words said do not mean much. The real meanings all come clear behind the words.

The front office had sent along the contract in triplicate, in mid-December. The typed figure shocked and angered him. They had given him the maximum cut allowable, the full twenty-five percent. He'd called Lew at his Texas place ten minutes after he ripped open the impressive envelope.

"Well, Wally, you got to look at it this way. That last-year figure, that was figured on a regular. Then you got that slump, and that Whitlock, he come up so good and strong, and that Kimberland was hitting, and so you were—well, reserved for half the season. Then they make out the budget and—"

"Nuts, Lew. This isn't a salary. It's more like a pension. I slumped and I came back. I pinch-hit a three-seventeen for you. I do a clown act on only two flies all year. I won't sign this damn thing.''

''Well, it's pretty tough, Wally. You don't sit where I sit. Before television they never got so cautious. Well, you sit tight. Let me see what I can do. But I don't think I can do much.''

Two weeks later, another set of contracts was mailed to him. Five percent of the cut had been restored. He had held out for a month, not communicating with them in any way. That month had been hell. Until Madge had said, ''Dear, I'm getting terribly tired of living with a bear. And it's all pride, you know. Not the money. We can get along. You want to play ball. You're afraid they'll let you go on waiver. Just sign, dear. Then you can prove they're wrong.''

It made sense. He felt a great weight lift off him when he dropped the signed contracts in the mail. And that was it—now. Prove they were wrong. Get out with the kids. Get the timing working. Get the fat off. Get that jump on the ball every time.

Madge drove him out and left him off the next morning. The town people had put new name signs on the lockers of the regulars. His name had been gaudily, lovingly printed and he had to grin at it.

Pilko, the squat, hairy catcher, patted him smartly across the pale winter softness of his waistline and said, ''Old butterball. Old mushmellow.''

''Still standing in your hole, Pilk?''

Pilko strained to stand on tiptoe. ''Say, Wally, that kid of mine. The boy. Thirteen, he is. And already an inch taller than his old man. A monster, he'll be.''

The kids up for their seasonal hack at the big time used the unnamed lockers and made as if they were not the least bit impressed with the large names around them. It was always that way. Always nonchalant, and most of them too smart to grandstand.

Wally Prews bundled himself up. He knew that Christy wouldn't bother him, that Christy would let him pace himself, lean the body down, harden the hands, toughen the legs, build up the wind. And, as always, when he started to jog around the outfield, he felt thick, middle-aged, sweaty and ridiculous. A bulky, overgrown child playing a solitary game with the grimness of all children who pretend.

Pilko ran with him for a time. On the far side of the field, one of the coaches was putting the kids through organized calisthenics. Sweat ran into Wally's eyes, making them sting. At the end of the session, one of Christy's men rubbed him down expertly. He was

two pounds lighter. Christy, himself, took care of the threat of a
blister on the side of his right heel.

Every night at the cabaña, he tumbled into the deepest of sleeps.
At first, he was waking up stiff and sore, taking minutes to work
his way out of bed. Then, that began to ease off. At the end of ten
days, he was down to one-ninety, where he belonged, and the sun
no longer reddened his brown neck.

Yet he knew he was not as relaxed as during other years. There
was a tension in him that erupted into anger too easily and too
often. He took his turn in the batting cage after batting-tee practice. A new kid was throwing them in. Wally measured his distance
from the plate with his bat, planted his feet in his wide, solid
stance, bat cocked. He hit two steaming line drives and then a pop-
up and then two fouls before he got hold of one in the sweetly
remembered way and dumped it out where he wanted it. The kid
had been throwing with an easy rhythm. On the next pitch, he
made a cute little hesitation. Wally didn't bother to swing. He
walked four steps toward the mound and said, "Okay, you pitched
a no-hitter. We won thirty to nothing. Now relax and throw."

"I'm sorry, Mr. Prews," the kid said.

The formality of the address shocked Wally. He went back and
got hold of several more before Quinn motioned him out. He
jogged out through the hole between first and second and took
right field, picking up the glove Whitlock had tossed aside as he
came in, and feeling an unreasonable annoyance with Whitlock for
not holding the glove, tossing it to him as they jogged past one
another.

Annoyance kept him full of adrenalin, and when Whitlock hit a
sharp line drive into short right, Wally charged it hard, snapped it
off the bounce and practiced a peg to the plate. The pitcher cut it
off, but not before Wally saw, with satisfaction, that it was
straight, true and fast.

When they played the first exhibition game, splitting up into two
teams and opening the stands to the public, Wally was pleased by
the hand he got. He got two at bat before relinquishing his position
to Kimberland. He struck out once and doubled once, driving in a
man from first, a new man who ran as if his pants were on fire.

Even then, he couldn't shake off the constant irritation, and he
told himself that he was sore because he was being purchased at
cut rates this year. It certainly wasn't because he could see that
both Kimberland and Whitlock were just as hot as during the last
half of the previous season.

The first scheduled exhibition was with the Giants from the other league. Wally started in right. He played three innnings but only got one at bat because it was Hearn throwing and he was rough. In his one time at bat, he hit the second ball pitched into a corner for a stand-up double and died there. He knew he had looked good in the field. He threw out Mays when Mays tried to stretch a single into a double. He made a good, long, running catch of a ball that some new kid got a fat piece of, and drew applause on the catch.

But after he came out, he sat sour on the bench, big shoe against the Coke machine, watching without any stir of interest. He knew that Madge was aware of his sourness, and he had seen the little ways in which she had tried to raise his spirits. He tried to respond, and knew his laughter was leaden.

At the end of one day, as he was combing his shower-wet hair over the fifty-cent bald spot, Lew came up behind him and said, "You and Madge, you two going to be home later on?"

"Sure, Lew. Stop on over. Bring Alice."

"Just me. She's got something on."

Wally didn't like the expression on Lew's face. It was too elaborately casual. He made himself smile. "Come on over any time. We'll be there."

Lew came just after dusk. He stood by the screen door and listened to the sound of the Gulf and said, "I stayed on the beach one year. Well, I like to died for not sleeping. Too damn noisy."

"How about a drink, Lew?" Madge asked him.

Lew folded his lean old body into a chair. "Now, if you got a cold brew . . ."

When they were all seated, Lew, looking peculiarly shy, said, "Well, I thought you ought to have a chance to put your two cents in this thing, Madge. Wally's been playing for me a long time."

"Eight seasons, Lew," Madge said quietly. "This will be the ninth."

"Or it won't be the ninth," Wally heard himself say.

"Well, that opens it up," Lew said, a little sharpness in his voice. "I been on the phone a lot. Trading talk. I'll keep the other club out of this. Just say this much. They haven't finished better than fifth in the last four years. They got outfield weakness and power weakness. And they got a kid we want where we're shaky, over there on third. I think maybe we use you for bait and they bite, Wally."

"Then go ahead. Don't come around apologizing in advance."

"You've been one damn miserable man ever since you showed up here, Prews," Lew said.

"I've been playing good ball."

"I know that. I didn't expect that."

Wally stared at him. "That's a hell of a funny thing to say!"

"I don't see how it is. Now, take last year. You were going good. Then you got so hot about whether or not you'd show up good enough to get in another year as a regular that you slumped off. Now, you come down here with a big chip on your shoulder and go around biting on people because already you're wondering about next year. Be honest, Wally Prews. Talk up. Aren't you thinking on next year?"

Wally looked down at his big hands. "Maybe I am, Lew," he said.

"You've got a nice business of your own. You've had a lot of years of ball. You were never a sour guy. What's your trouble now, Wally?"

Wally glanced at Madge and then looked down again. He wanted to put his finger on the trouble. He said the only thing he could think of. "It—it just doesn't seem to be any fun any more, Lew."

"I figured that. You always played hard. You were always a tough competitor. Now you're fighting yourself and me. You keep it up and you're going to slump worse than last year. Wally, why don't you make this the last year? Only you and me and Madge has to know it. Stop fighting yourself. You do that and I won't trade you. Maybe I'm a little superstitious about you. I've done pretty good in those eight seasons."

Next year, he thought. Watch from the stands. No hard swing and good gutty crack, and the ball sailing high as that great crowd sound came; no running hard for first and then seeing it go and slowing to that jog trot, taking off the cap after you round third. But, also, none of that drawn-down, sick weariness during the hot tag end of the season; none of forcing of muscles which have lost resilience. And Madge would not have to face the brittle, feline politeness of the other baseball wives. It would be down in the record book and all over.

He looked over at Madge. Her eyes were steady. Her expression told him nothing. "It's up to you, Wally," she said quietly.

"But how do you feel?"

"I want what you want. If it isn't any fun any more . . ." She shrugged.

He looked at Lew and then back at Madge. "This will be the last season, Lew," he said. And he saw the gladness in Madge's eyes, quickly masked.

Lew got up and cuffed him on the shoulder. "Okay, Wally. So now I'm fresh out of bait and we don't get that fast feller on third the way I wanted."

They heard him drive away. "Let's take a walk down the beach, honey," Wally said.

They walked on the hard sand where the tide had gone out. The last year. It was funny how thinking about it took weights off him. He held her hand as they walked. The last year in ball. The word had been given. He did not want to change it. And he had a feeling that he would be hot, and stay hot—substituting the ball sense and experience of eighteen years for Whitlock's younger legs, Kimberland's powerful swing. And no slump this year, because it was the last, with everything on the line.

He grunted and it was a sound that was half laugh, half pain.

"Darling?" she said.

"That old carp. That scavenger. All his talk about superstition. Don't you get it? He gets a good year out of me, maybe the best yet if I can keep lucky. Then next year, either Whitlock or Kimberland goes into my slot."

She stopped there, turned to face him. "But, Wally, does that mean you won't . . ."

He took her by the shoulders and turned her a little so that the moonlight was more clearly against her face. There was a feeling of rest, of peace, within him. And love for her.

"This is a fat old man playing his last year, Madge. And it might even be fun again, like they tell you it should be. It's a game, isn't it?"

She smiled in moonlight. "I guess I better be kissed."

So he did, and they walked back to the cabaña through the wave sounds, his big arm around her, their moonlight shadows sharp and clear on the white Florida sand.

THE UMPIRE'S REVOLT

Paul Gallico

SURELY THERE WILL be none to whom our national pastime is meat and drink who will have forgotten Cassaday's Revolt, that near catastrophe that took place some years ago. It came close not only to costing the beloved Brooklyns the pennant and star pitcher Rafe Lustig his coveted $7,500 bonus, but rocked organized baseball to its foundation.

The principal who gave his name and deed to the insurrection, Mr. Rowan (Concrete) Cassaday, uncorruptible, unbudgeable chief umpire of umpires of the National League, was supposed to have started it all. Actually, he didn't.

It is a fact that newspapers which focus the pitiless spotlight of publicity upon practically everyone connected with baseball, from magnate to bat boy, have a curiously blind side when it comes to umpires. They rarely seem to bother about what the sterling arbiters are up to, once the game is over.

Thus, at the beginning of this lamentable affair, no one had the slightest inkling that actually something had been invented capable of moving the immovable Concrete Cassaday, before whose glare the toughest player quailed and from whose infallible dictum there was no reprieve. That something was a woman, Miss Molly McGuire, queen of the lovely Canarsie section of Brooklyn, hard by fragrant Jamaica Bay.

The truth was, when umpire Cassaday went acourting Molly McGuire of a warm September night and sat with her on the stoop

288

of the old brownstone house where she lived with her father, the retired boulevard besomer, Old Man McGuire, he was no longer concrete, but sludge. When the solid man looked up into the beautifully kept garden of Molly's face with its forget-me-not eyes, slipperflower nose, anemone mouth, and hair the gloss and color of the midnight pansy, you could have ladled him up with a spoon.

Old Man McGuire, ex-street-cleaning department, once he had ascertained that Cassaday could not further his yearning to become the possessor of a lifetime pass to Ebbets Field, such as are owned by politicians or bigwigs, left them to their wooing. However, he took his grief for assuaging—since he considered it something of a disgrace that his daughter should have taken up with that enemy of all mankind, and in particular the Brooklyns, an umpire—to the Old Heidelberg Tavern, presided over by handsome and capable Widow Katina Schultz.

This was in a sense patriotic as well as neighborly and practical, since everyone knew that blond widow Schultz was engaged to be married to Rafe Lustig, sensational Brooklyn right-hander. Rafe had been promised a bonus of $7,500 if he won twenty-two games that season, which money he was intending to invest in Old Heidelberg to rescue it and his ladylove from the hands of the mortgage holders.

There was some division of opinion as to the manner in which Rowan Cassaday had acquired the nickname "Concrete." Ballplayers indicated that it referred unquestionably to the composition of his skull, but others said it was because of his square jaw, square shoulder, huge square head and square buttocks. Clad in his lumpy blue serge suit, pockets bulging with baseballs, masked and chest-protected, he resembled nothing so much as, in the words of a famous sports columnist, a concrete—ah—shelter.

Whatever, he was unbudgeable in his decisions, which were rarely wrong, for he had a photographic eye imprinting an infallible record on his brain, which made him invaluable.

You would think it would have been sufficient for Molly, one hundred and three pounds of Irish enchantress, to have so solid and august a being helplessly in love with her. But it was also a fact that Molly was a woman, a creature who, even when most attractive and sure of herself, sometimes has to have a little tamper with fate or inaugurate a kind of test just to make certain. Molly's tamper, let it be said, was a beaut.

It was a sultry evening in mid-September, with the Dodgers a game or two away from grabbing the banner, and the Giants, Cards and Bucs all breathing down their necks. Molly perched on the top step of the stoop, with Concrete adoring her from three below. Old Man McGuire still sat in the window of the front parlor, collarless, with his feet on the open window ledge, reading *The Sporting News*.

Miss McGuire, who had attended the game that afternoon, looked down at her burly admirer and remarked casually, "Rowan, dear, do you know what? I've been thinking about the old blue serge suit you always wear on the ball field. It's most unbecoming to you."

"Eh?" Cassaday exclaimed, startled, for he had never given it so much as a thought. For years, the blue serge suit, belted at the back, with oversize patch pockets and the stiff-visored blue cap, had been as much a part of him as his skin.

"Uh-huh! It makes you look pounds heavier and yards broader, like the old car barns back of Ebbets Field. My girl friend who was with me at the game was saying what a pity, on account of you were such a fine figure of a man. Can't you wear something else for a change, Rowan, darling?"

A bewildered expression came into Cassaday's eyes and he stammered, "Wear s-something else? Molly, baby, you know there's nothing I wouldn't do for you, but the blue serge suit is the uniform and mark of me trade!"

"Oh, is it?" she asked, and stared down at him in a manner to cause icicles to form about his heart. "So you don't care about my being humiliated, sitting up there in the stands with my girl friend on Ladies' Day? And anyway, who said you had to wear it? Is there any rule about it?"

"Sure," replied Cassaday. "There must be—I mean there ought to—that is, I'd have to look it up." For he was suddenly assailed with the strangest doubt. If there was any man who was wholly conversant with the rules and regulations of baseball, it was he, and he could not recall at that moment ever having seen one that applied to his dress. "What did you have in mind, darling?"

"Why, just that it's a free country and you're entitled to wear something a little more suitable to your personality, a man with a fine build like yours."

"Do you really think so, then?"

"Of course I do. When you bend over to dust off the plate at the start of the game, every eye in the park is on you, and I won't have my friends passing remarks about your shape. Next Monday when the Jints come to Ebbets Field, I'll expect to see you dressed a little more classy."

Cassaday fluttered feebly once more, "It would be against all precedent, Molly. You wouldn't want———"

"What I don't want is to see you in that awful suit again, either on or off the field," Molly concluded finally for him. "And I don't think I wish to talk about it any longer. But remember. I'll be at the game next Monday."

Concrete Cassaday, the terror of the National League, looked up at Molly McGuire and cooed, "Give us a kiss, Molly. I'm crazy about you."

"I don't know that I shall, naughty boy."

"Molly, baby, there's nothing I wouldn't do for you."

"I guess I'm crazy about you, too, honey."

With a pained expression on his wizened jockey's face, Old Man McGuire arose, descended the stoop and headed for Old Heidelberg, never dreaming at the moment the importance of what he had overheard.

I will refresh your memory as to some of the events of that awful Monday, when the Brooks trotted onto the cleanly outlined Ebbets Field diamond against the hated Giants. Big Rafe Lustig, who had won twenty-one games, and had warmed up beautifully, took the mound to win his twenty-second game. This would clinch the $7,500 bonus destined for the support of the tottering Old Heidelberg and just about put Brooklyn out of reach in the scamper for the rag down the homestretch.

Umpires Syme and Tarbolt had already taken up their stations at first and third. The head of the Giant batting order was aggressively swinging three war clubs. The batteries had been announced. Pregame tension was electric. Into this, marching stolidly from the dugout onto the field, looking neither right nor left, walked the apparition that was Concrete Cassaday.

He wore gray checked trousers, a horrid mustard-colored tweed coat with a plaid check overlay in red and green. His shirt was a gray-and-brown awning stripe worn with an orange necktie. From his pocket peered a dreadful Paisley handkerchief of red and yellow. On his head he wore a broad flat steamer cap of Kelly green with a white button in the center. Concrete Cassaday, at the behest of his lady love, and, no doubt, some long-dormant inner urge to express himself, had let himself go.

This sartorial catastrophe stalked to the plate, turned the ghastly cap around backward like a turn-of-the-century automobilist, and against a gasping roar that shook the girders of the field dedicated to Charlie Ebbets, called, "Play ball! Anybody makes any cracks is out of the game!"

Unfortunately, the storm of cheers and catcalls arising from the stands at the spectacle drowned out this fair warning, and Pat Coe, the manager, advancing on Cassaday with, "What the hell is this,

Cassaday—Weber and Fields?'' found himself thumbed from the premises before the words were out of his mouth.

Rafe Lustig, who had the misfortune to possess a sense of humor, fared even worse. With a whoop, he threw the ball over the top of the grandstand and, clutching at his eyes, ran around shouting, ''I'm blind! I'm blind!'' evoking roars of laughter until he fetched smack up against the object of his derision, who said, ''Blind, are you, Rafe? Then ye can't pitch. And what's more, as long as I'm wearing this suit, you'll not pitch! Now beat it!''

Too late, Rafe sobered, ''Aw, now, Concrete, have a————''

''Git!''

Wardrobe or no wardrobe, when Cassaday said, ''Git!'' they got.

Slidey Simpson, the big, good-natured Negro first baseman, said, ''Who-ee-ee, Mr. Cassaday! You sure enough dressed up like Harlem on Sunday night.''

''March!'' said Concrete.

Slidey marched with an expression of genuine grievance on his face, for he had really meant to be complimentary. Butts Barry, the heavy-hitting catcher, merely whinnied like a horse and found himself heading for his street clothes; Harry Stutz, the second baseman, was nailed making a rude gesture, and banished; Pads Franklin, the third baseman, went off the field for a look on his face; Allie Munson was caught by telepathy, apparently doing something derogatory all the way out in left field, and was waved off.

Sheltered by the dugout, the Giants somehow avoided the disaster that was engulfing the Brooklyn team. By the time Pat Coe managed to send word from the dressing room to lay off Cassaday and play ball, the Brooks fielded a heterogeneous mob of substitutes, utility infielders and bench-warmers including a deaf-and-dumb pitcher newly arrived from Hartford, whom the joyous and half-hysterical Giants proceeded to take apart.

Heinz Zimmer, the president of the club, had been thrown off the field by Cassaday for protesting, and was on the telephone to the office of the league president, who, advised of potential sabotage and riot at Ebbets Field, and the enormity of Cassaday's breach of everything sacred to the national sport, was frantically buzzing the office of the high commissioner of baseball.

Down on the diamond, the Giants were spattering hits against all walls and scoring runs in clusters; the fickle fans were hooting the hapless Dodger remnants. The press box was in an uproar. Photographers shot Cassaday from every angle, and even in color. All in all, it was an afternoon of the sheerest horror.

There was just one person in the park who was wholly and thoroughly pleased. This was Miss Molly McGuire.

You well remember the drama of the subsequent days, when the example set by umpire Cassaday spread to other cities in both leagues, indicating that the revolt had struck a sympathetic chord in many umpirical hearts.

Indeed, there did not appear to be an arbiter in either circuit but seemed to be sick unto death of the blue serge suit. Ossa piled upon Pelion as reports came in from Detroit that Slats Owney had turned up in Navin Field in golf knickers and a plaid hunting cap; that in Cleveland, Iron Spine McGoorty had discarded his blue serge for fawn-colored slacks and a Harry Truman shirt, and that Mike O'Halloran had caused a near riot in the bleachers at St. Louis by appearing in white cricket flannels and shirt and an Old School tie.

As the climax to all this came the long-awaited ruling from the office of the high commissioner, a bureau noted from the days of Kenesaw Mountain Landis for incorruptible honesty. It was a bombshell to the effect that, after delving into files, clippings and yellowing documents dating back to the days of Abner Doubleday, there was no written rule of any kind with regard to the garb that shall be worn by a baseball umpire.

As far as regulations or possible penalties for infractions were concerned, an umpire might take the field in his pajamas, or wearing a ballet tutu, a pair of jodhpurs, a sarong or a set of hunting pinks complete with silk topper, and no one could penalize him or fine him a penny for it.

While the fans roared with laughter, the press fulminated and Rafe Lustig continued not to occupy the mound for Brooklyn; Concrete Cassaday, still hideously garbed, went on to render his impeccable decisions as the shattered Dodgers staggered under defeat after defeat, and no one knew just what to do.

A rule would undoubtedly have to be made up and incorporated, but the high commissioner was one who did not care to write rules while under fire. To force the maverick Cassaday back into his blue serge retroactively was not consonant with his ideas of good discipline and the best for the game. It was, as you recall, touch-and-go for a while. The revolt might burn itself out. And, on the other hand, it could, as it seemed to be doing, spread to the point where, by creating ridicule, it would do the grand old game an irreparable mischief.

That much you know because you remember the hoohaw. But you weren't around a joint in Canarsie known as The Old Heidelberg when a stricken old ex-asphalt polisher moaned audibly into his lager over the evil case to which his beloved Brooklyns had been brought because his wicked and headstrong daughter had seduced the chief of all the umpires into masquerading as a race-horse tout or the opening act at Loew's Flatbush Avenue Theater. And the sharp ears of a certain widow Katina Schultz, whose business was going out the window on the wings of Rafe Lustig's apparent permanent banishment from the chance to twirl bonus-winning No. 22, picked it up.

Miss Plevin, the secretary, entered the commissioner's office and said, "There's a Mrs. Schultz and a Mr. McGuire to see you, sir. They've been waiting all morning. Something to do with the Cassaday affair," she said.

"What?" cried the commissioner; now ready to grasp at any straw. "Why didn't you say so before? Send them in."

Mrs. Katina Schultz was a handsome blond woman in her thirties, with undoubted strength of character, not to mention of grip, for that was what she had on the arm of a small, unhappy-looking Irishman.

Holding firmly to him, Mrs. Schultz said, "Go on. Tell him what you told me down in the tavern last night."

With a surprising show of stubbornness, Old Man McGuire said, "I'll not! Oh, the shame of it will bring me to an early grave!"

"Oh, you are the most exasperating old man!" wailed Katina, and looked as though she were about to shake him. She turned to the commissioner and said, "My Rafe is losing his bonus, the Dodgers are blowing the pennant and he knows why Umpire Cassaday stopped wearing his blue suit. He says he wants a gold pass or something."

"Hah!" cried the commissioner. "If he knows any way to get Cassaday back into his blue serge suit, he can have a platinum pass studded with————"

Old Man McGuire managed to look as cunning as a monkey, but in a way also as pathetic. "Just plain gold, yer honor," he said. "A lifetime pass to Ebbets Field. I'm an old man and not long for this world."

"O.K. It's yours. Now what's the story?"

"It's me daughter, Molly, as good as betrothed to Rowan Cassaday, the Evil One fly away with all umpires. She put him up to it." And he told of what he had overheard that evening on the stoop.

"Good grief!" the commissioner exploded. "A woman behind it. I didn't know that umpires ever————I beg your pardon. See here, Mr. McGuire. Do you think that if your daughter persuaded Umpire Cassaday into the revolting—ah—unusual outfit, she might likewise persuade him out of it and back into————''

"With a nod of her head, he's that soft about her," Old Man McGuire replied. "But she won't."

"Why not?"

"She's a stubborn lass. Everybody in Canarsie is talking about her as the power behind Cassaday's Revolt. We've been at her, but she says Cassaday's within his rights and nobody but her can stop him. She's jealous over her influence with him, and it's gone to her head."

"H'm'm," mused the commissioner, "I see. And what is your interest in this affair, Mrs. Schultz?"

Katina explained the insoluble dilemma of the mortgage on Old Heidelberg, the $7,500 bonus, the fading season and Cassaday's ultimatum to Rafe Lustig.

The commissioner nodded. "Cassaday is a valuable umpire, perhaps the most valuable we have, even though a little headstrong. I should not like to lose him. Still, if we can't make a rule now to order him back into his uniform, perhaps we————" And here he paused as one suddenly riven with an idea.

Then he smiled quietly and said, "Go home, old man. Maybe you've earned your lifetime pass."

When they had left, he searched his drawer and gave Miss Plevin a telephone number to call. Electrical impulses surged through a copper wire, causing a bell to ring in a small office on Broadway in the Fifties with the legend SIME HOLTZMAN, PUBLICITY lettered on the grimy glass door.

"Sime, this is your old pal," said the commissioner, and told him what was on his mind.

At his end, Sime doodled a moment on a pad, chewing on a cigar, and then said, "Boy, you're in luck. I got just what you want. She's a real phony from Czechoslovakia and hasn't paid me for six months. Can she lay it on thick! She oozes that foreign charm that will drive any self-respecting American girl off her chump. You leave it to me, kid."

Thus it was that after the game the following afternoon, which the Bucs won from Brooklyn by the score thirteen runs to one, a flashy redhead, her age artfully concealed beneath six layers of make-up, sat in an even flashier sports roadster at the players' entrance to Ebbets Field, nursing a large bundle of roses, accompanied by Sime Holtzman and a considerable number of photographers.

When Umpire Cassaday, still in his rebel's outfit, mustard-colored coat, green cap and all, emerged, Sime blocked his path for the cameramen.

"Mr. Cassaday," Holtzman said, "allow me to present Miss Anya Bouquette of Prague, in Czechoslovakia. Miss Bouquette represents the Free Czechoslovakian Film Colony in the United States. They have chosen you the best-dressed umpire and she wishes to make the presentation————"

At this point, Umpire Cassaday found himself with a bunch of roses in his arms and Miss Bouquette, a fragrant and not exactly repulsive bundle of femininity, draped about his neck, cooing in a thick Slavic accent, "Oooo! I am so hoppy because you are so beautifuls! I geev you wan kees, two kees, three kees————

"I congratulates you, Mr. Cassaday!" she declaimed, accenting the second syllable. "In Czechoslovakia, thees costume would be the mos' best and would cotch all the girls for to marry. I am Czech. I love the United States and Freedom, and therefore I am loving you too. I geev you wan kees, two kees, three kees————"

Thereafter, wherever Umpire Cassaday was, Mademoiselle Bouquette and the photographers were never far away. Holtzman worked out a regular schedule, duly noted in the press: Morning in the Brooklyn Museum, where she taught him European culture; lunch at Sardi's; dinner at 21 with the attaché of the Free Czechs, where Miss Bouquette announced that all men ought to dress like Mr. Cassaday; and so on.

In the meantime, word leaked from the commissioner's office that while no rule forcing umpires to wear blue serge was contemplated at the moment, so high was the esteem and regard in which Umpire Cassaday was held that consideration was being given to the idea of making his startling outfit the official uniform for all umpires.

The climax came the next afternoon at Ebbets Field, where the Pirates were playing their last game before the Giants returned for a short series, the last of the season, and the one that would decide the pennant.

In a box back of home plate, resplendent in a set of white fox furs purchased on credit restored by the new-found publicity and covered with orchids, sat Mademoiselle Anya Bouquette. This time she had a horseshoe of carnations and a huge parchment scroll, gold-embossed and dangling a red seal.

Umpire Cassaday had just emerged from the dugout, headed for home plate, when Sime Holtzman had a finger in his buttonhole and was hauling him toward the field box. Concrete had time only for one bewildered protest, "What, again?" smothered by Holtz-man's "It's the Yugoslavs this time. They're crazy about your outfit. They've asked Miss Bouquette to present you with a scroll."

But upon this occasion the fans were ready. As Umpire Cassa-day, with ears slightly reddened, stood with the floral horseshoe about his neck and Mademoiselle Bouquette arose with the parch-ment scroll unfurled, the united fanry of Flatbush, Jamaica Bay, Canarsie, Gowanus and other famous localities began to chant in unison, with a mighty handclap punctuating each digit.

"I geev you wan kees, two kees, three kees————"

They had reached "eight kees," when a very small contretemps took place which was hardly noticed by anyone.

Four boxes away there sat a most exquisite-looking young lady, in a dark Irish way. Between the count of eight and nine kees, Miss Molly McGuire arose from her seat and marched from the prem-ises. As I said, very few noticed this. One of those who did, out of the corner of his eye, was Umpire Rowan (Concrete) Cassaday.

This was the game, as I remember, in which Umpire Cassaday made one of the few palpable miscalls of his career. Pads Franklin, the Brooklyn lead-off hitter, looked at a ball that was so far over his head that the Buc catcher had to call for a ladder to pull it down. Concrete called him out on a third strike.

It was again a sultry September night. On the top of the stoop of the brownstone house in Canarsie sat Molly McGuire, fanning her-self vigorously. Below her—many, many steps below her, almost at the bottom, in fact—crouched Rowan Concrete Cassaday, an unhappy and bewildered man, for he was up against the unsolv-able.

"But, Molly, darling," he was protesting. "I only wanted to make you and your girl friend proud of me. Gosh, wasn't I voted the best-dressed umpire by the Free Czechoslovakian Film Players and awarded a certificate by Miss Anya Bouquette herself to prove————"

Miss Molly McGuire's sniff echoed four blocks to the very edge of Jamaica Bay. "Rowan Cassaday! If you ever mention that wom-an's name in my presence again, our engagement is off!"

The square bulk of Umpire Cassaday edged upward one step. "But, Molly, baby, believe me. She doesn't mean a thing to me. I was only trying to please you, in the first place, by wearing some-thing snappy. Why, the commissioner is even thinking of making it the regular————"

Molly gave a little shudder at the prospect of Mademoiselle Bouquette forever buzzing around her too generous wildflower. "If
you want to please me, Rowan Cassaday, you'll climb right back
into your blue serge suit and cap again, and start looking like the
chief of all the umpires ought to look!"

"But, Molly, baby, that's what I was doing in the first place,
when you———"

"Then do it for me, darling! Tomorrow!"

A glazed look came into the eyes of Rowan Cassaday, as it does
into the eyes of all men when confronted by the awful, unanswerable, moonstruck logic of women. Nevertheless, he gained six
steps without protest, and was able thus to arrive back where he
had started from a hideous ten days ago—at the hem of her dainty
skirt. And thus peace descended once more upon Flatbush.

Remember that wonderful day—a Thursday, I believe it was—
when out from the dugout at game time marched that massive
concrete figure once more impregnably armored, cap-a-pie, in
shiny blue serge, the belted back spread to the load of league
baseballs stuffed in the capacious pockets.

What a cheer greeted his appearance, and then what a roar went
up as Rafe Lustig emerged from the dugout, swinging his glove
and sweater. The historic exchange between the two will never be
forgotten.

Rafe said, "Hi, Rowan."

Concrete replied, "Hi, Rafe."

What a day that was. How the long-silent bats of the Brooks
pummeled the unhappy Jints. How the long-rested arm of Rafe
Lustig, twirling out the $7,500-bonus game and the everlasting rescue of Old Heidelberg, tamed the interlopers from Manhattan, disposing of them with no more than a single scratch hit. How the
word spread like wildfire through the cities of the league that Cassaday's Revolt was over and blue serge once again was the order
of the day.

Witness to all this was a happy Molly McGuire in a box back of
home plate. Absent from the festivities was Mademoiselle Anya
Bouquette, who, it seems, could not abide blue serge, for it reminded her of gloomy Sunday and an unhappy childhood in
Prague, with people jumping off bridges.

And yet, if you looked closely, there was one difference to be
observed, which, in a sense, gave notice who would wear the pants
in the Cassaday household, came that day. For while indeed Concrete was poured back into the lumpy anonymity of the traditional
garments—serge cap, coat, tie, breeches—yet from the breast

pocket fluttered the tip of that awful red-and-yellow Paisley kerchief.

This was all that was left of Cassaday's Revolt. He had tasted individuality. He would never quite be the same again. But the object in his breast pocket remained unnoticed and unmentioned, except for the quiet smile of triumph reflected from the well-kept garden of the countenance of Miss Molly McGuire.

THE CELEBRATED NO-HIT INNING

Frederik Pohl

T HIS IS A TRUE STORY, you have to remember. You have to keep that firmly in mind because, frankly, in some places it may not *sound* like a true story. Besides, it's a true story about baseball players, and maybe the only one there is. So you have to treat it with respect.

You know Boley, no doubt. It's pretty hard not to know Boley, if you know anything at all about the National Game. He's the one, for instance, who raised such a scream when the sportswriters voted him Rookie of the Year. "I never *was* a rookie," he bellowed into three million television screens at the dinner. He's the one who ripped up his contract when his manager called him, "The hittin'est pitcher I ever see." Boley wouldn't stand for that. "Four-eighteen against the best pitchers in the league," he yelled, as the pieces of the contract went out the window. "Fogarty, I am the hittin'est *hitter* you ever see!"

He's the one they all said reminded them so much of Dizzy Dean at first. But did Diz win thirty-one games in his first year? Boley did; he'll tell you so himself. But politely, and without bellowing . . .

Somebody explained to Boley that even a truly great Hall-of-Fame pitcher really ought to show up for spring training. So, in his second year, he did. But he wasn't convinced that he *needed* the training, so he didn't bother much about appearing on the field.

Manager Fogarty did some extensive swearing about that, but he did all of his swearing to his pitching coaches and not to Mr.

300
=

Boleslaw. There had been six ripped-up contracts already that year, when Boley's feelings got hurt about something, and the front office were very insistent that there shouldn't be any more.

There wasn't much the poor pitching coaches could do, of course. They tried pleading with Boley. All he did was grin and ruffle their hair and say, "Don't get all in an uproar." He could ruffle their hair pretty easily, since he stood six inches taller than the tallest of them.

"Boley," said Pitching Coach Magill to him desperately, "you are going to get me into trouble with the manager. I need this job. We just had another little boy at our house, and they cost money to feed. Won't you please do me a favor and come down to the field, just for a little while?"

Boley had a kind of a soft heart. "Why, if that will make so much of a difference to you, Coach, I'll do it. But I don't feel much like pitching. We have got twelve exhibition games lined up with the Orioles on the way north, and if I pitch six of those that ought to be all the warm-up I need."

"Three innings?" Magill haggled. "You know I wouldn't ask you if it wasn't important. The thing is, the owner's uncle is watching today."

Boley pursed his lips. He shrugged. "One inning."

"Bless you, Boley!" cried the coach. "One inning it is!"

Andy Andalusia was catching for the regulars when Boley turned up on the field. He turned white as a sheet. "Not the fast ball, Boley! Please, Boley," he begged. "I only been catching a week and I have not hardened up yet."

Boleslaw turned the rosin bag around in his hands and looked around the field. There was action going on at all six diamonds, but the spectators, including the owner's uncle, were watching the regulars.

"I tell you what I'll do," said Boley thoughtfully. "Let's see. For the first man, I pitch only curves. For the second man, the screwball. And for the third man—let's see. Yes. For the third man, I pitch the sinker."

"Fine!" cried the catcher gratefully, and trotted back to home plate.

"He's a very spirited player," the owner's uncle commented to Manager Fogarty.

"That he is," said Fogarty, remembering how the pieces of the fifth contract had felt as they hit him on the side of the head.

"He must be a morale problem for you, though. Doesn't he upset the discipline of the rest of the team?"

Fogarty looked at him, but he only said, "He win thirty-one

games for us last year. If he had *lost* thirty-one he would have
upset us a lot more.''

The owner's uncle nodded, but there was a look in his eye all
the same. He watched without saying anything more, while Boley
struck out the first man with three sizzling curves, right on schedule, and then turned around and yelled something at the outfield.

"That crazy— By heaven," shouted the manager, "he's chasing
them back into the dugout. I *told* that—"

The owner's uncle clutched at Manager Fogarty as he was getting up to head for the field. "Wait a minute. What's Boleslaw
doing?"

"Don't you see? He's chasing the outfield off the field. He wants
to face the next two men without any outfield! That's Satchel
Paige's old trick, only he never did it except in exhibitions where
who cares? But that Boley—"

"This is only an exhibition, isn't it?" remarked the owner's
uncle mildly.

Fogarty looked longingly at the field, looked back at the owner's
uncle, and shrugged.

"All right." He sat down, remembering that it was the owner's
uncle whose sprawling factories had made the family money that
bought the owner his team. "Go ahead!" he bawled at the right
fielder, who was hesitating halfway to the dugout.

Boley nodded from the mound. When the outfielders were all
out of the way he set himself and went into his windup. Boleslaw's
windup was a beautiful thing to all who chanced to behold it—
unless they happened to root for another team. The pitch was more
beautiful still.

"I got it, I got it!" Andalusia cried from behind the plate, waving
the ball in his mitt. He returned it to the pitcher triumphantly, as
though he could hardly believe he had caught the Boleslaw screwball—after only the first week of spring training.

He caught the second pitch, too. But the third was unpredictably
low and outside. Andalusia dived for it in vain.

"Ball one!" cried the umpire. The catcher scrambled up, ready
to argue.

"He is right," Boley called graciously from the mound. "I am
sorry, but my foot slipped. It was a ball."

"Thank you," said the umpire. The next screwball was a strike,
though, and so were the three sinkers to the third man—though
one of those caught a little piece of the bat and turned into an into-
the-dirt foul.

Boley came off the field to a spattering of applause. He stopped under the stands, on the lip of the dugout. "I guess I am a little rusty at that, Fogarty," he called. "Don't let me forget to pitch another inning or two before we play Baltimore next month."

"I won't!" snapped Fogarty. He would have said more, but the owner's uncle was talking.

"I don't know much about baseball, but that strikes me as an impressive performance. My congratulations."

"You are right," Boley admitted. "Excuse me while I shower, and then we can resume this discussion some more. I think you are a better judge of baseball than you say."

The owner's uncle chuckled, watching him go into the dugout. "You can laugh," said Fogarty bitterly. "You don't have to put up with that for a hundred fifty-four games, and spring training, *and* the Series."

"You're pretty confident about making the Series?"

Fogarty said simply, "Last year Boley win thirty-one games."

The owner's uncle nodded, and shifted position uncomfortably. He was sitting with one leg stretched over a large black metal suitcase, fastened with a complicated lock. Fogarty asked, "Should I have one of the boys put that in the locker room for you?"

"Certainly not!" said the owner's uncle. "I want it right here where I can touch it." He looked around him. "The fact of that matter is," he went on in a lower tone, "this goes up to Washington with me tomorrow. I can't discuss what's in it. But as we're among friends, I can mention that where it's going is the Pentagon."

"Oh," said Fogarty respectfully. "Something new from the factories."

"Something very new," the owner's uncle agreed, and he winked. "And I'd better get back to the hotel with it. But there's one thing, Mr. Fogarty. I don't have much time for baseball, but it's a family affair, after all, and whenever I can help— I mean, it just occurs to me that possibly, with the help of what's in this suitcase— That is, would you like me to see if I could help out?"

"Help out how?" asked Fogarty suspiciously.

"Well— I really mustn't discuss what's in the suitcase. But would it hurt Boleslaw, for example, to be a little more, well, modest?"

The manager exploded, *"No."*

The owner's uncle nodded. "That's what I've thought. Well, I must go. Will you ask Mr. Boleslaw to give me a ring at the hotel so we can have dinner together, if it's convenient?"

It was convenient, all right. Boley had always wanted to see how the other half lived; and they had a fine dinner, served right in the suite, with five waiters in attendance and four kinds of wine. Boley kept pushing the little glasses of wine away, but after all the owner's uncle was the owner's uncle, and if *he* thought it was all right— It must have been pretty strong wine, because Boley began to have trouble following the conversation.

It was all right as long as it stuck to earned-run averages and batting percentages, but then it got hard to follow, like a long, twisting grounder on a dry September field. Boley wasn't going to admit that, though. "Sure," he said, trying to follow; and, "You say the *fourth* dimension?" he said; and, "You mean a time machine, like?" he said; but he was pretty confused.

The owner's uncle smiled and filled the wineglasses again.

Somehow the black suitcase had been unlocked, in a slow, difficult way. Things made out of crystal and steel were sticking out of it. "Forget about the time machine," said the owner's uncle patiently. "It's a military secret, anyhow. I'll thank you to forget the very words, because heaven knows what the General would think if he found out— Anyway, forget it. What about you, Boley? Do you still say you can hit any pitcher who ever lived and strike out any batter?"

"Anywhere," agreed Boley, leaning back in the deep cushions and watching the room go around and around. "Any time. I'll bat their ears off."

"Have another glass of wine, Boley," said the owner's uncle, and he began to take things out of the black suitcase.

Boley woke up with a pounding in his head like Snider, Mays, and Mantle hammering Three-Eye League pitching. He moaned and opened one eye.

Somebody blurry was holding a glass out to him. "Hurry up. Drink this."

Boley shrank back. "I will not. That's what got me into this trouble in the first place."

"Trouble? You're in no trouble. But the game's about to start and you've got a hangover."

Ring a fire bell beside a sleeping Dalmatian; sound the Charge in the ear of a retired cavalry major. Neither will respond more quickly than Boley to the words, "The game's about to start."

He managed to drink some of the fizzy stuff in the glass and it was a miracle; like a triple play erasing a ninth-inning threat, the headache was gone. He sat up, and the world did not come to an end. In fact, he felt pretty good.

He was being rushed somewhere by the blurry man. They were going very rapidly, and there were tall, bright buildings outside. They stopped.

"We're at the studio," said the man, helping Boley out of a remarkable sort of car.

"The stadium," Boley corrected automatically. He looked around for the lines at the box office but there didn't seem to be any.

"The *studio*. Don't argue all day, will you?" The man was no longer so blurry. Boley looked at him and blushed. He was only a little man, with a worried look to him, and what he was wearing was a pair of vivid orange Bermuda shorts that showed his knees. He didn't give Boley much of a chance for talking or thinking. They rushed into a building, all green and white opaque glass, and they were met at a flimsy-looking elevator by another little man. This one's shorts were aqua, and he had a bright-red cummerbund tied around his waist.

"This is him," said Boley's escort.

The little man in aqua looked Boley up and down. "He's a big one. I hope to goodness we got a uniform to fit him for the Series."

Boley cleared his throat. "Series?"

"And you're in it!" shrilled the little man in orange. "This way to the dressing room."

Well, a dressing room was a dressing room, even if this one did have color television screens all around it and machines that went *wheepety-boom* softly to themselves. Boley began to feel at home.

He blinked when they handed his uniform to him, but he put it on. Back in the Steel & Coal League, he had sometimes worn uniforms that still bore the faded legend *100 Lbs. Best Fortified Gro-Chick,* and whatever an owner gave you to put on was all right with Boley. Still, he thought to himself, *kilts!*

It was the first time in Boley's life that he had ever worn a skirt. But when he was dressed it didn't look too bad, he thought— especially because all the other players (it looked like fifty of them, anyway) were wearing the same thing. There is nothing like seeing the same costume on everybody in view to make it seem reasonable and right. Haven't the Paris designers been proving that for years?

He saw a familiar figure come into the dressing room, wearing a uniform like his own. "Why, Coach Magill," said Boley, turning with his hand outstretched. "I did not expect to meet you here."

The newcomer frowned, until somebody whispered in his ear. "Oh," he said, "you're Boleslaw."

"Naturally I'm Boleslaw, and naturally you're my pitching

coach, Magill, and why do you look at me that way when I've seen
you every day for three weeks?''

The man shook his head. "You're thinking of Granddaddy Jim,''
he said, and moved on.

Boley stared after him. Granddaddy Jim? But Coach Magill was
no granddaddy, that was for sure. Why, his eldest was no more
than six years old. Boley put his hand against the wall to steady
himself. It touched something metal and cold. He glanced at it.

It was a bronze plaque, floor to ceiling high, and it was embossed
at the top with the words *World Series Honor Roll.* And it listed
every team that had ever won the World Series, from the day
Chicago won the first Series of all in 1906 until—until—

Boley said something out loud, and quickly looked around to
see if anybody had heard him. It wasn't something he wanted
people to hear. But it was the right time for a man to say something
like that, because what that crazy lump of bronze said, down toward the bottom, with only empty spaces below, was that the most
recent team to win the World Series was the Yokohama Dodgers,
and the year they won it in was—1998.

1998.

A time machine, thought Boley wonderingly, I guess what he
meant was a machine that traveled in *time.*

Now, if you had been picked up in a time machine that leaped
through the years like a jet plane leaps through space, you might
be quite astonished, perhaps, and for a while you might not be
good for much of anything, until things calmed down.

But Boley was born calm. He lived by his arm and his eye, and
there was nothing to worry about there. Pay him his Class C league
contract bonus, and he turns up in Western Pennsylvania, all ready
to set a league record for no-hitters his first year. Call him up from
the minors and he bats .418 against the best pitchers in baseball.
Set him down in the year 1999 and tell him he's going to play in the
Series, and he hefts the ball once or twice and says, "I better take
a couple of warm-up pitches. Is the spitter allowed?''

They led him to the bullpen. And then there was the playing of
the National Anthem and the teams took the field. And Boley got
the biggest shock so far.

"Magill," he bellowed in a terrible voice, "what is that other
pitcher doing out on the mound?''

The manager looked startled. "That's our starter, Padgett. He
always starts with the number-two defensive lineup against right-
hand batters when the outfield shift goes—''

"Magill! I am not any *relief* pitcher. If you pitch Boleslaw, you *start* with Boleslaw."

Magill said soothingly, "It's perfectly all right. There have been some changes, that's all. You can't expect the rules to stay the same for forty or fifty years, can you?"

"I am not a *relief* pitcher. I—"

"Please, please. Won't you sit down?"

Boley sat down, but he was seething. "We'll see about that," he said to the world. "We'll just see."

Things had changed, all right. To begin with, the studio really was a studio and not a stadium. And although it was a very large room, it was not the equal of Ebbetts Field, much less the Yankee Stadium. There seemed to be an awful lot of bunting, and the ground rules confused Boley very much.

Then the dugout happened to be just under what seemed to be a complicated sort of television booth, and Boley could hear the announcer screaming himself hoarse just overhead. That had a familiar sound, but—

"And here," roared the announcer, "comes the all-important nothing-and-one pitch! Fans, what a pitchers' duel *this* is! Delasantos is going into his motion! He's coming down! He's delivered it! And it's *in there* for a count of nothing and two! Fans, what a pitcher that Tiburcio Delasantos *is!* And here comes the all-important nothing-and-two pitch, and—and—yes, and he struck him out! *He struck him out!* He struck him *out!* It's a *no-hitter,* fans! In the all-important second inning, it's a no-hitter for Tiburcio Delasantos!"

Boley swallowed and stared hard at the scoreboard, which seemed to show a score of 14–9, their favor. His teammates were going wild with excitement, and so was the crowd of players, umpires, cameramen, and announcers watching the game. He tapped the shoulder of the man next to him.

"Excuse me. What's the score?"

"Dig that Tiburcio!" cried the man. "What a first-string defensive pitcher against left-handers he *is!*"

"The score. Could you tell me what it is?"

"Fourteen to nine. Did you *see* that—"

Boley begged, "Please, didn't somebody just say it was a no-hitter?"

"Why, sure." The man explained: "The inning. It's a no-hit *inning.*" And he looked queerly at Boley.

It was all like that, except that some of it was worse. After three innings Boley was staring glassy-eyed into space. He dimly noticed that both teams were trotting off the field and what looked like a whole new corps of players were warming up when Manager Magill stopped in front of him. "You'll be playing in a minute," Magill said kindly.

"Isn't the game over?" Boley gestured toward the field.

"Over? Of course not. It's the third-inning stretch," Magill told him. "Ten minutes for the lawyers to file their motions and make their appeals. You know." He laughed condescendingly. "They tried to get an injunction against the bases-loaded pitchout. Imagine!"

"Hah-hah," Boley echoed. "Mister Magill, can I go home?"

"Nonsense, boy! Didn't you hear me? You're on as soon as the lawyers come off the field!"

Well, that began to make sense to Boley and he actually perked up a little. When the minutes had passed and Magill took him by the hand, he began to feel almost cheerful again. He picked up the rosin bag and flexed his fingers and said simply, "Boley's ready."

Because nothing confused Boley when he had a ball or a bat in his hand. Set him down any time, anywhere, and he'd hit any pitcher or strike out any batter. He knew exactly what it was going to be like, once he got on the playing field.

Only it wasn't like that at all.

Boley's team was at bat, and the first man up got on with a bunt single. Anyway, they *said* it was a bunt single. To Boley it had seemed as though the enemy pitcher had charged beautifully off the mound, fielded the ball with machinelike precision, and flipped it to the first-base player with inches and inches to spare for the out. But the umpires declared interference by a vote of eighteen to seven, the two left-field umpires and the one with the field glasses over the batter's head abstaining; it seemed that the first baseman had neglected to say "Excuse me" to the runner. Well, the rules were the rules. Boley tightened his grip on his bat and tried to get a lead on the pitcher's style.

That was hard, because the pitcher was fast. Boley admitted it to himself uneasily; he was *very* fast. He was a big monster of a player, nearly seven feet tall and with something queer and sparkly about his eyes; and when he came down with a pitch there was a sort of a hiss and a *splat*, and the ball was in the catcher's hands. It might, Boley confessed, be a little hard to hit that particular pitcher, because he hadn't yet seen the ball in transit.

Manager Magill came up behind him in the on-deck spot and

fastened something to his collar. "Your intercom," he explained. "So we can tell you what to do when you're up."

"Sure, sure." Boley was only watching the pitcher. He looked sickly out there; his skin was a grayish sort of color, and those eyes didn't look right. But there wasn't anything sickly about the way he delivered the next pitch, a sweeping curve that sizzled in and spun away.

The batter didn't look so good either—same sickly gray skin, same giant frame. But he reached out across the plate and caught that curve and dropped it between third base and short; and both men were safe.

"You're on," said a tinny little voice in Boley's ear; it was the little intercom, and the manager was talking to him over the radio. Boley walked numbly to the plate. Sixty feet away, the pitcher looked taller than ever.

Boley took a deep breath and looked about him. The crowd was roaring ferociously, which was normal enough—except there wasn't any crowd. Counting everybody, players and officials and all, there weren't more than three or four hundred people in sight in the whole studio. But he could *hear* the screams and yells of easily fifty or sixty thousand— There was a man, he saw, behind a plate-glass window who was doing things with what might have been records, and the yells of the crowd all seemed to come from loudspeakers under his window. Boley winced and concentrated on the pitcher.

"I will pin his ears back," he said feebly, more to reassure himself than because he believed it.

The little intercom on his shoulder cried in a tiny voice: "You will not, Boleslaw! Your orders are to take the first pitch!"

"But, listen—"

"Take it! You hear me, Boleslaw?"

There was a time when Boley would have swung just to prove who was boss; but the time was not then. He stood there while the big gray pitcher looked him over with those sparkling eyes. He stood there through the windup. And then the arm came down, and he didn't stand there. That ball wasn't invisible, not coming right at him; it looked as big and as fast as the Wabash Cannonball and Boley couldn't help it, for the first time in his life he jumped a yard away, screeching.

"Hit batter! Hit batter!" cried the intercom. "Take your base, Boleslaw."

Boley blinked. Six of the umpires were beckoning him on, so the intercom was right. But still and all—Boley had his pride. He said to the little button on his collar, "I am sorry, but I wasn't hit. He missed me a mile, easy. I got scared is all."

"Take your base, you silly fool!" roared the intercom. "He *scared* you, didn't he? That's just as bad as hitting you, according to the rules. Why, there is no telling what incalculable damage has been done to your nervous system by this fright. So kindly get the bejeepers over to first base, Boleslaw, as provided in the rules of the game!"

He got, but he didn't stay there long, because there was a pinch runner waiting for him. He barely noticed that it was another of the gray-skinned giants before he headed for the locker room and the showers. He didn't even remember getting out of his uniform; he only remembered that he, Boley, had just been through the worst experience of his life.

He was sitting on a bench, with his head in his hands, when the owner's uncle came in, looking queerly out of place in his neat pin-striped suit. The owner's uncle had to speak to him twice before his eyes focused.

"They didn't let me pitch," Boley said wonderingly. "They didn't want Boley to pitch."

The owner's uncle patted his shoulder. "You were a guest star, Boley. One of the all-time greats of the game. Next game they're going to have Christy Mathewson. Doesn't that make you feel proud?"

"They didn't let me pitch," said Boley.

The owner's uncle sat down beside him. "Don't you see? You'd be out of place in this kind of a game. You got on base for them, didn't you? I heard the announcer say it myself; he said you filled the bases in the all-important fourth inning. Two hundred million people were watching this game on television! And they saw you get on base!"

"They didn't let me hit either," Boley said.

There was a commotion at the door and the team came trotting in, screaming victory. "We win it, we win it!" cried Manager Magill. "Eighty-seven to eighty-three! What a squeaker!"

Boley lifted his head to croak, "That's fine." But nobody was listening. The manager jumped on a table and yelled, over the noise in the locker room:

"Boys, we pulled a close one out, and you know what that means. We're leading in the Series, eleven games to nine! Now let's just wrap those other two up, and—"

He was interrupted by a bloodcurdling scream from Boley. Boley was standing up, pointing with an expression of horror. The athletes had scattered and the trainers were using pliers and screw-drivers instead of towels and liniment. Next to Boley, the big gray-skinned pinch runner was flat on his back, and the trainer was lifting one leg away from the body—

"Murder!" bellowed Boley. "That fellow is murdering that fellow!"

The manager jumped down to him. "Murder? There isn't any murder. Boleslaw! What are you talking about?"

Boley pointed mutely. The trainer stood gaping at him, with the leg hanging limp in his grip. It was completely removed from the torso it belonged to, but the torso seemed to be making no objections; the curious eyes were open but no longer sparkling; the gray skin, at closer hand, seemed metallic and cold.

The manager said fretfully, "I swear, Boleslaw, you're a nuisance. They're just getting cleaned and oiled, batteries recharged, that sort of thing. So they'll be in shape tomorrow, you understand."

"*Cleaned,*" whispered Boley. "*Oiled.*" He stared around the room. All of the gray-skinned ones were being somehow disassembled; bits of metal and glass were sticking out of them. "Are you trying to tell me," he croaked, "that those fellows aren't fellows?"

"They're ball players," said Manager Magill impatiently. "Robots. Haven't you ever seen a robot before? We're allowed to field six robots on a nine-man team, it's perfectly legal. Why, next year I'm hoping the Commissioner'll let us play a whole robot team. *Then* you'll see some baseball!"

With bulging eyes Boley saw it was true. Except for a handful of flesh-and-blood players like himself the team was made up of man-shaped machines, steel for bones, electricity for blood, steel and plastic and copper cogs for muscle. "Machines," said Boley, and turned up his eyes.

The owner's uncle tapped him on the shoulder worriedly. "It's time to go back," he said.

So Boley went back.

He didn't remember much about it, except that the owner's uncle had made him promise never, never to tell anyone about it, because it was orders from the Defense Department, you never could tell how useful a time machine might be in a war. But he did get back, and he woke up the next morning with all the signs of a hangover and the sheets kicked to shreds around his feet.

He was still bleary when he staggered down to the coffee shop for breakfast. Magill the pitching coach, who had no idea that he was going to be granddaddy to Magill the Series-winning manager, came solicitously over to him. "Bad night, Boley? You look like you have had a bad night."

"Bad?" repeated Boley. "Bad? Magill, you have got no idea. The owner's uncle said he would show me something that would learn me a little humility and, Magill, he came through. Yes, he did. Why, I saw a big bronze tablet with the names of the Series winners on it, and I saw—"

And he closed his mouth right there, because he remembered right there what the owner's uncle had said about closing his mouth. He shook his head and shuddered. "Bad," he said, "you bet it was bad."

Magill coughed. "Gosh, that's too bad, Boley, I guess—I mean, then maybe you wouldn't feel like pitching another couple of innings—well, anyway, one inning—today, because—"

Boley held up his hand. "Say no more, please. You want me to pitch today, Magill?"

"That's about the size of it," the coach confessed.

"I will pitch today," said Boley. "If that is what you want me to do, I will do it. I am now a reformed character. I will pitch tomorrow, too, if you want me to pitch tomorrow, and any other day you want me to pitch. And if you do not want me to pitch, I will sit on the sidelines. Whatever you want is perfectly all right with me, Magill, because, Magill, I—hey! Hey, Magill, what are you doing down there on the floor?"

So that is why Boley doesn't give anybody any trouble anymore, and if you tell him now that he reminds you of Dizzy Dean, why, he'll probably shake your hand and thank you for the compliment —even if you're a sportswriter, even. Oh, there still are a few special little things about him, of course—not even counting the things like how many shutouts he pitched last year (eleven) or how many homes runs he hit (fourteen). But everybody finds him easy to get along with. They used to talk about the change that had come over him a lot and wonder what caused it. Some people said he got religion and others said he had an incurable disease and was trying to do good in his last few weeks on earth; but Boley never said, he only smiled; and the owner's uncle was too busy in Washington to be with the team much after that. So now they talk about other things when Boley's name comes up. For instance, there's his little business about the pitching machine—when he shows up for batting practice (which is every morning, these days), he insists on hitting against real live pitchers instead of the machine. It's even in his contract. And then, every March he bets nickels against anybody around the training camp that'll bet with him that he can pick that year's Series winner. He doesn't bet more than that, because the Commissioner naturally doesn't like big bets from ball players.

But, even for nickels, don't bet against him, because he isn't ever going to lose, not before 1999.

EBBETS FIELD

Jay Neugeboren

EDDIE GOTTLIEB moved into my neighborhood in the fall of 1955 and I knew right away we were going to become pretty good friends. I was in the eighth grade then, at P.S. 92, and Eddie was brought into my official class about two weeks after school had started. At that time I was going through what my parents called one of my "growing periods"—always talking out in class, making some wiseacre remark, or doing something stupid to get attention, and for this I'd been rewarded with a seat right in front of the teacher's desk, with nobody allowed to sit next to me.

There were no other empty seats in the room, so when our teacher, Mrs. Demetri, told us that we were going to get a new boy in our class I figured he'd be sitting next to me. Our official class hadn't changed much since first grade and it was always a big event when somebody new came into it. When I saw Eddie walk through the door behind Mr. Weiner, the assistant principal, though, my heart jumped. I could tell right away he was a good ballplayer. He was very tall and lanky—about six two then—with thick curly hair that reached down into the collar of his shirt. He sort of shuffled into the room, moving very slowly, his body swaying from side to side, his arms swinging freely. They were real long, coming down just about to his kneecaps. He kept staring at the floor, and when we all started laughing and giggling he must have thought we were laughing at him, because he blushed and fidgeted with his hands and feet a lot—what we were laughing at, though, was not the way

Eddie looked but at the way he looked coming in *behind* Mr. Weiner, and I think Mr. Weiner knew it, because his face got red and angry. He was only about five foot one or two and when he walked he took huge steps, almost as if he were goose-stepping. At lunchtime we would always prance around the schoolyard or the lunchroom, mimicking him, and the teachers would never try very hard to make us stop. He was already at Mrs. Demetri's desk, right in front of me, and Eddie was only a couple of steps away from the door when he whirled around and glared at him.

"What's taking you so long?" he demanded. "Come here!"

Then, I remember, Eddie grinned broadly and in two giant steps he was in front of Mr. Weiner, towering over him, standing at attention, still grinning. We broke into hysterics. Mr. Weiner glared at us and we stopped. "Now, young man," he said to Eddie, "wipe that grin off your face. What are you—some kind of gangling idiot?"

Eddie shrugged. "I don't know," he said.

We laughed again and Mr. Weiner turned on us. "All right then. Who wants to be the first to have a private conference in my office today?" he asked.

We shut up. Eddie was staring at the floor again. I could tell that he knew he had done something wrong—but it was obvious he didn't know what it was.

"What's that in your pocket?" Mr. Weiner asked him, pointing.

"A baseball."

"Let me see it."

Eddie put his lunchbag on my desk and twisted the ball out of his side pocket. He showed it to Mr. Weiner. When Mr. Weiner reached for it, though, Eddie pulled his hand away.

"Let me have it," Mr. Weiner demanded.

"No," Eddie said, and he put his hand behind his back, gripping the ball tightly. I could tell from the printing that it was an Official National League ball. It looked really beautiful!

"I said let me have it!"

Eddie shook his head sideways. "It's mine," he said. Everybody was perfectly quiet. I glanced across the room at Izzie and Corky and Louie. They were on the edges of their seats.

"Young man, you will let me have it by the time I count to three or I will know the reason why!"

"Do you promise you'll give it back?" Eddie asked.

Mr. Weiner blinked. "Do I *what*—?"

Eddie was looking at Mr. Weiner now, intently. "I gotta have it," he said. "I just *gotta!* I never go anywhere without it."

"We do not allow hardball playing in this school."

Eddie grinned then, as if everything were okay, and brought the ball out from behind his back. "I didn't know that," he said. "I'm sorry." He pushed the ball right in front of Mr. Weiner's face. We all gasped and Mrs. Demetri took a step toward them. "See—?" Eddie said, smiling. "It's got Campy's signature on it."

"Who?"

"*Campy!*" Eddie said.

"Who, may I ask, is Campy?"

"Campy—Roy Campanella—he catches for the Dodgers!" Eddie was excited now. "You know—"

"Of course," Mr. Weiner said. Then he smiled awkwardly. There was something about Eddie that had him mystified. You could tell. "Well, put that ball away and don't bring it to school again," he said. "This is your first day here, so I'll excuse you. But there are no second chances with me. Remember that."

When he left, Mrs. Demetri introduced Eddie to us. I applauded and most of the guys followed my lead. Mrs. Demetri didn't get too angry at me, though—in fact, after she gave Eddie the seat next to me, she put me in charge of getting him his books and making sure he knew where things were. Maybe she figured I'd be less trouble that way. At any rate, I was glad. The first thing I did was ask him where he'd gotten the baseball.

"I won it," he said.

"Where?"

"On Happy Felton's Knothole Gang."

"Really?"

Eddie nodded and I nearly exploded out of my seat. I remember, wanting to tell all the guys. The Knothole Gang was this show they had on television then that came on before all the Dodger games. Three or four guys who played the same position would get together with Happy Felton and one of the Dodgers down the right-field line and they'd be tested on different things. Then, at the end, the Dodger would pick one of the guys as a winner and give the reasons he'd picked him.

I asked Eddie a few more questions and then I began telling him about our baseball team, The Zodiacs. He said he'd read about us in Jimmy O'Brien's column in the *Brooklyn Eagle*.

"You got that good pitcher, don't you—and that crazy kid who brings a victrola to the games and plays the Star-Spangled Banner on it—right?"

"That's Louie," I said, pointing across the room. "He lives in my building. But we don't have the pitcher any more. He's in high school now. Izzie pitches for us most of the time this year."

We talked some more and I asked him if he wanted to play with us, as long as he was in our class now, and he said he'd love to, if we'd let him. Then I wrote out a note, telling all the guys that Eddie had won the baseball on Happy Felton's show and that he'd agreed to play on our team, and I passed it across the room to Louie. His face lit up, and he passed it on to Corky. By the time we got into the yard for lunch that day, Eddie was a hero, and the guys all crowded around him, asking about what Campy had said to him and about what team he had played on before and things like that.

I got to know Eddie pretty well during the next few weeks. He wasn't very bright—this was pretty obvious the first time Mrs. Demetri called on him to read something—and he was very quiet, but he would have done anything for you if you were his friend. All the guys liked him and we were pretty happy he had moved into our neighborhood. He was the kind of guy you wished you had for a brother. His father had died a couple of years before, and until he moved he'd been living in Boro Park with his mother. He never talked much about her or his home or what it had been like living in Boro Park, but we all knew the most important thing— that his family was *Orthodox*. The first time one of us said something to him about making the big leagues some day, he shook his head and said that he didn't think he ever would because he couldn't play or travel on Saturdays. When we brought up the names of other Jewish ballplayers who'd played—Hank Greenberg, Cal Abrams, Sol Rogovin, Sid Gordon, Al Rosen—he said that they hadn't come from families like his. He said it would kill his mother if any of his relatives ever found out about the things he did on Saturday—that he could hide most things as long as he wasn't living near them, but if he ever got his picture in the papers for doing something on Saturday, they'd know about it.

Eddie himself wasn't very religious—he played ball with us at the Parade Grounds on Saturdays—but he was determined not to hurt his mother, and I guess I could understand why at the time. I knew she worked to support the two of them, and that Eddie felt pretty bad toward her about moving from their old neighborhood. I guess he felt she had moved because of him. Still, even though he may have felt obligated to her in a lot of ways, it didn't stop him from *wanting* to be a big-league ballplayer. That was obvious.

1955 was the year the Dodgers beat the Yankees in the World Series, and Eddie came over to my house to watch the games on television. I don't think I've ever seen a guy get more excited than he did during the last game of that series. The Dodgers had one of their great teams then—Campy, Furillo, Robinson, Reese, Snider,

Hodges, Newcombe, Erskine—but the heroes of that last game were two other guys, Sandy Amoros and Johnny Podres. When Amoros made his famous catch of Yogi Berra's fly ball in the sixth inning and without hesitating turned and threw to Reese, who doubled up McDougald at first base, Eddie went wild. He couldn't sit down after that. He just kept walking around the room, pounding guys on the back, shaking our hands, and repeating again and again: "Did you see that catch? Boy, did you see that catch?"

We must have relived each inning of that series a hundred times during the rest of that year. I kept telling Eddie that since Podres —who had won the third and last games of the series—was only twenty-three years old, he'd still have plenty of years to pitch to Eddie when Eddie got to the Dodgers. Eddie always insisted it was an impossibility, but then Louie came up with another one of his bright ideas—if Eddie changed his name and grew a mustache some day, how would his relatives ever find out? Eddie liked the idea and that spring, for practice, Eddie used the name Johnny Campy when he played with our team.

We played in the Ice Cream League at the Parade Grounds and we did pretty well, even though we didn't win the championship. Eddie was fantastic. He batted over .400, was lightning on the bases, only made about two or three errors, threw out ten guys stealing, and did the one thing he did in no other place—he talked all the time. He'd be quiet until we got to the field, but the minute he put on his shin guards, protector, and mask, his mouth began moving a mile a minute, and he'd keep up the chatter the whole game. I loved to listen to him. "C'mon, Izzie babe," he'd yell, crouched behind the plate. "Chuck it here, chuck it here. Plunk it home to Campy, honey babe. Show 'em how, show 'em how. Plunk it home to Campy! This batter's just posin' for pictures. Let's go, babe. Plunk it home to Campy. . . ."

He was one of the greatest natural athletes I've ever seen—and not just in baseball, as we soon found out. Until he came to our school Izzie and I were generally considered the best basketball players of all the guys, but Eddie made us look like amateurs. We were only in the eighth grade then, but when we'd play in the schoolyard on weekends Eddie could hold his own with the high school and college boys.

He was skinny and got banged around a lot under the boards, but he was the most fantastic leaper I've ever seen. Lots of times, even when he was boxed out, he'd just glide up in the air, over everybody else, and pluck the ball out of the sky with those big hands of his. He could dunk the ball with either hand.

My parents knew how much I loved basketball and that summer, for the second straight year, they sent me to Camp Wanatoo, where Abe Goldstein, the Erasmus coach, was head counselor. I remember he got pretty upset when I told him that Eddie was supposed to go to Westinghouse—a vocational high school—instead of to Erasmus. Schoolyard reputations spread pretty fast in our neighborhood and he'd already heard about Eddie from a lot of the guys on his team. I explained to him about how Eddie's grades weren't too good, and about his mother.

When I got back from camp and saw Eddie, the first thing he told me was that he'd decided to go to Erasmus. He said that Mr. Goldstein had visited him and promised him and his mother that Eddie would get through high school—and that he could get him a scholarship to college. We spent a lot of time that fall playing in the schoolyard together, and Eddie got better and better. He'd spent the summer in the city, working as a delivery boy and helper in his uncle's butcher shop in Boro Park, and he'd developed a gorgeous fade-away jump shot that was impossible to stop. When we weren't playing, we'd sit by the fence in the schoolyard and talk about the guys on the Erasmus team or about the Dodgers— and we'd have long debates on whether it was better to get a college education and then play pro basketball or to forget about college and take a big bonus from a major-league baseball team.

That winter we played on a basketball team together in the *Daily Mirror* tournament and we probably would have won the championship, only in the big game for the Brooklyn title Eddie didn't show up until the last quarter. He went wild then, putting in shots from crazy angles, rebounding like a madman, stealing the ball, and playing his heart out—but we were fifteen points behind when he arrived and when the clock ran out we were still down by four. For weeks afterwards you could hardly talk to him, he was so upset. All of us told him to forget it, that we understood about his mother getting sick and him having to stay with her until the doctor came, but he still felt he'd let us down.

His mother got better, spring came, the baseball season started, and Eddie stopped coming to school almost completely. Any time the Dodgers were in town—except for the days our baseball team had a game or the afternoons he worked as a delivery boy for his uncle—Eddie would be at Ebbets Field. He was always trying to get me to come along with him, but I usually found one excuse or another not to. He kept telling me there was nothing to worry about. He said he knew somebody in the attendance office and that all we had to do was give him our programs and show up for homeroom period in the morning—the guy in the office would write in our names as absent on the sheets that went to the teachers whose classes we'd be cutting. He never seemed to get into any trouble and finally, in the middle of June, I told him I'd go with him.

We made up to meet in front of Garfield's Cafeteria, at the corner of Flatbush and Church, at 10:30, after second period. Eddie was there ahead of me and we got on the Flatbush Avenue bus and paid our fares. I kept looking around, expecting to see a teacher or a cop.

"Just act normal," Eddie told me. "And if anybody stops us, just put one of these on your head—" he reached into a pocket and pulled out two *yamulkas*—"and tell whoever asks you it's a Jewish holiday and that we go to Yeshiva. That always works."

When we got off the bus at Empire Boulevard, where the Botanic Gardens begin, we still had a couple of hours until the game started and I asked Eddie what we were going to do until then.

He smiled. "Follow me," he said.

I followed. I saw a few cops along the street, but none of them bothered us. Some old men were getting their boards ready, with buttons and pennants and souvenirs, and when we got to McKeever and Sullivan Place, where the main entrance was, a few guys were selling programs and yearbooks. We walked along Sullivan Place and Eddie stopped about halfway down the block, where the players' entrance was.

A minute later a taxi stopped at the curb and two big guys got out—I recognized them right away as Gil Hodges and Duke Snider. It really surprised me, I remember, to discover that we were as tall as both of them—taller than Snider.

"Any extra tickets?" Eddie asked.

"Sorry—not today, Eddie," the Duke said, and the two of them disappeared into the clubhouse.

I nearly died. "You mean you actually *know* them?" I asked.

"Sure," Eddie said. "Hell—I've been out here like this for three years now." He scratched at his cheek and tried to act nonchalant, but I could tell how proud he was that a Dodger had called him by name with me there. "I don't think they'll have any extras today, though—Milwaukee has a good team this year and there were probably lots of their friends wanting tickets."

"It's okay," I said, still flabbergasted. "I got a couple of bucks for tickets."

"We won't need 'em, I hope," he said. "If nobody has extras, we can try waiting in the gas station on Bedford Avenue. There's always a bunch of kids there, hoping to catch a ball, but they usually hit four or five out in batting practice. If we can get just one, the guy at the gate will let us both in—he knows me.''

"If not?"

He shrugged. "The bleachers. It's only seventy-five cents, and after about the second inning you can sneak into the grandstands.''

Some more Dodgers came by and they all smiled and said hello to Eddie, but none of them had any extra tickets. It didn't bother me. After a while I just followed Eddie's lead and said hello to the players also, saying things like "How're you doing, Carl? We're rooting for you!" to Furillo, or "How're you feeling today, Campy?" and I hardly believed it when some of the players would actually answer me. As I got more confidence I got braver—telling Pee Wee to watch out for guys sliding into second base, telling Karl Spooner that if he pitched he should keep the ball low and outside to Aaron—and after each group of guys would go into the clubhouse I'd slam Eddie on the back and punch him in the arm. "C'mon," I'd say to him, "pinch me right on the ass, buddy. Then I'll know it's true!" Eddie just kept grinning and telling me how stupid I'd been to wait this long to come to a game with him.

By 11:30, though, we still didn't have any tickets.

"We should of waited by the visiting team's entrance," Eddie said. "They hardly ever use up their passes—''

Then, as we started to walk toward Bedford Avenue, we saw this little guy come trotting up the street toward us. Eddie squinted.

"It's Amoros," he said. "Hey, Sandy—any tickets?" he called.

"Oh, man, I late today," Amoros said when he got to us, shaking his head back and forth. He reached into his wallet, handed us two tickets, and we wished him luck. Then he continued toward the players' entrance, running.

"Whooppee!" I shouted as soon as he was gone. "Amoros for Most Valuable Player!" I threw my arm around Eddie's shoulder and we ran down the street together, half dragging each other, until we got to the turnstile entrance. Then we stopped and strutted inside together, handing the guard the tickets as if it was something we did every day of the week. As soon as we were inside, Eddie yelled "Let's go!" and we raced under the arcade, laughing and giggling. The instant we saw the field, though, we stopped. The groundkeepers had just finished hosing down the base paths and the visiting team hadn't come out yet for batting practice. There was hardly anybody in the stands and the sight of the empty ball park seemed to sober us both up. To this day I don't think there's any sight that's prettier than a ball park before a game's been played. Watching on television all the time, you forgret how green and peaceful the field looks.

We had great seats that day, right over the Dodger dugout. They blasted the Braves, 9–1, with fourteen or fifteen hits, and we cheered and shouted like mad, especially when Amoros came to bat. I remember everything about the ball park that day, and I think I remember the things that happened off the field more than I do the actual game. I remember the Dodger Symphony marching around the stands, and Mabel swinging her cowbell, and Gladys Gooding singing the National Anthem and playing "Follow the Dodgers" on the organ, and the groundkeepers wheeling the batting cage back out to center field, and the people across Bedford Avenue watching from their roofs. I remember being surprised at how many guys our age—and even younger—had come to the game, and I remember how great I felt when I heard somebody calling my name and I turned around and saw Mr. Hager wave to me. I waved back at him and then told Eddie about him. Mr. Hager was a retired fireman who lived on my block. He went to every Dodger game and when they lost he always wore a black armband. When the Giants beat the Dodgers in the playoff in '51, nobody saw him for weeks afterwards, and then he wore the same black suit day in and day out until they won back the pennant in '52. Everybody in our neighborhood knew him and it was said that he got into at least two or three fights a week at Hugh Casey's bar on Flatbush Avenue. There were a lot of Dodger fans like him in those days.

Most of all, though, I remember how *good* I felt that day—just sitting with Eddie, eating peanuts and cheering and talking baseball. As it turned out, that was the last time I ever got to see a Dodger game. At the end of the season they announced that they were moving to Los Angeles.

I went to Camp Wanatoo again that summer and Eddie stayed in the city. His uncle had gotten him a job loading sides of beef into refrigerator cars and this helped build up his chest and shoulders and arms. In the fall everybody was predicting he'd be the next great basketball star at Erasmus—maybe even All-City in his sophomore year.

When the time came for varsity tryouts, though, he didn't show up. Nobody could figure it out. Two days later he stopped by my house at night and asked if I wanted to go for a walk. He looked terrible—his face was long and he seemed to have lost a lot of weight. At first I figured it had something to do with his mother, but when I asked him he shook his head.

"Nah," he said when we were downstairs. He sighed. "I guess you were wondering why I didn't try out for the team, huh?"

"Everybody was—" I said.

"I know. Mr. Goldstein called my house tonight and I had to tell him—that's why I came by your house. I wanted you to know before the other guys. Maybe you could tell them, so I don't have to keep repeating the story."

"Sure," I said. "What is it?"

"It's my damn heart," he said. I looked at him and he was biting the corner of his lower lip. Then he shook his head back and forth and cursed. "I can't play any more," he said. "The doctor said so." He stopped. "Jesus, Howie, what am I gonna *do?* What am I gonna do?" he pleaded. I didn't know what to say. "Shit," he said. "Just shit!" Then his body seemd to go limp. "C'mon, let's walk."

"How'd you find out?" I asked.

"Ah, since the summer I've had this pain in my chest and when it didn't go away I went to our family doctor. My mother telephoned him about a week ago and he told her. It's only a murmur —nothing really dangerous—but it means no varsity."

"Can't you play at all?"

"Oh, yeah—as long as I take it easy. I just have to get a lot of sleep, and whenever I feel any of this pressure building up in my chest I have to be sure to stop."

We walked for a long time that night—up Bedford Avenue all the way past Ebbets Field to Eastern Parkway, then back home along Flatbush Avenue, and most of the time neither of us said anything. What could you say?

I made the varsity that year and Eddie came to all the games, home and away. He worked five afternoons a week at his uncle's butcher shop now, but on Saturdays, when it was closed, he'd come down to the schoolyard and play a few games. He kidded around a lot, telling everybody to take it easy against him because of his heart, but he was still tremendous. I was already about an inch taller than he was, and a pretty good jumper, but he'd go up over me as if I had lead in my sneakers.

In about the middle of our junior year he quit school and went to work full-time as an assistant to his uncle. He kept coming to all the Friday night games, though, and sometimes when I didn't have a date, we'd go to Garfield's afterwards and then walk home together.

Eddie and I lost touch with each other during my first two years at college—I don't think I saw him even once—but when I was home for spring vacation during my junior year my mother told me he'd bought a half interest in Mr. Klein's kosher butcher shop on Rogers Avenue. I went over to see him the next morning and there he was, behind the counter. I stood outside for a while, watching him wait on customers, and then when the store was empty I went inside.

"Hey, Campy—!" I called. He was at the far end of the counter, cutting up some meat.

He turned around. "Jesus, Howie!" He wiped his hands on his apron and then we shook hands and pounded each other on the back. "Boy, it's good to see you. How've you been?"

"Pretty good," I said. "When did all this happen?" I asked, motioning around the store.

"C'mon next door to the candy store," he said, taking off his apron. "I'll get you a Coke—boy, it's been a long time!"

He got Mr. Klein out of the big walk-in freezer in the back and then we went next door and Eddie told me about how he'd saved up money while he was working for his uncle—with that and some insurance money his mother had put away after his father's death, he was able to buy a half interest from Mr. Klein, who was getting old and wanted to retire soon. By then Eddie could buy out the other half and the store would be his.

"How about you?" he asked. "How do you like college?"

"It's okay," I said.

"What are you studying?"

"Liberal arts."

"Oh, yeah?—What subjects?"

I laughed. "You don't have to sound interested," I said.

He shrugged, embarrassed. "Anyway, I follow your team in the papers all the time—the *Times* always prints box scores of your games. You did real well this year—second high scorer on your team, weren't you?" When I didn't answer, he punched me in the arm. "Ah, don't be modest—you're a good ballplayer, Howie. Bet you got all those pretty girls running after you, too—"

"We'll be playing in the Garden against N.Y.U. next year," I said. "I'll get you some tickets—you can bring a girl and maybe we'll double after or something—"

"Sure," he said. "I'm going with a girl now—real nice, you'd like her." He shrugged, then grinned. "I'll probably be a married man by this time next year—"

When we played in the Garden the next year I sent him two

passes, but I had to leave right after the game to get the bus that was taking us back to school that night. I got an invitation to his wedding right after that. It was scheduled for Christmas week, but I couldn't go because of a holiday tournament our team was playing at Evansville, Indiana. I called him when I came in for spring vacation and told him how sorry I was that I hadn't been there.

"Jesus, Howie," he said. "Forget it. How could you have been? You were in that tournament in Indiana. I followed the whole thing." He laughed. "My wife nearly slammed me because on the first day of our honeymoon I rushed out in the morning to get the papers to see how many points you'd scored."

We talked some more and then he asked me over to dinner. I accepted the invitation, but I felt funny about it. I suppose I was afraid we wouldn't have anything to talk about—or, what seemed worse, that we'd spend the entire evening reminiscing about things we'd done when we were thirteen or fourteen.

I was partially right—we did spend a lot of time reminiscing, but I didn't mind. Eddie and I filled each other in on what had happened to guys we'd grown up with—who was getting married, who had finished college, who had moved out of the neighborhood— and I had a great time. Susie was, as Eddie promised, a great cook. She'd graduated from high school and was in her last year of nurse's training—just right for Eddie, I thought. After supper, while she did the dishes, Eddie and I sat in the living room and talked. I told him how much I liked her and he smiled.

"She's good for me," he said, nodding. "I'll tell you something —because of her I'm even thinking of going back to high school evenings to finish up."

"Does she want you to?"

"She'd never say so, even if she did—she lets me make up my own mind. But I think she'd like it."

"Sounds like a good idea," I offered.

"Yeah—but when do I have time? Running the store by myself now, there's a lot of work—books—I have to bring home, and then I'm so tired after being on my feet all day, about all I can do in the evening is turn on the TV and watch the Yanks or the Mets." He sighed. "But we'll see. I'd like to finish up."

"How's your health been?" I asked.

"Fine," he said, shrugging. Then his eyes opened wide. "Jesus!" he exclaimed. "You don't know, do you?"

"Know what?"

"About my heart—" I must have looked scared then, because he started laughing at me. "Thank God Kennedy put through that draft exemption for married men," he said. "Otherwise I'd be carrying a rifle—"

"I don't understand. I thought—"

"It's a long story," he said, "but the short of it is there was never anything wrong with my heart." He stood up and paced around the room. "When I went for my army physical about a year and a half ago, they didn't find anything wrong with me. That's how I found out."

"But what about—?"

"Ah, that was just a thing my mother told me that the family doctor went along with," he said, stopping my question. "He was religious or something, I guess. I don't know. What's the difference now? Thinking back, I guess he *himself* never really told me outright I had a murmur—"

Susie came back into the room and I could tell she knew what Eddie had been telling me. She put her arms around his waist and hugged him.

"My God!" I exclaimed. "How could she—?"

He was about to say something, but then Susie looked at him and he changed his mind. "That's the way the ball bounces, I guess," he said, shrugging his shoulders, and I could tell he'd used the same expression before in similar situations. He kissed Susie on the forehead and held her close to him. "Anyway," he laughed, "if you're in pro ball you got to be away from your wife and kids half the year."

"But Christ, Eddie," I began. Susie glared at me and I stopped. Eddie sat down and nobody said anything for a while—then suddenly he started talking. "You know something," he said. "My business is pretty good. I mean, I'm making a good living and at least I'm not working for somebody else—but you know what I'd *really* like to do?" He leaned forward and rubbed his hands together. He looked at Susie and she smiled. "I'd like to coach kids. No kidding."

"He's terrific with them, Howie," Susie said. "Really—"

"I love it—I help out at the center sometimes, and with this team of kids from our block. Guess what they call themselves?— The Zodiacs!" We both laughed. "It's something how these things get passed down—"

We began reminiscing again and soon we were both telling Susie about the day we'd played hooky together and gone to Ebbets Field.

"Have you seen it since it's torn down?" Eddie asked. "They got these big apartment houses—"

"I've been there," I said.

"I have a girlfriend who lives in right field," Susie said. I glanced at her, puzzled. "The people all give their section of the development names according to the way the field used to be laid out," she explained. Then she laughed, but the laugh was forced and we knew it. Eddie and I tried to get up a conversation about the old ballplayers and what they were doing then—Hodges managing the Senators, the Duke still hanging on as a pinch hitter, poor Campy in a wheelchair since his crash, conducting interviews on TV between Yankee doubleheaders—but our hearts weren't in it anymore and there were a lot of long silences. After a while I said I had to get up early the next morning for a job interview. It wasn't even midnight. I thanked them for the dinner and I said I'd be in touch when I got back from school in June. Then when I was at the door, Eddie put his arm around my shoulder.

"I been thinking," he said. "How about you playing some three-man ball with an old married man before you go back to school?"

"Sure," I said.

I met Eddie at the schoolyard on Saturday morning and we played for a couple of hours. He wasn't as graceful as I'd remembered him, but he could still jump—only now he knew how to throw his weight around and use his elbows and body and shoulders. He was murder under the boards and deadly with his jump shot and rough on defense. We played against some pretty tough high school and college and ex-college ballplayers that day and Eddie was the best of us all. Between games we'd rest next to the fence together and Eddie would talk and joke and kid about the potbelly he was putting on. When we played, though, he didn't smile and he didn't talk. He played hard and he played to win.

GOD HIT
A HOME RUN

Robert Fontaine

L ONG AGO WHEN I was very young my mother and father and I moved to Canada, to the lovely city of Ottawa.

We settled down in one half of a double house, next door to my several unusual uncles, my grandfather, and my aunt Felice, all of whom spoke, as we did ourselves, a strange language. It was a mixture of corrupt French, literally translated idioms, and, in time, the salt of French-Canadian patois.

There are but few memories of the first years in Ottawa. They are only bright fragments, like the little pieces of colored glass in the small hallway window at the stair landing.

The time, however, that God hit a home run is very clear.

My father played the violin and conducted an orchestra for a two-a-day vaudeville theater, so he had little time for diversion. In what spare moments he had, he turned to baseball. In spite of his sensitive, debonair temperament, he loved the game. It refreshed him, perhaps, because it was so far from his métier.

I remember well how many times he begged my mother to go with him to the twilight games at Strathcona Park. There was just time for him to see a game between the end of the matinée and the beginning of the evening performance.

My mother seemed always too busy.

"I must get the dinner, you know," she would say, with the faint, calm, resigned, Presbyterian air she often assumed.

"Dinner!" my father would exclaim. "We will stuff our pockets with apples and cheese."

328

"What about the Boy?" my mother would ask.

My father would look at me.

"The Boy is already too fat! Regard him!"

"It is only," my mother would smile, "because he has his cheeks full of shortbreads."

If it was not dinner she had to cook, it was socks she had to darn or blouses she had to make for me, or the kitchen floor she felt the need of shining.

All this made my father quite sad, even though, at each invitation, my mother promised to accompany him "some other time." Still, he never abandoned the hope that he would, in time, have the warm joy of explaining the principles of the intricate game to her. I suppose he knew that she was proud of his artistic talents and he wanted her to be pleased with his athletic knowledge, too.

One warm Sunday in the summer, when I was five or six (who can remember precisely those early times of coming-to-life when every week is a year?), my mind was occupied with the American funny papers and the eccentric doings of one Happy Hooligan, he of the ragged, patched coat and the small tin can on the side of his head.

My father came into the room where my mother was dusting the china on the mantel and shining the golden letters on the sign that proclaimed: *Jesus Christ Is the Unseen Guest in This House.*

There was, by the way, nothing else to do in Ottawa on a Sunday in those days but to dust religious signs and plates on the mantel or to read the papers. All stores were closed. All theaters were closed. There was prohibition, too, as I recall, so there was not even a bar where one could sit and dream. True, one could go across the Inter-Provincial Bridge to Hull, in Quebec province, and return with a secret bottle of wine, but it could not be served in public.

No, Sunday was the Sad Day in Ottawa.

But to return to my father. He spoke to my mother with some hesitation: "The Boy and I . . . we . . . we go to a game of baseball."

My mother turned from the plates and regarded my father coldly.

"On Sunday?" she inquired.

My father ran his finger the length of his nose, a gesture which always indicated an attempt at restraint. Then he removed the band from his cigar as nonchalantly as possible.

"But naturally," he replied. "Do I have some other time to go?"

"You can go, as usual, to the twilight games."

My father bit off the end of his cigar.

"Bah!" he exclaimed. "Baseball for seven innings only is like a dinner without cognac at the end. It is like kissing the woman you love good night by blowing it from your fingers. No. Baseball in the shadows, when the stars are appearing, is not in the true spirit of the game. One must have the bright sun and the green grass."

My mother looked at my eager, shining face and then looked back at my father.

"What is wrong," she asked, smiling faintly, "with kissing a woman you love good night by blowing it from your fingers?"

My father put his arm around her and laughed.

"The same thing that is wrong," he said, "with making from sour cherries an apple pie."

"You can't make an apple pie from sour cherries."

"Eh bien, you can't kiss a woman good night this way . . . you can only kiss your fingers."

He touched his lips to the back of my mother's neck.

I coughed impatiently at this dallying. My mind was fastened firmly on baseball.

"Papa," I said anxiously, "we go now? Yes?"

"You come with us," my father said to my mother. "Eh? We will stuff our pockets with apples and cheese and make a picnic. Red wine, too, perhaps."

"And an onion," I said, loving onions.

"Some other time," my mother said hastily. "Certainly not on Sunday."

"Ah!" my father cried. "Always some other time. Do you promise some time soon?"

"Yes," my mother replied without much conviction. I suppose the thought of sitting on a hard bench for hours, watching that of which she knew nothing, frightened her. I felt, though, that in time my father's plaintive eagerness would win her over.

"Why," she questioned, as if to soften the blow, "do you not ask Uncle Louis or Uncle Felix?"

"Uncle Louis will be full and will chase butterflies across the diamond. Uncle Felix will wish to measure the speed at which the baseball arrives at the catcher. Besides, they are gone up the Gatineau to bring back the Boy's grandfather."

"Grandpa is coming?" I asked happily.

"Yes. He will stay next door as usual and sleep here."

I laughed. "Why is it that Grandpa stays next door and sleeps here?"

My father shrugged.

"When you are old you sleep where you wish."

My mother was at the window, fixing the small jars of ivy that stood there.

"It looks like a thunderstorm coming," she said. "Grandpa and the uncles will get wet. You and the Boy, too, should not go out in a thunderstorm."

Our entire family was frightened to death of thunderstorms. At the first deep roll in the Laurentian Hills or up the Gatineau we huddled together in one room until the sun broke through, or the stars.

My father spoke bravely, though, on this occasion: "It will probably follow the river."

He did not mention the fact that there were three or four rivers it might follow, all of which came, in the end, almost to our back yard.

"Look!" my mother exclaimed, as a white flash lit the horizon's dark clouds.

"Bah!" my father said nervously. "Heat lightning."

"To me," my mother countered solemnly, "it looks like chain lightning."

"Chain lightning . . . heat lightning . . . it is miles away, *n'est-ce pas?* It is not here, is it?"

"Maman," I begged, "let us go please, before the storm begins."

"Voilà, a smart boy!" my father said proudly, patting me on the head.

My mother sighed and adjusted the tiebacks of the curtains.

"Very well," she said sadly, "but you know what Louis says— he pays too dear a price for honey who licks it off thorns!"

"Honey . . . thorns," my father repeated, rolling his eyes unhappily. "It is baseball of which we speak now."

"All right," my mother said. "All right. Only, just be careful. Don't stand under trees or near cows."

"No," my father agreed, "no cows and no trees."

He kissed my mother gently on the lips, and I naturally understood there would be no further discussion. I put on my best straw sailor, a white hat with the brim curled up and with a black elastic under the chin to keep the bonnet from the fury of any possible gales.

My mother regarded me with sadness, tucking in the string of my blouse. It was as if I were soon to be guillotined.

"It just doesn't seem right," she said slowly, "on Sunday."

My father lit his cigar impatiently.

"We must be going," he announced hastily. "The game will commence before we arrive."

My father took my by the hand. My mother put her arms around me and hugged and kissed me. It was as if I was going away forever to become a monk.

"Be careful," she said.

"Yes, *Maman*," I said dutifully.

"And pull up your stockings," she added.

On the trolley car going up Rideau Street I was happy. The wind blew through the open, summer seats and the sun was not too warm.

It is true I should have been in Sunday school at my mother's Presbyterian church, learning about the Red Sea turning back. Instead, I was on my way to the very brink of hell. For Hull, where my father whispered confidentially we were going, was well known to be a place of sinful living, and the sulphur that drifted daily from the match factories was enough to convince me of the truth of the report.

"Papa," I asked, "is it true Hull is wicked?"

"Not in the part where they play baseball," my father assured me.

A faint flash of lightning startled me a little.

"Papa. I have fear Uncle Louis and Uncle Felix and Grandpa will be struck by lightning."

My father smiled.

"Louis and Felix are too fast for the lightning."

"And Grandpa?" I plucked nervously at the tight elastic under my warm chin.

"Grandpa is too close a friend of the Lord to suffer from such things."

I felt better after this. I reasoned that if the Lord was a friend of Grandpa, then Grandpa would no doubt see that nothing happened to Papa and me.

We changed cars presently and were soon crossing the bridge into Hull and the province of Quebec.

I looked down at the dirty, roaring falls that ran the factories.

"No sulphur," I observed.

"Not on Sunday," my father said.

This pleased me a great deal. On the one hand, Grandpa and the Lord were good friends. On the other hand, the Devil did not work on Sunday. I was in a splendid strategic position to deal with Evil.

We descended from the trolley on the main street of Hull.

"We can walk from here," my father informed me. "At the theater, they say it is not far out on this street."

Soon we found ourselves in the midst of hundreds of jabbering French-Canadians, all speaking so quickly and with such laughter and mockery that I could not follow them. The patois, too, was beyond my young understanding. What is more, every other building on the main street of Hull was one of swinging doors from which came the strong smell of ale, making my head dizzy.

"What do they say, Papa? What do they all say so fast?"

My father laughed.

"They say that Hull will beat Ottawa like a hot knife enters the butter! The pitcher of Hull will fan every batter of Ottawa. The batters of Hull will strike the ball every time into the Lachine Rapids, which is many, many miles away. In the end, they say, everybody will become full as a barrel of ale except the people from Ottawa. They will return home crying and drink lime juice and go to bed ashamed."

I clapped my hands happily at this foolishness which sounded like a fairy tale—the white balls flying by the hundreds, like birds, up the Lachine Rapids.

A man reeled by from a bar as I was pondering the flight of the baseballs. He began to shout loudly: "Hooray for Ottawa! Hull is full of pea soups. Down with Hull and the pea soups!"

The crowd picked him up and tossed him on high from group to group, laughing all the while, until, at last, he admitted Hull was the fairest city in all Canada and pea soup the most delicious dish.

I laughed joyfully. "It will be a good game, no?" I asked happily.

"Mais oui," my father chuckled. With the Hull and the Ottawa it is like with David and Goliath."

It had become quite cloudy and dark when we made our way through the grounds to the ancient wooden stand. In the gray distance the lightning continued to dance.

My father patted my head gently. "Heat lightning," he said uneasily.

"I know," I said. In spite of the fact that I knew Grandpa was a friend of the Lord and that the Devil had taken the day off, I nevertheless felt a little nervous. After all, I *had* skipped Sunday school for the first time. And we *were* so far from home!

My attention turned from the storm for a time as the Hull team began field practice amid great roars of approval that drowned out the rumbling thunder. The crowd began to chatter happily and proudly like many birds screaming in our back yard.

"All the world," I said, "speaks French here."

"Mais oui," my father agreed. "In Hull all the world is French. In Ottawa it is mostly English. That is why there is so much desire to fight with each other."

"And we," I asked curiously, "what do we speak, you and me?"

"Ha!" my father exclaimed, patting my knee, "that is a problem for the French Academy!"

Since I did not know what the French Academy was, I placed my small chin in my hands and watched the Ottawa team as it came out on the field.

Groans and jeers now filled the air. Bottles, legs of chairs, programs, and bad fruit were thrown on the field like confetti at a wedding.

Two umpires and several groundkeepers cleared away the debris. One of the umpires announced through a megaphone:

"Mesdames et messieurs, we are the hosts. They are the guests. They are from Ottawa, but that is not a sin. We cannot always help where we live. It is requested not to throw bottles while the game proceeds as this is not the fair way we shall win. I am born in Hull and also my wife and four children and I am proud of it. But I do my honest duty to make a fair game. God save the King! *Play ball!"*

The game went on evenly and colorlessly for five or six innings. The darkness of the afternoon turned a sulphur yellow and the air became filled with tension.

The rumble of thunder grew louder.

In the seventh inning the Ottawa pitcher singled and stood proudly on first base. The bat boy ran out with a sweater. This is, of course, the custom in the big leagues, so that the pitcher will not expose his arm to possible chills.

To Hull, however, it was a fine opportunity to start something.

"Sissy!" someone shouted.

"Si . . . sssssssssyyyyyyyyy!" The crowd made one long sound as if the wind were moaning. Most of them probably did not know what the word meant, but it had a pleasant sound of derision.

The pitcher, O'Ryan, stepped far off first base in an attempt to taunt the Hull pitcher to throw, which he did.

O'Ryan darted back safely, stood arrogantly on the white bag, and carefully thumbed his nose.

The crowd jeered.

O'Ryan removed his cap and bowed from the waist in sarcasm.

Once more bottles, legs of chairs, programs, and overripe fruit came down on the field like hailstones.

Again the umpire picked up his megaphone and spoke.

"Mes amis," he begged, "they are the guests . . . we are the hosts."

A tomato glanced off the side of his head; a cushion landed in his face. He shrugged his shoulders, brushed himself off, and ordered wearily: "Play ball!"

The next pitch was hit and it was accompanied by a violent peal of thunder which almost coincided with the crack of the bat.

O'Ryan started for second base and was forced to slide when the Hull second baseman attempted to force him out. The second baseman, with his spiked shoes, jumped on O'Ryan's hand.

The Ottawa pitcher was safe by many seconds, but the crowd shouted insistently: "Out! *Out!"* with such anger that the umpire hesitated but a moment and then waved the astonished and stunned Irishman off the field.

Two thousand French-Canadian noses were instantly thumbed.

O'Ryan stood up dazedly and regarded his maimed hand. He brushed the dust from his uniform and strode quietly to the Ottawa bench. There he picked up several bats, swung them together for a while, and selected his favorite.

He pulled down his cap firmly, walked calmly to second base, and, with only a slight motion, brought the bat down solidly on the head of the Hull second baseman.

This was the signal for a riot. Spectators, umpire, players, peanut vendors—all swarmed across the field in one great pitched battle. In the increasing darkness from the oncoming storm they were as a great swarm of hornets, moving around the diamond.

My father and I, alone, remained seated. We did not speak for a long time.

I began to wish I had gone to Sunday school to have the Red Sea divided, or that I had stayed home with *Maman* and Happy Hooligan. I was coming to believe that Grandpa was not so good a friend of the Lord as he pretended and that if the Devil did not work on Sunday he had assistants who *did*.

My father spoke, at length, with the hollow sound of sin: "Poor *Maman* would be angry if she knew, eh?"

"Mais oui," I mumbled, fearfully watching the lightning tear the sky.

Papa tried to be calm and to talk lightly.

"Ah, well," he remarked, "it is not always so simple, eh, to tell the heat lightning from the chain lightning?"

"Mais non," I muttered.

"Also, in this case, one can see the storm did not follow the river."

"It followed *us,*" I replied nervously, almost to myself.

"Well, we are safe here, no? We are, thank the good Lord, not in the melee. Here we are safe. When the fight is ended we will go home. Meanwhile we are safe. *N'est-ce pas?*"

"And the storm, Papa?" I queried, pulling my sailor hat down over my head as far as it would go.

"The storm," my father announced, as thunder sounded so loudly it shook the flimsy stand, "is mostly wind. It will blow itself away in no time."

I sighed. I will pray, I told myself. I will ask to be forgiven for going to the city of the Devil on Sunday. I will pray the good Lord forgive me, in the name of my grandfather, for forgetting to attend the opening of the Red Sea, also.

I had but managed to mutter: "Dear Lord . . ." when the sky, like the Red Sea, divided in two and there was hurled at us a great fiery ball, as if someone in heaven had knocked it our way.

Before I could get my breath, the dry, wooden stand was in flames.

"Dear Lord," I began again, breathlessly and hastily, "we are not so bad as all this . . . we only . . ." But my father had me by the hand and was dragging me swiftly on to the field.

By this time, the rioters had stopped banging heads and were wistfully watching their beloved stand disappear with the flames.

By the time we arrived home the storm was over and even the rain had stopped. We had been at a restaurant to eat and rest and had recovered a little when we faced *Maman*.

In fact *I* did not feel bad at all. I reasoned that the Lord had not been after my destruction but after the rioters who profaned his Sabbath with fighting. For if the Lord had been after me, He could, in His infinite wisdom, have made the ball come even closer.

"I told you we would have a thunderstorm," my mother said angrily.

"To me," my father replied meekly, "it looked like heat lightning."

"You know I don't like the Boy out in thunderstorms!"

"Ah, well, he is safe now. Eh, *bibi?* And Louis and Felix and Papa?"

"They are here."

"Good."

"A baseball game on Sunday is just not right," my mother went on, refusing to be deflected from the subject. "Look how pale and sick-looking you both are!"

My father coughed uneasily.

"Let us call down Grandpa and have some wine and short-breads. Let us forget the rest. No?" He kissed my mother. She turned to me, relented a bit, and smiled.

"Was it a good game?"

I clapped my hands together excitedly. "It was wonderful, *Maman!* Everything happened!"

"Wine and shortbreads," Papa interrupted nervously.

"What do you mean, everything happened?" my mother asked, glancing sidelong at Papa.

"I must go up and see my poor father," said Papa. "It is now many months . . ."

"One moment," my mother cautioned. She turned and motioned for me to sit on her knee. My father sank wearily into a chair.

"Well?" my mother urged.

It was too wonderful and exciting to keep!

"Maman," I exclaimed, "God hit a home run!"

My father groaned. My mother's eyes widened.

"He what?" she asked, pale.

The words came rushing out: "He hit a home run and He struck the grandstand with His powerful lightning and then the grandstand burned to very small pieces, all of a sudden, and this was because everybody was fighting on the Sabbath and . . ."

My mother let me down slowly from her knee.

"Is this true?" she said to my father.

My father shrugged and waved his delicate hands helplessly.

"A small fire. The stand in Hull is made of . . ."

My mother jumped to her feet.

"Where?"

My father lowered his eyes.

"Hull," he admitted slowly. "After all, they do not permit baseball on Sunday in Ottawa. If they permit you to breathe it is something. All the world knows that."

"Hull!" my mother whispered, as if it were a dreadful name. "Hull! No wonder! To take the Boy from Sunday school to Hull! And on Sunday! Hull!"

"Maman," I said, tears coming into my eyes, "I will speak to the Lord . . ."

"Go," said my mother, and she sounded like a voice from the heavens, "and wash your dirty face."

"Ma chère," my father said, trying to be pleasant, "does one always know where a storm will travel?"

"You," my mother ordered, "go wipe your shoes. Look at the mud you have tracked in!"

As Papa and I went our respective ways, heads bowed, we heard her whisper once more: "Hull!"

I knew then that she would never go to a baseball game with Papa. The memory of the Lord's home run which so barely missed us would remain, I thought, forever in her mind. She would know one of the places the Lord was going to strike and she would know now that His aim was very good, if not perfect.

THE
PINCH HITTERS

George Alec Effinger

T HE TELEPHONE RANG, and the noise woke me up. I reached across the bed to pick up the receiver. I was still half asleep, and something about the dimly lit hotel room disturbed me. I couldn't identify the trouble, though. "Hello?" I said into the phone.

"Hello? Is this Sandor Courane?" said an unfamiliar voice.

I didn't say anything for a second or two. I was looking across the room at the other twin bed. There was someone sleeping in it.

"Is this Sandor Courane?" asked the voice.

"It often is," I said.

"Well, if it is now, this is Norris."

I was silent again. Someone was claiming to be a very good friend of mine, using a voice that didn't belong to Norris. "Uh huh," was all that I said. I remembered that I hadn't been alone the night before. I was at a rather large science fiction convention, and I had met a rather nice young woman. The person in the other bed, still asleep, was a large man I had never seen before.

"Where are you?" asked the person who claimed to be Norris.

"In my room," I said. "What time is it? Who is this?"

"This is Norris Page! Have you looked outside?"

"Norris," I said, "I can't think of a single reason why I would waste the effort to walk across the room. And I don't know how to say this, but, uh, you don't sound at all like Norris, if you know what I mean. My clock says it's eight-thirty, and that's a rotten time to wake somebody up at a convention. So I think I'll just hang—"

"Wait a minute!" The voice was suddenly very urgent. Much more urgent than a voice generally gets at a science fiction convention. I waited. The voice went on. "Look out the window," it said.

"Okay," I said. I'm moderately obliging. I got up. I was wearing thin green pajamas, something I have never owned in my entire life. I didn't like that discovery at all. I walked quietly by the stranger on the other bed and peered through the slats of the venetian blinds. I stared for a moment or two, then went back to the telephone. "Hello?" I said.

"What did you see?" asked the voice.

"A bunch of buildings I've never seen before."

"It's not Washington, is it?"

"No," I said. "Who is this?"

"Norris. It's Norris. I'm in New York."

"Last night you were in Washington," I said. "I mean, Norris was here in Washington. Why don't you sound like Norris?"

There was a short, exasperated sound from the voice. "You know, you don't sound like you either. You're in Boston."

"Boston?"

"Yeah. And Jim is in Detroit. And Larry is in Chicago. And Dick is in Cleveland."

"I feel sorry for Dick," I said. I was born in Cleveland.

"I feel sorry for all of us," said Norris. "We're not us anymore. Look at yourself."

I did. Beneath the pajamas, my body had become large and hairy. My tattoo—I have an Athenian owl tattooed on my left forearm—was gone, and in its place was a skull with a dagger through its eye and a naked lady with an anchor and a snake. There were certain other pertinent revisions in the body. "Wow," I said.

"I've been up since six o'clock running this down," said Norris. "The five of us have been hijacked or something."

"Who did it?" I was feeling very unhappy about the situation.

"I don't know," said Norris.

"Why?" I was starting to feel very frightened about the situation.

"I don't know."

"How?"

"I don't know."

I was beginning to feel annoyed. "Since six o'clock, huh?" I said. "What *have* you found out?"

Norris sounded hurt. "I found you, didn't I? And Jim and Larry and Dick."

I got the same cold feeling at the base of my spine that I get when I have to have blood taken. "We're scattered all over the United States of America. Last night we were all in the same lousy hotel. What happened?"

"Take it easy." When Norris said that, I knew we were all in trouble. "It seems as though we've been, uh, transported back in time too."

I screamed, "What?"

"It's 1954 out there," said Norris.

I gave up. I wasn't going to say another word. When I started the day, I was sleeping very nicely. Every time I opened my mouth, it only encouraged Norris to tell me something else I didn't want to hear. I decided to clam up.

"Did you hear me?" he asked.

I didn't say anything.

"It's 1954 out there. You've been transported back and put in the body of, uh, wait a minute. I wrote it down, uh, Ellard Mac-Iver. Do you know who that is?"

I felt cold again. "Yes," I said, "he was a utility infielder for the Red Sox. In the fifties."

"Right. You have a game today against the Athletics. Lots of luck."

"What am I supposed to do?"

Norris laughed, I don't know why. "Play ball," he said.

"How do we get back?" I shouted. The man in the other bed grumbled and woke up.

"I haven't figured that out yet," said Norris. "I have to go. This is long distance. Anyway, this week you play the Tigers, and you can talk it over with Jim. He's in the body of, uh, this guy Charlie Quinn. Second base."

"Wonderful," I said. "Terrific."

"Don't worry," said Norris. "I have to go. I'll talk with you later." He hung up.

I looked at the phone. "Terrific," I muttered.

The other guy propped himself up in the other bed and said, "Shut up, Mac, will you?" I just stared at him.

I realized that I should have asked Norris whose body he was in. I shrugged. Maybe Jim would know.

A few days later we had the situation completely sorted out. It still didn't bring us any closer to solving the problem, but at least it was sorted out. This is the way it looked:

Famous Science Fiction Writer	In the Body of	Team	Position and Batting Average	
Sandor Courane (me)	Ellard MacIver	Boston Red Sox	Inf.	.221
Norris Page	Don Di Mauro	Chicago White Sox	Left Field	.288
Larry Shrader	Gerhardt "Dutch" Ruhl	New York Yankees	1B	.334
Dick Shrader	Marv Croxton	Cleveland Indians	Center Field	.291
Jim Benedetti	Charlie Quinn	Detroit Tigers	2B	.254

I didn't like it at all. Not batting .221 and being thirty-six years old (I'm not thirty-six, but MacIver was, and he was in danger of losing his job next spring, and if we didn't get home soon, I'd have to become a broadcaster or something).

That morning I went to the ballpark with my roommate. His name was Tony Lloyd, and he was a huge first baseman. Everyone on the team called him "Money." His most memorable attribute was explaining how Jackie Robinson wouldn't survive the walk from the clubhouse to the dugout if the National League had any men with guts over there. I didn't listen to him much. Anyway, we had a game scheduled for two o'clock, but the Red Sox were headed for a mediocre finish to the season and that meant that everybody was taking all kinds of extra practice and hustling around and pretending that they cared a hill of beans about the outcome of every game.

I, for one, was excited. I was scared out of my skin too, but I was excited. I followed Lloyd into Fenway Park—the gate guard gave me a nod, recognizing my borrowed body—and stood for a while in the dressing room, just staring at things. I'd always wanted to be a ballplayer when I was a kid, of course, and now . . .

And now I *was* a ballplayer. Sort of. A sort of ballplayer, a bench-warming antique of a ballplayer who was hitting just well enough to prove he was still alive. I wondered why, if I were going to be transmiggled through time and space, I couldn't have ended up in the body of, oh, Ted Williams, say, whose locker wasn't far from mine. I stared at him; I stared at everybody else; I stared at the towels; I stared at the soap; I stared at the contents of my locker. *My* locker. My locker as a member of a professional base-ball team. There were pictures of beautiful women taped to the inside of the door. There were parts of the uniform that I couldn't even identify. I had to watch a couple of other guys getting dressed to see how they worked. I think the guys noticed me watching.

After I got dressed I walked through the long, cool tunnel under the stands and emerged in the dugout. Before me was a vast, green, utterly beautiful world. Fenway Park. And they were going to let me go out there and run around on their grass.

I took my fielder's glove and trotted out toward second base. I know how to trot. I was in a little trouble once I reached where I was going. I said hello to men I didn't recognize. Someone else was hitting ground balls to us and we were lazily scooping them up. Well, anyway, *they* were; I was letting them hit me on the elbow, the knee, and twice on the chin.

"Hey, look at the old man," said some kid, backhanding a hot rocket of a grounder. "You going to be around next year, old man?"

I felt angry. I wanted to show that kid, but there wasn't anything I could show him, with the possible exception of sentence struc-ture.

"He'll be around," said another kid. "They're going to bury him out under center field." Another grounder came my way and it zipped between my feet and out onto the grass. The kids laughed.

Later I took some batting practice. This was 1954, of course, and the batting practice was pitched by a venerable old ballplayer whose name had been a legend when I was a boy. I told him that I wasn't feeling very well, and he took some of the stuff off his pitches. They were nice and easy, right over the plate every time, and I hit some liners around the stadium. I pretended that they would have been base hits in a real game. It felt great. After I finished, Ted Williams stepped in and demolished the bleachers.

And then the fun began. The game started. I vaguely remem-bered hearing a kind of pep talk from Lou Boudreau, the manager. I guess they played the "Star Spangled Banner," but I don't re-member that. And then, before I was even aware of what was happening, I was sitting in a corner of the dugout, watching, and we were in the third inning of the game. Frank Sullivan was pitching for us, and Arnie Portocarrero was pitching for Philadelphia.

Right then, if someone had asked me, I might have declined to go back to the seventies, back to typing up fantasies to pay my rent. Why should I? I could stay in 1954 and get paid to play baseball! Eisenhower was President. The space race wasn't even to the starting gate yet. Ernie Kovacs and Buddy Holly were still alive. I could win a fortune betting on things and waiting for Polaroid to split.

But no. I had a responsibility to the science fiction world. After all, science fiction might well do without me (just let it try), but Norris and Jim and Dick and Larry were here too, and I had to help my friends, if I could. But could I? Why were we here, what had zapped us more than twenty years into the past?

And then I had a terrifying thought. What all this meant was that more than twenty years in the future, in New Orleans, some man named Ellard MacIver, a failure of a baseball player with very little to recommend him, was sitting down at my typewriter and continuing my writing career. No! I couldn't bear it! If anyone was going to ruin my career, I wanted it to be me.

On Sunday night we rode the train out to Detroit. It was a rotten trip. I hadn't gotten into any of the three weekend games with Philadelphia, which was just as well. I was extra baggage to the Red Sox, carried along in case a hole opened up and swallowed four-fifths of the team down into the bowels of the earth. I was looking forward to talking with Jim. Sure, 1954 had its good points —I think I counted about six of them—but, all in all, I had decided that we had to get out of the mess somehow, and as soon as possible. I had a contract outstanding with Doubleday, and I didn't want Ellard MacIver writing that novel. If he did and it won a Hugo, well, I'd have to join the Navy or something.

Fortunately, Jim was in the same frame of mind. Jim is a great guy normally, but his situation was driving him crazy. He was supposed to be a second baseman, a starting second baseman, and he had fallen on his face three times trying to pivot on double-play balls. Also, his batting had gone into a slump (understandably enough), and he didn't like the body he had been put into. "You think the old one gave me trouble," he said, "this one complains if I eat Wheaties."

We had lunch at my hotel on the afternoon of the first game of the Detroit series, Tuesday. "Have you had any ideas about who's doing this to us?" I asked him.

"Is somebody doing this to us?" he asked.

I looked at him blankly for a moment. It hadn't occurred to me that all of this might be a function of the Universe, instead of an evil plot. That made me feel even worse. "Look," I said, "we have to believe that we can get out of this somehow."

Jim ate some more oatmeal. "Fine," he said, "we'll believe that. What next?"

"The next logical step is to assume that if this is being done to us, that *someone* is doing it."

Jim looked at me like he suddenly realized that I was just a bit dangerous. "That's not the most spectacular reasoning in the world," he said.

"Well, we have to make that assumption. It doesn't make any difference who it is. The main thing is that we flip things around the right way."

"Boy, do I hate this oatmeal," he said. "Wait. What if we flip things, and we end up somewhere else? I mean, like in the bodies of apple salesmen in the thirties. Don't do anything we'll regret."

"I won't," I said, because as yet I couldn't think of anything at all. "If anyone can figure this out, Larry can."

"Right," said Jim, smiling suddenly. "We'll let Larry figure it out. You and I write sort of surreal fantasies. Larry is the real nuts and bolts science fiction type. He'll know what to do."

"Right," I said. We finished eating and went out to the ballpark. I sat in the corner of the dugout during the game and watched Jim muffling around second base.

The next series was in Cleveland, my hometown. I thought about visiting my parents and seeing myself at seven years old, but the idea was vaguely repellent. I reminded myself that I'd have to see my younger brother at five years old, and that settled the matter. I went to a movie instead.

I talked with Dick several times, and he said that he'd heard from his brother, Larry. Larry is a good old rocketship and ray-gun kind of thinker, and we were counting on him to help us out of the predicament. "What do you think?" I asked Dick Shrader.

"Well," said Dick, doing something I'd never seen him do before—take a handful of chewing tobacco, mix it with bubble gum, and stuff it all in one cheek—"unless I have a bad slump the last few weeks, I stand a good chance of finishing over .300. I'm going to ask for thirty thousand next season."

"Dick," I said loudly, "you're not paying attention."

"Okay. Thirty-five thousand."

Clearly there would be no progress at all until the series in New York, when Larry and I could go over the matter in great detail. I guess, then, that I can skip the next several days. Not much happened, really, other than a series with the Orioles during which I got to bat (a weak ground-out), and I had an interview with a newspaperman who thought I was Jimmy Piersall.

Following the first game with the Yankees, Larry and I went to a small restaurant where he wouldn't be recognized. We ordered dinner, and while we waited we talked. "How do you feel about this guy Dutch Ruhl taking over your writing career?" I asked.

"Doesn't bother me," said Larry, gulping some beer. Larry breathes beer.

"Why not?" My hopes rose. I thought he had found a solution.

"Well, if we get out of this, there won't be any problem, right?" he said, swallowing some more beer.

"Right," I said.

"And if we don't get out of it, well, I'll just wait around and come up behind him and take my career back."

"That's twenty years from now!" I said.

Larry didn't look disturbed. "Think of all the ideas I'll have by then," he said. "I'll do 'Star Trek' in 1960, and *2001* in 1961, and *Star Wars* in 1962, and—"

"What are you going to do with Dutch Ruhl?"

Larry knocked back the last of the beer. "Was there a Dutch Ruhl writing science fiction when we left?"

"No."

"Then there won't be."

"But there was somebody in the body of Larry Shrader, maybe you, maybe not. How are you going to prove *you're* Larry Shrader?"

Larry looked at me as though I were in some way tragic. "All I need are my driver's license and my Master Charge."

"Got those with you?"

Now Larry looked tragic. "No," he said.

"Who could stand to gain from this?" I wondered, as Larry signaled for several more beers.

"Who?" he said, in a hollow voice.

"Who?" I said.

There was a slight pause, and then we looked at each other.

"Who could stand to gain from the sudden disappearance of, well, if I do say so myself, the cream of the newer generation, the hope and future of science fiction?" he said, a little smile on his lips.

"Well," I said, "apart from the Dean of Science Fiction . . ."

"In conjunction with the Most Honored Writer of Science Fiction," said Larry, laughing a little.

"Acting in concert with the Acknowledged Master of Science Fiction," I said.

"With the aid of two or three others we might name," said Larry.

"Why would they do this to us?" I asked.

"Why, indeed? It's the natural reaction of the old dinosaurs when they spot the first strange mammals bounding through their jungle. But it's a futile action."

"How did they do it?" I was still bewildered.

Larry was not. These things were always marvelously simple to his agile mind. That was why he was hitting .334 for the Yankees and I was chewing gum for the Red Sox. Larry was on his way to becoming a dinosaur in his own right. "They accomplished it easily enough," he said. "They got us here the same way we're going home. By typewriter."

"You mean—" I said, my eyes wide with astonishment.

"Yes," said Larry, "what *is* reality, anyway?"

Before the veal marsala came, we had the solution to our problem. We weren't vengeful, though, because we have to set the tone of the future. That's a heavy burden, but we carry it gladly.

"Now what?" said Larry, drinking some beer for dessert.

"Now we go home. We can go now, or we can wait around here in 1954 for a while, for a kind of vacation."

"We'll take a vote," said Larry, because he's a four-square kind of guy.

Well, we did take a vote, and we decided to go right home, because some of us had library books overdue. Getting home was simple. It was like Dorothy's Ruby Slippers—it was there all the time. We all gathered in Washington, because that's where we had last been together. We all sat together in a large suite in the same hotel where so many years in the future there would be a science fiction convention. We had Cokes and beer and pretzels and potato chips. We had the television on ("The Stu Erwin Show"), and we messed the room up some. "Remember," said Norris, "not one word about baseball. Only science fiction."

"Just science fiction," said Dick Shrader.

We started talking about money, of course. We talked about who was paying what, and that led to a discussion of editors. When we realized how violent our passions were growing we changed the subject to "The Future of Science Fiction," and then "Science Fiction and the Media," and then "Academia and Science Fiction." Just about then a short, heavy man came into the suite with a camera and took Larry's picture. The man sat down and listened.

We offered him some pretzels. We talked about "The Short Fiction Market," and two wild young women dressed like characters from a trilogy of novels came in to fill the bathtub with some viscous fluid. We didn't offer them pretzels. We talked about "Science Fiction as a Revolutionary Weapon," and two writers and an agent and four more fans came in, and it was getting noisy, and Jim called down for some ice, and I went into the hall, and more fans and more pros were coming toward the room, so I went to the elevator and went up to my room. I opened the door carefully. The light was on and I saw that there was someone else in the room. I was ready to turn away, but I saw that it was the same young woman who had been with me at the start of the adventure. I looked down, and of course I was in my old body (it's not *that* old, really, and it's a little worn, but it's mine) and everything was all right for the moment. We were victorious.

ALIBI IKE

Ring Lardner

HIS FIRST NAME was Frank X. Farrell, and I guess the X stood for "Excuse me." Because he never pulled a play, good or bad, on or off the field, without apologizin' for it.

"Alibi Ike" was the name Carey wished on him the first day he reported down South. O' course we all cut out the "Alibi" part of it right away for the fear he would overhear it and bust somebody. But we called him "Ike" right to his face and the rest of it was understood by everybody on the club except Ike himself.

He ast me one time, he says:

"What do you all call me Ike for? I ain't no Yid."

"Carey give you the name," I says. "It's his nickname for everybody he takes a likin' to."

"He mustn't have only a few friends then," says Ike. "I never heard him say 'Ike' to nobody else."

But I was goin' to tell you about Carey namin' him. We'd been workin' out two weeks and the pitchers was showin' somethin' when this bird joined us. His first day out he stood up there so good and took such a reef at the old pill that he had everyone lookin'. Then him and Carey was together in left field, catchin' fungoes, and it was after we was through for the day that Carey told me about him.

"What do you think of Alibi Ike?" ast Carey.

"Who's that?" I says.

"This here Farrell in the outfield," says Carey.

349

"He looks like he could hit," I says.

"Yes," says Carey, "but he can't hit near as good as he can apologize."

Then Carey went on to tell me what Ike had been pullin' out there. He'd dropped the first fly ball that was hit to him and told Carey his glove wasn't broke in good yet, and Carey says the glove could easy of been Kid Gleason's gran'father. He made a whale of a catch out o' the next one and Carey says "Nice work!" or some-thin' like that, but Ike says he could of caught the ball with his back turned only he slipped when he started after it and, besides that, the air currents fooled him.

"I thought you done well to get to the ball," says Carey.

"I ought to been settin' under it," says Ike.

"What did you hit last year?" Carey ast him.

"I had malaria most o' the season," says Ike. "I wound up with .356."

"Where would I have to go to get malaria?" says Carey, but Ike didn't wise up.

I and Carey and him set at the same table together for supper. It took him half an hour longer'n us to eat because he had to excuse himself every time he lifted his fork.

"Doctor told me I needed starch," he'd say, and then toss a shovelful o' potatoes into him. Or, "They ain't much meat on one o' these chops," he'd tell us, and grab another one. Or he'd say: "Nothin' like onions for a cold," and then he'd dip into the perfu-mery.

"Better try that apple sauce," says Carey. "It'll help your ma-laria."

"Whose malaria?" says Ike. He'd forget already why he didn't only hit .356 last year.

I and Carey begin to lead him on.

"Whereabouts did you say your home was?" I ast him.

"I live with my folks," he says. "We live in Kansas City—not right down in the business part—outside a ways."

"How's that come?" says Carey. "I should think you'd get rooms in the post office."

But Ike was too busy curin' his cold to get that one.

"Are you married?" I ast him.

"No," he says. "I never run round much with girls, except to shows once in a while and parties and dances and roller skatin'."

"Never take 'em to the prize fights, eh?" says Carey.

"We don't have no real good bouts," says Ike. "Just bush stuff. And I never figured a boxin' match was a place for the ladies."

Well, after supper he pulled a cigar out and lit it. I was just goin'
to ask him what he done it for, but he beat me to it.

"Kind o' rests a man to smoke after a good workout," he says.
"Kind o' settles a man's supper, too."

"Looks like a pretty good cigar," says Carey.

"Yes," says Ike. "A friend o' mine give it to me—a fella in
Kansas City that runs a billiard room."

"Do you play billiards?" I ast him.

"I used to play a fair game," he says. "I'm all out o' practice
now—can't hardly make a shot."

We coaxed him into a four-handed battle, him and Carey against
Jack Mack and I. Say, he couldn't play billiards as good as Willie
Hoppe; not quite. But to hear him tell it, he didn't make a good
shot all evenin'. I'd leave him an awful-lookin' layout and he'd
gather 'em up in one try and then run a couple o' hundred, and
between every carom he'd say he put too much stuff on the ball,
or the English didn't take or the table wasn't true, or his stick was
crooked, or somethin'. And all the time he had the balls actin' like
they was Dutch soldiers and him Kaiser William. We started out
to play fifty points, but we had to make it a thousand so as I and
Jack and Carey could try the table.

The four of us set round the lobby a wile after we was through
playin', and when it got along toward bedtime Carey whispered to
me and says:

"Ike'd like to go to bed, but he can't think up no excuse."

Carey hadn't hardly finished whisperin' when Ike got up and
pulled it.

"Well, good night, boys," he says. "I ain't sleepy, but I got
some gravel in my shoes and it's killin' my feet."

We knowed he hadn't never left the hotel since we'd came in
from the grounds and changed our clo'es. So Carey says:

"I should think they'd take them gravel pits out o' the billiard
room."

But Ike was already on his way to the elevator, limpin'.

"He's got the world beat," says Carey to Jack and I. "I've knew
lots o' guys that had an alibi for every mistake they made; I've
heard pitchers say that the ball slipped when somebody cracked
one off'n 'em; I've heard infielders complain of a sore arm after
heavin' one into the stand, and I've saw outfielders tooken sick
with a dizzy spell when they've misjudged a fly ball. But this baby
can't even go to bed without apologizin', and I bet he excuses
himself to the razor when he gets ready to shave."

"And at that," says Jack, "he's goin' to make us a good man."

"Yes," says Carey, "Unless rheumatism keeps his battin' average down to .400."

Well, sir, Ike kept whalin' away at the ball all through the trip till everybody knowed he'd won a job. Cap had him in there regular the last few exhibition games and told the newspaper boys a week before the season opened that he was goin' to start him in Kane's place.

"You're there kid," says Carey to Ike, the night Cap made the 'nnouncement. "They ain't many boys that wins a big league berth their third year out."

"I'd of been up here a year ago," says Ike, "only I was bent over all season with lumbago."

II

It rained down in Cincinnati one day and somebody organized a little game o' cards. They was shy two men to make six and ast I and Carey to play.

"I'm with you if you get Ike and make it seven-handed," says Carey.

So they got a hold of Ike and we went up to Smitty's room.

"I pretty near forgot how many you deal," says Ike. "It's been a long wile since I played."

I and Carey give each other the wink, and sure enough, he was just as ig'orant about poker as billiards. About the second hand, the pot was opened two or three ahead of him, and they was three in when it come his turn. It cost a buck, and he throwed in two.

"It's raised, boys," somebody says.

"Gosh, that's right, I did raise it," says Ike.

"Take out a buck if you didn't mean to tilt her," says Carey.

"No," says Ike, "I'll leave it go."

Well, it was raised back at him, and then he made another mistake and raised again. They was only three left in when the draw come. Smitty'd opened with a pair o' kings and he didn't help 'em. Ike stood pat. The guy that'd raised him back was flushin' and he didn't fill. So Smitty checked and Ike bet and didn't get no call. He tossed his hand away, but I grabbed it and give it a look. He had king, queen, jack and two tens. Alibi Ike he must have seen me peekin', for he leaned over and whispered to me.

"I overlooked my hand," he says. "I thought all the wile it was a straight."

"Yes," I says, "that's why you raised twice by mistake."

They was another pot that he come into with tens and fours. It was tilted a couple o' times and two o' the strong fellas drawed ahead of Ike. They each drawed one. So Ike throwed away his little pair and come out with four tens. And they was four treys against him. Carey'd looked at Ike's discards and then he says:

"This lucky bum busted two pair."

"No, no, I didn't," says Ike.

"Yes, yes you did," says Carey, and showed us the two fours.

"What do you know about that?" says Ike. "I'd of swore one was a five spot."

Well, we hadn't had no pay day yet, and after a wile everybody except Ike was goin' shy. I could see him gettin' restless and I was wonderin' how he'd make the get-away. He tried two or three times. "I got to buy some collars before supper," he says.

"No hurry," says Smitty. "The stores here keeps open all night in April."

After a minute he opened up again.

"My uncle out in Nebraska ain't expected to live," he says. "I ought to send a telegram."

"Would that save him?" says Carey.

"No, it sure wouldn't," says Ike, "but I ought to leave my old man know where I'm at."

"When did you hear about your uncle?" says Carey.

"Just this mornin'," says Ike.

"Who told you?" ast Carey.

"I got a wire from my old man," says Ike.

"Well," says Carey, "your old man knows you're still here yet this afternoon if you was here this mornin'. Trains leavin' Cincinnati in the middle o' the day don't carry no ball clubs."

"Yes," says Ike, "that's true. But he don't know where I'm goin' to be next week."

"Ain't he got no schedule?" ast Carey.

"I sent him one openin' day," says Ike, "but it takes mail a long time to get to Idaho."

"I thought your old man lived in Kansas City," says Carey.

"He does when he's home," says Ike.

"But now," says Carey, "I s'pose he's went to Idaho so as he can be near your sick uncle in Nebraska."

"He's visitin' my other uncle in Idaho."

"Then how does he keep posted about your sick uncle?" ast Carey.

"He don't," says Ike. "He don't even know my other uncle's sick. That's why I ought to wire and tell him."

"Good night!" says Carey.

"What town in Idaho is your old man at?" I says.

Ike thought it over.

"No town at all," he says. "But he's near a town."

"Near what town?" I says.

"Yuma," says Ike.

Well, by this time he'd lost two or three pots and he was desperate. We was playin' just as fast as we could, because we seen we couldn't hold him much longer. But he was tryin' so hard to frame an escape that he couldn't pay no attention to the cards, and it looked like we'd get his whole pile away from him if we could make him stick.

The telephone saved him. The minute it begun to ring, five of us jumped for it. But Ike was there first.

"Yes," he says, answerin' it. "This is him. I'll come right down."

And he slammed up the receiver and beat it out o' the door without even sayin' good-by.

"Smitty'd ought to locked the door," says Carey.

"What did he win?" ast Carey.

We figured it up—sixty-odd bucks.

"And the next time we ask him to play," says Carey, "his fingers will be so stiff he can't hold the cards."

Well, we set round a wile talkin' it over, and pretty soon the telephone rung again. Smitty answered it. It was a friend of his'n from Hamilton and he wanted to know why Smitty didn't hurry down. He was the one that had called before and Ike had told him he was Smitty.

"Ike'd ought to split with Smitty's friend," says Carey.

"No," I says, "he'll need all he won. It costs money to buy collars and to send telegrams from Cincinnati to your old man in Texas and keep him posted on the health o' your uncle in Cedar Rapids, D.C."

III

And you ought to heard him out there on that field! They wasn't a day when he didn't pull six or seven, and it didn't make no difference whether he was goin' good or bad. If he popped up in the pinch he should of made a base hit and the reason he didn't was so-and-so. And if he cracked one for three bases he ought to had a home run, only the ball wasn't lively, or the wind brought it back, or he tripped on a lump o' dirt, roundin' first base.

They was one afternoon in New York when he beat all records. Big Marquard was workin' against us and he was good.

In the first innin' Ike hit one clear over that right field stand, but it was a few feet foul. Then he got another foul and then the count come to two and two. Then Rube slipped one acrost on him and he was called out.

"What do you know about that!" he says afterward on the bench. "I lost count. I thought it was three and one, and I took a strike."

"You took a strike all right," says Carey. "Even the umps knowed it was a strike."

"Yes," says Ike, "but you can bet I wouldn't of took it if I'd knew it was the third one. The score board had it wrong."

"That score board ain't for you to look at," says Cap. "It's for you to hit that old pill against."

"Well," says Ike, "I could of hit that one over the score board if I'd knew it was the third."

"Was it a good ball?" I says.

"Well, no, it wasn't," says Ike. "It was inside."

"How far inside?" says Carey.

"Oh, two or three inches or half a foot," says Ike.

"I guess you wouldn't of threatened the score board with it then," says Cap.

"I'd of pulled it down the right foul line if I hadn't thought he'd call it a ball," says Ike.

Well, in New York's part o' the innin' Doyle cracked one and Ike run back a mile and a half and caught it with one hand. We was all sayin' what a whale of a play it was, but he had to apologize just the same as for gettin' struck out.

"That stand's so high," he says, "that a man don't ever see a ball till it's right on top o' you."

"Didn't you see that one?" ast Cap.

"Not at first," says Ike; "not till it raised up above the roof o' the stand."

"Then why did you start back as soon as the ball was hit?" says Cap.

"I knowed by the sound that he'd got a good hold of it," says Ike.

"Yes," says Cap, "but how'd you know what direction to run in?"

"Doyle usually hits 'em that way, the way I run," says Ike.

"Why don't you play blindfolded?" says Carey.

"Might as well, with that big high stand to bother a man," says Ike. "If I could of saw the ball all the time I'd of got it in my hip pocket."

Along in the fifth we was one run to the bad and Ike got on with one out. On the first ball throwed to Smitty, Ike went down. The ball was outside and Meyers throwed Ike out by ten feet.

You could see Ike's lips movin' all the way to the bench and when he got there he had his piece learned.

"Why didn't he swing?" he says.

"Why didn't you wait for his sign?" says Cap.

"He give me his sign," says Ike.

"What is his sign with you?" says Cap.

"Pickin' up some dirt with his right hand," says Ike.

"Well, I didn't see him do it," Cap says.

"He done it all right," says Ike.

Well, Smitty went out and they wasn't no more argument till they come in for the next innin'. Then Cap opened it up.

"You fellas better get your signs straight," he says.

"Do you mean me?" says Smitty.

"Yes," Cap says. "What's your sign with Ike?"

"Slidin' my left hand up to the end o' the bat and back," says Smitty.

"Do you hear that, Ike?" ast Cap.

"What of it?" says Ike.

"You says his sign was pickin' up dirt and he says it's slidin' his hand. Which is right?"

"I'm right," says Smitty. "But if you're arguin' about him goin' last innin', I didn't give him no sign."

"You pulled your cap down with your right hand, didn't you?" ast Ike.

"Well, s'pose I did," says Smitty. "That don't mean nothin'. I never told you to take that for a sign, did I?"

"I thought maybe you meant to tell me and forgot," says Ike.

They couldn't none of us answer that and they wouldn't of been no more said if Ike had of shut up. But wile we was settin' there Carey got on with two out and stole second clean.

"There!" says Ike. "That's what I was tryin' to do and I'd of got away with it if Smitty'd swang and bothered the Indian."

"Oh!" says Smitty. "You was tryin' to steal then, was you? I thought you claimed I give you the hit and run."

"I didn't claim no such a thing," says Ike. "I thought maybe you might of gave me a sign, but I was goin' anyway because I thought I had a good start."

Cap prob'ly would of hit him with a bat, only just about that time Doyle booted one on Hayes and Carey come acrost with the run that tied.

Well, we go into the ninth finally, one and one, and Marquard walks McDonald with nobody out.

"Lay it down," says Cap to Ike.

And Ike goes up there with orders to bunt and cracks the first ball into that right-field stand! It was fair this time, and we're two ahead, but I didn't think about that at the time. I was too busy watchin' Cap's face. First he turned pale and then he got red as fire and then he got blue and purple, and finally he just laid back and busted out laughin'. So we wasn't afraid to laugh ourselfs when we seen him doin' it, and when Ike come in everybody on the bench was in hysterics.

But instead o' takin' advantage, Ike had to try and excuse himself. His play was to shut up and he didn't know how to make it.

"Well," he says, "if I hadn't hit quite so quick at that one I bet it'd of cleared the center-field fence."

Cap stopped laughin'.

"It'll cost you plain fifty," he says.

"What for?" says Ike.

"When I say 'bunt' I mean 'bunt,' " says Cap.

"You didn't say 'bunt,' " says Ike.

"I says 'Lay it down,' " says Cap. "If that don't mean 'bunt,' what does it mean?"

" 'Lay it down' means 'bunt' all right," says Ike, "but I understood you to say 'Lay on it.' "

"All right," says Cap, "and the little misunderstandin' will cost you fifty."

Ike didn't say nothin' for a few minutes. Then he had another bright idear.

"I was just kiddin' about misunderstandin' you," he says. "I knowed you wanted me to bunt."

"Well, then, why didn't you bunt?" ast Cap.

"I was goin' to on the next ball," says Ike. "But I thought if I took a good wallop I'd have 'em all fooled. So I walloped at the first one to fool 'em, and I didn't have no intention o' hittin' it."

"You tried to miss it, did you?" says Cap.

"Yes," says Ike.

"How'd you happen to hit it?" ast Cap.

"Well," Ike says, "I was lookin' for him to throw me a fast one and I was goin' to swing under it. But he come with a hook and I met it right square where I was swingin' to go under the fast one."

"Great!" says Cap. "Boys," he says, "Ike's learned how to hit

Marquard's curve. Pretend a fast one's comin' and then try to miss it. It's a good thing to know and Ike'd ought to be willin' to pay for the lesson. So I'm goin' to make it a hundred instead o' fifty.''

The game wound up 3 to 1. The fine didn't go, because Ike hit like a wild man all through that trip and we made pretty near a clean-up. The night we went to Philly I got him cornered in the car and I says to him:

"Forget them alibis for a wile and tell me somethin'. What'd you do that for, swing that time against Marquard when you was told to bunt?''

"I'll tell you," he says. "That ball he throwed me looked just like the one I struck out on in the first innin' and I wanted to show Cap what I could of done to that other one if I'd knew it was the third strike.''

"But," I says, "the one you struck out on in the first innin' was a fast ball.''

"So was the one I cracked in the ninth," says Ike.

IV

You've saw Cap's wife, o' course. Well, her sister's about twict as good-lookin' as her, and that's goin' some.

Cap took his missus down to St. Louis the second trip and the other one come down from St. Joe to visit her. Her name is Dolly, and some doll is right.

Well, Cap was goin' to take the two sisters to a show and he wanted a beau for Dolly. He left it to her and she picked Ike. He'd hit three on the nose that afternoon—of'n Sallee, too.

They fell for each other that first evenin'. Cap told us how it come off. She begin flatterin' Ike for the star game he'd played and o' course he begin excusin' himself for not doin' better. So she thought he was modest and it went strong with her. And she believed everything he said and that made her solid with him—that and her make-up. They was together ever mornin' and evenin' for the five days we was there. In the afternoons Ike played the grandest ball you ever see, hittin' and runnin' the bases like a fool and catchin' everything that stayed in the park.

I told Cap, I says: "You'd ought to keep the doll with us and he'd make Cobb's figures look sick.''

But Dolly had to go back to St. Joe and we come home for a long serious.

Well, for the next three weeks Ike had a letter to read every day and he'd set in the clubhouse readin' it till mornin' practice was half over. Cap didn't say nothin' to him, because he was goin' so good. But I and Carey wasted a lot of our time tryin' to get him to own up who the letters was from. Fine chancet!

"What are you readin'?" Carey'd say. "A bill?"

"No," Ike'd say, "not exactly a bill. It's a letter from a fella I used to go to school with."

"High school or college?" I'd ask him.

"College," he'd say.

"What college?" I'd say.

Then he'd stall a wile and then he'd say:

"I didn't go to the college myself, but my friend went there."

"How did it happen you didn't go?" Carey'd ask him.

"Well," he'd say, "they wasn't no colleges near where I lived."

"Didn't you live in Kansas City?" I'd say to him.

One time he'd say he did and another time he didn't. One time he says he lived in Michigan.

"Where at?" says Carey.

"Near Detroit," he says.

"Well," I says, "Detroit's near Ann Arbor and that's where they got the university."

"Yes," says Ike, "they got it there now, but they didn't have it there then."

"I come pretty near goin' to Syracuse," I says, "only they wasn't no railroads runnin' through there in them days."

"Where'd this friend o' yours go to college?" says Carey.

"I forget now," says Ike.

"Was it Carlisle?" ast Carey.

"No," says Ike, "his folks wasn't very well off."

"That's what barred me from Smith," I says.

"I was goin' to tackle Cornell's," says Carey, "but the doctor told me I'd have hay fever if I didn't stay up North."

"Your friend writes long letters," I says.

"Yes," says Ike; "he's tellin' me about a ballplayer."

"Where does he play?" ast Carey.

"Down in the Texas League—Fort Wayne," says Ike.

"It looks like a girl's writin'," Carey says.

"A girl wrote it," says Ike. "That's my friend's sister, writin' for him."

"Didn't they teach writin' at this here college where he went?" says Carey.

"Sure," Ike says, "they taught writin', but he got his hand cut off in a railroad wreck."

"How long ago?" I says.

"Right after he got out o' college," says Ike.

"Well," I says, "I should think he'd of learned to write with his left hand by this time."

"It's his left hand that was cut off," says Ike, "and he was left-handed."

"You get a letter every day," says Carey. "They're all the same writin'. Is he tellin' you about a different ballplayer every time he writes?"

"No," Ike says. "It's the same ballplayer. He just tells me what he does every day."

"From the size o' the letters, they don't play nothin' but double-headers down there," says Carey.

We figured that Ike spent most of his evenins answerin' the letters from his "friend's sister," so we kept tryin' to date him up for shows and parties to see how he'd duck out of 'em. He was bugs over spaghetti, so we told him one day that they was goin' to be a big feed of it over to Joe's that night and he was invited.

"How long'll it last?" he says.

"Well," we says, "we're goin' right over there after the game and stay till they close up."

"I can't go," he says, "unless they leave me come home at eight bells."

"Nothin' doin'," says Carey, "Joe'd get sore."

"I can't go then," says Ike.

"Why not?" I ast him.

"Well," he says, "my landlady locks up the house at eight and I left my key home."

"You can come and stay with me," says Carey.

"No," he says, "I can't sleep in a strange bed."

"How do you get along when we're on the road?" says I.

"I don't never sleep the first night anywheres," he says. "After that I'm all right."

"You'll have time to chase home and get your key right after the game," I told him.

"The key ain't home," says Ike. "I lent it to one o' the other fellas and he's went out o' town and took it with him."

"Couldn't you borry another key off'n the landlady?" Carey ast him.

"No," he says, "that's the only one they is."

Well, the day before we started East again, Ike come into the clubhouse all smiles.

"Your birthday?" I ast him.

"No," he says.

"What do you feel so good about?" I says.

"Got a letter from my old man," he says. "My uncle's goin' to get well."

"Is that the one in Nebraska?" says I.

"Not right in Nebraska," says Ike. "Near there."

But afterwards we got the right dope from Cap. Dolly'd blew in from Missouri and was going to make the trip with her sister.

V

Well, I want to alibi Carey and I for what come off in Boston. If we'd of had any idear what we was doin', we'd never did it. They wasn't nobody outside o' maybe Ike and the dame that felt worse over it than I and Carey.

The first two days we didn't see nothin' of Ike and her except out to the park. The rest o' the time they was sight-seein' over to Cambridge and down to Revere and out to Brook-a-line and all the other places where the rubes go.

But when we come into the beanery after the third game Cap's wife called us over.

"If you want to see somethin' pretty," she says, "look at the third finger on Sis's left hand."

Well, o' course we knowed before we looked that it wasn't goin' to be no hangnail. Nobody was su'prised when Dolly blew into the dinin' room with it—a rock that Ike'd bought off'n Diamond Joe the first trip to New York. Only o' course it'd been set into a lady's-size ring instead o' the automobile tire he'd been wearin'.

Cap and his missus and Ike and Dolly ett supper together, only Ike didn't eat nothin', but just set there blushin' and spillin' things on the tablecloth. I heard him excusin' himself for not havin' no appetite. He says he couldn't never eat when he was clost to the ocean. He'd forgot about them sixty-five oysters he destroyed the first night o' the trip before.

He was goin' to take her to a show, so after supper he went upstairs to change his collar. She had to doll up, too, and o' course Ike was through long before her.

If you remember the hotel in Boston, they's a little parlor where the piano's at and then they's another little parlor openin' off o' that. Well, when Ike come down Smitty was playin' a few chords and I and Carey was harmonizin'. We seen Ike go up to the desk to leave his key and we called him in. He tried to duck away, but we wouldn't stand for it.

We ast him what he was all duded up for and he says he was goin' to the theayter.

"Goin' alone?" says Carey.

"No" he says, "a friend of mine's goin' with me."

"What do you say if we go along?" says Carey.

"I ain't only got two tickets," he says.

"Well," says Carey, "we can go down there with you and buy our own seats; maybe we can all get together."

"No," says Ike. "They ain't no more seats. They're all sold out."

"We can buy some off'n the scalpers," says Carey.

"I wouldn't if I was you," says Ike. "They say the show's rotten."

"What are you goin' for, then?" I ast.

"I didn't hear about it bein' rotten till I got the tickets," he says.

"Well," I says, "if you don't want to go I'll buy the tickets from you."

"No," says Ike, "I wouldn't want to cheat you. I'm stung and I'll just have to stand for it."

"What are you goin' to do with the girl, leave her here at the hotel?" I says.

"What girl?" says Ike.

"The girl you ett supper with," I says.

"Oh," he says, "we just happened to go into the dinin' room together, that's all. Cap wanted I should set down with 'em."

"I noticed," says Carey, "that she happened to be wearin' that rock you bought off'n Diamond Joe."

"Yes," says Ike. "I lent it to her for a wile."

"Did you lend her the new ring that goes with it?" I says.

"She had that already," says Ike. "She lost the set out of it."

"I wouldn't trust no strange girl with a rock o' mine," says Carey.

"Oh, I guess she's all right," Ike says. "Besides, I was tired o' the stone. When a girl asks you for somethin', what are you goin' to do?"

He started out toward the desk, but we flagged him.

"Wait a minute!" Carey says. "I got a bet with Sam here, and it's up to you to settle it."

"Well," says Ike, "make it snappy. My friend'll be here any minute."

"I bet," says Carey, "that you and that girl was engaged to be married."

"Nothin' to it," says Ike.

"Now look here," says Carey, "this is goin' to cost me real money if I lose. Cut out the alibi stuff and give it to us straight. Cap's wife just as good as told us you was roped."

Ike blushed like a kid.

"Well, boys," he says, "I may as well own up. You win, Carey."

"Yatta boy!" says Carey. "Congratulations!"

"You got a swell girl, Ike," I says.

"She's a peach," says Smitty.

"Well, I guess she's O. K.," says Ike. "I don't know much about girls."

"Didn't you never run round with 'em?" I says.

"Oh, yes, plenty of 'em," says Ike. "But I never seen none I'd fall for."

"That is, till you seen this one," says Carey.

"Well," says Ike, "this one's O. K., but I wasn't thinkin' about gettin' married yet a wile."

"Who done the askin', her?" says Carey.

"Oh, no," says Ike, "but sometimes a man don't know what he's gettin' into. Take a good-lookin' girl, and a man gen'ally almost always does about what she wants him to."

"They couldn't no girl lasso me unless I wanted to be lassoed," says Smitty.

"Oh, I don't know," says Ike. "When a fella gets to feelin' sorry for one of 'em it's all off."

Well, we left him go after shakin' hands all round. But he didn't take Dolly to no show that night. Some time wile we was talkin' she'd come into that other parlor and she'd stood there and heard us. I don't know how much she heard. But it was enough. Dolly and Cap's missus took the midnight train for New York. And from there Cap's wife sent her on her way back to Missouri.

She'd left the ring and note for Ike with the clerk. But we didn't ask Ike if the note was from his friend in Fort Wayne, Texas.

VI

When we'd came to Boston Ike was hittin' plain .397. When we got back home he'd fell off to pretty near nothin'. He hadn't drove one out o' the infield in any o' them other Eastern parks, and he didn't even give no excuse for it.

To show you how bad he was, he struck out three times in Brooklyn one day and never opened his trap when Cap ast him

what was the matter. Before, if he'd whiffed oncet in a game he'd
of wrote a book tellin' why.

Well, we dropped from first place to fifth in four weeks and we
was still goin' down. I and Carey was about the only ones in the
club that spoke to each other, and all as we did was to remind
ourself o' what a boner we'd pulled.

"It's goin' to beat us out o' the big money," says Carey.

"Yes," I says. "I don't want to knock my own ball club, but it
looks like a one-man team, and when that one man's dauber's
down we couldn't trim our whiskers."

"We ought to knew better," says Carey.

"Yes," I says, "but why should a man pull an alibi for bein'
engaged to such a bearcat as she was?"

"He shouldn't," says Carey. "But I and you knowed he would
or we'd never started talkin' to him about it. He wasn't no more
ashamed o' the girl than I am of a regular base hit. But he just can't
come clean on no subjec'."

Cap had the whole story, and I and Carey was as pop'lar with
him as an umpire.

"What do you want me to do, Cap?" Carey'd say to him before
goin' up to hit.

"Use your own judgment," Cap'd tell him. "We want to lose
another game."

But finally, one night in Pittsburgh, Cap had a letter from his
missus and he come to us with it.

"You fellas," he says, "is the ones that put us on the bum, and
if you're sorry I think they's a chancet for you to make good. The
old lady's out to St. Joe and she's been tryin' her hardest to fix
things up. She's explained that Ike don't mean nothin' with his
talk; I've wrote and explained that to Dolly, too. But the old lady
says that Dolly says that she can't believe it. But Dolly's still stuck
on this baby, and she's pinin' away just the same as Ike. And the
old lady says she thinks if you two fellas would write to the girl
and explain how you was always kiddin' with Ike and leadin' him
on, and how the ball club was all shot to pieces since Ike quit
hittin', and how he acted like he was goin' to kill himself, and this
and that, she'd fall for it and maybe soften down. Dolly, the old
lady says, would believe you before she'd believe I and the old
lady, because she thinks it's her we're sorry for, and not him."

Well, I and Carey was only too glad to try and see what we could
do. But it wasn't no snap. We wrote about eight letters before we
got one that looked good. Then we give it to the stenographer and
had it wrote out on a typewriter and both of us signed it.

It was Carey's idear that made the letter good. He stuck in somethin' about the world's serious money that our wives wasn't goin' to spend unless she took pity on a "boy who was so shy and modest that he was afraid to come right out and say that he had asked such a beautiful and handsome girl to become his bride."

That's prob'ly what got her, or maybe she couldn't of held out much longer anyway. It was four days after we sent the letter that Cap heard from his missus again. We was in Cincinnati.

"We've won," he says to us. "The old lady says that Dolly says she'll give him another chance. But the old lady says it won't do no good for Ike to write a letter. He'll have to go out there."

"Send him tonight," says Carey.

"I'll pay half his fare," I says.

"I'll pay the other half," says Carey.

"No," says Cap, "the club'll pay his expenses. I'll send him scoutin'."

"Are you goin' to send him tonight?"

"Sure," says Cap. "but I'm goin' to break the news to him right now. It's time we win a ball game."

So in the clubhouse, just before the game, Cap told him. And I certainly felt sorry for Rube Benton and Red Ames that afternoon! I and Carey was standin' in front o' the hotel that night when Ike come out with his suitcase.

"Sent home?" I says to him.

"No," he says, "I'm goin' scoutin'."

"Where to?" I says. "Fort Wayne?"

"No, not exactly," he says.

"Well," says Carey, "have a good time."

"I ain't lookin' for no good time," says Ike. "I says I was goin' scoutin'."

"Well, then," says Carey, "I hope you see somebody you like."

"And you better have a drink before you go," I says.

"Well," says Ike, "they claim it helps a cold."

THE
SEVENTH
BABE

A Novel by
JEROME CHARYN

I would like to thank Bill Crowley and the Boston Red Sox for letting me visit the tunnels and playing field of Fenway Park in August, 1978. Roaming through those tunnels helped me write this book.

Book One

RAGLAND
OF THE RED SOX

1

T HEY WERE THE laughing boys of the American League. Footloose imbeciles, they couldn't hit, they couldn't field, they couldn't run. These were the Red Sox of 1923. They'd bartered half their club to those rich kids, the Yankees of New York, who fattened themselves on Babe Ruth and other Boston throwaways.

The Sox had been a dynasty six years ago, with Harry Hooper, the Babe, and Sad Sam Jones. Then their owner, Hollis McKee, decided to break them up. He allowed that beer baron, Jacob Ruppert, to steal his best men away. The Sox became a talent farm for Ruppert's Yanks.

Managers quit on Hollis, or else they were fired. This year the Sox had Briggs Josephson, who'd played third for the Brownies before his ankles chipped, and hobbled him for life. Briggs never argued when Hollis wanted to sell a man. He fielded a team and detached himself from the fact that he had ragamuffins instead of ballplayers. What was the use of bringing a boy along? Hollis would give the boy to the Yanks if he showed the least bit of promise.

The boss saves a penny wherever he can.

Hollis avoided the expense of a Florida training camp. He

brought his team to Sackville Forest, a godforsaken hole on the other side of Hot Springs, Arkansas. It was still freezing in March. The Sox had to play on grass and rubble that were bitten with hoarfrost.

One day, when the frost disappeared from the ground, Briggs ran a pathetic tryout camp. Hollis pushed this on him. "You have to be kind to local talent. Give some of the rubes from down here a chance to play. People like that. It gives them a feeling of power, seeing their own boys scrappling with my Red Sox."

So Briggs went through the bother of watching a bunch of Arkansas rubes bat, field, and pitch. He didn't expect it to be anything more than a clown show. Briggs couldn't take his vengeance on the Yanks. But he could copy from them. He hired a hunchback named Scarborough as mascot and bat boy to the club. Scarborough was pretty old for a bat boy. It was hard to guess his age, with the seams under his eyes and that hump. But he had to be over forty. Briggs didn't care. He had a hunchback on his team, like the Yankees did.

The players despised this Scarborough. The Yankees could afford to travel with a freak. *Their* hunchback had brought them two pennants in a row. But Scarborough would only bring the Sox to perdition.

He was a helpful brute. He carried a load of bats on his shoulder and a bag of old, squashy balls for the Arkansas boys on tryout day. He encouraged them, giving them pointers on how to hit. It was comical, watching Scarborough swing a bat. He had a cross-handed grip; the hump would move down his back at the end of the swing, with his wrists knotted against themselves. "Babe Ruth," the Sox would scream. "Babe Ruth." But Briggs was pleased with him. It helped pass the time, having Scarborough around.

The rubes had no more finesse than the hunchback. Still, Briggs got all their names on a slip of paper. He wanted proof for Hollis that he'd kept his word and drilled every rube that came to him. The last boy at Briggs' tryout camp was a beanpole in a ripped flannel shirt. He was tall as Briggs, five-foot-ten or eleven, but he couldn't have weighed more than a hundred and thirty pounds. You could see how sharp his elbows were under that shirt.

"How old are you, son?"

"Seventeen," the boy said.

"Are you from these parts?"

"No sir. I come from Baltimore. I heard about this tryout the Sox were having, and . . ."

Briggs had to laugh. "You mean, the news got to Baltimore?" He nodded to his own men. "Heck, we must be getting famous."

They crowded up to the boy, Germany Stone, the team's first baseman, Hooks Poland, and Chicken Stallings. "What's your name?"

The beanpole looked at them. "Babe," he said. "Babe Ragland."

Briggs scratched his head; he couldn't get out from under the grizzly shadow of Babe Ruth. The Babe's disappearance from Boston had ruined the Sox. That big monkey was the rage of the whole frigging world. He'd turned the National League into a cemetery. It had no Babe Ruth. And the American League existed as a playpen for the big monk. It was Babe this, and Babe that, and now Briggs had Babe Ragland in the middle of Arkansas.

"Hey," Chicken Stallings said, "how many Babes they got in the big leagues?" He used his knuckles to count on. "There's the monkey himself. There's Babe Adams of Pittsburgh. Babe Winters, Babe Pinelli, Babe LeJeune . . . Briggsy, whatever happened to Babe Chicote?"

"The Giants picked him up."

"Well," the Chicken said, after counting twice and pointing to the beanpole. "This one's the seventh Babe. But I can't figure on it. He's all elbows, and them other Babes are big, round men."

Germany poked Ragland with a thumb. "Kid, don't you have a regular name? Is it George Herman Ragland Ruth?"

Briggs told Germany to leave the kid alone. "What's your position, son? Where do you like to play?"

"I'm a third baseman, Mr. Briggs."

He took a crusty leather mitt out of his shirt pocket. It was a fifty-cent glove. It had no cushioning in it. The glove couldn't have stopped a dying ground ball. Ragland put it over his right fist. The players looked back and forth between Ragland and his glove. They were waiting for Briggs to grab him up and hurl him out of Sackville Forest. There was no such thing as a lefty third baseman. There had never been. You couldn't perfect the double play throwing with your left hand; you'd lose a step every time you went into the hole between third and short, because you'd have to make a backhanded stab at the ball with that glove on your wrong hand. Christ, they didn't have to lecture Briggs about it. He was on the Brownies fifteen years, the best corner man in the league. But he didn't even holler at the kid.

Ragland went to third, and Briggs himself hit grounders to him.

The beanpole gobbled them up, and Briggs said, "Okay, I'll carry you."

His men couldn't believe it. "Briggsy, should we cover first and second for you? Don't you want to see if he can make the throw?"

"I saw enough," Briggs said.

"Briggsy, let him grab a bat. He could have a hernia, or a wooden leg."

"What do I need his bat for, Chicken, when I have you, Germany, and Hooks?"

The three of them walked away in disgust, but there was nothing strange about Briggs' choice. He promised Hollis that he'd keep one rube from the tryout camp. It would make the locals happy.

The team avoided Briggs' seventh Babe. A left-handed third baseman meant rotten luck, like a catcher with a missing pinkie. No one wanted him. So he had to room with the hunchback. The Sox wouldn't let him near the batter's cage while they were being drilled. Ragland took his batting practice alone, with Scarborough as his mate. The hunchback was a crazy hurler. He couldn't throw the ball overhand. That hump would get in the way. He had to use a sidearm delivery. The Sox would die laughing when they saw the brute throw. He would wrench his body, twist halfway around the world, to get that ball across the plate. Ragland would choke up on the bat, peer out at Scarborough and paw the ground like the great Ty Cobb, and smack the ball over Scarborough's head. The hunchback had to jump off the pitching hill and retrieve the ball.

They were a comedy team, Ragland and the hunchback. Briggs could always use a pair of clowns. That's how he justified holding on to a third baseman who wore his glove on the wrong hand. "It's early," Briggs assured himself. He was waiting for a good prospect to arrive. His scouts tramped east and west, looking for desirable boys. "Give me a young ballplayer who's alive, and I'll drop Ragland in a minute." But the prospects never showed. Better teams were grabbing them up. He shaved a knuckleballer from his lists who'd been recommended to him by his most reliable man in the Southwest. The knuckleballer was gray around the temples, although he swore to Briggs he hadn't turned twenty yet. His scouts were bringing grandfathers into camp.

Briggs got out of Arkansas with his club and went down to New Orleans. Hollis had arranged for the Red Sox to travel around the country in an exhibition series with the Boston Braves. The Braves were as feckless as the Sox. Both teams occupied the cellar in 1922. They were natural rivals: the eighth-place wonders of the American and the National League.

Briggs would have preferred to link up with his old club, the St.

Louis Browns. But the Brownies trained in Florida. They wouldn't have trekked to New Orleans for a series with the lowly Red Sox. The Boston teams were stuck with each other like a brotherhood of crippled cats.

The bleachers were empty when they played. The Pelicans, a minor-league club, owned New Orleans. The Pelicans outdrew them every game. If you didn't have George Herman Ruth, you couldn't even gather the mice into a ball park. Briggs tried to cancel the tour. Hollis wouldn't have it. "The Pelicans are shit-birds," he said. "We'll draw, you'll see. New Orleans was always a dumb baseball town."

How the hell would you know, Mr. Hollis McKee?

The fans had loved Briggs when he came to New Orleans in 1920 with the Browns. They didn't need Babe Ruth. The Pelicans wouldn't have dared to schedule a game while the Browns were in New Orleans. But Briggs only nodded to his boss. "It's a dung-hole, you're right. We'll do better in Mobile."

They surrendered New Orleans to the Pelicans and got on the Alabama Express. There wasn't any more tolerance for Boston baseball across the Louisiana line: they were flops in Mobile too. The Braves would drift in and out of ice-cream parlors searching for applejack and fickle wives. The Sox kept to their hotel. They grew mean in Alabama. The boredom of an idiotic rivalry had turned them in upon themselves. They were without the usual factions that other clubs displayed. Veterans didn't have to band together and thwart rookies that might take over their jobs. Rookies were hard to find.

But cliques did develop on the Red Sox. The team was split in two. College men and country boys. The country boys made up the weaker side. They were led by Germany Stone. Stone had Chicken Stallings, Hooks Poland, Nemo Leibold, and Frank Howe in his camp—utility infielders and journeymen pitchers, most of them. They didn't amount to very much.

College men dominated the club. Hollis McKee was a Dartmouth man, and he preferred to surround himself with college players. He might get rid of a baboon like Babe Ruth, but he would never give a college man away. Seaman Schupp was from Notre Dame. Briggs' fireballer, Sheriff Smith, had gone to Gettysburg College. Tilly Young held a Phi Beta Kappa key from the University of Alabama. Ross Barnett and Snake Attreau were sons of Princeton and Cornell. Alvin Critz had two years at Florida State. Blondy Cutshaw, Steve Dubec, and Garland James were Dartmouth men, like the boss.

The college men looked to Garland James. Garland played center field for the Sox. He stole thirty bases in '22, and hit seventeen triples. He was the last piece of artillery the Red Sox had. The Indians would have traded Smokey Joe Wood for him. The Browns offered Baby Doll Jacobson and cash. The Tigers would have let Hollis pick any two men on their roster for Garland James. Hollis refused them all.

Maybe it was the idea of being untouchable that turned Garland into such a brat. Five years ago, on the Washington Senators, he'd been a modest young man who learned how to blast triples and play the center field wall. Then Hollis brought him to the Red Sox, and now he was the bully of the club. He made life miserable for Briggs' country boys. He laughed at them in the dressing room, reminding everyone how illiterate Chicken Stallings was. "That chump can't read his own contract. Lord, he wouldn't wear shoes if Briggsy didn't make him." The Chicken would have to fight. He'd get a bloody nose, and Garland would walk away without a scratch on him. That's how it was with those Dartmouth men Hollis loved to buy. They'd rather punch you in the face than swing a bat.

Garland wasn't going to chase after whores in Mobile, Alabama, or drink bootlegged mountain whiskey. He would read Plato before a game, tell Germany and Hooks Poland how dumb they were, and then destroy the Boston Braves with doubles rifled off the left field wall. It gave him little pleasure. There wasn't a pretty girl around. Hollis would have done better to bring the circus into Mobile.

The teams crept up to Birmingham. They didn't sell enough tickets to pay for their hotel rooms. "Things will liven in Baltimore," Hollis told the Braves. "That's no dead rabbit town."

Both teams were glum when they arrived at Union Station. Garland wouldn't allow a porter near his bags. He made the hunchback bend over and grab them up. "Go on, Scarb'ruh. Bat boys gotta earn their keep. I'll give you a silver dollar, you ugly son of a bitch."

The Sox were staying at the Kernan Hotel, and Scarborough had to carry those bags up to Garland's room on the eleventh floor. He went downstairs with the silver dollar clutched inside his fist. He wanted to treat his roommate to a chocolate sundae at the Kernan's soda shop, but Babe Ragland wouldn't slurp ice cream that had come from Garland James' pocket. "Carrying his bags is one thing, but why did you take money from him? He thinks he's such hot pants. I could hit just as many triples as that college baby if Mr. Briggs would let me try."

And Ragland went up to his room. Scarborough followed the

surly boy upstairs after his fifth chocolate sundae. He was drunk on the juice of those maraschino cherries he had swallowed. His hump swayed in the halls of the Kernan Hotel. Ragland had to put him to bed. Scarborough had an idiotic luster in his eyes. "Rags, aint your people from Baltimore?"

"Stop mumbling, you, and go to sleep. You took a silver dollar and stuffed yourself with ice cream."

"I thought Baltimore was your home," Scarborough said. He was growing alert. The wine from the pickled cherries had begun to wear off. "I aint deaf. I heard you tell Briggsy you come from Baltimore. So why are you staying in a hotel when this is your own town?"

"Because I don't have people here. I went to the bad boys' school . . . like Babe Ruth."

Scarborough tossed his covers off the bed. The whole world knew about the Babe's origins. He was a foundling who'd gone to St. Mary's Reform School, where he studied how to be a tailor and throw fast balls and the curve.

"Rags, you mean you aint got a mother and a father? . . . you're one of them bastards the school took in?"

The hunchback got dressed before Ragland could determine what was in his crazy head. "Come on, Rags, we're going to St. Mary's."

"What for?"

"I want to see where you and the Babe went to school."

Ragland had to accompany him, or the hunchback would have beaten down the hotel walls. They climbed on the Wilkens Avenue trolley, a seventeen-year-old boy in a baseball cap and a forty-five-year-old brute with deep lines in his face. Passengers twisted their bodies away from Scarborough and the kid, who had the back of the trolley to themselves. In his excitement Scarborough dipped over the side of the car. You could see his hump ride in the air.

"How far is it?" he asked. "How far?"

Ragland told him. "The school's at the end of the line."

The trolley didn't waver its course. It bumped down Wilkens Avenue mile after mile. Passengers began to drop off from both sides of the trolley. They arrived at the bottom of some vacant hill in a deserted trolley car. They jumped off, then the conductor and his mate turned the trolley around on its axis; the wires crackled once, the trolley pole dipped and then stood upright, and the car made its return run into Baltimore.

Scarborough was confused. Rags had brought him to a waste-yard at the edge of town. "Look up there, you dope!"

Scarborough turned his head. He saw a brick monster with a

church at one side and a tower in the middle, all at the top of the hill. But he wasn't going to be tricked. "If it's a reform school, how come it doesn't have a fence?"

"They don't need fences, Mr. Scarborough. Where else does a bastard have to go?"

The hunchback seemed satisfied with that piece of news. "Well, Rags, take me up the hill. Show me them Catholic brothers what taught you how to play third with your left hand. They must do miracles at St. Mary's school."

Ragland refused to go. "I aint getting inside there again."

The hunchback stamped on the ground. "You took me this far. Can't I watch where the bastards eat and sleep?"

"No. The brothers don't take to visitors. It riles up the kids."

"You're no visitor, Rags. You're an alumnoos. You made the Red Sox, goddamn. The brothers can show you off. Who knows? They could be raising a team of lefty shortstops right this minute."

"You shut up."

They had to wait for another trolley to come and turn itself around, so they could ride up Wilkens Avenue to their hotel.

The Sox and the Braves began a five-game series at Black River Park. Spooks could have been on that field. There wasn't a stir when Garland hit the ball into the bleachers for his second home run of the day. Studying the flight of that ball must have reeducated the owner of the Red Sox, because Hollis McKee called off the series with the Braves.

"Thank God," Briggs said. "I'd like the men to stare at a human face once in a while."

They got out of the Kernan Hotel, cursing Black River Park and the ungrateful fans of Baltimore. The Braves were going to Pittsburgh to try their luck at Forbes Field, but the Sox went straight to Boston on the Seaboard Special. The team invaded the club car and finished twelve rye breads and every slice of roast beef on board the train. Briggs' men lumbered out of Back Bay Station with their bellies hanging low. A trolleybus brought them to the Sox's headquarters at the Brunswick Hotel on Brookline Avenue, opposite Fenway Park.

Ragland could see the flags on the stadium roof from his window. Fenway was a wall of red bricks on the Lansdowne Street side. The hunchback wanted to nap, but Ragland was the curious one right now. "This aint Mobile, Mr. Scarborough. It's Boston, home of the Sox. Why does every rabbit on the team live at this hotel? Don't they have sisters, girlfriends, wives? . . . what about you?"

Ragland heard a voice from under the quilt. "There's no such thing as a married man on the Red Sox. Oh, Hooks Poland was married once. His wife left him after three weeks. We're vagabonders. It's trains and hotels, trains and hotels."

"Could be. But I'm going to find a rooming house somewhere in Boston. I aint living across the street from Fenway Park."

"Go 'head. Landladies don't cotton much to ballplayers. They'll charge you double the rate and call you a bum. It's rookie fever you got. Rent your little old room with some widow on Marlborough Street. She'll fix you up with curtains. She'll make you pots of tea. You'll have to stand in line with twenty boarders to take a leak. You'll come back to us. The Brunswick's home-sweet-home for the Red Sox. It's always been that way."

Rags was getting furious with the hunchback. "*Always* been? How the hell would you know? The skipper only brung you to the Sox last year."

The furrows began to darken on Scarborough's head. He could have been eighty, looking at him. The sun poured into the room, but his face was in some deep hollow that had nothing to do with Boston weather and Boston time. Ragland felt ashamed.

"I know lots about them," Scarborough said. "Skipper told me."

Ragland tried to make amends. "What did you do, Mr. Scarborough, before the skipper picked you up?"

"I lumberjacked."

He's lying, like always, Ragland thought. How could he swing an ax with that hump sitting on his shoulder? Briggs must have swiped him out of the Boston freak show.

Ragland decided to live with the Sox. A team of bachelors was good enough for him. Briggs began to drill in earnest for Opening Day, and Ragland had to scamper around Fenway with the full squad. Briggs cut three pitchers and a utility man who couldn't turn over the double play. But he didn't break up his comedy act: that brute and the beanpole called Rags kept playing pepper ball in the shadow of older, established men. The Dartmouth faction wouldn't condescend to notice a rube at third base, and the country boys, Germany, Chicken, and Hooks, didn't needle him very much. Ragland could have been a groundkeeper for all they cared. No one bothered to breathe the word "rookie" at him, or nail his shoes to the clubhouse wall. Why razz a boy who didn't have a monkey's chance of getting into a game?

Garland read Plato in Greek and patrolled center field. He had no time to think up pranks against the hunchback. It was April, and Garland had to take care of his batting eye. The Indians were coming to town.

Opening Day was a disaster for the Sox. Cleveland's young right-hander, big George Uhle, shut Boston out. The Sox bought one hit, a scratch single that splintered Hooks Poland's bat. A famine at the plate wouldn't have angered manager Briggs. When big George Uhle had his "smoke," he could put anybody's bat to sleep. But the Sox had murdered themselves. Their infield behaved like four ruptured Chinamen. Alvin Critz made three errors at short. Germany Stone couldn't trap a ball in his first-baseman's mitt. Seaman Schupp and Snake Attreau collided on the grass.

Five thousand fans snickered and booed. It was the smallest Opening Day crowd in Red Sox history. Hollis McKee had spooked the turnstiles on Lansdowne Street. He made his Red Sox into the dogs of the American League.

But five thousand fans seemed like a mob to Babe Ragland, who sat in the dugout by himself, because the hunchback left him there. Scarborough wasn't simply the mascot who had to hang off the dugout roof and point his tongue at opposing teams until they couldn't stomach the sight of him. He was the bat boy as well, and he was forever shuffling on and off the field to bring this man or that man his favorite piece of wood. Garland James had ten differ-ent bats, and Scarborough had to remember which was which. He couldn't entertain the rookie, he couldn't sit still. He was sweating in April, on Opening Day.

Rags would have liked to help his roommate carry bats and rosin bags, and shinguards for the catcher, Tilly Young. But not even the obscurest man in the major leagues could fool with a bat boy once the warm-ups were over with. Baseball had its laws: players didn't tamper with the necessary flow of a nine-inning game. The bat boy had his special place. You didn't want to get him out of his groove. He could kill whatever string of luck you had.

Briggs had none. The Indians didn't have to worry about a brute and his rosin bags. They took four from the Sox. They were a contender this year. And they'd never catch the Yankees if they couldn't run over the boys from Fenway Park. Briggs went to his secret book on the Washington Senators. The Senators were weak-lings. But they had a stable infield, and that was enough. Boston could only manage one win out of five.

The Sox were deep in the cellar after nine frigging games. Briggs had to do something when the Tigers arrived. He took Snake At-treau off third base. The Boston faithful, those three thousand fans that had come to the park, couldn't remember a game without

Attreau. The Snake meant glory to them. He'd been on the championship clubs of '15, '16, and '18. He was the last of the Sox to know what a World Series was.

The Boston announcer, Weingarten, stood at home plate with his beautiful megaphone and didn't mention Attreau. Hollis had lured this chubby little man away from the Athletics. Bull Weingarten was the surest magaphone man in the league. His voice could carry to the roof in center field. He would yell the Boston lineup once and only once. He knew how to capitalize on the absence of a name. "Batting eighth for the Red Sox and playing third," Bull said, with that megaphone high in the air, "we have the seventh Babe. Not Babe Pinelli. Not Babe Winters. Not Babe LeJeune. Not Babe Adams. Not Babe Chicote. And not Babe Ruth. But our Babe. Babe Ragland of the Red Sox."

The fans yelled back, "Snake, Snake, Snake," but they couldn't get to Bull. He finished up and withdrew to his tiny chair on the foul side of first base.

That echo wouldn't cease. "Snake, Snake, Snake." It shook the dugout walls. Briggs sat on the bench with his legs crossed. "Heck," he said. The fans weren't going to make his lineup card for him. They could yell their heads off. Either Hollis found a decent crop of ballplayers and held on to them, or Briggs would be obliged to play that young freak, Ragland, at third. The Sox had a Chinaman's infield. So why shouldn't Briggs use a third baseman who did everything the opposite way?

But Briggs' juggling of his men couldn't ease Ragland's pain on that wretched infield grass. The beanpole hadn't expected to play. The skipper never revealed what was on his lineup card. Rags had to learn from the croaker, Bull Weingarten, that "the seventh Babe" was bumping Attreau off third. So he picked up his glove that was patched with Band-Aids and he ran out onto the field with Briggs' other men. The shortstop, Alvin Critz, set a wide corridor for himself and left Rags with a stingy bit of land around third base. Ragland hugged that coffin of dirt. It was the one protection he had. The fans were screaming for Snake Attreau, and unless he dug in with his spiked shoes, their voices would have sucked him off the grass.

The Tigers were coming to bat. Boston's fireballer, Sheriff smith, went into his windup. The ball disappeared inside the crook of his arm. The pitch was released, and the Tiger shortstop, Topper Rigney, swung at a ball that danced in around his knees. Rags was shivering in the jersey under his short-sleeved blouse. "God," he mumbled, "please, please, let him bang it to some other guy."

He heard a hollow pock that told him the ball wasn't going very far. Rigney hit a high popper into foul territory. Alvin Critz leered at Rags. "Chase it, you dope. That's yours." And Rags started to run. He didn't have his eye on the ball. But he could *feel* a crazy shadow on him. He ran headlong into the Tiger dugout on the third-base side of the field. He stuck his glove hand out. The ball plopped into it like a lazy egg. Rags tripped on the dugout stairs; he fell and his body twisted around, but the glove stayed over his head. The third-base ump scrutinized him and signaled that Topper was out.

Rags had scraped his leg on the concrete floor. The blood pounded like a savage in his skull, and for a moment Rags couldn't decide where he was. He could have fallen into a spider den. The Tigers didn't offer to pick him up. Ty Cobb and his ferocious men would have loved to spill Ragland's brains under the dugout bench. Whoever heard of such a catch? Only a baseball monkey would dive in among the Tigers for a foul ball.

Rags shook the dizziness from his head and pulled himself out onto the field again. He didn't hear the chant of "Snake" anymore. The Boston faithful, scattered in a park that could seat thirty thousand souls, had gone wild. "Rags," they screamed, "Rags, Rags, Rags." It was their fickleness that disturbed the manager in the home-team dugout. Briggs understood: one catch, and they forgot Snake Attreau.

Rags didn't see another ball in the next two innings. He came up to bat at the bottom of the third. Scarborough had given him a piece of wood to carry to the plate. That blond stick wiggled on Rags' shoulder. It seemed like a puny weapon to use against Detroit's big righthander, Herm Pillette. The enemy catcher, Larry Woodall, was singing to Pillette. "Dumb kid here, dumb kid here." It was a language some catchers employed to calm their battery mates and pester the hitters. Woodall's song got to Rags. His shoulder felt stuck. Pillette scorned him from the mound. How could Rags face up to a big guy standing on a hill?

That first pitch floated up near the letters on his blouse. Rags thought it would never arrive. His ankles crossed as he swiped at the dead air around home plate. The ball was in the catcher's glove. Herm had given him a slider to eat.

"No bat," Larry Woodall sang, while Pillette went to his fast ball. Rags heard a strange wind. He blinked once, and the umpire yelled "Strike two!"

Ragland would have liked to vomit into one of his red and white socks. He couldn't swing at a pitch he never saw. He waited until Herm was in his stretch. As the ball left Herm's fingers, Rags closed his eyes. That wind had a cleaner sound. He lunged with his blond stick. He could feel a sweet vibration in his wrists. Hell with Ty Cobb! Rags got a piece of the ball. It looped over the first baseman's head. Bodies were moving in the outfield when Rags opened his eyes. The seventh Babe had bought himself a hit. He dropped his bat and strutted to first base.

Briggs grew forlorn in the dugout. He was mumbling a prayer. Briggs believed that every baseball city had gods of its own. And he begged the gods of Boston that this crazy-handed kid at third wasn't *too* good, or Hollis McKee would send him away to the Yanks. Hollis only cared about his Dartmouth men, and Rags was no college beauty. He was a country boy from Baltimore, like Babe Ruth.

"Gods of Fenway," Briggs muttered to himself. "Let me have this boy."

2

The Fenway gods were kind to manager Briggs. They shielded Ragland from Hollis McKee. The gods saw to it that Hollis wasn't around when Rags made his miracle catch in the Tiger dugout. The owner's box behind third base was empty for the series with Detroit. Hollis had gone to New York with a case of Broadway fever. He was looking for backers to help him mount a musical comedy. It was to be called *Eveline,* and the idea of it swelled in Hollis, clutched at him, as it always did. *Eveline* was about baseball wives who banded together and consoled themselves while their husbands were on the road. Hollis couldn't have been dreaming of his own club. The Sox were without one legitimate baseball wife.

The unmarried bandits split four games with Detroit. Ragland's hitting leveled off; he had two more singles in his maiden series, and went three for twelve. It was his fielding that surprised. He didn't lose a step at third, crazy-handed as he was. He was more agile than Snake Attreau had ever been at turning over the double play. But Briggs still had his Chinaman's infield. Critz, Schupp, and Stone fell behind that maddening rhythm that flew out of the boy's hands. So what? The Boston faithful had told their friends about this Ragland boy. There were over ten thousand in the park for the last game of the series.

Rags swiped the left side of the infield from Alvin Critz. Alvin had to retreat into a small pocket in back of second base. He was lucky to have this end piece of his old corridor. It was pathetic to watch him now. Before Alvin could make that first push into motion, Rags was in the air.

Briggs' men, his coaches, his hunchback, and the tiny band of journalists that still went on the road with the Sox, met at Back Bay Station and waited for the Liberty Bell to arrive. The Sox had three cars. It wasn't a night train, and they didn't have to scramble for upper or lower berths. The Liberty Bell seemed to exist for the comfort of Garland James. Garl was adored by the journalists. They compared him to Tris Speaker, who had played center field for the Sox at the beginning of their glory days. "Yeah, I like Tris," Garland said. "But have you noticed boys? . . . the old Gray Eagle has lost a step. He can't swoop down on those fly balls like he once did."

"It's true," the journalists had to admit; at this moment, in 1923, Garland James of the Red Sox played the shallowest center field in the American League.

"What about the new kid, Garl? The busher who's replaced Attreau at third. Where the hell did he come from? He wasn't on the roster of any minor-league club."

"You mean Rags? The skipper picked him up in Arkansas. He was planting weeds somewhere. You don't have to worry about the Snake. He'll get his old job back."

The journalists were skeptical of anything to do with Attreau.

"We hear Hollis McKee has it in mind to dump the Snake. Hollis is working on it. He hasn't found a taker yet."

"Boys, somebody's been feeding you a dumb line. This Ragland is like those other beauties. They come up swinging a big bat, they feast on grounders all April long, and then they disappear. He won't last into May, I'm telling you."

The Liberty Bell made a special stop at Mott Haven, in the Bronx, where two small buses took the Red Sox to their hotel, the Concourse Plaza. The Plaza overlooked the new wonder of baseball, Yankee Stadium. The Yanks had been tenants at the Polo Grounds until John McGraw of the Giants kicked them out. So the Yankees moved across the Harlem River and established themselves in the Bronx. That sly Colonel, Jacob Ruppert, built a concrete stadium that dwarfed the Polo Grounds. The Sox had never played in the Colonel's white horseshoe. They were used to the wind blowing off the river and into the Polo Grounds. The stands would shake during a hard blow. Water would seep up through the clubhouse floor, and the Sox had to come onto the playing field in wet shoes.

The Colonel's horseshoe was warm and dry. The wind couldn't bite through concrete. The Yanks scorned the Harlem River. The only thing that river got to see was the curve of a thick, thick wall. The grass wasn't yellow, like Fenway grass. The pipes didn't gurgle and sweat. The numbers on the scoreboard in center field had a whiteness you could find in no other ball park. The Sox marched into the dugout in those gray knickers a team had to wear on the road, and they couldn't believe the wide girdle of Yankee Stadium. You had to twist your eyes to locate the uppermost deck of the grandstands.

Rags caught the hunchback muttering to himself. "What's in your head, Scarborough?"

"I'm counting straw hats."

"How many did you catch?"

"Half a million so far."

The Yanks had their murderer's row of Ruth, Bob Meusel, and Wally Pip. Then there were the "cousins" they inherited from the Sox: Jumping Joe Dugan, Wally Schang, Everett Scott, the Bambino himself, and four starting pitchers, Herb Pennock, Sad Sam Jones, Waite Hoyt, and Bullet Joe Bush. The Sox were left with Dartmouth boys and the dregs of both leagues.

Briggs searched for Hollis in Colonel Ruppert's box. Hollis wasn't in the park. He was still busy with his *Eveline*. "Good," Briggs spoke into the wall of the dugout. "Maybe he won't scalp us on this trip. We might get away from the Bronx without losing a man."

He could sense a furor in the crowd. Yankee partisans didn't give a damn about the third baseman Briggs had unraveled. He was just another kid to them, no matter what hand he picked for wearing his glove. But they were irate over the hunchback. They jeered at Scarborough the first time he emerged from the dugout. The Yanks had their own brute. His name was Henry, Henry Watteau. The crowd loved his savageries, his willingness to fight lemonade boys, raucous fans, and enemy players. Henry would wag his buttocks at any umpire who made a rotten call against his team. He was vicious with children and all kinds of girls. He had no respect for the women who had come to watch Babe Ruth with their parasols and their white gloves. They didn't belong in Yankee Stadium. Henry would shout into the box seats. "Hey, you slits up there, leave the Bambino alone. Don't you make eyes at him. The Bam can't concentrate with too many slits in the house."

Nothing enraged him more than the sight of another brute. Scarborough was an affront to his dignity. Boston had mocked the hump on his back by bringing that creature to town. He didn't intend to stand for it. Twice he tried to enter the Boston dugout and wrestle with Scarborough, and twice he had to be restrained.

"It's me or him," he warned Miller Huggins, the Yankee skipper, who was even more of a shrimp than Henry Watteau. Huggins would have waved Henry off the field and banished him to the clubhouse for the *whole* Boston series, but he couldn't go against the fans. They were having a perfect day adoring Henry and reviling the Boston brute. They hurled pop bottles at him the moment he wandered from the dugout. And Henry kept aiming practice balls at his head. The brute was terrified. With each step he took, he could have been broken for life.

The stadium had gone berserk. You couldn't get through an inning without another rumpus featuring Scarborough and Henry Watteau. The umpire had to act. He tossed both brutes out of the game. The fans hissed and then grew quiet as the hunchbacks were forgotten.

The Bambino slapped a long triple at the bottom of the sixth that fell into the alley off right center field. The fans marveled at the flurry of Ruth's ankles as he rounded second base. Rags watched, like everybody else. He could hear the churning music of that enormous body. The nostrils were widening in front of Rags. The Bambino yelled at him between snorts of his nose. "Look out, you're in my cocksucking way."

Rags didn't mean to challenge the Babe. He was watching the big man run, that's all. Those nostrils widened in deep anger. The Bambino knocked Rags down with a flick of his shoulder and continued on to third. The fans were delighted to see Ragland lying in the dirt with pebbles in his mouth.

The Babe was jovial once he got to third. He stood on that base with his belly rumbling under the stripes of his Yankee blouse. "Sorry, I decked you, kid. But this aint a traffic circle. It's fucking third base." Then he danced on the bag and took off his hat to the crowd.

Rags turned eighteen on the road. He passed his birthday with the hunchback in a Philadelphia hotel. Scarborough had smuggled a pint of rum into the room. "Wish I was eighteen," he said, with those marks on his face looking like battle sores.

"How old are you, Scarborough? Fifty? Forty-five?"

"I'm twenty-three."

Rags started to laugh, but a sadness gnawed at him. How could a grizzled brute, with seams and pits all over him, have the nerve to claim he was twenty-three? Did he pull himself out of his moth-

er's womb with a hump on his shoulder, a lot of sores, and a head
of thin gray hair? Rags had never seen the hunchback without his
clothes. Scarborough would undress in the bathroom, and come to
bed wearing an ancient brown robe. He wouldn't display the hump
to anybody.

"You don't look twenty-three."

"Well I am. All lumberjacks age pretty fast. Hell, a bat boy's
like being on vacation."

"How long were you a lumberjack?"

"Ten years."

Scarborough had trapped himself with a stupid lie. "Ten years?
That's nice. Did you go from the cradle to dropping trees?"

A rage was building under Scarborough's lip. His jaw began to
shiver in Ragland's face. "Don't give me any cradles. You can't
lumberjack before you get to be eleven."

It was silly trying to untwist the words of a brute. Rags drank
his rum in silence, while Scarborough searched for his disgusting
brown robe.

The rum didn't hurt. Rags got two hits the next day at Shibe
Park. He was like a scorpion in the field, robbing Philadelphia of
doubles and triples with that crazy throwing hand and his flimsy
glove.

The Sox returned to Boston in seventh place. There were articles about Rags in the *Herald,* the *Globe,* and the *Evening Transcript.* The *Globe* called him "a foundling who had made good."
For the *Herald* he was "that mysterious boy without a minor-
league record." The *Evening Transcript* proclaimed in thick black
type that Rags had jumped from an orphanage to the Red Sox. All
three papers likened him to Babe Ruth. Heroes out of Baltimore,
they said, and St. Mary's "college." George Herman Ruth and
Boston's seventh Babe.

The stories disgusted Rags, who had hidden himself from the
journalists and granted no interviews. He caught Scarborough near
the bat rack in the Boston dugout. "What told them bigmouths I
went to the bad boys' school?"

"Briggs."

"And who told Briggs?"

"Me," Scarborough said. "He's the skipper. He has a right to
know."

That rage against the journalists and their stories spilled out of
Rags. He grabbed the hunchback by his ear. "What I say to you is
private, understand? It's got nothing to do with Mr. Briggs or any
bigmouths from the *Globe.*"

The other men heard Scarborough howl, and they slapped their knees and delivered horselaughs at the spectacle of a dumb brute with a fist clamped to the side of his head. That horrible sniggering of the team killed the anger in Rags. He saw the veins stand in purple knots on Scarborough's temple, and he let go of the ear. He should have questioned Scarborough in the hotel room, and not around the bat rack, where college babies and country boys could laugh at them.

"Didn't mean it, Scarborough," Rags said. "I shouldn't have touched your ear."

The hunchback drew his crippled shoulder away from Rags, and pulled two "black beauties" out of the rack for Garland James. Rags felt a shiver when the Sox took the field. He wasn't in the mood to crouch like a monkey, with his arms dangling, and his legs splayed, so he could gobble up any grounder that spun in the grass. He was as much a bully as Garland was. "Orphan," he muttered, "orphan Rags," hoping to work his mind back into the game.

Mr. Briggs' old team was at the park, those tough guys from St. Louis. The Brownies owned the bases. They could run you to death, charging at an infielder with their spikes above your throat. It gave them pleasure to rip a man's cheek. The Brownies, with Dutch Schleibner, Homer Ezzell, Baby Doll Jacobson, and Hank Severeid, loved a good brawl. They twittered at Ragland from the steps of their dugout.

"Love a hunchback," they said, making noises with their mouths inside their fists. "How's your roomie, little orphan boy? Did you grease him right? Hey, Rags, does a hunchback taste like snow?"

Their evil clucking only got Rags to play. He went into that crouch of his and denied a bunt single to Baby Doll, galloping and throwing to first in one great blur of motion that was too pure an act for anyone on the Browns to comprehend. Baby Doll had dropped a perfect bunt, and the ball arrived at first base before he did. There was a silence in the dugout.

St. Louis couldn't get a ball through the hole. Rags was always there. So the Brownies looked to Garland James in short center field. *The college boy thinks he's the old Gray Eagle.* The bench climbed on Garl. "Hey, Tris Speaker, how you doing, Tris?" Dutch Schleibner drilled a double over Garland's head. Garland tripped and tore the seat of his pants while running for the ball.

The Browns had made him appear ridiculous. Garland didn't blame them. It was Rags who had shut him off from his natural boundaries in the field, Rags who was forcing him out of his shallow spot. No center fielder running with his mouth to the wall could compete with a crazy-armed kid.

Rags wasn't thinking of Garland or the Browns. He noticed two women in Hollis McKee's box. They were like witches with hair on fire. That's what the sun behind third did to redheaded girls. Rags could see the quiver of their eyebrows as they talked to Hollis. They didn't bother with parasols and straw hats. They let the sun fall on their eyes and their lips. They had beautiful, sharp noses and little ears, the girls with Hollis McKee. Rags went over to his bat boy after the Brownies were retired in the fifth. Scarborough was still gloomy with him. Rags kept his distance from Scarborough's ear. "Who are the girlies with Hollis?" he asked.

"Them's the Cottonmouths," Scarborough said. "They live on Beacon Hill."

"They twins, or something?"

"No, no. They're a mother and daughter team."

Rags couldn't believe it. "They look like they're both your age, Scarborough . . . twenty-three."

The hunchback made a fat lip. "Iva's fifteen. And her mama's thirty-five, I expect. Marylou."

"Which one's the mama?"

"She's in the middle."

"Her? She aint mama Cottonmouth. The other one's older, you ask me."

"You're blind," the hunchback said, starting to move away.

Rags pulled him back with a shout. "How come you know about their histories?"

"Everybody knows. They're Hollis' pets, them Cottonmouths. He brings them to Fenway all the time."

And Scarborough finally got away, carrying out a rosin bag for Germany Stone.

Rags would look and look for the Cottonmouths, mixing up mother and daughter in his head. Marylou had the smile of a girl; Iva pouted like the matrons of Beacon Hill. Red hair on a woman could inflame Rags and weaken him for baseball. Hollis' pets, the hunchback crooned. Rags had to take his eyes off the Cottonmouths.

There was dissension on the club. Garland had tolerated Rags while he was a curio, but now he was a rookie that refused to disappear. Garl had been wrong about the kid. Snake Attreau didn't get his old job back. The Snake and Nemo Leibold were sent to Washington for a pittance, a small bundle of cash. The skipper was giving them away. He picked up Ira Flagstead, a journeyman outfielder from Detroit, but he held with Babe Ragland at

third. All the catches Garl made, coming out from behind the flagpole in center field, grabbing balls off the tongue of his shoe, were
meaningless with the kid around. The Royal Rooters, those raving
boys in red coats, who abandoned the Sox after Hollis sold Babe
Ruth and butchered the club, were coming back. The Royal Rooters could get little solace at Braves Field. The Boston Nationals
had lost a hundred games in 1922. So the Rooters took up their old
seats at Fenway, near the Boston dugout, to watch that strange kid
Hollis had brought out of the hinterland. They were touched by
the story of a foundling Babe.

"Bastard" became their call word. The Rooters had nothing for
Garland James. He could stand in the outfield forever, in wind,
sun, or rain, and they wouldn't have noticed him. They had an
affliction for Dartmouth men. None of the Rooters had been to
college. It was sissified. They were from South Boston, where all
the "John Harvards" were afraid to go at night.

Garland felt undermined. Why should he let a busher from no-
where usurp his position on the club? He began to pester Briggs.
"It's trading time, skip, that's what I hear. Me for Baby Doll.
You'd better talk to the Browns."

"Don't be silly, Garl. Hollis wouldn't think of losing you in a
trade."

"Well, do something about the busher then. Take him off third."

"I can't, Garl. I don't have an infield without him."

"It's too bad, skip, because all the commotion that busher
makes, all his jumping around, is gonna ruin my batting eye someday. And we'll really be in trouble."

Garland had other resources than Mr. Briggs. If the busher
wouldn't stop his monkey dance, Garl had ways of quieting him.
He broke into Rags' locker and tore the kid's uniforms with a razor
blade. He filed down Rags' spikes to little stubs that belonged in
an old man's mouth. He put wounds in the kid's three bats, shaving their barrels until the polish was gone and you had naked wood,
with splinters on every side.

The kid tolerated these shreds and ruins. Rookies weren't supposed to bitch. They had to cow before veterans if they wanted to
stay alive. That was the law of the major leagues. But Garl's wrath
went outside the expected boundaries of baseball gear. He slapped
and kicked Scarborough for rooming with Rags, and then he stole
Scarborough's shirts, hats, and pants from the hotel and burned
them in a trash barrel at Fenway Park.

A day after this bonfire, he discovered that his two favorite bats
were missing. A groundkeeper located them for Garl. His "black
beauties" were now charred sticks. Somebody put them in the

same barrel Garl had used to burn Scarborough's pants. He moaned at the image of his two dead bats. No one had ever seen a Dartmouth man cry. "Who did it?"

"Me."

Rags was pointing to himself. "I don't think black wood becomes you, Mr. James. It gives you a bloated look when you swing at the ball. Blond wood, sir. I'll make you a present of blond wood."

Garland leapt on the boy and tried to tear off his mouth. His own allies had to pull him away. It was ten minutes to game time, and the Sox had to be out on the field. The fans would have despaired if Rags had gone to third with no mouth. "Busher," Garl said, "meet me in the tunnel after the game."

Rags told him, "I will." His mouth was still raw from where Garl had clutched at him. Rags probed with a finger. He spat out a tooth and dropped it in a handkerchief. Scarborough was horrified, but Rags smiled behind his sleeve.

"It brings you luck to give up a tooth like that."

"You'll give up half your mouth if you meet him in the tunnel. He learned boxing at Dartmouth."

"So what?"

The hunchback began to sway his head. "Don't you know about him and Ty Cobb? Cobb used to beat shit out of everybody in the league. He decked George Sisler. He hung a bloody lip on Babe Ruth. And Ping Bodie had to run from him. But Garl boxed him to a draw. I seen it. They both took black eyes last year in Detroit . . . now Cobb leaves him alone. Listen. Go into the other dugout after the game, and I'll get you your street pants."

"Hell no. I aint gonna hide."

"He'll murder you, Rags. He has the fists."

"Maybe," Rags said. "But don't you bring me my pants."

The kid played his game. He smothered the Brownies, who couldn't break the jinx Rags put on them. The kid was everywhere. You couldn't drag bunt, or loop the ball into shallow left field. He would stagger, twist, hop, and rise off his knees with *something* in his glove. The Rooters brought their trombones to the park. They serenaded Rags before and after each catch. And they sang to him from third base.

> *Ragland, Ragland,*
> *Our orphan's the best.*
> *No one can beat us*
> *No one at all,*
> *With our seventh Babe.*

Hearing that song must have disheartened the Browns. They left the field, losing four out of four to the lowly Red Sox. Those clowns from Boston had shot to fifth place. Scarborough kept urging Rags to sneak into the visitors' dugout. Rags stuck his fifty-cent glove into his back pocket and went down the steps of his own dugout and on into the runway. It was in this damp tunnel leading to the clubhouse that he was supposed to fight Garland James. Scarborough walked behind Rags, groaning a lot.

It was gray and windy in the tunnel. The hunchback had to sneeze. Garland stood in the middle of the tunnel with most of the Boston club. The country boys and the Dartmouth men had come together in their hatred for Rags. The Sox couldn't win without him, but Rags took all the attention away. He was a kid with freak hands and a crazy sense of where the ball would drop; he made the whole team look like silly dogs with nothing to do.

Garl rolled up the sleeves of his jersey, waiting for Rags. Alvin Critz and Tilly Young had become his handlers. They warmed his knuckles inside their baseball shirts. Chicken Stallings glinted evilly at Rags. Garl had mocked the Chicken for two years, cackling at him, calling him an illiterate bum, but the Chicken would rather have Garland on him than play with Rags. "Close his eyes, Garl. Then we'll see how many balls he grabs away from us."

There was a sad look to Garland James. He'd gotten over the fit of having his "black beauties" destroyed. He didn't shove the kid, push him into the wet, narrow walls of the tunnel that held drainage pipes for the grandstand over their heads. The tunnel always leaked.

"Busher, do you apologize for killin' my bats?"

"No."

The Chicken was overjoyed. "Put his head on backwards, Garl. You can do it."

"Shut up," Garland said. And his voice grew sweet again. "When I knock you down, kid, I'll give you the chance to get up. But don't expect too much."

Rags made two fists, and Garland waltzed around him, his body jumping with tremendous grace between the tunnel walls. At first he hit Rags with an open paw, as if the kid were a doll that had to be punished. Rags lunged with his left fist, but he couldn't smack Garland James. His miracle arms and legs abandoned him inside the tunnel. He poked at cloudy gray air. Garl feinted, slapped, and danced in his baseball shoes. The Dartmouth men laughed at all the blue welts Garl had raised near the kid's eyes. Soon Garl began to close his fists. "Mercy," the Chicken said, "now we'll have some fun."

Garl shortened his blows; knuckles flicked out at Rags, then drew back, like a hard, muscular tongue. You heard the crush against Ragland's face before those knuckles fell out of sight. Still, Garl wouldn't spend himself on Rags. He was listless today. He toyed with the kid, but he wouldn't go about annihilating him. The Sox's admiration for Garl turned to bitterness. They remembered how ferocious he'd been with Ty Cobb. He'd knocked Cobb down with a left hook that rattled the great man's teeth. And here he was waltzing with the kid.

Garl put down his fists. It disgusted him to paw at Ragland. He was Garland James of the Red Sox. He didn't fight bushers. "You can have him," he said to his mates. "I'm through." He walked into the clubhouse with his sleeves rolled up.

Chicken Stallings conferred with Seaman Schupp and the other college men. They wanted blood out of Rags, and they didn't get any. Garl had tricked them. He'd stirred them up, given them the promise of a good fight, and there was nothing to show.

Rags had a mouse in his eye and a swollen cheek, but they didn't need Garl for that. Any of them could have accomplished the same thing. They stood around the rookie and sneered. They had to have a piece of Rags, or they'd croak. "Rookie," the Chicken said, "you'd better get down on your knees and lick our shoes."

Rags was still in his boxing stance. "I aint licking your smelly shoes."

So they tore into him, eight of the Red Sox, swinging at the kid's ears, his mouth, and his brains. But they couldn't land a blow. That frigging hunchback crept between them and Rags. He spilled five of them to the ground, bumping them with the gnarl on his back. He threw Hooks Poland into the wall. He caught Seaman Schupp in his arms, gave him a deadly hug, and dropped him on a pile of Red Sox. He seized Tilly Young, hurled him into that dumb grayness, until Tilly screamed for his life. This wasn't Scarborough, their own private brute, the middle-aged boy with undeveloped legs who delivered bats and rosin bags to them. His shirt was torn. They noticed a powerful chest they hadn't conceived before. His crooked shoulder was equipped with long bands of muscle. He had veins in his forearm that popped around like a crazy eye. They fled from Scarborough, scattering into the clubhouse.

Rags felt the cuts on his face. Then he looked at the brute. He was bewildered. With the Red Sox gone out of the tunnel, Scarborough retreated into his torn shirt. He became a bat boy again, his nose pointing into the ground. Rags could have twisted Scarborough's ear this second, and the brute would only have shrieked.

"You are twenty-three," he said. "And you lumberjacked, you really did."

The brute wouldn't answer him. He returned to the dugout to wipe the bats clean and collect old balls and rosin bags from behind the bench.

3

There was nothing in the *Globe* about any fights in a tunnel at Fenway Park. Garland wouldn't tell the journalists he was feuding with Rags. He went back to reading Homer in the dugout. He didn't need the Red Sox for company. He had his favorite books of Sophocles. He lived at the Brunswick like everybody else, but without a roommate. Garl was the highest paid member of the Sox.

He was contemptuous of all the chuggerheads he had to meet day after day, country boys who had trouble with their own signatures. He'd gone to Dartmouth on a scholarship, as the son of an impoverished lawyer from Terre Haute. His father caught a chill and died in Garland's junior year. Garl dropped out of school. He went home to the Wabash River, having to support three younger brothers, a grandfather, and a mother who was afflicted with a nervous disease; she couldn't hear, talk, or chew. He signed a contract to play professional ball. He was earning ten thousand by 1923. Half of it went to support his brothers at Dartmouth, Princeton, and Cornell medical college. But his salary wasn't enough. Garl had to play in the winter leagues. He barnstormed on the Harry Heilmann All-Stars, a loose confederation of men who would tour the South and the Far West, taking on local colleges and nigger teams.

The All-Stars would end up in Cuba, going from province to province in a little red bus; they were the gringo wonders who never lost a game. The team would disperse in January. Garl drifted for a few weeks, and it would be time to head for training camp in Sackville Forest.

After he was through with the frigging Sox, Garl swore he'd go back to Dartmouth and finish his degree. Maybe he could stay on in New Hampshire, become the college coach, and teach a little Sophocles on the side. Then he wouldn't have to live at a baseball hotel with the likes of Scarborough, Ragland, and Chicken Stallings.

Garl was getting notes in his box at the Brunswick. They were written in a mad scrawl. He didn't have to peek at the letterhead: Boston, Louisburg Square. Garl recognized the bite of the ink. That Cottonmouth woman was courting him again. Garl knew all about the families of Beacon Hill: the Cantons, The Borgoynes, the Beebes, and the Cottonmouths. But he had no love for the "Hill" people. Their names could linger for a century. *His* father died an obscure man. Garl preferred the mud of the Wabash to Louisburg Square.

"Garland James," the woman wrote, "Garland James, Garland James, when will you visit me?" *When the boss stops bringing you to ball games, Marylou.* How was he supposed to truck around with Hollis' lady friends? It was Hollis who paid him ten thousand a year. He was indentured to his Dartmouth brother, Hollis McKee. *I'm that man's slave, Marylou.*

She was the beautiful one, making a bonnet out of her own red hair to sit high on her forehead. The woman was fond of poetry. Hollis would invite him up to the executive office, near the roofs of Fenway Park, and serve bathtub gin to Garl and Marylou. The boss would grab him by the shoulder. "Garl, you're the only goddamn ballplayer on the club. I'd throw the others to the rats, but I wouldn't trade you for half the St. Louie Browns."

He'd go on palavering like that, while the woman recited scratches of poetry. She'd confuse Robert Browning and William Blake, but the difference was, her palaver didn't come out silky and smooth. She'd flirt with him right under the boss' nose. "How many fraternities bid for you, Garland James? I'll bet you were a terrific catch. My late husband Judah was a Dartmouth man. That's where he and Hollis met, in a fraternity house. I'm a Bryn Mawr girl myself."

"I didn't have much time for fraternities, ma'am. I went out for the baseball team, and I had to work in the college laundry to survive."

Garl crumpled that letter he got. A perfume seemed to come off the paper and stick to his hand. Marylou's smell. The Cottonmouths weren't for him. He'd have felt out of place on the brick paths of Louisburg Square. Garl was tied to his baseball hotel.

He encountered Ragland in the hall. The kid's face hadn't healed. The marks on him were turning yellow. It was almost as if he wore a colored mask around his eyes. That's how symmetrical Garl's blows had been. They passed each other without offering the meagerest sign of hello. Garl was ashamed. He shouldn't have used his knuckles on a growing boy.

The kid was going out for a walk. He could have gone down

Boylston Street to the Public Garden, where children would have
begged for his autograph. Rags had a free afternoon. There was no
Sunday baseball in Boston. The city fathers had declared a day of
rest.

The Red Sox and the Braves would descend on the Public Garden, or the Common that was attached to it. They would arrive in
their baseball caps, seek out a particular spot, and wait for widows
and college girls to appear. But Rags wouldn't wait with them. He
preferred that wild park, the Back Bay Fens, near his hotel. The
park was overgrown with every sort of leaf; some of the leaves
were taller than Rags. It was a thick, marshy land, half wet, half
dry, with a snaky black pool that would often sink into the ground.
This pool was called the Muddy River.

Rags enjoyed following the obscure banks of that crazy river on
a Sunday afternoon. The Fens had become a lovers' lane used by
clever people from the Latin School and Boston University; they
enticed local girls into the marsh and undressed them as often as
they could. Rags would stumble upon these creatures during his
walks. He'd pardon himself and let them hide under some magnificent leaf.

On a Sunday in June he broke up a disturbance near the river
bank. Two young men were annoying a woman in a light blue
dress. They kept trying to drag her somewhere. They each took
hold of an arm and pulled. They didn't abandon their wretched
work even when they spotted Rags. They smiled at him and continued to pull.

Rags cracked one of them on the neck with his forearm. The
young man tottered for a moment and fell into the river. He
screamed his outrage at Rags and ran off with his friend, while the
young woman took off her hat. Red hair spilled onto her eyes. She
was a Cottonmouth.

"Marylou?" he said, noticing a tiny wrinkle at the corner of her
chin.

"I'm Iva. Who are you?"

"Ragland. I play for the Sox. I saw you sittin' with Mr.
McKee."

Iva was doubtful of him. "What happened to your eyes?"

"Had a fight . . . two weeks ago."

"Did Garland James beat you up?"

"No, no," Rags said. "He swung, I swung, and that was it."

"Don't be so proud," she told him. "Garland beats up everybody."

The daughter was beginning to anger him. "What are you doin'
in the Fens?"

"Looking for my mother," she said.

"Hell, why would your mother come to a swamp?"

"Why do you think?"

Rags didn't like the way she pouted at him, as if she were lecturing a turtle in the woods, some dumb, helpless beast that could be flopped over on its back and made to writhe.

"Miz Iva, I don't care if your mother sleeps in the swamp. It's the same to me."

"Sometimes she does," Iva said. "It depends on if she can convince her beau to come back to the house."

"What beau is that?"

"Any beau she can find."

Iva wasn't making much sense. "You mean your mother comes here to meet college boys?"

"She isn't that choosy. She takes what she can get."

"And them two guys on the river bank, they weren't after you. They were after your mama. Aint that right? They thought Miz Iva was Marylou."

"Yes," she said, "but you certainly yak a lot for a baseball player. Now will you help me look?"

They began slapping at the thickets for Marylou. All they did was upset lovers in the grass. They knocked through the Fens for an hour, their faces swollen red from the heat of their work. Iva took to mumbling.

"Mama isn't in her right mind when she comes here. She gets on the trolley and she goes for a ride. It's like walking in your sleep. The madness hits her. She falls into a dream. I wouldn't care. But men take advantage of her. They steal her shoes and her purse. She brings gigolos back to the house. They live with us for weeks. They work up a bill you wouldn't believe. Mama buys them everything. Hollis has to throw them out. He was daddy's best friend."

Rags tried to listen while he searched for traces of red hair.

Iva shook his arm. "Give it up, will you? When mama wants to hide, there's nothing I can do. Take me home, Mr. Ragland. I hate it in here. Mama can have her jungle. I'm soaked through and through."

Rags had never been on the far side of the Common. Iva brought him to an incredible hill of streets. He marched on cobblestones and sidewalks of burnt red brick. Iva's hill was divorced from the rest of town. It had nothing to do with baseball diamonds, Rags' hotel, or her mother's swamp. The air wasn't smelly on Iva's hill.

They turned a corner and were at a little park with statues

planted on the lawn. The park had a gate around it with different kinds of spears running along the top. Someone had stuck an apple into one of these spears; the apple bled a strange pink from its open wound. Iva wouldn't let him look at apple blood for very long. He had to follow her to a row of houses on the right side of the park. The front walls swelled in and out, and Rags saw a line of undulating windows and roofs.

"What is this place?"

Iva wiggled her jaw in deep contempt. "The Red Sox must live on Mars. Every beggar in the street knows about Louisburg Square."

"Beggar yourself," Rags said. "This is the first time I'm on this hill. I've got an occupation, Miz Iva. I play ball."

"Oh, shut up, and come inside," she said, and they walked into a house near the end of the row. Things had to be snug on Louisburg Square; no one alongside the little park ever heard of robbers and thieves. Iva could come and go. The door wasn't locked.

A butler seemed to jump out of the wall. He startled Rags. Iva whispered, "That's Rhys. Don't pay any attention to him. He used to be one of mama's beaus."

"Did she lift him from the swamp?"

"Not Rhys. Rhys is too refined. Mama discovered him in a coffee shop."

Then she shouted at the poor man. "Rhys, this is Mr. Ragland of the Red Sox. He's famous. Did you see his picture in the roto-gravure? . . . don't forget to tell me when mama gets back. Are you listening, Rhys?"

She was a savage girl. Rags felt sorry for the butler, who had to wear a black coat all the time and take abuse from Iva. The leaves of the parlor door split apart, and a woman in red silk came through the leaves.

"Mama, you're home!"

Marylou Cottonmouth didn't have a blemish on her face. She should have been the fifteen-year-old, not Iva. Iva was an irascible witch.

"Darling, why don't you ask your friend to stay and have tea with us?"

"He's not my friend, mama. He's that infant at third base. Don't you recognize him? Babe Ragland. Look at his eyes. Garland beat him up, and he won't admit it."

Marylou was distressed. Her mouth began to jump at the corners; Rags tried to soothe her. "It wasn't much of a fight, Miz Marylou. Garl didn't hurt me at all."

Her mouth was quiet again. She smiled at Rags. He went into

the parlor with Marylou and her savage daughter. There were
twelve sofas in the room. You could have sat the Red Sox and the
Browns and still had space for most of the American League.
Mother and daughter picked the same couch. Rags settled into a
love seat.

He heard the butler speak into a tube that was stuck in the wall.
"The best cakes, I said. Henrietta, we have a ballplayer in the
house."

A horrible squeak overtook the room; it was the din of ropes
being pulled somewhere behind the wall. Rhys opened a closet,
dropped his hands inside, and drew out an enormous silver tray.
This ceremony of movements was for Rags. The butler knew about
the kid's bastard days in Baltimore; the *Evening Transcript* had
told him that. He figured a bastard would be unconscious of ordinary household machines. So Rhys could give the illusion of con-
juring knives, spoons, napkins, and plates out of a hole in the wall.

A splotch appeared on Iva's cheek. The servant's trick had filled
her with spite. She hated Rags. How could a boy be so alert with
his hands and so thick in the head?

"Ragland, what's wrong? Haven't you ever seen a dumbwaiter?"

"I saw plenty of dumbwaiters. Don't you worry."

Marylou came between their squabble and defended Rags.

"Iva, don't be such a frightful pest. Pour Mr. Ragland some
tea."

Rags drank his tea from a china cup. He was careful not to slurp.
Marylou offered him an apricot tart. The crust broke in his fingers
after he'd nibbled off the edges of the tart. He eats like a rat, Iva
noticed.

But Marylou eased him out of the discomfort of having tart
slivers all over his lap.

"Do your friends call you Babe?"

"I only have one friend, Miz Marylou. He's a hunchback. And
he calls me Rags."

"Don't you have a Christian name?"

"That's it, ma'am. Babe."

"Well, that's the funniest Christian name I ever heard . . . I'm
sorry, Rags. I shouldn't have contradicted you."

"You don't have to be sorry. The brothers at St. Mary's always
said 'Babe' to me. 'Come here, Babe.' 'Go to sleep, Babe.' Things
like that. Maybe there's a different name on my birth certificate.
But it's hard to tell. Because nobody knows where that certificate
is. I'm a foundling, ma'am. The brothers picked me right off the
front step. I was two and a half."

"It must have been dreadful."

"Not so dreadful, ma'am. Them brothers raised me good. It was like having fifty parents, instead of one or two."

Rags finished his tea. "It's getting late for batting practice," he said.

Iva rose off her couch to nudge him under the ribs. "What are you talking about? Fenway Park is closed on Sunday."

"Not for us. The skipper likes to have a Sunday drill."

But it wasn't that simple for Rags to leave the house. He still had a ruined tart in his lap. He might have been stranded on the love seat for another hour if mama Cottonmouth hadn't stooped next to him and brushed off his knees.

"Say hello to Garl for me."

"I don't know if I can, Miz Marylou. We don't talk much. But I'll ask the hunchback to give him your regards."

"Never mind," Iva said, and she walked him out of the room, opening the twin leaves of the door and shutting them behind her and Rags, so she could have him to herself. She wasn't the kind of girl who would close her eyes and wait for a ballplayer's kiss. She climbed up on Rags' shoes, thrust her tongue into his mouth, explored most of his teeth, and he uttered a little moan, she pushed him out onto Louisburg Square. Then she strode back into the parlor and began to scream.

"Rhys, get out of here. I want to be with my mother. And Rhys, I don't like you making fun of my guests. Save your dumbwaiter tricks for the cook. Now scatter. It gives me a headache just to look at you."

That barbarous quality went out of Iva's voice soon as Rhys disappeared. But she'd already struck a terror in Marylou. Miz Iva was the mother of the house. Marylou was like a small, wayward sister who had to be chastised, pummeled, and kissed.

"Mama, why do you embarrass yourself? Does the whole world have to know you're in love with Garland James? You can't trust that Ragland boy. He's a liar. I don't believe anybody found him on the steps. The boy with no name. What a dumb story!"

Marylou had begun to sob. "But he has such a nice face."

"What's so nice about it? He never smiles. And he's always watching you. It's shrewd of him to play the dope. Then he can blabber all he wants, and nothing he says has to make sense."

The kid was glad to get out of Boston. Rags would never want to live between Miz Iva and Miz Marylou. But he couldn't stop thinking of the sweet belly Marylou had under the folds of her red silk. That belly made him wild.

The Sox were going on their Western swing, into St. Louis,
Cleveland, Chicago, and Detroit. Rags welcomed the cramped runway of a Pullman car. Whatever distanced him from the Cottonmouths had tô be good. But the kid was unable to sleep. As a
rookie he inherited the Pullman's upper berth; uppers always rattled louder than the lower berths. Rags had nightmares while he
cuddled against a jittery shelf in the wall. He would dream that
Marylou's belly exploded in his face, drenching him in ripe brown
blood. The explosion hurt. Marylou's blood came at him in hot
pellets. He would shake himself out of the dream, spread the curtain apart, climb down from his upper, paddle along the runway in
his bare feet, and sit in the washroom for the rest of the night.

He got to Cleveland with swollen red eyes. He bathed his head
in the clubhouse sink, put on his uniform, and destroyed the Tribe,
as he knocked down bullet-shots with his chest, picked the ball out
of the rough infield grass, and made the throw to first. Rags wasn't
the only one who produced for the Sox. The infield had begun to
mesh. Germany Stone loosened up at first; Seaman Schupp found
his niche again; Alvin Critz rediscovered the double play. They
learned to live with Rags. They managed their own territories and
gave the left side of the infield to him.

And then there was Garl. He punched out three hits in the opening game, and went back to the center-field wall to rob Tris
Speaker of a double. The Sox, with their meager pitching staff,
took three of four from the Tribe.

They jumped on Chicago and Detroit, winning nine games in a
row, and found themselves in second place. You couldn't laugh at
the Red Sox anymore. They were beating you with broken-bat
singles and the crazy glove they had at third. Rags was frustrating
the American League. What sort of book could you keep on such
a kid? *Boston's seventh Babe.*

Those bad boys of baseball, the St. Louis Browns, decided they
would choke off Rags and end the Boston winning streak. The
Brownies weren't like the Indians and the Tigers, who kept trying
to seek out a pedigree for Rags, a magical notebook that would list
Ragland's weaknesses and strengths. The kid had been born in
smoke and fire. He could probably field the ball when he was five
or six. Who cared what teams he had or hadn't played on? The
Brownies rode him from their bench. "McKee's little bastard,"
they said. "Orphan prick." The Brownie catcher, Hank Severeid,
would twitch at Rags from behind the plate. "Bastard here, bastard here . . . bastards can't buy a hit."

They sat in the dugout, sharpening their spikes. Brownie runners
would fly at Rags and aim for his throat. It was futile work. Rags

would twist his body away from those oncoming spikes and tag the runner on top of his head.

The Sox took the first game, 1 to nothing, on Sheriff Smith's breaking stuff and a triple by Garland James. St. Louis journalists mourned the Browns, and admired the "new" Red Sox. Boston had come out of the American League cellar to ravage the East and the West. Briggs Josephson took a corpse and stung it to life.

Chicken Stallings scoffed at the fancy words of St. Louis journalists, repeated to him by Germany Stone, since the Chicken couldn't read or write. "Who's a frigging corpse? We're winning because Garl's got a hot bat and we're having fun. That's all. It don't take a genius to find out." The Chicken brought a few "medicine bottles" of drugstore beer up to the Buckingham Hotel, and distributed them to the players. He was celebrating the pennant in June. "Lordy Lord, we're gonna grab Mr. Babe Ruth by the balls, and squeeze 'em, until the Yanks drop out of first."

Scarborough guzzled beer with the rest. The Sox had grown a bit kinder to him after the fracas in the tunnel. They didn't want to madden the brute, or they'd have to deal with the muscles under his shirt. So they said, "Hiya, Scarborough," and gave him beer to drink.

The sixth floor had become a Red Sox station in St. Louis. Ballplayers lingered there. The Sox owned the Buckingham on their trips to Sportsman's Park. You couldn't keep bimbos, journalists, and baseball nuts out of the hotel. Everyone wanted to traffic with a team that was in second place. Scarborough trundled down the hall, his brain thick with beer. He couldn't avoid the crowds of men and women who wiggled fingers at him. "That's the mascot. He brings them luck. Say, Scarborough, will you sign your name on my handkerchief?" The ink from his pen soaked through the handkerchief, turning "Scarborough" into a meaningless blot.

The hunchback was lonely for his room. It was better when the Sox lived in eighth place. Then the halls had nothing but ghosts in them. The door to his room was open. Scarborough peeked in. Rags stood with a man in a dark brown suit. They were shouting at each other. Rags had a strange music in his voice that the hunchback had never heard.

"Tell him *this* is school for me. I don't care what he thinks. I can earn a living. Yes, I wear pajamas in front of thirty thousand people, pajamas and high socks. And I run after a ball that can knock your head off if it hits you right. But the ball feeds me. My father can go to hell."

"You'd give up your inheritance for that? Cedric, your father could have you committed if he knew."

"How? I'm eighteen, and I signed a contract with the Boston Red Sox."

"But you used a false identity."

"So what? The Sox have lawyers too. They can legalize any name I like. I'm their third baseman, Mr. Griffey. And the Sox are on a winning streak. Don't you interfere."

Rags didn't have to look up. He could feel that brute at the door and also sniff him out. The hunchback had a long shadow and his own peculiar smell.

"Goodbye, Mr. Griffey. Thanks for the advice."

The man brushed past Scarborough as if the hunchback didn't have the right to exist. Scarborough frowned at Rags. "Who was that?"

"Some duffer I used to know."

"Why'd he call you Cedric?"

"Because that's the name the brothers pinned on me at the bad boys' school. But don't you ever use it. I'm not Cedric to anybody. You understand?"

"I don't have to understand. I'm no skunk. I wouldn't call you by a name you didn't like . . . you said something about a father to him. Whose father is that? Orphans aint supposed to have a dad."

"It's not your business," Rags said. "Who told you to stand by the door and snoop on people?"

"You aint the king here. It's my room as much as yours."

"Maybe I should learn from Garl and get a private suite when I'm on the road."

"You can't afford it," the hunchback snarled at him. "You're stuck with me, unless your dad is rich."

Rags walked out of the room, making the hunchback scream into the hall. "What about the chocolate sodas we were gonna have?"

"Not today," Rags said. "I'm sick of you."

The secret visitor in Rags' and Scarborough's room didn't hurt the Red Sox. The Brownies were in trouble. They couldn't shake the Boston infield loose. Ragland, Critz, and Schupp kept turning over the double play. The Sox denied the Brownies their favorite weapon: the drag bunt. The infield tightened like a fist around St. Louis. Rags would lunge into the grass and begin his submarine throw, with his chin near his shoes and the ball coming from behind one knee. The busher was eating them alive.

They were an ordinary team without their trick bunts. The
Brownies couldn't lay a ball near the third-base line. But how come
Rags *always* knew when they were going to bunt? Some dog of a
player or coach was swiping their signals from the dugout. Who
the hell could it be? The Brownies had a complex schedule of
crisscrossing signs. They could have fooled the Wizard of Oz with
the different monkey twitches they'd developed. But the Sox were
reading their every move. Boston could pull the meaningful
twitches out of all the insane nods that passed between the dugout
and the coaching boxes. It was like having a snake under your own
bench.

The Brownies scratched themselves and looked across the field:
one man on the Sox, and only one, had an intimate sense of their
dugout. It was the brute. Scarborough enjoyed special privileges
as bat boy of the Sox. He was forever hovering around home plate.
The brute must have carried a pair of extra eyes in his hump. He
was swindling the Brownies into the American League grave.

They revised their signals after the fourth inning. Baby Doll
Jacobson bunted for a base hit. Ken Williams was able to bring
him across. The Browns weren't finished. They scored again in
the eighth, and squeaked past the Sox, 2-1. This was the kind of
baseball they admired.

With their signals protected, they took three more from the Sox,
and dropped them back to third. On getaway day, the Sox crept
out of their hotel and rode to Union Station without muttering a
word to the people of St. Louis. They were a club whose winning
streak had deserted them.

Rags put on his last clean shirt and hurried over to that swamp
near the ball park, the Back Bay Fens. His heart trembled under
the pocket of his shirt as he pushed through leaves and wet grass.
He was like a sleepwalker on some hungry mission. Sweat poured
into his eyes. The mud sucked around his shoes. Alligators could
have been roosting in the swamp water. Rags wouldn't have noticed. He'd come for Miz Marylou.

He had to leave the swamp without her. Iva must have tricked
him: her mother didn't take the streetcar every day. She only went
looking for beaus on very special afternoons.

Thoughts of Marylou's belly swam through his mind. He forgot
about baseball and his talent for choking off the bunt. The beanpole was turning into a voluptuary. He wanted to lick the juices
out of Marylou's succulent navel. He'd watch for pieces of lint.

He found Scarborough sulking in their room. The hunchback
was distraught. The Brownies had unmasked him. Soon the entire

league would know why Mr. Briggs "brung" him into baseball. He was a frigging thief. Brutes made lousy bat boys because they called attention to themselves and slowed the game down with their temperamental walks from the dugout. You couldn't rely on them. They had a lazy character. Sometimes they could be surly. And they liked to snarl at children. But their sneakiness paid off. No one could steal an enemy's signals like a brute. They could peer into your dugout from behind their hump. Most brutes were blessed with freakish fields of vision. They could see around benches, and under a coach's shoes. Scarborough had been decoding signs—an ear twitch, nose pulls, handkerchiefs sticking out of a manager's pocket—for a season and a half. That was his value to the club.

Rags heard him sniffle. "Skipper's gonna fire me."

"No he's not."

"He is. I'm useless. I can't grab signals for him. The bastards got my number now. You think Mr. Cobb'll let me near the Tiger bench? They'll hoot at me."

"So what? They can't hide a signal from you, Scarborough. Not in their life. They can dummy things up for a while. It won't do them any good. You're the best swiper in the major leagues."

But he couldn't console the hunchback. Scarborough kept figuring his own doom. So Rags went down to the lobby, where he could watch the constant parade of men and women. People loved to be seen at a baseball hotel. Country boys like Chicken Stallings and Germany Stone would assemble in the lobby so that Red Sox fans could seek them out and pay homage to them. They would sit with bubble gum in their jaws and yap to the prettiest girls.

There was a strange perfume in the lobby, stronger than cheap cologne and the Chicken's sour breath. You could feel that special sweetness rising out of everybody's skin. It was pennant fever. It hadn't come to Boston in five years. The faithful wouldn't abandon the Red Sox. What was a four-game losing streak? The Sox had their magical infield. They were still a first-division club.

Rags had his lobby hat, an old homburg he borrowed from the hunchback and pulled down over his eyes. He didn't want pretty girls to wink at him and ask for his room number when he was crazy for Marylou. The homburg made him invisible. He could stare at the circus of people from under the brim of his hat.

He recognized Marylou's servant Rhys. The servant had just come away from the front desk. "Hey Rhys," the kid said, raising his homburg.

The servant didn't seem to know who he was. "Don't you remember? I'm Babe Ragland. The ballplayer. I had tea at Marylou's house.''

"Hiya, Mr. Ragland. How do you do?''

"You hang out at the Brunswick, huh Rhys, you old son of a gun?''

"I don't hang out anywhere,'' Rhys said. "I was delivering a note from the missus.''

"Is that note for me?''

Rhys gave a smirk. "The missus doesn't send notes to little boys . . . it's for Garland James.''

The servant fled from Rags, who pulled his homburg down again. Michaels, the house detective, caught him muttering to himself. *She sends notes to Garl, and nothing for Rags.*

Michaels took him by the shoulder. He figured Rags was some stray dog who was trying to park his dirty bones at the Brunswick. "Say, you bum, get out of here. We don't like your kind in the lobby.''

"It's me,'' Rags whispered, and he had to let Michaels peek under the hat.

"Sorry, Babe. We have to be careful, you know, or bums come in and take a nap. What's the story with the Tigers tomorrow? I have a dollar on you boys. For God's sake, will you please murder Ty Cobb?''

"Sure I will,'' Rags said, to get the house detective off his back. But he had small luck with the Tigers. He pushed, scratched, ate dry brown grass to get at the ball, and the Sox could only grab one win out of five. The wounds deepened on Scarborough's face. His eyes turned a dull yellow. The brute was in mourning at Fenway Park. The Tigers jumped up and down and twittered at him from their bench, making the hand signals of deaf and dumb mutes. "Scarborough honey, read my fingers, will ya? Lookee, here's the sign for 'hit and run.' ''

Briggs didn't scold the brute. It wasn't Scarborough's fault that the Brownies caught him in the act and snitched to the rest of the league. It would have happened sooner or later. Sign-swipers last a summer or two. They have a high mortality rate. Scarborough could still entertain a ball park if Briggs could pull him out of his sad sleep. But the fans didn't seem to mind. They liked a slumbering brute. It took their attention away from the scoreboard, and those big leads the Tigers were running up.

Briggs realized the bitter rule of baseball under Hollis McKee: win if you can, and give them a clown show if you can't. Scarborough would walk from the dugout with a stuttering gait. He seemed terrorstruck. His eyeballs would shrink into his head, and he had the look of a stunted child, lost in the middle of Fenway Park. The Royal Rooters composed a song for him.

> *You can have your Cobb*
> *And your Harry Heilmann*
> *Manush and Hooks Dauss mean nothing to us.*
> *We've got Scarrrrrborough*
> *Scarrrrrborough, Ragland, and James.*

But you couldn't please the brute. The words of the song would fall onto his back, and his hump would start to whimper. He was the most miserable hunchback in town.

Rags couldn't bear Scarborough's company. He had to get out of the hotel. And he went back to the swamp because he had nothing better to do.

He stumbled around in the grass, swamp flies attacking his nose and giant caterpillars plummeting on his head. It could have been the Amazon jungle growing across from Fenway Park, the water was so steamy and black, and the air populated with murdering bugs. The kid had to slap at himself, or have his face get eaten off. He couldn't find a single pair of lovers in the swamp grass. It was too frigging hot.

He didn't believe Marylou was in there. She'd have to be crazy to crawl through the Fens. The swamp was empty of beaus. Who could tell where the college boys were? Sailing on the Charles? Plucking a banjo in the Common? They wouldn't have gone into any Back Bay jungle in this weather, not even for Marylou.

He heard a crackle in the high leaves. Was it a swamp animal? Boston alligators? A summer fox? A hand parted the leaves in front of Rags. The leaves snapped back into place. But they couldn't hide whoever it was. Rags saw a curl of red hair. Then a woman's shoe. Mama Cottonmouth.

"Miz Marylou?"

Her face broke through the leaves. She had tiny balls of sweat on her upper lip. Hair flew over her head in a disintegrating bun that frightened Rags. He thought it was a bushel of snakes: red snakes about to uncoil. She dressed for the jungle in long skirts and a green satin belt. Her eyebrows wrinkled up for one terrible moment, and she was a madwoman with her gaze fixed on Rags. Then her eyebrows smoothed over and that brittleness went out of her face.

"I know you," she sang out in the voice of a coquette. "You're Harvard Jack."

Rags was going to shake his head and say, No, no, you have the wrong guy. I'm Babe Ragland, Miz Marylou. I came to Beacon Hill with your daughter. She has a big mouth. But he didn't want her eyebrows to knit again. He'd be her Harvard Jack.

He didn't have to coo at her, mouth little stories to make her get out of her clothes. She wasn't interested in the whereabouts of Harvard Jack. She took him into a grotto of leaves near the river bank, and she undressed, using her petticoat and her skirts as a blanket to protect them from the sharpest grass. He couldn't take his eyes off Marylou. She had beautiful freckles on her arms. Her buttocks were as perfect as a child's. Her breasts were lovely and small, the nipples pointing out at Rags in the wild leaves of the grotto. Her belly didn't have one unsightly crease.

She laughed at him. "Harvard Jack, do you always lie down in the bushes with your trousers on?"

In that fervor of watching Marylou, Rags forgot about himself. He shucked off pants, shirt, and underwear, letting these articles drop around him, in the folds of different leaves. He was embarrassed by his own erection. He'd never had such a swelling before. His glans stood like a forest onion with red and blue skin. He was amazed at all the colors the throb of blood could produce.

Marylou didn't shy away from him. She brought him down into her blanket of skirts. Her body seemed luminescent to him, as if any part of her could give off wonderful bits of light. Her cheekbones began to shine for Rags. Her fingers were in the tangle of hair at the back of his neck. She signaled her desire with scratches and strokes. He was able to enter Marylou without the slightest push. How did he get so far inside her belly? Crickets chirped in his skull. Caterpillars dropped. Flies burrowed into his shoulder. The grotto was beset with tiny animals. His body served as a frigging table for them. But he could hardly feel their bites. Who would have dreamed that he'd ever make love to Marylou?

"Harvard Jack," she said, with licks behind his ear. Her tongue was warm and delicious.

4

A blight arrived at Fenway Park. It was another plague year for the Red Sox. They lost eleven out of fourteen and fell into sixth place. Thank God Hollis McKee was preoccupied with his musical, *Eveline*. It was having its summer trial at Boston's Shubert Theatre, and Hollis would leave Fenway Park in the middle of a game and taxi over to Tremont Street, so he could bully his director and his stars hours before show time. Theatre critics worshiped his musical comedy about the sufferings of baseball wives. It didn't matter to them that Hollis' team was moving towards the cellar. The critics adored *Eveline*. Hollis had himself a hit.

That's why manager Briggs began to worry. His spies on the club told him Hollis was looking for Babe Ragland. The boss wanted Rags up in the executive suite. He only invited Dartmouth men upstairs to drink moonshine with him, unless he had some deal in his head. Then he'd grab you by the hand and give you to his "cousins" at Yankee Stadium. Briggs smelled disaster for the Sox. His infield would come apart without Ragland at third, and the plague year would be complete.

Rags climbed the great wooden stairs over the clubhouse. Secretaries passed him on the stairs and wouldn't even nod to him. He knocked on a door that had the word OWNER scratched into the glass. Hollis came out for him, and Rags followed the boss inside. He didn't notice one desk or file cabinet in the executive suite. They sat on upholstered chairs in what looked to Rags like a wide living room.

"Congratulations," Hollis said.

Rags figured the boss had to be drunk. But where was all the whiskey?

"What's Briggs paying you, son?"

"Eight hundred, Mr. McKee."

"That's a swindle," Hollis said. "Nine hundred's the minimum on my club."

"I know that. But a hundred goes for uniforms and extra food bills on the road."

"I don't care. This isn't Paducah. It's the Boston Red Sox. We're not fly-by-nights. You're in the major leagues. Tell Briggs I'm doubling your salary."

Rags shifted around on the plush seat of his chair.

"He won't believe it, sir, if it comes from me."

"He'll have to believe it," Hollis said. So Rags settled in. What could he do? The boss had declared a raise for him.

"Don't let her talk you into eloping, son. It would break her mother's heart. She's just a schoolgirl. It will have to be a long engagement. You can't have her until she's seventeen. Otherwise the engagement is off."

Mr. McKee was starting with that crazy jabber again. The kid was a rookie in the American League. He lived at the Brunswick Hotel. He played third for Mr. Briggs. He didn't know anything about "long engagements." He figured it was smart to nod his head. He got a big raise from the boss, and he didn't want to anger him.

"You won't let me down, will you, Babe?"

"No, sir."

"I'm a single man myself. Iva and Marylou are like family to me. I won't tolerate seeing them hurt. I was at Dartmouth with Iva's pa. We were sworn to one another. Bloodbrothers. You're a foundling, and I don't expect you to understand fraternity rites. But I hope you'll appreciate this. My brother Judah is long dead, and I'm watching out for him. I consider Iva to be my own child. She's stubborn as the devil. If Iva says she's going to marry a baseball player, that's what she'll do. Only I pity the man who doesn't take my advice. No whirlwind courtships, Babe. She's fifteen and a half."

The boss stood up, so Rags did the same thing. They crossed that living room together, and Hollis opened the door and accompanied him to the edge of the stairs. Rags had been maneuvered into something, and he couldn't say what. He was in love with mama Cottonmouth, not that redheaded daughter who said goodbye to you with her tongue and then tossed you into the street.

The skipper was waiting for him at the bottom of the stairs. "Well, kid, how did it go?"

"Fine," Rags said, as if he'd just stepped out of a foolish dream.

"Is Hollis sending you to the Yanks?"

"No."

"Are you sure you won't be in a Yankee uniform next season?"

"Nobody can be sure of that, Mr. Briggs. This is the major leagues. But the boss told me to remind you that I'm getting a raise. He's giving me double money, Mr. Briggs."

Briggs couldn't grasp the mandarin ways of Hollis McKee. The skipper had been begging Hollis for months to throw the kid a few extra dollars, and Hollis had refused. He was the stingiest owner in baseball. He made Briggs "steal" a hundred dollars from all the rookies, obliging them to pay for food money that should have come out of the owner's purse. Now Hollis had decided to double the kid's salary.

The skipper said, "Good luck," and Rags went into the clubhouse to put on Boston's colors and his baseball shoes.

Rags had a miserable afternoon. He bobbled the ball twice chasing bunts, and he couldn't buy a hit. But the Sox managed to win.

Garland James doubled to the left-field wall with a man on board, and they nosed out the Indians, 1–0.

It wasn't shaky arms and legs that produced the kid's errors. He couldn't concentrate on the Indians; his eyes kept wandering to the owner's box. Hollis had brought the Cottonmouths to the game. Rags watched Marylou clap after Garl had his double. She wore a pink dress, and she didn't seem like a woman who strolled in the jungle and lay down with Rags. She had precise halfmoons of powder on her cheeks: Marylou could have been a polite doll who'd come to cheer for the Red Sox and sip pink lemonade. But she had a hard time tilting the thermos jug. It was as big and clumsy as a cannon shell.

He made Scarborough deliver a note to Miz Iva. *Meet me at the corner of Ipswich and Van Ness after the game. Truly yours, Rags.*

Rags got there first. He threw a jacket over his uniform in the clubhouse, so he could hide under the lapels. The crowd was too busy flowing away from the ball park to stop and recognize Rags. He was safe on Ipswich Street.

Iva discovered him skulking behind his lapels. "You picked a dumb place to meet. Can't we go to a little shop and have iced coffee?"

"I don't want to have an iced coffee with you," Rags muttered. His jaw was clamped so hard, a whistling noise rushed through his teeth.

"Then what is it you do want, Mr. Ragland Rags?"

She had a nest of tiny agitated wrinkles that ran under one ear. Her face couldn't shine like Marylou's. She was the most rambunctious girl Rags ever saw.

"Why'd you tell the boss we was engaged?"

She drew her head away from Rags and let her nostrils flare out. "I can tell Hollis whatever I like."

"Sure you can. He's your new pa. But I aint part of your family, Miz Iva."

"Oh, but I'll bet you'd like to be . . . you'd marry my mother in a minute."

"Your mother? Who says? I only talked to her once . . . don't you remember the tea we had?"

"I remember," Iva said. Rags thought her nostrils were going to rip. "I remember somebody who kissed me at the door and then sneaked into the swamp with Marylou. You're a disgusting liar, Mr. Rags. I saw you down with her in the grass. You're vile when you're naked, do you know that?"

Rags' heart thumped under the jacket. His fingers had turned to lead. "Who told you to spy on us?"

"I wouldn't spy on ballplayer trash like you. My mother's a crazy woman, can't you tell? If I don't follow her, who will? I have to make sure she doesn't drown herself. You idiot, she's in love with Garland James. You could have been any man to her in that swamp. Some dumb college boy in knee-pants. Didn't you hear her call you 'Harvard Jack'?"

"Then what do you want to marry me for?"

"To punish you," she said, and she shouted other things at Rags, but he couldn't hear. His jacket fell off, and it was too late. People spotted his uniform. They milled around Rags, touching his Red Sox shirt. Their eyes were inflamed. Their mouths hung at every angle. "Babe, Babe, will you write a note to my daughter Bess? She'll be so thrilled."

He was stuck inside a fence of people. He couldn't see Iva now. She'd abandoned him to all his rooters. He'd have to put his name on souvenir hats, scorecards, Red Sox flags, children's bonnets. "Awright," he said. "Here we go . . . 'to darling Bess from Babe Ragland. July, 1923. Hi, Bess. Your daddy and I wish you grow up to be healthy and tall. It's good to have a tall woman in the house.' "

The kid was ruthless with the Indians in their next game. He took his wrath out on them, since those raw faces burning in the sun reminded him of Iva's red hair. He was like some weird angel who landed in the ball park to single out Tris Speaker's Indians and strike at them. The Tribe couldn't get near Rags' corner. The kid would run down men caught between second and third, stifle suicide bunts, and sidestep any jackass who hoped to barrel into him and knock the ball out of his glove. Seven Indians were stranded on second base.

Rags didn't have to dart looks at the owner's box. It was vacant this afternoon. No Hollis McKee, and no Cottonmouths to drink lemonade out of a cannon shell and clap for Dartmouth men. Hollis had gone to the Shubert with the Cottonmouths for a matinee performance of *Eveline*.

Iva and Marylou missed games three, four, and five with the Indians, who suddenly remembered how to play. They didn't have to squeeze past Babe Ragland. Doubles and triples brought their men home. The Tribe crushed Boston in the last three games of the series.   •

Briggs kept pulling cotton threads out of his baseball cap. The brim was nearly gone, most of it unraveled in the skipper's hand. The Sox were a game and a half out of the cellar. These men who once sat in second place, spitting on the Yankees and the Browns, had turned to spooks. They slipped away from the dugout like shadows on the run. Briggs had two live creatures left, Garland and the kid. But Garl was thinking of his retirement, when he could return to Dartmouth with his books of Sophocles; and Rags was obsessed with that jungle woman, Marylou, and her daughter who liked to breathe poison on him.

If the Cottonmouths wouldn't come to Fenway, he'd have to walk on cobblestones to find Louisburg Square. He crossed the Public Garden. He climbed Beacon Hill. And he knocked on Marylou's front door. He noticed funny things through the window. The furniture was draped with sheets. He had to knock again before that servant would open up for him. Rhys was surly with Rags. "It's an odd time for tea, old boy. We're locking up the house. Come back in October, if you like. I'll feed you dog biscuits. Don't you ever listen? We're locking up."

"Why?" Rags said.

"We're going to Tisbury town."

"Where's that?"

"My God, don't they civilize you during spring training? How can you live in Boston and be unaware of Tisbury and Edgartown? Tisbury's on the Vineyard, you little ape. The missus always summers there."

"Martha's Vineyard?" Rags said. "Why didn't you say so? I heard of Martha's Vineyard. The governor of Massachusetts has a house on that island. I read it in the *Globe*."

"I'm glad they still teach orphans how to read," the servant told him. "Now go home to your Fenway Park. We don't like ballplayers on the Hill."

He would have shut the door in Rags' face, but Iva heard the commotion from her room, and she came downstairs to shout at Rhys. "I told you not to despise my guests."

"He's not a guest. Who invited him?"

"I did, Rhys. Get out of here."

Iva befriended Rags in front of the servant, but she didn't invite him inside. "You should have come yesterday," she said. "I could have shown you around the garden, Mr. Rags, given you the grand tour. You have special privileges now that you're my fiancé."

Rags saved his most bitter rookie smile for the girl. "I didn't sign no paper that says we're fiancéd."

"Who cares? Hollis made up a press release for me and you. It will be in all the society pages next week. *Mrs. Judah Cottonmouth of Tisbury and Beacon Hill announces the engagement of her only daughter, Iva Louise, to Mr. Babe Ragland of the Red Sox. Mr. Ragland has no family to speak for him, and no Christian name. He was educated by monks at St. Mary's reform school, where he studied baseball, shirtmending, and Aeschylus.*"

"Aeschylus to you," Rags said, and he started to walk down the hill. Iva ran after him. She touched him softly on the sleeve. "I'm sorry, Rags. I didn't mean to poke fun at you."

"That's okay, Miz Iva. I know Aeschylus by heart. I should have told you. Garland sings it in the dugout before every game." He continued down the hill.

The kid was glad they'd gone off to Tisbury town. He had to suffer through a boring week of society columns about the Cottonmouths and him. He kept getting phone calls from an editor at the *Evening Transcript*. "No, Mr. Finnbar. No, no, no . . . the teaching brothers at St. Mary's brought me up. . . . What? How can I tell you where I was born? They didn't find me until I was three. . . . Goodbye, Mr. Finnbar."

His teammates would get on his back soon as he arrived at the clubhouse. "Look who's here. The Cottonmouth Kid. How does it feel to rob the cradle, Rags? Does Miz Iva have her bleeding spells? Or do girls start bleeding these days before they're eleven?"

It was Garl who told them to shut up.

"I can't read with all this noise, you chumps. Leave the kid alone."

Chicken Stallings said, "Hell, Garl. Can't we have some fun?"

You could feel Garl about to turn mean. His eyes began to flutter in his head. "Where'd you learn about the engagement, little man? In the comic strips? Is that how retarded ballplayers get the news? Does Germany do the translating? Or can you look at the pictures yourself?"

The Chicken slunk away from Garl and disappeared into the tunnel. Rags went over to Garl.

"You didn't have to defend me, Mr. James. I'm used to it by now. The Chicken doesn't bother me at all."

"I wasn't defending you," Garl said, lacing up his shoes. "I just wanted some quiet."

The fans must have seen the society pages, because they whistled and clapped when the kid ran down to third for fielding prac tice. But he didn't get any mercy from the White Sox. Their bench jockeys assembled in the dugout long before the game. They crowed at Rags. "How's the Babe? Don't you see the hair on his lip? The kid's been eatin' moon pie."

Rags stroked two singles and knocked in the run that beat Kid Gleason's Chisox. The Bosox seemed to come alive for a day or two. Then they dropped a doubleheader to Chicago, and they were still the beauties of seventh place.

The Bosox took a leap into the cellar once they got on the road. They went into Yankee Stadium and were booed for half an hour. The Yanks' hunchback, Henry Watteau, sidled up to Rags and said, "How many li'l ladies did you unflower last week, you friggin' Bluebeard?" And then he challenged Scarborough to a fight. Henry's antics were only a prelude to the games themselves. The Yanks must have had a lumberyard inside their dugout. They walloped Boston to death with their different bats. Ruth was on the bench half the time with a bad cold, but the Yanks didn't need him. They had Wally Pipp, Aaron Ward, and Henry Watteau. They took five straight from their Boston cousins.

The Sox hid out in their rooms at the Concourse Plaza. Scarborough sat with his chin on one knee. He was beginning to steal signals again from enemy clubs, but the brute lost his desire for chocolate sundaes. All he did off the field was blink his eyes and mope.

Rags screamed at him. "Damn your hide. What's the gorilla face for?"

"Who's gonna be my roommate after you go? Briggs will have to find another hunchback to stay with me. They'll say we're brothers and promote us as the Red Sox freaks."

"You're demented, Scarborough, that's what. Briggs aint hiring another hunchback. He's got you. You're enough for five teams. How can I go anywhere, huh? I'm on the road with you."

"But you'll be livin' with the Cottonmouths when the summer's gone."

"Not Babe Ragland. Not me. The papers are full of society tricks. I'm eighteen, Scarborough. They can scribble about my engagement until their noses fall off. I aint getting married until I'm fifty-three."

The brute was satisfied. He pulled on his chin, climbed off the bed, and invited Rags downstairs for sundaes at the Concourse Soda Shoppe.

Scarborough smiled with a spoon in his mouth. He had a mob of chocolate syrup between his ears. "Rags, did you watch me read the Yankee bench? You can't fool ol' Scarborough. Next time I'll knock Henry Watteau off his ass. The Yanks must have picked him up in a dog factory. Henry's retiring next year. He caught a hernia lifting them Yankee bats.''

"Will you stop yakking about Henry Watteau. He's just a miserable dwarf."

The brute's eyebrows bunched along his forehead. "Who's miserabler? Henry or me? Henry's got a wife and two little girls. He owns a garage in Des Moines. What have I got? A pair of swollen balls and a big hole in my pocket."

"Well, we'll be in Philadelphia tonight. So you think about swiping plays off Connie Mack.''

"That old man? I'll steal him blind."

Whatever Scarborough stole, it didn't help much. The A's devoured the Boston Red Sox. Briggs took his circus act to Washington, D.C., where the Senators proceeded to tear the Sox apart. Those funny boys, the clowns of Fenway Park, hadn't won a game on this Eastern trip. They returned to Back Bay Station and the Brunswick Hotel.

Michaels, the house detective, was barking at a kid in the lobby. The kid was in hiding. Rags couldn't see much of his face. He had a cap that came down over his ears and covered his mouth. The kid wore a wool vest in July and baggy pants that he must have found in a barrel of old clothes.

"Hey, runt," Michaels said, "I told ya to beat it. Don't come back again.''

"Michaels, lay off," Rags said.

"Jesus, Babe, do ya know this runt?"

The house dick apologized. "I'm awfully sorry. I figured he was a bum who lives in garbage cans." He shook the kid's hand. It disappeared inside Michael's paw. Rags shoved the kid along by his neck. A strand of red hair poked out of his shirt. The hunchback was watching him.

"How are you?" the kid said. "I'm Muggsy. I went to reform school with the Babe. We was on the same team. I'm a southpaw. I pitch for the Blue Sox of St. Mary's. Fella, did you notice my wing?''

"Shut up," Rags said. "And go on upstairs."

The kid took his cap off in the room. He shook his head and revealed a full scalp of red hair. The brute was mortified. "Rags, you brung a bimbo up to the room."

"What bimbo? That's my fiancée."

"Iva? She aint supposed to be up here. Michaels will have the shits. He'll say the two of us are soliciting on the sixth floor. Let her climb down the fire escape. Girl, be quick.''

Rags hushed the brute. "Damn you, Scarborough, will you lemme talk to her for a second." Then he turned to Miz Iva. "What's all this playacting about? Muggsy of the Blue Sox. I'm not one of your stupid servants. You should be on that island with your mother. Tisbury town. With the governor and all the other golden men.''

"I came up to Boston for a holiday. I hate the beaches and the sand. Dunes are for burying people.''

"Good, but why do you need this hotel? Your mama has a place. You could sleep at home.''

"The house is shut for the summer. You can't find a soul on Louisburg Square in July and August, except silly people who come looking for John Hancock's grave. I don't want to sleep in a big old house by myself. You'll have to put me up, Mr. Rags.''

Scarborough paced across the room, his hump rising and falling with the lunges of his body. "All we got is one lousy bed.''

"I don't mind. I can sleep in the middle.''

Scarborough was muttering now. "Chase her out . . . skipper's gonna suspend us for carrying a child.''

"Where am I gonna chase her to?" Rags said. "They still shanghai girls off the street. You want her to end up in some whore's alley? She's practically the boss' niece. Hollis will send us to Paducah if something happens to her. She can stay for the night, and then she goes back to Martha's Vineyard. Where'd you get your cap and pants, Miz Muggsy?''

"From a ragman on Scollay Square.''

"Well, he sure knows his merchandise. You look like a Chinaman's daughter, long as you hide the red hair. I'm hungry. Let's go down and eat.''

They had to skirt the house dick, who would have sniffed under Muggsy's disguise soon enough and yelled for the manager. They traveled in a line of three, Scarborough, Rags, and the girl-boy in cap and vest, moving furtively from place to place. They had mutton chops on Queensberry Street, and banana splits on Horaedan Way. They sat in a nickelodeon on Huntington Avenue and watched cowboys slug Indians, prairie dogs, and white buffalo for twenty-five minutes. The cowboys didn't lose a man. Scarborough yawned but Iva wasn't taking any hints: she wouldn't rush with them to the Brunswick and go to bed. "Show me a speakeasy.''

"What?''

"You know, a saloon.''

"We aint got time for saloons," Rags screamed. "We're playing ball tomorrow."

Iva stopped dead on Shattuck Street. Rags whispered to the brute. "Scarborough, where's the closest saloon?"

They crossed the trolley tracks and hiked to a bluestone house on Darling Street. The brute went up the steps alone, knocked on the door, and muttered a few words. "Humpty Dumpty and his friends. Three Joes from the ball park."

The door opened for Scarborough, who signaled down to Iva and Rags, and the three of them were scooped inside. They followed a man in a striped shirt through a long, narrow hall and into a half-empty bar that smelled of mahogany, beer, and nickel plate. The man said goodbye to "Humpty Dumpty" and returned to his post at the door.

Rags frowned at the brute. "How come you're Humpty Dumpty on Darling Street?"

"You can't get in without a dummy name. That's the way it works."

It must have been a baseball saloon, because Rags spotted five of the Boston Braves: Cotton Charles, Mickey O'Neill, Hod Ford, and two utility men. They smiled at Scarborough, saying, "Hiya, Hump, how's the Sox?" They winked at Muggsy, but they refused to look at Rags. The Boston Braves didn't talk to rookies in their favorite saloon.

Rags shrugged at their insult and ordered wine and soda water for Muggsy and himself. He didn't have to watch over the brute. Scarborough was lord of the saloon. He stole a cocktail shaker from the barman and filled it with gin. He drank from the shaker, with fat Humpty Dumpty lips.

The wine and soda water loosened Iva's tongue. She growled the words of a song she remembered from Hollis' show, using the drunken voice of a man.

> *Eveline, Eveline, won't you wait for me?*
> *I die on the road*
> *Thinking of you.*

Cotton Charles clapped from his table. "I know that," he said, wagging a finger at Muggsy. "That's the love song from *Eveline* . . . hey, Hump, your boss Hollis laid a blue egg. His show stinks."

"There's a show that stinks worse than *Eveline*," Rags said. "It's called the Boston Braves."

Cotton Charles leapt up in a fury. "This is a decent house. Bushers aint supposed to talk."

Rags had a fury of his own gnawing at him. His face was like a bloody hood. You could only see bits of his eyes. "I know who I am, Mr. Charles. I'm Babe Ragland, and I wear a rookie's glove. I always respect my betters. But I don't have to play a deaf mute in the company of a turd."

It was funny talk for a bastard, Scarborough figured to himself. How many orphans learned to speak like that? But the hunchback had other considerations. "Rags, there's five of them, and only two of us."

"Don't forget Muggsy. Muggsy can fight."

The barman didn't have to oversee any squabbling between the Red Sox and the Braves. He beckoned to the man in the striped shirt. The man touched Scarborough on the shoulder. "Sorry, Hump, your friend the busher will have to go."

Rags wasn't inclined to move, but Scarborough squeezed his calf under the table, and he chose not to ignore a direct signal from the brute. He got up with Muggsy and left the saloon. Scarborough came out a minute later, while Rags sulked on Darling Street.

"Why did you take that guff? I have quicker hands than any gorilla in a striped shirt."

"That gorilla happens to be from the Homicide Bureau. The saloon hires him as a sheriff once or twice a week."

"What kind of frigging world is this, where cops can become babysitters in a Boston speakeasy?"

"The same frigging world that stole Babe Ruth from us and turned the Sox into a cemetery."

"Who cares about Babe Ruth?" Muggsy said. "I'm tired. I have to get some sleep."

They brought her up to the room, but they didn't know how to arrange for Miz Iva. It baffled them to live with a girl. The toilet was out in the hall, and one of the Boston players might see her if she tried to undress in there. They would have to curtain off a little den for her in the room. Muggsy didn't need a den. She borrowed a pair of the brute's pajamas and undressed behind the window drapes. She had no trouble sleeping with the two men. Scarborough and Rags kept to the corners, and she occupied the middle zones of the bed.

Rags brooded in his pajamas. The Boston papers were swearing he had a fiancée. RAGLAND TO MARRY ICE HEIRESS' DAUGHTER (the Cottonmouths had made their money manufacturing ice). But it wasn't an engagement worth talking about. How can you have a fiancée and not be able to touch her pajama leg? He had to squeeze over to the lumpy end of the mattress, and anchor himself somehow, so he wouldn't fall off the bed.

He was foul-eyed in the morning. His temper started to flair. He woke his bedmates at half-past six and said, "It's time for orange juice." He stuck Iva behind the drapes and told her to get dressed.

"Hold your horses," she snapped at him, but she still pinned up her garter belt and put on her shoes. Scarborough's shirttails were sticking out. Rags wouldn't give him the chance to groom himself. They went over to a coffee shop on Huntington Avenue that was a landmark now, because Babe Ruth had eaten there every morning when he first came to the Sox. Ruth would order twenty strips of bacon and ten scrambled eggs, and cover everything with ketchup. Rags didn't have Ruth's appetite. The most he could suck on were three soft-boiled eggs. The owners of the shop were careful with him. The Sox may have been a team of vagabonds, but the kid was Boston's new sensation. They wouldn't slight the seventh Babe.

"Eggs, Mr. Ragland?"

"Yeah, eggs for all of us. And orange juice."

The three of them ate their eggs in silence. Rags' foulness began to lift. "Did you sleep well, Miz Muggsy?"

"Well enough, but one of you has long toenails. My ankles are scratched."

"That's me," Scarborough confessed. "It's unlucky to cut your toes. It could put us on a losing streak."

"Cut 'em," Rags said. "We can't lose any more than we're losing now."

They walked Muggsy to the motorbus that would take her to Woods Hole, where she could catch the ferry to her mother's island. She gave Rags and Scarborough each a loud kiss and got on the bus. "See you in September or October," she said from her piece of the window. The fragrance of her kiss was lost in the fumes of the motorbus. But Rags didn't forget the impression of her teeth and the wet smack of her lips. Muggsy's lips. He wouldn't have a fiancée to think about until October. Maybe the gossip columns would leave him alone.

5

Boston had two dead dogs on its hands, the Braves and the Sox. But you couldn't sweep them away. Dead as they were, the dogs had real properties: groundsmen and players, dirt and yellow grass, grandstands, scoreboards, a hundred thousand frankfurters, and a legion of lemonade boys. You had to let the dogs lie still, or the frankfurters would rot and the grass would run wild, invade the stands, and throw splinters into the brick walls. The fans learned how to live with these dogs of baseball, who had their own dogs' war; they were so far down in the losing columns, they seemed to exist outside the major leagues.

The faithful still had their sport. They took bets: who would be the first to lose a hundred games, the Red Sox or the Braves? Briggs didn't care what went on at Braves Field. He wasn't a frigging bookie, and he wouldn't condone such a stupid bet. He drilled his men harder than before. He would give them no free days. They fielded among themselves in empty ball parks, while their opposition ate turkey dinners or swam in country lakes.

He invoked baseball history to inspire the Sox. "Remember the Miracle Browns of 1914? I was on that club. We were in the cellar for a hundred and sixteen days. Then we started to climb. We went from last to fifth in the month that was left. We damn near murdered the league. We should have been in the Series, not those big elephants, the A's."

"Times was different," Chicken Stallings said. "The Brownies had you, skip. You're worth ten Connie Macks."

"But Boston has the kid . . . no one can wear Ragland's glove."

"He's a forkhander," the Chicken said. "Forkhanders always jinx a club. You think Connie Mack would hire a forkhander to play third?"

"He'd hire the kid faster than he'd hire you," Garl said, and he went back to his Latin and his Greek.

Pep talks and drills couldn't advance the Sox. They'd win and lose, lose and win. July leaked into August, and September landed on the Sox in eighth place. Briggs said goodbye to his men, warning them about the perils of winter baseball. "I'll kill the son of a bitch who breaks a leg in Havana. Go fishing, for God's sake, or look for a wife. Maybe I'll see you bums in Arkansas."

Then he climbed upstairs to the owner's suite. He expected the boss to fire him. The Sox were exactly where he'd found them two years ago: at the bottom of the well.

He couldn't understand what Hollis was smiling about. "Briggs, how much did you steal from me this summer?"

"I didn't steal one bloody dime."

"I'd say you stole six or seven thousand. Isn't that what I'm paying you? I'll have to check."

"You've been paying me six, Hollis. I ought to know my salary."

"That's what I said. *Six*. Well, what if I raised you to six and a half?"

Briggs had been with baseball too long to trust an owner's word on the last day of the season. "Are you asking me to come back next spring?"

"Of course I am. I know the rubes you've had to work with. We collect fodder from the rest of the league. You did the best you could."

Briggs told himself Hollis was a lunatic. *He sells his players and then blames the team.* But the skipper understood—Hollis' mind wasn't on baseball. The boss was dreaming of *Eveline*.

Briggs shook the boss' hand, but he'd forget baseball until a contract arrived in the mail. You couldn't tell what would happen in 1924. Some wise developer might turn Fenway into a skating rink. The Sox would disappear from baseball, and Boston would be a one-team town. Briggs scratched his jaw. God help a city that had to depend on the Boston Braves.

The Sox could have lost ten more games, and Hollis wouldn't have cared. Owning a ballclub was a fool's occupation. But he enjoyed seeing himself on the metal plate in Fenway's front wall. BOSTON AMERICAN LEAGUE BASEBALL COMPANY. HOLLIS MCKEE, PRESIDENT. Who else had twenty-five dummies in red and white suits that he could barter with, buy or sell any day of the week? It was like swapping toy soldiers. Hollis paid them, and they had to bite their tongues. He picked up as many Dartmouth men as he could. He was loyal to his college. But it wasn't only that. He didn't want to shame Boston with a band of shoeless country boys.

Besides, Hollis was an impresario, a man who created musical comedies. He'd have sold his Sox if the chance came along. It never did. No one would have the Red Sox. He offered them to the governor of Massachusetts, a friend of his. "Bob, let the Commonwealth take my boys. You can bicker over who to buy and who to sell at the Old State House."

The governor laughed, but he didn't want the Sox. Hollis winked at him. He was bringing *Eveline* to Broadway. *Eveline* would arrive at the Morosco in another week. It couldn't miss. It would make up for the half million he'd lost on his last two shows. He hired a special train to deliver him and ninety-five guests to Manhattan. There would be congressmen on board and the governor himself. They could close one eye when the whiskey went around. Hollis invited Garland James, Rags, and the Cottonmouths, who'd just come home from Tisbury. He didn't like ballplayers to mix with his theatrical friends. Garl and Rags were the only two Red Sox on the train.

Rags had to buy monkey clothes for the launching of *Eveline*. He sat in a boiled shirt, with a collar that pinched his neck, and a tie that nearly strangled him. A servant (it was Rhys) traveled down the aisles of the car, ladling quantities of hot rum with a golden spoon that he would dip into a great wooden vat on wheels. A flame sputtered in the middle of the vat, and filled the car with a sulfurous smell. Rags had to sneeze. He wiped his nose with a towel that he lifted from the servant's pocket. He kept sneaking looks at Marylou. She wore a marvelous black cape that only covered half her body. Capes were getting shorter and shorter that year.

She couldn't have noticed Rags. All she did was stare at Garl. "Garland James, why don't you ever come to see us on Beacon Hill?"

"It's not that simple, ma'am. It's hard to visit when you're playing ball."

"But the season's over."

"Not for me, Miz Marylou. I go barnstorming next week with the Heilmann All-Stars."

"That's not the reason," she exclaimed. She was getting bolder with Garl. "You always have a good story."

"I'll try to come, ma'am. I will. I'll pack a day early if I can." Then he excused himself and went into the washroom. Rags followed him in there. Something bothered the kid. He hadn't received a single invitation to join a barnstorming club. What was wrong with him? He had better hands than most third basemen, and nobody wanted him. Even Chicken Stallings had gotten a bid. The Chicken was going to play with Bob Meusel and Babe Ruth.

He unwound that death knot of a tie, dipped his fingers in the water basin, and said to Garl, "Can Harry Heilmann use another hand at third, Mr. James?"

"I don't think so, kid, but I'll ask."

Garl noticed Ragland's sullen eyes.

"You didn't get a bid, did you?"

"I guess I could play winter ball in some outlaw league."

"That would be dumb. You could get fined for doing that. Keep away from the outlaws."

The outlaw leagues were made up of professionals who had been suspended for life by the commissioner of baseball, Judge Kenesaw Mountain Landis. The Judge declared that whoever played with them, or was seen in their presence, would be subject to a hundred-dollar fine. The fines were impossible to revoke, since the owners themselves had little power over the Judge.

"Don't worry," Garl said. "You'll get your bid. But you'll have to sit out a year. Heilmann won't take on a rookie, no matter how spectacular he is. That's the rule."

"Funny rule, if it keeps a man from playing."

"I didn't invent baseball, kid. It happens to everybody. Don't bitch. Harry Heilmann wouldn't even look at me until I was in my third year."

Rags shrugged his shoulders in the gloomy light. "What am I gonna do all winter if I can't play?"

"Run around the Public Garden . . . I don't know."

They walked out of the washroom together and rejoined the Cottonmouths. Iva was peculiar with him. She'd lost that playfulness she had when she'd come to the Brunswick in men's pants. He called her "Miz Muggsy," and she didn't say a thing.

A row of private cabs met Hollis' train in New York. The cabs crawled up Seventh Avenue like a funeral procession and dropped Hollis' ninety-five guests outside the Morosco Theatre. Rags had a seat up front with other members of the "Boston party." The governor of Massachusetts clapped hands with anyone who came his way. Rags failed to see how the governor could gather votes in New York. But politics was a crazy business.

A woman sitting behind Rags touched him on the shoulder. "Oh, my God, aren't you Babe Ragland of the Red Sox?"

There was no use denying who he was in a public theatre. "Yes, ma'am. I'm the Babe."

"Haven't the Yankees gotten around to buying you yet?"

"I'd rather play for the Sox, ma'am. Does New York City have a wild park like the Fens? A park with alligators and rats that can fly? I'll stay in Boston and live near the swamp."

Rags felt the point of a shoe attack him on the shin. It was Iva's doing. She had the seat next to him. She shouted into his ear. "Do you flirt with any old witch who recognizes your face?"

"I wasn't flirting," Rags said. "Just being polite." But he hunched down in his seat, so other women would find it difficult to tap him on the shoulder. The lights gave three flickers of warning and went out. Ushers barred the aisles to latecomers. The theatre grew still. Rags heard a couple of bassoons. The band was striking up the overture to *Eveline*.

The kid didn't have an ear for music. The fiddlers in the band could have scratched on wooden boards, and it would have been the same to him. He was thinking about the stupid winter he'd have to spend playing pepper ball with Scarborough in the room. He wondered if the hotel would let him swing a bat in the halls.

It could have been a hundred years of overtures. The fiddlers scratched and scratched. He'd have sworn his hair was turning gray inside the Morosco. Had Hollis rigged the thing? Were you supposed to collapse and die before the end of *Eveline?*

The fiddlers stopped. The curtains spread apart with the sound of rattling wind. Nine men in Red Sox uniforms pranced onto the stage. No one could ever believe they were from the majors. Their chests were much too puny. Rags could see the paint on their lips from the third row. Nothing was rumpled about them. Their hands looked soft; they should have been gnarled, with broken knuckle joints. Their uniforms had been pressed before the show.

They were a frigging chorus line that danced and chattered into song. Rags cocked his head, but he couldn't unravel the words. The dancing was too loud. Skinny men in baseball hats pushed themselves and shouted gibberish that only a cossack could have understood. It made no sense, the Red Sox singing Russian songs.

Then the hero arrived. He was fatter than the rest.

> *Eveline, Eveline, won't you wait for me?*
> *I die on the road*
> *Thinking of you.*

There were sniggers behind Rags. The theatre began to empty, and it was still the first act. Hollis was stuck with a fat man who swooned a lot.

The second act was devoted to Eveline and her gang of baseball wives. They could have been hens out of the Boston poultry markets; the red kerchiefs they wore shivered like chicken necks. Their shrill voices brought no sympathy for them. They complained about husbands who took to the road and left them to lie in an idle bed. People hissed openly now.

The third act united Eveline and the fat hero. They performed their duet, kissing, touching, singing with the chorus of men and wives. It was much too late. The charm had gone out of *Eveline*. They were singing in a graveyard. Hollis' own guests had deserted him. There were under twenty spooks in the theatre for the final kiss. Hollis had a stubborn actress playing Eveline's part. She insisted on her curtain calls. She came through the curtain with her eyebrows twitching like the devil. Rags clapped for her. What else could he do?

It was the first and last performance of *Eveline* in New York. Hollis had sunk a fortune into the show. His backers were ready to sue. Hollis had been precipitous with their money, they said. *Eveline* should never have gone to the Morosco. It would have died in Boston if Hollis hadn't paid certain newspapermen to puff the show. Hollis swore it was a lie. "I don't tamper with the critics." He hadn't lost faith in *Eveline*. It needed more work, that's all.

His actors quit. Hollis assembled a new cast. He went into rehearsal at Boston's Colonial Theatre. The papers stood behind him. "A little patching here and there, and *Evy* will be a wonderful show." No backers came forth with additional money. Hollis sank another fifty thousand into *Eveline*, and then he had to tell his actors and actresses to go home.

He consoled himself with a piece of undeniable truth: he still had his Red Sox. "I'm president of a baseball company. Those moneylenders can't grab the Sox away from me."

But it didn't cheer him up. Hollis had nothing but turkeys in his yard: a bum show about the Red Sox and the bums themselves. He was the town fool. Men he didn't even know sang snatches of *Eveline* to him on the street.

> *Evy, Evy, stay with me.*
> *It's hell in Chicago*
> *Grief in Detroit*
> *Without my darlin' wife.*

The boss went into seclusion. He exchanged no words with his employees. He locked his door at Fenway and retired to his rooms at the Ritz-Carlton Hotel. Hollis cast aside the small dignities of his station. He wouldn't put on a robe for the busboy who brought in his afternoon paper, his coffee, and his rye toast. He would stand in his underwear and look out at the Public Garden. Hollis' rooms were on the twelfth floor, and he could see all the way to Charlestown from his window.

Those heartless bastards in New York. I'll rewrite Eveline *myself. I'll play Ferdie Wills. I can sing.* Ferdie Wills was the ballplayer-husband and hero of the show.

The busboy would watch over Hollis while he was in a stupor at the window. "More coffee, Mr. McKee?"

Hollis turned his head. "Rory, can you dance?"

"Dance, sir? No."

"It's a pity. I could have used you in *Eveline*."

He ate his suppers in his room. He didn't go near any of the five Boston clubs that had him on their membership lists. He would have been bored to death discussing the ups and downs of baseball with merchants and vestrymen who'd never been on the road with the Sox, and hadn't endured spring training at Sackville Forest. He could visit one of the bordellos on Gloucester Street. But whores were a chatty lot. Hollis was a little more anonymous without his clothes. Yet the girls always recognized him by the incision he had across his belly, where his appendix had been removed as a child. They called him the man with the scar. The man with the scar was rich. He owned the Boston Red Sox. The whores would only ask him about Garland James if he went to Gloucester Street. They loved his dark handsomeness. "Why don't you bring your center fielder, Mr. McKee? We'll play catch with him. We'll be careful he doesn't bend his thing."

Sometimes, in a panic, he would pray that Judah Cottonmouth was still alive. Judah had been his one good friend. They'd survived the snobberies of Old Boston together, became mavericks, choosing Dartmouth over Harvard, Amherst, and Williams. Judah could make him laugh. He'd throw spinach under the table at the Algonquin Club. He'd piss in the same urinal with Hollis' ballplayers. They'd lie with a single whore half the night, ravage her, grow bored, ravage her again, drop cigar ashes on her belly, stuff a hundred dollars in her quim. He'd go on mourning Judah. How many bloodbrothers could a man have?

Hollis went walking after dark. He'd climb down the back stairs, so he wouldn't have to nod like a monkey on the elevator, and he'd exit from the hotel on Newbury Street. It was past the shopping hour. Bostonians had gone home to have their baked beans. Hollis could travel on foot without being sneered at. He was forty-one years old. He'd had three hits on Broadway. An American League franchise belonged to him. He was the man who sold Babe Ruth. Money turned to clay in his fists, kindergarten clay, red, blue, and yellow. He could twirl a million dollars out of that clay, and then lose it all. His existence seemed poisoned to him. *Eveline* was his only passion.

Foolishly, his walk had taken him near the Brunswick Hotel. He couldn't avoid Babe Ragland. The kid had gone out for an ice-cream soda. He was crossing Brookline Avenue. "Ragland, hello."

Rags hadn't seen the boss in a month. Hollis had deep gray circles under his eyes. He could have been a wax man who decided to wiggle his arms and talk.

"Have you been laying in for winter, Ragland, or what?"

"They wouldn't let me barnstorm, Mr. McKee. I'm stuck in Boston."

"So am I," Hollis said. "Here, I'll sign my name on a card, and you can play billiards at my club. Stay with billiards, and the winter will go fast."

Rags took the little card that was offered him. "Thank you, Mr. McKee, but I don't play billiards. Baseball's what I like. Me and Scarborough have been throwing the ball around. The hotel empties in November. So there's lots of room for us."

"How's your fiancée?"

"Miz Iva? She don't have much time for me now. She's studying poetry at school."

"Well, you wouldn't want to marry a girl who didn't get good grades, would you, Ragland?"

"I guess not," Rags said.

"Good boy. Don't you catch the sniffles. Winter colds are hard to get rid of, and I'll need you at third. You're not a rookie anymore. Remember that. Briggs isn't the only expert in this town. I can measure what a man is worth." He pumped Rags' hand, said, "See you in Arkansas, son," and went right on with his walk.

It was a dog's winter in town. The hunchback would go to speakeasies and tank up as often as he liked, but Rags didn't have the urge to drink. He would arrive at Fenway in battered cleats, shout until the gatekeeper let him in, and he'd run on frozen dirt. That was his occupation, except for pepper games with the hunchback. He figured cotton would start to grow in his head if the calendar didn't shake loose and come to February, so he could pack for Arkansas.

Once, deep in November, Miz Iva came looking for him at the hotel. She wasn't Miss Muggsy now. She wore a green blazer and long woolen socks. The green showed well with her hair. She was a day student at Miss Drabble's School for Girls on Chestnut Street.

"Funny you should remember me," Rags said. "I thought the engagement is off."

"That's a lie. Miss Drabble works us like donkeys, or I'd make you court me every night."

"How'd you get up to the room? Didn't the house dick notice you was a girl?"

"Oh, him? He's blind. Where's your roommate?"

"Drinking whiskey somewheres."

She stood Rags against the wall and kissed him with the full resources of her mouth. Rags couldn't say why his hands began to crawl. They were inside the blazer and under her blouse. Her breasts hardened to Rags' touch. They were much more swollen than Marylou's.

"My leg hurts," she bawled at him. "Are you going to undress me standing up?"

Rags grew aware of his fingers and he pulled away from Iva's blouse. "What if Scarborough comes back?"

"We'll give him a few nickels and tell him to blow."

Iva shed everything she had and went under the covers with Rags. He sat on her, chewing her back, his erection jumping up her spine. "You'd better not go in, Rags. Mama will kill me if I'm not a virgin when I get to the house."

The blood twisted in Rags' ears, and his penis turned profoundly blue, but he didn't penetrate Miz Iva. All that touching in bed seemed like torture to Rags. Iva began to dress in half an hour. "I'll visit you, sweetheart, soon as I can. And don't you ever think we're not engaged."

Rags had to walk around with a blue penis; thank God the swelling went down, or he couldn't have played pepper ball in the room. The snows had come to Boston when Iva knocked on his door again. She met Rags in a pair of filthy boots. He had to crouch in front of her and tug at the heels before her boots would come off. He sweated in the cold from all the pulling he had to do (steam at the Brunswick was an irregular affair). They accomplished the ritual of undressing themselves. They had their rigid play under the covers, kissing and a scrape of hands. Rags' knees shivered with lust. He had the same blue prick. "Couldn't we get married tonight?"

"Don't be a silly boy. Miss Drabble doesn't take wives into her school. And we'd need a home. I'm not living at the Brunswick Hotel."

"What kind of home can you get on a Red Sox salary?"

Iva stared at him as if he were the Boston idiot. "Hollis makes allowances for married men."

"He's already paying me double," Rags said.

"Who cares? Mama and him will provide for us."

But there was no more talk of houses and stipends for married players. It was the last he saw of Iva in the winter of 1923. Rags hiked up and down the halls for exercise. It was much too bitter outside to run in Fenway Park. He was more of a bachelor now than somebody's fiancé. He dined in soup kitchens with bums from the railroad yards. The brute had his speakeasies. Iva had her school. Rags went into winter shock. He could invent the sound of a ball rushing through dry yellow grass. That sound preserved whatever sanity he had left.

By February he was a frozen stick. He stuttered and blinked. The house detective would have hurled him into the street if he didn't know it was Rags under all that stubble on his chin. "Mr. Ragland, you look sorrowful, if you ask me. You have to prepare your mind for the Boston winter. It takes some disciplining. You crawl under your own skin like the grizzly bear, and one eye sleeps while the other's awake. That's the trick. You can die in Boston if you don't follow the grizzly bear."

"You should have told me that in October. I might have learned from it. But that's okay. We're going to Arkansas."

"Best of luck. I hope you boys get to the top. I'd like to make a pile on you. Only Hollis McKee'd have to disappear before that happens. That man's ruined us all."

Scarborough and Rags were the first scrubs to arrive at Sackville Forest. Icicles hung from their window at the team's boarding-house. The hammock on the front porch was stiff as a dead man's arm. The playing field sat under a curtain of ice. "Where the hell are the Red Sox?" Rags groaned. "Aint this the month of February?"

Rags had insulted the brute. "Mister, I know what month I'm living in. Skipper's smarter than us, that's all. He can sniff the air in these parts. He'll open camp when the weather's right."

The Sox began to dribble into town, one by one, with red eyes, long beards, and shaggy tails. Since when did Arkansas pirates break into the major leagues? They could have been hill people down from the Ozarks for a look at the civilized life of a baseball camp. But there was no baseball camp. Nothing but red eyes and shaggy tails. Chicken Stallings still had the trace of a sunburn on his nose. He blabbered about his times with Babe Ruth.

"Me and the Babe socked the hell out of them coons in Havana. The Babe won't bat against a colored boy until he crosses himself. They're devils on the mound. All you can see is them nigger eyes. The Babe asked for an extra thousand in Havana, and he got it. I didn't have trouble swinging against the coons. I hit three triples one day, off the blackest man on this earth. I figured how to get to him. I just didn't look at his eyes."

"You must have paid that coon to sweeten the ball," Tilly Young said. "You never hit a triple in your life."

But you couldn't train on Chicken's stories, or Tilly's rebukes. Then, as the boys grew surly feasting eyes on each other, Briggs appeared. He was a fox about the weather: the ice had begun to crack on the playing field. He stood quiet for a few days and wouldn't stir from the boardinghouse; then he ordered the Sox to get into their practice suits. They didn't play ball. They chopped through the ice with their bats, and that was the opening of Briggs' camp at Sackville Forest in 1924.

One man was late: Garl missed the ice-chopping ceremonies. He didn't play pepper on the muddy field. The "A" and "B" squad teams began without him. Rookies were invading Sackville Forest. Rags was insufferable to them. He'd developed a mean sophomore streak. His own bitterness surprised him. Why was he so quick to jump on those rooks? "Hey, busher, tie your shoes. This aint Paducah. It's the Red Sox training grounds."

The hunchback would scowl when he saw Rags join up with the Chicken or Germany Stone to taunt a new kid.

"You sure have a lean memory, brother Rags. Those country boys stuck you in the ribs during your rookie days."

"That's baseball," Rags said. "That's how it goes."

"Who says you have to keep up that shit?"

"I do. Ask Briggs. You'd rot to hell in Arkansas if you didn't have a few rookies to make you laugh . . . hey, where's Garl?"

"Garl knows how to find us. He'll get here when it's ripe for him to come."

So Rags went to the boardinghouse and picked the icicles off his window; the hunchback had ruined his taste for rookie-busting. The Sox looked scruffier than last year's team. Rags was waiting for Garl. Garl would pull these bushers together, create the Bosox of 1924.

He arrived in camp the first week of March. having walked out of some Nicaraguan jungle. The clothes were peeling on his back. His hands were scarred. But he didn't have winter fat on him. Garl came ready to play. The Chicken could brag about Babe Ruth. But it was kid stuff. The Babe would go wherever he was adored. His suite of followers lived at the best hotels in Havana and San Juan. He didn't hack out baseball diamonds with a machete and field a team of mestizos, convicts, and Nicaraguan Indians, like Garland James. Ruth barnstormed in white pants, with golf clubs and his own personal caddie, and enough ketchup and mustard to last him through the winter. Grown men and women would pay a dollar a head to watch him swing from his ankles. He was the most beloved giant in the world.

Garl was just a center fielder with a last-place team. He had seventeen triples in 1923 and batted .311, but he didn't hit more than five home runs. He wasn't beautiful when he struck out, like the Babe could be, his ankles hooked, and his body twisting into an incredible corkscrew machine. Garl only struck out eleven times.

His barnstorming was a different thing. Reporters didn't follow him. No one kept a record of his hits. He didn't have mustard raids and ketchup fights. He started in October with the Heilmann All-Stars, snaking down to Florida, leapfrogging across the provinces of Cuba, and ended winter baseball on his own. Who could be sure how many mestizos he converted to the game?

It didn't matter now. The Sox had him in short center field. The other outfielders wouldn't bump around, or crack a tooth with Garl there, signaling them away from the ball.

The ice lifted off Sackville Forest that week of Garl's arrival; tiny green stubs broke out of the muddy earth, as if Garl had come onto the playing field at midnight and put them in the ground. The Sox had a miraculous planter on their club. The rookies idolized him. "Can you show me how to grab the bat, Mr. James? I'm not getting any wood."

"Take a wider grip. You're not Babe Ruth."

The rookies kept away from Ragland, who guarded his terrain at third. You couldn't field with Rags. He ate up every grounder that fell within twenty yards of him. "Hey, you bushers, get out of my friggin' territory." The Sox didn't need a left fielder in Arkansas. Rags could chase down any fly that got to the left-field wall. But he wouldn't move into Garland's spot. He avoided center field.

He began drinking moonshine with the country boys. The Chicken took him into their irascible club. He wasn't a "kid" on the Bosox anymore. He was Babe Ragland. The country boys made room for him on the porch. They needed a strong ally against the Dartmouth men, who still dominated the Red Sox. Rags was replacing Germany Stone as their leader. They didn't bring up his obscure birth. Suppose he was an orphan. A bastard couldn't hurt, and who else among them would stand up to Garl? Something made them uneasy. They couldn't have Rags without the brute, and they detested Scarborough. "I can swallow as many bastards as you can find," the Chicken muttered to himself. "A freak of nature is something else. That has to be the unluckiest son of a bitch in the United States."

But Scarborough didn't intend to join their pack. He wouldn't run with bullies and practical jokers, who victimized cats, dogs, and any poor kid who came for a tryout with the Sox. The hunch-back roomed with Rags, but otherwise he was alone.

That same mysterious man, a certain Mr. Griffey, who'd argued with Rags in St. Louis and called him "Cedric," showed up at camp. He was a persistent bird, this Mr. Griffey. He kept stalking Rags. He would drink soda pop, rent a chair from the boarding-house, and watch Ragland play. He wasn't living in Sackville Forest. He'd come every morning from someplace else. Maybe the bird had a bungalow at Hot Springs.

The brute wouldn't spy on Rags, but he couldn't help hearing them scream.

"You've had your fun, your little immersion in baseball," the man said to Rags. "Now it's got to end. Your father won't tolerate much more of this."

"He'll have to tolerate it, Mr. Griffey. I'm not grubbing here. I'm on salary. I'd rather be a third-stringer than have to shine my father's shoes."

"Who said anything about shoes? Cedric, your father doesn't want you to beg. But his patience is being used up. I'm warning you. Get out of this wretched mud hole, resign on your own, or else . . ."

Rags must have had some moonshine in him. He grabbed ol' Griffey by the bottom of his coat, twisted all that material, and threw him down the boardinghouse steps. Griffey stopped haunt-ing Sackville Forest. And Rags continued to laze on the porch with the dumbest part of the team.

Then the lord of the Red Sox came to town. Hollis had two showgirls with him, Nancy and Edna Mae. He was breaking them into the musical business, he said. They sat on his lap, took mousy bites out of his eyebrows, and spoke in baby language, but these girls had a feeling for the hierarchy of a baseball club. They would only flirt with Dartmouth men and the seventh Babe. Hollis pun-ished them with a slap on their knuckles soon as they went near Rags. "That boy's engaged. He's going to marry my dead friend's little girl."

"But he's a honey, Mr. McKee. I'll bet he's wild as hell."

"It's not for you, Edna Mae. He has to save all that wildness for his wife."

The girls were only a decoration for Hollis. He hadn't come to Arkansas to philander with Nancy and Edna Mae. He was looking to arrange an exhibition series for his Red Sox.

"Hollis," Briggs said. "I know Emma Raines. She'd tour with us."

"Who's this Emma?"

"She owns the Cincinnati Colored Giants with her husband Carl."

"You must be out of your skull," Hollis said. "Mix my boys with a nigger outfit? Those Giants play too rough."

"It's only a tour, Hollis. I could advise Emma to take it slow."

"Slow, huh? I heard what they did to the Cardinals the year before last. Crippled half their men. You can keep your Colored Giants. We'll stick to the college circuit."

"Excuse me, Hollis, but we won't draw shit."

"We'll draw," Hollis said. "Just you wait a while."

The boss was right. His Sox went to Fayetteville for a five-game series with the U. of Arkansas and sold out the park. The fans had heard of Briggs' sophomore wonder, and they wanted to see him catch and throw. What other team had a lefty at third? They weren't disappointed in Rags. They saw a whirlwind cover third base. That body would leap out of nowhere to untwist a line drive and turn the double play.

The Sox were on fire in all the college towns. They sold out wherever Hollis could book a game. But a band of crows was following them around. Rags saw these crows. They had a Buick with an open top. The Buick's sides were made of mahogany. The crows would rest on this mahogany and watch Briggs' team. They never paid admission. They would park their Buick across from the playing field and eat out of paper bags. They had the pinkest gums in Kentucky, where the Sox were right now. They could have been Negro undertakers. All the crows wore dark suits.

Rags went to Scarborough. "Who are these guys?"

"Sockamayocks."

"Talk plain, will you? What's a sockamayock?"

"They're scrubs from the Cincinnati Colored Giants."

"Why the hell are they following us?"

"It's an honor, Rags. They must be scouting you."

"You crazy? I'm with the Red Sox. I aint signing with no Colored Giants. Are they figuring to steal me away?"

Scarborough smiled at Rags' stupidity. "That's how sockamayocks make their living. Sometimes they act as scouts. It means you aint a kid anymore. The Colored Giants have heard of you, and they're aiming to copy your style. They do that with everybody in the big leagues who's more than a little good. They got a man who plays like Hornsby, a man who plays like Heilmann and a man who plays like Garl. It's an act with them. They stop a game after five innings and pretend they're Heilmann and Cobb. There's a nigger on the Giants that you'd swear was Babe Ruth."

"How come you're such an expert on the Cincinnati Giants?"

"Skipper took us to see them play, that's how come."

"Well, if they're imitating people, they must be clowns."

"They have to clown to stay alive," Scarborough said. "The Cincinnati Giants are the best team in baseball. Ask Mr. Briggs. Even the sockamayocks in that car could tear the hell out of us."

"Undertakers couldn't beat the Red Sox. If you're so cushy with them, why don't you ask the sockamayocks if they want to play?"

The brute slouched in front of Rags. "I wish I could. The boss wouldn't let us into a game with them. He says it'll hurt our image if the Sox are caught on the same field with the Cincinnati Giants."

They didn't have to argue about it. The crows disappeared. Rags didn't need sockamayocks around him to play. He dazzled every little town and humiliated all the college babies.

Book Two

BOSTON AND THE COPPER KID

6

THE SOX OPENED in Philadelphia that year. They'd feasted on college pitching for over a month, and they expected the A's to lie down for them like the U. of Arkansas had done. The A's trimmed them, 5–2. Hollis was still in a cheerful mood. The Sox made a bundle for him on their spring tour. He could lose one to the A's. So what? His men turned around and buried the Athletics, 13–3. Garl homered into the roof, and Rags had a pair of doubles. The Sox split four games and got out of Philadelphia.

They didn't come home to an empty house. The Royal Rooters were at Back Bay Station to welcome Rags and the Red Sox. They brought xylophones and straw hats that their wives had painted red. Briggs had never seen the station so packed. *They're forgetting Babe Ruth, they're forgetting Babe Ruth.* Hollis dreamed of turnstiles. The idea of dollars at the gate got him to quit brooding over the failure of *Eveline*. He planned on thirty thousand for Opening Day at Fenway Park.

Those red-hatted Boston zealots serenaded Rags with a song, beating out the music on their xylophones with little wooden claws.

> *You can keep your Yankees and your Browns*
> *We have the true boy*
> *He can hop and skip*

Our Babe's a grownup now
Red Sox, Red Sox, 1924

The Royal Rooters would have carried Rags to his hotel, but he wouldn't allow it. "Thanks," he said. "I've got my own two feet." He kept giving his autograph away as he proceeded through the station.

There was a party for the Sox at the Brunswick Hotel. The manager had ordered wieners and a tub of sauerkraut from Jacob Worth & Co. Rags nibbled on a wiener and announced he was going to bed. The dark hadn't come to Boston yet. It was two o'clock in the afternoon, and Rags had a troubled sleep. Lizards crawled on his body. His toes were in muddy water. He must have stepped into the Boston swamp. Only Rags would dream of the Fens on his first day back. What was he trying to do? Walk across the swamp? He could hear sobbing in the Fens. The sobbing grew louder. It wrenched inside his head. Were the lizards crying for him? The sobs had a tremor that didn't seem strange. Rags opened his eyes.

The brute was sitting on the bed. His face was wet. A shudder went through the hump on his back. He was holding a newspaper. But he didn't look down at the words. He mewled something to Rags.

Rags couldn't understand him because of the sobs the brute was making. "What are you crying about?"

"You aint nothin' but a two-star fake. Talking to me like you come out of an orphanage when you're a college baby, like the rest."

Rags spread open the front page of the *Evening Transcript*. A headline barked out at him from the top. RICHES TO RAGS.

"Who wrote that shit?"

There was no name under the headline, just a photograph of Rags wearing his freshman beanie at Amherst College. And a caption that said he was Cedric Tannehill, the son of a copper millionaire.

The sight of that hump moving up and down on Scarborough's back filled Rags with loathing for himself. "You must think I'm the dumbest man in America," Scarborough said.

"Scarborough, I had to lie . . . it was the only way I could get on the team."

"I'm your roommate. You didn't have to lie to me."

"I would have told you, I swear."

But the brute turned his back on him. Rags got into his clothes

and crept out the door. He barreled through the lobby with such a
hard look that no one dared yell "Cedric" at him. He invaded the
Transcript's offices on Washington Street. He stood in the ancient
city room, with slow-eyed reporters and copyboys snoring behind
a multitude of desks. Rags woke them with a frightful scream.
"I'm Babe Ragland. Who wrote this about me?"

The reporters stared up at him while the copyboys ducked out
of the room.

"Take me to the son of a bitch."

The reporters rubbed their eyes and began to have a faint recol-
lection of Rags.

"Will you answer me? Where's the yellow bastard who's been
monkeying with my life?"

The reporter closest to Ragland gave a shrug.

"Hell, Babe. The story came to us. We don't know how."

"You'd better start remembering," Rags said, "or I'll finish this
place. I'm pretty good at throwing desks out the window."

Two night watchmen arrived. They had giant billy clubs, and
badges pinned to their chest. They couldn't grit their teeth at Rags.
They were Irishmen from Columbus Park, and the loyalest of Red
Sox fans. "For the love of God, Babe, will you go home now? The
rat who says you're Tannehill will stew in Hell. Let one lad desert
you at the ball park, and we'll chop off his nose."

Rags grumbled out a smile. The watchmen wouldn't let him
depart until he scratched "Babe Ragland" on their billies. The
copyboys had come back. Rags waved goodbye and left the *Evening Transcript*.

Babe Ruth was in town. He'd come for Opening Day with the
hunchback, Henry Watteau, and all the other Yanks. There wasn't
a seat to buy. Hollis stuck the overflow crowd in "Duffy's Cliff,"
that sharp embankment in left field named for Duffy Lewis. The
great Duff didn't need a piece of leather on his hand. He carried
an extra shoe. He climbed that crazy hill from 1910 to 1917 and
chased fly balls under the tongue of his third shoe. Not even Garl
could equal that.

You couldn't find a Yankee fan in the overflow on "Duffy's
Cliff." The Boston faithful wouldn't have allowed mongrels and
halfwits among them. They didn't sing a word about Babe Ruth.
They had a Babe of their own, and it wasn't important now if he
was a bastard, or the son of a millionaire. The *Globe* could scream
whatever it liked this morning. Copper magnate? Marcus Tannehill? King of the Southwest? What did the faithful know about
copper and the Southwest?

They mocked Ruth during Yankee batting practice. And they were furious at Henry Watteau. The Yankee hunchback was going to retire at the end of the month. Henry had a weak heart. He crouched in the dugout as much as he could. But a mascot had to do more than hide. Henry had to go onto the field and face those Boston lunatics. They called him "Babe Ruth's little man," because he would bring out bicarbonate of soda in a tall glass whenever the Bambino had one of his monster bellyaches.

It frightened him to be on Boston land. Henry could feel the pounding of his heart. He thought it would break through his ribs and leave him with a bloody wound inside his jersey. Baseball had never been kind to its brutes. It would pit one hunchback against the other. Henry could see an evil glint from the Boston dugout. Scarborough's eyes were burning into him. He didn't have the energy this year to frighten little girls and make a fist at Scarborough. Damn the Boston brute!

Scarborough wasn't thinking of Henry Watteau. *Tannehill* was in his head. The Sox had planted a college baby in his room. They'd stuck him with a rich boy, a rich boy who tells lies. The hunchback looked around: there wasn't any furor in the dugout. No one seemed disturbed by Rags' masquerade. The Dartmouth men snubbed him as much as they ever did. Could Rags talk Sophocles, like Garland James? He was still a fresh kid who had bumped their own man, Snake Attreau, off third base. And what about the country boys? They didn't shy away from Rags. The country boys were in awe of him; their new leader had gone to college. They didn't have to take guff from ol' Garl. Amherst was as fine a place as Dartmouth and Cornell.

Scarborough couldn't accomplish much on his own silly steam. Who would side with him? He didn't catch the skipper scolding Rags. He was one man against his roommate, Cedric, the copper kid. He felt a pair of baseball knickers brush past him. The knickers belonged to Rags.

"Aint you gonna talk to me ever again?"

The brute was furious. "Don't give me that rookie palaver. Orphans use *aint*. Not you. Nobody says aint at Amherst anymore."

Rags had to take the field with the rest of the Sox. There was a maddening roar soon as his head emerged from the dugout. "Rags, Rags, Rags." He trotted alongside the Red Sox announcer, Bull Weingarten, who was carrying his megaphone up to home plate. He had to shout at Bull to make himself heard over that constant roaring of his pet name.

"Listen, Bull, I'm still Babe Ragland. If you call me Cedric in front of everybody, I'll jam that foghorn down your throat."

Bull's eyelashes fluttered in the Boston wind. "We'll settle this in the tunnel," he told Rags. Bull was sixty-three. He had the strongest tonsils in baseball, but he couldn't have danced in the tunnel with an eighteen-year-old kid.

Rags could tell the stupid thing he'd done. Bull wouldn't scorn a Red Sox player. He wasn't disloyal to Rags. The kid said, "I'm sorry. I shouldn't have . . ."

He went to third base with his shoulders hanging down. "Rags, Rags, Rags. We love Rags." That roaring couldn't revive him. Who was he? Cedric Tannehill, or the seventh Babe? His roomie slept on a little hump at the edge of the mattress, as far from Rags as it was humanly possible to be.

Bull Weingarten startled Rags out of his dreamy condition. Bull stood near home plate with his feet spread apart and spit into that leather funnel. He was the only announcer on this earth who could quiet a Boston crowd. Even "Duffy's Cliff" stopped quacking and listened to the Bull. He went through the Yankee batting order without much of a stir from the boys and girls of Fenway Park. The fans had lost interest in jeering Babe Ruth.

Bull took the Boston names out of his vest pocket. "Batting first for Boston and playing second base is Seaman Schupp, our kid from Notre Dame." He knew how to string out a man's title, Bull did. The crowd was going crazy.

"Batting second and playing shortstop is Old Reliable, Alvin Critz." Then it was Tilly Young and his Phi Beta Kappa key; Garland James of Dartmouth, the clean-up man. "Batting fifth and playing first base is the boy from Ronkonkoma, New York, Germany Stone."

Bull had the park in his grip. He wiped his mouth with a handkerchief and raised his funnel again. "Batting sixth and playing third is the sophomore sensation, Babe Ragland out of Baltimore and the St. Mary's orphan school league."

A peculiar bedlam broke out in "Duffy's Cliff." You could see the snaky rhythm of six thousand shoulders, as the men and women on that hill began to scream like demented cats. "We got an orphan here." The whole stadium picked it up.

"Orphan, orphan, we got an orphan here."

The fans had defied the newspaper stories. They believed in their little bastard. Rags' shoulders straightened. He began to smile. *I'm Ragland. I play third.*

Bull called out the tail end of the lineup and trotted away with his leather funnel. Rags went into his familiar crouch at third, swinging on his knees, his head low, his knuckles in the dirt. The Yankees hooted at him from the dugout steps. "Talk to us, Cedric baby. How's the copper market? Can you buy us some shares? Tell us, do orphans like to play with copper shit?''

Rags didn't care. He had ''Duffy's Cliff'' behind him. He went to his left for a mean chopper and threw out the Yankee's first man, Whitey Witt. He turned to look into the owner's box. The Cottonmouths weren't there. Hollis sat by himself this afternoon.

He wished Miz Iva and Miz Marylou had come to smile at him and scream *orphan* with his other fans. But he could hit without his fiancée. He socked the ball into ''Duffy's Cliff'' in the fourth inning. It was a ground-rule double that drove in Alvin and Garl, and put the Sox ahead, 2–0.

Babe Ruth tripled in the seventh with none away. ''Kid,'' he yelled to Rags. ''Fuck the newspapers. They're out to get orphans like us.''

Kinship with Rags couldn't help the Babe. The Yankees left him stranded on third. When he came up to bat in the ninth, he grimaced and touched his belly. It was a signal for Henry Watteau to arrive with a glass of bicarb. The Babe drank it and belched to the crowd. He was still Babe Ruth, and you could afford to love him a little when your team was two runs ahead. But that love didn't include Henry Watteau. The fans took out their hatred for the Yanks on poor Henry.

''Drink poison, you shrimp.''

Popcorn boxes rained down on the brute. Those that thumped against his back did no harm. But when the sharp edge of a box landed in his face, Henry would go down on his knees. He had a gash along his nose, and different cuts on his ears. Blood trickled onto his Yankee blouse. None of the Yanks jumped off the dugout steps to shield the brute and bring him to safety. He wobbled into the dugout on his own and collapsed against the water fountain. He had a gray froth on his tongue. The Yanks forgot to notice him. He was their brute, that's all. They were watching the Babe.

He slapped the ball into the sky over third. It was heading for ''Duffy's Cliff.'' Rags waved off his left fielder, Steve Dubec, and began to chase the ball. He ran on stubble and grass, his elbows pumping at his sides. His knickers were like long white leaping stones in the sun. He got to ''Duffy's Cliff,'' reached in with his hand, and pulled that ball out of the overflow.

Ruth said ''shit'' to Boston. The kid had robbed him of a double. He crossed the infield on his famous pigeon toes, muttering to himself. He didn't see Henry lying near the water fountain. The Bambino was in a rage. He'd lost to the fucking Red Sox in Fenway Park.

7

The Yankee brute woke with his own sad image staring into his face. He wanted to scream for his life. Scarborough was in the same room with him, sitting near his bed. The Boston brute had discovered Henry Watteau in the Yankee dugout and got the Red Sox trainer to call an ambulance. That was three days ago. Henry had gone from the emergency ward to the only private room at Boston City Hospital. The room overlooked a tiny yard where chickenpluckers worked on a mountain of feathers. But Henry hadn't noticed the view. He'd been delirious, moaning, spitting, crying, and begging Red Sox fans to leave him in peace. Now he had Scarborough with him. And it was like a horrible sore, having a fellow brute to look at up close.

"Where's my wife?"

"I called her," Scarborough said. "She's coming on the bus."

Henry sat up in bed, scowling at his double. "You make me sick, you know that? It gives me chest pains just to look at you."

"You aint such a pleasant sight yourself, little man."

Henry began to chuckle. "How long have we been goin' at each other in the ball parks? Two summers? Did I ever bite you on the ear? Lemme see? I'd have bitten them flappers off by now if I didn't have a bad heart. Get out of the game, I'm telling you. Go live in a circus. It's better than being a baseball freak."

"Ah, it aint so bad with the Red Sox . . . hey, Watteau, don't you worry about this room. The Babe is paying for it."

"Ragland is paying for this room?"

"Your Babe," Scarborough said. "Not mine. He'd be here with you, only the Yanks have gone to Cleveland. I heard him say to the hospital, 'Put it on my tab. Henry gets the works.' "

Henry seemed a little miffed. "Didn't he say, 'Sky's the limit'?"

"Yeah, I think so. 'Sky's the limit for Henry Watteau.' "

"That's the Babe all right. He's always saying, 'Sky's the limit.' A heart of gold that man has. Heart of gold."

Scarborough stood up. "Hey, Watteau, I better get out before the nurses find me with you. I aint supposed to be here more than a minute."

"Did you really call my wife?"

"She's coming on the bus."

The Boston brute met Ragland in the hall. The kid was carrying a wand of pink and yellow flowers for Henry Watteau. "Gimme them daisies," Scarborough said. "Visitors aint allowed." He snatched the flowers away with a mean swipe of his fist. And he went back into Henry's room, shutting the door on Rags.

The kid wandered up Commonwealth Avenue to the Brunswick Hotel. He had to wear a cap over his eyes, or he would have been mobbed in the street. It might have been Ruth, Ruth, Ruth, everywhere else in the civilized world, but Rags was the beloved kid of Boston.

He had a guest in his room: Miz Iva had sneaked upstairs in her uniform from Miss Drabble's School for Girls.

"Why didn't you come over to the house?"

"Nobody invited me," Rags said.

"They don't have to. You're my fiancé."

"I can't come over. Your mother must hate my guts for telling her I was an orphan without a Christian name."

"Oh, I never believed that hogwash. Mama knew it was a lie."

She shed her blazer and her high green socks. Her hips had broadened over the winter, and her breasts seemed rounder to Rags. Iva was turning into Marylou. Rags had such a swollen penis, he could hardly get out of his pants. But she continued that same peculiar lovemaking of last fall. They weren't allowed to touch each other below their bellybuttons. It exhausted Rags to lie with her and pet, while his glans tightened like a powerful bolt and his own erection became unbearable to him.

"How come you didn't write to me from Arkansas?" she said.

"I can't spell."

"Hogwash. They wouldn't let a nonspeller into Amherst."

The veins pulsed and pulsed on Rags' prick.

"Cedric, what's the matter?"

"Don't call me that. I'm Cedric to my father, and nobody else."

"Well, whoever you are, you have a green face."

"It's part of my complexion," Rags said, grabbing for his clothes.

Iva squeezed into Rags' double bed. "I want to hug some more."

Too bad. Hugging you makes my prick stand up and whistle blood. "I can't, Miz Iva. You see, it's lousy for my batting eye."

"What is?"

"This staying in bed so long. I start looking at the ceiling, and I notice crazy blue spots, and the skipper says it can kill your eyes."

"He's a bigger idiot than you are," Iva said, but she got into her green socks. "I'm not going back to Miss Drabble's in the fall. I'm tired of her silly school. Rags, let's get married in July."

"Yeah, sure, July," Rags said, making her dress in a hurry. Iva wouldn't leave off kissing him. The kid had to shove her out the door. Then he dropped his pants, waddled over to the sink, and poured cold water on his burning blue prick. Petting was for dogs, he told himself. But he had to admit that Miz Iva was developing a beautiful bust.

The Sox went on the road mired in seventh place. They couldn't move up or down. The White Sox were the new niggers of the American League. Boston stomped on them and did nothing else. There was a hole everywhere you looked. Sheriff Smith destroyed the Yankees and the Browns with his fireball and his wicked change of pace. But the rest of the staff was composed of knuckle-heads like Frank Howe and Chicken Stallings, who had no pepper in their arms. Seaman Schupp was going stale at second base; Alvin Critz dragged his toes at short; Steve Dubec mumbled to himself in the outfield and missed ordinary fly balls; and Tilly's knees began to wobble behind the plate. The skipper could rely on four men: his fireballer, Sheriff Smith, his center fielder, Garland James, his third baseman, Rags, and Scarborough, his clown. Enemy fans loved to hiss at the Boston brute. Scarborough would climb the dugout wall and howl back at them. The brute enjoyed himself. He was the last surviving hunchback in the major leagues.

But he worried about the kid.

He wouldn't talk to Ragland. Ragland had broken the rules. Only a busher would be reckless enough to deceive his roommate. A roomie was as sacred as a wife. Still, Scarborough couldn't ignore what was true: the kid's lies had gotten him into trouble.

It was all right for visiting teams to call you the millionaire's boy. You could suffer through the worst sort of ridicule at home. Rags had the Boston faithful behind him. They sang to him from the stands and "Duffy's Cliff." He was the orphan they loved.

But who would sing for him on the road? The crowd paid its money to see Boston's left-handed wonder at third, the kid who liked to invent fables about himself. These fans weren't kind to him. They'd watch Ragland, but they wouldn't clap. Sometimes they'd clap for Garl, because they admired his footwork in center field; Garl didn't turn his body into a pretzel to come up with the ball; Garl didn't tell orphan's tales.

Christ, why did he have to copy off Babe Ruth?

Scarborough wished Rags had stolen another man's history. If he'd come into camp as a simple rookie called Rags, a millionaire father wouldn't have caused him so much grief. Who would have cared about the piles of copper in a kid's past? Now he couldn't outrun his own lies.

The bench jockeys feasted on him whenever Boston came to town. They razzed him in Chicago, they razzed him in St. Louis, they razzed him in Detroit. The Chisox were the worst offenders, because they were a bitter, frustrated team, stuck in the cellar, with the Red Sox sitting just on top of them, a game and a half away. They couldn't dislodge Boston. The Red Sox would bump them around. So they took their revenge on the kid.

The Chisox had a special party of buffoons, utility men who warmed the bench and could go at Rags all game. They were a party of four: Bibb Wallace, Shano Roth, Harvey Leonard, and Mike Welch. They would swagger on the dugout steps and yell across the infield at Rags. They'd heard somewhere that the kid's father had a limp, so Harvey Leonard came onto the field dragging his right foot and shouted, "Gimme copper, gimme copper," until the first-base ump chased him back into the dugout. Then Bibb Wallace began his routine. He swiped the announcer's megaphone and serenaded Rags. "Cedric Tannehill, son of Marcus the millionaire, tell us who your mama is. Aint she the Queen of Sheba?"

"My mother's dead," Rags repeated to himself and charged across the infield to get at Bibb. Tilly, Alvin, and Seaman Schupp had to take him by the belt and hurl him to the ground. The umpire seized the megaphone and tossed Bibb out of the game. Rags sent Chicken Stallings into the Chicago dugout with a message for the buffoons: he would meet with them in their own tunnel after the game and settle his accounts.

The White Sox chortled over the message. If the buffoons could break one of Ragland's legs, Chicago might climb out of the cellar. But those Chisox should have thought about the game. The Boston Sox whipped them 5–2, and Chicago was a whole foot deeper in the cellar after nine innings of play.

The Red Sox were chortling now. They drank warm beer smuggled in from a speakeasy at the Wentworth Street corner of Comiskey Park. It was getaway day and Scarborough was collecting all the bats and the team's traveling bags. He couldn't find the kid. "Where's Ragland?"

"You talking to me?" the Chicken said. "Rags has a date in the Chicago tunnel."

"What kind of date?"

"He went to knock the shit out of the White Sox and he said he didn't need no help from us."

Scarborough ran out of the clubhouse. *Some team I'm on. It sucks up beer and won't protect a man.* He had to go through the visitors' tunnel to get back onto the playing field. Mice scuttled around his shoes. *It's a lively ball park.* The players' tunnels in

Chicago were as foul and windy as the tunnels at Fenway Park. Each tunnel had a urinal on its south side, so the men wouldn't have to hike to the clubhouse in the middle of the game to relieve their bladders. Scarborough wondered who cleaned the urinals here: the wind carried the smell of piss straight to his nose.

He went from the tunnel into the visitors' dugout, climbed the steps and crossed the infield with its balding grass, sneaked into the Chicago dugout, littered with old tobacco pouches and peanut shells, and ducked his head into the home tunnel with its familiar smell of stale piss. He pulled out the two bats he was carrying in his baseball knickers. But the Chicken had been right. Rags didn't need help from a hunchback. He was boxing the four buffoons. It was a curious match. They could land eight blows to his two. But they were the bloody ones, not the kid. They tried to hit him with their windmill rights and lefts. The kid would waltz around and jab each of them on the nose.

"Hiya, Scarborough," he laughed, winking at the brute.

"Jesus, don't turn your head," Scarborough shouted into the tunnel. But it was too late. Bibb Wallace had clipped Rags in the ear. That ear began to bleed, and the kid's eyes were going blurry. Scarborough moved closer with his bats. The kid wouldn't let him into the fight. He danced until his head cleared, and then he finished the buffoons with punches that seemed to arrive from no place the buffoons could tell.

He didn't learn that boxing in the street.

The kid had science on his side; Rags laid out the buffoons on the tunnel floor. The rest of the White Sox had to bite their rage, watching him from the clubhouse stairs. They were still determined to break one of the kid's legs. They came down the stairs in a fighter's crouch.

Scarborough twirled his bats. "Don't get cute. You Chisox are gonna have a hard time fielding a club what's got dents in their skulls."

They wouldn't attack a moron with a bat in each hand. The Chisox dragged off the four buffoons and withdrew to their clubhouse.

"Lemme see that ear?" Scarborough said to the kid.

"The ear's all right. It stopped whistling on me."

"You sure are God's gift to the Red Sox," Scarborough told him. "You lied about the boxing, too. Pretending to fight Garl last year like you didn't know the first thing about closing a fist."

"Hell," Rags said. "Boxing was the rage at Amherst. Everybody did it."

"I'll bet you did it better than most. Mister, you could fight with Ty Cobb and win."

Scarborough wasn't angry any more. Standing against the whole Chicago team had made them roomies again. They would have gone to the nearest drug store for a honeymoon of chocolate sodas, but they had to rush back to the clubhouse and make the sleeper back to Boston.

Rags went from furor to furor.

His wedding banns had been published in the *Evening Transcript*. He was supposed to marry Miz Iva at Salem Street's Old North Church on the last Sunday in July. The wedding banns sounded like a goddamn batting order. He could imagine Bull Weingarten croaking it out through his leather funnel. "Cedric Tannehill, known as Babe Ragland to his Red Sox fans, and Iva Cottonmouth, daughter of Marylou Wilks Cottonmouth and Judah Cottonmouth, deceased . . ."

He went to Iva's house on the Hill. That servant, Rhys, was short with him, but Rags pushed his way through. Iva's mama opened her parlor door to see what the tumult was about. She looked confused. "Harvard Jack?" she said.

"No, it's Babe Ragland, your intended son-in-law. Where's Miz Iva?"

"I'm here," she said, coming out from behind her mother's wing.

"I'd like to have a talk with you in private."

Marylou gave over the parlor to them, and Rags prowled that room of sofas, drapes, and chairs.

"I wish I didn't have to read about my life all the time in the Boston *Transcript*. Who says we're getting married in July?"

"We agreed on it, you dope."

"When?"

"Last month . . . in your room at the baseball hotel."

"I don't remember that."

Rags sat down on the sofa, far from the girl. "Are you moving in with us at the Brunswick?"

"Don't be silly. We'll live with mama. In this house."

"I can't," Rags said. "I have a roommate, and I'm not going to desert him."

"You want to bring a bat boy into this house?"

"He's sensitive," Rags said. "He'll die if he has to live alone."

Iva's nose began to twitch; she was unbelievably pretty in her schoolgirl's blouse. "All right. He can live downstairs. Mama has an extra room in back of the kitchen."

Rags hadn't expected her to give in so easily. "Shouldn't you ask your mother first?"

"No!" she screamed at him. "A bargain is a bargain. But he can't be your best man."

"Best man?" Rags said. "What best man?"

"At the wedding, you silly goose. Mama won't stand for it. She wants Garl."

"Garl's no friend of mine. Who's getting married, anyway? Why should Garl be my best man?"

"Take it or leave it," Iva said. You couldn't outtalk this girl. Rags was only a kid who stepped on yellow grass in front of third base. "If your hunchback is going to live in this house, then Garland has to be best man. Hollis has already straightened it out with him."

"How did the boss get into this frigging pie? He's the one who told me I couldn't marry you until you were seventeen."

"Hollis changed his mind."

"That's swell of him," Rags said, moving to a different sofa. "Does Hollis own a piece of the *Transcript?* How come they picked the beginning of the season to swear I had a father, unless Hollis wanted to build a crowd for Opening Day? . . . is that why you're marrying me? Because my pa is rich?"

Iva stood up and began to swing at Rags. He bobbed away from her fists without having to shuffle his feet. A girl couldn't hit Rags. He'd knocked out four men at Comiskey Park. She was crying now, and he pitied her girlish swings. So he let her smack him once.

"You can go to the devil with your father and his copper fields. My father was twice as rich. His people used to manufacture all the ice in Massachusetts."

"That's what they'll say," Rags muttered. "Copper is marrying ice."

The two leaves of the parlor door began to shake. The leaves split and Miz Marylou walked in. "Children, what's going on?" She came over to Iva and whispered in her ear. Then she walked out, shutting the leaves behind her.

"Mama's writing invitations," Iva said, her cheeks flushed with embarrassment and a purple rage. "How many guests do you figure your pa will bring?"

"He won't bring a soul. There's no use inviting him. He won't come to my wedding. My father thinks I'm a bum."

"We can survive without him." She took Rags by the hand and led him behind a sofa. Iva undid all her buttons.

"Suppose your mother comes in again?"

"What if she does. Fiancées are allowed to kiss."

Rags shivered inside himself. *Oh, Lord, lemme marry this girl
so we can end the petting stuff. I can't take too much more of it.*
He wouldn't refuse Miz Iva. He kissed her behind the sofa and felt
that bursting in his pants.

The Sox were on the road again through the first half of July.
Rags caught it in every big-league town. Dugouts devoted themselves to mocking the kid. The jabber never ceased. They had a
new item to torture him about: Cedric's bride. "Where you having
the honeymoon, Cedric? In a dollhouse?" A sucking noise would
rise off the dugout steps and grow shrill as it carried across the
infield and got to Rags. But he smiled at the monkeys on the steps.
Scarborough had given him good advice.

"They'll eat you to death if you have rabbit ears. You gotta
learn to ignore them dodobirds. If they see you stutter and blink,
they'll ride on you and ride, until your hands are jelly and you've
got nothin' in your knees. Then the dodos will really start to peck.
They can pick out your eyes with their songs. So you play your
position and give them the old horse laugh. That can aggravate a
dodo. They'll start dropping off their bench."

The kid put a knuckle in his mouth. "Where the hell did you get
all this? You've only been with the Sox three years."

"A bat boy gets to see a lot. He's like a second catcher on the
field. You ask Mr. Briggs."

The kid didn't have to ask. He smiled at the dodos in the dugout,
hugged the line at third, and made himself deaf to their twittering.
You could find more gruesome things than dodobirds on a bench.
The Sox had come to St. Louis in the middle of a heat wave. The
temperature climbed to a hundred and six. The grass burned under
your feet at Sportsman's Park. You played with a dry mouth. Your
shirt clung to your back. The fans begged for shade. They deserted
the open pavilion in right field, walked along the roof, and settled
in the upper decks somewhere, shouting at the lemonade boys to
hurry. But the park was out of lemonade. The Brownies couldn't
satisfy their fans' lust for a cold drink.

They were listless on the field, those Browns, a team that had
dropped to fifth place. Their bark and their swagger meant little in
the heat. Sheriff Smith struck out Baby Doll Jacobson four times
in a single afternoon. Urban Shocker, the Brownies' thirty-three-
year-old ace, kept firing up doubles to Garl. Rags hit one of his
few home runs. The Sox bombed St. Louis, 12–6.

But they had no relief outside Sportsman's Park. You could have fried a whole hog on the ceiling of Rags' and Scarborough's room at the Buckingham Hotel. The wallpaper crackled and spit an ugly brown glue. When the shutters were open, the heat scorched everything in sight. The kid's bat case turned blond in St. Louis. The hair fell out of his shoe brush. The buttons to the coat he left out of the closet yellowed on him. And the room sealed up like a coffin, with the shutters closed.

The Red Sox weren't going to sleep at the Buckingham in that bloody weather. They soaked all their sheets in the bathtub and went downstairs in their underpants, with the sheets draped over themselves, like outriders of the Ku Klux Klan. They got to the park across from the Buckingham, curled into a bench, and tried to sleep.

There was a constant traffic from the park to the hotel, as the sheets began to dry. The manager, the house detective, and the St. Louis police didn't interfere with this pilgrimage of the Sox. It was an old baseball practice to wear wet sheets in the park.

Rags and the brute found a quiet bench near the duck pond. The ducks were too lazy to move; they rested at the side of the pond, with their necks out of the water. They looked at the white sheets of the two Red Sox without disturbing themselves. One small duck slapped its head around to take a drink of water. And the pond was still again.

The brute slowly fell into a dream. His hump twitched under the sheet, and his eyes rolled back into his head. Rags didn't know if he should wake the brute or not. *What's it hurting him to dream?*

But the kid himself couldn't get to sleep. The Brownies and their dodobirds didn't stick. His mind went off St. Louis. He was thinking of his wedding march and the church on Salem Street. The kid would take a wife in seven days. Iva was down in Martha's Vineyard with her mama and Rhys. They'd have to cut their summer short and open the house on Louisburg Square for the wedding party. He could kiss that baseball hotel goodbye. Rags and his roomie were going to live on Beacon Hill.

His petting days were over. She couldn't tell a husband where to touch. He'd have that girl, only Miz Iva would be Mrs. Ragland now. Wife of the seventh Babe. He was nineteen years old. His mother had died of pneumonia when he was six. He'd had nurses, aunts, and tutors to watch over him. And his own servant, a colored boy named Charles. Charles ran away once, and he was whipped for it. His father's handyman whipped him in front of Cedric. Then they held his mouth open, took a razor, and slashed his gums. That was a lesson for runaways. Colored boys didn't disappear after their gums were slashed. Rags couldn't forget that long zip of blood where the razor had gone into Charles' mouth. But Charles did run away again. They found him dead. A few miles from his father's properties, outside Abilene. He didn't have a mark on him. Do colored boys die of fright?

Cedric Tannehill.

Rags poked his head out from under the sheet. The brute was snoring, that hump riding low on his back. Were the Brownies in the park, trying to plague the kid?

Cedric Tannehill.

He didn't spot Baby Doll Jacobson behind a tree. He looked down into the pond. Could a sleeping duck quack the name of Rags' birthright?

Cedric Tannehill.

Was it the colored boy, Charles, come back to haunt him for his father's misdeeds?

"Charlie, is that you? I'm Ragland now. Cedric died at Amherst College."

He saw a cane beat in the grass. The cane was as deliberate as a man's shoe. Rags couldn't be wrong about its swish.

"Pa?"

His father wore a bowler and a dark brown suit in the boiling night. He didn't have his factotum with him, Griffey the lawyer. Marcus Tannehill, the copper millionaire, had come alone to St. Louis.

"Pa, should I run upstairs and get you a sheet? You'll roast in your winter suit."

Marcus had Rags' bony jaw. Except for his limp, which he'd gotten twenty years ago in a mining accident and gave his body an uncertain thrust, he could have been a slightly older brother to Rags, another third baseman for the Red Sox. He was left-handed, like the kid.

"Pa, did Griffey get our schedule for you? How did you know the Sox were in St. Louis? I hit one off Urban Shocker this afternoon. The dope challenged me with his sinkerball. I got it with the sweet end of my bat."

Marcus jabbed the hunchback with his cane. It made a little twist in the sheet. But Scarborough didn't give up his snoring.

"Pa, I'm getting married! At the Old North Church. On Sunday. Did the Cottonmouths write to you? Pa, will you come?"

Marcus hopped away on the end of his cane. He passed bench after bench of ballplayers in wet sheets. You'd think it was Rags who was chugging along on a stiff leg.

The brute woke up.

"My pa was here."

Scarborough rubbed his eyes. "Your pa? What did he say?"

"He wouldn't talk to me, but he touched you with his cane."

"I didn't feel it," Scarborough said.

"Well, he touched you. I can show you the spot."

Rags pointed to the little twist in Scarborough's sheet. It could have been the impression that a finger would make. "That don't look like no cane mark to me. I aint a man of cotton. You think I wouldn't feel a stick goin' in? You dreamed it."

"No, he was in the park with both of us."

"It's hot, you're scared of getting married, and you dreamed it. Good night." And Scarborough went under his sheet.

8

Judah Cottonmouth was dead, and his little girl had no man to give her away. So Hollis McKee had to become the "father" of the bride. He ran the wedding like a baseball club. He scolded ushers and vestrymen and the four schoolgirls from Miss Drabble's who attended to the bride. Miss Drabble herself wouldn't come to a schoolgirl's wedding. She was always furious when one of her girls ran off to church with a man. It finished your career at Miss Drabble's. She wouldn't allow married women to corrupt her school with the mark of sexual intercourse upon them.

Hollis was glad the crazy old witch had decided not to come. It gave him one less person to worry about. The church was packed, and Hollis had to find pews for everybody. The governor was there. His Excellency couldn't afford to boycott the wedding of the most popular kid in Massachusetts, even though this Ragland had a tainted history. He was an orphan with a millionaire father in his past. His Excellency had to side with the rabble. They could vote him out of office if he didn't swear allegiance to the seventh Babe, like any Royal Rooter. His kissed the little missus, Iva Ragland Tannehill Cottonmouth (the girl would be heavy with names), posed for photographers from the society pages, but he couldn't locate the president of the Red Sox. Hollis was in the sacristy, crying for his long dead college brother, who hadn't lived long enough to see his little girl marry the Babe.

"Ah, Judah boy, we'd have put some team together. I wouldn't have sold that big baboon to the Yankees if you'd been there to shout at me. But I got us another Babe. Jesus, can he go to his left. And I made him your son-in-law."

Two churchwardens stumbled into the sacristy. They didn't give

Hollis a chance to wipe his eyes. He scowled at them. "What's wrong?"

"We'll have to close the doors, Mr. McKee. There's five thousand people out on Salem Street. The church will fall down on them. We can't hold that many people."

"Those are Red Sox fans," Hollis said. "They've come to the Babe's wedding. They won't break into your precious church. Let them have the sidewalk. I don't want any doors shut in their face."

The two wardens had to slip out of the sacristy on their toes and let the Babe's fans mill in front of the Old North Church, while Hollis composed himself and went into the chapel. Most of the wedding party could leave through a side door. A fleet of Chryslers waited for them on top of Snowhill. But Rags wouldn't sneak out of church. His fans had stood for three hours on Salem Street. So he walked to the front of the chapel with his bride, his roommate, and his best man.

The crowd yelled and jumped at the first sight of Rags. Iva was alarmed. She'd never experienced the crush of so many people. But they adored the kid. And they allowed a small hollow to exist between Rags and themselves. "God bless you, Babe. We hope you and the little woman live to be a hundred."

Rags felt ridiculous in the opera hat Hollis made him wear at his own wedding. He sallied into the crowd, smiled at babies, shook hands, and returned to his bride. The brute had to step behind her and hold up all the trains of her wedding gown. Garland acted as a local magistrate for the bride and groom. He would grab an elbow here and there, give a gentle tug, and get his people through.

They traveled out of the North End, with hundreds sticking to them. It had the look of a sacred hike. They picked up stragglers, bums, and half the Quincy baseball team at New Sudbury Street. These pilgrims arrived on Louisburg Square, which was already mobbed with curiosity seekers, Harvard men, followers of the Babe, and bohemians from the bottom of the Hill.

Garl managed to sheriff the four of them into the house. The bridesmaids fell on Miz Iva and began to devour her neck. They occupied a whole corner of the house and took to giggling with obscene smirks on their faces. Rags threw his opera hat into the closet.

The governor collared Scarborough and tried to feel him out on the possibility of Republican strongholds at Fenway Park. Would His Excellency be booed by the fanatics of South Boston if he appeared in Hollis' box? Scarborough wouldn't commit himself. Bat boys didn't tinker with politics.

Marylou kept staring at Garl. A kind of hysteria crept up in her and colored her throat because of his nearness to her. She wished it had been a double wedding. Rags and Iva. Garl and Marylou. The center fielder was quiet, beautiful, and lean.

"Would you care for some fruit punch, Mr. James?"

Garl wouldn't flirt. He had all the reticence of an Indiana man. He wasn't stupid about the qualities she had: hips and ankles and a slow, silvery speech. But Marylou was linked with the boss in a way that was difficult to tell. She was half daughter, half mistress and companion to Hollis McKee.

"Thank you, ma'am, but I don't drink punch."

Garl would have run away from this house. But he was sworn to protect Ragland on his wedding day. He had squired Rags in and out of the Old North Church. He purchased the opera hat. He'd carried the wedding ring. Now the Sox had a legitimate husband on the roster. He was beginning to like this kid from Amherst, St. Mary's, and who knows where. He caught Rags mumbling to himself.

"Ragland, it's your party and you're supposed to smile."

"Who's the little man with Hollis?"

"Finnbar of the *Evening Transcript*. Noel's in charge of the society page."

"I figured that," Rags said.

Noel Finnbar wore a blue vest. His hands darted in and out of his cuffs as he talked to Hollis McKee. Rags waited until Hollis went into another room before he descended upon the society editor. Noel jumped. Rags had a frown line in the middle of his face.

"Where'd you get that picture of me in my freshman college hat?"

"What picture, Babe?" Noel Finnbar said, as if Rags had a Chinaman's voice.

"The one you printed in your rotten paper . . . on the goddamn front page."

"You'll have to ask our features man."

"You can take your features man and chew on his foot," Rags said. "Listen, Finnbar, if you start in on me again, I'll find you at the *Transcript* and show you what it means to have a bloody head."

The kid waltzed away from Noel Finnbar. But he couldn't have any peace. Marylou's servant patted him on the shoulder.

"You're booked at the Ritz-Carlton. The missus reserved the bridal suite."

The kid had to ask him, "What for?"

"For your honeymoon, Mr. Rags."

"Ballplayers don't get a honeymoon, Rhys. The Tigers'll be in Fenway tomorrow."

"The rooms are for tonight."

The bridesmaids wept as Miz Iva packed her pajamas in a small overnight bag. Rags wouldn't take a thing. They were five minutes from the Ritz-Carlton. He could always come back for extra underwear.

Scarborough had already moved in. His quarters were downstairs, in an alcove off the kitchen. It would be the first night in over a year that the two of them had slept apart. Rags could say goodbye to Hollis and Garl and the governor of Massachusetts, but it seemed silly to shake hands with his own roommate. So he shrugged to the brute, that's all, and left the house with Iva and her long wedding train. The skirts trailed on the cobblestones, because she didn't have Scarborough to hang on to them and hold them up. The bride and groom walked down Chestnut Street, entered the Public Garden, people shouting, "Babe and Iva . . . Iva and Babe," crossed the footbridge, came out on Arlington Street, with Rags shaking the dust and bits of grass off Iva's skirts, and checked into the Ritz-Carlton Hotel as Mr. and Mrs. Babe Ragland of the Boston Red Sox and Beacon Hill.

It was the only place in Boston where people didn't make a fuss over him. Pashas and kings had stayed at the Ritz. The kid wasn't even batting .300 this year. He was a sophomore with a crazy glove.

No one laughed at his wedding tie, or the girl's incredible train. The elevator boys were dressed in the Carlton shade of blue. They wore white gloves. And they drove their cars up and down. The motors purred for them. Iva didn't feel any jolts.

Rags was put on the fifteenth floor. You couldn't find a loose tack in the carpeting. The doorknobs were made of green glass. Rags did a reckoning of the bridal suite. "It's bigger than the clubhouse. And it's got a view."

They could see the dome of the State House, half of Beacon Hill, and the bend in the Charles from the windows of their sitting room. A magnum of champagne stood in a large silver bell near one window. "Did mama do that?" Iva wanted to know.

"Na, it comes with the place."

"Who says?"

Rags picked a little card out of the ice in the silver bell. The card had the hotel's emblem on it, embossed in blue: a lion looking sideways, with its tongue sticking out.

"See, it's from the Ritz!"

Iva looked in all the closets. Rags had a difficult time opening the champagne. "Son of a bitch." The cork shot up to the ceiling, and a blue smoke emerged from the bottle. Rags filled two long-stemmed champagne glasses, but Iva refused to drink.

"You have to make a toast."

The kid scratched his head.

"I drink to love and no more petting."

Iva was chagrined. "I want something better than that."

"Well, what about a life together in your mama's house, with Scarborough under the stairs?"

"Stop joking," she said, but she took a sip and started to laugh. The bowl of the champagne glass was too big for Iva's mouth; she had to clamp her teeth into the glass and suck up champagne. Bubbles got into her nose. Iva had a spell of hiccups. Rags frightened her with a horrible face, and the girl was cured.

They decided to have their honeymoon meal right in the sitting room. Rags pressed a buzzer in the wall, and a waiter arrived. "We'll have this and this . . . and this," they said, shoving their fingers along the menu. The waiter returned with a tray that could have come off a battleship. Bride and groom sampled sturgeon and roe, a *crudité* of carrots, broccoli, and blood tomatoes, sweetbreads under glass, lobster in whiskey sauce, grasshopper pie, and cherries jubilee. The kid rang for a second bottle of champagne.

"Me and my pa always used to eat like this," Rags said. "He took me everywhere."

"He's a louse," Iva said. "He never answered mama's invitation."

"I told you he wouldn't come . . . and don't call pa a louse. I disappointed him and left college like a bum."

"He should be proud of you. The Sox wouldn't keep a bum on third base. Where the hell did you grow up? In a monk's house?"

"Tucson and Texas," Rags said, his tongue growing heavier and heavier with each gulp of champagne. "I learned baseball from the niggers on my father's ranch. They didn't have any uniforms. Just neckerchiefs. It was the blue neckerchiefs against the red. But they sure could play. And they didn't have the big leagues sitting on their backs, teaching them how to hit and field the ball. If a lefty took a liking to third, nobody stopped you. They had lefty catchers, lefty shortstops, and everything. Those red and blue neckerchiefs could have pissed on the Sox."

"Don't you say a bad word about Hollis' team. Hollis is my goduncle."

Rags blinked at her. "What's a goduncle?"

"It's like a godfather, but not so sticky and tight."

"Well, those neckerchiefs were all goduncles to me."

"It's not the same," Iva said. "Hollis raised me and my mother after my father dropped dead."

"How could he raise your mother when she's already a woman?"

"Mama's less than a child."

The kid was too bewildered to answer her right away. He drank champagne, and drizzled all over his wedding pants. "Didn't your mother go to Bryn Mawr?"

"Mama couldn't spell Bryn Mawr if her life depended on it. She was my father's servant wench."

Rags sat in his wet pants and blinked at Miz Iva.

"Mama's a po' girl from Jackson, Mississip, who ran away from home. She landed in New England, a kitchen maid at my father's fraternity. She was Hollis' wench too. They shared her with five or six more fraternity brothers."

"Why did your father marry her then?"

"He wanted to shock the Cottonmouths, I guess. He brought his own whore to Beacon Hill and made her his wife."

"It's a dumb lie," Rags said. "Who told you this cock and bull story?"

"Mama did," Iva was sniffling now. "We're famous for the peculiar weddings in our family."

"What's so peculiar about us?"

"Nothing, nothing at all. A girl who can't finish high school and a boy who's ashamed to let his father know he's on the Red Sox."

Rags felt a ringing in his head. He was sick of so much blab. "Let's go into the other room."

The kid didn't leer at his wife. He took her sweetly by the hand and they both wobbled into the bedroom in a duckfooted walk. The blue drapes had been pulled for them. Only a magician could solve the honeymoon bed. It seemed to have a hundred coverlets and feather pillows on its summer quilt.

Rags couldn't undress the wife.

He grappled with Iva's wedding gown, leaning on her in his woozy condition. His fingers slipped off her buttons and her stays. "Lemme do it," she croaked, falling onto the bed.

The kid watched her unravel herself. *I won't have a blue prick tonight*. He tore at his wedding clothes, imprisoned in his cuffs. Iva had to come to him naked and unbutton the poor kid. Her body was smooth against his gruff ballplayer's skin. The back of his neck was freckled and dark where the sun beat down upon him behind third base. His thighs were bruised. His hands were gnarled from the smack of so many balls. He felt like a tortoise next to the wife.

They flung off the pillows, pulled away the coverlets, and got the bed down to its basic quilt. They crept inside and started to kiss. *Cedric's dead. Cedric's dead. I'm Babe Ragland. I have a wife.* He explored between her legs with his bumpy wrist. Iva sang her delight with a gentle moaning that tasted like silk in Rag's mouth. He went into her and moved against her hips with the slow, contented rhythm of a rocking horse. Then he pulled out.

She looked up at him, her cheeks swollen with raw animal surprise. "Where's the blood?" he said.

Rags wasn't a dope. He spent six months at Amherst, where he studied the laws of male and female anatomy. "A virgin's supposed to bleed."

"I did my bleeding." Iva sat up, her nose flaring out at Rags.

"Who was it that made you bleed?"

"None of your business."

A rage caught hold of him; he took her by the arms and squeezed. "Who was it?"

"Rhys," she said, as if to bite him with a single word.

"You put me off for a goddamn year, you lie to me with your virgin stories, and that bum is crawling into your bed."

"I didn't lie. It happened last week . . . at Martha's Vineyard. He was drunk with mama, and I was getting curious . . . I thought you wouldn't like me if I didn't know what to do. So I asked him to teach me, and he did . . . "

Rags got into his clothes; his collar was rumpled, his shirttails stuck out, and his wedding tie lay on him like an evil tongue.

"Where are you going?"

"For a walk. Some husband I am. I have to wait on line for sloppy seconds with my own wife . . . Rags gets in after Rhys."

And she couldn't keep him from marching out the door. He was rude to the elevator boy. "Take me downstairs," Rags shouted in the boy's face.

He galloped across the Public Garden with his tails wrapped around one leg. He wore a jackal's grin when he arrived on Louisburg Square. He stood outside his new home, remembering that the Cottonmouths didn't bother to lock up at night. Rags let himself in.

Was the servant downstairs with Scarborough, or upstairs with Marylou? He climbed up to the bedrooms on the second floor. He knocked and knocked until he found Rhys hiding in Marylou's bed.

The kid dragged him out of the pillows. He'd ruined their sleep. He could smell their lovemaking on the two of them.

"Mister, you shouldn't have monkeyed with my wife."

He wasn't out to murder Rhys. He smashed the servant around the kidneys with no more than half his might. But he didn't know how to stop. He punched and kicked, and the servant began to swallow his own blood. Marylou's wailing couldn't get him off Rhys. He felt a hand go under his crotch. He was lifted off the ground like a common potato sack and hurled into a chair.

No ordinary man could have done that to him. It was the brute. Scarborough came upstairs in his pajamas to see what the noise was about. He had Marylou fetch a basin of water and a towel, and he administered to Rhys. He washed the blood away, inspecting all the marks Rags had put on him. Rhys curled his head behind Scarborough's knee.

"You know what that bum did?" Rags said. "He taught my wife how to·screw."

"You just got married today. So he couldn't have taught her when she was your wife."

Rags didn't like the way a hunchback reasoned. Scarborough should have been kinder to him.

"Who cares when it was. She was still my fiancée. I ought to twist his neck."

He couldn't get the brute to look at him straight. Then Scarborough gave him the old familiar scowl that one roommate reserves for another.

"Raggsy, you're on your honeymoon. Go back to the Ritz."

Book Three

WINTER BALL WITH THE HARRYS

9

IT WAS A DOG'S LIFE.

A bride who'd been punctured by another man; a mother-in-law who lay down with boys in the swamp because she loved Garland James and couldn't have him; a roommate who lived in a rat's hole two floors under Rags. And all the kid ever wanted to do was play ball.

He had a father who was richer than the whole American League. *Who's your pa, little boy? My pa is copper and beef. Copper and beef.* Marcus Tannehill mined copper in Arizona and Colorado and had a cattle ranch in Texas to amuse himself with. The ranch could have swallowed up ten Boston swamps and twenty Beacon Hills. The kid developed a dinosaur's eye for open spaces. And a coyote's ear. Baseball seized hold of his senses. It wasn't a series of rituals between men in flannel suits. It was wild play. Rags defined himself against the territory of an infield and the smack of horsehide on wood like a prairie animal. His instinct was to lunge for that ball, grit his teeth, and throw.

At fifteen he played Texas baseball behind his father's back, pretending he was a bullrider's boy from Abilene who did every-thing with his left hand. But Griffey, his father's lawyer-toad, was on to him, and he had to give it up after a month. Marcus tutored him at home and sent him East to Amherst College, thinking to cure him of his baseball habits and his coyote smells. The kid stayed long enough to learn how to box, and study a little Greek, then he jumped to Arkansas.

It wasn't a silly act. The Red Sox were the most desperate team in baseball, and he knew he could get into their tryout camp. *I'm Babe Ragland*. Why couldn't the kid be an orphan like Mr. Ruth? He'd read so many stories about the bad boys' school in Baltimore, he could mutter *St. Mary's* by heart.

Now he wished somebody would put him in that bad boys' school and hide him from reporters, baseball owners, and the Cottonmouths. He was the most miserable husband on earth.

He searched for Garl in the clubhouse, with that dog's look on his face. His gums seemed bitter yellow inside his mouth. Garl was astonished over the change in Rags. He'd heard of recent bridegrooms falling apart, but yellow gums were new to him.

"Mr. James, is Harry Heilmann going to treat me like a rookie again? . . . can I play on his winter team?"

Garl didn't bother to ask what was putting winter into Ragland's mind. He told him outright about Harry. "I've inherited the Heilmann All-Stars. Harry's given up barnstorming as a winter career. He's got a sick shoulder. He'll go to California to hunt and fish."

The kid suddenly went shy. His back hunched over like the brute's, and he said in a low voice, "Will you carry me, Mr. James?"

Garl intended to offer third base to Homer Ezzell of the Browns, but he couldn't refuse a kid who had the dirty gray eyes of an injured wolf. "I'll carry you."

The kid's mouth curled up into a narrow grin. "What about Scarborough?"

"Yeah," Garl said, "I can always use a bat boy. I'll carry him too. But his expenses will have to come out of your own pocket."

"Sure thing," the kid said, and he was less of a hunchback now. It was the first time in Garl's life that a major leaguer looked so happy about the prospects of a barnstorming trip. You had to play in chickencoops all over the countryside and eat every sort of shit. He felt sorry for the Babe. Garl wouldn't live in that house on Louisburg Square. It was filled with Cottonmouth spooks. Rags shouldn't have moved in with that crazy mama. Why didn't he push the girl out and bring her someplace else? The Brunswick had plenty of bridal suites.

Rags was in a gay mood crossing Commonwealth Avenue. He'd solved his winter for himself. He was going to barnstorm with an all-star team.

He met the brute walking on Acorn Street. Scarborough was wearing Rags' opera hat. A Russian seamstress had fixed up a swallow-tailed coat for him that softened the lines of his hump. These were his Beacon Hill clothes.

"You're with the Red Sox," Rags muttered, "not a team of cockatoos. You can throw your new duds in the closet. We won't be here in October."

"We going around the world, Raggsy?"

"Better than that. We're playing in the winter leagues."

The swallow-tailed coat must have had a miraculous seam because Scarborough's hump swelled out from under the lining. "Why do we have to step in dirt when we got Beacon Hill to climb?"

"I had to beg Garl to take us on, and you want to wear your fancy hat and smile at all the swell people . . . don't come."

"I didn't say I wasn't coming . . . when do we pack?"

"Soon as the season's over."

He went in to have a talk with the wife. Mrs. Ragland was quiet as he delivered his song on winter baseball. "Give me a chance to play with a decent infield. Garl wouldn't carry fools like Alvin Critz. My wing gets frozen if I lay still from October to February. I have to catch the ball."

She was a baseball wife like the girls in *Eveline*. Only sixteen, and her husband was ready to crawl away.

"Can I go with you, Rags?"

"Wives don't barnstorm," the kid said. "We'll be living in dirtwater towns, playing niggers and all. We'll probably have to sleep on the grass."

"Will you come home for Christmas?"

"I'll try."

September dribbled out for the kid. Boston was still locked in seventh place. The kid held back; he wasn't going to burn his legs completely for the Sox. He had to save a little stuff for the Heilmann All-Stars.

He was disappointed when he saw the actual team. Garl had Topper Rigney of Detroit to play short, and ancient Zack Wheat in the outfield, but the rest of the All-Stars was a skunk's list: third-stringers, like Chappie Gruel and Steve Bumpo, who would have had a hard time making the Red Sox. Garl couldn't afford to carry more than two or three front-line men on the All-Stars. Come October and November, the country was deluged with all-star teams. There was the Rogers Hornsby All-Stars, the George Sisler Americans, the Babe Ruth All-Stars, the Rabbit Maranville Kings, and the Harry Heilmann All-Stars who had to go without Harry this year.

But the kid would have played for a circus, rather than spend another winter in Boston. He fled his Beacon Hill bride in a yellow and green barnstorming bus. Garl had rented this old bus for the team. He was manager, player, and entrepreneur, and his own booking agent. It wasn't so easy to book behind Rabbit Maranville and Babe Ruth. The Harry Heilmann All-Stars had to grab whatever they could. Bookings were slight until the Cincinnati Colored Giants rescued them.

Garl got the Cincinnati Giants by default: no other all-star team would barnstorm with them. The Giants were too rough. Rabbit Maranville always kept a hundred miles between himself and "them Cincinnatis." The Giants were known to chew up baseball men. They were like a wrecking company. They'd fight a whole town if you insulted them on the field, and ride off, leaving you to sit in the debris.

But those crazyheads could draw a crowd. People came to hiss at the Colored Giants. Garl didn't have much of a choice. He had to connect with the Giants, or get out of winter baseball. So he gambled with the bones of his men. Garl was the eldest son; and the burden of his family fell upon him. He had a disabled grandfather, a brood of maiden aunts, a sick mom, and three brothers who hadn't finished their schooling yet.

He pointed his bus driver towards Maryland, where he was supposed to rendezvous with the Colored Giants. Rags was confused about the wanderings of the bus. "Didn't we make the wrong turn? This isn't the road to Cincinnati?"

"Not so loud," the brute said. "You'll set the men to thinking. And they'll all start to twitch."

"Let them twitch. Shouldn't we head for the Giants' home park?"

"Raggsy, we aint hooking up with the St. Louis Browns. This is nigger baseball. The Cincinnati Giants don't have a park. Colored boys have to sneak onto a field if they expect to play."

"Then why call yourself the Cincinnati Giants?"

"Because that's built into their name. They have to pretend to people that they have some kind of home."

"Do the Cincinnati Giants ever play in Cincinnati?"

"Probably not. The Philadelphia Black Eagles don't even know where Philadelphia is. You'll learn."

"There's nothing to learn," Rags said. "It's crazy, that's all."

The bus hit upon a fleet of Buicks outside Annapolis, seven autocars with wooden hulls and no roofs. It was a baseball caravan: the players and worldly goods of the Cincinnati Colored

Giants. Their boss, Carl Raines, stood at the front of the caravan
with his arms akimbo and frowned at the yellow and green bus. He
was a small man with a wizened face.

"We're in trouble," Scarborough whispered to Rags.

"How come?"

"His wife Emma aint with the team. She must have run off with
the local milkman. Carl's gonna give us hell."

The All-Stars clambered out of the bus, stretching their knees
after the ride down from Boston. The Giants stuck to their autocars. They were the most aristocratic niggers Rags had ever met.
Where were the sockamayocks, those second-stringers who had
scouted Rags in Arkansas? Rags couldn't find one sockamayock
among the Colored Giants. They ignored the All-Stars with their
ill-tempered eyes, as if a team of worthless fellows had come to
play with them.

"Don't you pick an argument with these sassy niggers," Scarborough said. "Just smile, or they'll scowl you into the grave.
They practice voodoo, Carl and his black sons of a bitch."

Raines shook his head at Garland. "Looks like we'll have to
carry you on the road, young fella. You aint got much of a drawing
card without ol' Harry Heilmann. Harry take sick?"

"No, he went fishing in California."

The little man produced a bitter, raucous laugh for the Colored
Giants. "You hear that? Harry went fishing in California. He left
his All-Stars to try and feed themselves. Mister, without Harry
you a pile of shit."

"We have enough," Garl said.

"Who you got? Topper and Zack and little Steve Bumpo. They
couldn't bring out the horseflies."

"We have the kid, Babe Ragland."

Raines laughed so hard, a shiver went through his body. "Fella,
I got four lefty third basemen sitting in my hind car. I use them to
sweep up after the games."

"The kid can play his spot," Garl said. Raines and seven cars of
Giants couldn't irritate him.

"Pharaoh'll eat him up," the little man said. "He'll cry and beg
for lessons after he watches the Pharaoh do his tricks. But I aint
sure Pharaoh Yarbull will come onto the field with you. White
folks make him sneeze a lot."

"Who's this Pharaoh guy?" the kid asked the brute.

"Their top dog."

"Does he pitch?"

"He plays anywhere the Giants need him."

"Point him out to me."

"Never point at a nigger. It means you want to fight."

"Am I allowed to scratch my ass without insulting the Cincinnati Giants? I won't disturb Mr. Yarbull. He can talk to me with his bat and glove."

"He'll talk you into the bleachers," Scarborough said. "If he could put on some whiteface and pitch and field for the Sox, we'd have took the pennant this year."

"That's good to know. When do we get to play these miracle boys?"

"Soon," Scarborough said. His mournful looks disgusted Rags. The brute was all curled up. Rags had played with niggers on his father's ranch. He understood the flamboyances of their game. Niggers liked to shave a ball with a piece of emery cloth, or nick it with the tooth on a belt buckle, so the ball would hop at you out of the corner in ways you couldn't predict. You had to stare back at the nigger on the mound and swing under the crooked eye of the ball with one tiny flick of the bat. You could use their own stuff against them; the ball would carom off the bat with the same peculiar hop. Otherwise you'd be swinging all day, and you couldn't go near that nigger pitch.

The seven Buicks began to make sense: little Carl was carrying a small country of men. He had an umpire, a witch doctor, wandering carpenters and groundkeepers, and fourteen Giants. The groundkeepers set up a baseball diamond in a field across from the bus. They labored like fools with their trowels and their scythes, while the carpenters built a grandstand near first base. They'd turned a stinking field into a diamond in forty-five minutes. That little man had magicians on his side.

The Buicks became a dressing room for the Giants. They ventured out in uniforms of snug gold and white. The All-Stars wore a dumpy gray that seemed like woolen underwear next to the Cincinnati colors.

The little man chided Garl. "Lord alive, I'm ashamed to be around you scruffy boys."

"I forgot to bring my washerwoman along," Garl told him. "I picked the darkest uniforms I could find."

The little man said something about "mud pies," and he sent his pretty Giants into the neighboring villages to drum up business for both teams. The Giants brought placards with them that announced "A Colossal Baseball Match Between the World Champion Cincinnati Giants and those Great Contenders, the Harry Heilmann All-Stars of the White American League." The witch doctor, a sickly man called Samuel Sharn, blessed their trip. Rags couldn't say what kind of mumbo jumbo this Samuel used on the Giants. But it worked. Five thousand Marylanders followed Carl's gold-clad pitchmen back to that temporary diamond in the field.

The Giants didn't have to go to their emery boards. They walloped the All-Stars, 15–1, without doctoring a single pitch. Yam Murray was on the mound for them, and he got to the Harry Heilmanns with his cunning and his smoke. But it wasn't bats and pitching arms that really interested the kid. He didn't care how many black Walter Johnsons and George Sislers the Giants had. It was their fielding that stupefied Rags. The Giants were like rubbery extensions of the ball. Those bodies must have been made of liquid and glue. There were no false jumps, no extra moves to satisfy the crowd. The Giants wouldn't shimmy on their diamond.

Pharaoh Yarbull was at third for them. The Pharaoh threw with his left hand. He went into the hole deeper and faster than Rags ever could. And he skewered line drives out of the air with a whirling motion that would have been impossible to see if he hadn't worn a gold stripe.

The fans expected a baseball circus, and all they got was nigger magic. The Giants would clown for an inning, as Muley Jones mimicked the patter of Babe Ruth's little feet, and the Pharaoh charged a suicide bunt like Ragland himself might do, with his elbows pumping hard, and then they'd return to their natural game of destroying the Harry Heilmanns. They didn't chortle once. They took their win without much glee. It was almost a secret among themselves how good they were.

The Marylanders still enjoyed the show. "Them monkeys sure can dance." And they pitied the All-Stars who had to take on baboons without Harry to enliven their attack. The fans returned to their villages resigned to the reality of an evil world, where black devils couldn't lose.

Even the Harry Heilmanns weren't disgruntled about what had happened in the field. The Harrys went their nine innings. They drove in a run. They didn't shout "nigger" at the coons. They swung their bats and stayed polite. Rags was the only one who seemed upset. The kid walked over to Chappie Gruel and snarled at him.

"You fell asleep on us."

"I didn't sleep," Chappie said. "I played. Ask anybody."

"I don't have to ask. The next time you snore in the middle of a game, I'll kick your teeth in."

Garl stepped between Chappie and the kid. "I do the managing here, Mr. Ragland. You'd better apologize to Chappie."

If the kid wrestled with his manager, and kicked Chappie in the mouth, he could say goodbye to the Harrys and go back to Boston and the wife. It would be a winter of Beacon Hill. He'd have to count the blue shutters on Acorn Street to get some exercise.

"Didn't mean it about kicking your teeth," he mumbled, looking at his shoes.

"That's okay," Chappie said. "Hell, they aint nothin' but a bunch of crazy niggers. You can't beat them, so why kill yourself? But I don't snore when I'm in a game."

"Yes you do," Garl said. "The kid was right. You lie down on us again, Chappie, and I swear I'll strap you to the bus. The Harry Heilmanns aren't a juggling act. I play to win."

Garl had to find a boardinghouse to hold his men for the night. But he didn't see the Giants go scrambling for accommodations. They pitched their hotel under that grandstand the team's carpenters had made.

"You're welcome to bunk with us," the boss of the Giants said. "We got plenty of room."

It would have been like sleeping in a cave for Garl. "Thanks, but we'll try the boardinghouses."

"Suit yourself. Only mind this. The punkies are mean in these parts. Maryland's got the worst bedbugs and flies in America."

Garl should have listened to that little man. The boardinghouse he picked for the Harrys was overloaded with lice. They lived in the wallpaper, loving all the glue, but when Garl brought his men around, the lice ate through the walls to feast on Harry Heilmanns. The sound of ballplayers scratching themselves invaded the boardinghouse. The Harrys crawled out of their blankets and spent the night in sitting chairs.

The Giants were ready for them in the morning. Their pitchmen had assembled another big crowd from the next group of villages. These Marylanders heard about the whipping the "coon team" delivered to the white Harrys. And they'd come to watch the slaughter all over again. They didn't have to hoot at the blacks, since it wasn't a legitimate series in their eyes. Any nigger diamond was perfect for a carnival.

Chappie Gruel stroked his knees and hopped around in left field. No one could accuse him of snoring now. But a sockamayock like Chappie couldn't change the complexion of a baseball war. Pharaoh Yarbull stationed himself in center field and brought down whatever the Harrys could sock over the pitcher's head. He went into the trees for a long fly ball off Garland's bat. And he was like a fifth infielder who could guard the blind spots in back of second base. The Pharaoh doubled twice, and smashed a wicked ball through the fingers of Rags' glove. The Giants took the Harry Heilmanns, 17–2.

They also played in the afternoon. The pitchmen had already located a different crowd. Yarbull must have been restless; he moved to first base. He grabbed pop flies for his catcher, and stretched his body for throws that should have gone into the grandstand. There was no one person in the white leagues to compare with him. He was Garland James in the morning, George Sisler in the afternoon. In addition to that, he was Pharaoh the enchanter, who could step out of the ordinary workings of time, and appear to float while he was making the most savage and impossible leap; the Pharaoh could trim down his moves and translate them into absolute energy. It came with a price. He forced his body beyond what other men could do. But that terrifying tension he induced in the field had aged him. The Pharaoh was old at twenty-five. The muscles around his knees had begun to knot. He would have spasms in his thighs as he slept with his mates under the grandstand. The witch doctor had to unknot his legs every morning, or the Pharaoh couldn't have walked to first base. The skin near his eyes was pinched back, as if the Pharaoh wore a mask to cover that pain of his, and deaden it to the crowd.

The Giants won the afternoon game, 12–2. It was turning into a ritual for the kid, where the Giants would score at will and allow the Harrys a run or two. Their owner must have reckoned that a shutout might humiliate the boys in the stands. It wasn't good business to make the whites look like complete monkeys. The Harrys had to have some little streak, back-to-back hits in an early inning, so the Marylanders wouldn't start to yawn.

The kid brooded over this. He wasn't going to be a hankie in Pharaoh Yarbull's back pocket that you could mop your head with and stuff away whenever you liked. The Harrys were becoming invisible. The Giants blew on them, and plotted the course of each game. Rags felt like the negligible partner in a slow, killing dance. He intended to stop the Colored Giants.

He cornered Garl near the bus and begged him for a decent crop of men. "We can't win with the ginks you hired."

"Should I telegraph George Sisler to come rescue us? I can barely meet the payroll as it is."

"Who said anything about George? You could wire Tilly and Sheriff Smith . . . "

"The Sheriff won't play with colored boys, and Tilly has bad knees. Any more suggestions?"

The kid went to Scarborough, who'd become coach and trainer

to the Harrys, bandaging this man and that, and signaling for a suicide squeeze from his foot of grass behind first base.

"Scarborough, you have to try some voodoo on them, or we can forget about winning a game."

"I can't voodoo them. I don't know how."

"Then learn," Rags said. "Steal from their witch doctor, that guy they call Sam."

So the hunchback set out to voodoo the Cincinnati Giants. He would strut alongside their team, throwing up his hump at them. He would mumble incantations over their drinking water. He would crook his pinkie at the Pharaoh, wherever the Pharaoh happened to play.

The Giants laughed at his silly work. But Samuel Sharn was outraged. The witch doctor shuffled near the brute's tiny coaching box. "Don't you fuck with me. I'll put boils on Mr. Garland's ass. I'll bring the plague to you Harrys. You'll be shitting frogs out of your guts."

Samuel couldn't frighten the brute. Scarborough still displayed his hump to the Cincinnati Giants, and he would hex the Pharaoh as often as he could. The witch doctor wasn't conspicuous about his retaliation rites. He had no flagrant magic to offer up. He was a sickly man who didn't carry devils in his socks. But the plague did arrive. The Harry Heilmanns began to hog the little outhouse the carpenters had erected behind the stands. The whole team came down with the flux. The Harrys would rush from the diamond to the outhouse, from the outhouse to home plate. Chappie Gruel was too weak to hold a bat. Steve Bumpo quit the Harrys, traveled down to Cape Charles, and jumped into the Chesapeake, hoping a swim would cure him of his stomach fever. Zack Wheat went home to Missouri.

Garl was left with eight men. He had to put the brute on first base. Scarborough was agile enough. He gave up his voodoo to concentrate on trapping the ball in his mitt. It amused the villagers for a day to have a hunchback struggle on the diamond, but the war between the Giants and the Harrys had begun to lose its shine. The carpenters dismantled their benches in the field, the groundkeepers destroyed the diamond they had landscaped out of ordinary dirt and grass, and the caravan crossed over to Virginia. Garl tagged along.

The Harrys dropped nineteen games in a row; they hadn't crept within five runs of the Giants. Their lot didn't improve once they reached the Virginia line. The Cincinnatis camped outside Fredericksburg, creating a new diamond and putting up a pile of seats.

The pitchmen gandered about with their placards, hauling in fresh villagers to watch a baseball war that had become a bloodless affair. The Harrys seemed shackled to the Giants and their movable diamond. They lost another dozen games, with lopsided scores. It was like a theatre piece performed over and over again, with innings instead of acts. Rags was stuck inside a drama the Giants had prepared for him. Yarbull went from position to position, and Rags chewed lima beans and dust.

Garl couldn't dwell on the scores. He had to produce beds for the Harrys without too many lice. The kid got to live with bugs in his pants. Someone had tracked him to the team's Virginia boardinghouse. He had a caller on the telephone. His wife. He could hear her sniffle all the way from Beacon Hill.

"I miss you, Rags. Will you come for Christmas?"

"I'll try."

He knocked on the manager's door. "Excuse me, Skipper Garl. Have you been telling certain folks where we are?"

"Our schedule isn't a secret, kid. I promised Hollis I'd keep in touch."

"Have you changed your mind about Sheriff Smith?"

"I told you. The Sheriff doesn't play with colored boys."

"Then we'll lose and lose and lose. The Cincinnatis own us, skip. We're more than cousins to them. We're a team of babies for the Giants."

Rags shouldn't have despaired so much. A peculiar fate caught up with the Giants at Fredericksburg. Emma, the boss' wife, had left her milkman, whoever it was, and come back to the Giants. She was a high yellow woman of thirty or so, with reddish brown hair and a soft neck that reminded you of the dents and veins in a dish of cream. Her scowls were prettier than most people's smiles. She had long fingers, a fine back, and her hips held close to the denims she wore. She was half owner of the Cincinnati Giants.

She could turn Carl into a crazy man. The boss jumped up and down. He raged at her for abandoning him, and then he started to blubber. He was helpless around his wife, who could disappear as often as she pleased. His body became a gnarled thing with Emma in the caravan. His love for her twisted into a hatred that he tore out of his own skin.

It demoralized the team to watch Carl suffer like that. Yarbull made his first error in forty games. Yam Murray's sinkerball didn't come forking down at the batter with its usual breeze.

"Call the Sheriff," Rags shouted in Garl's ear. "I'll pay for his goddamn trip. He can tolerate niggers for half a day. We'll send

him back to sweet Georgia after nine innings. Garland, I'd like to
win one game. . . . ''

The Sheriff arrived on a Monday in November. His forehead
puckered when Rags kissed him on the cheek, to show what a joy
it was to have Sheriff Smith on the Harry Heilmanns. The Sheriff
wiped off that kiss with the length of his sleeve. ''Shit, Garland, I
said I'd strike out coons for you, but I didn't agree to getting kissed
. . . show me those Cincinnatis.''

The Giants were aware of Sheriff Smith. They knew all about
his smoke. The Sheriff had twenty-five wins for the seventh-place
Sox. They snorted at him from the wooden hulls of their Buicks,
pretending to shiver over his size. Then they scrambled onto the
diamond. Their criers had already declared the pitching duel of the
century, between Yam Murray of the Giants and Sheriff Smith.
They lured nine or ten thousand to the field. Carl had to put the
overflow near the foul lines. Pharaoh was the shortstop this afternoon.

The Harrys looked pathetic in their dirty grays. The Sheriff gave
them an extra man, so Garl could pull the brute off first base. Rags
told him not to. ''He'll bring us luck, skip. Leave him there.''

''When did Scar'bruh win for us?''

''He'll win today.''

Rags mustered whatever totems he could think of. He wore his
socks inside out. He twisted his belt around, so the buckle was
over his arse. he ate pieces of thread off his unwashed blouse. And
he had a brute on first to protect the Harrys from Samuel Sharn.
He reckoned that Scarborough's hump would behave like a lightning rod and drink up the Giants' voodoo.

The kid could feel that nigger logic after four weeks of bedbugs
and lice. The blood they took from Rags enlightened him. It was
no haphazard, scrambling war between the teams, with independent fight-outs in all the different villages. Carl the bossman was
stingy as hell. He told his Giants not to give a game to the Harry
Heilmanns. Beat them, beat them, beat them, from Maryland to
Floridy. Walk like Babe Ruth, diddle a bit, let the Pharaoh have
his nine positions, but never, never lose.

The kid made his stand outside Fredericksburg, with Scarborough, Sheriff Smith, Topper Rigney, Garland James, and the sockamayocks. The Giants weren't alarmed. Emma had bitten into
their playing style, because of the hold she had on Carl. But you
could bust the seams on their golden baseball pajamas and tie one
of Pharaoh's hands, and they'd still devour the Harrys.

The game began as a replica of all the others. Yam hid his smoke

for an inning and allowed the Harrys a string of hits. Topper doubled into the grass behind first. Ragland squeezed him over to third
with a bunt to the pitcher's box that he ran out for a Chinaman's
single. Garland homered to put the Harrys three ahead. The Giants
did nothing but smile. They enjoyed this little rally that Yam provoked with a lazy thumb. He tightened his fist and struck out the
next three batters, using his sinkerball.

The Sheriff whistled on his strut to the mound. "Where's my
pillow, Garland? No gang of coons can slap this ol' Sheriff for
three runs."

Pharaoh was the leadoff man. The Giants didn't share the white
leagues' theory of a "balanced" attack. They wouldn't save their
sluggers for the middle of the batting order. The heaviest hitters
came at you first.

But this was Sheriff Smith, who had made war on Cobb, Sisler,
Heilmann, and Ruth. He wouldn't concede an inch of batting room
to any man. He dusted Yarbull for trying to crowd home plate.
Then he leaned back and threw his fireball. Yarbull socked it into
the trees. Fast as he was, Garl didn't have the chance to spear that
ball. It traveled over fences and stray cows, into a neighboring
pasture, five hundred feet away, and then fell out of sight.

The Sheriff shrugged his right wing. "That's the last ball them
coons will touch with a bat." He laid his smoke on the Giants and
put them out, one, two, three.

The game went another five innings without a hit. Then the
Pharaoh strung a frozen rope that knocked off the bill of Scarborough's cap and continued on into right field for a stand-up triple.
Muley Jones came up to bat. The Sheriff had struck him out twice
with fireballs and slow curves. He was convinced that no coon in
the world could solve his change of pace. The Sheriff spun a drop
pitch and Muley drilled it into the hole. Rags hadn't watched and
watched the Pharaoh out of idleness. He leapt with both feet, his
torso acting like a javelin, and snared that ball as it sank around
his shoestrings. The Pharaoh had committed himself, lunging for
home, and he couldn't get back to third.

Carl stood near the overflow with his wife. Emma had to smile
for any kid who could catch Pharaoh Yarbull running to the wrong
base. Carl had an attack of bitterness. "That aint no white man
out there. He plays like a nigger."

Bossman Carl went to his witch doctor. "What's the matter with
you, Sam'l? We two runs behind, and them sisters are standing on
their feet."

"Mr. Carl, the hunchback is in my way."

"Lay him low with the measles, I don't care."

"Lord, I tried. But I can't work around the pimple on his back. He's got Satan someplace in his shoulder."

"Forget the hunchback and you bring a storm down on the Harrys. Aint you got your root?"

"Yes, sir, Mr. Carl."

"Then go to it. I want them Harrys to play in mud."

Samuel Sharn had manufactured rain dozens of times with the root he kept in a jar. It was his grandmother's root and it had never failed him. Samuel was the number one rootworker in the nigger leagues. He walked behind the grandstand, sneaked into the outhouse, closed the door, and worked that root, shaking and shaking the jar until the sky turned black. But the storm didn't break over the Harry Heilmanns. None of the Harrys got wet. It rained everywhere except on that baseball diamond. The grandstand flooded and people began to disappear. The Giants had the Harrys and themselves and no more paying customers. They finished out their innings in an isolated field. The boss cursed the witch doctor and his temperamental root that rained on him but wouldn't rain on the Harry Heilmanns. His wife was beautiful with wet brown hair. She stood in Samuel's rain and licked at it with her mouth. The boss had a miserable pinch in his groin.

He put his hope in Yarbull. The Pharaoh had one more at bat coming to him. You couldn't fool him with any goddamn fireball. The Pharaoh could murder slow stuff too.

Garland crouched near a stone wall at the end of the field and waited for the pitch. The Sheriff threw a junk ball at the Pharaoh that came in knee-high. Yarbull didn't have to look at it. He whipped his bat around, swinging from the heels, and clubbed that ball. The rain slowed it down, Samuel's rain, the rain that should have wrecked the Harrys. Garl didn't wander more than a dozen feet from the stone wall. "Goodbye, Pharaoh." He ran towards the diamond, signaling to the other Harrys. He had the victory ball in his glove.

10

The kid arrived on Beacon Hill two days after Christmas. He missed the candlelighting ceremony and the caroling that marked every Christmas eve at Louisburg Square. The first thing he did was throw Marylou's servant down into the kitchen area. "I'll ring you when I want you, Rhys. This is your home while I'm in the house. Stay out of the bedrooms, you understand?'' Then he kissed Iva and said hello to his mother-in-law.

Iva was huffy with him. ''You have a fine sense of Christmas, don't you, Rags? Mama and I had to light candles for you. There's supposed to be a man in the house on Christmas eve.''

''You had your mama's servant,'' Rags said, with spittle on his tongue.

''Don't you talk about him . . . where's Scarborough?''

''He went to Cuba with the team. Garl wouldn't give him Christmas off. He's too valuable to us. He breaks nigger voodoo spells.''

''Don't you say nigger to me. It's not polite.''

Her body was hard when Rags took her to bed. It was as if he hadn't gotten out from under Samuel's root. Iva could have been some votive creature. Her hips moved, but her presence seemed to have vanished from him. Iva girl wasn't there with Rags.

''Are you finished?'' she said, with her eyes on the wall.

He got up, feeling a rage against the Cottonmouths. He grabbed Iva by the wrist and flung her out of the room. He couldn't bring a terror into her eyes.

''Are we going for a walk without our clothes? It's too late for caroling.''

''You'll carol in your mama's bed.''

He could see the imprint of a smile on the wife. ''Is that what you want, Rags?''

They went naked into her mama's bedroom. Mother and daughter looked at each other without the slightest blush. Rags had his way with them. Marylou didn't complain. She whispered ''Harvard Jack'' in his ear.

Iva watched.

Ballplayers have such sharp hands and feet. Rags could cut you with his body, claw between mama and the girl. The bride was thinking to herself: my mother's insane. Mama and her Harvard Jacks! Iva had a husband who was late for Christmas. He'd rather play ball than live with her. *Baseball, baseball.* She'd married a glove and a pair of flannel pants. The kid dug a home for himself around third base. He wouldn't take Iva on the road. She was dumb ''Eveline,'' the baseball wife. Raggsy could have been a sailor. He went from port to port with his winter and summer teams. Was she supposed to do needlework while the hero was away? Or join a lending library? He shouldn't have brought her into mama's room. Oh, she'd do his bidding. She could be Raggsy's little doll. But dolls can scratch too. And she'd find a way to scratch that kid.

Rags was lonelier than he'd ever been, lonelier than Tucson, lonelier than Abilene, where his companions were bulls and nigger cowboys with neckerchiefs, gloves, and splintered bats. He couldn't make his bed with the Cottonmouths. Their love screams tormented him, their breath was like a killer perfume; he listened to the pounding of their hearts with a chill in his entrails. He got dressed while the Cottonmouths were asleep.

He ran to South Station with his equipment bag, shirts and underpants rolled between his bats. He was a ballplayer, not a husband with two redheaded wives. His desire froze in him. Curled against mama and daughter only half an hour ago, he couldn't reach into their vitals. It was like touching the dead. The kid had too many selves in that house. Ragland, Cedric, Harvard Jack. Everybody and nobody all at once. Would someone tell the kid who he was? He could catch a baseball in either fist. That's as much as he knew.

He was recognized on the "Beeline Express" to Miami. It comforted him to play Ragland again. To talk baseball with businessmen and honeymooners. To sing about the Red Sox and the Harry Heilmanns. To declare how the Harrys had beaten the Colored Giants on a rainy Monday in November with a hunchback at first. "They couldn't live with that one defeat. Sure, they whipped us plenty after that. We didn't come close. But it wasn't the same thing. We scratched the Giants, 3–1, on their own diamond, and they couldn't forgive themselves."

He got to Key West and took the mail boat to Havana. There was nothing unfamiliar about the bottle-shaped harbor he landed in. The old Spanish town was crazy for *beisbol*. Twelve American teams, black and white, had been working Cuba for a month. They had a World Series in Havana, Camagüey, and on the Isle of Pines. But there was a major disappointment among the fans. The Cubans loved the Yanquis, and what did they get? Rabbit Maranville, Rogers Hornsby, and a team that borrowed Harry Heilmann's name. Babe Ruth was in Puerto Rico that year. His winter contract didn't have Cuba in it. He was fat and muddy-eyed, but he still pulled in a thousand dollars a game, because the Juanitos adored his strikeouts as much as his home runs.

Rags couldn't locate his own team. The Harrys had dispersed throughout the provinces, and were playing in various winter leagues. He found Chappie Gruel in an American bar on the Calle O'Reilly. Chappie had a broken foot. He and the kid didn't get along, but Chappie was glad to see another Harry Heilmann. They drank rum all afternoon.

"Chappie, what happened to the foot?"

"Christ, they don't have grass in this country. You have to run on hard red clay. It's a miracle I didn't break my neck."

"Where's Garl?"

"In Camagüey, fielding a team of nigger farmers."

"Did he take Scarborough along?"

"Na . . . your roomie's out of baseball."

Rags figured the rum had gone to Chappie's broken foot and was feeding him with lies. "He's given it up, I'm telling you. The brute got married."

"That's impossible. I've only been away two and a half weeks."

"Well, he took the vows. Married a mulatto woman, I think. Nobody's seen the bride, but I'm told he discovered her while she was working on her back."

"Chappie, what's his address?"

Chappie sucked up more rum and gargled his throat with a grin on his face. "Can't tell you, kid. The brute swore me to silence. He's afraid of you. Says you'd scream at him for picking out a wife."

"Can't you give me a hint, or do I have to walk the whole island?"

"He's in the sailors' district," Chappie said. "You'd better wear your uniform. It's a rotten part of town, but they might have pity on a baseball man."

So Rags put on his filthy grays with HARRY HEILMANN sewn across the chest, and he wandered into the *barrio marino,* near the Havana seawall. It was a district of whores, sailors, pirates, Turks, male prostitutes, and starving old men. The *calles* looked as if they'd been eaten by a pack of wild boars. He passed wine cellars that could have housed coffins too. The smell of piss and old men's pants was everywhere. A bride and groom couldn't have walked abreast in those alley streets. But no one ruffled the kid. A gringo baseball player could go wherever he liked, as long as he wore a suit of magical pajamas.

He met a colonel on horseback, galloping through the narrow, crooked *calles.* The colonel saluted Rags and yelled *Yanqui boy* at him. He saw two infants leading a turtle around on a leash. He mumbled the choppy pidgin Spanish he could remember from his days in Old Tucson. *"Beisbol. Hunchyback. Jorobado. Bruto. Monstrosamente."*

The infants neglected their turtle to go with Rags. They led him to an alleyway stuck between two streets and left him there. Rags looked up at a building that had a few brittle balconies and line after line of hollowed-out floors. A tribe of bats collected on one window and slept with their noses pointing down. Rags woke the bats with a shout.

"Hey, roomie, show yourself."

The bats flew onto another window but couldn't settle into any permanent sleep.

"Scarborough, do I have to come up for you?"

The brute appeared on the topmost balcony. He wore his baseball knickers and nothing else. His hump rose like a marvelous welt out of his shoulder blades. Sweat gleamed from the muscles on his arms.

"Raggsy, go away."

Six or seven brats accompanied him on the balcony. Two were blond, and the rest were dark-skinned. They clutched Scarborough's hands and thighs and screamed "Papá, papá." Then the bride came out. She was a Negro woman with delicate bones in her face. She could have been twenty-five or forty. How could Rags tell the age of a woman on a balcony wall?

The brute seemed to have a murderous temper now.

"It's all right for you to get married, aint it, Rags? What about me? . . . go away. You're scaring my kids."

Rags followed the seawall out of the sailors' district. He returned to the Calle O'Reilly. He had nowhere else to go. He sat at the American bar two days and two nights. Chappie Gruel must have fled to one of the bars across the street. Rags shaved in the toilet and lived on plantain milk and rum. He would have waited out the winter on O'Reilly Street if Garl hadn't come for him.

"Chappie says all you do is shit and eat."

"You paying him to spy on me?"

"No. That little skunk feels sorry for you."

"I brought my equipment bag. Who are we playing next?"

"The season's over, kid. You'll have to swing your bat in a dead park. It's January, and I'm going on my vacation."

Rags wiped the rum off his mouth with a finger. "Take me with you, Garl."

"I don't need a partner where I'm going."

The kid seemed tied to that bar stool with some terrible loss of spirit. Garl couldn't abandon him to the tourists and the barflies. He held Rags under the shoulder and lifted him off the stool. "Okay, sockamayock, you can come with me."

Rags was like a helpless baby who had to be spun through the streets. He found himself near the seawall again, in another part of sailor town. Garl had put him on a fishing boat. The kid heard rough talk between Garl and the tillerman. But the tillerman stayed on the boat. Rags reached down with a tin can and tried to taste the sea water. Garl twisted his head back and threw the can away. They broke out of the harbor, with the tillerman grumbling at them.

The kid had lost his sense of time and place. He knew they were on the water. His cuffs were growing wet. He wanted to play fungo in the boat, but Garl ordered him to keep quiet.

"Garland, do we have to sail around the pirate coves?"

Piratas, he told the tillerman, and the tillerman laughed at the crazy gringo in the *beisbol* suit.

He took them into the half-deserted territory of Quintana Roo. It was a dumping ground for undesirables and political prisoners from Honduras, Mexico, and Guatemala. The tillerman was happy to get rid of his cargo of two baseball idiots.

Garl didn't pull Rags inland. They lived on the beach. It was a funny idea of a vacation for the kid. You couldn't even find a lizard in that dumb gray sand. Zombies walked the beach, men with eyes that didn't jut from the middle of their heads. They went up the beach and down, in a line that never varied. One of the zombies had a little scar under both ears.

"Who is that gink?"

"Shut up," Garl said. "He's a friend of mine. He used to be the governor of a goddamn state in Honduras until his party ruined itself. They forgot to steal some miserable election."

"If he's such a friend, how come he doesn't talk?"

Garl shook his head in disgust. Rags had to be the most ignorant boy in the territory.

"Governor Hermosa can't talk. The opposition ripped out his tongue and put him on Quintana Roo. They couldn't kill the old man. He had too many relatives around."

"How do you know the history of Honduras?" Rags said.

"If you come every winter you learn what it's like."

Garl left the beach for an hour and came back with stores of food and three handsome women. He couldn't have rented these women if they hadn't been in disgrace with their own village. They were fornicators, drunkards, and foulmouths whose husbands had deserted them and taken other brides. But the kid didn't find them wanting in any way. They jabbered in their native tongue, cooked a splendid turtle soup, and hugged the three men (Rags, Garl, and the silent governor), with absolute devotion.

The *beisbol* began to drift out of Rags. He could have wintered at Quintana Roo for the whole twelve months of the year. February was coming, and Garl touched the kid on the shoulder while he was sleeping with one of the disgraced wives. "We have to go. It's time for Arkansas."

"Hell, Garl, why don't we fuck baseball camp and stay right here?"

"I have a family to support . . . and if I don't bring you to Sackville Forest, Hollis will stick my pay envelope in his mouth and chew on it."

They said goodbye to the governor with a wave of the hand, and Garl returned the three women, who cried at the loss of such stupendous and agreeable men. The village took the wives back and waited for other beachcombers and ballplayers to rent these foulmouthed women.

The players' camp was in a shamble when Garl and the kid arrived at Sackville Forest. The Sox were without a manager. Briggs Josephson had jumped the club. Hollis never sent him a contract, thinking to whittle down his salary for 1925. The Brownies hired him away. Hollis swore to blackball him and sue the American League if he couldn't get satisfaction. He was readying an appeal to Kenesaw Mountain Landis, the high commissioner of baseball. But he dropped the subject of Briggs' piracy the minute he saw Garland.

"Mercy on us. I don't have to bring in a new man. You're my player-manager, Garl. That's three thousand extra in your pocket."

How could Garl refuse? He'd rather manage the Sox, and be their tyrant, than play under someone else. But he had no illusions about where the Sox would go. He'd have to fight like a crazed horse to keep them out of the cellar in 1925.

Meanwhile, Hollis frowned at the kid, who still wore his winter grays. "Get out of those stinking pants. You're with the Red Sox, or did you forget?"

He was down on Ragland this year. He knew about the troubles between Iva and the kid. And he blamed Rags.

The kid dragged himself to the Red Sox boardinghouse. There was another man's trousers in his room. And a baseball cap. The brute had beat Rags to Arkansas.

"Son of a bitch," Rags said, with his first smile in Sackville Forest. "I thought you were finished with us. Chappie told me that."

"He's a liar," Scarborough said. "I'm the Boston bat boy. I never miss a training camp."

"What about that woman on the balcony?"

Scarborough began to hide his chin. "She's my winter wife."

"We ought to celebrate," Rags said. "It's an event, isn't it, when roomies meet after a month? Let's see if we can dig up chocolate sundaes in this rabbit town."

The kid's wife showed up on the bus from Hot Springs. Hollis had arranged for the trip. He was the girl's "goduncle," and he had the right to mend her marriage. He found a separate bungalow for Iva and Rags, away from the boardinghouse.

The reconciliation didn't work. The girl had come for revenge on the husband who took her mama and her into bed, had his fill, and disappeared. She waited until Rags went with Hollis and Garl and Sheriff Smith to talk baseball in Hollis' private bungalow. Then she strolled up to the boardinghouse in her spring coat. The country boys were sitting on the porch. Chicken Stallings sensed that she had nothing on under the coat. He watched the play of her calves on the porch steps. The outline of her buttocks was clear and true under the green of her coat. "Your man aint in this house," the Chicken said. "He's with the boss . . . in the far shack."

"I know," Iva said, and she continued into the boardinghouse. The country boys whistled to themselves. "Somebody's getting some poontail," the Chicken muttered. And he sneaked behind the girl.

She'd gone up to the hunchback's room. She didn't shut the door. She began to unbutton her coat. Scarborough couldn't take his eyes off those fingers twirling around the buttons. He wanted to scream his head off, so the blood would break in him and turn him blind. How could he miss the red patch between her legs?

Iva walked over to the brute. She remembered lying next to him and Rags in their room at the baseball hotel, when she came up from Tisbury town the summer before last. The brute had shivered all night, his erection putting a tent in their mutual blanket. He wouldn't disobey her now.

His tongue grew into a fat toad. He was an imbecile with hot hands pulling on his baseball shirt. She undid his belt, kneeled, and suddenly his knickers were on the floor.

The brute was making love to Raggsy's wife. Her body glowed under him. She had a cat's eyes. The hump on his back had gone away. He bent perfectly into the wife. She didn't rush the brute. Iva stayed with his frenzy, held him while he moaned and fell weak against her side. He'd come out of her. He moved off the bed and sat hunched in the corner.

The Chicken had been watching from the door. He'd seen the

ripples on Scarborough's back, the muscles that snaked down from his neck while he was stuck to Miz Iva. But the girl was free, waiting on the bed, with lots of room between her thighs. The Chicken let his suspenders drop. Rags wasn't his leader anymore. The kid stopped fighting for the country boys. Hadn't he come into camp with their enemy, Garland James? Rags had jumped over to the Dartmouth crowd. So why couldn't the Chicken enjoy his wife?

Iva ruffled her forehead when he climbed on top of her, but she didn't refuse. Then it was Germany Stone at the door, with one or two Dartmouth men, Hooks Poland, and a full array of country boys. They stood on line for the girl. The Chicken had her twice.

The brute was muttering in the corner when Garl came in. He slapped at his own players, punched all the Red Sox in the room until he was near the bed. Iva had a deep glaze on her throat. She didn't recognize Garland. She thought he was another country boy who would get on top. He began to shove her into her coat. The brute stared up from his corner. His eyes touched on Garl for one terrible moment. He could have been in Egypt. All his sensibility had fled from the room.

Garl noticed that shriveled body, but he couldn't attend to the brute. He'd have a civil war on his hands if he didn't get Iva out of there. He gathered her belongings and drove the girl to Hot Springs. He didn't tell Hollis. Garl was manager of the Sox, and he understood the laws of training camp; a team fell apart every time a player's wife began serving other men.

It didn't take the kid very long to discover what went on in the boardinghouse. The boy who took care of the linen was fond of Rags and he ratted on the country boys. "Sorry, Mr. Ragland, but half the club had your missus."

Rags didn't ask about his wife. "Where's Scarborough?"

"Dunno," the boy said. "He run off somewheres. She took him first. I saw them from the window."

The country boys locked themselves inside their rooms. Rags didn't bang on the doors and challenge them to a boxing duel. He went searching for the brute.

He looked in all the little shacks around the playing field. He broke into deserted bungalows. Then he walked into the woods of Sackville Forest. It was a few acres of short, twisted trees and ancient bear dens. The kid went from tree to tree, calling "Scarborough, Scarborough."

The brute was there. He couldn't have heard Raggsy's calls. He had smoke in his head. The smoke licked at him with a hot tongue.

He stumbled in and out of bear dens, thinking of ways to destroy himself. He might have been a collector of mushrooms, with a finger on his back that twitched in the presence of hyenas and poisonous toadstools. But there was hardly a mushroom in these woods, or a hyena. That hump twitched with a sense of its own disaster. A roomie shouldn't fuck a wife. *I had Miz Iva. Sin, sin.*

The brute stepped out of his pants. He carried them in one arm and began to sock at trees. *Shitface. Whoreboy. Fuck. Fuck. Fuck.*

The kid spotted two naked legs dangling near the ground. Rags charged for those legs like an uncurled snake. The brute had tried to hang himself with his own baseball knickers, knotting them to the branch of a tree. His hump had saved him. His neck was too strong. It wouldn't break on a stunted tree in Sackville Forest. He was gagging, with slime on his tongue, when Rags pulled him down.

The kid tried to stroke his ear, comfort him, but Scarborough let out a shriek. It could have been an orphan wailing, or a lunatic.

"Don't cry," Rags said. "It wasn't your fault. She was only getting back at me. I got crazy in that house. I put Iva and her mama in the same bed."

Slowly the brute got onto his feet and followed Rags out of the woods, but he wouldn't let the kid touch him, steer him, or hold him around the waist.

Book Four

THE BAD BOY OF BASEBALL

11

THE KID GOT his old room back at the Brunswick Hotel. He and Scarborough slept under the same summer quilt. Beacon Hill fell out of their vocabulary. But it's a fickle thing to discard a baseball wife. The Royal Rooters had been fond of the kid's bride. They brought xylophones to the park, and beat out little tunes on their pieces of wood. The devotion of 1924 was gone. They'd turned cool to Rags.

He wasn't that familiar bastard, who'd stop a ball with his kidneys or his head to accomplish the double play. He was a mean kid now. He didn't acknowledge their songs. He seemed removed from the Boston infield. He never spoke a word to Alvin Critz. He growled at umpires. He'd have shoving wars with enemy catchers near home plate. He knocked down Muddy Ruel of the Washington Senators. The fans sided with Muddy in this war. Muddy was two inches shorter than Rags. And he had a rotten leg.

Garl fined the kid thirty bucks. He couldn't allow rhubarbs like that to happen. He wasn't raising bandits on the field. He had to hold a team together. But his Sox were pathetic without the kid. Whatever spirit they had burst out of his crazy glove.

He yelled at Rags in front of the team. "I don't care whose tongue you bite after a game. You don't attack a man when people are around. Save your feuding for the tunnel. Is that clear?"

The kid nodded in a perfunctory way. Garl had the mind to pull on Rags' nose. That might wake him up. Yet he had to go soft with

481

him. He understood the kid's torment. Rags was a veteran at nine-teen, a bastard with a live dad, a baseball tramp, and a husband who'd returned to bacheloring.

Garl whispered to the brute behind the kid's back. "Scarb'ruh, he can't fight everybody in the American League. His brains will be rolling around in the dirt. We haven't seen Detroit. What if he starts with Ty Cobb?"

"Cobb's an old man," the brute said, with a thin smile. "Rags can bust his face."

"Cobb's not *that* old, Mr. Scarb'ruh. Anyway, if the kid hurts a finger, he's useless to me. Calm him down, for Christ's sake. Take him to the picture show. Introduce him to a couple of whores. I'd rather he come down with the clap, than have to hear about his fights."

"I'm his roomie, skip. I aint no sorcery man. I can't stick his anger in a bottle and drown it in the Charles."

Garl thought of hiring a detective to watch over Rags. What's the good? He'd hit the detective in the jaw, and Garl would have to beg the local magistrate not to impound his third baseman. This time, when he received a note from Marylou in his hotel box, he decided not to ignore it. Maybe she could help him with the kid. He wouldn't march to her house on the Hill, because it was spooked with Cottonmouths, but he asked the bellboys at the Brunswick to show her up to his room.

She wouldn't discuss the kid. "I don't have any influence over my daughter, Mr. James. You'll have to ask her about the mar-riage."

"I'm in a pickle, Miz Marylou. I wouldn't want Rags to say I'm tinkering with his life. You see, ma'am, he's not surviving too well on his own, and . . . ."

"Doesn't he have a roommate?"

"Sure, but Scarb'ruh isn't the same as a wife."

The skipper was too involved in the running of his team to notice any signs of agitation in Marylou. Why was she shivering in Garl's sunny room? The hair whipped around her head like a serpent's rod. Her eyes went a bitter color as she stood close to Garl. He had Ragland in his mind. How could he tame the kid? He never heard the muttering in his ear.

"What, Miz Marylou?"

The words came like small intense bites from her mouth. "Would you like to undress me, Mr. James?"

She was beautiful with the sunlight burning in every hollow of her cheek. Garl couldn't place his own desire. He should have kissed her on the mouth, and spent the afternoon with the lady of Beacon Hill. Baseball strategy had turned him into an invalid and a fool. He didn't call out to her when she left him there, with his infield problems and his concern about the Tigers who were arriving tomorrow.

She'd had small luck with her men, Miz Marylou. A husband who died on her almost out of spite. That Judah. He felt her ass when she was a kitchen maid at his fraternity house. Judah got down on his knees in front of his brothers and proposed to her. They laughed and laughed, the Dartmouth boys and Judah dragged her to Beacon Hill to show off his kitchen maid–wife. His slut, he said. But she had a child with him. Hollis was more of a father than Judah was. Hollis taught Iva how to ice-skate. And Judah went and strangled on a chicken bone.

Marylou was in love with a baseball man. Quiet Garl. So serious. With three brothers in college. How many times could she offer herself? She might as well hear the frogs croak in the Fens. She'd find herself a frog lover if she could. Frogs were reliable. They didn't plead baseball. They croaked their songs and shook the mud off their backs. But she couldn't be sure. Maybe frogs had their own baseball league in the swamp. And they sang about their batting averages, just the way some men did.

I'll marry the frog in center field.

Garl didn't give another thought to Marylou. His team dropped three in a row to Detroit. Ragland challenged half the Tiger bench. He almost pushed Ty Cobb into the dugout wall. The great man was ready to fight. Cobb had lost his old handsomeness. He no longer had the look of a hawk. That sharp face of his was a matter of history. He developed jowls, and his ears were two puffy twists of flesh from all the knuckles he'd taken in his life.

Rags spit on the ground, near the great man's feet. "I don't fight grandfathers," he said, and he walked away from Ty Cobb. The great man threw himself at Rags, but the kid spun around and pushed Cobb off with an elbow.

The golden days were finished. Fans had stopped booing Ty Cobb. The American League had a new battler: Ragland of the Red Sox. He didn't have to struggle with a thirty-eight-year-old man. He added to his reputation by spurning Cobb's offer to fight.

He did go into the tunnel with Heinie Manush and Frank O'Rourke. He knocked Heinie senseless and chipped O'Rourke's teeth. He was the bad boy of baseball.

Christ, Garl figured to himself. I should have bloodied his head when I had him in the tunnel two years ago. Then he might have given up the habit of using his fists on other people.

Garl's telephone rang. It was Hollis McKee who wanted him. "Garland, have you heard from Marylou?"

"I talked to her last week . . . about Ragland."

"Well, she's missing, Garl."

"Missing? I don't understand."

"What's wrong with you? The woman disappeared."

Boston's fire companies worked with the police to find Marylou. Boats from the harbor patrol were raised onto fire trucks and shuttled over to the Fens. A dredging operation was begun in that wild park. The police had up to fifty boats in the water, dragging the marshland and the different pieces of the Muddy River for Marylou's corpse. They discovered an armada of sunken bottles, strangled cats and dogs, the bones of certain prehistoric fish, but nothing that resembled a woman or any of her clothes.

"I'll bet my thirty years in politics that the missus aint at the bottom of that lake," the mayor of Boston declared. The Republicans at the State House weren't so sure.

The police slapped and slapped at the water, while the Sox went on the road. Rags climbed on the dugout roof at Yankee Stadium and offered to take on twenty thousand fans. Altogether, or one at a time. He'd slug the women too, he said. Scarborough had to pull him down.

Rags fought with the A's and the Washington Senators. Fans assumed the practice of bombing him with soda pop while he was at third. It became routine for the ump to call time-out, so the bottles could be carted off the field. The booing didn't discourage Rags. He was batting .328. His mother-in-law was still missing from Boston and the rest of the world.

Two days after the police removed all their material from the Fens, Marylou rose to the top of that marshy water. She had weeds on her and cuts along her face. Her body was bloated with gas. But she wasn't unbeautiful. Nothing could damage that red hair.

The Boston papers screamed about Marylou:

HEIR TO ICE FORTUNE FOUND DEAD
POLICE EXPLORE POSSIBILITY OF FOUL PLAY
MURDER, SUICIDE, OR BIZARRE ACCIDENT?
WHAT WAS RAGLAND'S MOTHER-IN-LAW DOING IN A SWAMP?

The Sox returned to Boston with all that crazy news. Rags didn't stop off at his hotel. He rushed from South Station to Louisburg

Square. The front door wasn't locked. He stood in the main hall and started to yell.

"Iva? It's me . . . I'm sorry about your ma."

She came halfway down the stairs with her mother's servant. Rhys was carrying a blunderbuss, a pistol with a long snout. He couldn't keep it still. It wavered in his hand, like a frozen squirrel come alive. "You, get out of here."

"I'm talking to my wife," Rags said, starting up the stairs.

"So help me, I'll shoot."

The servant's teeth were chattering. Rags walked up to the blunderbuss, and pushed into it with his chest.

"Iva, I've come home . . . Scarborough doesn't have to live with us . . . maybe I could find a house . . ."

Iva didn't lunge for the pistol. She wouldn't splatter Rags against her wall. She pulled back her arm and brought him down to the bottom of the stairs. It took five hard slaps.

"Don't you ever come to this house again, Mr. Rags. You're not my husband anymore."

"Iva, I . . ."

She locked the door on him, and the kid stood on the salmon-colored bricks of Louisburg Square with bumps on his face. *That girl knows how to slap.*

12

The bad boy of baseball only got worse. He broke Pinky Hargrave's mouth under the grandstands of Sportsman's Park. He would have gone through the Brownies' roster and destroyed that team, with his Amherst boxing style. You couldn't gang up on the kid, trap him at the players' exit, and teach him a lesson with bats, fists, and spikes on a shoe, because the hunchback would get behind Rags and cover for him. And no bat or shoe in the world could penetrate that boil of armored skin and bone on Scarborough's shoulder.

Briggs Josephson had helped the Brownies climb to second place, but they wouldn't last the season if Ragland tore apart their infield, their outfield, and all their battery mates. Rags' old skipper left a message for the kid to come to a speakeasy opposite Sportsman's Park. It could have been a ploy to finish off Rags before he got out of St. Louis. The kid wouldn't bring Scarborough along. He went into the speakeasy by himself.

It must have been a haven for Brownie addicts, hoodlums, and gambling men. They scowled at Rags from the tables and the bar. He wasn't surprised. It was an enemy camp wherever he walked in St. Louis. Briggs ushered him into a private room. You had to be careful with Kenesaw Mountain Landis. The high commissioner had informers in each baseball town. And Briggs didn't like to be accused of tampering with another team's third baseman.

"Hiya, kid."

They drank soapy beer. Rags' old skipper smiled at him. "I won't be able to field a team pretty soon. Do me a favor, huh? Leave me nine men who can stand on their feet."

"It's not my fault," Rags said. "Tell your bench to lay off . . . I'll make them silly in the head if they go on riding me."

"Ah, what's a few goddamn words."

"Briggsy, they can spread shit about me. I don't care. But tell them not to mention my wife, my pa, and my mother-in-law who drowned. You don't hit a guy's family. It's dirty business."

"Rags, you owe me one."

"How's that?"

"I brought you into the league, remember? I found you in Arkansas, a lefty third baseman, and I carried you right away."

"Then you ran to St. Louis, and you forgot to take me with you."

Briggs looked into the beer mug. "You bonehead, I didn't forget. I'm dealing for you. I offered Gene Robertson and Baby Doll. Your skipper has to clear it with Hollis McKee."

"I won't walk without Scarborough. He has to be included in the deal."

Briggs swirled his beer, until it foamed up like a mug of warm piss. "Heck, I could have had Scarborough ages ago. But he dropped the same damn story. 'You take my roomie, or you can't have me.' "

They shook hands over the cloudy beer. "Stop causing trouble. I can't use a prizefighter on the Browns. And don't breathe a word until you get to Fenway, or you'll queer it for us."

Rags kept his mouth shut on the sleeper to Boston, but he had to spill *something* to his roommate. "Scarborough, we're going to live right near the Mississippi. Garl's trading for me and you. He's giving us away to the Browns."

"Don't be so sure," Scarborough whispered.

"I'm sure," Rags whispered back. "When did Briggsy ever lie?"

Garland didn't approach him after batting practice. Rags

winked, but the skipper kept a stone face. The kid had to corner
Garl in the dugout, while the rest of the Sox had gone up the stairs
to shed their practice uniforms.

"Skip, don't you have some news for me?"

"What about?"

"I thought Baby Doll was coming to Boston, and I was heading
for the Browns."

There wasn't a stir in that stone face.

"I thought so too. I tried to deal you. That's a fact. You're
ruining my club with those fists of yours. Baby Doll was just a
throw-in. He's thirty-four. I wanted Gene Robertson. He'll give
me the glove I need at third."

Garl stopped talking, and Rags followed him around the dugout.
"Well, what happened?"

"Hollis killed it . . . I can't say why. The deal made sense. Robertson's a ballplayer. You're a frigging shark. But Hollis isn't letting you out of the bag."

Rags strode through the tunnel in a fury and took those four
flights to the executive suite. He knocked on Hollis' door, the glass
rattling against his fist. "It's me. Ragland. The kid."

Hollis chased his secretary out, and Rags had that giant office
for the president of Boston baseball and himself.

"Trade me to the Browns," he said.

"No."

"I hate it here."

"Good."

"I'll split your fucking club. Believe me. I'll punch every man
you got."

"That's fine."

"Why won't you give me to St. Louis? Robertson can play
third."

"I know that. He hit .319 last year. He's got the hands. And he
isn't a lefty freak. But I want you in this graveyard. You're going
to die with the Red Sox. You son of a bitch, you murdered Marylou."

Rags jumped across the room and grabbed Hollis by the lapels.
"I don't give a shit whose boss you are. You didn't buy my tongue,
Mr. McKee. Marylou drowned. So don't say murderer to me."

"You broke her heart when you abandoned little Iva."

The kid dropped Hollis into a chair. "Mister, her heart was
broken long before that. I'd swear Dartmouth was the place. When
you and Iva's pa grabbed her for yourselves. Play with the country
girl. Eat her up. Tell me, boss, how did you and that Judah Cotton-

mouth decide which one would marry her? Did you cut the deck for Marylou?''

"Get out of my sight," Hollis said, his body sinking into the chair. His lips were a ghostly color.

"I'm not finished with you."

The kid seized the armrests of the chair and dragged Hollis up close to him. "Have you been touching pinkies with my father's lawyer? It's funny, isn't it, that the *Transcript* should shout Tannehill, Tannehill, last year, just before Opening Day. Griffey got to you, didn't he?''

"Yes," Hollis spit from the middle of his chair.

"You held on to the story, and you leaked it to Noel Finnbar. You got pictures of me at Amherst, the ones I sent to my pa, and you made Noel promise not to print them until you gave the word . . . lovely bastard that you are."

"I did what any owner would do."

"Mister, you don't have to trade little Cedric. I'll play for you. But if you ever come near me, on the field, and off the field, I'll wring your miserable neck. . . . ''

Rags turned aside from his enemies in the American League. He wouldn't fight with the Browns, or hurl insults at the Cleveland bench. He began to make war on the Sox. He didn't single out those bumpkins who had enjoyed the pleasures of his wife. That was a forgotten part of his war games. He took retribution on the whole roster of Hollis McKee. He bent Chicken Stallings' thumb, so the sockamayock couldn't pitch for a week. He insulted his own catcher, saying that Tilly Young ought to have a rocking chair. Tilly came from the U. of Alabama, where insults could fire a man's blood. He offered the kid a chance to apologize. Rags said no, and Tilly went to box the kid's ears back. He couldn't find the kid's ears. Rags dropped him with two vicious blows to the cheek. The catcher's tongue was split.

Garl had to put a stop to this crazy bloodbath. Who was next? Would the kid chirp at Seaman Schupp, or go after Alvin Critz? Garl suspended him for twenty-five days. Rags couldn't wear his glove on the field. He couldn't swing a bat. He had to warm the bench.

"Touch one more man, Ragland, and you're finished for the year."

The words came bitter to Garland's mouth. He'd butchered the Red Sox by suspending Rags. The guts were torn out of the Boston infield. He had to try a busher at third, a boy from Michigan named

Mark Travers. A rookie glove couldn't improve the Sox. Boston was so busy snoring in the cellar, it might fall out of the American League.

The brute became an emissary for Garl. "Skipper says he'll reinstate you if you promise to keep your knuckles inside your pocket."

"Tell him to blow."

And Rags sat on the Boston bench, with a wide girth between him and the other players. He wouldn't give any tips to Mark Travers. The fans were pulling for the new boy. But Travers seemed a bit shy of those pellets that were aimed for his skull. He would duck under a line drive, and he didn't have that third baseman's instinct to throw his chest into the path of an oncoming ball.

"You could sure use Gene Robertson," Rags would say to Garl. "Can't you twist Hollis' arm a little? The Sox are gonna be in baboonville in another month. Trade me to the Browns."

"I'd resign before I did that. You have your bench, Mr. Ragland. That's where you belong."

Rags stuck his knee out and tripped the fireballer, Sheriff Smith. Garl helped the Sheriff to his feet and then he looked at Babe Ragland. "You've been crying for this, haven't you? . . . meet me in the tunnel."

Rags shrugged off Garl's invitation. "I won't fight with my skipper. It's rotten baseball."

"Well, you'll have to pass over my body if you want to get to the clubhouse. I'm tired of your shit."

"Garl, you haven't punched a soul in two years. You're out of practice. You aim at my nose, and you'll be hitting wind."

"Try me, you arrogant prick."

The hunchback threw his hands over his eyes. But he couldn't get his sorrow to go down. He knew all along it would come to this. Sophocles and the bad boy of baseball. He wasn't sure who to pity. Garl or Rags? He'd have a pair of losers in the tunnel, that much he understood.

He appealed to Rags. "You can still back off. Make believe he's Mr. Cobb."

"How? Garl doesn't have bushy ears. He's the best outfielder in the East."

The Sox were exuberant. They'd have their revenge. No man could survive the skipper's combinations. His left was as wicked as his right. Scarborough had a different sense of things. He wanted to run from Boston and hide in some dark well.

The Sox lost to Cleveland, 7–2, and the players scrambled down the dugout steps and through the tunnel door. Rags stayed on the bench. He held his jaw in one fist. He liked Garland James. Garl had sailed with him to Quintana Roo. He couldn't have had his winter vacation without the skip. It was Hollis he was after, not Garl. Hollis McKee, who bought and sold players and country girls. Rags didn't have any desire to punch the skip.

"You can wait here until they dress."

It was Scarborough standing over him.

"That's no good. Garl means what he says . . . come on."

They walked into the tunnel, past the water fountain and the urinal, felt the dampness and the wind, and Rags began to warm his knuckles. Garl stood alone, midway up the tunnel. He wouldn't let the Sox hover close to him. They had to crouch on the clubhouse stairs.

Garl went into his boxing stance. Rags would have smirked at any other man. The Dartmouth position was a silly way to box. It followed the rules of 1905, that declared you had to display as little of yourself as possible. Narrow the target. Give your man nothing to hit. But the Dartmouth position cramped up your body. It couldn't induce that lightning in your elbow. It belonged to the grandfathers of a New Hampshire college town.

Amherst boxing was much less orthodox. It allowed you to spin off from the heel, and to lower and raise your center of gravity. You couldn't absorb a punch as well as any Dartmouth man. But you didn't have to. The Amherst style was to hit and run.

"Are you ready, kid?"

The first blow was off Garland's fist. It struck Ragland on the left nostril. The force of it threw the kid into the tunnel wall. The edge of his nose was pushed in. Rags pawed at the nostril, wiping the blood away. "Pretty, Garl. Going to my blind side."

The skipper snarled at him, "I didn't ask you for a commentary. *Fight.*"

Six short blows landed on Garl. For a minute Scarborough believed the kid was using different pairs of fists. Garl shortened his own punches. He knew how to flick at a man. But he couldn't land with Rags' frequency.

Humping Jesus! In all his misery, Scarborough was amazed. A fist would shoot out and die in the murky wind. There was so much weaving of bodies, you couldn't be sure where Amherst ended and Dartmouth began. Rags' head seemed disconnected from his feet. It was like watching two skeletons in baseball pajamas who had some missing joints. But their dance was starting to kill.

Garl wouldn't surrender to a boy. He could have taken all the cuffs to his eyebrows and his ears, only his knees twisted out from under him. He gave back whatever he could. Flurries of blows would pass between Garl and the kid. He couldn't get around that Amherst defense. Rags would coil and uncoil in front of Garl. Their blouses were ripped. They were carrying shreds on their shoulders. It wasn't fear that Garl could smell. It was dampness and piss. He would have punched and punched until September arrived and the season was over. He couldn't lay this kid on the tunnel floor. Rags had wires in his torso, instead of tissue and bone. You hit him, and he would spring back at you just as hard.

Garl's left eye was closed. He had to stare at a target that jumped all the time. The skip was angry at himself. He couldn't tame the bad boy. The walls were sliding onto him. Garl didn't give up his punches, even as he fell. His own flurries had beaten him. And those tiny Amherst jabs. The skip sat on his rump, with five or six gaps in his mouth.

The kid had lost just as many teeth. Rags was mystified when Garl disappeared. His fists were clenched. They pushed at where Garl's face should have been. He didn't know what else to do. Someone directed his shoulder towards the clubhouse. "You decked him, Raggsy. It's over now. . . . "

Scarborough had turned the kid around. He was as confused as any bat boy with a double ordeal. He had allegiances to his skipper and his roommate. But he couldn't help both of them. The kid was moving up the stairs, shoving Red Sox away. His shirt was like a series of rough bandannas that spilled down his back. His knees showed through his pants. One ear was so bloody, you would have sworn the lobe was gone. But he hadn't stumbled yet. So the brute took off his own jersey, rinsed it in the water fountain, and applied it to the bumps on Garland's head.

The skip blinked the blood and salt from his eyes. "I can see you, Chicken. You don't have to lean all over me."

"It ain't the Chicken," Scarborough said. "It's your bat boy, skip. Now be quiet, or you'll hurt the blisters on your tongue."

"He's the worst cocksucker in the league," Garl said. "He's crazy mean, but he can box. I'm glad he didn't fight with Cobb. He'd have butchered the old man from Detroit."

"How do you know?"

A tooth dropped out while Garl laughed from his plot of land in the tunnel. "Scarb' ruh, you sure are hard to please. You have the goddamn evidence. Look at me . . . am I on my ass, or not?"

And he coughed another tooth into the palm of his hand.

13

The kid wouldn't go on the road with his team. Why should he warm the Sox's bench in Chicago, St. Louis, and Detroit? But those Dartmouth blows to the head must have softened his reasoning skills. He forgot that the bat boy had to travel with Hollis' men. The kid remained at the Brunswick without his roommate. It saddened him not to have the brute under his quilt. Scarborough was the last man in Massachusetts he could hold a conversation with. He grinned like a wounded jackal at everybody else.

Michaels, the house detective, knocked on his door. "You have a visitor, Babe."

"Is it a redhead?" Rags was thinking of his wife.

"Na, it's some coon. Says he's a friend of yours. Sorry, Babe, we couldn't let him sit in the lobby . . . people might be upset. But I wouldn't chase out a friend. I don't care how black he is. He's waiting for you outside the porter's room."

The elevator took Rags under the lobby. He found the porter's room and said hello to Carl Raines of the Cincinnati Colored Giants.

"How's the Cincinnatis, Mr. Carl?"

"We're raking it in. There's no such thing as a bad year for my club."

"Should we find a soda shop? The Brunswick has funny ideas about its meeting places."

"This'll do." Carl said. He was the boss of the Giants, and no baseball hotel could get under his skin. "I hear you're on the outs with Hollis . . . and Garl is giving you a rest. Would you like to play for me?"

Old Carl's beautiful wife, Miz Emma, must have turned him crazy. Rags loved the Giants, but white men couldn't play on a nigger team in the United States.

"I have a contract with the Sox, Mr. Carl."

"That don't concern us. You can jump the American League . . . how much is Hollis paying you?"

"Five thousand."

"I'll pay you six."

"It's not the money, Mr. Carl. I'd like to get out of Boston, but I can't. I'm signed to Hollis McKee. I wouldn't run out on the Red Sox."

"Love a duck," Carl said. "Do the white man's jig. That McKee will hump you blind. You got no future at Fenway Park. That's what my medicine man told me."

"You mean Samuel Sharn, the witch? Hell, he couldn't even make the rain fly on us."

"Rain's a tricky business, little Rags. But Sam'l's good with futures. You ain't got none."

The kid returned to his room and mulled over the witch doctor's words. Scarborough had stronger magic than Samuel Sharn. So he went to the brute's speakeasy on Darling Street. "It's Ragland," he shouted through the peephole in the door. "Humpty Dumpty's pal."

The bouncer let him in.

"How's the Hump, Mr. Ragland?"

"He's on the road . . . with the Sox."

The bouncer's name was Herman, and he said, "It's a pity. We enjoy having the Hump around."

The bar area was packed with assorted shysters, floozies, and members of the Boston Braves, who were at home this week. These Braves, led by Cotton Charles, wouldn't acknowledge that Boston had another team. They were in fifth place this year. Cotton already had twenty-five doubles. A third baseman for the lowly Sox was less than invisible at the Darling Street saloon.

The kid sat at a table by himself. He drank soda water and white wine.

"That stuff's for grandmothers," Cotton Charles shouted to his mates. "Water and wine . . . hey, kid, is it true Garl caught the syph in Mexico last winter? Aint that why he's swinging a crippled bat?"

The saloon was cosier than Rags' hotel, and he didn't want to be banished from Darling Street for slapping Cotton Charles.

"Kid, what happened to your mouth? You have enough holes in there to park a bus."

One of the shysters told Cotton to shut up. He was wearing an orange suit. He had pink buttons on his vest and bold, bold stripes. He came over to Rags and introduced himself as Billy Rogovin.

"I'm Rags. I play for the Sox."

"I know. You're the kid with the magic glove."

"The magic's dead. I can't even walk onto the field."

Rogovin had gentle eyes. He seemed misplaced in an orange suit. Rags couldn't tell. Maybe Rogovin needed a shyster's uniform on Darling Street.

"The Sox are crazy to give up on you," Rogovin said. "They'll be stuck in the cellar for the next twenty years."

"Ah, it wasn't Garland's fault. He had to sit me down. I was scavenging. . . . "

"How do you scavenge on a ball club?"

"It's easy. You beat up your own men."

"They probably deserved it. That owner of yours has a habit of collecting bums."

Rags and Rogovin had an afternoon of soda and wine. Their faces turned red. The shyster wobbled in his orange suit. "Come on. I'm taking you on a buying trip."

They clumped across the city, from Darling Street to Scollay Square. They passed tattoo artists, ten-cents-a-dance ballrooms for Army and Navy men, photo shops, a shooting gallery, boys who stood outside the burlesque houses, waiting for a peek, toothless old bums who did favors for prostitutes, wives who searched for missing husbands, and husbands with wives who'd gone to Scollay and never came back. Rogovin seemed to know all of them.

The distraught husbands would surround Rogovin and touch him on his orange suit. He had to push their hands away. But he didn't scream at them. They were customers of his.

"I'll find her, Sol. I'm working on it. I'll need another few dollars."

"I already paid you ten."

"Ten? Ten can't even get me into the alleys. You think I can shop around for every bitch who runs from Somerville and Braintree? It'll cost you, Sol, and it takes time."

Rogovin led Rags into a clothing shop on Brattle Street. He bought silk pajamas for himself and cajoled Rags into an orange suit. He shouted for the tailor, who had to crawl under Rags and put chalk marks on crotch, shoulders, and cuffs. The tailor asked for six days.

Rogovin turned his gentle eyes on him. "Do it now."

The tailor shrugged and went to his sewing machine, while Rags stood around in his underwear.

"Rogovin, I'm not on salary this month. I can't pay for this."

"Who says pay? It's a gift. If we're gonna become brothers, you gotta dress like me."

They walked away from Brattle Street in twin suits. "Fucking Hymie, he's a dog's tailor," Rogovin said, plucking loose hairs off Rags' orange sleeve.

The kid didn't get back to his hotel until three in the morning. The telephone rang soon as he opened the door. St. Louis was on the line. The long-distance operator prattled in his ear. Then he heard Scarborough's voice.

Rags shouted into the phone. "Hiya, Hump."

"Since when am I Hump to you?"

"Ah, I was at your saloon . . . on Darling Street. That's your nickname over there. . . ."

"Raggsy, are you all right?"

"Sure," the kid said. "I made a friend while you're traveling with Garl and the Sox. I went to Scollay with him and he dressed me up in an orange suit."

There was a pause in the wires. "Who is this friend?"

"Don't get jealous, Hump . . . you're my roomie for life. They call him Rogovin, and he hangs out at Darling Street."

"I never heard of no Rogovins," the brute said. "Be careful, will you, Rags?"

"Guess what? The Colored Giants offered me a job . . . old Mr. Carl came to the hotel and said I should quit the Sox and go with him."

"What did you tell the man?"

"Shit, Garl benched me and all . . . but I wouldn't desert my team."

The operator started prattling how three minutes were up, and Scarborough had to get off the line from St. Louis. Rags fell asleep with the telephone in his hand. He dreamt of his roommate. They were fishing from their windowsill at the Brunswick, and all they could lure into the room with their rope and their hooks were pairs of dirty pajamas. The pajamas might have been old players' uniforms. Rags flung them out the window.

He had coffee and eggs after he woke. He trotted to Darling Street in his orange suit. The bouncer winked at him. "You're spiffy today, Mr. Ragland."

He put a silver dollar into the bouncer's paw. "Thank you, Herman."

The bar was empty. Drinkers wouldn't arrive until noon. But Rogovin was there, eating an egg out of a cup. He looked unhappy, with thick, frozen circles under his eyes. The kid would have sworn that Rogovin had never gone to sleep. Who knows where his bedroom was? The egg revived him. The yoke dripping onto his chin shook off some of Rogovin's gloom.

"Rags, when are they gonna lift that suspension and let you play?"

"After the Sox get back from St. Louis. . . ."

"We're brothers now, you and me."

"I guess so," the kid said, with his morning smile. "Humpty and Dumpty with the same orange suit."

"Rags, your brother's in a rotten hole . . . I've been betting on the Sox to lose, and . . . "

"That's a sure bet. The Sox are two and eighteen without me."

"I know, but I need a little more leverage."

"What kind of leverage, Billy boy?"

"Your glove."

The kid's eyes began to narrow.

"If you could fake a step, slow down a bit going for the ball, I'd have that leverage I need."

"I play to win," the kid said. "But don't worry. We're shitbirds this year. My glove can't change that."

Rogovin still had egg yoke on his chin. "You're right. Rags, forget about what I said . . . I was only asking for a friend."

They marched to Scollay again, took off their orange suits, and slept with a team of Portuguese whores at a house on Franklin Avenue; Rags was grateful to his new brother. It was the first woman he'd had since those dishonored wives who lived with him on Quintana Roo. Later, they had pig's knuckles and Bavarian cream pie in the sunken part of the dining room at Jacob Worth & Co. Then they walked home to Darling Street.

Rags couldn't avoid the Boston Braves.

It was nighttime; Cotton Charles and his flunkies had half the saloon for themselves. They didn't bother the kid once they saw Rogovin with him, although Cotton smirked at the twin suits. The brothers had whiskey and orange juice at an end table. The bar ran out of juice, so they drank the whiskey with a little water on the side.

"Rags, who's the worst bum on the Red Sox?"

"Chicken Stallings. He can't throw the ball, and he likes to make lip farts in the shower."

"Let's get him on the phone . . . and I'll warn him not to fart with his lips."

"The Chicken's in St. Louis. At the Buckingham."

Rogovin escorted Rags to the bar's private phone. He got the operator to ring St. Louis and the Buckingham Hotel.

"Chicken? It's me. Babe Ragland . . . I'm in Boston, where do you think? . . . A pal of mine wants to say hello."

The kid handed the phone to Rogovin and waltzed back to his table. He had to go around Cotton Charles. Then Rogovin appeared.

"Billy, did you tell him no more lip farts?"

"I certainly did."

"Isn't he the biggest cluck you ever talked to in your life?"

"The biggest," Rogovin said, and he dug a swollen envelope into the kid's pocket.

"Billy, what's that?"

"A thousand fish. Do me a favor. Hold it for me. I don't trust the bastards in this place. They might lift it out of my pants. But they wouldn't touch you. You're the Babe . . ."

"I'll hold it, Billy. It's just like Wells Fargo inside my pocket."

He walked around with Rogovin's money for two days. Rogovin never called for it. Rags couldn't find him on Darling Street.

"Where's Billy?" he asked Herman the bouncer.

Herman shrugged. "Billy boy does the sly every now and then. But he always comes back."

Rags had company at his hotel. It was the brute himself. Scarborough had returned to Boston ahead of the club. His face was more shriveled than it had ever been. Rags felt sorry for the brute. Scarborough had turned into an ancient, sobbing five-year-old dwarf.

"I shouldn't have left you here . . . I should have said, 'Skipper, suspend me too, because Raggsy don't know beans outside of baseball.' "

"Who says? I know boxing, I know bulls, I know Scollay Square. Can I help it if Hollis started humping me?"

"Mister, you humped yourself. When you walk with gamblers, you gotta pay the price."

"Who's a gambler?"

"That gink you put on the phone with Chicken Stallings. The gink offered Chicken ten thousand if he could get the Sox to blow any two games with the Tribe. Chicken squealed. Now Hollis knows, and Garl knows, and everybody is burning mad. Chicken swears the gink gave you a goddamn envelope for the Sox. A 'sweetener' he called it. Is that true?"

Rags took the envelope out of his pocket. "Sweetener? Rogovin asked me to hold this for him. He said it would be safer in my pants."

Scarborough was reluctant to feel the envelope. He shuddered at its thickness and shook his head at Rags. "Did anybody see the moolah change hands?"

"Yeah, half the Boston Braves."

Scarborough groaned. He wrapped the envelope in a towel, and hid the towel under the mattress, where the maids wouldn't have bothered to dust. Then he dragged the kid to Darling Street.

Humpty Dumpty didn't have his old sway at the saloon. The bouncer wouldn't let him in.

"Sorry, Hump, the vice squad's been here. Your boy's a no-no in this town . . . tell the Babe to pack his valise and run to Colorado."

"Herm," Scarborough said, "who's this Rogovin?"

The bouncer closed the door on Humpty Dumpty. Humpty sat on the stoop.

"Somebody set you up. Rags, was it your father? . . . would he give you the royal screw?"

"Pa wouldn't connive with shysters like Billy Rogovin. He'd steal the Red Sox away from Hollis and send me down to the minors. . . . Billy said he was my brother. He shouldn't have fingered me with a gambler's envelope."

Scarborough climbed off the stoop. "He's probably a small-time Yid from Henchman Street. He sits with the gamblers at Fenway and he stooges for the cops. We'll never find him."

Rags rubbed the material of his orange suit. "I know a guy who can lead us to Billy."

"Who? The captain of the North End horse patrol?"

"No. The tailor that widened the crotch on these pants I'm wearing."

They sneaked into the clothing store on Brattle Street. Rags went up to the tailor. "Hymie, it's Ragland . . . how do you like me in your masterpiece?"

The tailor shrank from him.

"Don't you remember? Billy Rogovin brought me in . . . and you let out the crotch and fixed the cuffs on your sewing machine."

"This aint my merchandise," the tailor said, with contempt for Rags and his orange suit. "I don't put cheesecloth on my customers' backs."

He grabbed one of the kid's sleeves and tore it with his fists.

"Cheesecloth. I told you."

Rags would have pitched Hymie over his sewing machine, but Scarborough touched the kid's undamaged sleeve and led him out of the store.

"The rat's gone into the sewers. It's too late to flush him out. We gotta take care of you. The Judge's coming in tomorrow with the team."

"Which judge is that?"

Scarborough rolled his eyes to indicate what a rube the kid was.

"Mountain Landis himself, the emperor of baseball. You'll get the full inquisition in Hollis' office. Play the nigger to him. Be his Uncle Tom. Yes him to death, you hear? Promise you'll report any gambler who winks his eye at you. And maybe, just maybe, you'll get off the ineligible list in a couple of years. Figure 1926 or '27. But for God's sakes, burn that orange suit."

Rags wore his player pajamas to Hollis' suite. He had to go upstairs all by himself. Bat boys weren't allowed in the front office. Furniture had been shoved around to satisfy the Judge. Hollis prepared a courtroom for Kenesaw Mountain Landis. An oak table served as the Judge's trial bench. You couldn't approach that table without a nod from him.

The Judge could have used Rogovin's Brattle Street tailor. Landis had teethmarks on his cuffs; they were bitten and frayed. His high collar had gone yellow against his scrawny neck. He was a small, frail man in a musty suit. The emperor of baseball clutched an old cane with rubber bands around the nob. If he flicked the rubber bands, it was a sign that he was getting impatient with you. He had a sharp beak, lots of silver hair, and a bulge in his jaw. The son of a bitch was chewing tobacco at Rags' inquisition.

He had Chicken Stallings, Cotton Charles, Hollis McKee, and the skipper on his left side. They sat in simple chairs. Hollis was like any other witness before the Judge. He'd lost the rights to his room. No president of the Red Sox could upstage Kenesaw Mountain Landis.

The Chicken leered at Rags. Cotton played with his fingers. Garl was the only one who seemed sad and uncomfortable in the emperor's court. He understood the ridiculous wrath of the Judge. Landis had come to Boston on the same train with the Sox. But he was too pure to mingle with them. The Judge rode in the engineer's caboose.

He let Hollis talk first. "Commissioner, the Babe kept busting people in the mouth. You couldn't go anywhere without Ragland having a fight. He got to be a real hyena. He attacked my Red Sox . . . beat up his own manager, didn't he, Garl?"

Garl wouldn't go along with his boss and savage the kid. "Rags had a bad marriage, Judge. It turned him wild. . . . "

The emperor began to flick his rubber bands. "A bad marriage is no excuse for hitting a man . . . continue, Mr. McKee."

"Well, we couldn't have a hyena on the field. We had to sit him down . . . and he made more trouble for himself and the team. We have gamblers at Fenway, Commissioner. Every ball park does. But my Red Sox wouldn't throw a game. Ask the Chicken here. He blew the whistle on Ragland and his friends."

The Chicken was in his glory. He'd been a journeyman pitcher since 1917, with enough stuff on the ball to strike out Harry Heilmann every other year. Garl would use him in the late innings, when the Sox were ten runs behind or ten runs ahead. But now the Chicken would get his reward. He could declare his righteousness to the Judge. He rambled on and on, how he thwarted the gamblers in their attempt to bribe the Sox. ". . . Commissioner, he says there's money in it for you, ten thousand to spread across the board, and I say to Raggsy's pal, you go to hell. I hung up on him and I went straight to Hollis."

Then Cotton Charles sang to the Judge about the telephone call from Darling Street and the envelope Rogovin gave to the kid after the call was over. But he couldn't snitch on Rags without revealing his own trips to the speakeasy. The Judge's silver eyebrows curled up at him. "What were you doin' around bootleggers and gamblers, Mr. Charles?"

Cotton had to recant while his nostrils twitched and his ears were going gray. "It was just a hangout. I didn't talk to bootleggers, sir."

Mountain Landis mashed the tobacco inside his jaw. "Promise you'll never go near a speakeasy again."

"Hope to die if I ever do," Cotton said, with a look of misery settling between his gray ears.

"I fine you a hundred dollars for sittin' with bootleggers, Mr. Charles. But I'm not an ungrateful man. I'll rescind that fine and thank you for helping us shuck those gamblers out of baseball."

The emperor turned his eyebrows on Rags. The kid stepped forward. His knees were prickly from having to stand so long in one spot.

"I know your father, young man. I wouldn't want to shame his only son . . . Cedric Tannehill, did you put Chicken Stallings on the phone with a gambler?"

"I'm the Babe," Rags muttered. But the emperor couldn't have heard.

"Speak up," Landis shouted at the kid.

"Judge," Garl said. "He's twenty years old . . . the best third baseman the Sox ever had. Whatever he did, he was acting out of ignorance."

The Judge went to his rubber bands. He didn't like busybodies in his court. "The boy has a tongue, sir. I'll beg you to be silent. We don't need interpretations of the law."

Garl stared back at the silver eyebrows. He wasn't frightened of the Judge. The owners had elected him emperor after the White Sox lay down to the Cincinnati Reds and threw the World Series of 1919. Landis ruled from a tiny office in Chicago, with the single word COMMISSIONER on his door. He could descend upon any clubhouse and lecture players for an hour on the evils that might befall them. Whiskey and gambling were the two great sins. He

had his private box at every ball park. He went from city to city in
the engineer's caboose, high priest, emperor, and tyrannical god.

Garl didn't own a baseball team and he didn't have to bow to
the Judge. Landis was a prick. But Garl couldn't help Rags through
the emperor's court.

"Young Cedric, did you put Stallings on the phone?"

Rags was growing muddled on his feet. *Who's young Cedric?
I'm the seventh Babe.*

"Billy was my friend . . . why couldn't he say a few words to
the Chicken?"

"So you admit it. You gave the phone to a gambler. And in
return, he paid you off. Cedric, where's the money?"

Rags took the envelope out of his baseball knickers. Landis
seized the envelope, stuck his fingers in, and counted ten hundred-
dollar bills.

"Billy said hold it for him . . . there were some creeps in the
saloon."

The emperor frowned. "Young Cedric, you consorted with gamblers, you aided and abetted them in a bribery scheme, and took
filthy lucre from their hands . . . are you sorry for what you did?"

Garl should have thrown Rags onto the floor and got him to cry
in front of the Judge. You had to soothe the white-haired god,
stroke him to sleep But the kid wouldn't bend.

"Are you sorry?"

"No."

"Then I'll have to punish you . . . Cedric Tannehill, as of this
moment, the sixteenth of June, 1925, I declare you ineligible to
play. You will not be allowed to enter any ball park in the major or
the minor leagues. Do you understand? Baseball is finished with
you."

Rags left the emperor's court, trudged down the stairs, thinking,
No more Red Sox, no more Babe, and walked out of Fenway Park.

Book Five

RAGS AND THE CINCINNATI GIANTS

14

H E COULD HAVE BEEN a bullrider, or a copper engineer, like his pa, with Amherst, Tucson, and Abilene behind him. He'd have chatted with lawyers, had his own Mr. Griffey to watch over his affairs. Then he'd have taken a wife. Not a girl who'd sleep with the Red Sox. But a bride from Old Tucson, in a marriage that Griffey would have arranged. His pa would have come to the wedding, given Cedric a copper mine or two. The kid would have been safe among the Tannehills.

I don't want that.

His was leather, air, and horsehide on a ball. He was knickers and dirty brown grass, the first twist of a double play. He couldn't live apart from a baseball diamond. He was married to a fifty-cent glove.

Copper wasn't his birthright. *No.* He hadn't slept in any cradle in his father's house. He was born in a pile of mud near the pitcher's box. A baseball baby. Orphan Rags. And somebody had stolen his birthright from him. Now he'd have to go and hide in the nigger leagues.

Scarborough blubbered when he saw Rags' face. He didn't have to hear the news: hollow eyes told him everything. The emperor had chased Rags, put him on the permanent ineligible list.

"He scratched you out of the game, didn't he?"

The kid's shoulders slumped under his Red Sox shirt.

502

"Raggsy, couldn't you play up to that old man? He didn't have a nickel's worth of evidence against you. Did he produce Billy Rogovin? Where's the famous gambler?"

"Who cares," Rags said. "I'm joining the Cincinnati Giants."

"What about Scarborough?"

"Hell, the Judge isn't after you. You can stay. You're still the Sox's bat boy."

"Aint we roomies?" Scarborough said.

"I have to play with niggers. You don't. Whoever heard of anybody banning himself from the big leagues? I won't let you do it."

"It's a free country," Scarborough said. "We'll have to give notice to the hotel and buy ourselves a car."

Scarborough didn't have to worry about the hotel; the Brunswick wanted Rags out. Any night was soon enough. The press had announced Landis' decision: FENWAY AND OTHER PARKS TO CLOSE THEIR DOORS ON THE BABE; RAGLAND BARRED FOR LIFE; CONNECTION WITH GAMBLERS HINTED AT; BOSTON POLICE WON'T ENTER COMMISSIONER'S BAILIWICK.

Rags didn't blink until he looked at Noel Finnbar's column. Finnbar called Rags a wifebeater and a rogue. BAD BOY STRIKES OUT. Rags reached for the baseball bat he always kept in the room. "I'm gonna knock some wood on Finnbar's head."

The brute struggled with him and grabbed the bat away. "Go on. It'll be wonderful with them photographing you in your jailhouse pajamas."

Scarborough resigned from the Sox, and they bought a three-year-old Hudson sedan. Rags was shunned by his teammates. Sheriff Smith wouldn't shake the kid's hand. Alvin Critz turned from him in the lobby. But Garland came up to the room. The skip seemed much more devastated than Rags or the brute. His team was dying on him. But it wasn't only that. The Judge had ruined a twenty-year-old boy. The kid would have to play with outlaws, or use another name on the field.

"Ah, don't you worry, skip. Me and the Hump are joining up with the Giants."

Garl stared at Rags as if he'd just been unwired. "John McGraw is tough, but he won't take on the commissioner of baseball. Don't have fantasies of playing in New York."

"Not New York," the kid said. "The Cincinnati Giants."

The skipper went pale in the mouth. "You won't live out the year . . . if the Cincinnatis don't kill you, the fans will."

"Hell, Garl, me and the Hump'll fight them all, back to back."

You couldn't dissuade the boy. Garl took him and the brute by their shoulders and squeezed, then he helped them carry down their bags. They got into the Hudson, with Scarborough behind the wheel.

"So long, skip."

And they drove out of Boston to marry up with the Giants.

They crossed seven states. They stopped at fairgrounds, circuses, cow pastures, and village greens. The brute tried the friends he had in baseball. No one could tell him where the Cincinnatis were.

The Hudson was eating up gasoline, and the kid grew disgusted with the search. "They're gone, those Cincinnatis . . . disappeared."

"How do you know? Maybe Carl Raines took them on a Cuban tour."

"You're crazy. Carl wouldn't run to Havana in June. He'd save it for February. I'll bet the Giants got into a fight with some town like Springfield or Decatur, and the town chewed them alive."

"Bushwah. Decatur couldn't beat up the Cincinnati Giants."

"They're gone, wiped out. Scarborough, suppose we wiggled ourselves into one of the outlaw leagues along the Rio Grande? It's a natural. There's Texas baseball in my blood."

"You think the old man would let you do that? He'll hunt you down. The emperor's got agents everywhere. You can hide with a Negro club, and that's it."

"I'm going to the Rio Grande."

But they got stalled outside of Louisville. Scarborough began to shudder in the driver's chair. He had to use every bit of force coming down from his crooked shoulder, or the Hudson would have gone off the road.

"I can smell him," Scarborough said.

"Who?"

"That magician. Samuel Sharn. The Cincinnatis have got to be close. . . ."

Scarborough sniffed the air and arrived at a country barn. All Rags could see was a battered yellow bus. Where were those Buicks with mahogany on the outside?

Bossman Carl walked out of the barn.

"If it aint the bad boy himself . . . and Mr. Scarborough. Didn't I tell you Sam'l doesn't lie? Ditch the Red Sox, he said. And the Red Sox ditched you. I'm not sure I fancy having a renegade on my club. I'll give ya two thousand for the rest of the year."

"You promised me six."

"That was before the Judge demoted you. You aint worth much to me now. I can pick up an outlaw any time I want. Two thousand . . . and the hunchback has to blow. Sam'l won't tolerate him. He can't work his root with Mr. Scarborough around."

"Well, good luck to the Cincinnatis," Rags said. "Scarborough, are we on the road to Texas?"

Scarborough didn't move. "You ought to think about his proposition, Rags. I can always lumberjack."

"The heck with him and his Giants. Let's go."

Carl sprang in front of the sedan. "Three thousand . . . and we'll settle on a price for Scarborough."

They got out of the Hudson and peeked into the barn. "Where's Pharaoh?" The barn was filled with sockamayocks. "Where's Yam Murray?"

Carl began to curse and spit. "Pharaoh jumped the Cincinnatis. He's with the Black Barons. Yam's with the Memphis ABCs. Muley Jones went over to the Buckeyes. There's a players' war going on."

"No wonder you came begging to my hotel. You lost your fucking team. And your seven Buicks, where are they?"

Carl stared at the ground. "Had to hock them for a while. They were getting too conspicuous. A town would spot my cars and say, 'It's them troublemakers, the Giants.' They'd send the sheriffs down on our scalps. So we switched to a bus."

"You don't need Samuel Sharn," Rags said. "You have your own liar's root. You're in the poorhouse. You sold your cars, or you couldn't eat. . . ."

The witch doctor came stumbling out of the barn. He must have been whiskey mad, because the sight of Scarborough nearly riled him to death. He stamped his feet, brought up a dark blue bile, and began to whirl around the Hudson. Then he stopped to crook his finger at the brute. "Send him away, Mr. Carl. My liver is churning. My bladder is gone. I'm a ghost. My piss'll be black by tonight. I'll join the players' war, Mr. Carl, if you don't get that hump out of here."

"Go back into the barn," the bossman said. "Nobody's gonna steal a witch doctor off a losing team. Sam'l, this is the only home you got."

It must have made sense to the medicine man; he scampered into the barn with all the sockamayocks.

The boss' carpenters and groundsmen had also deserted him in the players' war. So the sockamayocks had to build a diamond and a grandstand for Carl. And they didn't have that magical way with a hammer, a trowel, and a scythe. The stands were lumpy down the middle, and the diamond had potholes near third base. The kid began to wonder if the holes were meant for him.

He was advertised as Mr. Babe Ragland, Refugee of the White American League, The Boy Who Was Driven out of Baseball by Kenesaw Mountain Landis, And Is Now a Fixture at Third Base for the Cincinnati Giants. Fans came to watch the black monkeys and their "fixture," Babe Ragland.

Rags got curious when the bossman didn't move from his barn. The Cincinnatis had run out of local villages to play. Scarborough told the kid not to ask. "It's probably got something to do with his wife."

Then, after the diamond lay empty for a week, Carl declared that Emma was supposed to meet him at the barn, and he wouldn't budge until his woman arrived.

The sockamayocks grew irritable living inside a barn like dairy cows. They couldn't attack their own boss, so they turned against Rags and the brute. "Randolph, you see them hug last night? My, my, they is a lovin' couple. There's more touchin' between those two than with Emma and Mr. Carl."

"Suck a tit," Rags said to the twenty sockamayocks, and they came at him with big nails, shovels, and scythes. Rags didn't jump out of the barn. He stood with Scarborough. They had their fists, Scarborough's hump, and a pair of Louisville Sluggers.

Carl was sleeping in the bus with Samuel, and he didn't hear that disturbance from the barn. The sockamayocks began to swish the scythes. Rags and the brute knocked at those blades with their Sluggers. The kid had a gash in his arm from a falling scythe. But three sockamayocks were on the floor, groaning, with bumps on their heads.

"Seventeen more to go."

The scythes kept swishing at them. A boom exploded through the barn. The ceiling buckled over the sockamayocks, who swore that heaven and hell had descended upon the Cincinnati Giants. It was Emma Raines with a Colt revolver in her hands. She could steady that Colt as fine as any cowboy Rags could remember from his father's ranch.

"Go on," she said. "Carl's brave skunks, trying to cut up two little men."

The sockamayocks backed into a corner of the barn. They dropped their scythes and the other weapons they were carrying. They wouldn't take on Miz Emma, with or without her Colt.

"Thank you, ma'am," Rags said, shy around that beautiful woman who had Marylou's hair and creamy yellow skin. But she'd already gone out to wake her husband Carl.

A brittle truce was declared between the sockamayocks and the whites. Actually, it was Emma who forced a pact on the Giants. She had her husband vacate the barn and shove off for Tennessee. The sockamayocks would go with Samuel on the bus; Emma and Carl would ride in the white man's Hudson. Carl served as navigator. He sat up front, digging his fingers into different maps, while Scarborough steered. Emma and Rags had the back of the Hudson to themselves.

The kid forgot his wife and his lost pa and his dead career in the majors. The heated perfume that rose off Emma cured Rags of his ills. She would smile at him, kick off one shoe, and curl her toes under the Hudson's floor rug and Rags' foot, so her husband couldn't see. That woman had more fondling power in the twigs of her feet than any whore Rags had run into at Scollay Square. They couldn't pet or clutch hands in front of Carl, but the kid's blood was beginning to cook from all the caressing his ankles got before they reached the Great Smoky Mountains, where Carl decided to pitch camp.

The sockamayocks slapped at the grass, rolled a few dozen rocks, and built their crooked diamond on a hill outside Newport, Tennessee. Then they turned to hawking with placards on their chests, and sold the Giants in mountain villages. Carl had a crowd again. People were coming to hiss at the outlaw.

Rags solved the difficulty of playing on a hill. He ran along with the slant in the ground and took any ball off the weirdest hops. But the kid paid a price; he lost the feel of Emma's toes. How could she crawl into the Hudson with Rags, when Carl and the sockamayocks and hundreds of villagers were around on the hill?

"Take me to New Orleans," she sang in his ear.

The kid was forlorn. "I can't, Miz Emma . . . I have to play."

She stuck to the Giants for a week, lived in the Smoky Mountains with her husband Carl, and then she disappeared. Carl's face wrinkled up, the kid bobbled a few, but the Giants were winning on their Tennessee hill.

A man with a satchel came up to Rags on a Saturday, wearing a black mourner's suit. He'd noticed Rags in the Cincinnatis' pants and shirt. "I'm awfully sorry, but can you direct me to Cedric Tannehill? . . . he calls himself the Babe. Isn't he on your team?"

"What are you sorry for, Mr. Giffey?"

"My God, is that you?" Griffey said. Rags had dirt around his eyes and a sneer, and Griffey thought he was looking at a sockamayock.

"Hey Griffey, is my pa gonna buy off the Judge and put me back on the eligible list? Tell him to forget it. I'd rather play for the Giants."

"Cedric, your father is dead."

A shiver went from his throat and continued down to his knees, and the kid nearly fell. Griffey caught him by an elbow. Rags shook himself free. The shiver had gone out of him.

"My pa wasn't even sixty. Why should he die?"

"It was sudden. He collapsed . . . no one could revive him."

The kid's shoulders began to heave, and he turned from Griffey, so his father's lawyer wouldn't catch him in the act of crying.

The kid stood with his knuckles in his eyes. He'd wet the collar of his gold and white baseball shirt. He realized the lawyer had business to discuss. Griffey wouldn't have brought his satchel to Tennessee for a simple death call. The lawyer may have been a toad for the Tannehill copper pits, but he wasn't a brute. He felt awkward with a satchel full of papers around a grieving boy.

"Cedric, I could come another time. . . ."

"Na," the kid said. "We can go to my office." And he led Griffey into the back seat of the Hudson. The lawyer removed an enormous folder with sleeves that opened out like an accordion; there were envelopes stuffed into every sleeve.

"When did pa die?"

"A month ago," Griffey said, fiddling with the sleeves.

Rags grabbed the folder away; envelopes spilled onto the floor and made a pyramid around Griffey's feet. Griffey darted for the envelopes.

"Leave 'em there . . . pa dies and it takes you a month to bring the news? I ought to hang you up by your funeral coat and let the bullfrogs jump into your mouth."

"Cedric, we couldn't find you, I swear. . . . "

"Griffey, you could find anybody. I never heard of a soul escaping you."

"We had searchers out," Griffey said in his own defense. "We offered a big reward . . . Cedric, you're on a phantom team."

"You don't have to tell me that. Phantoms and sockamayocks and outlaws like me."

"I only discovered yesterday where the Cincinnatis were."

Griffey scooped up the envelopes, and Rags signed papers until his shoulder hurt. He wouldn't read any of the jabber written on them. That was for Griffey, not the kid. "I suppose pa cut me out for skipping Amherst and playing ball."

"On the contrary. You're president of Tannehill Copper . . . I grant you, it doesn't mean all that much. Your father's industries are run by an independent board. But he wouldn't disown you. You can draw a monthly stipend if you come to Tucson. And the ranch, the ranch is yours . . . you can't sell it, or trade livestock, but you can live on it whenever you like. . . . "

"Thanks, Griffey," the kid said, "but I don't think I'll get to Abilene."

"There's one more problem," Griffey said, turning shy. "You've inherited me. I'm your lawyer now."

"Well, if I can use a lawyer, Griffey, I'll give a yell. Until then you can push your rump to Tucson and sit on all that copper dust."

A regret began to eat at Rags after the lawyer was gone. *Should have asked him about pa.* He approached the witch doctor. "Samuel, how strong is that root of yours?"

"Stronger than angels and devils," Samuel said, showing off.

"What exactly can it do?"

"Curse the living and raise the dead."

"I want you to raise up my pa for me . . . I'll give you twenty bucks."

The witch doctor was contemptuous of the kid's offer. "Keep them twenty bucks. I don't work my root for cash. Any rootman does that, he's worth shit. Mr. Rags, you aint said a kind word to me before today. And you brung that Scarborough into camp. Why should I raise white folks for you?"

Even a lesser magician could have smelled the kid's disease: that lumpy, pathetic twist of Rags' body made Sam'l aware how heartsore he was. Samuel agreed to work his root. "I can't promise you nothin'. But I'll try. Come on with me."

Rags followed the magician into the bus. Samuel found his root, which was in an old, cloudy jar, and he disappeared into the Tennessee woods with Rags.

He crouched near a rock and worked his root, fondling the outside of the jar. He chanted something that came out muddled to the kid. Who could understand a witch's tongue? The sky turned dark over the kid's head. A wind blew in the trees. The woods must have been full of owls. He saw their green eyes. They hopped along the branches, hooting at him. Rags wasn't going to be mocked by a company of owls. He swung at the branches with his throwing arm.

"Concentrate on your pa," the rootworker said.

It's a lie. Samuel can't raise a bean.

Sam worked and worked that root. It looked like he was bleeding his own jar.

The hooting stopped and a figure tumbled out of the forest haze. "Pa?"

It was a woman, dressed in swamp weeds and a torn blouse. Marylou. The magician had conjured up a Cottonmouth. She swayed next to Rags in her damp clothes. Samuel hid behind the rock.

Her hair fell like rat tails around her shoulders. She smiled at Rags' uniform, the gold braiding of the Giants on his chest. "Harvard Jack," she said.

The kid had asked for his father, but he wouldn't refuse what he got. Rags didn't know how to talk to a ghost, so he blinked and pushed with his tongue.

"Why did you go and drown yourself, Miz Marylou?"

"Garl wouldn't marry me."

"There's other men."

"Of course," she said, wiggling her rat tails. "Rotten lovers and a mean son-in-law. God gave them all to me."

She turned from him and ran deeper into the woods. Rags begged her to wait. He didn't feel as lonely with her rat tails around. But she wouldn't heed the kid.

"I'll have the swamps if I can't have Garland James," she said. "I'm going home."

Rags took the magician out from behind his rock. Samuel had a disappointed grin. "It aint my fault. No sir. That root sure is stubborn, Mr. Rags. It just wouldn't raise your pa."

"That's all right," the kid said, putting his arm around the magician. "I was glad to see Miz Marylou."

15

The Giants prospered in Tennessee. Pharaoh Yarbull jumped back to the team. He could have earned more if he'd stayed with the Black Barons. But he wasn't happy with their kind of ball. They didn't fuss and fight and build their own diamonds. Pharaoh preferred the hurly-burly of the Cincinnati Giants. A few days after Yarbull, Yam Murray returned. Then Moses Cutshaw, Muley Jones, and Swimmy Welles.

The players' war was over. Pharaoh had cut out its heart. Carl began sending the sockamayocks away. His seven Buicks arrived from Atlanta on their own mysterious run. His carpenters were showing up, and his former groundsmen. Carl scolded them, called them traitors and skunks, but he took them in. Now he could afford to laugh at the kid.

"Where'm I gonna put you?" he said, stroking his chin. "Pharaoh's the best third baseman in town."

"Put me on the bench," Rags said. "I've been there before."

But the Pharaoh wouldn't allow it. "Give him third, Mr. Carl. I like playing short this time of year."

With Yarbull around, the kid didn't dwell so much on his father and Marylou's ghost. Rags had the perfect team he'd always wanted. With Pharaoh, Yam, and Swimmy Welles, there wasn't a weak spot on the Giants. They had bats, they had brains and gloves. None of them smirked at the kid's white hands. They sucked Rags into their scheme of liquid motion. Legs and arms would melt around a ball. Nothing got through.

The diamond became a prison camp for enemy runners. Swimmy Welles would leap into the air over second, tag the runner, and throw before you realized he'd ever had the ball in his glove. He'd hide the catch by twisting his body away from the runner and the fools in the stands. But he was only a trickster compared to the man at short.

Yarbull wasn't double-jointed like Swimmy Welles. He didn't have to bend his shoulder back to lure a runner off the bag. He would leave you stranded wherever you were. The Pharaoh was an antelope on mud and grass. The Giants would shout to one another: "Is Yarbull puttin' on his hooves today?" He wouldn't have been human without the letters on his shirt. The batter would swing, and a bar of gold would pass in front of your eyes. That was Pharaoh on the move.

The witch doctor kept him alive. Yarbull's knees would buckle after a game. He would fall onto the diamond, and lie there, spasms going up and down his legs like malicious snakes under the skin, as if Yarbull had contracted epilepsy of the calves and thighs. Samuel would run out to him with a blanket and his root. He would place the root jar near Yarbull's left cheek, wrap him in the blanket, and draw those evil snakes out of his legs.

There wasn't another rootworker in the business that could touch Samuel Sharn. He was the medicine man of the Cincinnati Giants and he could scorn his brother magicians, with their pathetic, shriveled roots. "Nobody can piss on Sam. I brung a white lady to life for three minutes."

The boss of the Giants had everything: Yarbull, Rags, and a magician. "Niggers," he announced to his club, "we aint goin' to Puerto this winter. The Buckeyes and the ABCs can have their Havanas. The Giants are stickin' to the United States."

It was after World Series time, and the barnstorming teams shunned the little man. Harry Heilmann had come back to play with his All-Stars, and he wouldn't consider arranging a post-season match with the Giants. The Judge had warned Harry never to go near a team that had Babe Ragland on its roster. Landis sent his agents down to reason with Mr. Carl. "Get rid of the Babe, and we'll find some competition for you." The boss didn't throw them out of camp. He had his financial stakes to consider.

Pharaoh had to knock on the bossman's shoulder. "Mr. Carl, that's a honey of a third baseman we got. I'd lose a step at short if you gave me a colored boy."

Carl shut the doors of his Buick to the emperor's agents. "What you mean, fuckin' with my roster. The emperor aint got no business here. Mr. Rags stays with me."

The Cincinnatis were the only team in baseball that had defied the emperor and won. College towns, villages, and industrial teams outside organized baseball were eager to scrap with the Colored Giants. They wanted an eyeful of Pharaoh and the Boston outlaw.

Rain, sheriffs, and the emperor of baseball couldn't halt the Cincinnati Giants. Samuel appeased the rain gods with his root. He could calm the worst storm, or push it over to another hill. If the rain did fall on the Giants, Sam would point to Scarborough. "It's him. The gods won't listen to my root, when we got a crippleback in camp."

Carl told his magician to shut up. The boss was satisfied. He could live with an occasional storm. If he fooled with Scarborough, Rags would walk off the field. Then the Pharaoh would bitch at him and start a second players' war. And Carl would have to give up his Buicks again. His ankles swelled on him every time he rode in a bus.

Let the rain gods get even with Carl a little for carrying a brute. They could blow as much as they liked, as long as they didn't steal his Giants away. Carl had the "winningest" team in baseball. He called the World Series a mockery in the placards he hung on his criers and his scouts. He challenged the Cardinals of 1926 to play Yarbull and the kid. "Hornsby aint nothin' but a big fat hen. I'll offer him two free games in a World Series with my Giants."

He knew the Judge would never allow the World Champions to play another series with a nigger team, even if the niggers didn't have a kid named Rags, so he could bark and bark. "I'll let my outfield snore in the grass. They won't touch wood with Yam Murray on the hill."

Carl had plenty of placards and plenty of blab. He didn't give a hoot about Rogers Hornsby. He was worried about Yarbull's knees. The spasms were getting worse. His carpenters had to build a stretcher to carry the Pharaoh off the field. Yarbull wouldn't budge until the fans had gone home.

Carl snapped at his magician. "Go to your root, Sam'l. You're not shakin' it as much as you could."

The magician was hurt. "You see how skinny I am, Mr. Carl. I'm working that root day and night for the Pharaoh. He runs during the game, don't he? When's the last time Yarbull missed a ball? My root can't fix him after innings is over. His knees are shot. The Buckeyes got a rootworker. Try him."

Carl wouldn't forsake Samuel Sharn. You didn't swap magicians in the nigger leagues. You might steal one off the ABCs if your witch doctor happened to die. But whoever worked a trade would bring boils, mosquitoes, and the flux to his men.

"Do your best, is all. If we lose the Pharaoh, we'll have to ride down the Mississippi, slappin' baseballs on a barge."

Three men stole Rags from the Giants. They waited until Scarborough was asleep. Then they opened the back door of the Hudson, taped Rags' mouth, wrapped him in a blanket, and carried him to another automobile.

Rags couldn't tell how many hours he was on the road with his kidnappers. They didn't feed him once. They kept the blanket over him when they pushed Rags out of the car. He had a short elevator trip. He was shoved into a chair. The blanket fell off.

The emperor of baseball had kidnapped him. Rags was in Chicago. He sat across from that cruel old man.

The Judge offered him steak and fried potatoes. The kid was hungry. He chewed on some steak with the Judge. It must have still been dark outside, or else those agents couldn't have smuggled him into Landis' Chicago office.

"Would you like a cigar?" Landis said.

"No thanks, Judge . . . why'd you bring me here?"

"You're a stupid young man. You think you can run from me in the Negro leagues? I heard your father died, and I wanted to give you a second chance."

"What kind of second chance?"

"To go back to your wife and the Red Sox."

"What's my wife to you?"

"Oh, we've been watching her . . . I have agents in all the cities. She spends her summers on an island with somebody named Rhys."

Rags would have strangled that old emperor if the three kidnappers hadn't been with Landis in the same little room.

"My wife wasn't in the majors, Judge . . . you tell your men to quit following her."

"Then come to your senses, Cedric Tannehill."

The emperor grabbed his cane and thumped it against the floor. The room shook, and those silver eyebrows on the Judge almost leapt out at Rags.

"If you're feuding with Hollis, that's all right," the Judge said. "You don't have to play for him. I'll get you a spot on the Browns. Just sign a paper declaring you won't mess with gamblers again. Is that so hard to do?"

"Keep your Browns," the kid said. "I already have my spot."

The Judge looked at him. "Stubborn mule. I can reach into nigger baseball . . . I'll throw a boycott around your precious team."

"Bushwah. You can't hurt the Colored Giants."

The kidnappers took Rags out of the office and pummeled him a bit. He had to wear tape on his mouth and a blanket over his head. But they didn't abandon the kid. They brought him home to the Giants and disappeared in their car.

Rags wandered over to the Hudson. The brute wasn't inside. Scarborough came up to him after a while.

"Raggsy, where you been?"

"I had my morning walk," the kid said.

"That's nice . . . a morning walk in the middle of the afternoon. You missed the first game. I was worried about you. Carl's been screaming. You'd better get into your suit. . . ."

He shouldn't have lied to the Hump. But he didn't want to retell the whole kidnapping story. It made him sick to think about the Judge.

There was an army of troublemakers in the stands for the afternoon game. They threw bottles down at the Giants and yelled evil things to Rags. The kid wondered if the Emperor had hired them to stalk the team.

The troublemakers didn't fare too well. Yarbull got out of his stretcher to lead the Cincinnatis up into the stands. He had carpenters, coaches, and players with him. They knocked seventy-five men out of the grandstands. The Giants had to depart before the sheriffs arrived. But no one stalked them after that.

Only Rags had crazy lions in his sleep. The lions were on a beach. Someone had shaved their heads. Ribs showed through the deep hollows in their backs. They had an infielder's crooked paws. Give them jerseys and golden hats, and they could have played for the Giants.

Who could have dreamed of such lions? Comical beasts, their awkward bodies sinking into wet sand. They moaned like walruses. Then Rags recognized the beach. It was Tisbury town, where he'd never been. The lions were on one sandy wall. A redhead came over from her house to feed the stupid things. She wasn't wearing any clothes. She gave them gruel out of a smelly pot, sticking her fingers into their mouths. It was the kid's wife. The lions belonged to her. They were Iva's beasts, and they loved to eat from her fingers, lapping the gruel off her knuckle joints. And it horrified the kid. His wife going naked in front of lions. They could see the beard between her legs. Who knows what kind of lustful thoughts a lion could have?

The kid felt a hand on him. Scarborough peered over the front seat. "Raggsy, you having a nightmare? You cried in your sleep."

"It was nothing," the kid said. "A dumb dream." And he pulled up his knees into his ordinary sleeping position. He didn't give a damn about lions with infielders' claws.

They circled the country for a year and a half, those Cincinnatis, drawing crowds wherever they could sculpt a diamond. A yellow woman with a bruised eye showed up at the camp they had near the Snake River, in Idaho. Carl grew agitated. It was Miz Emma. He didn't have the nerve to ask her about those missing eighteen months. It was the longest Emma had been gone from him.

Carl turned witless. He couldn't run the team. Yarbull had to care for the Cincinnatis, lying on his back. He sent hawkers out with placards and told each man who would sit and who would play. Then the boss recovered his wits.

Rags was in a deeper funk. He could smell Emma Raines upriver and downriver too. He couldn't stop thinking of her skin and her reddish brown hair. He lay in his bed on the back seat of the Hudson, with spasms that were almost as bad as the Pharaoh's. The brute would call to him from the front of the car. "Should I give you my blanket, Raggsy?"

"How's a blanket gonna cure me? I'll have to borrow Sam's root."

But the kid survived without a witch doctor. Emma crawled into the Hudson with him one night, and the spasms went away. She didn't have to fondle Rags with her toes anymore. Carl wasn't in the front seat. She hugged and kissed the third baseman. He watched her body in the moonlight. He loved how her ass jutted out, and the soft pull of her kneecaps that were like tiny animals trained to rub against the kid.

"What happened to your eye?"

"I got hit," she said.

"By what? A squirrel, or a circus bear?"

"By a man," she said.

The kid started to put on his socks. "I'll kill him . . . right now."

She laughed. "It was a thousand miles from here."

"I don't give a turd about that."

He was into his clothes before she could protest. Rags wouldn't take off his socks again until she told him the man's name.

"Marshall Glove."

"I'll remember that."

And he found that snuggling spot in her shoulder where he could fall asleep. Emma was there in the morning, hugging him still.

"Don't you have to sneak back to Carl?"

"Why? He knows about us. I'd run to New Orleans if I couldn't stay with you. He'd rather have me in Idaho."

So Emma lived in the Hudson with Rags. It was her bedroom and her couch. The kid didn't hear the boss complain. Rags had his usual berth with the Giants.

It was Scarborough who began to grumble. *How can you have a roomie when there's a woman in the back seat?* The brute was like an extra wife. He listened to the sounds of their caressing, and then he took the kid aside.

"Raggsy, you think Carl would give me a few weeks off?"

"Where you going, Hump?"

"To visit Claudine in Havana."

"Who's Claudine?"

"My winter wife."

"This is July, you dope. Cuba's like an oven."

He couldn't hold on to Scarborough. The brute got Carl's permission to leave, and Rags had the Hudson for Emma and himself. He loved that high yellow woman, slept with her, ate with her, but he developed a slight twitch in his shoulder when Scarborough forgot to come back. It was the last days of September, and he was lonely for the brute.

The Giants had traveled down to Louisiana, and Emma began her whispering act. "Take me to New Orleans."

"I'll take you," Rags said, "when their police chief lets us in."

The police chief of New Orleans promised to string up Giants in Jackson Park if he saw one gold uniform near his parish.

"I didn't ask the team to take me . . . I'm asking you."

Rags withstood her whispering into the month of October. He looked for signs of Scarborough, and when Scarborough didn't come, he said for the sake of argument, "Carl will fire me if I hop to Orleans with you."

"He won't," she said. "The Giants are half mine. . . ."

Emma drove the kid and his Hudson from Baton Rouge to the Parish of Orleans. She parked on Iberville Street, a few blocks above the French Quarter. The Creoles wouldn't live so far up on Iberville. It was a nigger street at this end. It had mansions with peeling walls, empty lunch houses, and retired whore "cribs." The whores were driven out by the Navy in 1917. The whores didn't starve. They moved down to the Mississippi, in the Vieux Carré.

Emma took him through a gate in a high wall on Iberville Street. They walked round and round a patio and landed in a little house that was shut off from the street. They could have entered another parish, walking round that patio. There were shutters on every window in the house.

"Emma, did you borrow this cottage for us?"

"I didn't have to. It belongs to me."

She went marketing and returned with pots of food, while the kid dusted off tables and chairs with his elbow. They had yellow rice, shrimp, peppers, and red beans that Emma cooked on her stove, and then they made love in a real live bed. It wasn't like scratching around in the back seat of the Hudson, with nowhere to put your arms and legs. They had sixty hours to themselves, behind the shutters. Rags snored without the rhythms of third base in his head. Baseball couldn't spook him on Iberville Street.

"Emma, what's the best restaurant in town? . . . not the biggest, just the best."

She laughed at him. "Are you tired of my cooking so quick?"

"I want to go out with you . . . what's the best place?"

"Victoire's on Burgundy Street . . . but they don't let brown-skins in there. You'll have to pick out fish bones by yourself."

"We'll see," the kid said.

"Honey, it aint smart for us to stroll into the Quarter together. Trust me. . . ."

But the kid had decided on Victoire's. So Emma fixed her hair and put on a green dress, and the kid found a reasonable suit of clothes in his traveling bag. Emma pressed the trousers for him.

They walked hand in hand to Burgundy Street and stood in line outside Victoire's. The Creoles next to him did nothing but stare.

"Honey," she whispered, "we'd better scat. They'll bring the cops down on us."

"They're only staring because you're beautiful in your green dress."

Emma realized how crazy the kid was. But she wouldn't shame him in front of the Creoles and drag him from Burgundy Street. The line brought them closer and closer to Victoire's door. Emma anticipated the moment when Victoire himself would point at the sidewalk and say no to her. He liked to greet his customers at the door.

Victoire smiled when Rags and Miz Emma approached. Lord of Egypt and Jerusalem, Victoire hugged the kid and shook Emma's hand. "M'sieu le Babe," he said.

The kid was known in New Orleans.

Emma wasn't a prophet. How could she tell Rags was a hero to the Creoles, who loved baseball but despised its American commissioner and his despotic ways? The Creoles considered Rags one of them, a boy who had been shoved into a stateless society by the whims of a heartless judge.

They had the center table at Victoire's. M'sieu le Babe and Emma drank wine at Victoire's expense. Everything was on the house. Rags noticed a slight red tinge in the wine glasses of the Creoles.

"What's that?"

"Cassis," Emma said.

"White wine and cassis," he told the waiter.

Rags wanted pompano. The waiter shook his head. "Sorry, M'sieu, no pomp. The fishermen are lazy. They won't go out and catch pomp in the fall."

Rags had broiled trout, and Emma had redfish. Victoire drank a glass of wine with them, and asked the Babe to please come in January when they would have pompano for him, and the fishermen weren't so lazy. The Creoles were too proud to beg autographs from Rags. The waiters had to do it for them. Victoire gave up some of his finest linen to satisfy the Creoles. Rags scribbled on a dozen napkins. "To all my pals in New Orleans, Babe Ragland, October 17, 1927."

Another man came up to him. He was short and stumpy, but he didn't have a waiter's black sleeves. It was Roland Shakespeare, the police chief of New Orleans. "Shucks, Babe, when I put that edict out on the Giants, I didn't mean you. It's a delight, Babe, a pure delight, having you in town."

Rags had to sign a napkin for him. "To Chief Shakespeare, from the Boston outlaw."

The Chief chuckled over that. "People here is wishing the Judge drops dead . . . enjoy your meal, son."

Rags began to whistle after they got back to Iberville Street. "Didn't we chew on good fish? That's no lie."

Somebody knocked on Emma's window. Rags heard her talk through the wooden slats. Her back humped while she talked. The cassis had mellowed the kid. "That a friend? Honey, invite him in. . . ."

A dandy in a pink collar and yellow shoes marched into the little house with a pair of henchmen behind him. The henchmen wore ugly pieces of metal on their fists.

"Hi," the dandy said. "I'm Marshall Glove, and you must be Ragland, the baseball bandit that took my old lady into Victoire's and had a little trout . . . Emma, you should have told me you was back in New Orleans. That aint nice to ol' Marsh."

It was Marshall Glove who'd socked Emma and put that mouse under her eye. The kid hadn't forgotten that. He began to sneer. "You sure look pretty in your yellow shoes. Does it give you courage when you have to beat on a woman?"

Marshall didn't throw his henchmen at Rags. He stuck a dash of white powder into his nostrils and wouldn't say a word until he snorted three times, and the powder went up the tubes of his nose. It was the loudest snorts the kid had ever heard. The snorts weren't new to him. Carl's sockamayocks would snort cocaine though rolled-up paper dollars, but none of them had such quantities of powder to toss around and spill.

Marshall smiled. "Just because Chief Shakespeare kissed your skinny ass, it doesn't mean you own the bayou. Be a good boy and lemme borrow Emma for an hour. I'll bring her home, I promise. . . ."

"You're not borrowing shit."

Emma moved in front of Rags, so the henchmen's iron knuckles would fall on her instead of him. "Honey, let me go with Marsh. I won't stay long. . . ."

But Emma could see that dopey male pride burn through Rags. His head was like a cabbage shot with blood. He'd get himself killed in New Orleans. Emma took her Colt out of the kitchen drawer.

Marshall had a waxiness in his eyes. It had nothing to do with cocaine. "Baby, that's my gun. I gave it to you. . . ."

"That won't hurt my trigger finger, Marsh. I can still shoot your ears off."

He made a slow move towards Emma. She cocked the revolver and lined the barrel up with Marshall's left ear. Marsh didn't waste a threat on Emma and Rags. He went out onto the patio with his henchmen and disappeared from Iberville Street.

Rags hunched into a corner of the little house. "Who's this Marshall Glove?"

"A sportin' man. A gambler, a thief, and a pimp."

The kid had a dread of asking her things. He didn't want to know about Emma's times with Marsh. She locked all the shutters and took the kid into her arms and stroked his eyes.

"I'm a crib baby," she said. "I was born in a whorehouse attic on Robertson Street. My mama had the same yellow skin. I worked in a bagnio since I was old enough to crawl. It was a sportin' house for colored people. No whites was allowed. But it was high class. We had nigger planters and all. I would run pitchers of wine into the bedrooms and watch the girls milk a man's prick to see if he had the clap."

"How old were you?" the kid asked.

"Five or six."

"Well, I don't want to hear any more."

Rags shut his eyes. "How'd you meet Carl?"

"He was visiting Stalebread's, the bagnio where my mama raised me . . . the Giants had more clout in them days. They didn't bust up cities so much, and the cops would let them in. They were a little unrefined for Stalebread's, but the landlady liked baseball men. She thought they were minstrels, or something. Carl kidnapped me out of the bagnio after his first look. I was thirteen. He married me the next day, in front of a nigger priest and all."

"What about your mama?"

Emma giggled as she remembered Robertson Street. "Mama was glad to get rid of me. She didn't want no competition. I had hair in the right places, and the sweetest tits. . . . "

"Didn't it make you cuckoo being with so many men?"

"One prick's as good as another," Emma rasped, and then she started to retreat from her own rough talk. "I was happy with Carl . . . but he got so jealous . . . how can you be a wife, a child, and a woman to one man?"

They kept to the upper ranges of Iberville Street. Every hovel they passed had a shuttered door. Emma wouldn't have him wander down to the Vieux Carré. Franklin was the dividing line. The streets below Franklin belonged to Marsh. They were safe up around these hovels.

"Can't we go to Victoire's again?"

"He invited you in January for pompano. If you eat there now, he won't let you pay, and he'll get resentful. That's how the Creoles are. They have codes that even they can't understand."

New Orleans was too complicated for the kid. Creoles and gamblers and Shakespeare the Chief. He holed up in Emma's alley. He had her warm body at night, and curling against her, with the skin of her shoulder in his mouth, he didn't look for anything else. Palm trees grew in the courtyard. They were lusher than the Boston Fens. He had a jungle in his woman's yard, and no swamp water to drown in.

They toured the nigger streets and visited a row of cemeteries. The cemeteries were strange to Rags. People were buried above the ground in vaults that reminded him of brick ovens. The ovens had begun to corrode. Most of the writing on their faces was in French. The kid found a pirate's grave with a poem on it:

> *Intrépide guerrier sur la terre et sur l'onde*
> *Il fut dans cent combats signaler sa valeur*
> *Et ce nouveau Bayard, sans reproche et sans peur,*
> *Aurait pu sans trembler voir s'écrouler le monde*

Emma told him what it said. "The pirate Dominique fought in a million battles and could have watched the end of the world without shivering once."

"How'd you learn all that French growing up in a whorehouse?"

"This aint Cincinnati, you chump. It's Creole country."

The kid hiked on brown cemetery grass that could have been the Boston infield.

"My mama's buried in here," she said, and she led him to another aisle of oven graves in the cemetery across the street. The oven had no marker on it.

"It's the brownskins' vault. The whores had their own funeral society. Girls from Stalebread's go into the upper shelf."

Now Rags had a sense of the living and the dead in New Orleans. His muscles began to knot after a few more days, and his eyelids drooped.

"Look at you," she said. "A person would swear I gave you the gleet."

"What's the gleet?"

"The syph and the clap rolled into one . . . you're a baseball junkie is what you are. Rags, I can cure you of it. The midwife at Stalebread's taught me some gris-gris. She was our voodoo woman."

"It won't work," he said, but he had to do something about his shivers and his sweats. She cut the heart out of a turtle she bought on Villere Street and boiled it in a pot. She applied the gray, bloodless heart like a compress over Rags' belly. It drew the baseball poison out of him. He didn't shiver for a whole night. But the shivers came back in the morning.

Emma had to go to a voodoo shop in the Vieux Carré. She sprinkled a red dust inside his armpits and sang a little prayer about cat whiskers and the intestines of a pig. The shivering left him and returned, like before. He grabbed her hand when she wanted to try another voodoo shop.

"I can't stay here . . . Emma, please. We'll go to Carl. I'll be his goddamn slave if he'll let us live in the Hudson like married folks. Come with me to the Giants."

"Not now," she said. "Honey, I'll join you in a while."

The kid drove up Iberville Street and got out of New Orleans.

16

It wasn't the sockamayocks of 1925, a team that had gone invisible during the players' war, and shrank into the earth with their battered yellow bus. The kid had no trouble finding a caravan of seven Buicks. The '27 Giants were the idols of backwater villages all along the Gulf. No one talked of Ruth, Lazzeri, and Gehrig in Biloxi, Mississip. It was "that wild nigger gang" the Biloxians wanted to catch, boys that could hack out a diamond in the swamps and put on a baseball show.

The kid wondered at it: a baseball diamond in the midst of alligators and mud. The Giants were absolute engineers; they could solve any problem that had to do with foul lines and the pitcher's hill. They could have floated a diamond under the shabbiest bridge, or let a river run past second base.

Carl wasn't greedy. He gave third back to the outlaw and didn't mention his wife. The Buicks would have sunk forever without the pontoons the Giants built. The team was snug in its swamp home.

The Giants had to wear galoshes on the field; the magician frightened alligators with his root, or they would have eaten every base, but so what? The fans were coming in. And the blue swamp gas that made everybody cough seemed good for Yarbull's knees. The Pharaoh didn't take to his stretcher after a game. He could run off the diamond like any other Giant.

Biloxians enjoyed the notion that a team of niggers would carry a white brute. Scarborough returned from Havana. The kid had a roommate again.

"How's Claudine?"

The hunchback was playing deaf.

"I asked you about your winter wife."

Scarborough shrugged unhappily. "She has a new man. . . . "

"I thought you married her in church."

"Claudine aint no whore. She takes all her men to church. She's got wedding papers for nine husbands. I gave her a hundred dollars . . . for her kids."

"Is that a special fund for bastards, orphans, and love babies?"

"It's my money," Scarborough said. "I can do what I want."

And they settled into their usual life of peace and irascible talk inside the Hudson.

Nigger baseball took Rags out of any specific order of time. Seasons didn't count. Winter and summer meant the same thing: baseball diamonds in the hinterland, Carl and his hawkers scrambling for games. February looked no different from July. The Cincinnatis searched out warm, leafy spots, away from sheriffs' offices, and near a village or two. The kid was waiting for Emma to show. It was 1929. Or did he have the wrong year? Scarborough was better with calendars. Scarborough kept up. The brute would feed Rags baseball stories.

"Hollis McKee lost the Sox. He had to sell out. They were gonna throw him into receivership."

The kid shrugged at the news. Emma was what he cared about. He was miserable in the back seat, without her hands to stroke his eyes. He considered a journey to Iberville Street whenever the Giants played near the Gulf. But he was terrified somehow. He couldn't tell what he would meet behind her shutters. Marshall Glove, or another man? He wasn't scared of Marsh and those boys with the iron knucks. He was scared of Emma Raines and the look she might give him. If she turned cool to Rags, the kid would die.

"Raggsy, you know it's bullshit about Babe Ruth. He went to St Mary's, but he wasn't an orphan . . . he had a mom and a dad. It's in all the papers. His dad owned a bar, and that monkey would steal from the till. So they tossed him into the bad boys' school. And he'd say, 'I'm too ugly for my pa to visit.' It must have rattled the monk. When he got to the big leagues, he told everybody he was a bastard."

"You can't put him in jail for that. It's not a crime."

"I know, but the rest of the league's been jumping on his tail, shouting, 'Bastard, bastard, bastard. . . .' "

Rags had a vision of Iberville Street, and he lost most of what the brute was telling him. But he did hear the name "Garl."

"What's that about Garland climbing the flagpole in center field?"

"It was a trick he had before you came to the Sox. He would hide behind that pole and shimmy right up to the middle if the ball was coming his way. He'd stiff-arm that ball and do his 'flag' catch. But he twisted his foot last year and fell down the pole. Garl aint with Boston anymore."

"Did the Brownies pick him up?"

"I don't think so."

"Then he must have gone back to Dartmouth to study Greek."

"No. Garl's disappeared."

"Who told you that?"

"Hooks Poland. He opened a hobby shop in Shreveport. I bumped into him yesterday on the road."

"You sure Garl isn't at Dartmouth under another name?"

"Raggsy, Hooks wouldn't lie to me. The skipper's disappeared."

"I know where he went," Rags muttered. "Hey, are we in 1930?"

The brute figured he had Rip van Winkle for a roommate. Rags must have gone into a great snore since he returned from New Orleans.

"We're in 1931," Scarborough said, not wanting to plague the kid.

"And what month is it?"

"Rags, people have been out of work for two fuckin' years . . . half the country is living on apples and water, and you juggle baseballs and run around with cardboard over your eyes . . . it's June. Wake up, and don't be such a jackass. You're twenty-six, and you already have a gray hair on your head."

Rags wandered through the bushes and found a country store. The store had a telephone. It took him twenty minutes to get an operator on the line and another ten to place his call to Tucson. He heard her squabble with the receptionist at his father's company. "I have a collect call for Mr. Martin Griffey from Cedric Tannehill. Will you accept the charges, hon?"

The receptionist had never heard of Cedric, and the kid had to break into the conversation. "I'm the president of Tannehill Copper," he growled. "Get me Griffey right away. . . . "

After five more squabbling minutes, Rags screaming he was president, president, Griffey took the call.

"I was with a client," Griffey said. "You should have given me a little warning. . . . "

"Didn't you say you were my lawyer now?"

"Be reasonable, Cedric. You haven't been in touch for so long. . . . "

"Well, I need you, Griff. Find me a small college in Massachusetts or New Hampshire that could use a Greek teacher and a baseball coach."

"You do have a charming way about you, Cedric . . . I suppose I could find this miracle college in a year or two."

"Have it by tomorrow, Griff." And the kid hung up.

He got a booking out of Galveston to Quintana Roo. He must have been on a smuggler's run. The ship stank of whiskey, and the sailors carried machine guns. But they all remembered the American League.

"Rags, I saw you play the Indians in 1925. What a glove!"

Being sailors, they were curious about the fist a third baseman had. They examined the rough claws on his throwing hand. He drank rum with them out of their private stock and took target practice aboard the *Sweet Marie*. The machine gun turned hot and shivered in his arms. But he did destroy two straw hats and the captain's old pajamas. He borrowed a dinghy from the pirates, and they dropped him in the water about a mile from Quintana Roo. They were wary of other pirates, who jumped out like flying snakes at any ship that touched near the coast.

So the kid thanked the good pirates and rowed his dinghy onto the beach at Quintana Roo. The beach wasn't as deserted as it had been during his last vacation. It had the same dumb sand that couldn't support a lizard or a cockroach. But it was congested with human beings. They weren't the zombies of 1925, kind old men with bald spots and vacant looks, exiled governors and poets and conquistadors. These were a rough band of men. The rats had come to Quintana Roo. The beachcombers were vicious this year.

They carried sticks and cumbersome knives that they shook at Rags. He wasn't to join their party. They babbled in some devil's tongue and fought among themselves for what little food was around: inland berries, roots, nuts, chewable leather. You couldn't see too many faces under the thick beards they wore. How was the kid supposed to uncover Garl?

He shouted at these ratty men.

"It's the Babe, Garl. I'm on Quintana Roo."

No one bothered to answer him. They continued their babble of tongues, and menaced him with their sticks and knives.

Rags developed a kind of intuition on that dumb gray sand. Garl was hiding with these rats, he was somewhere in that body of beachcombers. He didn't want to expose himself to Rags.

The kid stomped up and down, yelling "Pharaoh, Harry Heilmann, Hollis McKee." He was getting hungry. But he couldn't borrow a nut or a root off these terrible men.

Garl, I understand. I remind you of baseball too much. I'm your own fucking history that you came here to outrun.

Didn't the brute say Rags was twenty-six? That single gray hair in his scalp had to mean something. Rags was no orphan in the sand. He'd wrestled baby bulls on his father's ranch. He'd hit seven home runs in the major leagues. He could survive on Quintana Roo.

He went searching for berries and nuts. The hinterland was even more godforsaken than the beach. What happened to the village where Garl had found an adulterous wife for Rags? The kid returned to the beach with one sickly root. It seemed like a prize to the starving beachcombers, who were making ready to dismember Rags with their knives. The knives never touched Rags. Garl picked this moment to reveal himself. He was as ratty as the rest, with a long brown beard, but he began hurling beachcombers into the sand. The entire gang fled from this loco who turned on his own people for a boy with a root.

"Shit, Garl, you didn't have to lose your friends on account of me. I would have socked a few of 'em before they whittled me down with their pieces of tin."

Garland chuckled under that beard, and the kid recognized his old skipper.

"I hear you fell off the flagpole," Rags said.

"Who told you that?"

"Scarborough did. He got it from Hooks Poland."

"Hooks was always a blabbermouth," Garl said. "What the hell are you doing in this miserable place?"

"I've come to bring you out of Quintana Roo."

"Why? Are you offering me a spot with the Giants? I'm finished with baseball. Rags, I've paid my dues. I can live on a beach. My mother is dead, my grandpa is gone, and my three brothers are out of school."

"What happened to Dartmouth and Greek?"

Garl began to sputter words from a play called *Philoctetes*.

The kid answered him in Greek. "They do that finger talk at Amherst too . . . I had a whole month of Sophocles."

"Well, Sophocles can sleep without Garland James," Garl said. "I'll pick roots in the territories and swallow sand. . . . "

"No you won't. I'm not leaving by myself. We don't have the Boston tunnel, Garl, but we can fight up and down the beach . . . until I drag you off Quintana."

"I have fifty friends over there with knives. I think they'd side with me."

"Maybe. You buried a dozen heads in the sand. Those beach rats might not forget so fast . . . Garl, there's a college in New Hampshire named Calliope that's looking for a Greek and Latin scholar and baseball coach. Guess what? They've decided on you. . . . "

Garl scratched his cheek.

"I inherited my father's company," the kid said. "I have some pull. But that's not it, Garl. You beat out all the contenders by a country mile. There's not another scholar in the world who went to Dartmouth, studied Greek, played center field, and skippered the Red Sox. . . . "

They broke the kid's root and sucked on the bitter ends for nourishment.

"Garl, where's that village with the bad wives?"

"They moved into the interior. They couldn't stand the smell of so many gypsies on the beach . . . how's the Colored Giants?"

"Going at six hundred games a year . . . I'm in love with Carl's wife. She lives in New Orleans now. She won't stay with the Giants."

"If you can take me off Quintana, why can't you steal her from New Orleans?"

"She's got a pistol, Garl. She'll shoot me in the nose."

"Who says you need a nose to play third?"

Rags couldn't answer the scholar. They got into the dinghy and started to row. The kid had made arrangements with the pirate ship. He wagged his shirt for half an hour until the good pirates appeared and picked them out of the sea.

17

The Giants had snaked over to Mississippi while the kid was down in the Yucatán rescuing Garl. He discovered his own Hudson outside Hattiesburg, but where was the baseball diamond? The

Giants were in mourning. They didn't go around in gold and white. They had dusty black suits and nigger chapeaus, hats that were snug on their foreheads and hid one eye. They weren't in a talking mood.

The kid had to slide into the Hudson and catch Scarborough in the front seat. The brute also wore black.

"Hump, what's going on? I left a team and come back to a funeral station."

"Mrs. Carl is dead."

That name didn't draw blood at first. *Mrs. Carl? Who's that?* Then the kid remembered who Mrs. Carl was. "Emma Raines?" he said, and his lip turned swollen. He went to Carl.

The bossman lay in the head Buick, with his body in the frozen attitude of a corpse. It took him a while to unbend himself and respond to the kid. They smoked a reefer together. The cigarette didn't take Carl from his sorrows, but it did get him to talk.

"The police come looking for me . . . they found Emma in her yard with a necktie on her that was a little too tight. They don't keep a body long in Louisiana . . . they put her in the whore's vault, where her mama is . . . on the nigger side of the cemetery."

"Who strangled her, Carl?"

"The cops wouldn't tell, but it must have been her fancy man . . . the gambler she was living with."

"Marshall Glove?"

"I never heard his name," Carl said, and he grew corpselike again.

The kid ran to the Hudson and tried to push Scarborough off the front seat. "Get out, Hump. I'm goin' to Orleans to kill a man."

"Who?"

"The gambler, Marshall Glove . . . I'm sure he strangled Emma Raines."

"Nobody arrested him, Raggsy. If he's a gambler, he's got an in with the police. Kill him, and you'll die in New Orleans."

"It's none of your business."

"Who says? Roomies don't have secrets. Your business is my business . . . where does he live, this Marshall Glove?"

"I don't know."

"Some murderer you are . . . come on, I'll help you find Marshall Glove. But don't you kill him. Just break his bones a little . . . that way you won't have a murder charge sittin' on your head."

"Who taught you so much about criminal justice, huh Hump?"

Scarborough took the wheel. "It aint criminal justice. It's common sense. . . . "

They left the Hudson behind a watermelon shed in the French Market. Rags crossed the railroad tracks and stood on the levee, watching the slow brown run of the river. There were rafts and houseboats for sale near the Toulouse Street wharf.

"Wish we could buy a houseboat," Rags said. "I'd park it downriver, and then we'd have a home somewhere."

The brute dragged him from the levee. "Houseboat, my eye. After we finish with Glove, you won't be able to rent a frog off the river."

"How are you gonna get to Marsh?" Rags said. "With your hump?"

"You'll see," the brute muttered. They walked from bottle shop to bottle shop on St. Philip Street. Girls hung out from the balcony windows with nothing on, and showed their pudendas to Rags and the brute. Scarborough wouldn't stop for a look. At the fifth or sixth bottle shop he found a dwarf. He signaled to Rags, telling him to stay on the street. Rags could smell peaches and horseshit in the Vieux Carré. The brute came out smiling from the bottle shop.

"Glove lives on Barracks Street . . . but it's no use trying to catch him there. He hangs out at a gambler's den on Dumaine. Two in the morning is the best time to parlay with him. He goes out for a piss in the street and a friendly poke with the ladies."

"Hump, do you have a detective's license? How did you learn all this?"

"From the dwarf. Little guys like to help each other out."

"Let's go to Victoire's. It's not the right time for pompano, but we can have the best trout in New Orleans."

They waited on line outside Victoire's window. Rags couldn't understand why the Creoles on line with him inched their bodies away from the brute. Victoire wasn't at the door to greet his customers. Had the restaurant changed hands? A different Creole stood watch. He seemed reluctant to let Rags and Scarborough into the restaurant. He pointed to a card in the window that claimed gentlemen had to be properly attired after dusk. The kid was in his baseball shirt.

"Where's Victoire?" Rags growled.

The Creole shrugged. "The old man has been dead for a year. His son hardly comes to the restaurant."

"Don't you recognize me? I'm Babe Ragland. I defied the Judge. . . ."

It meant nothing to this man. The Creoles had forgotten the kid. Then a waiter peeked through the door. "Ah, M'sieu le Babe." He brought them into the restaurant but they had to sit at an end table, next to the cashier. The waiter produced a scarf and a coat for Rags. He bent over and whispered to the kid. "It's your friend. The Creoles are superstitious, M'sieu. Hunchbacks frighten them out of their wits."

"Should we leave the table?"

"No, no. Victoire would return from the dead and cut off our tongues if we offended you."

Rags ordered white wine and cassis. The brute liked that pink taste in his mouth. He had two halves of a blood-red Texas grapefruit, chicken gumbo, and a crabmeat casserole. The name *Victoire* was printed on his water glass. A fan with wooden blades spun over his head, stopped, and spun. He could see his own ears in the mirror on the wall. The mirror had hooks for a gentleman's umbrella. The grandfather clock behind the cashier's booth wouldn't toll the hour. The chimes stood still.

A Creole lady stared at her pocket watch. "Darlin', it's ten minutes till nine."

The kid had his trout. He sucked on the lemon that came with the fish. "Good for the teeth," he said. "It stops yellow scurvy."

Scarborough was annoyed at the kid's arrogance. "Any dumbbell knows that."

They paid the bill and sneaked out of their hidden corner. Rags left the coat and scarf on his chair. Conversation stopped when the two of them passed among the Creoles.

They still had hours to kill.

"Hump, we'll go to Marsh's sportin' club and feel the place out. . . ."

"What if he recognizes you?"

"He'll be too busy making dollars and sniffing nose powder."

They didn't hop on a trolley to Dumaine. They decided to walk. They couldn't avoid the "crib" girls of Conti Street. Haggard women would leap out at them from windows and low balconies. They were more interested in the brute than in Rags. "Hello, Hot Papa, want a good ride?"

Scarborough wouldn't flirt with them or examine their tits.

They followed him down the street. "Half a dollah, half a dollah, and you can go round the world. . . ."

The brute had to give them the change in his pocket, or they would have torn pieces of his flesh. He cursed the whores of the Vieux Carré.

"It's not their fault," Rags said. "The Navy chased them out of their own District. So they relocated, and got new cribs. Emma told me that. . . ."

"Well, I don't like it much when painted women touch me in the street."

They arrived at Marshall's hangout, the Royal Fox. It was part speakeasy, sporting house, and gambling den. The Fox had a cherrywood bar, competing nests of whores and pimps, cocaine dealers, river rats, smugglers, gamblers, and the impoverished sons of Creole sugar men. It also had a pit near the bar for wrestling and boxing matches, and dog fights. The champion boxer of New Orleans, a Cajun named Mario, stood in the pit without his clothes. His ears had been chewed off. A nostril was gone. He had dents in his skull that were as deep as a human hand. His back was ribbed with scars that read like some crazy scripture. Who would want to challenge such a man?

Marshall Glove stood near Mario, with wads of paper money and gamblers' notes stuck in his fist. He was the main betting man at the Fox.

"We're out of luck," the kid said. "What if this Mario is his bodyguard?"

"Uh, uh," Scarborough said. "The gambler is bettin' against the Cajun."

"Well, show me the man Marsh is bettin' for?"

A roly-poly woman started to undress. Rags had assumed she was a barmaid. People called her Alice. She didn't have a line on her gentle face. All her pubic hair had been cropped. Alice's cunt inflamed the brute. He couldn't take his eyes from that baldness between her legs.

The river rats told Scarborough that Alice was ruined for life. She'd gotten on the bad side of certain voodoo mistresses in the French Quarter, and the mistresses laid a curse on her: they "sealed her up" so that no man could enter Alice.

The brute said he didn't care. He'd find a way of loving her if she would marry him. He'd ask her after the fight.

"There aint gonna be nothin' left to ask," the rats said. "She won't have arms, she won't have legs . . . she'll be a puddle of water and shit. No one can beat the Cajun."

"What odds are you giving?" Scarborough said to the river rats.

"Eighteen to one."

He bet a dollar on Alice.

She went into the pit with Mario the Cajun. There wasn't a referee to watch over them. It was a curious fighting they did. They could only box and wrestle with one hand, because they had to attack and cover their genitals at the same time. The Cajun was a head taller than Alice, and his reach was almost double. He could slap and kick at her before she got close. But it wasn't Amherst vs. Dartmouth at the Royal Fox. Alice didn't have to depend on any science and rules of fisticuffs. She took the slaps and kicks. Her mouth turned bloody. The Cajun laughed at his fat target. He could have danced in the pit and waited for Mardi Gras to come. Alice couldn't absorb every one of his blows.

Mario drank a glass of beer in the middle of the fight. The rats applauded when he belched out an aria for them. They begged him to finish Alice. They wanted their money. So the Cajun resumed his kicking act. Alice's skin went black around the knees. Mario got careless. He slapped at her with both hands. Alice burrowed in like a bulldog and caught him where he was hung. The Cajun screamed. He jumped into the air, his neck muscles quivering, and fell out of the pit. His handlers might have revived him. But it was too late. The laws of the house wouldn't let Mario reenter the pit.

The brute collected his eighteen dollars and went over to Alice, who sat on the cherrywood bar with her legs open. The rats had lied to him. Alice wasn't sealed.

"Ma'am, would you consider marrying me?"

Alice figured the brute wanted to rent her for half an hour. "Sure, honey," she said. "I'm tired right now. I'll marry ya tomorrow."

The brute returned to the river rats. You could see his discouragement in the twitching of his shoulder. His hump had dropped a whole mile. How could he marry her tomorrow when he'd have to run like the devil from New Orleans?

It was only midnight. They'd have to hover near the bar until Marsh strolled out for his two A.M. piss.

That dwarf on St. Philip Street knew his man. Marshall didn't stir. Then, at the stroke of two, he walked out of the Royal Fox with fat Alice, who had gotten dressed in the meantime.

"Damn," the brute said, *"she's* his bodyguard." But he wouldn't disappoint the kid. He'd have to jump on his espoused wife and wrestle with her, or the kid would never reach Marshall Glove.

They slinked behind Marsh and Alice. The gambler turned around. He thought the two men were out to steal his money. He gave these two men to Alice. She stood with her hands on her hips. "Go on home, little boys."

She didn't recall Scarborough. He could have been any hunchback on the street. The brute tried to rush her. He leapt at Alice.
She plucked him out of the air and threw him into the gutter, with
the dead cats, the garbage, and the shit. He rolled over, slid off a
dead cat, and rushed her again.

The kid had his chance. While Alice was busy flinging Scarborough everywhere, Rags got to Marshall Glove. He climbed on
Marshall's back, clung to him, and socked him in the kidneys. He
could hear Scarborough shout.

"Don't go for the head . . . you'll kill him, you'll kill him . . .
don't go for the head."

Even in his fury to hit Marsh, the kid followed Scarborough's
instructions. He socked the gambler into the sidewalk, going for
the kidneys, the back, the shoulders, and the heart. Alice couldn't
help her boss. The brute was like a small octopus. As far as she
hurled that slippery man, the faster he would rush her. She'd try a
different strategy. Break off his miserable hump. She hadn't reckoned on that tough bark under his shirt and coat. She held him in
her arms, but she couldn't snap off any piece of him. He wiggled
out of her grip, and using his hump as a battering ram, he knocked
her into the street. Alice was stunned. She'd destroyed the Cajun
tonight. She couldn't believe a common hunchback would humiliate her.

"Raggsy, are ya through with the gink?"

The kid sat over Glove, and pulled on the gambler's scarf. "Did
you enjoy strangling Miz Emma, you son of a bitch?"

Glove's eyes dropped back into his head. It was like pulling on
a blind man. The gambler mumbled something. What if the kid had
been wrong, and some mad Creole murdered Emma in her patio?
"Marshall, it's me . . .Ragland, the baseball player. . . ."

He couldn't get Marshall to admit a thing. The gambler began to
shudder on the sidewalk. Was it cocaine fever, or guilt over Emma
Raines? Rags climbed off of him. "Hump, let's go."

The kid was running somewhere. The brute had to follow. He
waved to Alice sitting in the garbage. Where was east and where
was west? The kid was going the wrong way. The Hudson was
parked near the Mississippi River.

"Raggsy, this Alice aint gonna lie down in garbage too long.
She'll send an army after us . . . where the hell are ya running
to?"

The kid wouldn't answer him. He called to a flower girl outside
a bagnio on Dauphine Street. The flower girl couldn't have been
more than six or seven. What was she doing here so early in the
morning? The kid demanded all her goods. He didn't settle on a

price. Rags wouldn't bargain down a six-year-old girl. He put twenty dollars into her hand and grabbed a hill of half-dead flowers. The brute had to walk with a rotten sweetness in his nose.

Rags took him into a graveyard with knobby walls. The graveyard had brick houses in it. The kid stumbled from row to row, searching for a particular house. There wasn't much of a moon in New Orleans, and Rags had to squint into the shadows under and over the bricks. He paused, stooped, and put the fucking daisies at the bottom of a house with a crumbling roof. "Emma's inside."

Scarborough pulled Rags away from Emma's brick house. They took a wide, circular route down to the levee. The Hudson was still there.

"Raggsy, stop dreaming on your toes. We got gamblers and fat ladies after us." Scarborough shook his head. He stowed Rags in the Hudson and got behind the wheel.

"Jesus, don't you want to play for the Giants?"

Book Six

BOSSMAN
AND MAGICIAN

18

T HE SCYTHES LAY DEAD in the Buicks. The grass was un-
shorn. The groundkeepers hadn't cleared a line for first
base, and they didn't grow a hill for Yam Murray. Carl
wandered in and out of his Buick in bedroom slippers. The boss
was incoherent most of the time. His speech jumped from whore-
houses to curve balls and Mississippi mud. He would rant and cry
and threaten his players, and then talk of "lending" the team to
Pharaoh.

Worst of all, the magician had run off and left his root behind. It
was unheard of to function in the nigger leagues without a witch
doctor to chase the storms into another district, cast a spell on
your enemies, and heal the lame.

Samuel hadn't committed a senseless act. It was shrewd of him
to go. The Giants had deteriorated in front of his eyes, fallen to a
nothing club, and who would be blamed for it? Samuel Sharn.
They couldn't hire another magician. No dependable witch doctor
would come to the Giants.

Pharaoh met with Swimmy and Yam. They offered the root to
Scarborough. The hunchback wouldn't hear of it.

"I'm a bat boy, trainer, and first baseman," he said. "I won't
fuck with clouds."

"Can't you do a little magic with your hump?" Swimmy asked.

"I aint got voodoo in my blood. I wouldn't know how to talk to
a root."

"I'll be your magician," Rags said, and he took the root jar into the Hudson's back seat. Then he pointed to his chest. "This magician swears Texas is for us. We have to hold down until Carl recovers his head."

"Where in Texas is that, magician Rags?"

"Gents, we're goin' to Abilene."

It was seven dirty Buicks and a Hudson that arrived at his father's ranch. The foreman didn't know what to make of it. He never saw so many niggers leaning out of automobiles. Was it a minstrel show coming through central Texas? He had enough scatterguns and Colts behind him to let these niggers fly like gooney birds up into the Panhandle.

The foreman had to hesitate. There were two white boys in the Hudson sedan. A skinny fella and a brokeback. The skinny one got out of the car.

"Where's the owner of this cattle farm?"

"Aint your business," the foreman told him.

"I'm making it my business," Rags said. The scatterguns were raised to the level of his neck. But Rags wouldn't back off.

"Look at me, you . . . I'm Cedric Tannehill. And this is my fuckin' place."

The foreman and his ranch hands slapped their knees. They chuckled so hard, their scatterguns wavered and dipped. A gun went off. Rags thought he was standing on top of an earthquake. The boom split the ground under him, and turned the kid deaf for a minute.

"Liar," the foreman said. "Cedric wouldn't bring niggers to his daddy's house . . . he's in Boston playing for those Red Sox."

An old black cowboy in leather pants came up to Rags, sniffed at him, and hugged him around the shoulders.

The foreman scolded the black cowboy. "Benjamin, what the hell are you doin' now?"

Rags smiled. "How are you, Benjy?"

"Still walkin', Mr. Cedric," the cowboy said.

Rags turned to the foreman. "Jack Tarr, you were always a scumsucker and a prick."

And the foreman had to eat crow. He'd failed to recognize young Tannehill around niggers and a brokeback. It was still confusing to him. Had the shines taken over Boston? Did the Red Sox go black? He muttered to his own nigger cowboy. "Benjy, what team is this?"

"Don't you know, captain? The Cincinnati Colored Giants, champeens of the world."

Jack Tarr would have broken into guffaws, but he couldn't insult this millionaire kid, who had come out of the dust with seven jalopies and a run-down sedan. *The Cincinnati Colored Giants*. What could you do about these eccentric millionaire sons? Old Mr. Marcus died with the grit of copper on his tongue. There was a man. Drink his whiskey and sit on a bull's back. And the son plays catch with niggers.

"Cedric, we got your father's room all prepared for you . . . the team can bed down in the number-two barn."

"Thanks, Jack, but I'll sleep in the barn with the Giants."

Jack couldn't have a Tannehill breathing cowshit. He had to relent. "Aint no bother. There's room for everybody in the big house."

So the Cincinnatis stopped being nomads for a while and moved onto the ranch. The Spanish maids and cooks prepared a hundred flapjacks for the Cincinnatis alone. Jack Tarr took his food at the opposite end of the table. The ranch was suddenly a lonesome place.

Rags wouldn't sleep in his father's bed. He occupied his old room in the northwest corner of the house. Scarborough shared the room with him.

The kid wouldn't have his breakfast without the old black cowboy. "Mr. Yarbull, this is the man who taught me how to hold a bat . . . Benjy, where are those other guys? . . . Clarence, Dummy, and Spot . . . with their neckerchiefs . . . bullriders who could hit and field."

"They're gone, Mr. Cedric. Clarence is in El Paso. Dummy joined another outfit. Spot's dead. . . ."

Yarbull looked across the table at Rags. "Why'd you come to the Giants when you have all this? . . . flapjacks, clean sheets, and enough bulls to keep every shorthorn in the state of Texas happy."

"I'm a ballplayer," the kid said. "I don't breed bulls." And he finished his breakfast without mentioning baseball again.

Carl didn't regain his wits at the ranch. He cried in his room and clutched the few articles of Emma's that he had: a kerchief, a ripped dress, a bottle of toilet water that was going scummy, a pair of whore's stockings he kept around ever since he lifted Emma from that bagnio in New Orleans. But his mind wouldn't crawl back to the Cincinnati Giants.

Rags went to Yarbull. "He's not getting any better . . . and we can't rebuild the team if we stay off the road and live in this house. How can you barnstorm from a Texas ranch?"

"We need lights," the Pharaoh said.

Rags blinked at him.

"The best nigger teams are carrying their own lights these days. The Monarchs started that. Now the ABCs have them, the Memphis Sox, the Nashville Elites . . . we won't survive if we can't fit night games into our schedule."

"How much would it cost?"

"I aint no accountant, but the ABCs might sell us their lights."

It took Yarbull thirteen phone calls to find out.

"We can have their lights, their poles, and their generator for a thousand dollars cash."

The kid didn't have a thousand on him. He had to telephone his Santa Claus, Martin Griffey of Tucson and Tannehill Copper.

"The Giants are in trouble, Griff. We can't operate without a portable lighting system. It'll take a thousand in cash. Am I entitled to a loan? Or do I have to beg for it?"

"You'll get your money, Cedric . . . off the books. I wouldn't want your phantoms to play in the dark."

"I have one more problem, Griff. The boss of the Giants is out of his mind. Would Tannehill Copper like to buy a baseball club?"

"I'll discuss it with the board, but to tell you the truth, I don't think we'll go into baseball this year."

"Then I'll have to buy the Giants. What would you say we're worth?"

"That depends. What have you got?"

"We got plenty . . . Pharaoh Yarbull, for instance. He's the black George Sisler. . . . "

"Can he break into the major leagues?"

"Don't fool with me, Griff . . . you know he can't play in the majors . . . and I've been barred for life."

"Cedric, give the crazy man who owns the Giants two hundred dollars. That's a fair price."

"Listen, Griff. The phantoms have rolling stock . . . seven Buicks and a Hudson sedan."

"What vintage? How old are the cars?"

"Ten years old, I suspect. . . ."

"That'll add another two hundred to your baseball company. I'd say the Giants are worth four hundred dollars on the open market. . . ."

"Then you'll have to lie a bit . . . stretch the inventory, Griff. You know how. And give Carl Raines twelve hundred for his Giants."

"That's robbery," the lawyer said.

"Who cares? I'm president of Tannehill Copper. I have to have a little leeway."

There were no documents to sign. Nothing could be transferred over to the kid. Carl had ruled by fiat. His ownership didn't come from a piece of paper. Rags stuck Griffey's twelve hundred dollars into an empty tobacco tin and gave it to the black cowboy to hold for Mr. Carl. "You take care of that man, Benjy. I'm leaving him on the ranch. He was like a pa to me . . . I stole his wife for a few weeks. I'm sorry for that. . . ."

And the Giants got out of central Texas to pick up their lights from the ABCs. Rags saw a converted fire truck with ladders on the sides and a gasoline generator sitting on top, and some shaky poles and strings of light bulbs.

The kid was dubious about the lights. Pharaoh reassured him. "The deal was made nigger to nigger, boss. They wouldn't burn us. We got a first-class system, you'll see."

"Shouldn't we test the stuff?"

"Boss, we can't insult the ABCs."

The Cincinnatis rode off with their lights; the poles rattled and the fire truck leaked. Every Giant, from the carpenters and groundkeepers to the players, the hunchback, and the magician-boss, had to cradle light bulbs in his lap. Glass shivered and popped on the bumpy roads. Rags cursed Yarbull, the ABCs, and his new lights. He should have been a farmer, not the entrepreneur of a wandering baseball club.

They camped in a small desert patch outside Colorado Springs. The groundsmen left their scythes in the Buicks. There wasn't enough grass to monkey with. They threw up a diamond in the middle of the desert floor. The carpenters stuck the poles into the ground, screwed in the lights, stretched out the cable lines that snaked from pole to pole, and hid the fire truck in deep center field.

Their placards had lured a team of deaf mutes into camp. Rags could let his generator sleep during the afternoon. The mutes played ferocious ball. They lied, cheated, and wanted to fight Swimmy Welles. They had six thousand of their brothers in the stands. Scarborough was amazed. "There must be a whole army of mutes in Colorado Springs."

The Giants had to beat them twice, or the mutes wouldn't go home. The kid had strawberries on his legs from the way those rough little bastards slid at him. He ate a can of sardines and prepared for the night game that was scheduled with a bunch of semipros.

The semipros arrived at six o'clock. They were bandits and out-casts from a dozen leagues. Not one of them had a decent baseball jersey. Rags didn't care. He was more interested in his lights.

A carpenter went into the bowels of the fire truck and switched the generator on. The fire truck shook; ladders fell off. A noise came out of the truck that was like the scream of a hundred women. Rags had to hold his ears, but Yarbull hadn't tricked him. The truck was alive. It fed the cables and the poles, and produced a terrific blaze of light. The Cincinnatis had a second afternoon on the diamond.

They were destroying the semipros, who showed themselves to be sickly bandits. But the generator had a coughing fit after the third inning. The fire truck stopped shivering, and the lights went dead. Rags swore he'd sue the ABCs. Carpenters hopped about. The Giants' golden uniforms looked like strips of lead in the dark. The generator began to cough again. There was a hiss around the poles. The lights blazed up. The Giants finished murdering the semipros.

Yarbull's legs.

Rags couldn't cure them with a generator and a string of lights. He didn't have Samuel Sharn to pack the Pharaoh's brittle knees with a variety of ointments, spices, and medicinal gums. The kid had to be his own magician. Scarborough would give the Pharaoh rubdowns between innings, and wait with him until he was carried off the field. But these were temporary measures. Rags was the only one who could go to the root.

He concealed himself in the back seat of the Hudson, sang to the root jar, and stroked it with his claws. The Pharaoh hit three home runs. The Cincinnatis gaped at Rags. The new bossman was a regular witch. Swimmy found the solution. Rags was crazy enough to work nigger magic with a white man's claws.

Yarbull didn't have to lie down in the stretcher more than two hours a day. He could twist around faster than he ever could. But Rags didn't trust himself as a magician. Yarbull's eyes were old. The skin near his lips was tough as shoe leather. His hairline seemed to push right into his skull.

He was leaping for a ball in another game with the mutes, and you could hear his body rip. It was like the grinding of ferocious teeth, as if an invisible shark had cut through his legs and into his groin. He dropped to the ground in a swoon.

The kid ran to the Hudson. The root jar revived the Pharaoh. His tongue was hornier than a toad's head. Rags scooped water into the Pharaoh's mouth with his own magician's hand.

"We'll get a doctor," the kid said.

The Pharaoh said no. All he needed was a carpenter and the

kid's root. He'd wear stilts under his baseball pajamas. "Boss, you'll have to put me on third . . . I can hold the base line, and that's about it."

"Who'll play short for us" the kid blubbered, thinking of Yarbull's ripped knees.

Pharaoh got his smile back. The horniness had gone out of his tongue. "Don't bellyache," he said. "You'll have to be the shortstop, Mr. Rags."

So they worked a switch. Yarbull stood on his carpentered legs. He was like a snowman in gold and white. He didn't melt. But he couldn't do more than stretch an arm or hop on those stilts under his pajamas. Rags had to cover the Pharaoh's ground. He scrambled after bunts and jumped out at balls that flew over third. But no one could say the Giants didn't have Yarbull in the field.

He couldn't go for singles anymore. How can you beat out a hit with boards taped to your legs? It was a home run or nothing for Pharaoh Yarbull. He would sock the ball into the next prairie and hobble around the bases. That was Yarbull's only chance.

It didn't hurt the Giants. They won with that snowman on third, and crept into 1934, while other nigger teams dropped out of sight. The big leagues were also having a troublesome year. Babe Ruth was thirty-nine, and the Yanks had become the old men of organized baseball. The Cardinals took the World Series from Detroit. Their ace, Jerome "Dizzy" Dean, had put together a barnstorming act with his brother Paul. The Dean brothers weren't afraid of Mountain Landis. They met with Rags on the sly and agreed to appear once with the Cincinnatis for a purse of two thousand dollars. The game site was a pasture outside Enid, Oklahoma, where Landis' agents were unlikely to come.

"What happens if we lose?" Scarborough asked.

"I'll have to hock the team . . . or cry to Santa Claus, Martin Griffey."

"Suppose you cry to Santa a little too often?"

"We'll have to risk that," the kid muttered. "Now go and tape up Yarbull's legs."

The Dizzy Dean All-Stars arrived in a huge traveling van. The van had a washroom and couches for Dizzy and Paul. The Dean boys liked to rest their arms on the road. The All-Stars that hopped out of the van didn't impress the kid. They were the usual sockamayocks. He couldn't have told you their names. Rags had already been out of the majors nine and a half years.

The sockamayocks were a decoration Dizzy could afford. He won thirty games this year, and he also had his brother Paul. He was six feet two, and when he came over the hill with his long right arm, batters had to sing a prayer. His smoke was the best in the league, but he didn't have to depend on it. He had a slider and a screwball that broke into your cuffs, or disappeared altogether. He could turn that horsehide into a "ghost."

If Dizzy liked you, he'd let you call him Jerome. He was twenty-three years old, and he'd been following the Cincinnati Giants since he was a boy in Arkansas. He worshiped Pharaoh Yarbull and Yam Murray, and he was fond of Swimmy Welles and the kid. He swore he'd learned half his stuff from Yam.

But Yam was nearing fifty. He couldn't compete with Jerome and Paul. He had to go to his emery board because even a socka-mayock can buy a lucky hit.

The game started at four in the afternoon. Paul shouted to his brother. "You be tender with the Giants, Jerome. We aint got insurance for broken skulls."

Dizzy went through the Giant batting order and struck out all nine men. Rags noticed a piece of wind. He could smell the ball. It seemed to drop around his toes. He couldn't accuse Jerome's umpire. Rags had his three cuts. The ball looped and looped and was gone.

Yarbull might have hit the great Jerome. But he was handicapped. He couldn't push his elbows very far with those stilts he was carrying. He had to taper his swing, or fly on his ass.

Fucking Jerome, the kid sang to himself. The Dean brothers wouldn't have bet two thousand dollars on a team of sockama-yocks if they weren't sure Pharaoh was wearing stilts. The money was in their pocket. They could have Yam scrape the ball, and tickle it with his emery paper. The sockamayocks would get to him after a while. All they needed was a run.

But old Yam Murray surprised the Deans. He made those sock-amayocks slap the ball on the ground. Swimmy and Rags gobbled everything out of the grass.

Rags had his generator switched on at seven o'clock. It was the nineteenth inning. Not a single son of a bitch had reached first base. The sirens, those crazy women inside the fire truck, began to wail. They couldn't disturb Jerome. He put down Giant after Giant with his screwball, his sinker, and his smoke. He ate a candy bar between innings. He would have gone back to the hill and pitched until morning if he had to.

Yam was dying on his feet. His arm had stiffened up, his knees had withered to a kind of paste. Rags fed him sardines and water. The brute seized Yam's shoulders and rubbed and rubbed.

They got him to pitch again.

The sirens wailed.

The lights in the outfield began to dim.

The diamond was turning gray. Yam couldn't see his catcher's fist.

The wailing from the truck inspired Rags. He had Scarborough pinch-hit for Muley Jones. Dizzy peered down at Scarborough from the hill. He winked to his brother Paul. It was the bottom of the twenty-fifth. Jerome hadn't pitched to a hunchback in his years with the Cards. He was searching for a reliable target. Should he throw to that bubble the brute had on his back? Or aim for the gold letters on Scarborough's chest? His smoke couldn't harm the brute, and his sinker bounced in front of the plate. He walked Scarborough in five pitches. The hunchback ruined his perfect game.

The sirens had blessed the Giants. After twenty-four innings they had a man on first. But Rags couldn't take Scarborough's hand and lead him around the bases. How could they bring him home?

Rags swallowed wind for the tenth time. Jerome struck him out. It was the Pharaoh's turn. Yarbull took off one of the stilts. He had to have the opportunity to bend a knee. The stilt he wore was a peg leg now. It anchored him to the plate, but it didn't poison the cut of his bat. Jerome went over the hill and gave Yarbull a screwball to eat.

The clap of wood on horsehide was the sweetest sound Rags could hear. Scarborough scampered to second. He stopped, coughed, touched his heart. Rags waved him to third. "Go on, Hump, go. . . ." The sockamayocks looked and looked for that ball in the outfield. The dim lights baffled them. They tripped and stumbled and climbed in and out of gopher holes as the brute jumped on home plate. His head was blue from all the running he did.

"Shucks," Dizzy said to Paul. "Yarbull tricked us. Aint a damn thing wrong with his legs. . . ."

The Pharaoh was lying on the ground. The tremble of the bat had traveled like a shock wave through his body. The remaining stilt dropped off. He was in a cold, cold shiver. Muley Jones carried Yarbull into his Buick. Rags poked his face in the window. He'd won two thousand from Jerome and Paul, but he seemed miserable.

"I'm fine, Mr. Rags," Yarbull said. "I think I'll sleep a little." And he managed to pull down the Buick's window shade.

The caravan drove to a spot near the 'Bama state line. They were outside a village of sheds and cardboard houses. You could sniff the burning of pork. It was Yarbull's hometown. He wouldn't go into the village with the Giants. He got out of the Buick and stood on the road with his bossman-magician.

"Stop worrying, Mr. Rags. I won't get lost."

He couldn't hit and field any longer on those ravaged knees. And he wasn't going to watch the Giants play while living in a stretcher. Yarbull rubbed his cheek.

"I started playing for money when I was twelve. I had three road wives, and my main woman is in this here town. We got five kids . . . it wasn't those stilts that put an end to me. I could have played with my whole body in wood. But I'm sick of it. A man likes to hold his children more than once a year. Please don't wait with me, boss. Some nigger will pass by and bring ol' Pharaoh into town. You'll frighten him . . . a white man and a pack of Buicks."

So the kid left Yarbull on the road and took off with his caravan of Cincinnati Giants.

Rags went back to third base, and the Giants got themselves a new shortstop, a seventeen-year-old boy named Ira Sharp. He was surly and began to fight other Giants until Scarborough cured him of the habit by flinging Ira over the roof of the Hudson one day. The boy respected his elders after that. He developed good hands and feet. He could charge the ball and throw his face in the dust. Other nigger teams began to court Ira Sharp. The Homestead Grays wanted him for their spot in the Negro National League. They offered to triple his salary. Ira wouldn't jump to the Grays. "I'm with the white magician," he said. "I play for Mr. Ragland and his Colored Giants."

But no amount of magic could thrust a calendar into the kid's head. "Hump, what year is this?"

"1937."

Scarborough had become the bookkeeper-first baseman of the Giants. "You're thirty-two," he said.

"Thirty-two? We got years and years to play. . . ."

The root jar kept the Giants strong. The kid was a powerful magician. He could pull sheriffs and the Judge's lackeys off a baseball diamond. He could turn a swarm of locusts away. He could heal cuts and wounds. But why had Scarborough begun to limp?

"What's the matter?"

"A charley horse," the brute said.

But he was coughing and breathing hard at first base.

"I'm sittin' you down, Hump. Tend to the books. That's enough."

"I'm a first baseman," Scarborough said. Rags was in a pickle. How could he bench his own roommate?

Scarborough coughed up blood after a game and wobbled towards the Hudson. The brute was giddy. He shoved his narrow hips like a wild boy, gassed on some strange wine. He labored, knee over knee, frightened that Rags would find the spots of blood on his baseball shirt. *Nobody's benching the Hump.*

He had a fist inside his back. The fist had a mouth, and the mouth was full of teeth. It clawed under his shoulder, and ripped his chest. *Raggsy, aint I cute at first base? I helped you beat Dizzy Dean. You can't throw strikes to a hunchback. That's the truth.*

He couldn't make it to the Hudson. His knees twisted out. The kid ran to where the brute had fallen. Scarborough was dead.

The magician got his root. He leaned over Scarborough, kissed him, and fondled the jar. Not one nerve in Scarborough twitched. "Hump," Rags said, "get up, get up, get up. . . ."

He threw the jar into the dirt. It wouldn't break. Swimmy picked up the jar and put it back in the Hudson. Then he grabbed the kid's arms and led him away from the corpse.

19

Disaster struck the Giants. Locusts ate the wood off a Buick. Diamonds would freeze up and split along the baselines. Storm clouds followed the team. Bullfrogs would leap out of the mud to plague the magician and his men. Swimmy stubbed his toe, trying to avoid the frogs.

All these visitations only served to harden Rags. He would slip on a frog's head, roll in the mud, and denounce the root. The Giants had to plead with the magician. "For God's sake, boss, don't mock that thing. It's got legs and arms like any nigger man. You can't beat the devil without Sam'l's jar. . . ."

So Rags took out the jar to save his team. He wouldn't fondle it. But he did rub the sides a little. The storm clouds disappeared. The frogs burrowed into the mud and left the Giants alone. Without his knowing it, Rags grew kinder to the root. Hairs sprouted on one of its three forks. These were the only blossoms a root could have.

Rags would have been satisfied with a simple ghost. It didn't have to carry the brute's smell. Just give it a voice and the beginnings of a hump. Rags sang to the jar.

They were outside Des Moines. The groundsmen had combed the earth. There wasn't a split in the diamond. The local all-stars had challenged the Giants. Swimmy, Ira, and Rags performed seven double plays.

A brute came loping out of the stands. He wore a homburg, but no felt hat with green feather and a beautiful crown could hide his twisted back. It was Scarborough, Scarborough in fancy clothes. Rags got his wish. He had Scarborough's ghost on a hill outside Des Moines.

He hugged the little man and kissed him on the forehead. "Hump, how does it feel to be dead?"

The brute had a sour face. "Lay off, will ya?"

It wasn't Scarborough's voice. But Rags had to consider the alterations of heaven and hell. He hugged the little man again.

"Jesus, will you give a guy some air? Are you crazy, or what?"

The joy began to drop from Rags. The brute had a crow's-foot at the end of each eye. Scarborough's wrinkles were terrific, but they weren't so severe. He hadn't looked seventy when he was with the Giants.

The kid was talking to Henry Watteau, Babe Ruth's old bicarbonate of soda boy. He'd flourished in the last fifteen years. His handkerchief was pure silk.

"Ragland, where's your brute?"

"Gone," the kid said. "He had a hemorrhage and a heart attack on the same day."

Watteau lifted his hat. "I told him to get out of baseball. It's a killer for us . . . you can't live long with a toadstool sitting on you that squeezes your heart every minute."

Brother, how did you survive?

"I got nineteen garages," Watteau said. "And two diners. Ragland, I'm worth a million . . . I owe it all to the Babe. The sweetest man what ever lived, Mr. George Herman Ruth. I come out of the hospital and he gives me a grubstake . . . heart of gold. Say a bad word about him and you get a kick in the balls. . . ."

He presented Rags with his signature on a little card. "That's worth a free meal at one of my diners. But do me a favor. Don't bring the coons."

Rags tore up the card after Watteau left the diamond. The kid wouldn't eat without his giants.

He didn't die at third base. A lefty couldn't hurl that ball around the horn the way a righty could. But Ragland hugged the line like no other human being in the majors, the minors, or the nigger leagues. He was the white Pharaoh Yarbull, without Yarbull's stilts. It didn't matter that he had a glaze in his eye, that he would think and think of his roomie while he covered the bag. "Come on, Hump . . . where the hell are you?" The glaze didn't interfere with his glove.

A world of Scarboroughs could have tumbled in the kid's head, and he still would have completed the throw to first. He lived in the Hudson on cans of sardines. He heard mumblings about some kind of war. His Amherst days hadn't deserted him. He'd studied maps of China and Japan.

Ira was kidnapped from the Giants. It had nothing to do with a scalping party in the nigger leagues. The shortstop was going overseas. Swimmy Welles was safe. He had a wife and three kids. But he had to scribble out an itinerary for his draft board in St. Louis. The War Department was asking him to stay in touch.

The Cincinnatis began to lose their evil reputation. Towns and villages had gotten gentler to the Giants. Baseball was good for the home front. Rags was allowed to parade his men on village greens. Schools lent their diamonds to him, as long as the Giants showered somewhere else. Rags thought the schools were crazy. The Giants hadn't showered in three years. It was their habit to bathe in the nearest stream.

But this new glory did nothing for Rags. Town life was no comfort to him. He missed the Hump. He didn't want another roommate. Swimmy would have moved into the front seat, but the kid preferred to live alone inside the Hudson.

Once, in a fit of isolation, when he would have been happy to give the team over to Yam, he showed up at an Army induction center in Hannibal, Missouri. He had the gold and white of the Giants on his chest. His face was wild, as if an animal had come in off the street. You couldn't have guessed his age. He was like some mad, ancient boy walking in his own fever.

The Army nurses humored him as he stood on line.

"Can we get you a cup of tea?"

"Get me into the war first."

The medical examiners didn't have to listen to his heart. They peeked at those claws of his. They hadn't encountered a normal person with such gnarled hands. It was a mystery. The nails were black. The knuckles had horns on them. The fingers themselves bent in curious ways. Every joint must have been broken once or twice.

"I can catch a baseball," Rags said. "Why couldn't I throw a hand grenade?"

The examiners thanked him for coming around. They couldn't accept cripples in this man's Army.

Rags went to a soda shop and had five chocolate sundaes. The soda clerk studied his gloom. "Mister, I can get you as much tail as you want."

There was a one-room whorehouse right above the soda shop. The kid marched upstairs. Why couldn't he rest with a woman for an hour or two? He wasn't unkind to whores. Hadn't he been in love with a crib baby, Miz Emma Raines?

He knocked on the door.

"Honey, come on in. . . ."

Two women were sitting on a bed in flesh-colored peignoirs. The kid turned sly. He looked again. It was a woman and a girl. Their faces were suspiciously alike. God, a mother and daughter team in Hannibal. All he could think of was red hair. *Iva and Marylou*. He ran out of the whorehouse shrieking to himself.

He heard a familiar tune outside the soda shop.

Eveline, Eveline, won't you wait for me?

Rags stepped across the street.

He was on the sidewalk of the Hannibal Playhouse. He saw posters for *Eveline*. Hallelujah! Hollis' play about baseball wives had come to Hannibal. A hit on Broadway, the posters declared. *The miracle of '42*. But he couldn't find Hollis' name.

The kid paid half a dollar to walk in on the matinee. This wasn't the same *Eveline* Hollis had brought to the Morosco in 1923. The actors who played the Red Sox were much leaner in Missouri. Their blouses were ragged. Their shoes were unlaced. The kid could have died. These weren't fat boys out of any acting school. They were the original ragamuffins, Hollis' team of orphans and fools. Ferdie Willis, Eveline's husband and the hero of the play, could have been Chicken Stallings, or the kid himself. He had the rough, garbled voice of a ballplayer:

Evy, Evy, stay with me.
It's hell in Chicago
Grief in Detroit
Without my darlin' wife.

The kid couldn't control himself. He was sobbing by the middle of the second act.

Fortune stuck with the Giants. It wasn't on account of the hairs in a root jar. The magic was in the receipts Rags collected at the end of every Giant game. The war had made them popular. Those phantoms, the Cincinnati Colored Giants, were pushed into American history.

They appeared at schools, colleges, big city stadiums, and prison farms. Convicts were their greatest fans. These embezzlers, murderers, and thieves remembered Pharaoh and old Carl.

"Where's the hunchback . . . where's Carl's wife?"

The phantoms were playing a team of convicts inside the penitentiary at Springfield, Massachusetts, when the kid recognized his lost brother, Billy Rogovin, among the population. Rogovin wasn't wearing his orange suit. He had gray pajamas in the prison yard. He tried to sink back into the crowd of convicts.

It was the sixth inning, and Rags had interrupted the game to grab hold of Billy. The gambler from Darling Street had aged. His lips were pudgy. He was like a fat, rotting toad without his orange suit. Where were the prison tailors? Couldn't they have found other pajamas for Billy to wear?

No one considered it strange that Rags should talk to a convict. The trusties and prison guards didn't interfere with the owner of the Colored Giants. The kid held Billy by his pajama tops.

Rags didn't have to query him, or repeat old, old stories. Billy volunteered to mumble the truth. "Your boss Hollis . . . he paid me to fuck you out of the American League. . . ."

"Thanks, brother Bill."

The Giants didn't have Ira Sharp to plug their hole at short. They had to jump around like Chinese bandits to beat the jailbirds, 2–1.

The caravan stopped in Weymouth. It couldn't have been five hours since the Giants collected their bats and said goodbye to the warden at Springfield. A man in a twill suit rapped on the window of the Hudson with his ring.

"Babe Ragland, I'd like a word with you."

Rags welcomed him into the car.

"I'm Howard Pile . . . from the commissioner's office."

Howard Pile had the most beautiful hands in Weymouth. His nails were pink as an Alabama sky, and he didn't have the slightest bump or horn on any of his knuckles.

"You work for the Judge?"

"Yes, sir, and he's mighty sorry what happened to you, son."

Son? Who's calling me son?

"What the hell does that rascal want from me, Mr. Pile?"

"We're conducting an investigation against Hollis McKee . . . we'd like you to help. You'll have to file some papers against your old boss . . . we can't put you on the active list until that man Hollis goes before the Judge."

"Active list?"

"The Judge means to reinstate you . . . let you play again in the American League."

"What year are we in, Mr. Pile?"

"I don't understand . . . year? This is 1943."

Rags didn't have the Hump to calculate for him.

"Is it May or June?"

"Son, it's the middle of August."

"I must be thirty-eight . . . they'll laugh at me. Grandpas can't bust into a training camp."

"There's a war on. Teams are dying for third basemen."

The kid threw that agent out of the Hudson. Then he sat on top of him and started to bite Howard's ear. It was a bullrider's trick, something he'd learned from wrestling baby bulls on his father's ranch.

It was lucky for Howard that the carpenters were close. They kept the caravan in tiptop condition, banging dents out of twenty-five-year-old Buicks, and sealing up cracks in the mahogany with some kind of paste.

"Mr. Rags, that's a man lying under you . . . you'll bite his ear off and we'll have to run to Missouri."

Rags let Howard go. "You tell the Judge I don't need redemption from him."

The carpenters applied Mercurochrome to the agent's ear.

"How'd you learn so fast that I talked to Billy Rogovin? Does the emperor have spies in the Springfield pen? I'll handle Hollis McKee on my own. . . ."

The Giants had a free day in Boston. The kid wouldn't visit the Fens. He wasn't afraid of alligators rising out of the swamp. It was something else. He didn't want to meet Marylou's ghost. He went to the Ritz-Carlton in his gold baseball suit and asked for Hollis McKee. The clerks shrugged their shoulders. They didn't remember Hollis at the Ritz.

A bellboy who must have been fifty winked at Rags.

"You'll find him in Scollay Square . . . try the Mackerel bar on Franklin Avenue. That's his new address."

Rags handed the bellboy a paper dollar. "Hollis lives at a bar?"

"Why not? He's a whiskey bum."

The kid walked down to Scollay. He had to go through the Mackerel twice before he could spot Mr. McKee. Hollis didn't have a tooth in his mouth. He sat with an empty glass and sucked on his cheeks. The kid had a bottle of whiskey brought to Hollis' table. The bum drank and drank.

"Hollis, look at me. . . ."

Those raw whiskey eyes took Rags in.

"The gracious son-in-law," he said. "The lefty comes home to Boston. . . ."

"Dumbhead, I was your property, your kid at third . . . you sabotaged your own team when you hired Billy Rogovin to set me up. Why did you do such a crazy thing?"

The whiskey eyes began to clear. "I wanted you out, out for good . . . you destroyed my poor dead brother's girls."

"Go on, drag in Judah Cottonmouth's ghost . . . poor dead brother." Rags wished he had his root on him. That jar couldn't find the Hump, but maybe it would bring Hollis' bloodbrother into the Mackerel, so Rags could look at those Dartmouth twins, Hollis and Judah Cottonmouth, and decide which one was the bigger prick. "I ought to hang you from the ceiling . . . you created Iva and Marylou . . . you slept with the mother and turned the daughter into a nagging child."

Hollis clutched the bottle and cursed Rags with whiskey on his tongue. He was in a panic. He'd guzzled and slobbered so much, most of the bottle was gone. The kid ordered a second bottle for the whiskey bum.

"Hollis, you should be rich . . . *Eveline* is everywhere."

"I sold my rights to it for a hundred dollars . . . I'm glad. It was a stupid show. *Evy, Evy, stay with me. . . .*"

"Hollis, where's my wife?"

The bum started to grin. "She's down the block."

"What's Iva doing on Franklin Avenue? . . . it's August. Iva should be in Tisbury town."

"She gave up the vineyard years ago . . . she was living with her mama's servant. You remember Rhys . . . he squeezed the last penny out of her and ran off to Rio with a banker's wife. . . ."

"What happened to the house on Beacon Hill?"

"She lost that too . . . Iva's come to Scollay, like the rest of us . . . can you blame her when she has a husband who wears knickers all the time? . . . I should have sold *Eveline* to you . . . changed the third act, put in material about the orphan who abandons his wife . . . gives her to Rhys."

Rags lifted the bum out of his chair. He could have hurled him across the Mackerel. It wouldn't have cost Hollis. The bum had no more teeth.

Customers watched a man rise over a table. It was no whiskey dream. The magician's forearms kept Hollis up in the air.

"What's Iva's address?"

"Who knows? She works at the hash house two doors to the left. . . ."

The kid put Hollis back in his chair. How could you take your revenge on a twisted root of a man? He went to Iva's hash house, the Harbinger Inn. The shock of her red hair made Rags shiver in his gold and whites. She was behind the counter, feeding sailors and bums. The pout lines had disappeared from her face. Delivering ten-cent hamburgers to the bums, she had all the concentration of a dutiful child.

Iva looked up and saw a grown man in pajamas. She thought he was a Negro from the way he had shuffled in; it was only the standard crouch of the Cincinnati Colored Giants, a gesture of suspicion and a pattern of flight that were necessary for a team that lived on the run. The kid walked and moved like any other Giant. His eyes were hidden from her. His jaw slanted away from the counter.

Iva recognized the meaning of his pajamas: a baseball player. She stared hard at the slant of his jaw. It wasn't a Negro who had come in for the twenty-cent special: coffee and baked beans. No. It was the seventh Babe. Cedric Tannehill Rags. She rushed out at him with a meat chopper in her hand, muttering, "Baseball, baseball, baseball. . . ." The kid ran for his life.

Iva blamed her goduncle. Ragland would never have found her on his own. He couldn't see past third base. Hollis must have led Rags to the Harbinger Inn. Iva took her apron off and went to Hollis' perch at the Mackerel.

She was convinced that both of them had been born under the same tree. They were wastrels. Iva and the old man. They'd pissed their fortunes away. Hollis lost his team and backed one abominable show after the other. And Iva had her gigolo, Rhys. Funny, she didn't even like to kiss that man. But she gave him everything. It was only Cottonmouth cash. It didn't keep her mother from drowning in the swamp. What could it do for Iva?

"Hollis McKee, why did you tell that baseball player where I was?"

The goduncle grinned at her. "I thought it was about time Scollay had a marriage broker."

"Well, do your brokering for someone else. I've had enough husbands in my life."

"Iva girl, you were only married once. . . ."

"Don't talk. You didn't have a third baseman in your house."

"But I had him on my team. That was worse. I could never stand a fanatic. He would have played for free if I'd let him . . . will you buy some whiskey for an old gent?"

"No, but I'll feed you a hamburger if you'll get the hell out of the Mackerel and go down the block with me."

Hollis wouldn't leave his perch. So Iva had to bring the hamburger to him. But a toothless man couldn't swallow a whole patty of meat. Iva mashed it for him with a spoon. Then she had to go back to her job. The sailors and bums at the Harbinger Inn wanted their hamburgers and bowls of soup.

20

Ragland learned how to follow the railroad tracks. The Giants would go from one whistle-stop to another. It was good business. You could always find a team of grandfathers, school boys, and military rejects in a railroad town. The kid began to wonder why so many of these towns put diamonds up near a churchyard. Was it recreation for the dead? It bothered Swimmy Welles to blink at tombstones all the time. Rags got used to it. Why should he care if the dead yearned to watch phantoms in gold and white?

The Giants caused a miracle in Maryland, Kansas: the Chicago Limited hadn't stopped at Maryland for over twenty-five years. People collected around the engineer's caboose. It was painted red and Denver gray. The engineer himself stepped down from the caboose. He asked for Cedric Tannehill.

The town of Maryland didn't have any Cedric Tannehills to give away. "He's with the nigger team," the engineer said.

Townsmen brought the engineer into the Giants' camp. The engineer looked at Rags. "Cedric Tannehill?"

"Who wants him?" the kid said with a scowl.

"Judge Landis."

"Tell him to go suck on an egg."

"He's been riding for a week now, young man . . . he had to call the president of the railroad. You think it's so easy to make a special stop? It was a favor to the Judge. The president of a railroad's got small power these days. The goddamn government runs this line. . . ."

"Maybe I ought to snitch on you and the Judge."

"You are an ungrateful young man," the engineer told Rags. "The Judge is sick . . . and he's been waiting to see you."

"Let him wait . . . that son of a bitch threw me out of baseball."

But the kid was foxy when it came to the Giants. He realized a red caboose was handsomer than a ballclub. The Cincinnatis would have to crawl into the churchyard and sleep while the Chicago Limited was around. So Rags went along with the engineer.

He climbed up into the caboose.

The caboose looked like a rich man's den. It had rugs and drapes and a small cherrywood bar that could have come from the Royal Fox, that sporting house where Rags saw the Cajun lose to fat Alice, when the Hump was still alive. Rags had to peek into the corners to find Judge Landis. The emperor lay on a reclining chair, with blankets over his legs. You couldn't have recognized the Judge without his silver scalp. The rest of him was puny and dry.

Rags came up close; he would have sworn some dead Indian was underneath the blankets. But dead Indians don't cry. Rags couldn't mistake the sobbing of that old emperor man.

"Something hurt, Judge?"

Landis wiped his eyes with the ragged edge of his sleeve. The emperor didn't have a decent handkerchief.

"It's seeing you in that colored boy's suit, and knowing I'm the cause. . . ."

"Well, don't let that bother you, Judge. I like the Cincinnati Giants."

". . . I was hasty. I didn't stop to think it could be Hollis trying to ruin a player of his. Cedric, can you forgive this old crackpot . . . I'm a pompous, self-righteous ass."

"Nothing to forgive, Judge. I would have been miserable if I had to stay with the Sox."

The emperor began to sob again. "I have twenty years of reports on you . . . my men shouldn't have hounded you so much. But they did reach that gambler . . . what the hell is his name?"

"Billy, Billy Rogovin."

"They discovered him in jail . . . why didn't you let us prosecute dirty Hollis?"

"I couldn't, Judge. It's got to do with family. That's personal business between Hollis and me."

But the sobbing didn't stop.

"Shit, Judge, don't cry . . . I forgive you."

A blanket had fallen off. Rags stooped, got the blanket in his gnarled hand, and covered up the emperor's knees. Then he walked out of the caboose.

Mustard and buttermilk, that's my diet. I can't swallow anything hard.

The Judge couldn't have told you if he was having a dream on a railroad car. He'd done a lot of crying lately. It was like a rheumatism attack. They called him baseball czar. Do czars have chilly feet? Son of bitches, who else had preserved the national sport? He'd made an outlaw of this Ragland. But what else could he do?

He had to bite at every gambler who approached a ball park, or the game would sink into the muck again. It was gambling, or baseball. You couldn't have both.

He remembered Ragland's hands. *Loved to watch that kid.* The first and last lefty in the corner. The seventh Babe. Imbecile. Why hadn't he suspected Hollis McKee? Anybody who mixes baseball and musical comedies can't be good.

The train left in a quarter of an hour. But that miracle happened twice. The Chicago Limited stopped at Maryland station on its return run. It was heading for Albuquerque. The Giants hadn't gone out of Kansas yet. They were at the diamond near the churchyard when the train stopped. The engineer signaled from the caboose. Half the town rushed over. The emperor of baseball was dead.

"Went in his sleep . . . like a baby. Give that news to young Cedric. He'll want to know."

The townsmen ran to the diamond and interrupted a game between the Giants and the military rejects.

"Ah," Rags said, after hearing about the Judge. "He wasn't such a bad egg."

The game started up, and Rags socked the ball into the churchyard for a home run. He felt jittery as he hopped around the bases. Something roared in his ears: it was the sound of the emperor crying, under the whistle of a train.

Rags sat out the last two innings. The Giants could take on military rejects without the Babe.

No one had to tell Rags the war was over.

A boy in military shoes met the caravan near St. Cloud. Ira Sharp had been returned to the Giants. The shortstop got out of his military shoes. He went deep into the hole to deny a base hit to the Black Pygmies of St. Cloud, Eau Claire, and Duluth (the Pygmies had to represent three towns in order to survive).

It was almost like having the Pharaoh again, only this Pharaoh threw with his right hand. He could sock triples, steal second base, hold cannonballs in his glove. The Giants didn't keep any stats; the number of strikeouts and double plays meant nothing to a phantom team. Yet Ira had to be batting .600 on the road. Rags couldn't remember when his shortstop had less than two hits in a game.

A man was following them around. He watched the Giants in Omaha, Beatrice, Hastings, and North Platte. He saw them in little stadiums and under the Giants' own lights. When there was an overflow crowd, he would stand behind the fire truck in deep center field that carried the old gasoline generator. He couldn't have ignored the sirens inside the truck, the crazy voices that generator provoked, the sound of shrieking women.

Rags caught him near the truck. It was Howard Pile, the commissioner's man. What the hell did he want? Landis was dead.

Howard started to shake. The kid had to grab his shoulders and give a pull, or Howard might have had a seizure in center field. "Howard, I promise not to bite your ear off. Why are you following us?"

He handed Rags a card that had the nose and cheeks of an Indian on it, the emblem of the Boston Braves.

"I'm a scout," he said. "We're looking for colored boys. . . ."

"Why?"

"The Dodgers are picking up Negroes like crazy and hiding them in their farm teams. . . ."

"What the hell for?"

"Son, this isn't 1922 . . . you're gonna have an explosion of colored boys in the major leagues. We'd like to take Ira Sharp off your hands, give you three thousand for his contract. . . ."

"I don't have contracts with my men. You can deal with Ira yourself."

Ira wouldn't go.

"Mr. Rags, who needs the Boston Braves? Only an idiot would give up the Colored Giants."

"Well, idiots are growing smart this year . . . take the man's money, Ira. The nigger leagues are shrinking fast."

He argued with Ira for three days, until Ira grew depressed.

"Don't you like me any more, Mr. Rags?"

"Like you? Next to Pharaoh, you're the sweetest shortstop I ever had. . . ."

"Then why are you working so hard to get rid of me?"

"Because. They're scumsuckers in the major leagues, but that's where you belong. Now will you go with the man?"

Ira left with Howard Pile, and the phantoms had a broken team. Rags put a sockamayock on short. He had no one else. The big leagues were grabbing away all the good nigger prospects.

The sockamayock owned a pair of wooden feet. Rags and Swimmy Welles had to dive into that hole at short. Rags' knees would whistle. A peculiar wind would blow through him as he hopped around the infield.

Soon I'll be like the Pharaoh, and I'll have to play on stilts.

The kid went to his root. He caressed the jar and sang to it. "Baby, if my knees give out, we'll land in a pile of shit."

The whistling stopped. The kid developed a healing glue in his knees. He had the stamina of a rookie boy. He rode bulls at third base. He ran after prairie dogs. He snorted and tumbled in the grass.

Swimmy had to caution him. "Boss, you aint no chicken. Slow down a little."

"Bushwah," Rags said. He ran onto the field and tossed a bullet to first base. The fire truck shrieked at him. The sirens started to yackety-yak. He could hear a constant word under the scattered breath of their song. They didn't throw the Hump's name at him. These women had a different shriek. *Iva, Iva, Iva.*

He went back to the root. "Tell those bitches to leave me alone."

He began to dread night games and the grinding of the generator. The sirens were eating him up. They were the true magicians. They could beguile him with their music, trick him with a roar. Scarborough spoke to him out of the fire truck. The bitches had faked his voice.

"Raggsy, go to your wife."

The kid's body rattled at third. He would have poured lead in his ears to drown that music. Let the sirens mock him. He loved Scarborough's voice.

". . . where are you, you little guy?"

"Raggsy, go to your wife."

"Have a heart, will you? . . . she chased me with a goddamn cleaver. The woman would have turned me into chopped meat."

Swimmy watched his boss hold a conversation with himself. Mr. Rags was overworked. The big leagues were kidnapping niggers all over the place. The Giants would be reduced to an old folks' home for sockamayocks and aging outlaws. But how could Swimmy tell his boss to shut up and play?

The mumbo jumbo didn't hurt the Giants. Whatever passed between Raggsy and the fire truck, he still chased ground balls. He would sing to Scarborough and claw a high chopper out of the air.

The Giants should have been going into their winter act. It was November, but they didn't shoot for the bayou country. The caravan pushed east. The sirens were charting the Cincinnatis' course. The groundsmen had to sculpt their diamonds on hills of snow. The kid could frighten blizzards away with his root, but he couldn't take care of freezing weather. The sirens purred their undersong in the cold. *Iva, Iva, Iva.* The Giants had to wear extra shirts.

Rags got to Boston on the last day of the blizzard. He only had his baseball shoes, and Scollay was adrift in a white field that snaked along the streets just like the Mississippi going around the bend of New Orleans. The kid arrived at the Harbinger Inn with snow on his head.

Iva growled when she saw those silly pajamas on Rags, and his wet stockings. She didn't reach for that butcher knife behind the counter. His face was hollow, as if he'd lost his cheeks somewhere in the blizzard. She gave him a cup of soup. He drank the soup with frosty hands and said hello.

Some bums at the counter began to paw Miz Iva. She was used to it. She slapped them on their dirty gloves. The bums didn't like having the kid around. He was an intruder in their hash house. They pawed Miz Iva again. The kid seized them by their collars and shoved them into the wall.

"Don't get rough," Iva said. "They're old men."

The kid apologized. He picked up the bums, dusted off their pants, and returned them to the counter.

"Where's Scarborough?" she asked.

"Dead," the kid told her.

"Do you have another roommate?"

"No."

She couldn't say why he seemed handsome in his pajamas. He was skinny as ever. But that pile of bones appealed to her in some crazy fashion.

He began to stutter. His lips were cold. Miz Iva had to help him out.

"Are you proposing to me?"

Rags could hear the bitterness in her voice. "No, ma'am . . . I'm looking for a roommate, that's all."

She smiled and took her apron off.

"I'll be your roommate," she said.

She announced to no one in particular that she was quitting her job. The bums blinked at her. Scollay was turning upside down. You couldn't depend on a coffee girl anymore. It would be a miserable winter for them. Miz Iva grabbed her coat and said, "Henry, Tom, Victor, Paul, you be good . . . I'll come back and spank you if you don't behave."

Then she walked into the blizzard with that pajama man and the bums started to cry.

Book Seven

GLORY, GLORY
AND THE BROWNS

21

R AGGSY HAD A new partner inside the Hudson, a different kind of brute. An ex-waitress with red hair, a bride from some lost century, a wife who wasn't a wife. She gobbled sardines with the kid. She sewed patches on his uniform. But she wouldn't sleep with him.

He didn't quarrel. He didn't push. He didn't climb over to her portion of the car. She would have thrown a shoe in his face. All he could do was sniff her red hair. Miz Iva wouldn't peek into an old ballplayer's heart. She was a roommate with her own territories. She hadn't promised to kiss and fondle Rags. There was nothing about husbands and wives in her "contract" with the Giants.

Rags was like a rookie with a blue prick. The magician couldn't seduce Miz Iva; she'd have none of him. He didn't go to his root; the jar was next to worthless on women with red hair.

He had the back of the Hudson to himself at night, and more than Iva to disturb his head. The rolling stock was falling apart. A Buick had to be junked in Topeka. The fire truck had a terrible cough. But the kid couldn't replace his rolling stock. Santa Claus was gone. Griffey died the same year as the Judge. How could Rags ring up lawyers in Tucson he didn't even know?

The caravan was losing its tail. But Rags kept the Giants. He wouldn't let go. And he learned how to exist with that brute in the front seat. His desire shrank into his gold and whites. His prick turned a natural color. The blueness wasn't there.

A telegram caught up with him in Battle Creek. It had lots of numbers on it and crooked lines. He could read the words *St. Louis Browns*. But he couldn't deal with the crooked lines. "Iva, what's this?"

"The Brownies want you to join up. . . ."

Rags giggled to himself. "Maybe they think I'm a colored short-stop . . . tell them Ira Sharp went to the Braves."

"They know who you are . . . they're offering you ten thousand dollars to finish the season with them."

"Lunatics," Rags said. He was ready to tear that yellow paper in his fists. "What name is on it?"

"Briggs Josephson."

"Is Briggsy still managing the Browns?"

Iva squinted at the telegram. "He's the owner now."

"They're paying me money to pick up with them in June?"

"Husband, it's July. . . ."

How come I'm her husband when she reads a telegram?

Rags got the long-distance operator to dial St. Louis. The Brownies were on the road. A clerk in the front office gave him their schedule.

Rags took off his gold and whites. He felt peculiar in civilian pants. "Iva, I can fix our rolling stock for ten thousand . . . get a few light bulbs. Will you take care of the club while I'm away."

"Of course," she said. "What am I supposed to do?"

"Make sure we have enough sardines . . . Swimmy will do the rest."

He left the Hudson with Miz Iva, grabbed a Buick, and drove to New York City. He found Briggs in his private suite at the Concourse Plaza. The old skipper's back had gone crooked. He walked with a cane now. And this was the sweetest third baseman the Browns would ever know. He tortured the American League with his bat and his glove before he went over to Hollis' Red Sox and discovered Babe Ragland in the middle of Arkansas.

They gave each other a third baseman's hug.

"You bum, didn't I say you'd come to the Browns? . . . heck, Rags, where you been?"

"Everyplace and no place, boss."

"Goddammit, we need your glove."

"I'm an outlaw . . . they won't let me into Yankee Stadium."

Briggs looked at him. "Bushwah. The Judge cleared you right before he died."

"Who's gonna be my roommate?" the kid asked.

"Don't be silly. You'll room with me. And when we get to St.

Louis we'll have a Babe Ragland Day. Free bats for the first two thousand kids. How does it feel to be a rookie all over again?''

"Is Ty Cobb still around? I don't think I'm strong enough to fight that son of a bitch."

"Did you know the truth about Cobb? His mother shot his father in the head when Ty was a boy. She mistook him for a burglar. Ty loved the old man, and it turned him mean."

It made the kid sorrowful to hear about Cobb's mom and dad. "I'm tired," he said. He took a nap in Briggs' suite.

He must have been Rip van Winkle, like Scarborough once said, because Rags didn't even know night games had come to the American League. He was issued a uniform by the Browns' equipment boy. It had a number on the back. He was Mr. 12 of St. Louis. You didn't wear knickers anymore. The Brownie pajamas dropped below the calf and narrowed at the knee. You couldn't fly in them.

Iva had circled the year 1949 in the kid's pocket calendar. Rags had to be coming on forty-five. Wasn't that old for a rookie? What was he doing on the Browns? One glance at his teammates and Rags knew why. Briggs had to be desperate. His Browns were the modern dogs of baseball.

Nine men on stilts could have clobbered them.

Rags didn't linger in the clubhouse. He walked through the tunnel at Yankee Stadium and borrowed a mitt off a left-handed brother on the Browns. He didn't like the gloves of 1949: the fingers were banded together, and the pocket was webbed. You could have squeezed a grapefruit in a glove like that.

He sat out the first three innings, while the Yankees climbed on the Browns for six runs. They had DiMaggio, Henrich, Woodling, Rizzuto, and Jerry Coleman. The names meant little to Rags. What could Rip van Winkle declare about the wonders of white baseball?

He couldn't find a single colored man among the Yankees and the Browns. Were they hiding their crop of niggers on some baseball farm? Would the niggers revolt and start a new players' war? How could Rags tell?

He didn't complain when they put him in the field. He wished he had his generator with him. The kid preferred his own lights. The glare from the roof bit into his eyes. He took his familiar monkey crouch. He stabbed at ground balls. People didn't notice his crazy left hand. He was a journeyman infielder, recently arrived on the Browns. Who would have remembered that other Babe Ragland?

He scratched a single and struck out twice. He looked into the Yankee dugout. Where was Henry Watteau.

Rags didn't travel to Boston on any train with the Browns. He rode in his Buick and avoided the Brunswick Hotel. The Red Sox had moved out years and years ago. They were rich men who lived in the suburbs of Boston during the hot months. The Browns had inherited the Sox's old hotel.

The kid couldn't stay there. He had a grievance against this hotel. The Brunswick had turned on him in 1925, after the Judge threw Rags out of organized baseball. He slept in the Buick.

Night games were still unpopular in Boston. The kid was grateful for that. He wouldn't have a rotten glare in his eyes. But the gods of Fenway had done terrific damage to the park. "Duffy's Cliff" was gone: left field lay completely flat. It couldn't have supported a hill of toads. And what had happened to Garl's old spot? Center field seemed forlorn without a flagpole. It was a naked pie of dirt and grass.

Loudspeakers hurled the kid's name through Fenway Park. Did they fire Bull Weingarten? Bury his horn in left field? Such loudspeakers wouldn't mention the kid's past. Rags was forgotten history. Jesus, how many Babe Raglands could there have been?

He started for the Browns. What was forty-five to the kid? He had the legs. He dove towards the line and took a double from Birdie Tebbetts. He twisted left and right, charged suicide bunts, raced into shallow left field.

The Sox scratched their heads: who is that funny old man? Do the Brownies have any more amazing grandpas? Dom, will they lend us one? Isn't that loony throwing with his left hand?

Rags didn't get much pleasure out of it. A wind blabbered through his skull. He heard Bull Weingarten's voice. *Batting sixth for the Browns and playing third base, out of the Negro leagues, our former bad boy who bloodied many noses in his three years with us, Ragland himself, the seventh Babe.*

He wouldn't jump the Browns without telling Briggs. He had to go into the Brunswick Hotel to find the bossman. The lobby had fallen to shit. No wonder the Sox fled from here. It was a haven for parasites, roaches, and bums. Whores barked from the lobby chairs. The kid wouldn't have been surprised to meet shysters in orange suits. A bellboy touched his shoulder. "Good to see you, Babe. It aint been much of a hotel without you and Mr. Scarborough."

Rags couldn't remember him. Didn't bellboys ever leave their jobs?

"Are you Stanley?" There must have been a Stanley at the Brunswick.

"No, I'm Ned."

He shook the bellboy's hand. "Good to see you, Ned."

And he went up to Mr. Briggs. The old skipper seemed disappointed that Rags couldn't stay with the Browns. "Aw, we could have had some fun . . . a Babe Ragland Day. You deserve it, kid. The American League pissed on your head."

"It's only yellow water, skip. You can blow it off when it dries."

Fenway hadn't spooked the kid. He just didn't care about the major leagues.

He raced like the devil to Battle Creek. Rags had only been gone six days. He got into his team's pants and shook off the dourness of Boston and New York.

"Iva," he said, "I'm sorry . . . I couldn't hold on to that ten thousand. I like Briggs. But the Browns aint for me."

Iva was an independent girl. She could have run the Giants without Mr. Ragland. Hadn't she grown up on baseball? Sat with her mother in Hollis' box at Fenway Park? She would have stolen Rags' pajamas and installed herself at third with his little glove if she had to. Lefty, righty, it didn't matter to her. She could throw either way. She invited herself into the back of the Hudson after they finished a can of sardines.

The kid was surprised when the wife's hand went under his shirt. He could have yodeled to her from the back seat for half a century and she wouldn't have listened to his songs. You had to wait until the girl made up her mind to crawl in with you.

It took twenty-six years.

She held his roughened body. He was all skin and bones, a wire tuned to jump in the grass. She'd missed her roommate Rags. She didn't mind being married to a man with a glove. *Don't call me Eveline*. She wasn't a baseball widow out of Hollis' musical show. She lived with her husband in an automobile. Miz Iva was part of the team. She went on the road with the Cincinnati Giants.

They kissed and scratched, like the children they used to be. Rags had tender claws.

Book Eight

NEW MAN IN THE NATIONAL LEAGUE

22

THEY WERE A couple of barnstormers.

Rags would lie down with his wife, his gnarled fingers in her red hair. They had no interest in a permanent home, with pantry shelves and potatoes in the ground. Iva could make her pantry under the seat. They had the front and back of Raggsy's Hudson.

The kid was glad he got out of white baseball. He couldn't understand its habits and hidden rules. The majors were buying up colored ballplayers, and then these ballplayers turned invisible. How long could you hold them on a baseball farm? The kid didn't have to worry. Colored ballplayers began to leave the farm. Rags heard Swimmy Welles talk of Luke Easter, Monte Irvin, Sam Jethroe, Don Newcombe, Larry Doby, Willie Mays, and Ira Sharp, who was now a shortstop with the Braves.

The kid was approached by the Negro National League. Teams were drying up, and they wanted Rags to be the new man in "organized" nigger baseball. They never would have come to him if their league hadn't been in such rotten shape. The bossmen of the National League had scoffed at the Giants, called them desperadoes and trash. But those bossmen needed the desperadoes to stay alive.

"Hell," Rags said. "I'll play with them. It's no skin off my ass."

He liked the idea of having tournaments with the Black Yankees, the Pittsburgh Stars, and the Philadelphia Elites. "Maybe I'll get into a World Series before we die."

But it was a crazy, helter-skelter league. Rags couldn't be sure who would show up to play. Teams would move in and out, join other leagues, lose players, crumple, and start up again. The Pittsburgh Stars became the Jersey Bisons, and ran off to the Negro American League.

The kid managed to squeeze in seven games. He was back at Yankee Stadium to battle the nigger Yanks. There couldn't have been more than a thousand faces in that cavern. The kid scowled at empty seats. He couldn't perform in a graveyard. Balls rocketed over his head. He didn't turn over a single play. He had cotton wool inside his bat. He hit baby balls to the pitcher's box. But he wasn't as feckless as the Black Yanks. He forced his men to keep awake, and they drubbed the Yankees, 6–0.

He resigned from the National League.

The league would have grown thin with or without the Cincinnati Giants. The bossmen couldn't compete with Willie Mays. They'd had Ragland for a minute, and nobody else. Would Ted Williams jump to the Negro National League?

Nigger ball began to suffocate. It couldn't survive on its own bitter sweat. A few mavericks remained. But how could they support their magicians, their lights, and their players' sardines? Only the Giants wouldn't give it up. Rags had his root jar and his wife. The Hudson died on him somewhere in 1954. The kid moved into a Buick.

He had the fire truck soldered and stitched. Ladders would break. Fenders would disappear. He'd crawl under the truck and stroke its stomach with the root. The Giants would have perished without their lights.

They were baseball dinosaurs, the last of the barnstorming teams. You couldn't find another crew like them. Their money bag was low. Rags couldn't promise his men anything more than a share of sardines. His eyes would hurt him off the field. Miz Iva drove the Buick.

But the kid had his spot. He ate ground balls. He went into the hole, his glove snapping like the meanest turtle in America. He was Ragland of the Colored Giants. If he had a dizzy spell, he would blink twice and then sock a triple over a barn or a chicken-coop. Iva had to rub his legs in a vinegar solution to burn away the charley horses.

The Cincinnatis built a stretcher for their boss. Sometimes they had to carry him off the field. The wife would come with her vinegar and roll up the kid's pajamas. He'd shut his eyes and think of Yarbull, the Mississippi River, Texas, and the Hump. He had a ball club. No one could make him retire to his father's ranch. He'd have to buy lemons to go with the sardines. He didn't want his men to suffer from yellow scurvy.

The kid opened his eyes.

He wasn't a Brownie or a Red Sock. Rags hated schedules and choochoo trains. He had more fun in the heartland. With his desperadoes. His legs twitched from the wife's vinegar solution. When the twitching stopped he stood on one knee and broke the stretcher his men had made. It bothered Rags to be surrounded by sticks of wood. Those sticks reminded him of the Pharaoh's career. "I'm too young to start wearing stilts."

He rolled his knickers down and walked away.

Elbows and claws.

He was an old wizard in kneepants, defying nature with a root. By every conceivable law the Giants should have vanished, and their magician corralled somewhere with grandpas. Only madmen and children would have persisted with all that barnstorming in the mud. Who cared about the Cincinnati Giants? You couldn't get more than fifty people at a game. *Fuck the receipts.*

The dinosaurs went from town to town. The old hurly-burly was gone. They were lucky to finish a game. Baseball was a disease in the magician's head. Incurable by now. He'd have played fungo in the grass if no other team would walk onto the field with his Giants. High schools were better equipped than Ragland's men. They didn't have to survive on sardines. The Cincinnatis were stitched together like their own fire truck. They wore patches on every sleeve. They would come into town with soot on their faces from a long, long ride. Refugees from nowhere. You would have thought fifty sheriffs had been chasing them. But no one was on their tail except that bossman-magician. *Play your game,* he said. He didn't bother to send out hawkers and criers. What the hell is a crowd? He had Miz Iva and his lights.

He came to Arkansas with his men.

The wizard wanted to see Sackville Forest one last time. There wasn't a trace of that old Boston tryout camp. Sackville Forest was sinking into the ground. It had a few huts and a grocery store. Rags couldn't find the Sox's boardinghouse. It must have blown away.

Iva prepared a big pot of beans for the desperadoes. The smell of her cooking brought a gang of old men out of their huts. They weren't vagabonds, like the Giants. They were citizens of Sackville Forest. But they didn't refuse the beans Iva offered them.

The wizard got into a conversation with the old men, who were amused by the threadbare gold and whites the Giants wore.

"I guess the Sox ruined your town," the wizard said.

"How you mean?"

"When they pulled out and went to Florida."

None of these old men could recall the Red Sox.

"It's that demon what killed us," they said. "We got a monster in the forest."

"What does he look like?"

"He's small and rough . . . and he knocks you on your ass. He's good to little kids. But little kids can't run no town."

"Does he have an odd shape?" the wizard asked.

"Who can tell? He bumps you so fast."

Rags ventured into the woods. He had to fight through a thicket of low, twisted trees, with branches slapping against his neck. He shouted at the trees.

"You in there, Scarborough? Are you the guy who scared this town to death?"

But the demon wouldn't come to him.

The wizard tumbled into a bear den. He was up to his belly in dry leaves.

He saw ten sharp toenails dangling over his head.

The monster of Sackville Forest was hanging from a tree outside the bear den. It was Scarborough. He'd strung himself up by his baseball pants. His neck was all blue. But he wasn't gagging, or spitting blood. He smiled at the wizard.

"Remember me?"

Rags was afraid to look. "Doesn't it hurt? . . . hanging like that. . . ."

He tried to pull Scarborough down, but he couldn't reach those ten sharp toes. The baseball gods were punishing Rags for being greedy and playing so long. They'd brought back Scarborough's ghost without any nigger root. The kid was powerless. He'd have to watch Scarborough hang. He couldn't save the Hump this time.

"Raggsy, don't worry. It only hurts when I yawn."

"Why are you spooking this place?"

"I feel like it," the demon said.

"Don't you want to climb down and talk to me?"

"I can talk from up here."

Rags was confused. Did the demon count as Scarborough? Or was it a dumb masquerade? But the kid would rather have this Scarborough, than no Scarborough at all.

Scarborough's tree began to shake. Rags heard a bitter laugh. "Pretzelhead, you should retire your glove. You're blind, you know that? The Cincinnatis are a piece of shit."

The baseball pants ripped from the tree, and Scarborough

jumped into the bear den with Rags. "You wanna wrestle, or box?"

The kid wouldn't fight with his roomie. He didn't care what kind of demon Scarborough had become.

"I can take your little Amherst jabs," Scarborough said, flicking his paws into the wizard's face.

"You think I'm Garl, huh? You can't punch me into no tunnel floor."

He barreled into Rags. The wizard was up to his belly in leaves again.

This aint Scarborough.

The monster turned gentle all of a sudden.

"I didn't mean to deck you, Raggsy. I had a fit. It's hard meeting your roomie after you been living alone in the woods."

"Hump, I could camp around here if you like . . . keep the Giants in this state."

"Na," Scarborough said. "Don't come to Sackville no more . . . I'll have to bump you, Raggsy. That's my job."

How did Scarborough get to be such a demon? Was it the kid's fault? Some curse that baseball had put on him? Was it better to bump people and hang from trees as the monster of Sackville Forest, or lie dead in the ground? Even a wizard couldn't answer that.

Scarborough leapt out of the bear den with a crazy somersault.

"Goodbye, Raggsy."

The kid couldn't hope to follow him. He had to work with his claws to scale the bear den's high crooked wall. He didn't go chasing Scarborough. What's the use?

Rags left that tiny forest. He nodded to the old men around Iva's pot and ate the leftovers. The wizard chewed and chewed.

The gods of baseball could go to hell. The kid was glad he saw Scarborough in the woods. But he wouldn't haunt the brute. He took his dinosaurs out of Sackville Forest.

Call him devil. The Hump didn't care. He owned these woods. He was ferocious. He banged into ladies and old men who put their feet inside his forest. He was Scarborough, first baseman and lumberjack, formerly of the Red Sox and the Giants.

He couldn't tell you how he got here. He was playing first for Raggsy when he dropped to the ground. He woke with leaves on his forehead. His body ached. He didn't have any compulsion to look for the Giants. He was like a forest animal now. He'd have wrestled foxes and bears if these animals had been around. The woods were empty of them. He could only prey on people.

He recognized this forest the minute he woke. It was the same woods where he tried to hang himself years and years ago, when he was still with the Sox. The devils must have stolen him from first base. They didn't have to instruct the brute in the art of being nasty. He bumped whoever came close. But he couldn't get baseball out of his head.

He *knew* Rags would come. He had to wait until the root jar turned cloudy enough and Rags felt the urge to bring his desperadoes. The Hump put on a show for his roommate, pretending to swing from a tree.

Who was the bigger magician, Raggsy or the Hump? He heard himself cry. It was a rough, snorting sound. Something a bear would make. He had a new wish. To get out of the forest and recapture first base. But he was bound up in these woods. Doomed to bump into people until the whole of Arkansas disappeared from the earth.

He should never have given up lumberjacking to join the Sox. The devils couldn't steal a lumberjack. But the hell with it. He wouldn't have met Raggsy without Briggs and the Sox. He was Scarborough, Scarborough, bumping with his body and holding baseball inside his head.

He'd shove his brains out onto the road, taste the leather on his mitt. Who could stop him? Devils couldn't order him around. He'd have his first base in the woods. The hidden Giant, running, jumping, knocking into trees.

Book Nine

ON A FIELD IN HOLYOKE, MASSACHUSETTS

23

DRINK YOUR HONEY and hot milk, Mr. James.''
Fuck off.
Garl wasn't impolite to the fat nurse. He sipped the beverage she had prepared for him. He was seventy-nine years old. His three baby brothers had put him in Holyoke House last year. Garl paid the bills. He had a small pension and something of a bank account. His brothers would phone him from time to time, ask him about the pain in his legs, but they wouldn't come to Holyoke. It was too far away. Shem was a lawyer. Laurence was a brain surgeon. Theodore was a stock and bond man who was retiring to the Florida Keys.

How could Garl have been close with his brothers? He played ball summer and winter to see them through college. Shem, Laurence and Theodore established themselves, made long careers, and Garl was happy for his brothers. He spilled the honey and hot milk into a flower bowl after the fat nurse had gone.

There was Red Sox fever in Holyoke and all of Massachusetts. Boston sat on top of the American League, thirteen games ahead of its rivals. The orderlies at the nursing home remembered that Garl had once played center field for the Sox. So they considered him an expert on anything to do with the club.

"What about Yaz? Jesus, he'll be thirty-nine this month. . . . And Jim Rice? Can you believe that man's power? . . . and who's a better catcher than Carlton Fisk? . . . the Boomer at first and

Hobson in the corner . . . banging in a hundred and twelve runs . . ."

"His arm is weak," Garl said.

The orderlies looked at the old man. "You crazy? He's a god-damn hero . . . going with a hurt shoulder."

"Bushwah, he can't make the throw."

"Wise guy, who won the Man of the Year Award, Hobson or you?"

They had a conference among themselves. They didn't want to rile the old man. They heard how he fell off a flagpole fifty years ago. They were crafty with Garl, leading him away from the current Sox.

"Who's the best third basemen you ever saw?"

They figured he'd say Brooks Robinson, Billy Cox, or Graig Nettles, their enemy on the Yanks.

"Pharaoh Yarbull. No one could chew his glove."

The orderlies were mystified. "What team was he on?"

"The Cincinnati Colored Giants."

He was spiteful and shrewd, this old man, reaching into the nigger leagues to arrive at a third baseman that none of them could have known about.

"Was your Pharaoh a righty or a lefty at the plate?"

"He hit from the left side," Garl said.

"Then he had to change hands when he took the field."

"No, he was lefty all the way."

The orderlies knew their baseball. They weren't toys for any flagpole man. A lefty third baseman? Only niggers would tolerate such a freak. "How did he go around the horn with that left hand? He'd have to be an acrobat."

"He could go around the horn, through the horn, anywhere you like."

Demented. They had to feed orange juice to an old fool. They began to doubt he'd ever been on the Sox.

"Who's your next choice, old man?"

"Babe Ragland."

"Was he a lefty too?" they tittered.

"All the way."

"With the Black Yankees, or what?"

"Ragland was with the Red Sox."

A fury began to grow inside the orderlies. In a different year they might have ripped off his clothes and allowed him to bake on the lawn. Why should they give a crap? Boston was destroying the American League. The old man could invent all the lefty third basemen he wanted. Would they forget a Babe Ragland if he'd held down third for the Sox? They scratched their heads and pulled fiercely on their chins. "Hey, there was a guy . . . he came up from an orphanage, hit a lot of singles, and was thrown out of baseball by the commissioner himself."

"That's the Babe. . . ."

This obscure mouse was better than Cox and Nettles and their own Butch? Demented. They'd have to keep the old man from climbing another flagpole. They wrapped the blood pressure cuff around his arm, squeezed the bulb, took four individual readings, put a check on the old man's chart, laughed to themselves. *Babe Ragland, Babe Ragland,* and told Garl to stick to a diet of lettuce and orange juice.

He was glad when they removed their trays and bottles and cuffs. They didn't torture him at Holyoke House. But he despised the charts, the hot milk, and the sound of their blood-pressure bulb. His legs had caved in, and that's the reason his brothers conspired to get him into a nursing home, so Garl would stop falling in the street. He refused to sit in a wheelchair. He had a cane, and he would hobble about. But mostly he stuck to his room.

He'd been forty years a baseball coach and master of Greek at a college in the Hampshire hills. Garl had never married. Women stayed with him. He would hug their bodies at night. But nothing seemed to last. He was ashamed to admit that he'd forgotten them. It wasn't the fault of his dotage. Garl remembered every busher he had played with. And one redhead. Marylou. Her lips would peck at him in his sleep. Old man as he was, he would eat off her body. Look for freckles on her shoulder.

He was a hunter in a nursing home, killing off old taboos. Garl had fucked himself. He'd denied the redhead and starved whatever passion there was in him. He should have married Marylou, taken her off the roster at Fenway Park, severed her from Hollis McKee. Garl always had the good excuse. He was a gypsy ballplayer with a family to support. How could he anger Hollis?

He lost Marylou to the swamps. He'd enter his eighties with the mark of her lips on him: a tired center fielder married to a redhead in his sleep when he could have had a waking-time wife. He was a constant boarder, living in hotels, rooming houses, and a nursing home. His wandering had brought him here, to Holyoke House. Hot milk and honey.

There was a tumult downstairs. A convict was loose in the nursing home. It sounded unreasonable to Garl. What would a convict be doing at Holyoke?

"Hiya, skip."

He did see a man in a convict's suit. Was it for halloween? Impossible. It was August now. The man reminded Garl of his brother Shem. Shem wouldn't come to Massachusetts.

The convict began to keen at him. He was reciting garbled bits of Sophocles . . . a freshman could have done a better job. The convict mixed up Ajax and the wound in Philoctetes' leg.

Garl wouldn't correct him. He liked how this convict sang in Greek.

"Babe, you son of a bitch. You scared the hell out of everybody."

Ragland was wearing the pajamas of the Cincinnati Colored Giants. The orderlies had sneaked upstairs with huge frying pans. They were ready to pounce on the kid.

"Go away," Garl screamed at them. The orderlies disappeared.

"Shit, I was only trying to visit you, Garl."

"People aren't used to the old-fashioned uniforms, kid."

The kid had to be seventy, or seventy-two. His back wasn't curled over. He didn't have wattles on his neck. His fingers were hooked and powerful: the proper claws of any third baseman.

"Babe, what's up? You didn't come all the way from Alabama or Wyoming to visit an old brother you once knew on the Red Sox and the Harry Heilmanns. . . ."

"Ah, we're having an exhibition with some boys from Amherst summer school . . . a night game, Garl. And it's in the field next door. I was hoping you might come down and watch."

Garl jumped out of bed. He put on a shirt and pants and grabbed hold of his cane. He hobbled behind Rags.

"I could carry you. It wouldn't be difficult."

"I can walk."

Garl met the orderlies on the stairs. "Come on with us," he said. "We're going to a night game."

Three orderlies, Rags, and Garl passed the nurses' office and ducked away from Holyoke House. It was a party of five scratchy men. The Babe led his party to a field across the road. The Amherst summer-school team was waiting for the boss of the Colored Giants. These scrappling, big-necked boys were anxious to beat the ass off a band of country niggers. But the Cincinnatis had gone half white. Garl stared at them and recognized the kid's dilemma: these Giants were the rejects of a hundred tryout camps. "Sockamayocks," Garl said.

The kid agreed. "You take what you can get, skip."

Where were those landscape artists, the men who could sculpt a baseball diamond on any field? The kid had four lumpy bases, crooked foul lines, a batting cage with holes and wounds in the metal fabric, and a pitcher's station that looked like dirt off a chickencoop.

Garl noticed an ancient fire truck in deep center field, a rat's nest of cables, and lighting poles that gave the impression of giant toothpicks in the ground. The fire truck had bronchitis. It coughed a lot. What about the Cincinnatis' mahogany Buicks? There were only three of them left, and the mahogany was bitten off. The Buicks seemed naked to Garl.

A redhead came out of the Buick. Garl had to go to his cane, or he would have flopped into the grass. *Marylou*. He prayed some local god would toss a curtain over him, so he wouldn't have to see that red hair. He put an elbow in front of his face. The beautiful witch was no longer satisfied to peck him in his sleep. She followed Garl out of the nursing home. Who could say what unholy thing she'd do to him in the field?

"Since when are you so shy, Garland James? You used to look at my mother."

Ah, it was only the girl. Marylou was dead.

"Sorry, Miz Iva, I didn't realize you were traveling with the team."

"You know Raggsy. He can't survive without a roommate."

Both of them laughed.

Shouldn't the girl have some gray specks in her hair? She had to be seventy, or sixty-nine? Did you kick old age in the pants when you traveled with the Giants?

And who was on the hill for them, warming up his right arm? Yam Murray's hundred-year-old shadow? Garl's legs were twisted and all, but pathetic kneecaps couldn't interfere with his eagle eye: he spotted the emery board in the pitcher's glove.

Garl hobbled over to Rags. "Don't confuse a sick old man. Who's working for you on the hill? If it's not Yam Murray, it has to be his son."

"Wrong," Rags said. "It's his grandson."

"What's his name?"

"Yam Murray."

"Jumping Jesus," Garl said. "Whole generations of Yams . . . he kicks like his grandpa. And I like the way he goes into the stretch. Rags, are you holding him prisoner? . . . why isn't he in the majors now?"

"Shoulder trouble," the kid said. "He screwed around with knuckleballs and got himself hurt. The Dodgers had to let him go. It's all right. He can pitch for me."

The kid couldn't blab too long. He had to play his spot. He
lumbered off to third. The Amherst boys chuckled as he went into
his crouch. They hadn't figured the boss would be part of the Giant
infield. They could blow him down with the wind from their bats.
They shouted to him, "Pop, do you have disability insurance?"

The kid told them to play ball.

"Then bring up the lights . . . it's black around home plate."

"Sorry," the kid said, and he signaled to the sockamayock in
center field. The center fielder ran behind the fire truck. Garl heard
a hiss. The poles shook in the ground. A light with a soft blue haze
burned all over the diamond. This blue didn't hide the base paths;
it was as if a mellow fog had rolled onto the field at noon time.

The summer-school team was satisfied.

Yam kicked from the mound and threw his emery ball into the
cuffs of the first batter. He chopped at the pitch and banged a hard
grounder into the hole. It would have gone through the shortstop,
but the old man at third angled his body and it became a fucking
knife that could stab a ground ball, recover itself, and hit the first
baseman with a strike.

"He learned that from the Pharaoh," Garl said with a scowl.
The Amherst boys shrugged. It had to be the night for graybeards.
How else could you explain the catch? The orderlies touched Garl
on his shirt. "Who is that old geezer?"

"Babe Ragland."

Two more innings of play and Garl had converted them.

"He's the best," the orderlies whispered. ". . . tell Nettles to
move over, or Ragland will make the All-Star team."

The kid hopped, twisted, tossed strikes from between his legs.
Amherst barely had the courage to go on with the game.

Garl could swear his kneecaps were on the mend. He was dancing near the third-base line. He listened to a crazy knock from the
fire truck. The knock turned into a song. Women were serenading
him from inside the truck. *Go with the Giants, go with the Giants.*
Garl assumed his blood pressure was running high.

The sockamayocks beat Amherst summer school, 11–1. The
center fielder switched off the lights. The truck was calm again.

The sockamayocks moved about the field like busy ants. They
unearthed the lighting poles and carried them to the truck, dismantled the batting cage, picked up the pillow-bases and stored them
in a Buick.

While Garl rocked on his feet, the orderlies were growing tense.
They'd have to include Babe Ragland in their "immortals" list,
put him ahead of Billy Cox, but what about the fat nurse? She
would scream at them if she discovered that Mr. James had fled

Holyoke House to watch college boys, scamps, niggers, and old men play on a warty field.

"Garland baby, we'd better shuffle back to the house."

Garl stared at the orderlies. "I have to say goodbye to the kid."

That medicine from the fire truck, the generator-song, had begun to wear off. Garl felt a burning in his leg. The flagpole injury was flaring up. Was it bravura or stupidity to fall off a pole in center field? Whenever the umps tossed him out of a game, Garl would sit near the piss trough at the neck of the tunnel and relay his signals to the bench. He was the captain of piss and manager of the Red Sox. Did he drop from that pole out of spite, after his brothers' education had been finished?

What could he declare about his own folly? That he loved Greek and the foolishness of cramming Sophocles into the skulls of boys? That he wanted his center field without the rigmarole and politics of a major-league club? He hadn't falled off any pole. He'd jumped. To cripple himself and shout "fuck you" to Hollis.

"Skip, what's the matter?"

The Babe was standing in dusty pajamas.

"Rags, you should have left me on Quintana Roo . . . I'd have had a ripe old age among those bandits, eating shrubs and roots. I'm not partial to nursing homes . . . honey is bad for your teeth."

"Why don't you come with us?"

"I wasn't trained to be a bat boy, Mr. Ragland. . . ."

"I could give you center field."

"How?" Garl muttered. "With a dead knee . . . and a stick in my glove hand?"

"I'd rather have Garland James on one leg than any sockama-yock . . . if the knee acts up, you can always manage the Giants. I have enough to do at third."

Crazy team. Crazy fire truck. Would they like him in Colorado when he turned eighty-six? He got into the Buick with Iva and Rags. Four sockamayocks sat in the back. Iva drove.

The orderlies were dumbfounded as the caravan took off. The Giants had kidnapped *their* old man. They chased the Buicks and the fire truck down the road. It went on for half a mile, until the wind was out of them. It was a fool's errand. They couldn't outrun a caravan. They'd have to return emptyhanded to Holyoke House.

They argued, pushed each other on the road. A furor was upon them to think up a story. How do you tell a nurse that you lost one old man? *Vanished.* That's the word. The old man had vanished on a walk in the fields. They could afford to whistle. Who cared about a nurse? They had their story now.

Also by V. S. Naipaul

NONFICTION

India: A Wounded Civilization

The Overcrowded Barracoon

The Loss of El Dorado

An Area of Darkness

The Middle Passage

FICTION

Guerrillas

In a Free State

A Flag on the Island

The Mimic Men

Mr. Stone and the Knights Companion

A House for Mr. Biswas

Miguel Street

The Suffrage of Elvira

The Mystic Masseur

A Bend in the River

A Bend
in the River

V. S. NAIPAUL

Alfred A. Knopf
New York 1979

THIS IS A BORZOI BOOK
PUBLISHED BY ALFRED A. KNOPF, INC.

Copyright © 1979 by V. S. Naipaul

All rights reserved under International and Pan-American
Copyright Conventions. Published in the United States by
Alfred A. Knopf, Inc., New York. Distributed by Random
House, Inc., New York.

LIBRARY OF CONGRESS CATALOGING IN PUBLICATION DATA

Naipaul, Vidiadhar Surajprasad.
A bend in the river.

I. Title.
PZ4.N155BE   [PR9272.9.N32]   823'.9'14   78-21591
ISBN 0-394-50573-5

Manufactured in the United States of America

FIRST EDITION

FC14
12/04 PS

Contents

A Bend in the River

ONE

The Second Rebellion

1 The world is what it is; men who are nothing, who allow themselves to become nothing, have no place in it.

Nazruddin, who had sold me the shop cheap, didn't think I would have it easy when I took over. The country, like others in Africa, had had its troubles after independence. The town in the interior, at the bend in the great river, had almost ceased to exist; and Nazruddin said I would have to start from the beginning.

I drove up from the coast in my Peugeot. That isn't the kind of drive you can do nowadays in Africa—from the east coast right through to the centre. Too many of the places on the way have closed down or are full of blood. And even at that time, when the roads were more or less open, the drive took me over a week.

It wasn't only the sand drifts and the mud and the narrow, winding, broken roads up in the mountains. There was all that business at the frontier posts, all that haggling in the forest outside wooden huts that flew strange flags. I had to talk myself and my Peugeot past the men with guns—just to drive through bush and more bush. And then I had to talk even harder, and shed a few more bank notes and give away more of my tinned food, to get myself—and the Peugeot—out of the places I had talked us into.

Some of these palavers could take half a day. The top man would ask for something quite ridiculous—two or three thousand dollars. I would say no. He would go into his hut, as though there was nothing more to say; I would hang around outside, because there was nothing else for me to do. Then after an hour or two I would go inside the hut, or he would come outside, and we would settle for two or three dollars. It was as Nazruddin had said, when I asked him about visas and he had said that bank notes were better. "You can always get into those places. What is hard is to get out. That is a private fight. Everybody has to find his own way."

As I got deeper into Africa—the scrub, the desert, the rocky climb up to the mountains, the lakes, the rain in the afternoons, the mud, and then, on the other, wetter side of the mountains, the fern forests and the gorilla forests—as I got deeper I thought: But this is madness. I am going in the wrong direction. There can't be a new life at the end of this.

But I drove on. Each day's drive was like an achievement; each day's achievement made it harder for me to turn back. And I couldn't help thinking that that was how it was in the old days with the slaves. They had made the same journey, but of course on foot and in the opposite direction, from the centre of the continent to the east coast. The further away they got from the centre and their tribal area, the less likely they were to cut loose from the caravans and run back home, the more nervous they became of the strange Africans they saw about them, until at the end, on the coast, they were no trouble at all, and were positively anxious to step into the boats and be taken to safe homes across the sea. Like the slave far from home, I became anxious only to arrive. The greater the discouragements of the journey, the keener I was to press on and embrace my new life.

When I arrived I found that Nazruddin hadn't lied. The place had had its troubles: the town at the bend in the river was more than half destroyed. What had been the European suburb near the rapids had been burnt down, and bush had grown over the ruins; it was hard to distinguish what had been gardens from what had been streets. The official and commercial area near the dock and customs house survived, and some residential streets in the centre. But there wasn't much else. Even the African *cités* were inhabited only in corners, and in decay elsewhere, with many of the low, box-like concrete houses in pale blue or pale green abandoned, hung with quick-growing, quick-dying tropical vines, mattings of brown and green.

Nazruddin's shop was in a market square in the commercial

area. It smelt of rats and was full of dung, but it was intact. I had bought Nazruddin's stock—but there was none of that. I had also bought the goodwill—but that was meaningless, because so many of the Africans had gone back to the bush, to the safety of their villages, which lay up hidden and difficult creeks.

After my anxiety to arrive, there was little for me to do. But I was not alone. There were other traders, other foreigners; some of them had been there right through the troubles. I waited with them. The peace held. People began coming back to the town; the *cité* yards filled up. People began needing the goods which we could supply. And slowly business started up again.

Zabeth was among the earliest of my regular customers. She was a *marchande*—not a market woman, but a retailer in a small way. She belonged to a fishing community, almost a little tribe, and every month or so she came from her village to the town to buy her goods wholesale.

From me she bought pencils and copybooks, razor blades, syringes, soap and toothpaste and toothbrushes, cloth, plastic toys, iron pots and aluminum pans, enamel plates and basins. These were some of the simple things Zabeth's fisherfolk needed from the outside world, and had been doing without during the troubles. Not essentials, not luxuries; but things that made ordinary life easier. The people here had many skills; they could get by on their own. They tanned leather, wove cloth, worked iron; they hollowed out large tree trunks into boats and smaller ones into kitchen mortars. But to people looking for a large vessel that wouldn't taint water and food, and wouldn't leak, imagine what a blessing an enamel basin was!

Zabeth knew exactly what the people of her village needed and how much they would be able or willing to pay for it. Traders on the coast (including my own father) used to say—especially when they were consoling themselves for some bad purchase—that everything eventually had its buyer. That wasn't so here. People were interested in new things—like the syringes, which were a surprise to me—and even modern things; but their tastes had set around the first examples of these things that they had accepted. They trusted a particular design, a particular trademark. It was useless for me to try to "sell" anything to Zabeth; I had to stick as far as possible to familiar stock. It made for dull business, but it avoided complications. And it helped to make Zabeth the good and direct businesswoman that, unusually for an African, she was.

She didn't know how to read and write. She carried her complicated shopping list in her head and she remembered what she had paid for things on previous occasions. She never asked for credit—she hated the idea. She paid in cash, taking the money out from the vanity case she brought to town with her. Every trader knew about Zabeth's vanity case. It wasn't that she distrusted banks; she didn't understand them.

I would say to her, in that mixed river language we used, "One day, Beth, somebody will snatch your case. It isn't safe to travel about with money like that."

"The day that happens, Mis' Salim, I will know the time has come to stay home."

It was a strange way of thinking. But she was a strange woman.

"Mis'," as used by Zabeth and others, was short for "mister." I was mister because I was a foreigner, someone from the far-off coast, and an English-speaker; and I was mister in order to be distinguished from the other resident foreigners, who were *monsieur*. That was, of course, before the Big Man came along and made us all *citoyens* and *citoyennes*. Which was all right for a while, until the lies he started making us all live made the people confused and frightened, and when a fetish stronger than his was found, made them decide to put an end to it all and go back again to the beginning.

Zabeth's village was only about sixty miles away. But it was some distance off the road, which was little more than a track; and it was some miles in from the main river. By land or by water it was a difficult journey, and took two days. By land during the rainy season it could take three. In the beginning Zabeth came by the land way, trekking with her women assistants to the road and waiting there for a van or truck or bus.

When the steamers started up again, Zabeth always used the river; and that wasn't much easier.

The secret channels from the villages were shallow, full of snags, humming with mosquitoes. Down these channels Zabeth and her women poled and often pushed their dugouts to the main river. There, close to the bank, they waited for the steamer, the dugouts full of goods—usually food—to be sold to people on the steamer and the barge the steamer towed. The food was mainly fish or monkey, fresh or *boucané*—smoked in the way of the country, with a thick black crust. Sometimes there was a smoked snake or a smoked small crocodile, a black hunk barely recognizable for what it had been—but with white or pale pink flesh below the charred crust.

When the steamer appeared, with its passenger barge in tow, Zabeth and her women poled or paddled out to the middle of the river and stood at the edge of the steamer channel, drifting down with the current. The steamer passed; the dugouts rocked in the swell; and then came the critical moment when the dugouts and the barge came close together. Zabeth and her women threw ropes onto the lower steel deck of the barge, where there were always hands to grab the ropes and tie them to some bulkhead; and the dugouts, from drifting downstream and against the side of the barge, began moving in the other direction, while people on the barge threw down pieces of paper or cloth on the fish or the monkey they wanted to buy.

This attaching of dugouts to the moving steamer or barge was a recognized river practice, but it was dangerous. Almost every trip the steamer made there was a report of a dugout being overturned somewhere along the thousand-mile route and of people being drowned. But the risk was worth taking: afterwards, without labour, as a *marchande* selling goods, Zabeth was towed up the river to the very edge of the town, uncoupling her dugouts by the ruins of the cathedral, a little before the docks, to avoid the officials there, who were always anxious to claim some tax. What a journey! Such trouble and danger to sell simple village things, and to take other goods back to the people of her village.

For a day or two before the steamer came there was a market

and a camp in the open space outside the dock gate. Zabeth became part of this camp while she was in the town. If it rained she slept in the verandah of a grocery or a bar; at a later date she put up in an African lodging house, but in the beginning such places didn't exist. When she came to the shop there was nothing in her appearance that spoke of her difficult journey or her nights in the open. She was formally dressed, wrapped in her cotton in the African style that by folds and drapes emphasized the bigness of her bottom. She wore a turban—a piece of downriver style; and she had her vanity case with the creased notes she had got from people in her village and people on the steamer and barge. She shopped, she paid; and some hours before the steamer sailed again her women—thin, short, bald-looking, and in ragged working clothes—came to take the goods away.

This was a quicker journey, downriver. But it was just as dangerous, with the same coupling and uncoupling of the dugouts and the barge. In those days the steamer left the town at four in the afternoon; so it was deep night when Zabeth and her women came to where they had to cast off from the steamer. Zabeth took care then not to give away the entrance to her village. She cast off; she waited for the steamer and the barge and the lights to disappear. Then she and her women poled back up or drifted down to their secret channel, and their nighttime labour of poling and pushing below the overhanging trees.

Going home at night! It wasn't often that I was on the river at night. I never liked it. I never felt in control. In the darkness of river and forest you could be sure only of what you could see— and even on a moonlight night you couldn't see much. When you made a noise—dipped a paddle in the water—you heard yourself as though you were another person. The river and the forest were like presences, and much more powerful than you. You felt unprotected, an intruder.

In the daylight—though the colours could be very pale and ghostly, with the heat mist at times suggesting a colder climate— you could imagine the town being rebuilt and spreading. You could imagine the forests being uprooted, the roads being laid across creeks and swamps. You could imagine the land being made part of the present: that was how the Big Man put it later, offering us the vision of a two-hundred-mile "industrial park" along the river. (But he didn't mean it really; it was only his wish to appear a greater magician than any the place had ever known.) In daylight, though, you could believe in that vision of the future. You could imagine the land being made ordinary, fit for men like yourself, as small parts of it had been made ordinary for a short while before independence—the very parts that were now in ruins.

But at night, if you were on the river, it was another thing. You felt the land taking you back to something that was familiar, something you had known at some time but had forgotten or ignored, but which was always there. You felt the land taking you back to what was there a hundred years ago, to what had been there always.

What journeys Zabeth made! It was as though she came out each time from her hidden place to snatch from the present (or the future) some precious cargo to take back to her people— those razor blades, for instance, to be taken out from their packets and sold one by one, miracles of metal—cargo that became more precious the further she got from the town, the nearer she got to her fishing village, the true, safe world, protected from other men by forest and clogged-up waterways. And protected in other ways as well. Every man here knew that he was watched from above by his ancestors, living forever in a higher sphere, their passage on earth not forgotten, but essentially preserved, part of the presence of the forest. In the deepest forest·was the greatest security. That was the security that Zabeth left behind, to get her precious cargo; that was the security to which she returned.

No one liked going outside his territory. But Zabeth travelled without fear; she came and went with her vanity case and no one molested her. She was not an ordinary person. In appearance she was not at all like the people of our region. They were small and slight and very black. Zabeth was a big woman with a coppery complexion; there were times when this copper glow, especially on her cheekbones, looked like a kind of make-up. There was something else about Zabeth. She had a special smell. It was strong and unpleasant, and at first I thought—because she came from a fishing village—that it was an old and deep smell of fish. Then I thought it had to do with her restricted village diet. But the people of Zabeth's tribe whom I met didn't smell like Zabeth. Africans noticed her smell. If they came into the shop when Zabeth was there they wrinkled their noses and sometimes they went away.

Metty, the half-African boy who had grown up in my family's house on the coast and had come to join me, Metty said that Zabeth's smell was strong enough to keep mosquitoes away. I thought myself that it was this smell that kept men away from Zabeth, in spite of her fleshiness (which the men here liked) and in spite of her vanity case—because Zabeth wasn't married and, so far as I knew, lived with no man.

But the smell was meant to keep people at a distance. It was Metty—learning local customs fast—who told me that Zabeth was a magician, and was known in our region as a magician. Her smell was the smell of her protecting ointments. Other women used perfumes and scents to attract; Zabeth's ointments repelled and warned. She was protected. She knew it, and other people knew it.

I had treated Zabeth so far as a *marchande* and a good customer. Now that I knew that in our region she was a person of power, a prophetess, I could never forget it. So the charm worked on me as well.

2　Africa was my home, had been the home of my family for centuries. But we came from the east coast, and that made the difference. The coast was not truly African. It was an Arab-Indian-Persian-Portuguese place, and we who lived there were really people of the Indian Ocean. True Africa was at our back. Many miles of scrub or desert separated us from the upcountry

people; we looked east to the lands with which we traded—
Arabia, India, Persia. These were also the lands of our ancestors.
But we could no longer say that we were Arabians or Indians or
Persians; when we compared ourselves with these people, we felt
like people of Africa.

My family was Muslim. But we were a special group. We were
distinct from the Arabs and other Muslims of the coast; in our
customs and attitudes we were closer to the Hindus of north-
western India, from which we had originally come. When we had
come no one could tell me. We were not that kind of people. We
simply lived; we did what was expected of us, what we had seen
the previous generation do. We never asked why; we never recorded. We felt in our bones that we were a very old people; but
we seemed to have no means of gauging the passing of time.
Neither my father nor my grandfather could put dates to their
stories. Not because they had forgotten or were confused; the
past was simply the past.

I remember hearing from my grandfather that he had once
shipped a boatful of slaves as a cargo of rubber. He couldn't tell
me when he had done this. It was just there in his memory,
floating around, without date or other association, as an unusual
event in an uneventful life. He didn't tell it as a piece of wickedness or trickery or as a joke; he just told it as something unusual
that he had done—not shipping the slaves, but describing them
as rubber. And without my own memory of the old man's story I
suppose that would have been a piece of history lost forever. I
believe, from my later reading, that the idea of rubber would
have occurred to my grandfather at the time, before the First
World War, when rubber became big business—and later a big
scandal—in central Africa. So that facts are known to me which
remained hidden or uninteresting to my grandfather.

Of that whole period of upheaval in Africa—the expulsion of
the Arabs, the expansion of Europe, the parcelling out of the
continent—that is the only family story I have. That was the sort
of people we were. All that I know of our history and the history
of the Indian Ocean I have got from books written by Europeans. If I say that our Arabs in their time were great adven-

turers and writers; that our sailors gave the Mediterranean the lateen sail that made the discovery of the Americas possible; that an Indian pilot led Vasco da Gama from East Africa to Calicut; that the very word *cheque* was first used by our Persian merchants—if I say these things it is because I have got them from European books. They formed no part of our knowledge or pride. Without Europeans, I feel, all our past would have been washed away, like the scuff marks of fishermen on the beach outside our town.

There was a stockade on this beach. The walls were of brick. It was a ruin when I was a boy, and in tropical Africa, land of impermanent building, it was like a rare piece of history. It was in this stockade that the slaves were kept after they had been marched down from the interior in the caravans; there they waited for the dhows to take them across the sea. But if you didn't know, then the place was nothing, just four crumbling walls in a picture-postcard setting of beach and coconut trees.

Once the Arabs had ruled here; then the Europeans had come; now the Europeans were about to go away. But little had changed in the manners or minds of men. The fishermen's boats on that beach were still painted with large eyes on the bows for good luck; and the fishermen could get very angry, even murderous, if some visitor tried to photograph them—tried to rob them of their souls. People lived as they had always done; there was no break between past and present. All that had happened in the past was washed away; there was always only the present. It was as though, as a result of some disturbance in the heavens, the early morning light was always receding into the darkness, and men lived in a perpetual dawn.

The slavery of the east coast was not like the slavery of the west coast. No one was shipped off to plantations. Most of the people who left our coast went to Arabian homes as domestic servants. Some became members of the family they had joined; a few became powerful in their own right. To an African, a child of the forest, who had marched down hundreds of miles from the interior and was far from his village and tribe, the protection of a foreign family was preferable to being alone among strange and unfriendly Africans. This was one reason why the trade went on long after it had been outlawed by the European powers; and why, at the time when the Europeans were dealing in one kind of rubber, my grandfather could still occasionally deal in another. This was also the reason why a secret slavery continued on the coast until the other day. The slaves, or the people who might be considered slaves, wanted to remain as they were.

In my family's compound there were two slave families, and they had been there for at least three generations. The last thing they wanted to hear was that they had to go. Officially these people were only servants. But they wanted it known—to other Africans, and to poor Arabs and Indians—that they were really slaves. It wasn't that they were proud of slavery as a condition; what they were fierce about was their special connection with a family of repute. They could be very rough with people they considered smaller fry than the family.

When I was young I would be taken for walks in the narrow white-walled lanes of the old part of the town, which was where our house was. I would be bathed and dressed; they would put kohl on my eyes and hang a good-luck charm around my neck; and then Mustafa, one of our old men, would hoist me on his shoulders. That was how I took my walk: Mustafa displaying me on his shoulders, displaying the worth of our family, and at the same time displaying his own trusted position in our family. There were some boys who made a point of taunting us. Mustafa, when we ran into these boys, would set me down, encourage me to speak insults, would add to these insults himself, would encourage me to fight, and then, when things became too hot for me, would lift me out of reach of the boys' feet and fists and place me again on his shoulders. And we would continue our walk.

This talk of Mustafa and Arabia and dhows and slaves might sound like something out of the *Arabian Nights*. But when I think of Mustafa, and even when I hear the word "slave," I think of the squalor of our family compound, a mixture of school yard and back yard: all those people, someone always shrieking, quantities of clothes hanging on the lines or spread out on the bleaching stones, the sour smell of those stones running into the smell of the latrine and the barred-off urinal corner, piles of dirty enamel and brass dishes on the washing-up stand in the middle of the yard, children running about everywhere, endless cooking in the blackened kitchen building. I think of a hubbub of women and children, of my sisters and their families, the servant women and their families, both sides apparently in constant competition; I think of quarrels in the family rooms, competitive quarrels in the servants' quarters. There were too many of us in that small compound. We didn't want all those people in the servants' quarters. But they weren't ordinary servants, and there was no question of getting rid of them. We were stuck with them.

That was how it was on the east coast. The slaves could take over, and in more than one way. The people in our servant houses were no longer pure African. It wasn't acknowledged by the family, but somewhere along the line, or at many places along the line, the blood of Asia had been added to those people. Mustafa had the blood of Gujarat in his veins; so had Metty, the boy who later came all the way across the continent to join me. This, though, was a transferring of blood from master to slave. With the Arabs on our coast the process had worked the other way. The slaves had swamped the masters; the Arabian race of the master had virtually disappeared.

Once, great explorers and warriors, the Arabs had ruled. They had pushed far into the interior and had built towns and planted orchards in the forest. Then their power had been broken by Europe. Their towns and orchards disappeared, swallowed up in bush. They ceased to be driven on by their idea of their position in the world, and their energy was lost; they forgot who they were and where they had come from. They knew only that they were Muslims; and in the Muslim way they needed wives and more wives. But they were cut off from their roots in Arabia and could only find their wives among the African women who had once been their slaves. Soon, therefore, the Arabs, or the people who called themselves Arabs, had become indistinguishable from Africans. They barely had an idea of their original civilization. They had the Koran and its laws; they stuck to certain fashions in dress, wore a certain kind of cap, had a special cut of beard; and that was all. They had little idea of what their ancestors had done in Africa. They had only the habit of authority, without the energy or the education to back up that authority. The authority of the Arabs—which was real enough when I was a boy—was only a matter of custom. It could be blown away at any time. The world is what it is.

I was worried for the Arabs. I was also worried for us. Because, so far as power went, there was no difference between the Arabs and ourselves. We were both small groups living under a European flag at the edge of the continent. In our family house when I was a child I never heard a discussion about our future or the future of the coast. The assumption seemed to be that things would continue, that marriages would continue to be arranged between approved parties, that trade and business would go on, that Africa would be for us as it had been.

My sisters married in the traditional way; it was assumed that I, too, would marry when the time came and extend the life of our family house. But it came to me while I was quite young, still at school, that our way of life was antiquated and almost at an end.

Small things can start us off in new ways of thinking, and I was started off by the postage stamps of our area. The British administration gave us beautiful stamps. These stamps depicted local scenes and local things; there was one called "Arab Dhow." It was as though, in those stamps, a foreigner had said, "This is what is most striking about this place." Without that stamp of the dhow I might have taken the dhows for granted. As it was, I learned to look at them. Whenever I saw them tied up at the waterfront I thought of them as something peculiar to our region, quaint, something the foreigner would remark on, something not quite modern, and certainly nothing like the liners and cargo ships that berthed in our own modern docks.

So from an early age I developed the habit of looking, detaching myself from a familiar scene and trying to consider it as from a distance. It was from this habit of looking that the idea came to me that as a community we had fallen behind. And that was the beginning of my insecurity.

I used to think of this feeling of insecurity as a weakness, a failing of my own temperament, and I would have been ashamed if anyone had found out about it. I kept my ideas about the future to 'myself, and that was easy enough in our house, where, as I have said, there was never anything like a political discussion. My family were not fools. My father and his brothers were traders, businessmen; in their own way they had to keep up with the times. They could assess situations; they took risks and sometimes they could be very bold. But they were buried so deep in their lives that they were not able to stand back and consider the nature of their lives. They did what they had to do. When things went wrong they had the consolations of religion. This wasn't just a readiness to accept Fate; this was a quiet and profound conviction about the vanity of all human endeavour.

I could never rise so high. My own pessimism, my insecurity, was a more terrestrial affair. I was without the religious sense of my family. The insecurity I felt was due to my lack of true religion, and was like the small change of the exalted pessimism of our faith, the pessimism that can drive men on to do wonders. It was the price for my more materialist attitude, my seeking to occupy the middle ground, between absorption in life and soaring above the cares of the earth.

If the insecurity I felt about our position on the coast was due to my temperament, then little occurred to calm me down. Events in this part of Africa began to move fast. To the north there was a bloody rebellion of an upcountry tribe which the British seemed unable to put down; and there were explosions of disobedience and rage in other places as well. Even hypochondriacs sometimes have real illnesses, and I don't think it was my nervousness alone that made me feel that the political system we had known was coming to an end, and that what was going to replace it wasn't going to be pleasant. I feared the lies—black men assuming the lies of white men.

If it was Europe that gave us on the coast some idea of our history, it was Europe, I feel, that also introduced us to the lie.

Those of us who had been in that part of Africa before the Europeans had never lied about ourselves. Not because we were more moral. We didn't lie because we never assessed ourselves and didn't think there was anything for us to lie about; we were people who simply did what we did. But the Europeans could do one thing and say something quite different; and they could act in this way because they had an idea of what they owed to their civilization. It was their great advantage over us. The Europeans wanted gold and slaves, like everybody else; but at the same time they wanted statues put up to themselves as people who had done good things for the slaves. Being an intelligent and energetic people, and at the peak of their powers, they could express both sides of their civilization; and they got both the slaves and the statues.

Because they could assess themselves, the Europeans were better equipped to cope with changes than we were. And I saw, when I compared the Europeans with ourselves, that we had ceased to count in Africa, that really we no longer had anything to offer. The Europeans were preparing to get out, or to fight, or to meet the Africans halfway. We continued to live as we had always done, blindly. Even at this late stage there was never anything like a political discussion in our house or in the houses of families I knew. The subject was avoided. I found myself avoiding it.

I used to go twice a week to play squash in the squash court of my friend Indar. His grandfather had come from the Punjab in India to work on the railway as a contract labourer. The old Punjabi had done well. When he had worked out his contract he had settled on the coast and become a market money-lender, lending twenty or thirty shillings a time to stall-keepers in the market who ran short and depended on these small loans to buy their goods. For ten shillings lent this week twelve or fifteen had to be returned the next. Not the best kind of business; but an active man (and a tough man) could increase his capital many times over in a year. Well, it was a service, and a living. And more than a living. The family had become very grand. They had become merchant bankers in an unofficial way, staking small prospecting companies, staking trading ventures to India and Arabia and the Persian Gulf (still in the Arab dhows of the postage stamp).

The family lived in a big compound in an asphalted yard. The main house was at the far end; there were smaller houses at the side for members of the family who wished to live by themselves, other houses for the servants (proper servants, hire-and-fire people, not limpets like ours); and there was the squash court. Everything was surrounded by a high ochre-washed wall, and there was a main gate with a watchman. The compound was in a newer part of the town; I didn't think it was possible to be more exclusive or protected.

Rich people never forget they are rich, and I looked upon Indar as a good son of his money-lending or banking family. He was handsome, careful of his appearance, and slightly effeminate, with something buttoned up in his expression. I put that expression down to his regard for his own wealth and also to his sexual anxieties. I thought he was a great brothel man on the sly and lived in fear of being exposed or catching some disease.

We were having cold orange juice and hot black tea after our game (Indar was already concerned about his weight), when he told me he was leaving. He was going away, going to England to a famous university to do a three-year course. It was like Indar, and his family, to announce important news in this casual way. The news depressed me a little. Indar could do what he was doing not only because he was rich (I associated going abroad to study with great wealth), but also because he had gone right through our local English-language college until he was eighteen. I had left when I was sixteen. Not because I wasn't bright or didn't have the inclination, but because no one in our family had stayed at school after sixteen.

We were sitting on the steps of the squash court, in the shade. Indar said in his quiet way, "We're washed up here, you know. To be in Africa you have to be strong. We're not strong. We don't even have a flag."

He had mentioned the unmentionable. And as soon as he spoke I saw the wall of his compound as useless. Two generations had built what I saw; and I mourned for that lost labour. As soon as Indar spoke I felt I could enter his mind and see what he saw—the mocking quality of the grandeur, the gate and the watchman that wouldn't be able to keep out the true danger.

But I gave no sign that I understood what he was talking about. I behaved like the others who had infuriated and saddened me by refusing to acknowledge that change was coming to our part of the world. And when Indar went on to ask, "What are you going to do?" I said, as though I didn't see any problem, "I'll stay. I'll go into the business."

It wasn't true at all. It was the opposite of what I felt. But I found that I was unwilling—as soon as the question had been put to me—to acknowledge my helplessness. I instinctively fell into the attitudes of my family. But with me the fatalism was bogus; I cared very much about the world and wished to renounce nothing. All I could do was to hide from the truth. And that discovery about myself made the walk back through the hot town very disturbing.

The afternoon sun fell on the soft black asphalt road and the tall hibiscus hedges. It was all so ordinary. There was as yet no danger in the crowds, the broken-down streets, the blank-walled lanes. But the place was poisoned for me.

I had an upstairs room in our family house. It was still light when I got back. I looked out over our compound, saw the trees and greenery of the neighbouring yards and open spaces. My aunt was calling to one of her daughters: some old brass vases that had been taken out to the yard to be scoured with limes hadn't been taken back in. I looked at that devout woman, sheltered behind her wall, and saw how petty her concern with the brass vases was. The thin whitewashed wall (thinner than the wall of the slave stockade on the beach) protected her so little. She was so vulnerable—her person, her religion, her customs, her way of life. The squalling yard had contained its own life, had been its own complete world, for so long. How could anyone not take it for granted? How could anyone stop to ask what it was that had really protected us?

I remembered the look of contempt and irritation Indar had

given me. And the decision I came to then was this. I had to break away. I couldn't protect anyone; no one could protect me. We couldn't protect ourselves; we could only in various ways hide from the truth. I had to break away from our family compound and our community. To stay with my community, to pretend that I had simply to travel along with them, was to be taken with them to destruction. I could be master of my fate only if I stood alone. One tide of history—forgotten by us, living only in books by Europeans that I was yet to read—had brought us here. We had lived our lives in our way, done what we had to do, worshipped God and obeyed his commandments. Now—to echo Indar's words—another tide of history was coming to wash us away.

I could no longer submit to Fate. My wish was not to be good, in the way of our tradition, but to make good. But how? What did I have to offer? What talent, what skill, apart from the African trading skills of our family? This anxiety began to eat away at me. And that was why, when Nazruddin made his offer, of a shop and business in a far-off country that was still in Africa, I clutched at it.

Nazruddin was an exotic in our community. He was a man of my father's age, but he looked much younger and was altogether more a man of the world. He played tennis, drank wine, spoke French, wore dark glasses and suits (with very wide lapels, the tips of which curled down). He was known among us (and slightly mocked behind his back) for his European manners, which he had picked up not from Europe (he had never been there), but from a town in the centre of Africa where he lived and had his business.

Many years before, following some fancy of his own, Nazruddin had cut down on his business on the coast and begun to move inland. The colonial boundaries of Africa gave an international flavour to his operations. But Nazruddin was doing no more than following the old Arab trading routes to the interior; and he had fetched up in the centre of the continent, at the bend in the great river.

That was as far as the Arabs had got in the last century. There they had met Europe, advancing from the other direction. For Europe it was one little probe. For the Arabs of central Africa it was their all; the Arabian energy that had pushed them into Africa had died down at its source, and their power was like the light of a star that travels on after the star itself has become dead. Arab power had vanished; at the bend in the river there had grown up a European, and not an Arab, town. And it was from that town that Nazruddin, reappearing among us from time to time, brought back his exotic manners and tastes and his tales of commercial success.

Nazruddin was an exotic, but he remained bound to our community because he needed husbands and wives for his children. I always knew that in me he saw the prospective husband of one of his daughters; but I had lived with this knowledge for so long that it didn't embarrass me. I liked Nazruddin. I welcomed his visits, his talk, his very alienness as he sat downstairs in our drawing room or verandah and spoke of the excitements of his far-off world.

He was a man of enthusiasms. He relished everything he did. He liked the houses he bought (always bargains), the restaurants he chose, the dishes he had ordered. Everything worked out well for him, and his tales of unfailing luck would have made him intolerable if he didn't have the gift of describing things so well. He made me long to do what he had done, to be where he had been. In some ways he became my model.

He was something of a palmist, in addition to everything else, and his readings were valued because he could do them only when the mood took him. When I was ten or twelve he had given me a reading and had seen great things in my hand. So I respected his judgment. He added to that reading from time to time. I remember one occasion especially. He was on the bentwood rocker, rocking unsteadily from the edge of the carpet onto the concrete floor. He broke off what he was saying and asked to see my hand. He felt the tips of my fingers, bent my fingers, looked briefly at my palm, and then let my hand go. He thought for a little about what he had seen—it was his way, thinking about what he had seen rather than looking at the hand all the time—and he said, "You are the most faithful man I know." This didn't please me; it seemed to me he was offering me no life at all. I said, "Can you read your own hand? Do you know what's in store for you?" He said, "Don't I know, don't I know." The tone of his voice was different then, and I saw that this man, for whom (according to his talk) everything worked out beautifully, really lived with a vision of things turning out badly. I thought: This is how a man should behave; and I felt close to him after that, closer than I did to members of my own family.

Then came the crash which some people had been quietly prophesying for this successful and talkative man. Nazruddin's adopted country became independent, quite suddenly, and the news from that place for weeks and months was of wars and killings. From the way some people talked you might have believed that if Nazruddin had been another kind of person, if he had boasted less of his success, drunk less wine and been more seemly in his behaviour, events would have taken another turn. We heard that he had fled with his family to Uganda. There was a report that they had driven through the bush for days on the back of a truck and had turned up panic-stricken and destitute at the border town of Kisoro.

At least he was safe. In due course he came to the coast. People looking for a broken man were disappointed. Nazruddin was as sprightly as ever, still with his dark glasses and suit. The disaster appeared not to have touched him at all.

Usually when Nazruddin came to visit, efforts were made to receive him well. The drawing room was given a special cleaning, and the brass vases with the hunting scenes were polished up. But this time, because of the belief that he was a man in trouble, and therefore ordinary again, just like us, no one had tried hard. The drawing room was in its usual state of mess and we sat out on the verandah facing the yard.

My mother brought tea, offering it not in the usual way, as the shamefaced hospitality of simple folk, but behaving as though she was performing some necessary final rite. When she put the tray down she seemed about to burst into tears. My brothers-in-law gathered around with concerned faces. But from Nazruddin —in spite of that tale about the long-distance ride on the back of a truck—there came no stories of disaster, only stories of continuing luck and success. He had seen the trouble coming; he had pulled out months before it came.

Nazruddin said: "It wasn't the Africans who made me nervous. It was the Europeans and the others. Just before a crash people go crazy. We had a fantastic property boom. Everybody was only talking about money. A piece of bush costing nothing today was selling for half a million francs tomorrow. It was like magic, but with real money. I got caught up in it myself, and nearly got trapped.

"One Sunday morning I went out to the development where I had bought a few lots. The weather was bad. Hot and heavy. The sky was dark but it wasn't going to rain; it was just going to stay like that. The lightning was far away—it was raining somewhere else in the forest. I thought: What a place to live in! I could hear the river—the development wasn't too far from the rapids. I listened to the river and looked up at that sky and I thought: This isn't property. This is just bush. This has always been bush. I could scarcely wait for Monday morning after that. I put everything up for sale. Lower than the going price, but I asked to be paid in Europe. I sent the family to Uganda.

"Do you know Uganda? A lovely country. Cool, three to four thousand feet up, and people say it's like Scotland, with the hills. The British have given the place the finest administration you could ask for. Very simple, very efficient. Wonderful roads. And the Bantu people there are pretty bright."

That was Nazruddin. We had imagined him done for. Instead, he was trying to excite us with his enthusiasm for his new country, and asking us to contemplate his luck yet again. The patronage, in fact, was all on his side. Though he never said anything openly, he saw us on the coast as threatened, and he had come that day to make me an offer.

He still had interests in his old country—a shop, a few agencies. He had thought it prudent to keep the shop on, while he was transferring his assets out of the country, to prevent people looking at his affairs too closely. And it was this shop and those agencies that he now offered me.

"They aren't worth anything now. But they will be again. I really should be giving it to you for nothing. But that would be bad for you and for me. You must always know when to pull out. A businessman isn't a mathematician. Remember that. Never become hypnotized by the beauty of numbers. A businessman is someone who buys at ten and is happy to get out at twelve. The other kind of man buys at ten, sees it rise to eighteen and does nothing. He is waiting for it to get to twenty. The beauty of numbers. When it drops to ten again he waits for it to get back to eighteen. When it drops to two he waits for it to get back to ten. Well, it gets back there. But he has wasted a quarter of his life. And all he's got out of his money is a little mathematical excitement."

I said, "This shop: assuming you bought at ten, what would you say you were selling it to me for?"

"Two. In three or four years it will climb up to six. Business never dies in Africa; it is only interrupted. For me it is a waste of time to see that two get up to six. There is more for me in cotton in Uganda. But for you it will be a trebling of your capital. What you must always know is when to get out."

Nazruddin had seen faithfulness in my hand. But he had read me wrong. Because when I accepted his offer I was in an important way breaking faith with him. I had accepted his offer because I wanted to break away. To break away from my family and community also meant breaking away from my unspoken commitment to Nazruddin and his daughter.

She was a lovely girl. Once a year, for a few weeks, she came to the coast to stay with her father's sister. She was better educated than I was; there was some talk of her going in for accountancy or law. She would have been a very nice girl to marry, but I admired her as I would have admired a girl of my own family. Nothing would have been easier than to marry Nazruddin's daughter. Nothing, to me, would have been more stifling. And it was from that stifling as well as from everything else that I drove away, when I left the coast in the Peugeot.

I was breaking faith with Nazruddin. Yet he—a relisher of life, a seeker after experience—had been my exemplar; and it was to his town that I drove. All that I knew of the town at the bend of the river I had got from Nazruddin's stories. Ridiculous things can work on us at moments of strain; and towards the end of that hard drive what was often in my head was what Nazruddin had said about the restaurants of the town, about the food of Europe and the wine. "The wines are Saccone and Speed," he had said. It was a merchant's observation. He had meant that even there, in the centre of Africa, the wine had come from the shippers on our east coast, and not from the people on the other side. But in my imagination I allowed the words to stand for pure bliss.

I had never been to a real European restaurant or tasted wine —forbidden to us—with any pleasure; and I knew that the life Nazruddin had described had come to an end. But I drove through Africa to Nazruddin's town as to a place where this life might be re-created for me.

When I arrived I found that the town from which Nazruddin had brought back his tales had been destroyed, had returned to the bush he had had a vision of when he had decided to sell. In spite of myself, in spite of all that I had been told about recent events, I felt shocked, let down. My faithlessness hardly seemed to matter.

Wine! It was hard to get the simplest food; and if you wanted vegetables you either got them out of an old—and expensive— tin, or you grew them yourself. The Africans who had abandoned the town and gone back to their villages were better off; they at least had gone back to their traditional life and were more or less self-sufficient. But for the rest of us in the town, who needed shops and services—a few Belgians, some Greeks and Italians, a handful of Indians—it was a stripped, Robinson Crusoe kind of existence. We had cars and we lived in proper houses—I had bought a flat over an empty warehouse for almost nothing. But if we had worn skins and lived in thatched huts it wouldn't have been too inappropriate. The shops were empty; water was a problem; electricity was erratic; and petrol was often short.

Once for some weeks we were without kerosene. Two empty oil barges had been shanghaied by people downriver, towed as river spoil to a hidden creek, and converted into living quarters. The people here liked to scrape their yards down to the red earth, to keep away snakes; and the steel decks of the barges provided an ideal living surface.

On those keroseneless mornings I had to boil my water on an English-made cast-iron charcoal brazier—part of my shop stock, intended for sale to village Africans. I took the brazier to the landing of the external staircase at the back of the house, squatted and fanned. All around me people were doing the same; the place was blue with smoke.

And there were the ruins. *Miscerique probat populos et foedera jungi.* These Latin words, whose meaning I didn't know, were all that remained of a monument outside the dock gates. I knew the words by heart; I gave them my own pronunciation, and they ran like a nonsense jingle in my head. The words were carved at the top of a block of granite, and the rest of the granite was now bare. The bronze sculpture below the words had been torn away; the jagged little bits of bronze that remained anchored in the granite suggested that the sculptor had done banana leaves or palm branches at the top, to frame his composition. I was told that the monument had been put up only a few years before, almost at the end of the colonial time, to mark sixty years of the steamer service from the capital.

So almost as soon as it had been put up—no doubt with speeches about a further sixty years of service—the steamer monument had been knocked down. With all the other colonial statues and monuments. Pedestals had been defaced, protective railings flattened, floodlights smashed and left to rust. Ruins had been left as ruins; no attempt had been made to tidy up. The names of all the main streets had been changed. Rough boards carried the new, roughly lettered names. No one used the new names, because no one particularly cared about them. The wish had only been to get rid of the old, to wipe out the memory of the intruder. It was unnerving, the depth of that African rage, the wish to destroy, regardless of the consequences.

But more unnerving than anything else was the ruined suburb near the rapids. Valuable real estate for a while, and now bush again, common ground, according to African practice. The houses had been set alight one by one. They had been stripped— before or afterwards—only of those things that the local people needed: sheets of tin, lengths of pipe, bathtubs and sinks and lavatory bowls (impermeable vessels, useful for soaking cassava in). The big lawns and gardens had returned to bush; the streets had disappeared; vines and creepers had grown over broken, bleached walls of concrete or hollow clay brick. Here and there in the bush could still be seen the concrete shells of what had been restaurants (Saccone and Speed wines) and nightclubs. One nightclub had been called "Napoli"; the now meaningless name, painted on the concrete wall, was almost bleached away.

Sun and rain and bush had made the site look old, like the site of a dead civilization. The ruins, spreading over so many acres, seemed to speak of a final catastrophe. But the civilization wasn't dead. It was the civilization I existed in and in fact was still working towards. And that could make for an odd feeling: to be among the ruins was to have your time-sense unsettled. You felt like a ghost, not from the past, but from the future. You felt that your life and ambition had already been lived out for you and you were looking at the relics of that life. You were in a place where the future had come and gone.

With its ruins and its deprivations, Nazruddin's town was a ghost town. And for me, as a newcomer, there was nothing like a social life. The expatriates weren't welcoming. They had been through a lot; they still didn't know how things were going to turn out; and they were very nervous. The Belgians, especially the younger ones, were full of resentments and a sense of injustice. The Greeks, great family men, with the aggressiveness and frustrations of family men, kept to their families and their immediate friends. There were three houses that I visited, visiting them in turn on weekdays for lunch, which had become my main meal. They were all Asian or Indian houses.

There was a couple from India. They lived in a small flat that smelled of asafoetida and was decorated with paper flowers and brightly coloured religious prints. He was a United Nations expert of some sort who hadn't wanted to go back to India and had stayed on doing odd jobs after his contract had expired. They were a hospitable couple and they made a point (I feel for religious reasons) of offering hospitality to frightened or stranded foreigners. They spoilt their hospitality by talking a little too much about it. Their food was too liquid and peppery for me, and I didn't like the way the man ate. He bent his head low over his food, keeping his nose an inch or two away from his plate, and he ate noisily, slapping his lips together. While he ate like this his wife fanned him, never taking her eyes off his plate, fanning with her right hand, resting her chin on the palm of her left hand. Still, I went there twice a week, more for the sake of having somewhere to go than for the food.

The other place I went to was a rough, ranch-like house that belonged to an elderly Indian couple whose family had all gone away during the troubles. The yard was big and dusty, full of abandoned cars and trucks, the relics of a transport business in colonial days. This old couple didn't seem to know where they were. The bush of Africa was outside their yard; but they spoke no French, no African language, and from the way they behaved you would have thought that the river just down the road was the Ganges, with temples and holy men and bathing steps. But it was soothing to be with them. They didn't look for conversation, and were quite happy if you said nothing, if you ate and ran.

Shoba and Mahesh were the people I felt closest to, and I soon thought of them as friends. They had a shop in what ought to have been a prime commercial position, opposite the van der Weyden Hotel. Like me, they were migrants from the east and refugees from their own community. They were an extraordinarily good-looking couple; it was strange, in our town, to find people so careful of their dress and appearance. But they had lived too long apart from their fellows and had forgotten how to be curious about them. Like many isolated people, they were wrapped up in themselves and not too interested in the world outside. And this beautiful couple had their days of tension. Shoba, the lady, was vain and neurotic. Mahesh, the simpler partner, could be in a state of anxiety about her.

That was my life in Nazruddin's town. I had wanted to break away and make a fresh start. But there are degrees in everything, and I felt burdened by the bareness of my days. My life was unconstricted, but narrower than it had ever been; the solitude of my evenings was like an ache. I didn't think I had the resources to last. My comfort was that I had lost little, except time; I could always move on—though where, I didn't yet know. And then I found I couldn't move. I had to stay.

What I had feared would happen on the coast came to pass. There was an uprising; and the Arabs—men almost as African as their servants—had been finally laid low.

I first heard the news from my friends Shoba and Mahesh, who had got it from the radio—that expatriate habit of listening to the BBC news was something I had not yet got into. We treated the news as a secret, as something that had to be kept from the local people; this was one occasion when we were glad there was no local newspaper.

Then newspapers from Europe and the United States came to various people in the town and were passed around; and it was extraordinary to me that some of the newspapers could have found good words for the butchery on the coast. But people are like that about places in which they aren't really interested and where they don't have to live. Some papers spoke of the end of feudalism and the dawn of a new age. But what had happened was not new. People who had grown feeble had been physically destroyed. That, in Africa, was not new; it was the oldest law of the land.

Letters eventually came from the coast—in a batch—from members of my family. They were cautiously written, but their message was plain. There was no place for us on the coast; our life there was over. The family was scattering. Only old people would stay on in our family compound—a quieter life there, at last. The family servants, burdensome to the end, refusing to go away, insisting on their slave status even at this time of revolution, were being split up among the family. And one of the points of the letters was that I had to take my share.

It was not for me to choose whom I wanted; apparently I had

already been chosen by someone. One of the boys or young men from the servant houses wanted to get as far away from the coast as possible, and he had been firm about being sent "to stay with Salim." The boy said he had always had "a special liking for Salim," and he had made such a fuss that they had decided to send him to me. I could imagine the scene. I could imagine the screaming and the stamping and the sulking. That was how the servants got their way in our house; they could be worse than children. My father, not realising what other people in the family had written, simply said in his letter that he and my mother had decided to send someone to look after me—he meant, of course, that he was sending me a boy to look after and feed.

I couldn't say no: the boy was on his way. That this boy had "a special liking" for me was news to me. A better reason for his choice of me was that I was just three or four years older than he was, unmarried, and more likely to put up with his wandering ways. He had always been a wanderer. We had sent him to the Koranic school when he was small, but he was always running off somewhere else, in spite of beatings by his mother. (And how he screamed in the quarters, and how his mother shouted—both of them overdoing the drama, trying to get as much attention as possible from the rest of the compound!) He was nobody's idea of a house servant. With bed and board always provided, he was more a man about town, friendly and unreliable and full of friends, always willing, always offering to help, and never doing a quarter of what he promised.

He turned up at the flat one evening in one of Daulat's trucks, not long after I had got the letters saying that he had been sent. And my heart went out to him: he looked so altered, so tired and frightened. He was still living with the shock of events on the coast; and he hadn't liked the journey across Africa at all.

He had done the first half of the journey by the railway, which travelled at an average speed of ten miles an hour. Then he had transferred to buses and finally to Daulat's trucks: in spite of wars, bad roads and worn-out vehicles, Daulat, a man of our community, maintained a trucking service between our town and the eastern frontier. Daulat's drivers helped the boy past the various officials. But the mixed-race man about town from the coast was still African enough to be unsettled by his passage through the strange tribes of the interior. He couldn't bring himself to eat their food, and he hadn't eaten for days. Without knowing it, he had made in reverse the journey which some of his ancestors had made a century or more before.

He threw himself into my arms, converting the Muslim embrace into a child's clinging. I patted him on the back, and he took this as a signal to scream the place down. Right away, between screams and bawls, he began telling me about the killings he had seen in the market at home.

I didn't take in all that he was saying. I was worried about the neighbours, and trying to get him to tone down the screaming, trying to get him to understand that that kind of showing-off slave behaviour (which it partly was) was all right on the coast, but that people here wouldn't understand. He was beginning to go on a little bit, too, about the savagery of the *kafar*, the Africans, behaving as though my flat was the family compound and he could shout anything he wanted about people outside. And all the time Daulat's friendly African loader was coming up the external staircase with luggage—not much, but in many small, awkward pieces: a few bundles, a wickerwork laundry basket, some cardboard boxes.

I broke away from the bawling boy—to pay attention was to encourage him—and I dealt with the loader, walking out with him to the street to tip him. The bawling in the flat upstairs died down, as I had expected; solitude and the strangeness of the flat were having their effect; and when I went back up I refused to hear any more from the boy until he had had something to eat.

He became quiet and correct, and while I prepared some baked beans and cheese on toast he brought out, from his bundles and boxes, the things that had been sent me by my family. Ginger and sauces and spices from my mother. Two family photographs from my father, and a wall print on cheap paper of one of our holy places in Gujarat, showing it as a modern place, though: the artist had put in motorcars and motorbikes and bicycles and even trains pell-mell in the surrounding streets. It was my father's way of saying that, modern as I was, I would return to the faith.

"I was in the market, Salim," the boy said, after he had eaten. "At first I thought it was just a quarrel around Mian's stall. I couldn't believe what I was seeing. They were behaving as though knives didn't cut, as though people weren't made of flesh. I couldn't believe it. At the end it was as if a pack of dogs had got into a butcher's stall. I saw arms and legs bleeding and lying about. Just like that. They were still there the next day, those arms and legs."

I tried to stop him. I didn't want to hear more. But it wasn't easy to stop him. He went on about those cut-off arms and legs that belonged to people we had known since we were children. It was terrible, what he had seen. But I was also beginning to feel that he was trying to excite himself to cry a little bit more after he had stopped wanting to cry. I felt that it worried him to find that from time to time he was forgetting, and thinking of other things. He seemed to be wanting to thrill himself again and again; and this disturbed me.

In a few days, though, he thawed out. And the events of the coast were never spoken of again. He settled down more easily than I expected. I had expected him to go sulky and withdrawn; I had thought, especially after his unhappy journey, that he would have hated our backward town. But he liked it; and he liked it because he was himself liked, in a way he hadn't been before.

Physically he was quite different from the local people. He was taller, more muscular, looser and more energetic in his movements. He was admired. The local women, with their usual free ways, made no secret of finding him desirable—calling out to him in the street, and stopping and staring with wicked, half-smiling (and slightly crossed) eyes that appeared to say: "Consider this a joke, and laugh. Or take it seriously." My own way of looking at him changed. He ceased to be one of the boys from the servant houses. I saw what the local people saw; in my own eyes he became more handsome and distinctive. To the local people he wasn't quite an African, and he aroused no tribal uneasiness; he was an exotic with African connections whom they wanted to claim. He flourished. He picked up the local language fast, and he even got a new name.

At home we had called him Ali or—when we wanted to suggest the special wild and unreliable nature of this Ali—Ali-wa ("Ali! Ali! But where is this Ali-wa?"). He rejected his name now. He preferred to be called Metty, which was what the local people called him. It was some time before I understood that it wasn't a real name, that it was just the French word *métis*, someone of mixed race. But that wasn't how I used it. To me it was only a name: Metty.

Here, as on the coast, Metty was a wanderer. He had the bedroom just across the passage from the kitchen; it was the first door on the right as you came in from the landing of the external staircase. I often heard him coming in late at night. That was the freedom he had come to me for. But the Metty who enjoyed that freedom was a different person from the boy who had arrived bawling and screaming, with the manners of the servant house. He had quickly shed those manners; he had developed a new idea of his worth. He became useful in the shop; and in the flat, his wandering habits—which I had dreaded—kept his presence light. But he was always there, and in the town he was like one of my own. He lessened my solitude and made the empty months more bearable—months of waiting for trade to start up again. As, very slowly, it was beginning to do.

We fell into the routine of morning coffee at the flat, shop, separate lunches, shop, separate evenings. Man and master sometimes met, as equals with equal needs, in the dark little bars that began to appear in our town, signs of reawakening life: rough little cells with roofs of corrugated iron, no ceilings, concrete walls painted dark blue or green, red concrete floors.

In one such place Metty put the seal on our new relationship one evening. When I entered I saw him dancing fantastically— slim-waisted, narrow-hipped, wonderfully made. He stopped as soon as he saw me—his servant's instinct. But then he bowed and made a show of welcoming me as though he owned the place. He said, in the French accent he had picked up, "I must do nothing indecent in front of the *patron*." And that was precisely what he went on to do.

So he learned to assert himself. But there were no strains between us. And he became, increasingly, an asset. He became my customs clerk. He was always good with the customers and won me and the shop much goodwill. As an exotic, a licensed man, he was the only person in the town who would risk making a joke with Zabeth, the *marchande* who was also a sorceress.

That was how it was with us, as the town came to life again, as the steamers started to come up again from the capital, once a week, then twice a week, as people began coming back from the villages to the *cités* in the town, as trade grew and my business, which had stood for so long at zero, climbed (to use Nazruddin's scale of ten) back up to two, and even gave me glimpses of four.

3   Zabeth, as a magician or sorceress, kept herself from men. But it hadn't always been so; Zabeth hadn't always been a magician. She had a son. She spoke of him sometimes to me, but she spoke of him as part of a life she had put behind her. She made that son seem so far away that I thought the boy might be dead. Then one day she brought him to the shop.

He was about fifteen or sixteen, and already quite big, taller and heavier than the men of our region, whose average height was about five feet. His skin was perfectly black, with nothing of his mother's copper colour; his face was longer and more firmly modelled; and from what Zabeth said I gathered that the boy's father came from one of the tribes of the south.

The boy's father was a trader. As a trader, he had travelled about the country during the miraculous peace of the colonial time, when men could, if they wished, pay little attention to tribal boundaries. That was how, during his travels, he and Zabeth had met; it was from this trader that Zabeth had picked up her trading skills. At independence, tribal boundaries had become important again, and travel was not as safe as it had been. The man from the south had gone back to his tribal land, taking the son he had had by Zabeth. A father could always claim his child; there were any number of folk sayings that expressed this almost universal African law. And Ferdinand—that was the name of the boy—had spent the last few years away from his mother. He had gone to school in the south, in one of the mining towns, and had been there through all the troubles that had come after independence, especially the long secessionist war.

Now for some reason—perhaps because the father had died, or had married again and wished to get rid of Ferdinand, or simply because Zabeth had wished it—Ferdinand had been sent back to his mother. He was a stranger in the land. But no one here could be without a tribe; and Ferdinand, again according to tribal custom, had been received into his mother's tribe.

Zabeth had decided to send Ferdinand to the lycée in our town. That had been cleaned up and got going again. It was a solid two-story, two-courtyard stone building in the colonial-official style, with wide verandahs upstairs and downstairs. Squatters had taken over the downstairs part, cooking on fire stones in the verandah and throwing out their rubbish onto the courtyards and grounds. Strange rubbish, not the tins and paper and boxes and other containers you would expect in a town, but a finer kind of waste—shells and bones and ashes, burnt sacking —which made the middens look like grey-black mounds of sifted earth.

The lawns and gardens had been scuffed away. But the bougainvillaea had grown wild, choking the tall palmiste trees, tumbling over the lycée wall, and climbing up the square pillars of the main gate to twine about the decorative metal arch where, in letters of metal, was still the lycée motto: *Semper Aliquid Novi*. The squatters, timid and half-starved, had moved out as soon as they had been asked. Some doors and windows and shutters had been replaced, the plumbing repaired, the place painted, the rubbish on the grounds carted away, the grounds asphalted over; and in the building which I had thought of as a ruin there had begun to appear the white faces of the teachers.

It was as a lycée boy that Ferdinand came to the shop. He

wore the regulation white shirt and short white trousers. It was a simple but distinctive costume; and—though the short trousers were a little absurd on someone so big—the costume was important both to Ferdinand and to Zabeth. Zabeth lived a purely African life; for her only Africa was real. But for Ferdinand she wished something else. I saw no contradiction; it seemed to me natural that someone like Zabeth, living such a hard life, should want something better for her son. This better life lay outside the timeless ways of village and river. It lay in education and the acquiring of new skills; and for Zabeth, as for many Africans of her generation, education was something only foreigners could give.

Ferdinand was to be a boarder at the lycée. Zabeth had brought him to the shop that morning to introduce him to me. She wanted me to keep an eye on him in the strange town and take him under my protection. If Zabeth chose me for this job, it wasn't only because I was a business associate she had grown to trust. It was also because I was a foreigner, and English-speaking as well, someone from whom Ferdinand could learn manners and the ways of the outside world. I was someone with whom Ferdinand could practise.

The tall boy was quiet and respectful. But I had the feeling that that would last only while his mother was around. There was something distant and slightly mocking in his eyes. He seemed to be humouring the mother he had only just got to know. She was a village woman; and he, after all, had lived in a mining town in the south, where he must have seen foreigners a good deal more stylish than myself. I didn't imagine him having the respect for my shop that his mother had. It was a concrete barn, with the shoddy goods spread all over the floor (but I knew where everything was). No one could think of it as a modern place; and it wasn't as brightly painted as some of the Greek shops.

I said, for Ferdinand's benefit as well as Zabeth's, "Ferdinand's a big boy, Beth. He can look after himself without me."

"No, no, Mis' Salim. Fer'nand will come to you. You beat him whenever you want."

There was little likelihood of that. But it was only a way of speaking. I smiled at Ferdinand and he smiled at me, pulling back the corners of his mouth. The smile made me notice the neatness of his mouth and the sharp-cut quality of the rest of his features. In his face I felt I could see the starting point of certain kinds of African masks, in which features were simplified and strengthened; and, with memories of those masks, I thought I saw a special distinction in his features. The idea came to me that I was looking at Ferdinand with the eyes of an African, and that was how I always looked at him. It was the effect on me of his face, which I saw then and later as one of great power.

I wasn't happy about Zabeth's request. But it had to be assented to. And when I swung my head slowly from side to side, to let them both know that Ferdinand was to look upon me as a friend, Ferdinand began to go down on one knee. But then he stopped. He didn't complete the reverence; he pretended that something had itched him on that leg, and he scratched the back of the knee he had bent. Against the white trousers his skin was black and healthy, with a slight shine.

This going down on one knee was a traditional reverence. It was what children of the bush did to show their respect for an older person. It was like a reflex, and done with no particular ceremony. Outside the town you might see children break off what they were doing and suddenly, as though they had been frightened by a snake, race to the adults they had just seen, kneel, get their little unconsidered pats on the head, and then, as though nothing had happened, run back to what they were doing. It was a custom that had spread from the forest kingdoms to the east. But it was a custom of the bush. It couldn't transfer to the town; and for someone like Ferdinand, especially after his time in the southern mining town, the child's gesture of respect would have seemed old-fashioned and subservient.

I had already been disturbed by his face. Now I thought: There's going to be trouble here.

The lycée wasn't far from the shop, an easy walk if the sun wasn't too hot or if it wasn't raining—rain flooded the streets in no time. Ferdinand came once a week to the shop to see me. He came at about half past three on Friday afternoon, or he came on Saturday morning. He was always dressed as the lycée boy, in white; and sometimes, in spite of the heat, he wore the lycée blazer, which had the *Semper Aliquid Novi* motto in a scroll on the breast pocket.

We exchanged greetings, and in the African way we could make that take time. It was hard to go on after we had finished with the greetings. He offered me nothing in the way of news; he left it to me to ask questions. And when I asked—for the sake of asking—some question like "What did you do at school today?" or "Does Father Huismans take any of your classes?" he gave me short and precise answers that left me wondering what to ask next.

The trouble was that I was unwilling—and very soon unable—to chat with him as I would have done with another African. I felt that with him I had to make a special effort, and I didn't know what I could do. He was a boy from the bush; when the holidays came he would be going back to his mother's village. But at the lycée he was learning things I knew nothing about. I couldn't talk to him about his school work; the advantage there was on his side. And there was his face. I thought there was a lot going on behind that face that I couldn't know about. I felt there was a solidity and self-possession there, and that as a guardian and educator I was being seen through.

Perhaps, with nothing to keep them going, our meetings would have come to an end. But in the shop there was an attraction: there was Metty. Metty got on with everybody. He didn't have the problems I had with Ferdinand; and it was for Metty that Ferdinand soon began to come, to the shop and then to the flat as well. After his stiff conversation in English or French with me, Ferdinand would, with Metty, switch to the local patois. He would appear then to undergo a character change, rattling away in a high-pitched voice, his laughter sounding like part of his speech. And Metty could match him; Metty had absorbed many of the intonations of the local language, and the mannerisms that went with the language.

From Ferdinand's point of view Metty was a better guide to the town than I was. And for these two unattached young men the pleasures of the town were what you would expect—beer, bars, women.

Beer was part of people's food here; children drank it; people began drinking from early in the morning. We had no local brewery, and a lot of the cargo brought up by the steamers was that weak lager the people here loved. At many points along the river, village dugouts took on cases from the moving steamer; and the steamer, on the way back to the capital, received the empties.

About women, the attitude was just as matter-of-fact. Shortly after I arrived, my friend Mahesh told me that women slept with men whenever they were asked; a man could knock on any woman's door and sleep with her. Mahesh didn't tell me this with any excitement or approval—he was wrapped up in his own beautiful Shoba. To Mahesh the sexual casualness was part of the chaos and corruption of the place.

That was how—after early delight—I had begun to feel myself. But I couldn't speak out against pleasures which were also my own. I couldn't warn Metty or Ferdinand against going to places I went to myself. The restraint, in fact, worked the other way. In spite of the changes that had come to Metty, I still regarded him as a member of my family; and I had to be careful not to do anything to wound him or anything which, when reported back, would wound other members of the family. I had, specifically, not to be seen with African women. And I was proud that, difficult though it was, I never gave cause for offence.

Ferdinand and Metty could drink in the little bars and openly pick up women or drop in at the houses of women they had got to know. It was I—as master of one man and guardian of the other—who had to hide.

What could Ferdinand learn from me? I had heard it said on the coast—and the foreigners I met here said it as well—that Africans didn't know how to "live." By that was meant that Africans didn't know how to spend money sensibly or how to keep a house. Well! My circumstances were unusual, but what would Ferdinand see when he considered my establishment?

My shop was a shambles. I had bolts of cloth and oilcloth on the shelves, but most of the stock was spread out on the concrete floor. I sat on a desk in the middle of my concrete barn, facing the door, with a concrete pillar next to the desk giving me some feeling of being anchored in that sea of junk—big enamel basins, white and blue-rimmed, or blue-rimmed with floral patterns; stacks of white enamel plates with squares of coarse, mud-coloured paper between the plates; enamel cups and iron pots and charcoal braziers and iron bedsteads and buckets in zinc or plastic and bicycle tires and torchlights and oil lamps in green or pink or amber glass.

That was the kind of junk I dealt in. I dealt in it respectfully because it was my livelihood, my means of raising two to four. But it was antiquated junk, specially made for shops like mine; and I doubt whether the workmen who made the stuff—in Europe and the United States and perhaps nowadays Japan—had any idea of what their products were used for. The smaller basins, for instance, were in demand because they were good for keeping grubs alive in, packed in damp fibre and marsh earth. The larger basins—a big purchase: a villager expected to buy no more than two or three in a lifetime—were used for soaking cassava in, to get rid of the poison.

That was my commercial setting. There was a similar rough-and-ready quality about my flat. The unmarried Belgian lady who had lived there before had been something of an artist. To her "studio" atmosphere I had added a genuine untidiness—it was like something beyond my control. Metty had taken over the kitchen and it was in a terrible state. I don't believe he ever cleaned the kerosene stove; with his servant-house background, he would have considered that woman's work. And it didn't help if I cleaned the stove. Metty wasn't shamed: the stove soon began to smell again and became sticky with all kinds of substances. The whole kitchen smelled, though it was used just for making morning coffee, mainly. I could scarcely bear to go into the kitchen. But Metty didn't mind, though his bedroom was just across the passage from the kitchen.

You entered this passage directly from the landing of the external staircase, which hung at the back of the building. As soon as you opened the landing door you got the warmed-up, shut-in smell of rust and oil and kerosene, dirty clothes and old paint and old timber. And the place smelled like that because you couldn't leave any window open. The town, run down as it was, crawled with thieves, and they seemed able to wriggle through any little opening. To the right was Metty's bedroom: one look showed you that Metty had turned it into a proper little servant's room, with his cot, his bedding rolls and his various bundles, his cardboard boxes, his clothes hanging on nails and window catches. A little way down the passage, to the left, after the kitchen, was the sitting room.

It was a large room, and the Belgian lady had painted it white all over, ceiling, walls, windows, and even window panes. In this white room with bare floorboards there was a couch upholstered in a coarse-weave, dark-blue material; and, to complete the studio–sitting room effect, there was an unpainted trestle table as big as a Ping-Pong table. That had been spread over with my own junk—old magazines, paperbacks, letters, shoes, rackets and spanners, shoe boxes and shirt boxes in which at different times I had tried to sort things. One corner of the table was kept clear, and this was perpetually covered by a scorched white cloth: it was where Metty did his ironing, sometimes with the electric iron (on the table, always), sometimes (when the electricity failed) with the old solid flatiron, a piece of shop stock.

On the white wall at the end of the room was a large oil painting of a European port, done in reds and yellows and blues. It was in slapdash modern style; the lady had painted it herself and signed it. She had given it pride of place in her main room. Yet she hadn't thought it worth the trouble of taking away. On the floor, leaning against the walls, were other paintings I had inherited from the lady. It was as if the lady had lost faith in her own junk, and when the independence crisis came, had been glad to go.

The bedroom was at the end of the passage. It was for me a place of special desolation, with its big fitted cupboards and its very big foam bed. What anticipations that bed had given me, as it had no doubt given the lady! Such anticipations, such an assurance of my own freedom; such letdowns, such a sense of shame. How many African women were hustled away at difficult hours—before Metty came in, or before Metty woke up! Many times on that bed I waited for morning to cleanse me of memory; and often, thinking of Nazruddin's daughter and the faith of that man in my own faithfulness, I promised to be good. In time that was to change; the bed and the room were to have other associations for me. But until then I knew only what I knew.

The Belgian lady had attempted to introduce a touch of Europe and home and art, another kind of life, to this land of rain and heat and big-leaved trees—always visible, if blurred, through the white-painted window panes. She would have had a high idea of herself; but judged on its own, what she had tried to do wasn't of much value. And I felt that Ferdinand, when he looked at my shop and flat, would come to the same conclusion about me. It would be hard for him to see any great difference between my life and the life he knew. This added to my nighttime glooms. I wondered about the nature of my aspirations, the very supports of my existence; and I began to feel that any life I might have anywhere—however rich and successful and better furnished—would only be a version of the life I lived now.

These thoughts could take me into places I didn't want to be. It was partly the effect of my isolation: I knew that. I knew there was more to me than my setting and routine showed. I knew there was something that separated me from Ferdinand and the life of the bush about me. And it was because I had no means in my day-to-day life of asserting this difference, of exhibiting my true self, that I fell into the stupidity of exhibiting my things.

I showed Ferdinand my things. I racked my brains wondering what to show him next. He was very cool, as though he had seen it all before. It was only his manner, the dead tone of voice he used when he spoke to me. But it irritated me.

I wanted to say to him: "Look at these magazines. Nobody pays me to read them. I read them because I am the kind of person I am, because I take an interest in things, because I want to know about the world. Look at those paintings. The lady took a lot of trouble over them. She wanted to make something beautiful to hang in her house. She didn't hang it there because it was a piece of magic."

I said it in the end, though not in those words. Ferdinand didn't respond. And the paintings were junk—the lady didn't know how to fill the canvas and hoped to get away with the rough strokes of colour. And the books and magazines were junk—especially the pornographic ones, which could depress me and embarrass me but which I didn't throw away because there were times when I needed them.

Ferdinand misunderstood my irritation.

He said one day, "You don't have to show me anything, Salim."

He had stopped calling me mister, following Metty's lead. Metty had taken to calling me *patron*, and in the presence of a third person, could make it sound ironical. Metty was there that day; but Ferdinand, when he told me I wasn't to show him anything, wasn't speaking ironically. He never spoke ironically.

I was reading a magazine when Ferdinand came to the shop one afternoon. I greeted him and went on with the magazine. It was a magazine of popular science, the kind of reading I had become addicted to. I liked receiving these little bits of knowledge; and I often thought, while I read, that the particular science or field I was reading about was the thing to which I should have given my days and nights, adding knowledge to knowledge, making discoveries, making something of myself, using all my faculties. It was a good feeling; from my point of view, it was as good as the life of knowledge itself.

Metty was at the customs that afternoon, clearing some goods that had arrived by the steamer a fortnight before—that was the pace at which things moved here. Ferdinand hung about the shop for a while. I had felt rebuked by what he had said about not showing him things, and I wasn't going to take the lead in conversation. At last he came to the desk and said, "What are you reading, Salim?"

I couldn't help myself: the teacher and the guardian in me came out. I said, "You should look at this. They're working on a new kind of telephone. It works by light impulses rather than an electric current."

I never really believed in these new wonder things I read about. I never thought I would come across them in my own life. But that was the attraction of reading about them: you could read article after article about these things you hadn't yet begun to use.

Ferdinand said, "Who are they?"

"What do you mean?"

"Who are the 'they' who are working on the new telephone?"

I thought: We are here already, after only a few months at the lycée. He's just out of the bush; I know his mother; I treat him like a friend; and already we're getting this political nonsense. I didn't give the answer I thought he was expecting. I didn't say, "The white men." Though with half of myself I felt like saying it, to put him in his place.

I said instead, "The scientists."

He said no more. I said no more, and deliberately went back to reading. That was the end of that little passage between us. It was also, as it turned out, the end of my attempts to be a teacher, to show myself and my things to Ferdinand.

Because I thought a lot about my refusal to say "the white men" when Ferdinand asked me to define the "they" who were working on the new telephone. And I saw that, in my wish not to give him political satisfaction, I had indeed said what I intended to say. I didn't mean the white men. I didn't mean, I couldn't mean, people like those I knew in our town, the people who had stayed behind after independence. I really did mean the scientists; I meant people far away from us in every sense.

They! When we wanted to speak politically, when we wanted to abuse or praise politically, we said "the Americans," "the Europeans," "the white people," "the Belgians." When we wanted to speak of the doers and makers and the inventors, we all—whatever our race—said "they." We separated these men from their groups and countries and in this way attached them to ourselves. "They're making cars that will run on water." "They're making television sets as small as a matchbox." The "they" we spoke of in this way were very far away, so far away as to be hardly white. They were impartial, up in the clouds, like good gods. We waited for their blessings, and showed off those blessings—as I had shown off my cheap binoculars and my fancy camera to Ferdinand—as though we had been responsible for them.

I had shown Ferdinand my things as though I had been letting him into the deeper secrets of my existence, the true nature of my life below the insipidity of my days and nights. In fact, I—and all the others like me in our town, Asian, Belgian, Greek—were as far away from "they" as he was.

That was the end of my attempts to be a teacher to Ferdinand. I decided now simply to let him be, as before. I felt that by giving him the run of the shop and the flat I was keeping my promise to his mother.

The rainy-season school holidays came, and Zabeth came to town to do her shopping and to take Ferdinand back with her. She seemed pleased with his progress. And he didn't seem to mind exchanging the lycée and the bars of the town for Zabeth's village. So he went home for the holidays. I thought of the journey downriver by steamer and dugout. I thought of rain on the river; Zabeth's women poling through the unlit waterways to the hidden village; the black nights and the empty days.

The sky seldom cleared now. At most it turned from grey or dark grey to hot silver. It lightened and thundered much of the time, sometimes far away over the forest, sometimes directly overhead. From the shop I would see the rain beating down the flamboyant trees in the market square. Rain like that killed the vendors' trade; it blew all around the wooden stalls and drove people to shelter under the awnings of the shops around the square. Everyone became a watcher of the rain; a lot of beer was drunk. The unsurfaced streets ran red with mud; red was the colour of the earth on which all the bush grew.

But sometimes a day of rain ended with a glorious clouded sunset. I liked to watch that from the viewing spot near the rapids. Once that spot had been a little park, with amenities; but all that remained of the park was a stretch of concrete river wall and a wide cleared area, muddy in rain. Fishermen's nets hung on great stripped tree trunks buried among the rocks at the edge of the river (rocks like those that, in the river, created the rapids). At one end of the cleared area were thatched huts; the place had become a fishing village again. The sinking sun shot through layers of grey cloud; the water turned from brown to gold to red to violet. And always there was the steady noise of the rapids, innumerable little cascades of water over rock. The darkness came; and sometimes the rain came as well, and to the sound of the rapids was added the sound of rain on water.

Always, sailing up from the south, from beyond the bend in the river, were clumps of water hyacinths, dark floating islands on the dark river, bobbing over the rapids. It was as if rain and river were tearing away bush from the heart of the continent and floating it down to the ocean, incalculable miles away. But the water hyacinth was the fruit of the river alone. The tall lilac-coloured flower had appeared only a few years before, and in the local language there was no word for it. The people still called it "the new thing" or "the new thing in the river," and to them it was another enemy. Its rubbery vines and leaves formed thick tangles of vegetation that adhered to the river banks and clogged up waterways. It grew fast, faster than men could destroy it with the tools they had. The channels to the villages had to be constantly cleared. Night and day the water hyacinth floated up from the south, seeding itself as it travelled.

I had decided to let Ferdinand be. But in the new term I noticed a change in his attitude to me. He was less distant with me, and when he came to the shop he wasn't so anxious to leave me for Metty. I thought that his mother might have given him a talking to. I thought also that though he had been cool when he had gone to his mother's village for the holidays, he had probably been shocked by his time there—how, I wondered, had he spent the days?—and no longer took the town, and the life of the town, for granted.

The truth was simpler. Ferdinand had begun to grow up, and he was finding himself a little bit at sea. He was of mixed tribal heritage, and in this part of the country he was a stranger. He had no group that was really his own, and he had no one to model himself on. He didn't know what was expected of him. He wanted to find out, and he needed me to practise on.

I could see him now trying on various characters, attempting different kinds of manners. His range was limited. For a few days after Zabeth came to town for her goods, he might be the son of his mother, the *marchande*. He would pretend to be my business associate, my equal, might make inquiries about sales and prices. Then he might become the young African on the way up, the lycée student, modern, go-ahead. In this character he liked to wear the blazer with the *Semper Aliquid Novi* motto; no doubt he felt it helped him carry off the mannerisms he had picked up from some of his European teachers. Copying one teacher, he might, in the flat, stand with crossed legs against the white studio wall and, fixed in that position, attempt to conduct a whole conversation. Or, copying another teacher, he might walk around the trestle table, lifting things, looking at them, and then dropping them, while he talked.

He made an effort now to talk to me. Not in the way he talked to Metty; with me he attempted a special kind of serious conversation. Whereas before he had waited for me to ask questions, now it was he who put up little ideas, little debating points, as though he wanted to get a discussion going. It was part of the new lycée character he was working on, and he was practising, treating me almost as a language teacher. But I was interested. I began to get some idea of what was talked about at the lycée— and I wanted to know about that.

He said to me one day, "Salim, what do you think of the future of Africa?"

I didn't say; I wanted to know what he thought. I wondered whether, in spite of his mixed ancestry and his travels, he really had an idea of Africa; or whether the idea of Africa had come to him, and his friends at school, from the atlas. Wasn't Ferdinand still—like Metty, during his journey from the coast—the kind of man who, among strange tribes, would starve rather than eat their strange food? Did Ferdinand have a much larger idea of

Africa than Zabeth, who moved with assurance from her village
to the town only because she knew she was especially protected?

Ferdinand could only tell me that the world outside Africa
was going down and Africa was rising. When I asked in what way
the world outside was going down, he couldn't say. And when I
pushed him past the stage where he could repeat bits of what he
had heard at the lycée, I found that the ideas of the school discussion had in his mind become jumbled and simplified. Ideas of
the past were confused with ideas of the present. In his lycée
blazer, Ferdinand saw himself as evolved and important, as in
the colonial days. At the same time he saw himself as a new man
of Africa, and important for that reason. Out of this staggering
idea of his own importance, he had reduced Africa to himself;
and the future of Africa was nothing more than the job he might
do later on.

The conversations that Ferdinand, in this character, attempted
with me had a serial quality, because he wasn't always well
briefed. He took a discussion up to a certain point and then
dropped it without embarrassment, as though it had been a language exercise in which he would do better next time. Then,
returning to old ways, he would look for Metty and leave me.

Though I was learning more of what went on in the lycée (so
quickly colonial-snobbish again), and what went on in the mind
of Ferdinand, I didn't feel I was getting closer to him. When I
had considered him a mystery, distant and mocking behind his
mask-like face, I had seen him as a solid person. Now I felt that
his affectations were more than affectations, that his personality
had become fluid. I began to feel that there was nothing there,
and the thought of a lycée full of Ferdinands made me nervous.

Yet there was the idea of his importance. It unsettled me—
there wasn't going to be security for anyone in the country—and
it unsettled Metty. When you get away from the chiefs and the
politicians there is a simple democracy about Africa: everyone is
a villager. Metty was a shop assistant and a kind of servant;
Ferdinand was a lycée boy with a future; yet the friendship between the two men was like the friendship between equals. That
friendship continued. But Metty, as a servant in our family

house, had seen playmates grow into masters; and he must have felt himself—with his new idea of his worth—being left behind again.

I was in the flat one day when I heard them come in. Metty was explaining his connection with me and the shop, explaining his journey from the coast.

Metty said: "My family used to know his family. They used to call me Billy. I was studying bookkeeping. I'm not staying here, you know. I am going to Canada. I've got my papers and everything. I'm just waiting for my medical."

Billy! Well, it was close to Ali. Canada—that was where one of my brothers-in-law had gone; in a letter I received shortly after Metty joined me I had heard about the anxiety of the family about that brother-in-law's "medical." That was no doubt where Metty had picked up the talk about Canada.

I made a noise to let them know I was in the flat, and when they came into the sitting room I pretended I had heard nothing.

Not long after this, on an afternoon of settled rain, Ferdinand came to the shop and abruptly, wet and dripping as he was, said, "Salim, you must send me away to America to study."

He spoke like a desperate man. The idea had burst inside him; and he clearly had felt that if he didn't act right away, he might never act. He had come through the heavy rain and the flooded streets; his clothes were soaked. I was surprised by the abruptness and the desperation, and by the bigness of his request. To me, going abroad to study was something rare and expensive, something beyond the means of my own family.

I said, "Why should I send you to America? Why should I spend money on you?"

He had nothing to say. After the desperation and the trip through the rain, the whole thing might just have been another attempt at conversation.

Was it only his simplicity? I felt my temper rising—the rain and the lightning and the unnatural darkness of the afternoon had something to do with that.

I said, "Why do you think I have obligations to you? What have you done for me?"

And that was true. His attitude, since he had begun to feel towards a character, was that I owed him something, simply because I seemed willing to help.

He went blank. He stood still in the darkness of the shop and looked at me without resentment, as though he had expected me to behave in the way I was behaving, and had to see it through. For a while his eyes held mine. Then his gaze shifted, and I knew he was going to change the subject.

He pulled the wet white shirt—with the lycée monogram embroidered on the pocket—away from his skin, and he said, "My shirt is wet." When I didn't reply, he pulled the shirt away in one or two other places and said, "I walked through the rain."

Still I didn't reply. He let the shirt go and looked away to the flooded street. It was his way of recovering from a false start: his attempts at conversation could end with these short sentences, irritating observations about what he or I was doing. So now he looked out at the rain and spoke scattered sentences about what he saw. He was pleading to be released.

I said, "Metty is in the storeroom. He will give you a towel. And ask him to make some tea."

That was not the end of the business, though. With Ferdinand now, things seldom ended neatly.

Twice a week I had lunch with my friends Shoba and Mahesh in their flat. Their flat was gaudy and in some ways like themselves. They were a beautiful couple, certainly the most beautiful people in our town. They had no competition, yet they were always slightly overdressed. So, in their flat, to the true beauty of old Persian and Kashmiri carpets and old brassware they had added many flimsy, glittery things—crudely worked modern Moradabad brass, machine-turned wall plaques of Hindu gods, shiny three-pronged wall lights. There was also a heavy carving in glass of a naked woman. This was a touch of art, but it was also a reminder of the beauty of women, the beauty of Shoba—personal beauty being the obsession and theme of that couple, like money for rich people.

At lunch one day Mahesh said, "What's got into that boy of yours? He's getting *malin* like the others."

"Metty?"

"He came to see me the other day. He pretended he had known me a long time. He was showing off to the African boy he had with him. He said he was bringing me a customer. He said the African boy was Zabeth's son and a good friend of yours."

"I don't know about good friend. What did he want?"

"Metty ran away just when I was beginning to get angry, and left the boy with me. The boy said he wanted a camera, but I don't think he wanted anything at all. He just wanted to talk."

I said, "I hope he showed you his money."

"I didn't have any cameras to show him. That was a bad business, Salim. Commission, commission all the way. You hardly get your money back in the end."

The cameras were one of Mahesh's ideas that had gone wrong. Mahesh was like that, always looking for the good business idea, and full of little ideas he quickly gave up. He had thought that the tourist trade was about to start again, with our town being the base for the game parks in the east. But the tourist trade existed only in the posters printed in Europe for the government in the capital. The game parks had gone back to nature, in a way never meant. The roads and rest houses, always rudimentary, had gone; the tourists (foreigners who might be interested in cut-price photographic equipment) hadn't come. Mahesh had had to send his cameras east, using the staging posts that were still maintained by people like ourselves for the transport (legal or otherwise) of goods in any direction.

Mahesh said, "The boy said you were sending him to America or Canada to do his studies."

"What am I sending him to study?"

"Business administration. So he can take over his mother's business. Build it up."

"Build it up! Buying a gross of razor blades and selling them one by one to fishermen."

"I knew he was only trying to compromise you with your friends."

Simple magic: if you say something about a man to his friends, you might get the man to do what you say he is going to do.

I said, "Ferdinand's an African."

When I next saw Ferdinand I said, "My friend Mahesh has been telling me that you are going to America to study business administration. Have you told your mother?"

He didn't understand irony. This version of the story caught him unprepared, and he had nothing to say.

I said, "Ferdinand, you mustn't go around telling people things that aren't true. What do you mean by business administration?"

He said, "Bookkeeping, typing, shorthand. What you do."

"I don't do shorthand. And that's not business administration. That's a secretarial course. You don't have to go to America or Canada to do that. You can do that right here. I am sure there are places in the capital. And when the time comes you'll find you want to do more than that."

He didn't like what I said. His eyes began to go bright with humiliation and anger. But I didn't stay for that. It was with Metty, and not me, that he had to settle accounts, if there were accounts to be settled.

He had found me as I was leaving to play squash at the Hellenic Club. Canvas shoes, shorts, racket, towel around my neck—it was like old times on the coast. I left the sitting room and stood in the passage, to give him the chance to leave, so that I could lock up. But he stayed in the sitting room, doubtless waiting for Metty.

I went out to the staircase landing. It was one of our days without electricity. The smoke from charcoal braziers and other open fires rose blue among the imported ornamental trees— cassia, breadfruit, frangipani, flamboyant—and gave a touch of the forest village to a residential area where, as I had heard, in the old days neither Africans nor Asians were permitted to live. I knew the trees from the coast. I suppose they had been imported there as well; but I associated them with the coast and home, another life. The same trees here looked artificial to me, like the town itself. They were familiar, but they reminded me where I was.

I heard no more about Ferdinand's studies abroad, and soon he even dropped the bright-young-lycée-man pose. He began trying out something new. There was no more of that standing against the wall with crossed legs, no more walking around the trestle table and lifting and dropping things, no more of that serious conversation.

He came in now with a set face, his expression stern and closed. He held his head up and moved slowly. When he sat on the couch in the sitting room, he slumped so far down that sometimes his back was on the seat of the coach. He was languid, bored. He looked without seeing; he was ready to listen, but couldn't be bothered to talk himself—that was the impression he tried to give. I didn't know what to make of this new character of Ferdinand's, and it was only from certain things that Metty said that I understood what Ferdinand was aiming at.

During the course of the term there had come to the lycée some boys from the warrior tribes to the east. They were an immensely tall people; and, as Metty told me with awe, they were used to being carried around on litters by their slaves, who were of a smaller, squatter race. For these tall men of the forest there had always been European admiration. Ever since I could remember there had been articles about them in the magazines— these Africans who cared nothing about planting or trade and looked down, almost as much as Europeans, on other Africans. This European admiration still existed; articles and photographs continued to appear in magazines, in spite of the changes that had come to Africa. In fact, there were now Africans who felt as the Europeans did, and saw the warrior people as the highest kind of African.

At the lycée, still so colonial in spite of everything, the new boys had created a stir. Ferdinand, both of whose parents were traders, had decided to try out the role of the indolent forest warrior. He couldn't slump around at the lycée and pretend he was used to being waited on by slaves. But he thought he could practise on me.

I knew other things about the forest kingdom, though. I knew that the slave people were in revolt and were being butchered back into submission. But Africa was big. The bush muffled the sound of murder, and the muddy rivers and lakes washed the blood away.

Metty said, "We must go there, *patron*. I hear it is the last good place in Africa. *Y a encore bien, bien des blancs côté-qui-là.* It have a lot of white people up there still. They tell me that in Bujumbura it is like a little Paris."

If I believed that Metty understood a quarter of the things he said—if I believed, for instance, that he really longed for the white company at Bujumbura, or knew where or what Canada was—I would have worried about him. But I knew him better; I knew when his chat was just chat. Still, what chat! The white people had been driven out from our town, and their monuments destroyed. But there were a lot of white people up there, in another town, and warriors and slaves. And that was glamour for the warrior boys, glamour for Metty, and glamour for Ferdinand.

I began to understand how simple and uncomplicated the world was for me. For people like myself and Mahesh, and the uneducated Greeks and Italians in our town, the world was really quite a simple place. We could understand it, and if too many obstacles weren't put in our way we could master it. It didn't matter that we were far away from our civilization, far away from the doers and makers. It didn't matter that we couldn't make the things we liked to use, and as individuals were even without the technical skills of primitive people. In fact, the less educated we were, the more at peace we were, the more easily we were carried along by our civilization or civilizations.

For Ferdinand there was no such possibility. He could never be simple. The more he tried, the more confused he became. His mind wasn't empty, as I had begun to think. It was a jumble, full of all kinds of junk.

With the arrival of the warrior boys, boasting had begun at the lycée, and I began to feel that Ferdinand—or somebody—had been boasting about me too. Or what had been got out of me. The word definitely appeared to have got around that term that I was interested in the education and welfare of young Africans.

Young men, not all of them from the lycée, took to turning up at the shop, sometimes with books in their hands, sometimes with an obviously borrowed *Semper Aliquid Novi* blazer. They wanted money. They said they were poor and wanted money to continue their studies. Some of these beggars were bold, coming straight to me and reciting their requests; the shy ones hung around until there was no one else in the shop. Only a few had bothered to prepare stories, and these stories were like Ferdinand's: a father dead or far away, a mother in a village, an unprotected boy full of ambition.

I was amazed by the stupidity, then irritated, then unsettled. None of these people seemed to mind being rebuffed or being hustled out of the shop by Metty; some of them came again. It was as if none of them cared about my reactions, as if somewhere out there in the town I had been given a special "character," and what I thought of myself was of no importance. That was what was unsettling. The guilelessness, the innocence that wasn't innocence—I thought it could be traced back to Ferdinand, his interpretation of our relationship and his idea of what I could be used for.

I had said to Mahesh, lightly, simplifying matters for the benefit of a prejudiced man: "Ferdinand's an African." Ferdinand had perhaps done the same for me with his friends, explaining away his relationship with me. And I felt now that out of his lies and exaggerations, and the character he had given me, a web was being spun around me. I had become prey.

Perhaps that was true of all of us who were not of the country. Recent events had shown our helplessness. There was a kind of peace now; but we all—Asians, Greeks and other Europeans—remained prey, to be stalked in different ways. Some men were to be feared, and stalked cautiously; it was necessary to be servile with some; others were to be approached the way I was approached. It was in the history of the land: here men had always been prey. You don't feel malice towards your prey. You set a trap for him. It fails ten times; but it is always the same trap you set.

Shortly after I had arrived Mahesh had said to me of the local Africans: "You must never forget, Salim, that they are *malins*." He had used the French word, because the English words he

might have used—"wicked," "mischievous," "bad-minded"—
were not right. The people here were *malins* the way a dog chasing a lizard was *malin*, or a cat chasing a bird. The people were *malins* because they lived with the knowledge of men as prey.

They were not a sturdy people. They were very small and slightly built. Yet, as though to make up for their puniness in that immensity of river and forest, they liked to wound with their hands. They didn't use their fists. They used the flat of the hand; they liked to push, shove, slap. More than once, at night, outside a bar or little dance hall, I saw what looked like a drunken pushing and shoving, a brawl with slaps, turn to methodical murder, as though the first wound and the first spurt of blood had made the victim something less than a man, and compelled the wounder to take the act of destruction to the end.

I was unprotected. I had no family, no flag, no fetish. Was it something like this that Ferdinand had told his friends? I felt that the time had come for me to straighten things out with Ferdinand, and give him another idea of myself.

I soon had my chance, as I thought. A well-dressed young man came into the shop one morning with what looked like a business ledger in his hand. He was one of the shy ones. He hung around, waiting for people to go away, and when he came to me I saw that the ledger was less businesslike than it looked. The spine, in the middle, was black and worn from being held. And I saw too that the man's shirt, though obviously his best, wasn't as clean as I had thought. It was the good shirt he wore on special occasions and then took off and hung up on a nail and wore again on another special occasion. The collar was yellow-black on the inside.

He said, "Mis' Salim."

I took the ledger, and he looked away, puckering up his brows.

The ledger belonged to the lycée, and it was old. It was something from near the end of the colonial time: a subscription list for a gymnasium the lycée had been planning to build. On the inside of the cover was the lycée label, with the coat of arms and the motto. Opposite that was the principal's appeal, in the stiff and angular European handwriting style which had been passed down to some of the Africans here. The first subscriber was the governor of the province, and he had signed royally, on a whole page. I turned the pages, studying the confident signatures of officials and merchants. It was all so recent, but it seemed to belong to another century.

I saw, with especial interest, the signature of a man of our community about whom Nazruddin had talked a great deal. That man had had old-fashioned ideas about money and security; he had used his wealth to build a palace, which he had had to abandon after independence. The mercenaries who had restored the authority of the central government had been quartered there; now the palace was an army barracks. He had subscribed for an enormous amount. I saw Nazruddin's signature—I was surprised: I had forgotten that he might be here, among these dead colonial names.

The gymnasium hadn't been built. All these demonstrations of loyalty and faith in the future and civic pride had gone for nothing. Yet the book had survived. Now it had been stolen, its money-attracting properties recognized. The date had been altered, very obviously; and Father Huismans's name had been written over the signature of the earlier principal.

I said to the man before me, "I will keep this book. I will give it back to the people to whom it belongs. Who gave you the book? Ferdinand?"

He looked helpless. Sweat was beginning to run down his puckered forehead, and he was blinking it away. He said, "Mis' Salim."

"You've done your job. You've given me the book. Now go." And he obeyed.

Ferdinand came that afternoon. I knew he would—he would want to look at my face, and find out about his book. He said, "Salim?" I didn't acknowledge him. I let him stand. But he didn't have to stand about for long.

Metty was in the storeroom, and Metty must have heard him. Metty called out: "Oo-oo!" Ferdinand called back, and went to the storeroom. He and Metty began to chat in the patois. My temper rose as I heard that contented, rippling, high-pitched sound. I took the gymnasium book from the drawer of my desk and went to the storeroom.

The room, with one small barred window set high, was half in darkness. Metty was on a ladder, checking stock on the shelves on one wall. Ferdinand was leaning against the shelves on another wall, just below the window. It was hard to see his face.

I stood in the doorway. I made a gesture towards Ferdinand with the book and I said, "You are going to get into trouble."

He said, "What trouble?"

He spoke in his flat, dead way. He didn't mean to be sarcastic; he really was asking what I was talking about. But it was hard for me to see his face. I saw the whites of his eyes, and I thought I saw the corners of his mouth pulling back in a smile. That face, that reminder of frightening masks! And I thought: Yes—what trouble?

To talk of trouble was to pretend there were laws and regulations that everyone could acknowledge. Here there was nothing. There had been order once, but that order had had its own dishonesties and cruelties—that was why the town had been wrecked. We lived in that wreckage. Instead of regulations there were now only officials who could always prove you wrong, until you paid up. All that could be said to Ferdinand was: "Don't harm me, boy, because I can do you greater harm."

I began to see his face more clearly.

I said, "You will take this book back to Father Huismans. If you don't, I will take it back myself. And I will see that he sends you home for good."

He looked blank, as though he had been attacked. Then I noticed Metty on the ladder. Metty was nervous, tense; his eyes betrayed him. And I knew I had made a mistake, saving up all my anger for Ferdinand.

Ferdinand's eyes went bright, and the whites showed clearly. So that, at this terrible moment, he seemed like a comic in an old-time film. He appeared to lean forward, to be about to lose his balance. He took a deep breath. His eyes never left my face. He was spitting with rage; his sense of injury had driven him mad. His arms hung straight and loose at his sides, so that they seemed longer than usual. His hands curled without clenching. His mouth was open. But what I had thought was a smile was no smile at all. If the light had been better I would have seen that at the beginning.

He was frightening, and the thought came to me: This is how he will look when he sees his victim's blood, when he watches his enemy being killed. And climbing on that thought was another: "This is the rage that flattened the town."

I could have pushed harder, and turned that high rage into tears. But I didn't push. I thought I had given them both a new idea of the kind of man I was, and I left them in the storeroom to cool down. After some time I heard them talking, but softly.

At four o'clock, closing time, I shouted to Metty. And he, glad of the chance to come out and be active, said, *"Patron,"* and frowned to show how seriously he took the business of closing up the shop.

Ferdinand came out, quite calm, walking with a light step. He said, "Salim?" I said, "I will take the book back." And I watched him walk up the red street, tall and sad and slow below the leafless flamboyants, past the rough market shacks of his town.

4 Father Huismans wasn't in when I went to the lycée with the book. There was a young Belgian in the outer office, and he told me that Father Huismans liked to go away for a few days from time to time. Where did he go? "He goes into the bush. He goes to all those villages," the young man—secretary or teacher—said, with irritation. And he became more irritated when I gave him the gymnasium book.

He said, "They come and beg to be admitted to the lycée. As soon as you take them in they start stealing. They would carry away the whole school if you let them. They come and beg you to look after their children. Yet in the streets they jostle you to show you they don't care for you." He didn't look well. He was pale, but the skin below his eyes was dark, and he sweated as he talked. He said, "I'm sorry. It would be better for you to talk to Father Huismans. You must understand that it isn't easy for me here. I've been living on honey cake and eggs."

It sounded as though he had been put on an especially rich diet. Then I understood that he was really telling me he was starving.

He said, "Father Huismans had the idea this term of giving the boys African food. Well, that seemed all right. There's an African lady in the capital who does wonderful things with prawns and shellfish. But here it was caterpillars and spinach in tomato sauce. Or what looked like tomato sauce. The first day! Of course, it was only for the boys, but the sight of it turned my stomach. I couldn't stay in the hall and watch them chew. I can't bring myself to eat anything from the kitchens now. I don't have cooking facilities in my room, and at the van der Weyden there's this sewer smell from the patio. I'm leaving. I've got to go. It's all right for Huismans. He's a priest. I'm not a priest. He goes into the bush. I don't want to go into the bush."

I couldn't help him. Food was a problem for everybody here. My own arrangements were not of the happiest; I had had lunch that day with the couple from India, in a smell of asafoetida and oilcloth.

When, a week or so later, I went back to the lycée I heard that just two days after our meeting the young Belgian had taken the steamer and gone away. It was Father Huismans who gave me the news; and Father Huismans, sunburnt and healthy after his own trip, didn't seem put out by the loss of one of his teachers. He said he was glad to have the gymnasium book back. It was part of the history of the town; the boys who had stolen the book would recognize that one day themselves.

Father Huismans was in his forties. He wasn't dressed like a priest, but even in ordinary trousers and shirt there was something about him of the man apart. He had the "unfinished" face which I have noticed that certain Europeans—but never Arabs or Persians or Indians—have. In these faces there is a baby-like quality about the cut of the lips and the jut of the forehead. It might be that these people were born prematurely; they seem to have passed through some very early disturbance, way back. Some of these people are as fragile as they look; some are very tough. Father Huismans was tough. The impression he gave was of incompleteness, fragility, and toughness.

He had been out on the river, visiting some villages he knew, and he had brought back two pieces—a mask and an oldish wood carving. It was about these finds that he wanted to talk, rather than about the teacher who had gone away or the gymnasium book.

The carving was extraordinary. It was about five feet high, a very thin human figure, just limbs and trunk and head, absolutely basic, carved out of a piece of wood no more than six to eight inches in diameter. I knew about carving—it was one of the things we dealt in on the coast; we gave employment to a couple of carving families from a tribe who were gifted that way. But Father Huismans dismissed this information when I gave it to him, and talked instead of what he saw in the figure he had picked up. To me it was an exaggerated and crude piece, a carver's joke (the carvers we employed did things like that sometimes). But Father Huismans knew what the thin figure was about, and to him it was imaginative and full of meaning.

I listened, and at the end he said with a smile, *"Semper aliquid novi."* He had used the lycée motto to make a joke. The words were old, he told me, two thousand years old, and referred to Africa. An ancient Roman writer had written that out of Africa there was "always something new"—*semper aliquid novi.* And when it came to masks and carvings, the words were still literally true. Every carving, every mask, served a specific religious purpose, and could only be made once. Copies were copies; there was no magical feeling or power in them; and in such copies Father Huismans was not interested. He looked in masks and carvings for a religious quality; without that quality the things were dead and without beauty.

That was strange, that a Christian priest should have had such regard for African beliefs, to which on the coast we had paid no attention. And yet, though Father Huismans knew so much about African religion and went to such trouble to collect his pieces, I never felt that he was concerned about Africans in any other way; he seemed indifferent to the state of the country. I envied him that indifference; and I thought, after I left him that day, that his Africa, of bush and river, was different from mine. His Africa was a wonderful place, full of new things.

He was a priest, half a man. He lived by vows I couldn't make; and I had approached him with the respect that people of my background feel for holy men. But I began to think of him as something more. I began to think of him as a pure man. His presence in our town comforted me. His attitudes, his interests, his knowledge, added something to the place, made it less barren. It didn't worry me that he was self-absorbed, that he had been indifferent to the breakdown of one of his teachers, or that he scarcely seemed to take me in while he was talking to me. To me that was part of his particular religious nature. I sought him out and tried to understand his interests. He was always willing to talk (always looking away slightly) and to show his new finds. He came a few times to the shop and ordered things for the lycée. But the shyness—that wasn't really shyness—never left him. I was never easy with him. He remained a man apart.

He explained the second motto of the town for me—the Latin words carved on the ruined monument near the dock gates: *Miscerique probat populos et foedera jungi.* "He approves of the mingling of the peoples and their bonds of union": that was what the words meant, and again they were very old words, from the days of ancient Rome. They came from a poem about the founding of Rome. The very first Roman hero, travelling to Italy to found his city, lands on the coast of Africa. The local queen falls in love with him, and it seems that the journey to Italy might be called off. But then the watching gods take a hand; and one of them says that the great Roman god might not approve of a settlement in Africa, of a mingling of peoples there, of treaties of union between Africans and Romans. That was how the words occurred in the old Latin poem. In the motto, though, three words were altered to reverse the meaning. According to the motto, the words carved in granite outside our dock gates, a settlement in Africa raises no doubts: the great Roman god approves of the mingling of peoples and the making of treaties in Africa. *Miscerique probat populos et foedera jungi.*

I was staggered. Twisting two-thousand-year-old words to celebrate sixty years of the steamer service from the capital! Rome was Rome. What was this place? To carve the words on a monument beside this African river was surely to invite the destruction of the town. Wasn't there some little anxiety, as in the original line in the poem? And almost as soon as it had been put up the monument had been destroyed, leaving only bits of bronze and the mocking words, gibberish to the people who now used the open space in front as a market and bivouac, with their goats and crated hens and tethered monkeys (food, like the goats and hens), for the two days or so before the steamer sailed.

But I was glad I didn't speak, because to Father Huismans the words were not vainglorious. They were words that helped him to see himself in Africa. He didn't simply see himself in a place in the bush; he saw himself as part of an immense flow of history. He was of Europe; he took the Latin words to refer to himself. It didn't matter that the Europeans in our town were uneducated, or that there was such a difference between what he stood for in his own life and what the ruined suburb near the rapids had stood for. He had his own idea of Europe, his own idea of his civilization. It was that that lay between us. Nothing like that came between me and the people I met at the Hellenic Club. And yet Father Huismans stressed his Europeanness and his separateness from Africans less than those people did. In every way he was more secure.

He wasn't resentful, as some of his countrymen were, of what had happened to the European town. He wasn't wounded by the insults that had been offered to the monuments and the statues. It wasn't because he was more ready to forgive, or had a better understanding of what had been done to the Africans. For him the destruction of the European town, the town that his countrymen had built, was only a temporary setback. Such things happened when something big and new was being set up, when the course of history was being altered.

There would always have been a settlement at that bend in the river, he said. It was a natural meeting place. The tribes would have changed, power would have shifted, but men would always have returned there to meet and trade. The Arab town would have been only a little more substantial than the African settlements, and technologically not much more advanced. The Arabs, so far in the interior, would have had to build with the products of the forest; life in their town wouldn't have been much more than a kind of forest life. The Arabs had only prepared the way for the mighty civilization of Europe.

For everything connected with the European colonization, the opening up of the river, Father Huismans had a reverence which would have surprised those people in the town who gave him the reputation of being a lover of Africa and therefore, in their way of thinking, a man who rejected the colonial past. That past had been bitter, but Father Huismans appeared to take the bitterness for granted; he saw beyond it. From the ship-repair yard near the customs, long neglected and full of junk and rust, he had taken away pieces of old steamers and bits of disused machinery from the late 1890s and laid them—like relics of an early civilization—in the inner courtyard of the lycée. He was especially pleased with a piece that carried, on an oval steel plate, the name of the makers in the town of Seraing in Belgium.

Out of simple events beside that wide muddy river, out of the mingling of peoples, great things were to come one day. We were just at the beginning. And to Father Huismans colonial relics were as precious as the things of Africa. True Africa he saw as dying or about to die. That was why it was so necessary, while that Africa still lived, to understand and collect and preserve its things.

What he had collected from that dying Africa lay in the gun room of the lycée, where the antiquated rifles of the school cadet corps used to be kept in the old days. The room was as big as a classroom and from the outside looked like one. But there were no windows, only tall panelled doors on two sides; and the only light was from a bare bulb hanging on a long cord.

When Father Huismans first opened the door of that room for

me, and I got the warm smell of grass and earth and old fat, and had a confused impression of masks lying in rows on slatted shelves, I thought: This is Zabeth's world. This is the world to which she returns when she leaves my shop. But Zabeth's world was living, and this was dead. That was the effect of those masks lying flat on the shelves, looking up not at forest or sky but at the underside of other shelves. They were masks that had been laid low, in more than one way, and had lost their power.

That was the impression only of a moment, though. Because in that dark, hot room, with the mask smells growing stronger, my own feeling of awe grew, my sense of what lay all around us outside. It was like being on the river at night. The bush was full of spirits; in the bush hovered all the protecting presences of a man's ancestors; and in this room all the spirits of those dead masks, the powers they invoked, all the religious dread of simple men, seemed to have been concentrated.

The masks and carvings looked old. They could have been any age, a hundred years old, a thousand years old. But they were dated; Father Huismans had dated them. They were all quite new. I thought: But this one's only 1940. I was born in that year. Or: This is 1963. That was when I came here. While this was being made I was probably having lunch with Shoba and Mahesh.

So old, so new. And out of his stupendous idea of his civilization, his stupendous idea of the future, Father Huismans saw himself at the end of it all, the last, lucky witness.

5 Most of us knew only the river and the damaged roads and what lay beside them. Beyond that was the unknown; it could surprise us. We seldom went to places off the established ways. In fact, we seldom travelled. It was as though, having come so far, we didn't want to move about too much. We kept to what we knew—flat, shop, club, bar, the river embankment at sunset.

Sometimes we made a weekend excursion to the hippopotamus island in the river, above the rapids. But there were no people there, just the hippopotamuses—seven of them when I first used to go, three now.

We knew the hidden villages mainly by what we saw of the villagers when they came to the town. They looked exhausted and ragged after their years of isolation and want, and seemed glad to be able to move about freely again. From the shop I used to see them idling about the market stalls in the square, gazing at the displays of cloth and ready-made clothes, and wandering back to the food stalls: little oily heaps of fried flying ants (expensive, and sold by the spoonful) laid out on scraps of newspaper; hairy orange-coloured caterpillars with protuberant eyes wriggling in enamel basins; fat white grubs kept moist and soft in little bags of damp earth, five or six grubs to a bag—these grubs, absorbent in body and of neutral taste, being an all-purpose fatty food, sweet with sweet things, savory with savory things. These were all forest foods, but the villages had been cleaned out of them (the grubs came from the heart of a palm tree); and no one wanted to go foraging too far in the forest.

More and more of the villagers who came as visitors remained to camp in the town. At night there was cooking in the streets and the squares. On the pavements below shop awnings, symbolic walls were put up around sleeping spaces—low fences of cardboard held between stones or bricks, or lengths of string tied (like the ropes of a miniature boxing ring) to sticks kept upright by cairns of stones.

From being abandoned, the town began to feel crowded. It seemed that nothing could stop the movement of people from the villages. Then, from the great unknown outside the town, came the rumour of a war.

And it was the old war, the one we were still recovering from, the semi-tribal war that had broken out at independence and shattered and emptied the town. We had thought it over and done with, the passions burnt out. There was nothing to make us think otherwise. Even local Africans had begun to talk of that time as a time of madness. And madness was the word. From

Mahesh and Shoba I had heard dreadful stories of that time, of casual killings over many months by soldiers and rebels and mercenaries, of people trussed up in disgusting ways and being made to sing certain songs while they were beaten to death in the streets. None of the people who came in from the villages seemed ready for that kind of horror. Yet now it was all starting up again.

At independence the people of our region had gone mad with anger and fear—all the accumulated anger of the colonial period, and every kind of reawakened tribal fear. The people of our region had been much abused, not only by Europeans and Arabs, but also by other Africans; and at independence they had refused to be ruled by the new government in the capital. It was an instinctive uprising, without leaders or a manifesto. If the movement had been more reasoned, had been less a movement of simple rejection, the people of our region might have seen that the town at the bend in the river was theirs, the capital of any state they might set up. But they had hated the town for the intruders who had ruled in it and from it; and they had preferred to destroy the town rather than take it over.

Having destroyed their town, they had grieved for it. They had wished to see it a living place again. And seeing it come to a kind of life again, they had grown afraid once more.

They were like people who didn't know their own mind. They had suffered so much; they had brought so much suffering on themselves. They looked so feeble and crazed when they came out of their villages and wandered about the town. They looked so much like people needing the food and the peace that the town offered. But it was people like them, going back to their villages, who wished to lay the town low again. Such rage! Like a forest fire that goes underground and burns unseen along the roots of trees it has already destroyed and then erupts in scorched land where it has little to feed on, so in the middle of destruction and want the wish to destroy flared up again.

And the war, which we had thought dead, was all at once around us. We heard of ambushes on roads we knew, of villages attacked, of headmen and officials killed.

It was at this time that Mahesh said something which I remembered. It wasn't the kind of thing I was expecting from him—so careful of his looks and clothes, so spoiled, so obsessed with his lovely wife.

Mahesh said to me: "What do you do? You live here, and you ask that? You do what we all do. You carry on."

We had the army in our town. They came from a warrior tribe who had served the Arabs as slave-hunters in the region, and had later, with one or two nasty mutinies, served the colonial government as soldiers. So the pattern of policing was old.

But slaves were no longer required, and in post-colonial Africa everybody could get guns; every tribe could be a warrior tribe. So the army was discreet. Sometimes there were trucks with soldiers in the streets—but the soldiers never showed their weapons. Sometimes there was a ceremonial coming and going at the barracks—the palace built by the great man of our community, which now had women's washing hung out in the partitioned verandahs upstairs and downstairs (a Greek had the laundry contract for the soldiers' uniforms). The army was seldom more provocative than that. They couldn't afford to be. They were among their traditional enemies, their former slave prey; and though they were paid regularly and lived well, they were kept short of equipment. We had a new President, an army man. This was his way of policing the country and controlling his difficult army.

It made for a balance in the town. And a well-paid, domesticated army was good for trade. The soldiers spent. They bought furniture, and they loved carpets—that was a taste they had inherited from the Arabs. But now the balance in our town was threatened. The army had a real war to fight; and no one could say whether those men, given modern weapons again and orders to kill, wouldn't fall into the ways of their slave-hunting ancestors and break up into marauding bands, as they had done at independence, with the collapse of all authority.

No, in this war I was neutral. I was frightened of both sides. I didn't want to see the army on the loose. And though I felt sympathy for the people of our region, I didn't want to see the town destroyed again. I didn't want anybody to win; I wanted the old balance to be maintained.

One night I had a premonition that the war had come close. I woke up and heard the sound of a truck far away. It could have been any truck; it could even have been one of Daulat's, near the end of its hard run from the east. But I thought: That is the sound of war. That sound of a steady, grinding machine made me think of guns; and then I thought of the crazed and half-starved village people against whom the guns were going to be used, people whose rags were already the colour of ashes. This was the anxiety of a moment of wakefulness; I fell asleep again.

When Metty brought me coffee in the morning he said, "The soldiers are running back. They came to a bridge. And when they got to that bridge their guns began to bend."

"Metty!"

"I am telling you, *patron*."

That was bad. If it was true that the army was retreating, it was bad; I didn't want to see that army in retreat. If it wasn't true, it was still bad. Metty had picked up the local rumours; and what he said about the bending guns meant that the rebels, the men in rags, had been made to believe that bullets couldn't kill them, that all the spirits of the forest and the river were on their side. And that meant that at any moment, as soon as someone gave the correct call, there could be an uprising in the town itself.

It was bad, and there was nothing I could do. The stock of the shop—there was no means of protecting that. What other things of value did I have? There were two or three kilos of gold I had picked up in various little deals; there were my documents—my birth certificate and my British passport; there was the camera I had shown Ferdinand, but didn't want to tempt anyone with now. I put these things in a wooden crate. I also put in the wall print of the holy place my father had sent me by Metty, and I got Metty to put in his passport and money as well. Metty had become the family servant again, anxious, for the sake of prestige, even at this moment, to behave just like me. I had to stop him from throwing in all kinds of rubbish. We dug a hole in the yard just at the bottom of the external staircase—it was easy: no stones in the red earth—and buried the crate there.

It was early morning. Our back yard was so drab, so ordinary with sunlight and the smell of the neighbours' chickens, so ordinary with red dust and dead leaves and the morning shadows of trees I knew at home on the coast, that I thought: This is too stupid. A little later I thought: I've made a mistake. Metty knows that everything of value that I possess is in that box. I've put myself in his hands.

We went and opened the shop; I was carrying on. We did a little business in the first hour. But then the market square began to empty and the town began to go silent. The sun was bright and hot, and I studied the contracting shadows of trees and market stalls and buildings around the square.

Sometimes I thought I could hear the noise of the rapids. It was the eternal noise at that bend in the river, but on a normal day it couldn't be heard here. Now it seemed to come and go on the wind. At midday, when we shut the shop for lunch, and I drove through the streets, it was only the river, glittering in the hard light, that seemed alive. No dugouts, though; only the water hyacinths travelling up from the south, and floating away to the west, clump after clump, with the thick-stalked lilac flowers like masts.

I was taking lunch that day with the old Asian couple—they had had a transport business until independence, when business just stopped, and the rest of the family went away. Nothing had changed there since I had made the arrangement to have lunch with them twice a week. They were people almost without news, and we still had very little conversation. The view, from the verandah of the rough, ranch-like house, was still of abandoned motor vehicles, relics of the old business, rotting away in the yard. I would have minded that view, if it had been my business. But the old people didn't seem to mind or know that they had lost a lot. They seemed content just to live out their lives. They had done all that their religion and family customs had required them to do; and they felt—like the older people of my own family—that they had lived good and complete lives.

On the coast I used to grieve for people of our community who were like that, indifferent to what lay around them. I wanted to shake them up and alert them to danger. But it was soothing now to be with these calm old people; and it would have been nice, on a day like this, not to have to leave that house, to be a child again, protected by the wisdom of the old, and to believe that what they saw was true.

Who wanted philosophy or faith for the good times? We could all cope with the good times. It was for the bad that we had to be equipped. And here in Africa none of us were as well equipped as the Africans. The Africans had called up this war; they would suffer dreadfully, more than anybody else; but they could cope. Even the raggedest of them had their villages and tribes, things that were absolutely theirs. They could run away again to their secret worlds and become lost in those worlds, as they had done before. And even if terrible things happened to them they would die with the comfort of knowing that their ancestors were gazing down approvingly at them.

But this was not true of Ferdinand. With his mixed parentage, he was almost as much a stranger in the town as I was. He came to the flat in the afternoon, and he was wild, close to hysteria, possessed by all the African terror of strange Africans.

Classes had been suspended at the lycée; thoughts there were of the safety of the boys and the teachers. Ferdinand had decided that the lycée wasn't safe; he thought it would be one of the first places to be attacked if there was an uprising in the town. He had dropped all his characters, all his poses. The blazer, which he had once worn with pride as a young man of new Africa, he had discarded as dangerous, something that made him more a man apart; and he was wearing long khaki trousers, not the white shorts of the school uniform. He talked in a frantic way of returning to the south, to his father's people. But that was impossible—he knew it was impossible; and there was no question either of sending him downriver to his mother's village.

The big boy, almost a man, sobbed, "I didn't want to come here. I don't know anyone here. My mother wanted me to come. I didn't want to be in the town or go to the lycée. Why did she send me to the lycée?"

It was a comfort to us, Metty and myself, to have someone to comfort. We decided that Ferdinand was to sleep in Metty's room, and we dug out some bedding for him. The attention calmed Ferdinand down. We ate early, while it was still light. Ferdinand was silent then. But later, when we were in our different rooms, he and Metty talked.

I heard Metty say: "They came to a bridge. And all the trucks stalled and the guns began to bend."

Metty's voice was high-pitched and excited. That wasn't the voice he had used when he had given me the news in the morning. He was talking now like the local Africans, from whom he had got the story.

In the morning the market square outside the shop didn't come to life at all. The town remained empty. The squatters and campers in the street seemed to have gone into hiding.

When I went to Shoba and Mahesh's flat for lunch I noticed that their better carpets had disappeared, and some of the finer glassware and silver, and the crystal figure of the nude woman. Shoba looked strained, especially around her eyes, and Mahesh seemed more nervous of her than of anything else. Shoba's mood always dictated the mood of our lunch, and she seemed that day to want to punish us for the good lunch she had prepared. We ate for some time in silence, Shoba looking down at the table with her tired eyes, Mahesh constantly looking at her.

Shoba said, "I should have been at home this week. My father is sick. Did I tell you, Salim? I should have been with him. And it is his birthday."

Mahesh's eyes hopped about the table. Spoiling the effect of the words that I had found so wise, he said, "We'll carry on. It will be all right. The new President's not a fool. He isn't just going to stay in his house like the last man, and do nothing."

She said, "Carry on, carry on. That's all I've been doing. That's how I've spent my life. That's how I've lived in this place, among Africans. Is that a life, Salim?"

She looked at her plate, not at me. And I said nothing.

Shoba said, "I've wasted my life, Salim. You don't know how

I've wasted my life. You don't know how I live in fear in this place. You don't know how frightened I was when I heard about you, when I heard that a stranger had come to the town. I've got to be frightened of everybody, you know." Her eyes twitched. She stopped eating, and pressed her cheekbones with the tips of her fingers, as though pressing away a nervous pain. "I come from a well-to-do family, a rich family. You know that. My family had plans for me. But then I met Mahesh. He used to own a motorcycle shop. Something terrible happened. I slept with him almost as soon as I met him. You know us and our ways well enough to know that that was a terrible thing for me to do. But it was terrible for me in another way as well. I didn't want to get to know anybody else after that. That has been my curse. Why aren't you eating, Salim? Eat, eat. We must carry on."

Mahesh's lips came together nervously, and he looked a little foolish. At the same time his eyes brightened at the praise contained in the complaining words; yet he and Shoba had been together for nearly ten years.

"My family beat up Mahesh terribly. But that just made me more determined. My brothers threatened to throw acid on me. They were serious. They also threatened to kill Mahesh. That was why we came here. I watched for my brothers every day. I still do. I wait for them. You know that with families like ours certain things are no joke. And then, Salim, while we were here, something worse happened. Mahesh said one day that I was stupid to be watching out for my brothers. He said, 'Your brothers wouldn't come all the way here. They'll send somebody else.'"

Mahesh said, "That was a joke."

"No, that wasn't a joke. That was true. Anybody could come here—they could send anybody. It doesn't have to be an Asian. It could be a Belgian or a Greek or any European. It could be an African. How am I to know?"

She did all the talking at lunch, and Mahesh let her; he seemed to have handled this kind of situation before. Afterwards I drove him back to the centre of the town—he said he didn't want to take his car in. His nervousness disappeared as soon as we left

Shoba. He didn't seem embarrassed by what Shoba had said about their life together, and made no comment about it.

He said, as we drove through the dusty red streets, "Shoba exaggerates. Things are not as bad as she believes. The new man's no fool. The steamer came in this morning with the white men. You didn't know? Go across to the van der Weyden and you'll see a few of them. The new man might be a maid's son. But he's going to hold it together. He's going to use this to put a lot of people in their place. Go to the van der Weyden. It will give you an idea of what things were like after independence."

Mahesh was right. The steamer had arrived; I had a glimpse of it when we drove by the docks. It hadn't hooted and I hadn't looked for it earlier. Low-decked, flat-bottomed, it was almost hidden by the customs sheds, all but the top of the superstructure at the rear. And when I stopped outside Mahesh's shop, which was opposite the van der Weyden, I saw a number of army vehicles, and some civilian trucks and taxis that had been commandeered.

Mahesh said, "It's a good thing Africans have short memories. Go and have a look at the people who've come to save them from suicide."

The van der Weyden was a modern building, four stories high, concrete and straight lines, part of the pre-independence boom; and in spite of all that it had gone through, it still pretended to be a modern hotel. It had many glass doors at pavement level; the lobby had a mosaic floor; there were lifts (not reliable now); there was a reception desk with a pre-independence airline advertisement and a permanent *Hôtel Complet* ("No Vacancies") sign—which hadn't been true for some years.

I had expected a crowd in the lobby, noise, rowdiness. I found the place looking emptier than usual, and it was almost hushed. But the hotel had guests: on the mosaic floor there were about twenty or thirty suitcases with identical blue tie-on labels printed *Hazel's Travels*. The lifts weren't working, and a single hotel boy—a small old man wearing the servant costume of the colonial time: short khaki trousers, short-sleeved shirt, and a large, coarse white apron over that—had the job of taking the suitcases up the terrazzo steps at the side of the lift. He was working under the direct supervision of the big-bellied African (from downriver somewhere) who normally stood behind the reception desk cleaning his teeth with a toothpick and being rude to everybody, but was now standing by the suitcases and trying to look busy and serious.

Some of the hotel's new guests were in the patio bar, where there were a few green palms and creepers in concrete pots. The terrazzo floor here sloped from all sides to a central grille, and from this grille there always came, but especially after rain, a smell of the sewer. In this smell—not particularly bad now: it was dry and hot, a triangle of sunlight dazzled on one wall—the white men sat, eating the van der Weyden's sandwiches and drinking lager.

They wore civilian clothes, but they would have been a noticeable crowd anywhere. An ordinary bar crowd would have had some flabby types and would have been more mixed in age. These men were all in fine physical condition, and even the few grey-haired ones among them didn't look over forty; they could have passed as some kind of sports team. They sat in two distinct groups. One group was rougher-looking, noisier, with a few flashy dressers; two or three very young men in this group were pretending to be drunk, and clowning. The men in the other group were graver, cleaner-shaved, more educated in face, more conscious of their appearance. And you might have thought the two groups had accidentally come together in the bar, until you saw that they were all wearing the same kind of heavy brown boots.

Normally at the van der Weyden the hotel boys drooped around. The old ones, with their squashed and sour little faces, sat on their stools and expected only to be tipped, wearing their shorts and very big aprons like a pensioner's uniform (and sometimes, in their great stillness, hiding their arms below their aprons and looking like men at the barber's); the younger, post-independence boys wore their own clothes and chatted behind the counter as though they were customers. Now they were all alert and jumping about.

I asked for a cup of coffee, and no cup of coffee ever came to me more quickly at the van der Weyden. It was a tiny old man who served me. And I thought, not for the first time, that in colonial days the hotel boys had been chosen for their small size, and the ease with which they could be manhandled. That was no doubt why the region had provided so many slaves in the old days: slave peoples are physically wretched, half-men in everything except in their capacity to breed the next generation.

The coffee came fast, but the stainless steel jug the old man brought me had only a stale-looking trickle of powdered milk. I lifted the jug. The old man saw before I could show him, and he looked so terrified that I put the jug down and sipped the awful coffee by itself.

The men in the bar had come to do a job. They—or their fellows—had probably already begun. They knew they were dramatic figures. They knew I had come to see what they looked like; they knew the boys were terrified of them. Until this morning those hotel servants had been telling one another stories about the invincibility of their people in the forest; and those hotel servants were men who, given an uprising in the town, would have done terrible things with their small hands. Now, so quickly, they had become abject. In one way it was good; in another way it was pitiful. This was how the place worked on you: you never knew what to think or feel. Fear or shame—there seemed to be nothing in between.

I went back to the shop. It was a way of carrying on, and a way of passing the time. The flamboyant trees were in new leaf, feathery, a delicate green. The light changed; shadows began to angle across the red streets. On another day at this time I would have been starting to think of tea at the flat, squash at the Hellenic Club, with cold drinks afterwards in the rough little bar, sitting at the metal tables and watching the light go.

When Metty came in, just before four, closing time, he said, "The white men came this morning. Some of them went to the barracks and some of them went to the hydro." This was the hydroelectric station, some miles upriver from the town. "The first thing they did at the barracks was to shoot Colonel Yenyi. It was what the President asked them to do. He doesn't play, this new President. Colonel Yenyi was running out to meet them. They didn't let him talk. They shot him in front of the women and everybody. And Iyanda, the sergeant—he bought that bolt of curtain material with the apple pattern—they shot him too, and a few other soldiers as well."

I remembered Iyanda with his overstarched uniform, his broad face, and his smiling, small, malicious eyes. I remembered the way he had rubbed the palm of his hand over the cloth with the big red apples, the proud way he had pulled out the rolled-up notes to pay—such a small sum, really. Curtain material! The news of his execution would have pleased the local people. Not that he was a wicked man; but he belonged to that detested slave-hunting tribe, like the rest of the army, like his colonel.

The President had sent terror to our town and region. But at the same time, by terrorizing the army as well, he was making a gesture to the local people. The news of the executions would have spread fast, and people would already have become confused and nervous. They would have felt—as I began to feel— that for the first time since independence there was some guiding intelligence in the capital, and that the free-for-all of independence had come to an end.

I could see the change in Metty. He had brought quite bloody news. Yet he seemed calmer than in the morning; and he made Ferdinand calmer. Late in the afternoon we began to hear guns. In the morning that sound would have panicked us all. Now we were almost relieved—the guns were far away, and the noise was a good deal less loud than thunder, to which we were accustomed. The dogs were disturbed by the strange noise, though, and set up a barking that rolled back and forth, at times drowning the sound of the guns. Late sunlight, trees, cooking smoke: that was all we could see when we went out to the landii g of the external staircase to look.

No lights came on at sunset. There was no electricity. The machinery had failed again, or the power had been deliberately turned off, or the power station had been captured by the rebels. But it wasn't bad to be without lights now; it meant that at least there would be no uprising during the night. People here didn't like the dark, and some could sleep only with lights in their rooms or huts. And none of us—neither Metty nor Ferdinand nor myself—believed that the station had been captured by the rebels. We had faith in the President's white men. The situation, so confused for us in the morning, had become as simple as that now.

I stayed in the sitting room and read old magazines by an oil lamp. In their room Metty and Ferdinand talked. They didn't use their daytime voices or the voices they might have used in electric light. They both sounded slow, contemplative, old; they talked like old men. When I went out to the passage I saw, through the open door, Metty sitting on his cot in undershirt and pants, and Ferdinand, also in undershirt and pants, lying on his bedding on the floor, one raised foot pressed against the wall. In lamplight it was like the interior of a hut; their leisurely, soft talk, full of pauses and silences, matched their postures. For the first time in days they were relaxed, and they felt so far from danger now that they began to talk of danger, war and armies.

Metty said he had seen the white men in the morning.

Ferdinand said, "There were a lot of white soldiers in the south. That was a real war."

"You should have seen them this morning. They just raced to the barracks and they were pointing their guns at everybody. I never saw soldiers like that before."

Ferdinand said, "I saw soldiers for the first time when I was very young. It was just after the Europeans went away. It was in my mother's village, before I went to stay with my father. These soldiers came to the village. They had no officers and they began to behave badly."

"Did they have guns?"

"Of course they had guns. They were looking for white people to kill. They said we were hiding white people. But I think they only wanted to make trouble. Then my mother spoke to them and they went away. They just took a few women."

"What did she say to them?"

"I don't know. But they became frightened. My mother has powers."

Metty said, "That was like the man we had on the coast. He

came from somewhere near here. He was the man who made the people kill the Arabs. It began in the market. I was there. You should have seen it, Ferdinand. The arms and legs lying about in the streets."

"Why did he kill the Arabs?"

"He said he was obeying the god of Africans."

Metty had never told me about that. Perhaps he hadn't thought it important; perhaps it had frightened him. But he had remembered.

They went silent for a while; I had the feeling that Ferdinand was examining what he had heard. When they spoke again it was of other things.

The gunfire went on. But it came no nearer. It was the sound of the weapons of the President's white men, the promise of order and continuity; and it was oddly comforting, like the sound of rain in the night. All that was threatening, in that great unknown outside, was being held in check. And it was a relief, after all the anxiety, to sit in the lamplit flat and watch the shadows that electric lights never made; and to hear Ferdinand and Metty talk in their leisurely old men's voices in that room which they had turned into a warm little cavern. It was a little like being transported to the hidden forest villages, to the protection and secrecy of the huts at night—everything outside shut out, kept beyond some magical protecting line; and I thought, as I had thought when I had had lunch with the old couple, how nice it would be if it were true. If in the morning we could wake up and find that the world had shrunken only to what we knew and what was safe.

In the morning there came the fighter plane. Almost as soon as you heard it, before you had time to go out and look for it, it was overhead, flying low, and screaming at such a pitch that you barely felt yourself in possession of your body; you were close to a cutting-out of the senses. A jet fighter flying low, so low that you clearly see its triangular silver underside, is a killing thing. Then it was gone, and was soon hardly visible in the sky, white with the heat of the day that had just begun. It made a few more passes over the town, that one plane, like a vicious bird that wouldn't go away. Then it flew over the bush. At last it lifted, and just a little while later, at some distance, the missiles it had released exploded in the bush. And that was like the thunder we were used to.

It came back more than once during the week, that single plane, to fly low over the town and the bush and to drop its explosives at random in the bush. But the war was over that first day. Though it was a month before the army began to come back from the bush, and a full two months before the van der Weyden began to lose its new guests.

In the beginning, before the arrival of the white men, I had considered myself neutral. I had wanted neither side to win, neither the army nor the rebels. As it turned out, both sides lost.

Many of the soldiers—from the famous warrior tribe—were killed. And afterwards many more lost their guns and over-starched uniforms and the quarters they had spent so much of their money furnishing. The army was reorganized by the President, far away in the capital; in our town the army became more mixed, with men from many tribes and different regions. The men of the warrior tribe were turned out unprotected into the town. There were dreadful scenes at the barracks; the women wailed in the forest way, lifting their bellies and letting them drop heavily again. A famous tribe, now helpless among their traditional prey: it was as though some old law of the forest, something that came from Nature itself, had been overturned.

As for the starveling rebels of our region, they soon began to reappear in the town, more starved and abject, their blackened rags hanging on them, men who only a few weeks before had thought they had found a fetish powerful enough to cause the guns of their enemies to bend and to turn bullets to water. There was bitterness in their wasted faces, and for a little while they were withdrawn, like people slightly crazed. But they needed the town they had wanted to destroy; as Mahesh said, they had been saved from suicide. They recognized the new intelligence that ran the country from afar, and they returned to their old habit of obedience.

For the first time since I had arrived there was something like life at the van der Weyden. The steamers brought up not only supplies for the President's white men, but also very plump and fantastically dressed women from the downriver peoples, beside whom the women of our region, polers of dugouts and carriers of loads, looked like bony boys.

Eventually we were allowed to drive out to the dam and the hydroelectric station, near where there had been fighting. The installations were untouched; but we had lost one of our new nightclubs. It had been started by a refugee from the Portuguese territory to the south (a man avoiding conscription), and it was beautifully sited, on a cliff overlooking the river. It was a place to which we had just begun to get accustomed. The trees were hung with small coloured bulbs and we sat out at metal tables and drank light Portuguese white wine and looked at the gorge and the floodlit dam; it was like luxury to us, and made us feel stylish. That place had been captured by the rebels and pillaged. The main building was basic and very ordinary—walls of concrete blocks around an unroofed dance floor with a covered bar at one side. The walls still stood (though they had tried to set the concrete alight: there were fire marks in many places); but all the fittings had been destroyed. The rage of the rebels was like a rage against metal, machinery, wires, everything that was not of the forest and Africa.

There were signs of that rage in other places as well. After the earlier war a United Nations agency had repaired the power station and the causeway at the top of the dam. A metal plaque set on a small stone pyramid, some distance from the dam itself, recorded this fact. That plaque had been defaced, battered with some heavy metal piece, individual letters filed away. At the beginning of the causeway old cast-iron lamp standards from Europe had been placed as a decorative feature—old lamps at a site of new power. A pretty idea; but the lamp standards had also received a battering, and again attempts had been made to file away the lettering—the name of the nineteenth-century makers in Paris.

It was the rage that made an impression—the rage of simple men tearing at metal with their hands. And already, after only a few weeks of peace, with so many people from the villages hungry and scrounging in the town, it seemed far away, hard to imagine.

It was during these early days of the peace that Father Huismans went out on one of his trips and was killed. His death need never have been discovered; he could easily have been buried somewhere in the bush. But the people who killed him wanted the fact to be known. His body was put in a dugout, and the dugout drifted down the main river until it caught against the bank in a tangle of water hyacinths. His body had been mutilated, his head cut off and spiked. He was buried quickly, with the minimum of ceremony.

It was terrible. His death made his life seem such a waste. So much of his knowledge was buried with him, and what to me was more than knowledge—his attitudes, his relish for Africa, his feeling for the beliefs of the forest. A little bit of the world was lost with him.

I had admired him for his purity, but now I had to ask whether in the end it had been of value. A death like that makes us question everything. But we are men; regardless of the deaths around us we continue to be flesh and blood and mind, and we cannot stay with that questioning mood for long. When the mood went away I felt—what deep down, as a life-loving man, I had never doubted—that he had passed his time better than most of us. The idea Father Huismans had of his civilization had made him live his particular kind of dedicated life. It had sent him looking, inquiring; it had made him find human richness where the rest of us saw bush or had stopped seeing anything at all. But his idea of his civilization was also like his vanity. It had made him read too much in that mingling of peoples by our river; and he had paid for it.

Little was said about the way he had died. But the body had floated down the main river in a dugout and must have been seen by many people. Word got around the lycée. In our town Father Huismans had the reputation—though most people were rather vague about him—of being a lover of Africa; and some of the boys at the lycée were embarrassed and ashamed. Some were aggressive. Ferdinand—recovered from the days of fright, his wish to be back in his father's or mother's village—was one of the aggressive ones. I wasn't surprised.

Ferdinand said, "It is a thing of Europeans, a museum. Here it is going against the god of Africans. We have masks in our houses and we know what they are there for. We don't have to go to Huismans's museum."

"The god of Africans"—the words were Metty's, and Metty had got them from the leader of the uprising against the Arabs on the coast. I had heard the words for the first time that night when we heard the gunfire from the hydroelectric station and knew that we were safe. The words, occurring when they did, seemed to have released certain things in Ferdinand. Those days in the flat had been days of special crisis for Ferdinand, and he had ever since been settling into a new character. This one fitted, or made more sense. He was no longer concerned about being a particular kind of African; he was simply an African, himself, ready to acknowledge all sides of his character.

It didn't make him easier. He abandoned politeness; he became aggressive and perverse, over a secret nervousness. He began to stay away from the shop and flat. I expected that; it was his way of demonstrating, after the great fright of the rebellion, that he could do without me. But then one day Metty brought me a letter from Ferdinand, and the letter moved me. It was a one-sentence letter written in very big letters on a lined sheet roughly torn out from an exercise book, and sent without an envelope, the sheet just folded small and tight. "Salim! You took me in that time and treated me as a member of your own family. F."

It was his letter of thanks. I had given him shelter under my own roof, and to him, as an African, that hospitality was extraordinary and had to be acknowledged. But he didn't want to appear fawning or weak, and everything in the letter was deliberately crude—no envelope, the lined paper torn down one side, the very big and careless handwriting, the absence of the direct word of thanks, the "Salim!" and not "Dear Salim," the "F." and not "Ferdinand."

I found it funny and moving. Yet there was something ironical about the whole thing. The action which had drawn that softness from Ferdinand was the simple gesture of a man from the coast whose family had lived close, too close, to their servants, once their slaves, descendants of people snatched from this part of Africa. Ferdinand would have been outraged if he knew. Still, the letter, and his unapologetic new character, showed how far, as a man, he had rounded out. And that was what his mother, Zabeth, had had in mind when she brought him to the shop and asked me to look after him.

What Ferdinand had said about Father Huismans's collection, other people began to say. While he lived, Father Huismans, collecting the things of Africa, had been thought a friend of Africa. But now that changed. It was felt that the collection was an affront to African religion, and no one at the lycée took it over. Perhaps there was no one there with the knowledge and the eye that were required.

Visitors were sometimes shown the collection. The wooden carvings remained as they were; but in the unventilated gun room the masks began to deteriorate and the smell became more unpleasant. The masks themselves, crumbling on the slatted shelves, seemed to lose the religious power Father Huismans had taught me to see in them; without him, they simply became extravagant objects.

In the long peace that now settled on the town, we began to receive visitors from a dozen countries, teachers, students, helpers in this and that, people who behaved like discoverers of Africa, were happy with everything they found, and looked down quite a bit on foreigners like ourselves who had been living there. The collection began to be pillaged. Who more African than the young American who appeared among us, who more ready to put on African clothes and dance African dances? He left suddenly by the steamer one day; and it was discovered afterwards that the bulk of the collection in the gun room had been crated and shipped back with his belongings to the United States, no doubt to be the nucleus of the gallery of primitive art he often spoke of starting. The richest products of the forest.

TWO

The New Domain

6 If you look at a column of ants on the march you will see that there are some who are stragglers or have lost their way. The column has no time for them; it goes on. Sometimes the stragglers die. But even this has no effect on the column. There is a little disturbance around the corpse, which is eventually carried off—and then it appears so light. And all the time the great busyness continues, and that apparent sociability, that rite of meeting and greeting which ants travelling in opposite directions, to and from their nest, perform without fail.

So it was after the death of Father Huismans. In the old days his death would have caused anger, and people would have wanted to go out to look for his killers. But now we who remained—outsiders, but neither settlers nor visitors, just people with nowhere better to go—put our heads down and got on with our business.

The only message of his death was that we had to be careful ourselves and remember where we were. And oddly enough, by acting as we did, by putting our heads down and getting on with our work, we helped to bring about what he had prophesied for our town. He had said that our town would suffer setbacks but that they would be temporary. After each setback, the civilization of Europe would become a little more secure at the bend in the river; the town would always start up again, and would grow a little more each time. In the peace that we now had, the town wasn't only re-established; it grew. And the rebellion and Father Huismans's death receded fast.

We didn't have Father Huismans's big views. Some of us had our own clear ideas about Africans and their future. But it occurred to me that we did really share his faith in the future.

Unless we believed that change was coming to our part of Africa, we couldn't have done our business. There would have been no point. And—in spite of appearances—we also had the attitude to ourselves that he had to himself. He saw himself as part of a great historical process; he would have seen his own death as unimportant, hardly a disturbance. We felt like that too, but from a different angle.

We were simple men with civilizations but without other homes. Whenever we were allowed to, we did the complicated things we had to do, like the ants. We had the occasional comfort of reward, but in good times or bad we lived with the knowledge that we were expendable, that our labour might at any moment go to waste, that we ourselves might be smashed up; and that others would replace us. To us that was the painful part, that others would come at the better time. But we were like the ants; we kept on.

People in our position move rapidly from depression to optimism and back down again. Now we were in a period of boom. We felt the new ruling intelligence—and energy—from the capital; there was a lot of copper money around; and these two things—order and money—were enough to give us confidence. A little of that went a long way with us. It released our energy; and energy, rather than quickness or great capital, was what we possessed.

All kinds of projects were started. Various government departments came to life again; and the town at last became a place that could be made to work. We already had the steamer service; now the airfield was recommissioned and extended, to take the jets from the capital (and to fly in soldiers). The *cités* filled up, and new ones were built, though nothing that was done could cope with the movement of people from the villages; we never lost the squatters and campers in our central streets and squares. But there were buses now, and many more taxis. We even began to get a new telephone system. It was far too elaborate for our needs, but it was what the Big Man in the capital wanted for us.

The growth of the population could be gauged by the growth

of the rubbish heaps in the *cités*. They didn't burn their rubbish in oil drums, as we did; they just threw it out on the broken streets—that sifted, ashy African rubbish. Those mounds of rubbish, though constantly flattened by rain, grew month by month into increasingly solid little hills, and the hills literally became as high as the box-like concrete houses of the *cités*.

Nobody wanted to move that rubbish. But the taxis stank of disinfectant; the officials of our health department were fierce about taxis. And for this reason. In the colonial days public vehicles had by law to be disinfected once a year by the health department. The disinfectors were entitled to a personal fee. That custom had been remembered. Any number of people wanted to be disinfectors; and now taxis and trucks weren't disinfected just once a year; they were disinfected whenever they were caught. The fee had to be paid each time; and disinfectors in their official jeeps played hide and seek with taxis and trucks among the hills of rubbish. The red dirt roads of our town, neglected for years, had quickly become corrugated with the new traffic we had; and these disinfectant chases were in a curious kind of slow motion, with the vehicles of hunters and hunted pitching up and down the corrugations like launches in a heavy sea.

All the people—like the health officials—who performed services for ready money were energetic, or could be made so: the customs people, the police, and even the army. The administration, however hollow, was fuller; there were people you could appeal to. You could get things done, if you knew how to go about it.

And the town at the bend in the river became again what Father Huismans had said it had always been, long before the peoples of the Indian Ocean or Europe came to it. It became the trading centre for the region, which was vast. *Marchands* came in now from very far away, making journeys much more difficult than Zabeth's; some of those journeys took a week. The steamer didn't go beyond our town; above the rapids there were only dugouts (some with outboard motors) and a few launches. Our town became a goods depot, and I acquired a number of agencies (re-assuming some that Nazruddin had had) for things that until then I had more or less been selling retail.

There was money in agencies. The simpler the product, the simpler and better the business. It was a different kind of business from the retail trade. Electric batteries, for instance—I bought and sold quantities long before they arrived; I didn't have to handle them physically or even see them. It was like dealing in words alone, ideas on paper; it was like a form of play—until one day you were notified that the batteries had arrived, and you went to the customs warehouse and saw that they existed, that workmen somewhere had actually made the things. Such useful things, such necessary things—they would have been acceptable in a plain brown-paper casing; but the people who had made them had gone to the extra trouble of giving them pretty labels, with tempting slogans. Trade, goods! What a mystery! We couldn't make the things we dealt in; we hardly understood their principles. Money alone had brought these magical things to us deep in the bush, and we dealt in them so casually!

Salesmen from the capital, Europeans most of them, preferring to fly up now rather than spend seven days on the steamer coming up and five going down, began to stay at the van der Weyden, and they gave a little variety to our social life. In the Hellenic Club, in the bars, they brought at last that touch of Europe and the big city—the atmosphere in which, from his stories, I had imagined Nazruddin living here.

Mahesh, with his shop just across the road from the van der Weyden, saw the comings and goings, and his excitement led him into a series of little business ventures. It was strange about Mahesh. He was always on the lookout for the big break, but he could spend weeks on things that were quite petty.

He acquired at one time a machine for cutting out or engraving letters and numbers, and he acquired a stack of the very tough plastic plates on which the numbers or letters were to be engraved. His idea was to supply nameplates to the town. He practised at home; Shoba said the noise was terrible. Mahesh, in his flat and in his shop, showed off the practice nameplates as though it was he, rather than the machine, that had made the beautiful letters. The modernity and precision—and, above all, the "manufactured" look of the plates—really excited him, and he was sure it would excite everybody else as well.

He had bought the equipment from a salesman who had stayed at the van der Weyden. And it was typical of Mahesh's casual approach to business that when it came to getting engraving orders, he could only think of crossing the road back to the van der Weyden—reversing the trip of the salesman who had sold him the equipment. He had pinned all his hopes on the van der Weyden. He was going to redo the room numbers, all the *Hommes* and *Dames* signs, and he was going to affix descriptive plates on almost every door downstairs. The van der Weyden alone was going to keep him busy for weeks and pay back for the machine. But the van der Weyden owners (a middle-aged Italian couple who kept themselves in the background and hid behind their African front men) didn't want to play. And not many of us felt the need to have our names on triangular sections of wood on our desks. So that idea was dropped; that tool was forgotten.

Mahesh, broaching a new idea, liked to be mysterious. The time, for instance, he wanted to import a machine from Japan for cutting little flat wood sticks and spoons for ice cream, he didn't say so right out. He began by offering me a sample spoon in a paper wrapper which the salesman had given him. I looked at the little shoe-shaped spoon. What was there to say? He asked me to smell the spoon and then to taste it; and while I did so he looked at me in a way that made me feel that I was going to be surprised. There was no surprise: he was just demonstrating to me—something I must say I had never stopped to think about—that ice cream spoons and sticks shouldn't taste or smell.

He wanted to know whether there was a local wood which was like that nice Japanese wood. To import the wood from Japan with the machine would be too complicated, and might make the sticks and spoons cost more than the ice cream. So for some weeks we thought and talked about wood. The idea interested me; I got taken up with it, and began to look at trees in a different way. We had tasting sessions, smelling and tasting different kinds of wood, including some varieties that Daulat, the man with the trucks, picked up for us on his runs east. But then it occurred to me that it was important to find out—before the spoon-making machine came down—whether the local people, with their own tastes in food, were ready for ice cream. Perhaps there was a good reason why the ice cream idea hadn't occurred to anybody else; and we had Italians in the town, after all. And how was the ice cream going to be made? Where were the milk and the eggs?

Mahesh said, "Do you need eggs to make ice cream?"

I said, "I don't know. I was asking you."

It wasn't the ice cream that attracted Mahesh. It was the idea of that simple machine, or rather the idea of being the only man in the town to own such a machine. When Shoba had met him he had been a motorcycle repairman; and he had been so flattered by her devotion that he had not risen above that kind of person. He remained the man who loved little machines and electrical tools and saw them as magical means of making a living.

I knew a number of men like that on the coast, men of our community; and I believe people like that exist wherever machines are not made. These men are good with their hands and gifted in their own way. They are dazzled by the machines they import. That is part of their intelligence; but they soon start behaving as though they don't just own the machines, but the patents as well; they would like to be the only men in the world with such magical instruments. Mahesh was looking for the wonderful imported thing which he would own exclusively, the simple thing which would provide a short-cut to power and money. So that in this respect Mahesh was only a notch or two above the *marchands* who came to the town to buy modern goods to take back to their villages.

I used to wonder how someone like Mahesh had survived all that he had survived in our town. There was a kind of quiet wisdom or canniness there, no doubt of that. But I also began to feel that he had survived because he was casual, without doubts or deep anxieties, and—in spite of his talk of getting out to a better country (standard talk among us)—without deeper ambitions. He suited the place; he would have found it hard to survive anywhere else.

Shoba was his life. She told him—or by her devotion showed him—how fine he was; and I believe he saw himself as she saw him. Outside that, he took things as they came. And now in the most casual way, with almost no attempt at secrecy or guile, he became involved in "business" deals that frightened me when he told me about them. He seemed unable to resist anything that might be described as a business offer. And most of those business offers came to him now from the army.

I wasn't too happy with our new army. I preferred the men from the warrior tribe, for all their roughness. I understood their tribal pride and—always making allowance for that—I had found them straight. The officers of the new army were a different breed. No warrior code there; no code. They were all in varying ways like Ferdinand, and they were often as young as Ferdinand. They were as aggressive, but without Ferdinand's underlying graciousness.

They wore their uniforms the way Ferdinand had at one time worn his lycée blazer: they saw themselves both as the new men of Africa and the men of the new Africa. They made such play with the national flag and the portrait of the President—the two now always going together—that in the beginning I thought, after all that the country had gone through, and all that had happened to them, the officers, all the lucky accidents that had taken them where they had got, in the beginning I thought these new officers stood for a new, constructive pride. But they were simpler. The flag and the President's portrait were only like their fetishes, the sources of their authority. They didn't see, these young men, that there was anything to build in their country. As far as they were concerned, it was all there already. They had only to take. They believed that, by being what they were, they had earned the right to take; and the higher the officer, the greater the crookedness—if that word had any meaning.

With their guns and jeeps, these men were poachers of ivory and thieves of gold. Ivory, gold—add slaves, and it would have been like being back in oldest Africa. And these men would have dealt in slaves, if there was still a market. It was to the traders in the town that the army turned when they wished to clear their gold or, more especially, the ivory they had poached. Officials and governments right across the continent were engaged in this ivory trade which they themselves had declared illegal. It made smuggling easy; but I was nervous of getting involved, because a government that breaks its own laws can also easily break you. Your business associate today can be your jailer or worse tomorrow.

But Mahesh didn't mind. Like a child, as it seemed to me, he accepted all the poisoned sweets that were offered him. But he wasn't a child; he knew the sweets were poisoned.

He said, "Oh, they will let you down. But if they let you down, you pay up. That is all. In your costing you make allowances for that. You just pay. I don't think you understand, Salim. And it isn't an easy thing to understand. It isn't that there's no right and wrong here. There's no right."

Twice, miraculously interpreting a nonsense telephone call from him as an appeal for help, I had to take away things from his flat.

The first time, one afternoon, after some inconsequential talk from him about tennis and the shoes I had asked for, I drove to his flat and blew my horn. He didn't come down. He opened a window of his sitting room and shouted down to me in the street, "I'm sending the boy down with the tennis shoes for you. Right, Salim!" And, still standing before the window, he turned and shouted in patois to someone inside. " 'Phonse! Aoutchikong pour Mis' Salim!"—aoutchikong, from caoutchouc, the French word for rubber, being patois for canvas shoes. With many people looking on, the boy Ildephonse brought down something roughly wrapped in newspaper. I threw it on the back seat and drove off without hanging around. It turned out, when I examined it later, to be a bundle of foreign bank notes; and it went, as soon as it was dark, into the hole in the ground at the foot of my external staircase. To help Mahesh like this, though, was only to encourage him. The next time I had to bury some ivory. Burying ivory! What age were we living in? What did people want ivory for, apart from carving it—and not too well these days—into cigarette holders and figurines and junk like that?

Still, these deals made Mahesh money, and he acknowledged

my help and put me in the way of adding to my little store of gold. He had said that there was no right. It was hard for me to adapt to that; but he managed it beautifully. He was always cool and casual, never ruffled. I had to admire him for it. Though the casualness could lead him into situations that were quite ridiculous.

He said to me one day, with the mysterious, over-innocent manner he put on when he was about to tell about some deal: "You read the foreign papers, Salim. Are you keeping an eye on the copper market? What's it like?" Well, copper was high. We all knew that; copper was at the bottom of our little boom. He said, "It's that war the Americans are fighting. I hear they've used up more copper in the last two years than the world has used in the last two centuries." This was boom talk, salesmen's chat from the van der Weyden. Mahesh, just across the road, picked up a fair amount of that chat; without it, he might have had less idea than he had of what was happening in the world.

From copper he turned to the other metals, and we talked for a while, quite ignorantly, about the prospects for tin and lead. Then he said, "Uranium—what about that? What are they quoting that at now?"

I said, "I don't think they quote that."

He gave me his innocent look. "But it must be pretty high? A chap here wants to sell a piece."

"Do they sell uranium in pieces? What does it look like?"

"I haven't seen it. But the chap wants to sell it for a million dollars."

That was what we were like. One day grubbing for food, opening rusty tins, cooking on charcoal braziers and over holes in the ground; and now talking of a million dollars as though we had talked of millions all our lives.

Mahesh said, "I told the general it could be sold only to a foreign power, and he told me to go ahead. You know old Mancini. He is consul for quite a few countries here—that's a nice line of business, I always think. I went to see him. I told him straight out, but he wasn't interested. In fact, Mancini went crazy. He ran to the door and closed it and stood with his back against it and told me to get out. His face was red, red. Everybody's frightened of the Big Man in the capital. What do you think I should tell the general, Salim? He's frightened too. He told me he stole it from some top-security place. I wouldn't like to make an enemy of the general. I wouldn't like him to think I hadn't tried. What do you think I should tell him? Seriously, seriously."

"You say he's frightened?"

"Very frightened."

"Then tell him he's being watched and he mustn't come to see you again."

I looked in my science magazines and children's encyclopaedia parts (I had grown to love those) and read up on uranium. Uranium is one of those things we all hear about but not many of us know about. Like oil. I used to think, from hearing and reading about oil reservoirs, that oil ran in trapped underground streams. It was my encyclopaedia parts which told me that oil reservoirs were of stone and could even be of marble, with the oil in tiny pockets. It was in just such a way, I suppose, that the general, hearing of the immense value of uranium, had thought of it as a kind of super-precious metal, a kind of gold nugget. Mancini the consul, must have thought so too. My reading told me of tons and tons of ore that had to be processed and reduced—but reduced to hefty blocks.

The general, offering a "piece," might have been duped himself. But for some reason—Mahesh might have told him he was being watched—he never troubled Mahesh again. And not long afterwards he was posted away from our town. It was the method of the new President: he gave his men power and authority, but he never allowed them to settle in anywhere and become local kings. He saved us a lot of trouble.

Mahesh went on as coolly as before. The only man who had had a fright was Mancini, the consul.

That was what we were like in those days. We felt that there was treasure around us, waiting to be picked up. It was the bush that gave us this feeling. During the empty, idle time, we had been indifferent to the bush; during the days of the rebellion it had depressed us. Now it excited us—the unused earth, with the promise of the unused. We forgot that others had been here before us, and had felt like us.

I shared in the boom. I was energetic in my own modest way. But I was also restless. You so quickly get used to peace. It is like being well—you take it for granted, and forget that when you were ill, to be well again had seemed everything. And with peace and the boom I began to see the town as ordinary, for the first time.

The flat, the shop, the market outside the shop, the Hellenic Club, the bars, the life of the river, the dugouts, the water hyacinths—I knew it so well. And especially on hot sunny afternoons—that hard light, those black shadows, that feeling of stillness—it seemed without further human promise.

I didn't see myself spending the rest of my days at that bend in the river, like Mahesh and the others. In my own mind I separated myself from them. I still thought of myself as a man just passing through. But where was the good place? I couldn't say. I never thought constructively about it. I was waiting for some illumination to come to me, to guide me to the good place and the "life" I was still waiting for.

From time to time now letters from my father on the coast reminded me of his wish to see me settled—married to Nazruddin's daughter: that was almost like a family commitment. But I was less prepared than ever for that. Though it was a comfort on occasion to play with the idea that outside this place a whole life waited for me, all the relationships that bind a man to the earth and give him a feeling of having a place. But I knew that it wasn't like that really. I knew that for us the world was no longer as safe as that.

And again events caught up with my anxieties. There was trouble in Uganda, where Nazruddin had a cotton-ginning business. Uganda up till then had been the secure and well-run country Nazruddin had tried to excite us about, the country which received refugees from neighbouring countries. Now in Uganda itself a king was overthrown and forced to flee; Daulat brought back stories of yet another army on the loose. Nazrud-din, as I remembered, lived with the knowledge that, after all his luck, things were going to end badly for him; and I thought that his luck had run out now. But I was wrong; Nazruddin's luck was still with him. The trouble in Uganda didn't last; only the king suffered. Life there went back to normal. But I began to fear for Nazruddin and his family, and the idea of marriage to his daughter ceased to be the idea of a correct family duty. It became a more oppressive kind of responsibility, and I pushed it to the back of my mind as something I would face when I absolutely had to.

So in the midst of the boom I had my anxieties and became almost as dissatisfied and restless as I had been at the beginning. It wasn't only outside pressures, or my solitude and my temperament. It also had to do with the place itself, the way it had altered with the peace. It was nobody's fault. It was something that had just happened. During the days of the rebellion I had had the sharpest sense of the beauty of the river and the forest, and had promised myself that when the peace came I would expose myself to it, learn it, possess that beauty. I had done nothing of the sort; when the peace came I had simply stopped looking about me. And now I felt that the mystery and the magic of the place had gone.

In those days of fear I felt we had been in touch, through the Africans, with the spirits of the river and forest; and that everything had been full of tension. But all the spirits seemed now to have left the place, as, after Father Huismans's death, the spirits appeared to have left his masks. We had been so nervous of the Africans during those days; we hadn't taken any man for granted. We had been the intruders, the ordinary men, they the inspired ones. Now the spirits had left them; they were ordinary, squalid, poor. Without effort we had become, in a real way, the masters, with the gifts and skills they needed. And we were so simple. On the land now ordinary again we had arranged such ordinary lives for ourselves—in the bars and brothels, the night-clubs. Oh, it was unsatisfactory. Yet what else could we do? We did only what we could do. We followed Mahesh's motto: we carried on.

Mahesh did more than that. He pulled off a coup. He continued to consult catalogues, fill in coupons, write off for further information; and at last he found the package he had been looking for, the thing he could import whole and use as a short-cut to business and money. He got the Bigburger franchise for our town.

It wasn't what I was expecting. He had been running an odd little shop that dealt in ironmongery of various sorts, electrical goods, cameras, binoculars, lots of little gadgets. Hamburgers—Bigburgers—didn't seem to be his thing. I wasn't even sure that the town would go for Bigburgers. But he had no doubts.

He said, "They've done their market research and they've decided to make a big push in Africa. They have an area office now in one of the French places on the west coast. The chap came the other day and measured up and everything. They don't just send you the sauce, you know, Salim. They send you the whole shop."

And that was what they did. The crates that came up on the steamer in a couple of months did contain the whole shop: the stoves, the milk-shake machines, the coffee machine, the cups and plates, the tables and chairs, the made-to-measure counter, the stools, the made-to-measure wall panelling with the Bigburger design. And after all this serious stuff there were the toys: the Bigburger cruets, the Bigburger ketchup containers, the Bigburger menus and menu holders, and the lovely advertisements: "Bigburgers—The Big One—The Bigwonderful One," with pictures of different kinds of Bigburgers.

I thought the Bigburger pictures looked like smooth white lips of bread over mangled black tongues of meat. But Mahesh didn't like it when I told him, and I decided not to say anything disrespectful about Bigburgers again. Mahesh had been full of jokes about the project; but as soon as the stuff arrived he became deadly serious—he had become Bigburger.

Mahesh's shop was structurally quite simple, the standard concrete box of our town; and in no time the local Italian builder had cleared it of Mahesh's shelves, rewired, put in new plumbing, and fitted up a dazzling snack bar that seemed to have been imported from the United States. The whole prefabricated business did work; and it was great fun to be in Bigburger, to leave the sewer smells of the street, and the dust and the rubbish, and to step into this modern interior, with the advertisements and everything. So Mahesh did, after all, pull it off.

The prettiness had an effect on Shoba too. It made her energetic and brought out something of her family business talents. She organized the place and soon had it running smoothly. She arranged for the deliveries of meat from our new supermarket (the meat came from South Africa, like our eggs now) and she arranged with an Italian for the loaves. She trained the boys and worked out their schedules.

Ildephonse, the houseboy, was taken from the flat and given a Bigburger chef's cap and a yellow Bigburger jacket and put behind the counter. It was Mahesh's idea to give Ildephonse a label for his jacket with his name and the designation—in English, for the extra style—Manager. Mahesh did little things like that sometimes which showed you that, casual as he was, he knew instinctively how to operate in our town. He said he called Ildephonse the manager to ward off African resentment of the new, rich-looking place, and also to attract African customers. And he made a point of leaving Ildephonse in charge for some hours every day.

It was strange about Ildephonse, though. He loved his Bigburger costume and he loved his new job. No one was quicker and more friendly and more anxious to please than he was, when Shoba or Mahesh was around. They trusted Ildephonse; they boasted of their trust in him, in his presence. Yet as soon as he was left alone he became a different person. He went vacant. Not rude, just vacant. I noticed this alteration in the African staff in other places as well. It made you feel that while they did their jobs in their various glossy settings, they were only acting for the people who employed them; that the job itself was meaningless to them; and that they had the gift—when they were left alone, and had no one to act for—of separating themselves in spirit from their setting, their job, their uniform.

Bigburger was a success. The van der Weyden, across the road, was content to make money from its beds and rooms. The service and the kitchens there drove people out to look for food, and Bigburger was perfectly placed to capture that refugee trade. Bigburger attracted a lot of African officials and army people as well—they liked the décor and the modernity. So that Mahesh, from running a nondescript little hardware shop, found himself at the centre of things in our town.

All this happened quickly, in less than a year. Everything happened quickly now. It was as though everyone felt he had to make up for the lost years, or as though everyone felt that time was short, that the place might close down at any moment again.

Mahesh said to me one day, "Noimon offered me two million. But you know Noimon. When he offers two, you know it's worth four."

Noimon was one of our local big Greeks. The new furniture shop—doing fantastic business—was just one of his ventures. The two million he offered were local francs, which were thirty-six to the dollar.

Mahesh said, "I suppose your place is worth a lot now. Nazruddin offered it to me, you know. A hundred and fifty thousand. What do you think you'll get for it now?"

You heard that kind of property talk everywhere now. Everyone was totting up how much he had gained with the boom, how much he was worth. People learned to speak huge figures calmly.

There had been a boom before, just at the end of the colonial period, and the ruined suburb near the rapids was what it had left behind. Nazruddin had told a story about that. He had gone out there one Sunday morning, had thought that the place was bush rather than real estate, and had decided to sell. Lucky for him then; but now that dead suburb was being rehabilitated. That development or redevelopment had become the most important feature of our boom. And it had caused the big recent rise in property values in the town.

The bush near the rapids was being cleared. The ruins which had seemed permanent were being levelled by bulldozers; new avenues were being laid out. It was the Big Man's doing. The government had taken over all that area and decreed it the Domain of the State, and the Big Man was building what looked like a little town there. It was happening very fast. The copper money was pouring in, pushing up prices in our town. The deep, earth-shaking burr of bulldozers competed with the sound of the rapids. Every steamer brought up European builders and artisans, every airplane. The van der Weyden seldom had rooms to spare.

Everything the President did had a reason. As a ruler in what was potentially hostile territory, he was creating an area where he and his flag were supreme. As an African, he was building a new town on the site of what had been a rich European suburb —but what he was building was meant to be grander. In the town the only "designed" modern building was the van der Weyden; and to us the larger buildings of the Domain were startling—concrete louvres, pierced concrete blocks of great size, tinted glass. The smaller buildings—houses and bungalows —were more like what we were used to. But even they were on the large side and, with air conditioners sticking out in many places like building blocks that had slipped, looked extravagant.

No one was sure, even after some of the houses were furnished, what the Domain was to be used for. There were stories of a great new model farm and agricultural college; a conference hall to serve the continent; holiday houses for loyal citizens. From the President himself there came no statement. We watched and wondered while the buildings were run up. And then we began to understand that what the President was attempting was so stupendous in his own eyes that even he would not have wanted to proclaim it. He was creating modern Africa. He was creating a miracle that would astound the rest of the world. He was by-passing real Africa, the difficult Africa of bush and villages, and creating something that would match anything that existed in other countries.

Photographs of this State Domain—and of others like it in other parts of the country—began to appear in those magazines about Africa that were published in Europe but subsidized by governments like ours. In these photographs the message of the

Domain was simple. Under the rule of our new President the miracle had occurred: Africans had become modern men who built in concrete and glass and sat in cushioned chairs covered in imitation velvet. It was like a curious fulfilment of Father Huismans's prophecy about the retreat of African Africa, and the success of the European graft.

Visitors were encouraged, from the *cités* and shanty towns, from the surrounding villages. On Sundays there were buses and army trucks to take people there, and soldiers acted as guides, taking people along one-way paths marked with directional arrows, showing the people who had recently wished to destroy the town what their President had done for Africa. Such shoddy buildings, after you got used to the shapes; such flashy furniture —Noimon was making a fortune with his furniture shop. All around, the life of dugout and creek and village continued; in the bars in the town the foreign builders and artisans drank and made easy jokes about the country. It was painful and it was sad.

The President had wished to show us a new Africa. And I saw Africa in a way I had never seen it before, saw the defeats and humiliations which until then I had regarded as just a fact of life. And I felt like that—full of tenderness for the Big Man, for the ragged villagers walking around the Domain, and the soldiers showing them the shabby sights—until some soldier played the fool with me or some official at the customs was difficult, and then I fell into the old way of feeling, the easier attitudes of the foreigners in the bars. Old Africa, which seemed to absorb everything, was simple; this place kept you tense. What a strain it was, picking your way through stupidity and aggressiveness and pride and hurt!

But what was the Domain to be used for? The buildings gave pride, or were meant to; they satisfied some personal need of the President's. Was that all they were for? But they had consumed millions. The farm didn't materialize. The Chinese or the Taiwanese didn't turn up to till the land of the new model African farm; the six tractors that some foreign government had given remained in a neat line in the open and rusted, and the grass grew high about them. The big swimming pool near the building that was said to be a conference hall developed leaks and remained empty, with a wide-meshed rope net at the top. The Domain had been built fast, and in the sun and the rain decay also came fast. After the first rainy season many of the young trees that had been planted beside the wide main avenue died, their roots waterlogged and rotted.

But for the President in the capital the Domain remained a living thing. Statues were added, and lamp standards. The Sunday visits went on; the photographs continued to appear in the subsidized magazines that specialized in Africa. And then at last a use was found for the buildings.

The Domain became a university city and a research centre. The conference-hall building was turned into a polytechnic for people of the region, and other buildings were turned into dormitories and staff quarters. Lecturers and professors began to come from the capital, and soon from other countries; a parallel life developed there, of which we in the town knew little. And it was to the polytechnic there—on the site of the dead European suburb that to me, when I first came, had suggested the ruins of a civilization that had come and gone—that Ferdinand was sent on a government scholarship, when he had finished at the lycée.

The Domain was some miles away from the town. There was a bus service, but it was irregular. I hadn't been seeing much of Ferdinand, and now I saw even less of him. Metty lost a friend. That move of Ferdinand's finally made the difference between the two men clear, and I thought that Metty suffered.

My own feelings were more complicated. I saw a disordered future for the country. No one was going to be secure here; no man of the country was to be envied. Yet I couldn't help thinking how lucky Ferdinand was, how easy it had been made for him. You took a boy out of the bush and you taught him to read and write; you levelled the bush and built a polytechnic and you sent him there. It seemed as easy as that, if you came late to the world and found ready-made those things that other countries and peoples had taken so long to arrive at—writing, printing, universities, books, knowledge. The rest of us had to take things in stages. I thought of my own family, Nazruddin, myself—we were so clogged by what the centuries had deposited in our minds and hearts. Ferdinand, starting from nothing, had with one step made himself free, and was ready to race ahead of us.

The Domain, with its shoddy grandeur, was a hoax. Neither the President who had called it into being nor the foreigners who had made a fortune building it had faith in what they were creating. But had there been greater faith before? *Miscerique probat populos et foedera jungi*: Father Huismans had explained the arrogance of that motto. He had believed in its truth. But how many of the builders of the earlier city would have agreed with him? Yet that earlier hoax had helped to make men of the country in a certain way; and men would also be made by this new hoax. Ferdinand took the polytechnic seriously; it was going to lead him to an administrative cadetship and eventually to a position of authority. To him the Domain was fine, as it should be. He was as glamorous to himself at the polytechnic as he had been at the lycée.

It was absurd to be jealous of Ferdinand, who still after all went home to the bush. But I wasn't jealous of him only because I felt that he was about to race ahead of me in knowledge and enter realms I would never enter. I was jealous more of that idea he had always had of his own importance, his own glamour. We lived on the same patch of earth; we looked at the same views. Yet to him the world was new and getting newer. For me that same world was drab, without possibilities.

I grew to detest the physical feel of the place. My flat remained as it had always been. I had changed nothing there, because I lived with the idea that at a moment's notice I had to consider it all as lost—the bedroom with the white-painted window panes and the big bed with the foam mattress, the roughly made cupboards with my smelly clothes and shoes, the kitchen with its smell of kerosene and frying oil and rust and dirt and cockroaches, the empty white studio–sitting room. Always there, never really mine, reminding me now only of the passing of time.

I detested the imported ornamental trees, the trees of my childhood, so unnatural here, with the red dust of the streets that turned to mud in rain, the overcast sky that meant only more heat, the clear sky that meant a sun that hurt, the rain that seldom cooled and made for a general clamminess, the brown river with the lilac-coloured flowers on rubbery green vines that floated on and on, night and day.

Ferdinand had moved only a few miles away. And I, so recently his senior, felt jealous and deserted.

Metty, too, was like a man with preoccupations. Freedom had its price. Once he had had the slave's security. Here he had gained an idea of himself as a man to be measured against other men. That had so far brought him only pleasure. But now it seemed to have brought him a little bitterness as well. He seemed to be staying away from his friends.

He was full of friends, and all kinds of people came to the shop and the flat to ask about him. Or sometimes they sent others to ask about him. One such messenger I grew to recognize. She was like a very thin boy, the kind of girl you would see poling the dugouts, someone regarded by her people just as labour, a pair of hands. Hard work and bad food appeared to have neutered her, worn away her feminine characteristics, and left her almost bald.

She used to come for Metty at the shop, hanging around outside. Sometimes he spoke to her; sometimes he was rough with her. Sometimes he made as if to chase her away, bending down to pick up an imaginary stone, the way people did here when they wanted to frighten away a pariah dog. No one like the slave for spotting the slave, or knowing how to deal with the slave. This girl was among the lowest of the low; her status, in whatever African household she was, would have been close to that of a slave.

Metty succeeded in driving her away from the shop. But one afternoon, when I went to the flat after closing the shop, I saw her on the pavement outside, standing among the dusty hummocks of wild grass near the side entrance to our back yard. An ashy, unwashed cotton smock, wide-sleeved and wide-necked, hung loosely from her bony shoulders and showed she was wearing nothing else below. Her hair was so sparse her head looked shaved. Her thin little face was set in a frown which wasn't a frown but was only meant to say she wasn't looking at me.

She was still there when, after making myself some tea, and changing, I went down again. I was going to the Hellenic Club for my afternoon squash. It was my rule: whatever the circumstances, however unwilling the spirit, never give up the day's exercise. Afterwards I drove out to the dam, to the Portuguese nightclub on the cliff, now got going again, and had some fried fish there—I am sure they did it better in Portugal. It was too early for the band and the town crowd, but the dam was floodlit, and they turned on the coloured lights on the trees for me.

The girl was still on the pavement when I went back to the flat. This time she spoke to me. She said, "*Metty-ki là?*"

She had only a few words of the local patois, but she could understand it when it was spoken, and when I asked her what she wanted she said, "*Popo malade. Dis-li Metty.*"

Popo was "baby." Metty had a baby somewhere in the town, and the baby was sick. Metty had a whole life out there, separate from his life with me in the flat, separate from his bringing me coffee in the mornings, separate from the shop.

I was shocked. I felt betrayed. If we had been living in our compound on the coast, he would have lived his own life, but there would have been no secrets. I would have known who his woman was; I would have known when his baby was born. I had lost Metty to this part of Africa. He had come to the place that was partly his home, and I had lost him. I felt desolate. I had been hating the place, hating the flat; yet now I saw the life I had made for myself in that flat as something good, which I had lost.

Like the girl outside, like so many other people, I waited for Metty. And when, very late, he came in, I began to speak at once.

"Oh, Metty, why didn't you tell me? Why did you do this to me?" Then I called him by the name we called him at home.

"Ali, Ali-wa! We lived together. I took you under my roof and treated you as a member of my own family. And now you do this."

Dutifully, like the servant of the old days, he tried to match his mood to mine, tried to look as though he suffered with me.

"I will leave her, *patron*. She's an animal."

"How can you leave her? You've done it. You can't go back on that. You've got that child out there. Oh, Ali, what have you done? Don't you think it's disgusting to have a little African child running about in somebody's yard, with its *toto* swinging from side to side? Aren't you ashamed, a boy like you?"

"It is disgusting, Salim." He came and put his hand on my shoulder. "And I am very ashamed. She's only an African woman. I will leave her."

"How can you leave her? That is now your life. Didn't you know it was going to be like that? We sent you to school, we had the mullahs teach you. And now you do this."

I was acting. But there are times when we act out what we really feel, times when we cannot cope with certain emotions, and it is easier to act. And Metty was acting too, being loyal, reminding me of the past, of other places, reminding me of things I could scarcely bear that night. When I said, acting, "Why didn't you tell me, Metty?" he acted back for my sake. He said, "How could I tell you, Salim? I knew you were going to get on like this."

How did he know?

I said, "You know, Metty, the first day you went to school, I went with you. You cried all the time. You began to cry as soon as we left the house."

He liked being reminded of this, being remembered from so far back. He said, almost smiling, "I cried a lot? I made a lot of noise?"

"Ali, you screamed the place down. You had your white cap on, and you went down the little alley at the side of Gokool's house, and you were bawling. I couldn't see where you had gone. I just heard you bawling. I couldn't stand it. I thought they were doing terrible things to you, and I begged for you not to go to school. Then the trouble was to get you to come back home. You've forgotten, and why should you remember? I've been noticing you since you've been here. You've been very much getting on as though you're your own man."

"Oh, Salim! You mustn't say that. I always show you respect."

That was true. But he had returned home; he had found his new life. However much he wished it, he couldn't go back. He had shed the past. His hand on my shoulder—what good was that now?

I thought: Nothing stands still. Everything changes. I will inherit no house, and no house that I build will now pass to my children. That way of life has gone. I have lost my twenties, and what I have been looking for since I left home hasn't come to me. I have only been waiting. I will wait for the rest of my life. When I came here, this flat was still the Belgian lady's flat. It wasn't my home; it was like a camp. Then that camp became mine. Now it has changed again.

Later, I woke to the solitude of my bedroom, in the unfriendly world. I felt all the child's heartache at being in a strange place. Through the white-painted window I saw the trees outside— not their shadows, but the suggestion of their forms. I was homesick, had been homesick for months. But home was hardly a place I could return to. Home was something in my head. It was something I had lost. And in that I was like the ragged Africans who were so abject in the town we serviced.

7 Discovering the ways of pain, the aging that it brings, I wasn't surprised that Metty and myself should have been so close just at that moment when we understood that we had to go our separate ways. What had given the illusion of closeness that evening was only our regret for the past, our sadness that the world doesn't stand still.

Our life together didn't change. He continued to live in his room in the flat, and he continued to bring me coffee in the mornings. But now it was understood that he had a whole life outside. He altered. He lost the brightness and gaiety of the servant who knows that he will be looked after, that others will decide for him; and he lost what went with that brightness—the indifference to what had just happened, the ability to forget, the readiness for every new day. He seemed to go a little sour inside. Responsibility was new to him; and with that he must also have discovered solitude, in spite of his friends and his new family life.

I, too, breaking out of old ways, had discovered solitude and the melancholy which is at the basis of religion. Religion turns that melancholy into uplifting fear and hope. But I had rejected the ways and comforts of religion; I couldn't turn to them again, just like that. That melancholy about the world remained something I had to put up with on my own. At some times it was sharp; at some times it wasn't there.

And just when I had digested that sadness about Metty and the past, someone from the past turned up. He walked into the shop one morning, Metty leading him in, Metty calling out in high excitement, "Salim! Salim!"

It was Indar, the man who had first brought out my panic on the coast, confronted me—after that game of squash in the squash court of his big house—with my own fears about our future, and had sent me away from his house with a vision of disaster. He had given me the idea of flight. He had gone to England, to his university; I had fled here.

And I felt now, as Metty led him in, that he had caught me out again, sitting at my desk in the shop, with my goods spread out on the floor, as they had always been, and with my shelves full of cheap cloth and oilcloth and batteries and exercise books.

He said, "I heard some years ago in London that you were here. I wondered what you were doing." His expression was cool, balanced between irritation and a sneer, and it seemed to say that he didn't have to ask now, and that he wasn't surprised by what he had found.

It had happened so quickly. When Metty came running in

saying, "Salim! Salim! Guess who's here," I had at once had an idea that it would be someone we had both known in the old days. I thought it would be Nazruddin, or some member of my family, some brother-in-law or nephew. And I had thought: But I can't cope. The life here is no longer the old life. I cannot accept this responsibility. I don't want to run a hospital.

Expecting, then, someone who was about to make a claim on me in the name of family and community and religion, and preparing a face and an attitude for that person, I was dismayed to find Metty leading Indar into the shop, Metty beside himself with joy, not pretending now, but for that moment delighted to re-create something of the old days, being the man in touch with great families. And from being myself the man full of complaint, the man who was going to pour out his melancholy in harsh advice to a new arrival who was perhaps already half crushed— "There is no place for you here. There is no place here for the homeless. Find somewhere else"—from being that kind of man, I had to be the opposite. I had to be the man who was doing well and more than well, the man whose drab shop concealed some bigger operation that made millions. I had to be the man who had planned it all, who had come to the destroyed town at the bend in the river because he had foreseen the rich future.

I couldn't be any other way with Indar. He had always made me feel so backward. His family, though new on the coast, had outstripped us all; and even their low beginnings—the grand-father who was a railway labourer, then a market money-lender —had become (from the way people spoke) a little sacred, part of their wonderful story. They invested adventurously and spent money well; their way of living was much finer than ours; and there was their unusual passion for games and physical exercise. I had always thought of them as "modern" people, with a style quite different from ours. You get used to differences like that; they can even begin to appear natural.

When we had played squash that afternoon, and Indar had told me he was going to England to a university, I hadn't felt resentful or jealous of him for what he was doing. Going abroad, the university—that was part of his style, what might have been expected. My unhappiness was the unhappiness of a man who felt left behind, unprepared for what was coming. And my resentment of him had to do with the insecurity he had made me feel. He had said, "We're washed up here, you know." The words were true; I knew they were true. But I disliked him for speaking them: he had spoken as someone who had foreseen it all and had made his dispositions.

Eight years had passed since that day. What he had said would happen had happened. His family had lost a lot; they had lost their house; they (who had added the name of the town on the coast to their family name) had scattered, like my own family. Yet now, as he came into the shop, it seemed that the distance between us had remained the same.

There was London in his clothes, the trousers, the striped cotton shirt, the way his hair was cut, his shoes (oxblood in colour, thin-soled but sturdy, a little too narrow at the toes). And I—well, I was in my shop, with the red dirt road and the market square outside. I had waited so long, endured so much, changed; yet to him I hadn't changed at all.

So far I had remained sitting. As I stood up I had a little twinge of fear. It came to me that he had reappeared only to bring me bad news. And all I could find to say was: "What brings you to the back of beyond?"

He said, "I wouldn't say that. You are where it's at."

" 'Where it's at'?"

"Where big things are happening. Otherwise I wouldn't be here."

That was a relief. At least he wasn't giving me my marching orders again, without telling me where to go.

Metty all this while was smiling at Indar and swinging his head from side to side, saying, "Indar! Indar!" And it was Metty who remembered our duty as hosts. He said, "You would like some coffee, Indar?" As though we were on the coast, in the family shop, and he just had to step down the lane to Noor's stall and bring back the little brass cups of sweet and muddy coffee on a heavy brass tray. No coffee like that here; only Nescafé, made in the Ivory Coast, and served in big china cups. Not the same kind of drink: you couldn't chat over it, sighing at each hot sweet sip.

Indar said, "That would be very nice, Ali."

I said, "His name here is Metty. It means 'half-caste.' "

"You let them call you that, Ali?"

"African people, Indar. *Kafar.* You know what they give."

I said, "Don't believe him. He loves it. It makes him a great hit with the girls. Ali's a big family man now. He's lost."

Metty, going to the storeroom to boil the water for the Nes-café, said, "Salim, Salim. Don't let me down too much."

Indar said, "He was lost a long time ago. Have you heard from Nazruddin? I saw him in Uganda a few weeks ago."

"What's it like out there now?"

"Settling down. For how long is another matter. Not one bloody paper has spoken up for the king. Did you know that? When it comes to Africa, people don't want to know or they have their principles. Nobody cares a damn about the people who live in the place."

"But you do a lot of travelling."

"It's my business. How are things with you here?"

"It's been very good since the rebellion. The place is booming. Property is fantastic. Land is two hundred francs a square foot in some parts now."

Indar didn't look impressed—but the shop wasn't an impressive place. I felt, too, I had run on a little bit and was doing the opposite of what I intended to do with Indar. Wishing to let him know that his assumptions about me were wrong, I was in fact acting out the character he saw me as. I was talking the way I had heard traders in the town talk, and even saying the things they said.

I said, attempting another kind of language, "It's a specialized business. A sophisticated market would be easier in some ways. But here you can't follow your personal likes and dislikes. You have to know exactly what is needed. And of course there are the agencies. That's where the real money is."

Indar said, "Yes, yes. The agencies. It's like old times for you, Salim."

I let that pass. But I decided to tone the whole thing down. I said, "I don't know how long it's going to last, though."

"It will last as long as your President wants it to last. And no one can tell how long that will be. He's a strange man. He seems to be doing nothing at all, and then he can act like a surgeon. Cutting away some part he doesn't like."

"That's how he settled the old army. It was terrible, Indar. He sent a message to Colonel Yenyi telling him to stay at the barracks and to welcome the commander of the mercenaries. So he stayed on the steps in full uniform, and when they arrived he began to walk to the gate. They shot him as he walked. And everybody with him."

"It saved your bacon, though. I have something for you, by the way. I went to see your father and mother before I came here."

"You went home?" But I dreaded hearing about it from him.

He said, "Oh, I've been there a few times since the great events. It isn't so bad. You remember our house? They've painted it in the party colours. It's some kind of party building now. Your mother gave me a bottle of coconut chutney. It isn't for you alone. It is for Ali and you. She made that clear." And to Metty, coming back then with the jug of hot water and the cups and the tin of Nescafé and the condensed milk, he said, "Ma sent you some coconut chutney, Ali."

Metty said, "Chutney, coconut chutney. The food here is *horrible*, Indar."

We sat all three around the desk, stirring coffee and water and condensed milk together.

Indar said, "I didn't want to go back. Not the first time. I didn't think my heart could stand it. But the airplane is a wonderful thing. You are still in one place when you arrive at the other. The airplane is faster than the heart. You arrive quickly and you leave quickly. You don't grieve too much. And there is something else about the airplane. You can go back many times to the same place. And something strange happens if you go back often enough. You stop grieving for the past. You see that the past is something in your mind alone, that it doesn't exist in real life. You trample on the past, you crush it. In the beginning it is like trampling on a garden. In the end you are just walking on ground. That is the way we have to learn to live now. The past is here." He touched his heart. "It isn't there." And he pointed at the dusty road.

I felt he had spoken the words before, or had gone over them in his mind. I thought: He fights to keep his style. He's probably suffered more than the rest of us.

We sat, the three of us, drinking Nescafé. And I thought the moment beautiful.

Still, the conversation had so far been one-sided. He knew everything about me; I knew nothing about his recent life. When I had first arrived in the town I had noticed that for most people conversation meant answering questions about themselves; they seldom asked you about yourself; they had been cut off for too long. I didn't want Indar to feel that way about me. And I really wanted to know about him. So, a little awkwardly, I began to ask.

He said he had been in the town for a couple of days and was going to stay for a few months. Had he come up by the steamer? He said, "You're crazy. Cooped up with river Africans for seven days? I flew up."

Metty said, "I wouldn't go anywhere by the steamer. They tell me it's horrible. And it's even worse on the barge, with the latrines and the people cooking and eating everywhere. It's horrible-horrible, they tell me."

I asked Indar where he was staying: it had occurred to me that I should make the gesture of offering him hospitality. Was he staying at the van der Weyden?

This was the question he was waiting to be asked. He said in a soft and unassuming voice, "I'm staying at the State Domain. I have a house there. I'm a guest of the government."

And Metty behaved more graciously than I. Metty slapped the desk and said, "Indar!"

I said, "The Big Man invited you?"

He began to scale it down. "Not exactly. I have my own outfit. I am attached to the polytechnic for a term. Do you know it?"

"I know someone there. A student."

Indar behaved as though I had interrupted him; as though—

although I lived in the place, and he had just arrived—I was trespassing, and had no right to know a student at the polytechnic.

I said, "His mother's a *marchande*, one of my customers."

That was better. He said, "You must come and meet some of the other people there. You may not like what's going on. But you mustn't pretend it isn't happening. You mustn't make that mistake again."

I wanted to say: "I live here. I have lived through quite a lot in the last six years." But I didn't say that. I played up to his vanity. He had his own idea of the kind of man I was—and indeed he had caught me in my shop, at my ancestral business. He had his own idea of who he was and what he had done, the distance he had put between himself and the rest of us.

His vanity didn't irritate me. I found I was relishing it, in the way that years before, on the coast, as a child, I had relished Nazruddin's stories of his luck and of the delights of life here, in the colonial town. I hadn't slapped the desk like Metty, but I was impressed by what I saw of Indar. And it was a relief to put aside the dissatisfactions he made me feel, to forget about being caught out, and to give him a straight admiration for what he had made of himself—for his London clothes and the privilege they spoke of, his travelling, his house in the Domain, his position at the polytechnic.

To give him admiration, to appear not to be competing or resisting, was to put him at his ease. As we chatted over our Nescafé, as Metty exclaimed from time to time, expressing in his servant's manner the admiration which his master also felt, Indar's edginess wore off. He became gentle, full of manners, concerned. At the end of the morning I felt I had at last made a friend of my kind. And I badly needed such a friend.

And far from being his host and guide, I became the man who was led about. It wasn't all that absurd. I had so little to show him. All the key points of the town I knew could be shown in a couple of hours, as I discovered when I drove him around later that morning.

There was the river, with a stretch of broken promenade near the docks. There were the docks themselves; the repair yards with open corrugated-iron sheds full of rusting pieces of machinery; and some way downriver the ruined cathedral, beautifully overgrown and looking antique, like something in Europe —but you could only look from the road, because the bush was too thick and the site was famous for its snakes. There were the scuffed squares with their defaced and statueless pedestals; the official buildings from the colonial time in avenues lined with palmiste trees; the lycée, with the decaying masks in the gun room (but that bored Indar); the van der Weyden and Mahesh's Bigburger place, which were hardly things to show to a man who had been to Europe.

There were the *cités* and the squatters' settlements (some of them I was driving into for the first time) with their hills of rubbish, their corrugated dusty lanes, and a lot of old tires lying in the dust. To me the rubbish hills and the tires were features of the *cités* and shanty towns. The spidery little children that we had here did wonderful somersaults off those tires, running, jumping on the tires, and then springing high in the air. But it was nearly noon. There were no children doing somersaults when we drove by; and I realized that (after a monument with nothing on it, and pedestals without statues) I was literally just showing Indar a lot of rubbish. I cut short the tour at that point. The rapids and the fishermen's village—that had been incorporated into the State Domain; that he had already seen.

As we drove to the Domain—the intervening area, once empty, now filling up with the shacks of new arrivals from the villages: shacks which, in Indar's company, I seemed to be seeing for the first time: the red ground between the shacks stained with rivulets of black or grey-green filth, maize and cassava planted in every free space—as we drove, Indar said, "How long did you say you've been living here?"

"Six years."

"And you've shown me everything?"

What hadn't I shown him? A few interiors of shops and houses and flats, the Hellenic Club—and the bars. But I wouldn't have shown him the bars. And really, looking at the place with his eyes, I was amazed at the little I had been living with. And I had stopped seeing so much. In spite of everything, I had thought of the town as a real town; I saw it now as an agglomeration of shack settlements. I thought I had been resisting the place. But I had only been living blind—like the people I knew, from whom in my heart of hearts I had thought myself different.

I hadn't liked it when Indar had suggested that I was living like our community in the old days, not paying attention to what was going on. But he wasn't so far wrong. He was talking about the Domain; and for us in the town the Domain had remained only a source of contracts. We knew little of the life there, and we hadn't wanted to find out. We saw the Domain as part of the waste and foolishness of the country. But more importantly, we saw it as part of the President's politics; and we didn't want to become entangled with that.

We were aware of the new foreigners on the periphery of our town. They were not like the engineers and salesmen and artisans we knew, and we were a little nervous of them. The Domain people were like tourists, but they were not spenders—everything was found for them on the Domain. They were not interested in us; and we, thinking of them as protected people, looked upon them as people separate from the true life of the place, and for this reason not quite real, not as real as ourselves.

Without knowing it, and thinking all the time that we were keeping our heads down and being wise and protecting our interests, we had become like the Africans the President ruled. We were people who felt only the weight of the President's power. The Domain had been created by the President; for reasons of his own he had called certain foreigners to live there. For us that was enough; it wasn't for us to question or look too closely.

Sometimes, after Ferdinand had come to the town to see his mother during one of her shopping trips, I had driven him back to his hostel in the Domain. What I saw then was all that I knew, until Indar became my guide.

It was as Indar had said. He had a house in the Domain and he was a guest of the government. His house was carpeted and furnished showroom style—twelve hand-carved dining chairs, upholstered chairs in fringed synthetic velvet in two colours in the sitting room, lamps, tables, air conditioners everywhere. The air conditioners were necessary. The Domain houses, naked in levelled land, were like grander concrete boxes, with roofs that didn't project at all, so that at any hour of a bright day one wall, or two, got the full force of the sun. With the house there was also a boy, in the Domain servant costume—white shorts, white shirt and a white *jacket de boy* (instead of the apron of colonial days). It was the Domain style for people in Indar's position. The style was the President's. It was he who had decided on the costumes for the boys.

And in the strange world of the Domain Indar appeared to be well regarded. Part of this regard was due to the "outfit" to which he belonged. He couldn't quite explain to me what the outfit was that sent him on African tours—or I might have been too naïve to understand. But a number of people on the Domain seemed to belong to outfits that were as mysterious; and they looked upon Indar not as a man of our community or a refugee from the coast, but as one of themselves. It was all a little extraordinary to me.

These were the new-style foreigners whom we, in the town, had seen arriving for some time past. We had seen them putting on African clothes; we had noticed their gaiety, so unlike our own caution; their happiness with everything they found. And we had considered them parasites and half dangerous, serving some hidden cause of the President's, people we had to be careful with.

But now, being with them in the Domain, which in every way was their resort, and being admitted so easily to their life, their world of bungalows and air conditioners and holiday ease, catching in their educated talk the names of famous cities, I swung the other way and began to see how shut in and shabby and stagnant we in the town would have seemed to them. I began to get some sense of the social excitements of life on the Domain, of people associating in a new way, being more open, less concerned with enemies and danger, more ready to be interested and entertained, looking for the human worth of the other man. On the

Domain they had their own way of talking about people and events; they were in touch with the world. To be with them was to have a sense of adventure.

I thought of my own life and Metty's; of Shoba and Mahesh and their overheated privacy; of the Italians and Greeks— especially the Greeks—bottled up and tense with their family concerns and their nervousness of Africa and Africans. There was hardly anything new there. So to travel those few miles between the town and the Domain was always to make some adjustment, to assume a new attitude, and each time almost to see another country. I was ashamed of myself for the new judg- ments I found myself making on my friends Shoba and Mahesh, who had done so much for me for so many years, and with whom I had felt so safe. But I couldn't help those thoughts. I was tilting the other way, to the life of the Domain, as I saw it in the company of Indar.

I was aware, in the Domain, that I belonged to the other world. When I met people with Indar I found I had little to say. There were times when I thought that I might be letting him down. But there seemed to be no such thought in his head. He introduced me round as a friend of his family's from the coast, a member of his community. He didn't only want me to witness his success with the people of the Domain; he seemed to want me to share it as well. It was his way of rewarding me for my admira- tion, and I saw a delicacy in him that I had never seen on the coast. His manners were like a form of consideration; and how- ever small the occasion, his manners never failed. They were the manners of an impresario, a little bit. But it was also his old family style; it was as though he had needed security and admira- tion to bring it out again. In the artificiality of the Domain he had found his perfect setting.

We in the town could offer Indar nothing like the regard and the social excitements he enjoyed at the Domain; we could scarcely appreciate what he enjoyed there. With our cynicism, created by years of insecurity, how did we look on men? We judged the salesmen in the van der Weyden by the companies they represented, their ability to offer us concessions. Knowing such men, having access to the services they offered, and being flattered by them that we were not ordinary customers paying the full price or having to take our place in the queue, we thought we had mastered the world; and we saw those salesmen and representatives as men of power who had to be courted. We judged traders by their coups, the contracts they landed, the agencies they picked up.

It was the same with Africans. We judged them by their ability, as army men or officials in the customs or policemen, to do us services; and that was how they also judged themselves. You could spot the powerful in Mahesh's Bigburger place. They, sharing in our boom, and no longer as shoddy as they once were, wore gold as much as possible—gold-rimmed glasses, gold rings, gold pen-and-pencil sets, gold watches with solid gold wristlets. Among ourselves we scoffed at the vulgarity and pathos of that African lust for gold. Gold—how could it alter the man, who was only an African? But we wanted gold ourselves; and we regularly paid tribute to the Africans who wore gold.

Our ideas of men were simple; Africa was a place where we had to survive. But in the Domain it was different. There they could scoff at trade and gold, because in the magical atmosphere of the Domain, among the avenues and new houses, another Africa had been created. In the Domain, Africans—the young men at the polytechnic—were romantic. They were not always present at the parties or gatherings; but the whole life of the Domain was built around them. In the town "African" could be a word of abuse or disregard; in the Domain it was a bigger word. An "African" there was a new man whom everybody was busy making, a man about to inherit—the important man that years before, at the lycée, Ferdinand had seen himself as.

In the town, when they were at the lycée, Ferdinand and his friends—certainly his friends—were still close to village ways. When they were off duty, not at the lycée or with people like myself, they had merged into the African life of the town. Ferdinand and Metty—or Ferdinand and any African boy—could become friends because they had so much in common. But in the Domain there was no question of confusing Ferdinand and his friends with the white-uniformed servants.

Ferdinand and his friends had a clear idea of who they were

and what was expected of them. They were young men on government scholarships; they would soon become administrative cadets in the capital, serving the President. The Domain was the President's creation; and in the Domain they were in the presence of foreigners who had a high idea of the new Africa. Even I, in the Domain, began to feel a little of the romance of that idea.

So foreigners and Africans acted and reacted on one another, and everyone became locked in an idea of glory and newness. Everywhere the President's photograph looked down at us. In the town, in our shops and in government buildings, it was just the photograph of the President, the ruler, something that had to be there. In the Domain the glory of the President brushed off onto all his new Africans.

And they were bright, those young men. I had remembered them as little tricksters, pertinacious but foolish, with only a kind of village cunning; and I had assumed that for them studying meant only cramming. Like other people in the town, I believed that degree courses had been scaled down or altered for Africans. It was possible; they did go in for certain subjects—international relations, political science, anthropology. But those young men had sharp minds and spoke wonderfully—and in French, not the patois. They had developed fast. Just a few years before, Ferdinand had been incapable of grasping the idea of Africa. That wasn't so now. The magazines about African affairs —even the semi-bogus, subsidized ones from Europe—and the newspapers, though censored, had spread new ideas, knowledge, new attitudes.

Indar took me one evening to one of his seminars, in a lecture room in the big polytechnic building. The seminar was not part of any course. It was an extra, and was described on the door as an exercise in English-speaking. But more must have been expected from Indar. Most of the desks were taken. Ferdinand was there, in a little group of his own.

The biscuit-coloured walls of the lecture room were bare except for a photograph of the President—not in army uniform, but in a chief's leopard-skin cap, a short-sleeved jacket and a polka-dotted cravat. Indar, sitting below this photograph, began to speak, easily, about the other parts of Africa he had visited, and the young men were fascinated. Their innocence and eagerness were astonishing. In spite of the wars and coups they were hearing about, Africa was still to them the new continent, and they behaved as though Indar felt like them, was almost one of them. The language exercise turned into a discussion about Africa, and I could feel polytechnic topics, lecture topics, coming to the surface. Some of the questions were dynamite; but Indar was very good, always calm, never surprised. He was like a philosopher; he tried to get the young men to examine the words they were using.

They talked for a while about the coup in Uganda, and about the tribal and religious differences there. Then they began to talk more generally about religion in Africa.

There was some movement in the group around Ferdinand. And Ferdinand—not unaware of me—stood up and asked, "Would the honourable visitor state whether he feels that Africans have been depersonalized by Christianity?"

Indar did what he had done before. He restated the question. He said, "I suppose you are really asking whether Africa can be served by a religion which is not African. Is Islam an African religion? Do you feel that Africans have been depersonalized by that?"

Ferdinand didn't reply. It was as in the old days—he hadn't thought beyond a certain point.

Indar said, "Well, I suppose you can say that Islam has become an African religion. It has been on the continent for a very long time. And you can say the same for the Coptic Christians. I don't know—perhaps you might feel that those people have been so depersonalized by those religions that they are out of touch with Africa. Would you say that? Or would you say they are Africans of a special sort?"

Ferdinand said, "The honourable visitor knows very well the kind of Christianity I mean. He is trying to confuse the issue. He knows about the low status of African religion, and he knows very well that this is a direct question to him about the relevance or otherwise of African religion. The visitor is a gentleman sympathetic to Africa who has travelled. He can advise us. That is why we ask."

A number of desk lids were banged in approval.

Indar said, "To answer that question you must allow me to ask you one. You are students. You are not villagers. You cannot pretend you are. You will soon be serving your President and his government in different capacities. You are men of the modern world. Do you need African religion? Or are you being sentimental about it? Are you nervous of losing it? Or do you feel you have to hold on to it just because it's yours?"

Ferdinand's eyes went hard. He banged the lid of his desk and stood up. "You are asking a complicated question."

And "complicated," among these students, was clearly a word of disapproval.

Indar said, "You are forgetting. I didn't raise the question. You raised it, and I merely asked for information."

That restored order, put an end to the banging of the desk lids. It made Ferdinand friendly again, and he remained friendly for the rest of the seminar. He went to Indar at the end, when the boys in the *jackets de boy* pushed in chromium-plated trolleys and began serving coffee and sweet biscuits (part of the style the President had decreed for the Domain).

I said to Ferdinand, "You've been heckling my friend."

He said, "I wouldn't have done it if I had known he was your friend."

Indar said, "What are your own feelings about African religion?"

Ferdinand said, "I don't know. That's why I asked. It is not an easy question for me."

Later, when Indar and I left the polytechnic building to walk back to his house, Indar said, "He's pretty impressive. He's your *marchande*'s son? That explains it. He's got that little extra background."

In the asphalted space outside the polytechnic building the flag was floodlit. Slender lamp standards lifted fluorescent arms down both sides of the main avenue; and the avenue was also lit with lights at grass level, like an airport runway. Some of the bulbs had been broken and grass had grown tall around the fittings.

I said, "His mother's also a magician."

Indar said, "You can't be too careful. They were tough tonight, but they didn't ask the really difficult question. Do you know what that is? Whether Africans are peasants. It's a nonsense question, but big battles are fought about that one. Whatever you say you get into trouble. You see why my outfit is needed. Unless we can get them thinking, and give them real ideas instead of just politics and principles, these young men will keep our world in turmoil for the next half century."

I thought how far we had both come, to talk about Africa like this. We had even learned to take African magic seriously. It hadn't been like that on the coast. But as we talked that evening about the seminar, I began to wonder whether Indar and I weren't fooling ourselves and whether we weren't allowing the Africa we talked about to become too different from the Africa we knew. Ferdinand didn't want to lose touch with the spirits; he was nervous of being on his own. That had been at the back of his question. We all understood his anxiety; but it was as though, at the seminar, everyone had been ashamed, or fearful, of referring to it directly. The discussion had been full of words of another kind, about religion and history. It was like that on the Domain; Africa there was a special place.

I wondered, too, about Indar. How had he arrived at his new attitudes? I had thought of him, since the coast, as a hater of Africa. He had lost a lot; I didn't think he had forgiven. Yet he flourished on the Domain; it was his setting.

I was less "complicated"; I belonged to the town. And to leave the Domain and drive back to the town, to see the shacks, acres and acres of them, the rubbish mounds, to feel the presence of the river and the forest all around (more than landscaping now), to see the ragged groups outside the drinking booths, the squatters' cooking fires on the pavements in the centre of the town— to do that drive back was to return to the Africa I knew. It was to climb down from the exaltation of the Domain, to grasp reality again. Did Indar believe in the Africa of words? Did anyone on the Domain believe? Wasn't the truth what we in the town lived with—the salesmen's chat in the van der Weyden and the bars, the photographs of the President in government offices and in our shops, the army barracks in the converted palace of the man of our community?

Indar said, "Does one believe in anything? Does it matter?"

There was a ritual I went through whenever I had to clear a difficult consignment through the customs. I filled in the declaration form, folded it over five hundred francs, and handed it to the official in charge. He would—as soon as he had got his subordinates out of the room (and they of course knew why they had been asked to leave the room)—check the notes with his eyes alone. The notes would then be taken; the entries on the form would be studied with exaggerated care; and soon he would say, "C'est bien, Mis' Salim. Vous êtes en ordre." Neither he nor I would refer to the bank notes. We would talk only about the details on the declaration form, which, correctly filled, correctly approved, would remain as proof of both our correctness. Yet what had lain at the heart of the transaction would be passed over in silence, and would leave no trace in the records.

So, in my talks with Indar about Africa—the purpose of his outfit, the Domain, his anxieties about imported doctrines, the danger to Africa of its very newness, first ideas being caught most securely by new minds as sticky as adhesive tape—I felt that between us lay some dishonesty, or just an omission, some blank, around which we both had to walk carefully. That omission was our own past, the smashed life of our community. Indar had referred to that at our first meeting that morning in the shop. He said that he had learned to trample on the past. In the beginning it had been like trampling on a garden; later it had become like walking on ground.

I became confused myself. The Domain was a hoax. But at the same time it was real, because it was full of serious men (and a few women). Was there a truth outside men? Didn't men make the truth for themselves? Everything men did or made became real. So I moved between the Domain and the town. It was always reassuring to return to the town I knew, to get away from that Africa of words and ideas as it existed on the Domain (and from which, often, Africans were physically absent). But the Domain, and the glory and the social excitements of the life there, always called me back.

8 Indar said, "We are going to a party after dinner. It's being given by Yvette. Do you know her? Her husband, Raymond, keeps a low profile, but he runs the whole show here. The President, or the Big Man, as you call him, sent him down here to keep an eye on things. He's the Big Man's white man. In all these places there's someone like that. Raymond's a historian. They say the President reads everything he writes. That's the story anyway. Raymond knows more about the country than anyone on earth."

I had never heard of Raymond. The President I had seen only in photographs—first in army uniform, then in the stylish short-sleeved jacket and cravat, and then with his leopard-skin chief's cap and his carved stick, emblem of his chieftaincy—and it had never occurred to me that he might be a reader. What Indar told me brought the President closer. At the same time it showed me how far away I, and people like me, were from the seat of power. Considering myself from that distance, I saw how small and vulnerable we were; and it didn't seem quite real that, dressed as I was, I should be strolling across the Domain after dinner to meet people in direct touch with the great. It was strange, but I no longer felt oppressed by the country, the forest and the waters and the remote peoples: I felt myself above it all, considering it from this new angle of the powerful.

From what Indar had said I had expected that Raymond and Yvette would be middle-aged. But the lady—in black slacks in some shiny material—who came to meet us after the white-jacketed boy had let us in was young, in her late twenties, near my own age. That was the first surprise. The second was that she was barefooted, feet white and beautiful and finely made. I looked at her feet before I considered her face and her blouse, black silk, embroidered round the low-cut collar—expensive stuff, not the sort of goods you could get in our town.

Indar said, "This lovely lady is our hostess. Her name is Yvette."

He bent over her and appeared to hold her in an embrace. It was a piece of pantomime. She playfully arched her back to receive his embrace, but his cheek barely brushed hers, he never touched her breast, and only the tips of his fingers rested on her back, on the silk blouse.

It was a house of the Domain, like Indar's. But all the upholstered furniture had been cleared out of the sitting room and had been replaced by cushions and bolsters and African mats. Two or three reading lamps had been put on the floor, so that parts of the room were in darkness.

Yvette said, referring to the furniture, "The President has an exaggerated idea of the needs of Europeans. I've dumped all that velvety stuff in one of the bedrooms."

Remembering what Indar had told me, I ignored the irony in her voice, and felt that she was speaking with privilege, the privilege of someone close to the President.

A number of people were already there. Indar followed Yvette deeper into the room, and I followed Indar.

Indar said, "How's Raymond?"

Yvette said, "He's working. He'll look in later."

We sat down all three next to a bookcase. Indar lounged against a bolster, a man at ease. I concentrated on the music. As so often when I was with Indar on the Domain, I was prepared only to watch and listen. And this was all new to me. I hadn't been to a Domain party like this. And the atmosphere itself in that room was something I had never experienced before.

Two or three couples were dancing; I had visions of women's legs. I had a vision especially of a girl in a green dress who sat on a straight-backed dining chair (one of the house set of twelve). I studied her knees, her legs, her ankles, her shoes. They were not particularly well made legs, but they had an effect on me. All my adult life I had looked for release in the bars of the town. I knew only women who had to be paid for. The other side of the life of passion, of embraces freely given and received, I knew nothing of, and had begun to consider alien, something not for me. And so my satisfactions had only been brothel satisfactions, which hadn't been satisfactions at all. I felt they had taken me further and further away from the true life of the senses and I feared they had made me incapable of that life.

I had never been in a room where men and women danced for mutual pleasure, and out of pleasure in one another's company. Trembling expectation was in that girl's heavy legs, the girl in the green dress. It was a new dress, loosely hemmed, not ironed into a crease, still suggesting the material as it had been measured out and bought. Later I saw her dancing, watched the movements of her legs, her shoes; and such a sweetness was released in me that I felt I had recovered a part of myself I had lost. I never looked at the girl's face, and it was easy in the semi-gloom to let that remain unknown. I wanted to sink into the sweetness; I didn't want anything to spoil the mood.

And the mood became sweeter. The music that was being played came to an end, and in the wonderfully lit room, blurred circles of light thrown onto the ceiling from the lamps on the floor, people stopped dancing. What next came on went straight to my heart—sad guitars, words, a song, an American girl singing "Barbara Allen."

That voice! It needed no music; it hardly needed words. By itself it created the line of the melody; by itself it created a whole world of feeling. It is what people of our background look for in music and singing: feeling. It is what makes us shout "Wa-wa! Bravo!" and throw bank notes and gold at the feet of a singer. Listening to that voice, I felt the deepest part of myself awakening, the part that knew loss, homesickness, grief, and longed for love. And in that voice was the promise of a flowering for everyone who listened.

I said to Indar, "Who is the singer?"

He said, "Joan Baez. She's very famous in the States."

"And a millionaire," Yvette said.

I was beginning to recognize her irony. It made her appear to be saying something when she had said very little—and she was, after all, playing the record in her house. She was smiling at me, perhaps smiling at what she had said, or perhaps smiling at me as Indar's friend, or smiling because she believed it became her.

Her left leg was drawn up; her right leg, bent at the knee, lay flat on the cushion on which she sat, so that her right heel lay almost against her left ankle. Beautiful feet, and their whiteness was wonderful against the black of her slacks. Her provocative posture, her smile—they became part of the mood of the song, too much to contemplate.

Indar said, "Salim comes from one of our old coast families. Their history is interesting."

Yvette's hand lay white on her right thigh.

Indar said, "Let me show you something."

He leaned across my legs and reached up to the bookcase. He took out a book, opened it and showed me where I was to read. I held the book down to the floor, to catch the light from the reading lamp, and saw, among a list of names, the names of Yvette and Raymond, acknowledged by the writer of the book as "most generous of hosts" at some recent time in the capital.

Yvette continued to smile. No embarrassment or playing it down, though; no irony now. Her name in the book mattered to her.

I gave the book back to Indar, looked away from Yvette and him, and returned to the voice. Not all the songs were like "Barbara Allen." Some were modern, about war and injustice and oppression and nuclear destruction. But always in between there were the older, sweeter melodies. These were the ones I waited for, but in the end the voice linked the two kinds of song, linked the maidens and lovers and sad deaths of bygone times with the people of today who were oppressed and about to die.

It was make-believe—I never doubted that. You couldn't listen to sweet songs about injustice unless you expected justice and received it much of the time. You couldn't sing songs about the end of the world unless—like the other people in that room, so beautiful with such simple things: African mats on the floor and

African hangings on the wall and spears and masks—you felt
that the world was going on and you were safe in it. How easy it
was, in that room, to make those assumptions!

It was different outside, and Mahesh would have scoffed. He
had said, "It isn't that there's no right and wrong here. There's
no right." But Mahesh felt far away. The aridity of that life,
which had also been mine! It was better to pretend, as I could
pretend now. It was better to share the companionship of that
pretence, to feel that in that room we all lived beautifully and
bravely with injustice and imminent death and consoled ourselves with love. Even before the songs ended I felt I had found
the kind of life I wanted; I never wanted to be ordinary again. I
felt that by some piece of luck I had stumbled on the equivalent
of what years before Nazruddin had found right here.

It was late when Raymond came in. I had, at Indar's insistence, even danced with Yvette and felt her skin below the silk of
her blouse; and when I saw Raymond my thoughts—leaping at
this stage of the evening from possibility to possibility—were at
first only about the difference in their ages. There must have
been thirty years between Yvette and her husband; Raymond
was a man in his late fifties.

But I felt possibilities fade, felt them as dreams, when I saw
the immediate look of concern on Yvette's face—or rather in her
eyes, for her smile was still on, a trick of her face; when I saw the
security of Raymond's manner, remembered his job and position, and took in the distinction of his appearance. It was the
distinction of intelligence and intellectual labours. He looked as
though he had just taken off his glasses, and his gentle eyes were
attractively tired. He was wearing a long-sleeved safari jacket;
and it came to me that the style—long sleeves rather than short
—had been suggested to him by Yvette.

After that look of concern at her husband, Yvette relaxed
again, with her fixed smile. Indar got up and began fetching a
dining chair from against the opposite wall. Raymond motioned
to us to stay where we were; he rejected the chance of sitting next
to Yvette, and when Indar returned with the dining chair, sat on
that.

Yvette said, without moving, "Would you like a drink, Raymond?"

He said, "It will spoil it for me, Evie. I'll be going back to my room in a minute."

Raymond's presence in the room had been noted. A young man and a girl had begun to hover around our group. One or two other people came up. There were greetings.

Indar said, "I hope we haven't disturbed you."

Raymond said, "It made a pleasant background. If I look a little troubled, it is because just now, in that room, I became very dejected. I began to wonder, as I've often wondered, whether the truth ever gets known. The idea isn't new, but there are times when it becomes especially painful. I feel that everything one does is just going to waste."

Indar said, "You are talking nonsense, Raymond. Of course it takes time for someone like yourself to be recognized, but it happens in the end. You are not working in a popular field."

Yvette said, "You tell him that for me, please."

One of the men standing around said, "New discoveries are constantly making us revise our ideas about the past. The truth is always there. It can be got at. The work has to be done, that's all."

Raymond said, "Time, the discoverer of truth. I know. It's the classical idea, the religious idea. But there are times when you begin to wonder. Do we really know the history of the Roman Empire? Do we really know what went on during the conquest of Gaul? I was sitting in my room and thinking with sadness about all the things that have gone unrecorded. Do you think we will ever get to know the truth about what has happened in Africa in the last hundred or even fifty years? All the wars, all the rebellions, all the leaders, all the defeats?"

There was a silence. We looked at Raymond, who had introduced this element of discussion into our evening. Yet the mood was only like an extension of the mood of the Joan Baez songs. And for a little while, but without the help of music, we contemplated the sadness of the continent.

Indar said, "Have you read Muller's article?"

Raymond said, "About the Bapende rebellion? He sent me a proof. It's had a great success, I hear."

The young man with the girl said, "I hear they're inviting him to Texas to teach for a term."

Indar said, "I thought it was a lot of rubbish. Every kind of cliché parading as new wisdom. The Azande, that's a tribal uprising. The Bapende, that's just economic oppression, rubber business. They're to be lumped with the Budja and the Babwa. And you do that by playing down the religious side. Which is what makes the Bapende dust-up so wonderful. It's just the kind of thing that happens when people turn to Africa to make the fast academic buck."

Raymond said, "He came to see me. I answered all his questions and showed him all my papers."

The young man said, "Muller's a bit of whiz kid, I think."

Raymond said, "I liked him."

Yvette said, "He came to lunch. As soon as Raymond left the table, he forgot all about the Bapende and said to me, 'Do you want to come out with me?' Just like that. The minute Raymond's back was turned."

Raymond smiled.

Indar said, "I was telling Salim, Raymond, that you are the only man the President reads."

Raymond said, "I don't think he has much time for reading these days."

The young man, his girl now close to him, said, "How did you meet him?"

"It is a story at once simple and extraordinary," Raymond said. "But I don't think we have time for that now." He looked at Yvette.

She said, "I don't think anybody is rushing off anywhere right at this minute."

"It was long ago," Raymond said. "In colonial times. I was teaching at a college in the capital. I was doing my historical work. But of course in those days there was no question of publishing. There was the censorship that people pretended didn't exist, in spite of the celebrated decree of 1922. And of course in those days Africa wasn't a subject. But I never made any secret of what I felt or where I stood, and I suppose the word must have got around. One day at the college I was told that an old African woman had come to see me. It was one of the African servants who brought me the message, and he wasn't too impressed by my visitor.

"I asked him to bring her to me. She was middle-aged rather than old. She worked as a maid in the big hotel in the capital, and she had come to see me about her son. She belonged to one of the smaller tribes, people with no say in anything, and I suppose she had no one of her own kind to turn to. The boy had left school. He had joined some political club and had done various odd jobs. But he had given up all that. He was doing nothing at all. He was just staying in the house. He didn't go out to see anybody. He suffered from headaches, but he wasn't ill. I thought she was going to ask me to get the boy a job. But no. All she wanted me to do was to see the boy and talk to him.

"She impressed me a great deal. Yes, the dignity of that hotel maid was quite remarkable. Another woman would have thought that her son was bewitched, and taken appropriate measures. She, in her simple way, saw that her son's disease had been brought on by his education. That was why she had come to me, the teacher at the college.

"I asked her to send the boy to me. He didn't like the idea of his mother talking to me about him, but he came. He was as nervous as a kitten. What made him unusual—I would even say extraordinary—was the quality of his despair. It wasn't just a matter of poverty and the lack of opportunity. It went much deeper. And, indeed, to try to look at the world from his point of view was to begin to get a headache yourself. He couldn't face the world in which his mother, a poor woman of Africa, had endured such humiliation. Nothing could undo that. Nothing could give him a better world.

"I said to him, 'I've listened to you, and I know that one day the mood of despair will go and you will want to act. What you mustn't do then is to become involved in politics as they exist. Those clubs and associations are talking shops, debating societies, where Africans posture for Europeans and hope to pass as evolved. They will eat up your passion and destroy your gifts. What I am going to tell you now will sound strange, coming from me. You must join the Defence Force. You won't rise high, but you will learn a real skill. You will learn about weapons and transport, and you will also learn about men. Once you understand what holds the Defence Force together, you will understand what holds the country together. You might say to me, "But isn't it better for me to be a lawyer and be called *maître?*" I will say, "No. It is better for you to be a private and call the sergeant sir." This isn't advice I will want to give to anybody else. But I give it to you.' "

Raymond had held us all. When he stopped speaking we allowed the silence to last, while we continued to look at him as he sat on the dining chair in his safari jacket, distinguished, his hair combed back, his eyes tired, a bit of a dandy in his way.

In a more conversational voice, as though he was commenting on his own story, Raymond said at last, breaking the silence, "He's a truly remarkable man. I don't think we give him enough credit for what he's done. We take it for granted. He's disciplined the army and brought peace to this land of many peoples. It is possible once again to traverse the country from one end to the other—something the colonial power thought it alone had brought about. And what is most remarkable is that it's been done without coercion, and entirely with the consent of the people. You don't see policemen in the streets. You don't see guns. You don't see the army."

Indar, sitting next to Yvette, who was still smiling, seemed about to change the position of his legs prior to saying something. But Raymond raised his hand, and Indar didn't move.

"And there's the freedom," Raymond said. "There's the remarkable welcome given to every kind of idea from every kind of system. I don't think," he said, addressing Indar directly, as though making up to him for keeping him quiet, "that anyone has even hinted to you that there are certain things you have to say and certain things you mustn't say."

Indar said, "We've had an easy ride here."

"I don't think it would have occurred to him to try to censor you. He feels that all ideas can be made to serve the cause. You might say that with him there's an absolute hunger for ideas. He uses them all in his own way."

Yvette said, "I wish he would change the boys' uniforms. The good old colonial style of short trousers and a long white apron. Or long trousers and a jacket. But not that carnival costume of short trousers and jacket."

We all laughed, even Raymond, as though we were glad to stop being solemn. And Yvette's boldness was also like proof of the freedom Raymond had been talking about.

Raymond said, "Yvette goes on about the boys' uniforms. But that's the army background, and the mother's hotel background. The mother wore a colonial maid's uniform all her working life. The boys in the Domain have to wear theirs. And it isn't a colonial uniform—that's the point. In fact, everybody nowadays who wears a uniform has to understand that. Everyone in uniform has to feel that he has a personal contract with the President. And try to get the boys out of that uniform. You won't succeed. Yvette has tried. They want to wear that uniform, however absurd it is to our eyes. That's the amazing thing about this man of Africa—this flair, this knowledge of what the people need, and when.

"We have all these photographs of him in African costume nowadays. I must confess I was disturbed when they began to appear in such number. I raised the issue with him one day in the capital. I was shattered by the penetration of his answer. He said, 'Five years ago, Raymond, I would have agreed with you. Five years ago our African people, with that cruel humour which is theirs, would have laughed, and that ridicule would have destroyed our country, with its still frail bonds. But times have changed. The people now have peace. They want something else. So they no longer see a photograph of a soldier. They see a photograph of an African. And that isn't a picture of me, Raymond. It is a picture of all Africans.' "

This was so like what I felt, that I said, "Yes! None of us in the town liked putting up the old photograph. But it is different seeing the new photographs, especially in the Domain."

Raymond permitted this interruption. His right hand was being raised, though, to allow him to go on. And he went on.

"I thought I would check this. Just last week, as a matter of fact. I ran into one of our students outside the main building. And just to be provocative, I dropped some remark about the number of the President's photographs. The young man pulled me up quite sharply. So I asked him what he felt when he saw the President's photograph. You will be surprised by what he said to me, that young man, holding himself as erect as any military cadet. 'It is a photograph of the President. But here on the Domain, as a student at the polytechnic, I also consider it a photograph of myself.' The very words! But that's a quality of great leaders—they intuit the needs of their people long before those needs are formulated. It takes an African to rule Africa—the colonial powers never truly understood that. However much the rest of us study Africa, however deep our sympathy, we will remain outsiders."

The young man, sitting now on a mat with his girl, asked, "Do you know the symbolism of the serpent on the President's stick? Is it true that there's a fetish in the belly of the human figure on the stick?"

Raymond said, "I don't know about that. It is a stick. It is a chief's stick. It is like a mace or a mitre. I don't think we have to fall into the error of looking for African mysteries everywhere."

The critical note jarred a little. But Raymond seemed not to notice.

"I have recently had occasion to look through all the President's speeches. Now, what an interesting publication that would make! Not the speeches in their entirety, which inevitably deal with many passing issues. But selections. The essential thoughts."

Indar said, "Are you working on that? Has he asked you?"

Raymond lifted a palm and hunched a shoulder, to say that it was possible, but that he couldn't talk about a matter that was still confidential.

"What is interesting about those speeches when read in sequence is their development. There you can see very clearly what I have described as the hunger for ideas. In the beginning the ideas are simple. Unity, the colonial past, the need for peace. Then they become extraordinarily complex and wonderful about Africa, government, the modern world. Such a work, if adequately prepared, might well become the handbook for a true revolution throughout the continent. Always you can catch that quality of the young man's despair which made such an impression on me so long ago. Always you have that feeling that the damage can never perhaps be undone. Always there is that note, for those with the ears to hear it, of the young man grieving for the humiliations of his mother, the hotel maid. He's always remained true to that. I don't think many people know that earlier this year he and his entire government made a pilgrimage to the village of that woman of Africa. Has that been done before? Has any ruler attempted to give sanctity to the bush of Africa? This act of piety is something that brings tears to the eyes. Can you imagine the humiliations of an African hotel maid in colonial times? No amount of piety can make up for that. But piety is all we have to offer."

"Or we can forget," Indar said. "We can trample on the past."

Raymond said, "That is what most of the leaders of Africa do. They want to build skyscrapers in the bush. This man wants to build a shrine."

Music without words had been coming out of the speakers. Now "Barbara Allen" began again, and the words were distracting. Raymond stood up. The man who had been sitting on the mat went to lower the volume. Raymond indicated that he wasn't to bother, but the song went faint.

Raymond said, "I would like to be with you. But unfortunately I have to get back to my work. Otherwise I might lose something. I find that the most difficult thing in prose narrative is linking one thing with the other. The link might just be a sentence, or even a word. It sums up what has gone before and prepares one for what is to come. As I was sitting with you I had an idea of a possible solution to a problem that was beginning to appear quite intractable. I must go and make a note. Otherwise I might forget."

He began to move away from us. But then he stopped and

said, "I don't think it is sufficiently understood how hard it is to write about what has never been written about before. The occasional academic paper on a particular subject, the Bapende rebellion or whatever—that has its own form. The larger narrative is another matter. And that's why I have begun to consider Theodor Mommsen the giant of modern historical writing. Everything that we now discuss about the Roman Republic is only a continuation of Mommsen. The problems, the issues, the very narrative, especially of those extraordinarily troubled years of the later Republic—you might say the German genius discovered it all. Of course, Theodor Mommsen had the comfort of knowing that his subject was a great one. Those of us who work in our particular field have no such assurance. We have no idea of the value posterity will place on the events we attempt to chronicle. We have no idea where the continent is going. We can only carry on."

He ended abruptly, turned, and went out of the room, leaving us in silence, looking after where he had disappeared, and only slowly directing our attention to Yvette, now his representative in that room, smiling, acknowledging our regard.

After a little Indar said to me, "Do you know Raymond's work?"

Of course he knew the answer to that one. But, to give him his opening, I said, "No, I don't know his work."

Indar said, "That's the tragedy of the place. The great men of Africa are not known."

It was like a formal speech of thanks. And Indar had chosen his words well. He had made us all men and women of Africa; and since we were not Africans the claim gave us a special feeling for ourselves which, so far as I was concerned, was soon heightened by the voice of Joan Baez, turned up again, reminding us sweetly, after the tensions Raymond had thrown among us, of our common bravery and sorrows.

Indar was embraced by Yvette when we left. And I was embraced, as the friend. It was delicious to me, as the climax to that evening, to press that body close, soft at this late hour, and to feel the silk of the blouse and the flesh below the silk.

There was a moon now—there had been none earlier. It was small and high. The sky was full of heavy clouds, and the moonlight came and went. It was very quiet. We could hear the rapids; they were about a mile away. The rapids in moonlight! I said to Indar, "Let's go to the river." And he was willing.

In the wide levelled land of the Domain the new buildings seemed small, and the earth felt immense. The Domain seemed the merest clearing in the forest, the merest clearing in an immensity of bush and river—the world might have been nothing else. Moonlight distorted distances; and the darkness, when it came, seemed to drop down to our heads.

I said to Indar, "What do you think of what Raymond said?"

"Raymond tells a story well. But a lot of what he says is true. What he says about the President and ideas is certainly true. The President uses them all and somehow makes them work together. He is the great African chief, and he is also the man of the people. He is the modernizer and he is also the African who has rediscovered his African soul. He's conservative, revolutionary, everything. He's going back to the old ways, and he's also the man who's going ahead, the man who's going to make the country a world power by the year 2000. I don't know whether he's done it accidentally or because someone's been telling him what to do. But the mish-mash works because he keeps on changing, unlike the other guys. He is the soldier who decided to become an old-fashioned chief, and he's the chief whose mother was a hotel maid. That makes him everything, and he plays up everything. There isn't anyone in the country who hasn't heard of that hotel maid mother."

I said, "They caught me with that pilgrimage to the mother's village. When I read in the paper that it was an unpublicized pilgrimage, I thought of it as just that."

"He makes these shrines in the bush, honouring the mother. And at the same time he builds modern Africa. Raymond says he doesn't build skyscrapers. Well, he doesn't do that. He builds these very expensive Domains."

"Nazruddin used to own some land here in the old days."

"And he sold it for nothing. Are you going to tell me that? That's an African story."

"No, Nazruddin sold well. He sold at the height of the boom before independence. He came out one Sunday morning and said, 'But this is only bush.' And he sold."

"It could go that way again."

The sound of the rapids had grown louder. We had left the new buildings of the Domain behind and were approaching the fishermen's huts, dead in the moonlight. The thin village dogs, pale in the moonlight, their shadows black below them, walked lazily away from us. The fishermen's poles and nets were dark against the broken glitter of the river. And then we were on the old viewing point, repaired now, newly walled; and around us, drowning everything else, was the sound of water over rocks. Clumps of water hyacinths bucked past. The hyacinths were white in the moonlight, the vines dark tangles outlined in black shadow. When the moonlight went, there was nothing to be seen; the world was then only that old sound of tumbling water.

I said, "I've never told you why I came here. It wasn't just to get away from the coast or to run that shop. Nazruddin used to tell us wonderful stories of the times he used to have here. That was why I came. I thought I would be able to live my own life, and I thought that in time I would find what Nazruddin found. Then I got stuck. I don't know what I would have done if you hadn't come. If you hadn't come I would never have known about what was going on here, just under my nose."

"It's different from what we used to know. To people like us it's very seductive. Europe in Africa, post-colonial Africa. But it isn't Europe or Africa. And it looks different from the inside, I can tell you."

"You mean people don't believe in it? They don't believe in what they say and do?"

"No one is as crude as that. We believe and don't believe. We believe because that way everything becomes simpler and makes more sense. We don't believe—well, because of this." And Indar waved at the fishermen's village, the bush, the moonlit river.

He said after a time, "Raymond's in a bit of a mess. He has to keep on pretending that he is the guide and adviser, to keep himself from knowing that the time is almost here when he will just be receiving orders. In fact, so as not to get orders, he is beginning to anticipate orders. He will go crazy if he has to acknowledge that that's his situation. Oh, he's got a big job now. But he's on the slippery slope. He's been sent away from the capital. The Big Man is going his own way, and he no longer needs Raymond. Everybody knows that, but Raymond thinks they don't. It's a dreadful thing for a man of his age to have to live with."

But what Indar was saying didn't make me think of Raymond. I thought of Yvette, all at once brought nearer by this tale of her husband's distress. I went over the pictures I had of her that evening, ran the film over again, so to speak, reconstructing and reinterpreting what I had seen, re-creating that woman, fixing her in the posture that had bewitched me, her white feet together, one leg drawn up, one leg flat and bent, remaking her face, her smile, touching the whole picture with the mood of the Joan Baez songs and all that they had released in me, and adding to it this extra mood of moonlight, the rapids, and the white hyacinths of this great river of Africa.

9 It was on that evening, by the river, after he had spoken about Raymond, that Indar began to tell me about himself. The evening that had excited me had enervated and depressed him; he had become irritable as soon as we had left Yvette's house.

Earlier in the evening, as we had walked across to the house for the party, he had spoken of Raymond as a star, someone close to power, the Big Man's white man; but then, by the rapids, he had spoken of Raymond in quite another way. As my guide Indar had been anxious for me truly to understand the nature of life on the Domain, and his own position there. Now that I had seized the glamour of his world he was like a guide who had lost faith in what he showed. Or like a man who, because he had got someone else to believe, had felt he could let go of some of his own faith.

The moonlight that made me light-headed deepened his depression, and it was out of this depression that he began to speak. The mood of the evening didn't stay with him, though; the next day he had bounced back, and was like the man he had always been. But he was more ready to acknowledge his depression when it came; and what he outlined that evening he returned to and filled in at other times, when the occasion suited, or when he drifted back to that earlier mood.

"We have to learn to trample on the past, Salim. I told you that when we met. It shouldn't be a cause for tears, because it isn't just true for you and me. There may be some parts of the world—dead countries, or secure and by-passed ones—where men can cherish the past and think of passing on furniture and china to their heirs. Men can do that perhaps in Sweden or Canada. Some peasant department of France full of half-wits in châteaux; some crumbling Indian palace-city, or some dead colonial town in a hopeless South American country. Everywhere else men are in movement, the world is in movement, and the past can only cause pain.

"It isn't easy to turn your back on the past. It isn't something you can decide to do just like that. It is something you have to arm yourself for, or grief will ambush and destroy you. That is why I hold on to the image of the garden trampled until it becomes ground—it is a small thing, but it helps. That perception about the past came to me at the end of my third year in England. And oddly enough, it came to me beside another river. You've told me that I've led you here to the kind of life you've always felt you needed. It was something like that, too, that I began to feel beside that river in London. I made a decision about myself then. And it was as an indirect result of that decision that I came back to Africa. Though when I left it was my intention never to return.

"I was very unhappy when I left. You remember that. I tried to depress you—in fact, I tried to wound you—but that was only because I was myself so depressed. The thought of the work of two generations going to waste—it was very painful. The thought of losing that house built by my grandfather, the thought of the risks he and my father had taken to build up a business from nothing, the bravery, the sleepless nights—it was all very painful. In another country such effort and such talent would have made us millionaires, aristocrats, or at any rate secure for some generations. There it was all going up in smoke. My rage wasn't only with the Africans. It was also with our community and our civilization, which gave us energy but in every other way left us at the mercy of others. How do you rage against a thing like that?

"I thought when I went to England I would put all that behind me. I had no plans beyond that. The word 'university' dazzled me, and I was innocent enough to believe that after my time in the university some wonderful life would be waiting for me. At that age three years seems a long time—you feel that anything can happen. But I hadn't understood to what extent our civilization had also been our prison. I hadn't understood either to what extent we had been made by the place where we had grown up, made by Africa and the simple life of the coast, and how incapable we had become of understanding the outside world. We have no means of understanding a fraction of the thought and science and philosophy and law that have gone to make that outside world. We simply accept it. We have grown up paying tribute to it, and that is all that most of us can do. We feel of the great world,that it is simply there, something for the lucky ones among us to explore, and then only at the edges. It never occurs to us that we might make some contribution to it ourselves. And that is why we miss everything.

"When we land at a place like London Airport we are concerned only not to appear foolish. It is more beautiful and more complex than anything we could have dreamed of, but we are concerned only to let people see that we can manage and are not overawed. We might even pretend that we had expected better. That is the nature of our stupidity and incompetence. And that was how I spent my time at the university in England, not being overawed, always being slightly disappointed, understanding nothing, accepting everything, getting nothing. I saw and understood so little that even at the end of my time at the university I could distinguish buildings only by their size, and I was hardly aware of the passing of the seasons. And yet I was an intelligent man, and could cram for examinations.

"In the old days, after three years like that, and with some scraped-through degree, I would have returned home and hung up my board and devoted myself to the making of money, using the little half-skill I had picked up, the half-knowledge of other men's books. But of course I couldn't do that. I had to stay where I was and I had to get a job. I hadn't acquired a profession, you understand; nothing at home had pushed me in that direction.

"For some time the boys of my year at the university had been talking of jobs and interviews. The more precocious ones had even been talking about the interview expenses various companies paid. In the porter's lodge the pigeonholes of these boys were full of long brown envelopes from the University Appointments Committee. The dimmest boys were naturally the ones with the most varied prospects; they could be anything; and in their pigeonholes the brown envelopes fell as thick as autumn leaves. That was my attitude to those adventurous boys—slightly mocking. I had to get a job, but I never thought of myself as someone who would have to go through the brown-envelope adventure. I don't know why; I just didn't; and then, almost at the end of my time, with bewilderment and shame I realised that I had. I made an appointment with the Appointments Committee and on the morning put on a dark suit and went.

"As soon as I got there I knew my errand was fruitless. The Committee was meant to put English boys in English jobs; it wasn't meant for me. I realised that as soon as I saw the look on the face of the girl in the outer office. But she was nice, and the dark-suited man inside was also nice. He was intrigued by my African background, and after a little talk about Africa he said, 'And what can this great organization do for you?' I wanted to say, 'Couldn't you send me some brown envelopes too?' But what I said was: 'I was hoping you would tell me.' He seemed to find this funny. He took down my details, for the form of the thing; and then he tried to get a conversation going, senior dark suit to junior dark suit, man to man.

"He had little to tell me, though. And I had less to tell him. I had hardly looked at the world. I didn't know how it worked or what I might do in it. After my three unamazed student years, I was overwhelmed by my ignorance; and in that quiet little office full of peaceful files I began to think of the world outside as a place of horror. My dark-suited interviewer became impatient. He said, 'Good heavens, man! You must give me some guidance. You must have some idea of the kind of job you see yourself doing.'

"He was right, of course. But that 'Good heavens, man!' seemed to me affected, something he might have picked up in the past from someone his senior and was now throwing at me as someone lesser. I became angry. The idea came to me that I should fix him with a look of the utmost hostility and say, 'The job I want is your job. And I want your job because you enjoy it so much.' But I didn't speak the words; I didn't speak any words at all; I just gave him the hostile look. So our interview ended inconclusively.

"I became calmer outside. I went to the café where I used to go for coffee in the mornings. As a consolation, I bought myself a piece of chocolate cake as well. But then, to my surprise, I found I wasn't consoling myself; I was celebrating. I found I was positively happy to be in the café in the middle of the morning, drinking coffee and eating cake, while my tormentor fussed about with his brown envelopes in his office. It was only escape, and it couldn't last long. But I remember that half hour as one of pure happiness.

"After this I didn't expect anything from the Appointments Committee. But the man was, after all, a fair man; a bureaucracy is a bureaucracy; and a couple of brown envelopes did arrive for me, unseasonably, not as part of the autumn rush, choking the pigeonholes in the porter's lodge, but like the last dead leaves of the year, torn away by the gales of January. An oil company, and two or three other large companies with connections in Asia or Africa. With each job description I read, I felt a tightening of what I must call my soul. I found myself growing false to myself, acting to myself, convincing myself of my rightness for whatever was being described. And this is where I suppose life ends for most people, who stiffen in the attitudes they adopt to make themselves suitable for the jobs and lives that other people have laid out for them.

"None of those jobs came my way. There again I found myself amusing my interviewers unintentionally. Once I said, 'I don't know anything about your business, but I can put my mind to it.' For some reason this brought the house down—in this case it was a three-man board. They laughed, the oldest man leading the laughter and in the end even wiping away tears; and they dismissed me. With each rejection came a feeling of relief; but with each rejection I became more anxious about the future.

"Once a month or so I had lunch with a woman lecturer. She was about thirty, not bad-looking, and very kind to me. She was unusual because she was so much at peace with herself. That was why I liked her. It was she who made me do the absurd thing I am now going to describe.

"This lady had the idea that people like myself were at sea because we were men of two worlds. She was right, of course. But at the time it didn't seem so to me—I thought I saw everything very clearly—and I thought she had got the idea from some young man from Bombay or thereabouts who was trying to make himself interesting. But this lady also thought that my education and background made me extraordinary, and I couldn't fight the idea of my extraordinariness.

"An extraordinary man, a man of two worlds, needed an extraordinary job. And she suggested I should become a diplomat. That was what I decided to do, and the country I decided to serve—since a diplomat has to have a country—was India. It was absurd; I knew it was absurd, even while I was doing it; but I wrote a letter to the Indian High Commission. I got a reply, and was given an appointment.

"I went up to London by train. I didn't know London very well, and didn't like what I knew; and I liked it less that morning. There was Praed Street with its pornographic bookshops that didn't deal in real pornography; there was the Edgware Road, where the shops and restaurants seemed continually to be changing hands; there were the shops and crowds of Oxford Street and Regent Street. The openness of Trafalgar Square gave me a lift, but it reminded me that I was almost at the end of my journey. And I had begun to be very embarrassed by my mission.

"The bus took me down the Strand and dropped me at the curve of the Aldwych, and I crossed the road to the building that had been pointed out to me as India House. How could I have missed it, with all the Indian motifs on the outside wall? At this stage my embarrassment was acute. I was in my dark suit and my university tie, and I was entering a London building, an English building, which pretended to be of India—an India quite different from the country my grandfather had spoken about.

"For the first time in my life I was filled with a colonial rage. And this wasn't only a rage with London or England; it was also a rage with the people who had allowed themselves to be corralled into a foreign fantasy. My rage didn't die down when I went inside. There again were the Oriental motifs. The uniformed messengers were English and middle-aged; they clearly had been taken on by the old management, if you can call it that, and were working out their time under the new. I had never felt so involved with the land of my ancestors, and yours, and so far from it. I felt in that building I had lost an important part of my idea of who I was. I felt I had been granted the most cruel knowledge of where I stood in the world. And I hated it.

"It was a minor official who had written me. The receptionist spoke to one of the elderly English messengers, and he led me, with no great ceremony and a lot of asthmatic breathing, to a room that contained many desks. At one of these my man was sitting. His desk was bare, and the man himself seemed quite vacant and easy in his mind. He had small, smiling eyes, a superior manner, and he didn't know what I had come about.

"In spite of his jacket and tie he wasn't what I was expecting. He wasn't the kind of man I would have worn a dark suit for. I thought he belonged to another kind of office, another kind of building, another kind of city. His name was the name of his merchant caste, and it was easy for me to imagine him in a dhoti reclining against a bolster in a cloth shop in a bazaar lane, with his feet bare, and his fingers massaging his toes, rubbing off the dead skin. He was the kind of man who would say, 'Shirtings? You want shirtings?' and, barely moving his back from the bolster, would throw a bolt of cloth across the sheet spread on the floor of his stall.

"It wasn't shirtings that he flung across the desk at me, but my letter, the letter he had written himself, which he had asked to see. He understood that I was looking for a job and his small eyes twinkled with amusement. I felt very shabby in my suit. He said, 'You had better go and see Mr. Verma.' The English messenger, breathing heavily, and seeming to choke with every breath, led me to another office. And there he abandoned me.

"Mr. Verma wore horn-rimmed glasses. He sat in a less crowded office and he had many papers and folders on his desk. On the walls there were photographs, from the British days, of Indian buildings and Indian landscapes. Mr. Verma looked more worried than the first man. He was higher in the service; and he had probably taken the name Verma to conceal his caste origins. He was puzzled by my letter; but he was also made uneasy by my dark suit and university tie and he attempted in a half-hearted way to interview me. The telephone rang a lot and our interview never got going. At one stage, after talking on the telephone, Mr. Verma left me and went out of the room. He was away for a while and when he came back, with some papers, he seemed surprised to see me. He told me then that I should go to an office on another floor; and, giving me real attention for the first time, told me how to get there.

"The room I knocked at turned out to be a dark little ante-chamber, with a small man sitting before an old-fashioned standard typewriter with a wide carriage. He looked at me with something like terror—it was the effect of my dark suit and the tie, my man-of-two-worlds garb—and he calmed down only when he had read my letter. He asked me to wait. There was no chair. I remained standing.

"A buzzer rang, and the typist-secretary jumped. He seemed,

after this jump, to land on the tips of his toes; he very quickly drew his shoulders up and then down into a kind of cringe, making himself smaller than he already was; and with a curious long tiptoeing stride, a lope, he reached the great wooden doors that separated us from the room on the other side. He knocked, opened; and with his hunched gait, his prepared cringe, disappeared.

"My wish for the diplomatic life had by now vanished. I studied the large framed photographs of Gandhi and Nehru and wondered how, out of squalor like this, those men had managed to get themselves considered as men. It was strange, in that building in the heart of London, seeing those great men in this new way, from the inside, as it were. Up till then, from the outside, without knowing more of them than I had read in newspapers and magazines, I had admired them. They belonged to me; they ennobled me and gave me some place in the world. Now I felt the opposite. In that room the photographs of those great men made me feel that I was at the bottom of a well. I felt that in that building complete manhood was permitted only to those men and denied to everybody else. Everyone had surrendered his manhood, or a part of it, to those leaders. Everyone willingly made himself smaller the better to exalt those leaders. These thoughts surprised and pained me. They were more than heretical. They destroyed what remained of my faith in the way the world was ordered. I began to feel cast out and alone.

"When the secretary came back to the room, I noticed that he still walked on tiptoe, still cringed, still leaned forward. I saw then that what had looked like a cringe, that humping of the shoulders as he had jumped off his chair and loped across to the door, wasn't something he had put on, but was natural. He was a hunchback. This was a shock. I began confusedly to think back to my earlier impressions of the man, and I was in a state of confusion when he motioned me through the door into the inner office, where a fat black man in a black suit, one of our black Indians, was sitting at a big black table, opening envelopes with a paper knife.

"His shiny cheeks were swollen with fat and his lips appeared to pout. I sat down on a chair placed some distance away from his desk. He didn't look up at me and he didn't speak. And I didn't speak; I let him open his letters. Not an hour's exercise had he taken in his life, this devout man of the South. He reeked of caste and temple, and I was sure that below that black suit he wore all kinds of amulets.

"At last, but still not looking up, he said, 'So?'

"I said, 'I wrote in about joining the diplomatic service. I had a letter from Aggarwal and I came to see him.'

"Opening his letters, he said, '*Mister* Aggarwal.'

"I was glad he had found something we might fight about.

" 'Aggarwal didn't seem to know too much. He sent me to Verma.'

"He almost looked at me. But he didn't. He said, 'Mister Verma.'

" 'Verma didn't know too much either. He spent a long time with someone called Divedi.'

" 'Mister Divedi.'

"I gave up. He could outplay me. I said, wearily, 'And he sent me to you.'

" 'But you say in your letter you are from Africa. How can you join our diplomatic service? How can we have a man of divided loyalties?'

"I thought: How dare you lecture me about history and loyalty, you slave? We have paid bitterly for people like you. Who have you ever been loyal to, apart from yourself and your family and your caste?

"He said, 'You people have been living the good life in Africa. Now that things have got a little rough you want to run back. But you must throw in your lot with the local people.'

"That was what he said. But I don't have to tell you that what he was really talking about was his own virtue and good fortune. For himself the purity of caste, arranged marriage, the correct diet, the services of the untouchables. For everybody else, pollution. Everybody else was steeped in pollution, and had to pay the price. It was like the message of the photographs of Gandhi and Nehru in the room outside.

"He said, 'If you become a citizen of India, there are the examinations. We have arranged for them to be taken at some of the universities here. Mr. Verma should have told you. He shouldn't have sent you to me.'

"He pressed a buzzer on his desk. The door opened, and the hunchback secretary sent in a tall, thin man with bright, anxious eyes and a genuine cringe. The new man carried an artist's zip-up portfolio, and he had a long green woollen scarf wound about his neck, although the weather was warm. Without reference to me, with eyes only for the black man, he unzipped his portfolio and began taking out drawings. He held them one by one against his chest, giving the black man an anxious open-mouthed smile every time, and then looking down at what he was showing, so that, with his head bowed over his drawings, and with the cringe that was already there, he looked like a man doing penance, displaying one sin after another. The black man didn't look at the artist, only at the drawings. They were of temples and of smiling women picking tea—perhaps for some window display about the new India.

"I had been dismissed. The hunchback secretary, tense over his old, big typewriter, but not typing, his bony hands like crabs on the keys, gave me one last look of terror. This time, though, in his look I thought there was also a question: 'Do you understand now about me?'

"Walking down the steps, surrounded by the motifs of imperial India, I saw Mr. Verma, away from his desk again, and with more papers; but he had forgotten me. The idle merchant-caste man in the office downstairs remembered me, of course. I received his mocking smile, and then I went out through the revolving door into the London air.

"My crash course in diplomacy had lasted a little over an hour. It was past twelve, too late for the comfort of coffee and cake, as a sign in a snack bar reminded me. I set to walking. I was full of rage. I followed the curve of Aldwych to the end, crossed the Strand, and went down to the river.

"As I walked, the thought came to me: It is time to go home. It wasn't our town that I thought of, or our stretch of the African coast. I saw a country road lined with tall shade trees. I saw fields, cattle, a village below trees. I don't know what book or picture I had got that from, or why a place like that should have seemed to me safe. But that was the picture that came to me, and I played with it. The mornings, the dew, the fresh flowers, the shade of the trees in the middle of the day, the fires in the evening. I felt I had known that life, and that it was waiting for me again somewhere. It was fantasy, of course.

"I awakened to where I was. I was walking on the Embankment, beside the river, walking without seeing. On the Embankment wall there are green metal lamp standards. I had been examining the dolphins on the standards, dolphin by dolphin, standard by standard. I was far from where I had started, and I had momentarily left the dolphins to examine the metal supports of the pavement benches. These supports, as I saw with amazement, were in the shape of camels. Camels and their sacks! Strange city: the romance of India in that building, and the romance of the desert here. I stopped, stepped back mentally, as it were, and all at once saw the beauty in which I had been walking—the beauty of the river and the sky, the soft colours of the clouds, the beauty of light on water, the beauty of the buildings, the care with which it had all been arranged.

"In Africa, on the coast, I had paid attention only to one colour in nature—the colour of the sea. Everything else was just bush, green and living, or brown and dead. In England so far I had walked with my eyes at shop level; I had seen nothing. A town, even London, was just a series of streets or street names, and a street was a row of shops. Now I saw differently. And I understood that London wasn't simply a place that was there, as people say of mountains, but that it had been made by men, that men had given attention to details as minute as those camels.

"I began to understand at the same time that my anguish about being a man adrift was false, that for me that dream of home and security was nothing more than a dream of isolation, anachronistic and stupid and very feeble. I belonged to myself alone. I was going to surrender my manhood to nobody. For someone like me there was only one civilization and one place—

London, or a place like it. Every other kind of life was make-believe. Home—what for? To hide? To bow to our great men? For people in our situation, people led into slavery, that is the biggest trap of all. We have nothing. We solace ourselves with that idea of the great men of our tribe, the Gandhi and the Nehru, and we castrate ourselves. 'Here, take my manhood and invest it for me. Take my manhood and be a greater man yourself, for my sake!' No! I want to be a man myself.

"At certain times in some civilizations great leaders can bring out the manhood in the people they lead. It is different with slaves. Don't blame the leaders. It is just part of the dreadfulness of the situation. It is better to withdraw from the whole business, if you can. And I could. You may say—and I know, Salim, that you have thought it—that I have turned my back on my community and sold out. I say: 'Sold out to what and from what? What do you have to offer me? What is your own contribution? And can you give me back my manhood?' Anyway, that was what I decided that morning, beside the river of London, between the dolphins and the camels, the work of some dead artists who had been adding to the beauty of their city.

"That was five years ago. I often wonder what would have happened to me if I hadn't made that decision. I suppose I would have sunk. I suppose I would have found some kind of hole and tried to hide or pass. After all, we make ourselves according to the ideas we have of our possibilities. I would have hidden in my hole and been crippled by my sentimentality, doing what I was doing, and doing it well, but always looking for the wailing wall. And I would never have seen the world as the rich place that it is. You wouldn't have seen me here in Africa, doing what I do. I wouldn't have wanted to do it, and no one would have wanted me to do it. I would have said: 'It's all over for me, so why should I let myself be used by anybody? The Americans want to win the world. It's their fight, not mine.' And that would have been stupid. It is stupid to talk of *the* Americans. They are not a tribe, as you might think from the outside. They're all individuals fighting to make their way, trying as hard as you or me not to sink.

"It wasn't easy after I left the university. I still had to get a job, and the only thing I knew now was what I didn't want to do. I didn't want to exchange one prison for another. People like me have to make their own jobs. It isn't something that's going to come to you in a brown envelope. The job is there, waiting. But it doesn't exist for you or anyone else until you discover it, and you discover it because it's for you and you alone.

"I had done a little acting at the university—that had begun with a walk-on part in a little film somebody had made about a boy and girl walking in a park. I fell in with the remnants of that group in London and began to do a certain amount of acting. Not in any important way. London is full of little theatrical groups. They write their own plays, and they get grants from firms and local councils here and there. A lot of them live on the dole. Sometimes I played English parts, but usually they wrote parts for me, so that as an actor I found myself being the kind of person I didn't want to be in real life. I played an Indian doctor visiting a dying working-class mother; I did another Indian doctor who had been charged with rape; I was a bus conductor no one wanted to work with. And so on. Once I did Romeo. Another time there was an idea of rewriting *The Merchant of Venice* as *The Malindi Banker*, so that I could play Shylock. But it became too complicated.

"It was a bohemian life, and it was attractive at first. Then it became depressing. People dropped out and took jobs and you understood that they had had pretty solid connections all along. That was always a letdown, and there were times during those two years when I felt lost and had to fight hard to hold on to that mood that had come to me beside the river. Among all those nice people I was the only real dropout. And I didn't want to be a dropout at all. I'm not running these people down. They did what they could to make room for me, and that is more than any outsider can say for us. It's a difference in civilization.

"I was taken one Sunday to lunch at the house of a friend of a friend. There was nothing bohemian about the house or the lunch, and I discovered that I had been invited for the sake of one of the other guests. He was an American and he was interested in Africa. He spoke about Africa in an unusual way. He spoke of Africa as though Africa was a sick child and he was the parent. I later became very close to this man, but at that lunch he irritated me and I was rough with him. This was because I had never met that kind of person before. He had all this money to spend on Africa, and he desperately wanted to do the right thing. I suppose the idea of all that money going to waste made me unhappy. But he also had the simplest big-power ideas about the regeneration of Africa.

"I told him that Africa wasn't going to be saved or won by promoting the poems of Yevtushenko or by telling the people about the wickedness of the Berlin Wall. He didn't look too surprised. He wanted to hear more, and I realised I had been invited to the lunch to say the things I had been saying. And it was there that I began to understand that everything which I had thought had made me powerless in the world had also made me of value, and that to the American I was of interest precisely because I was what I was, a man without a side.

"That was how it began. That was how I became aware of all the organizations that were using the surplus wealth of the Western world to protect that world. The ideas I put forward, aggressively at that lunch, and more calmly and practically later, were quite simple ones. But they could only have come from someone like myself, someone of Africa, but with no use at all for the kind of freedom that had come to Africa.

"My idea was this. Everything had conspired to push black Africa into every kind of tyranny. As a result Africa was full of refugees, first-generation intellectuals. Western governments didn't want to know, and the old Africa hands were in no position to understand—they were still fighting ancient wars. If Africa had a future, it lay with those refugees. My idea was to remove them from the countries where they couldn't operate and send them, if only for a little while, to those parts of the continent where they could. A continental interchange, to give the men themselves hope, to give Africa the better news about itself, and to make a start on the true African revolution.

"The idea has worked beautifully. Every week we get requests from one university or the other where they would like to keep some kind of intellectual life going without getting involved in local politics. Of course, we've attracted the usual freeloaders, black and white, and we've run into trouble with the professional anti-Americans. But the idea is good. I don't feel I have to defend it. Whether it's doing any good as of now is another matter. And perhaps we don't have the time. You've seen the boys at the Domain here. You've seen how bright they are. But they only want jobs. They'll do anything for that, and that's where it may all end. There are times when I feel that Africa will simply have its own way—hungry men are hungry men. And that is when I can get very low.

"To work for an outfit like this is to live in a construct—you don't have to tell me that. But all men live in constructs. Civilization is a construct. And this construct is my own. Within it, I am of value, just as I am. I have to put nothing on. I exploit myself. I allow no one to exploit me. And if it folds, if tomorrow the people at the top decide we're getting nowhere, I've now learned that there are other ways in which I might exploit myself.

"I'm a lucky man. I carry the world within me. You see, Salim, in this world beggars are the only people who can be choosers. Everyone else has his side chosen for him. I can choose. The world is a rich place. It all depends on what you choose in it. You can be sentimental and embrace the idea of your own defeat. You can be an Indian diplomat and always be on the losing side. It's like banking. It is stupid setting up as a banker in Kenya or the Sudan. That was more or less what my family did on the coast. What do the banks say in their annual reports about those places? That many of the people are 'outside the monetary sector'? You're not going to be a Rothschild there. The Rothschilds are what they are because they chose Europe at the right time. The other Jews, just as talented, who went to bank for the Ottoman Empire, in Turkey or Egypt or wherever, didn't do so well. Nobody knows their names. And that's what we've been doing for centuries. We've been clinging to the idea of defeat and forgetting that we are men like everybody else. We've been choosing the wrong side. I'm tired of being on the losing side. I don't want to pass. I know exactly who I am and where I stand in the world. But now I want to win and win and win."

10 Indar had begun his story at the end of that evening at Raymond and Yvette's. He had added to it at different times later. He had begun his story on the first evening I had seen Yvette, and whenever I saw Yvette afterwards she was in his company. I had trouble with both their personalities: I could pin down neither.

In my mind I had my own picture of Yvette, and this never varied. But the person I saw, at different times of day, in different kinds of light and weather, in circumstances so different from those in which I had first seen her, was always new, always a surprise. I was nervous of looking at her face—I was becoming obsessed with her.

And Indar too began to change for me. His personality too had a dissolving quality. As he filled in his story he became in my eyes quite unlike the man who had presented himself in my shop many weeks before. In his clothes then I had seen London and privilege. I had seen that he was fighting to keep up his style, but I hadn't thought of his style as something he had created for himself. I had seen him more as a man touched by the glamour of the great world; and I had thought that given the chance to be in his world, I, too, would have been touched by the same glamour. In those early days I had often wanted to say to him: "Help me to get away from this place. Show me how to make myself like you."

But that wasn't so now. I could no longer envy his style or his stylishness. I saw it as his only asset. I felt protective towards him. I felt that since that evening at Yvette's—the evening which had lifted me up but cast him down—we had exchanged roles. I no longer looked on him as my guide; he was the man who needed to be led by the hand.

That perhaps was the secret of his social success which I had envied. My wish—which must have been like the wish of the people in London he had told me about, who had made room for him—was to clear away the aggressiveness and the depression that choked the tenderness I knew was there. I was protective towards him and towards his stylishness, his exaggerations, his delusions. I wished to keep all those from hurt. It saddened me that in a little while he would have to leave, to carry on with his lecturer's duties elsewhere. That was what, from his story, I judged him to be—a lecturer, as uncertain of his future in this role as he had been in his previous roles.

The only friends in the town I had introduced him to were Shoba and Mahesh. They were the only people I thought he would have had something in common with. But that hadn't worked. There was suspicion on both sides. These three people were in many ways alike—renegades, concerned with their personal beauty, finding in that beauty the easiest form of dignity. Each saw the other as another version of himself; and they were like people—Shoba and Mahesh on one side, Indar on the other —sniffing out the falseness in one another.

At lunch in their flat one day—a good lunch: they had gone to a lot of trouble: silver and brass polished, the curtains drawn to keep out the glare, the three-stemmed standard lamp lighting up the Persian carpet on the wall—Shoba asked Indar, "Is there any money in what you do?" Indar had said, "I get by." But outside, in the sunlight and red dust, he raged. As we drove back to the Domain, his home, he said, "Your friends don't know who I am or what I've done. They don't even know where I've been." He wasn't referring to his travels; he meant they hadn't appreciated the kind of battles he had fought. "Tell them that my value is the value I place on myself. There is no reason why it couldn't be fifty thousand dollars a year, a hundred thousand dollars a year."

That was his mood as his time at the Domain came to an end. He was more easily irritated and depressed. But for me, even during those racing days, the Domain remained a place of possibility. I was looking for a repeat of the evening I had had—the mood of the Joan Baez songs, reading lamps and African mats on the floor, a disturbing woman in black slacks, a walk to the rapids below a moon and drifting cloud. It began to feel like fantasy; I kept it secret from Indar. And Yvette, whenever I saw her, in harsher electric light or ordinary daylight, confounded me again and again, so different from what I remembered.

The days passed; the polytechnic term was over. Indar said goodbye abruptly one afternoon, like a man who didn't want to make too much fuss about a goodbye; he didn't want me to see him off. And I felt that the Domain, and the life there, had been closed to me forever.

Ferdinand too was going away. He was going to the capital to take up his administrative cadetship. And it was Ferdinand whom I went to see off on the steamer at the end of the term. The hyacinths of the river, floating on: during the days of the rebellion they had spoken of blood; on heavy afternoons of heat and glitter they had spoken of experience without savour; white in moonlight, they had matched the mood of a particular evening. Now, lilac on bright green, they spoke of something over, other people moving on.

The steamer had arrived the previous afternoon with its passenger barge in tow. It hadn't brought Zabeth and her dugout. Ferdinand hadn't wanted her to be there. I had told Zabeth this was only because Ferdinand was at the age when he wanted to appear quite independent. And this was true up to a point. The journey to the capital was important to Ferdinand; and because it was important, he wished to play it down.

He had always seen himself as important. But this was part of the new unsurprised attitude to himself that he had developed. From dugout to a first-class cabin on the steamer, from a forest village to the polytechnic to an administrative cadetship—he had leapt centuries. His passage hadn't always been easy; during the rebellion he had wanted to run away and hide. But he had since learned to accept all sides of himself and all sides of the country; he rejected nothing. He knew only his country and what it offered; and all that his country offered him he wished now to take as his due. It was like arrogance; but it was also a form of ease and acceptance. He was at home in every setting, he accepted every situation; and he was himself everywhere.

That was what he demonstrated that morning when I picked him up from the Domain to drive him to the dock. The change from the Domain to the shanty settlements outside—with their scattered plantings of maize, their runnels of filth and mounds of sifted rubbish—jarred more on me than on him. I would have preferred, being with him, and thinking of his pride, to ignore them; he spoke about them, not critically, but seeing them as part of his town. At the Domain, saying goodbye to people he knew, he had behaved like the administrative cadet; with me in the car he had been like an old friend; and then outside the dock gates he had become a reasonably happy, and patient, member of an African crowd, taken with the market bustle.

Miscerique probat populos et foedera jungi. I had long since ceased to reflect on the vainglory of the words. The monument had only become part of the market scene on steamer days. Through that crowd we now began to make our way, accompanied by an old man, feebler than either of us, who had taken possession of Ferdinand's suitcases.

Basins of grubs and caterpillars; baskets of trussed-up hens, squawking when they were lifted by one wing by the vendor or a prospective buyer; dull-eyed goats on the bare, scuffed ground, chewing at rubbish and even paper; damp-haired young monkeys, full of misery, tethered tightly around their narrow waists and nibbling at peanuts and banana skin and mango skin, but nibbling without relish, as though they knew that they themselves were soon to be eaten.

Nervous passengers from the bush, barge passengers, travelling from one far-off village to another, and being seen off by families or friends; the established vendors in their established places (two or three at the foot of the monument), with their box seats, cooking stones, pots and pans, bundles, babies; idlers, cripples and scroungers. And officials.

There were many more officials nowadays, and most of them appeared to be active in this area on steamer days. Not all of them were in police or army uniform, and not all of them were men. In the name of his dead mother, the hotel maid, "the woman of Africa," as he called her in his speeches, the President had decided to honour as many women as possible; and he had done so by making them government servants, not always with clear duties.

Ferdinand and myself and the porter made a noticeable group

(Ferdinand much taller than the men of the region), and we were stopped about half a dozen times by people who wanted to see our papers. Once we were stopped by a woman in a long African-style cotton dress. She was as small as her sisters who poled the dugouts in village creeks, and fetched and carried; her head was as hairless and looked as shaved; but her face had plumped out. She spoke to us roughly. She held Ferdinand's steamer tickets (one for the fare, one for the food) upside down when she examined them; and she frowned.

Ferdinand's face registered nothing. When she gave him back the tickets he said, "Thank you, *citoyenne*." He spoke without irony; the woman's frown was replaced by a smile. And that seemed to have been the main point of the exercise—the woman wanted to be shown respect and to be called *citoyenne*. *Monsieur* and *madame* and *boy* had been officially outlawed; the President had decreed us all to be *citoyens* and *citoyennes*. He used the two words together in his speeches, again and again, like musical phrases.

We moved through the waiting crowd—people made room for us simply because we were moving—to the dock gates. And there our porter, as though knowing what was to follow, dropped his load, asked for a lot of francs, quickly settled for less, and bolted. The gates, for no reason, were closed against us. The soldiers looked at us and then looked away, refusing to enter into the palaver Ferdinand and I tried to get going. For half an hour or more we stood there in the crowd, pressed against the gate, in the stinging sun, in the smell of sweat and smoked food; and then, for no apparent reason, one of the soldiers opened the gate and let us in, but just us, not anyone behind, as though, in spite of Ferdinand's tickets and my own dock pass, he was doing us a great favour.

The steamer was still pointing towards the rapids. The white superstructure, with the first-class cabins, just visible above the customs-shed roof, was at the stern end of the steamer. On the steel-plated deck below, just a few feet above the water, a range of iron-clad barrack-like structures ran all the way to the rounded bow. The iron barracks were for the lesser passengers.

And for passengers who were least of all there was the barge—tiers of cages on a shallow iron hull, the cages wire-netted and barred, the wire netting and bars dented and twisted, the internal organization of the cages hidden, lost in gloom, in spite of the sunlight and the glitter of the river.

The first-class cabins still suggested luxury. The iron walls were white; the timbered decks were scrubbed and tarred. The doors were open; there were curtains. There were stewards and even a purser.

I said to Ferdinand, "I thought those people down there were going to ask you for your certificate of civic merit. In the old days you had to have one before they let you up here."

He didn't laugh, as an older man might have done. He didn't know about the colonial past. His memories of the larger world began with the mysterious day when mutinous soldiers, strangers, had come to his mother's village looking for white people to kill, and Zabeth had frightened them off, and they had taken away only a few of the village women.

To Ferdinand the colonial past had vanished. The steamer had always been African, and first class on the steamer was what he could see now. Respectably dressed Africans, the older men in suits, the evolved men of an earlier generation; some women with families, everyone dressed up for the journey; one or two of the old ladies of such families, closer to the ways of the forest, already sitting on the floor of their cabins and preparing lunch, breaking the black hulls of smoked fish and smoked monkeys into enamel plates with coloured patterns, and releasing strong, salty smells.

Rustic manners, forest manners, in a setting not of the forest. But that was how, in our ancestral lands, we all began—the prayer mat on the sand, then the marble floor of a mosque; the rituals and taboos of nomads, which, transferred to the palace of a sultan or a maharaja, become the traditions of an aristocracy.

Still, I would have found the journey hard, especially if, like Ferdinand, I had to share a cabin with someone else, someone in the crowd outside who had not yet been let in. But the steamer was not meant for me or—in spite of the colonial emblems embroidered in red on the frayed, much laundered sheets and pillowcase on Ferdinand's bunk—for the people who had in the old days required certificates of civic merit, with good reason. The steamer was now meant for the people who used it, and to them it was very grand. The people on Ferdinand's deck knew they were not passengers on the barge.

From the rear end of the deck, looking past the lifeboats, we could see people going aboard the barge with their crates and bundles. Above the roof of the customs sheds the town showed mainly as trees or bush—the town which, when you were in it, was full of streets and open spaces and sun and buildings. Few buildings showed through the trees and none rose above them. And from the height of the first-class deck you could see—from the quality of the vegetation, the change from imported ornamental trees to undifferentiated bush—how quickly the town ended, what a narrow strip of the riverbank it occupied. If you looked the other way, across the muddy river to the low line of bush and the emptiness of the other bank, you could pretend that the town didn't exist. And then the barge on this bank was like a miracle, and the cabins of the first-class deck an impossible luxury.

At either end of that deck was something even more impressive—a *cabine de luxe*. That was what the old, paint-spattered metal plates above the doors said. What did these two cabins contain? Ferdinand said, "Shall we have a look?" We went into the one at the back. It was dark and very hot; the windows were sealed and heavily curtained. A baking bathroom; two armchairs, rather beaten up, and one with an arm missing, but still armchairs; a table with two shaky chairs; sconces with bulbs missing; torn curtains screening off the bunks from the rest of the cabin; and an air conditioner. Who, in that crowd outside, had such a ridiculous idea of his needs? Who required such privacy, such cramping comforts?

From the forward end of the deck came the sound of a disturbance. A man was complaining loudly, and he was complaining in English.

Ferdinand said, "I think I hear your friend."

It was Indar. He was carrying an unusual load, and he was

sweating and full of anger. With his forearms held out at the horizontal—like the fork of a fork-lift truck—he was supporting a shallow but very wide cardboard box, open at the top, on which he could visibly get no grip. The box was heavy. It was full of groceries and big bottles, ten or twelve bottles; and after the long walk from the dock gates and up all the steamer steps, Indar seemed to be at the end of all physical resource and on the verge of tears.

With a backward lean he staggered into the *cabine de luxe*, and I saw him drop—almost throw—the cardboard box on the bunk. And then he began to do a little dance of physical agony, stamping about the cabin and flexing his arms violently from the elbows down, as though to shake out the ache from all kinds of yelping muscles.

He was overdoing the display, but he had an audience. Not me, whom he had seen but was yet in no mood to acknowledge. Yvette was behind him. She was carrying his briefcase. He shouted at her, with the security that the English language gave him here, "The suitcase—is the bugger bringing the suitcase?" She looked sweated and strained herself, but she said soothingly, "Yes, yes." And a man in a flowered shirt whom I had taken to be a passenger appeared with the suitcase.

I had seen Indar and Yvette together many times, but never in such a domestic relationship. For a dislocating moment the thought came to me that they were going away together. But then Yvette, straightening up, and remembering to smile, said to me, "Are you seeing someone off too?" And I understood that my anxiety was foolish.

Indar was now squeezing his biceps. Whatever he had planned for this moment with Yvette had been destroyed by the pain of the cardboard box.

He said, "They had no carrier bags. They had no bloody carrier bags."

I said, "I thought you had taken the plane."

"We waited for hours at the airport yesterday. It was always coming and coming. Then at midnight they gave us a beer and told us that the plane had been taken out of service. Just like that. Not delayed. Taken away. The Big Man wanted it. And no one knows when he is going to send it back. And then buying this steamer ticket—have you ever done that? There are all kinds of rules about when they can sell and when they can't sell. The man is hardly ever there. The damned door is always locked. And every five yards somebody wants to see your papers. Ferdinand, explain this to me. When the man was totting up the fare, all the de luxe supplements, he worked the sum out twenty times on the adding machine. The same sum, twenty times. Why? Did he think the machine was going to change its mind? That took half an hour. And then, thank God, Yvette reminded me about the food. And the water. So we had to go shopping. Six bottles of Vichy water for the five days. It was all they had—I've come to Africa to drink Vichy water. One dollar and fifty cents a bottle, U.S. Six bottles of red wine, the acid Portuguese stuff you get here. If I had known I would have to carry it all in that box, I would have done without it."

He had also bought five tins of sardines, one for each day of the journey, I suppose; two tins of evaporated milk; a tin of Nescafé, a Dutch cheese, some biscuits and a quantity of Belgian honey cake.

He said, "The honey cake was Yvette's idea. She says it's full of nourishment."

She said, "It keeps in the heat."

I said, "There was a man at the lycée who used to live on honey cake."

Ferdinand said, "That's why we smoke nearly everything. Once you don't break the crust it lasts a long time."

"But the food situation in this place is appalling," Indar said. "Everything in the shops is imported and expensive. And in the market, apart from the grubs and things that people pick up, all you have are two sticks of this and two ears of that. And people are coming in all the time. How do they make out? You have all this bush, all this rain. And yet there could be a famine in this town."

The cabin was more crowded than it had been. A squat bare-footed man had come in to introduce himself as the steward of the *cabine de luxe*, and after him the purser had come in, with a towel over one shoulder and a folded tablecloth in his hand. The purser shooed away the steward, spread the tablecloth on the table—lovely old material, but mercilessly laundered. Then he addressed Yvette.

"I see that the gentleman has brought his own food and water. But there is no need, madame. We follow the old rules still. Our water is purified. I myself have worked on ocean liners and been to countries all over the world. Now I am old and work on this African steamer. But I am accustomed to white people and know their ways well. The gentleman has nothing to fear, madame. He will be looked after well. I will see that the gentleman's food is prepared separately, and I will serve him with my own hands in his cabin."

He was a thin, elderly man of mixed race; his mother or father might have been a mulatto. He had conscientiously used the forbidden words—*monsieur, madame*; he had spread a table-cloth. And he stood waiting to be rewarded. Indar gave him two hundred francs.

Ferdinand said, "You've given him too much. He called you *monsieur* and *madame*, and you tipped him. As far as he's concerned, his account has been settled. Now he will do nothing for you."

And Ferdinand seemed to be right. When we went down one deck to the bar, the purser was there, leaning against the counter, drinking beer. He ignored all four of us; and he did nothing for us when we asked for beer and the barman said, "*Terminé.*" If the purser hadn't been drinking, and if another man with three well-dressed women hadn't been drinking at one of the tables, it would have looked convincing. The bar—with a framed photograph of the President in chief's clothes, holding up the carved stick with the fetish—was stripped; the brown shelves were bare.

I said to the barman, "*Citoyen.*" Ferdinand said, "*Citoyen.*" We got a palaver going, and beer was brought from the back room.

Indar said, "You will have to be my guide, Ferdinand. You will palaver for me."

It was past noon, and very hot. The bar was full of reflected river light, with dancing veins of gold. The beer, weak as it was, lulled us. Indar forgot his aches and pains; a discussion he started with Ferdinand about the farm at the Domain that the Chinese or Taiwanese had abandoned trailed away. My own nervousness was soothed; my mood was buoyant: I would leave the steamer with Yvette.

The light was the light of the very early afternoon—everything stoked up, the blaze got truly going, but with a hint of the blaze about to consume itself. The river glittered, muddy water turned to white and gold. It was busy with dugouts with outboard motors, as always on steamer days. The dugouts carried the extravagant names of their "establishments" painted in large letters down their sides. Sometimes, when a dugout crossed a patch of glitter, the occupants were all silhouetted against the glitter; they appeared then to be sitting very low, to be shoulders and round heads alone, so that for a while they were like comic figures in a cartoon strip, engaged on some quite ridiculous journey.

A man teetered into the bar on platform shoes with soles about two inches thick. He must have been from the capital; that style in shoes hadn't reached us as yet. He was also an official, come to check our tickets and passes. Not long after he had teetered out, panic appeared to seize the purser and the barman and some of the men drinking at tables. It was this panic that finally distinguished crew and officials, none of them in uniform, from the other people who had come in and palavered for their beer; and it meant only that the steamer was about to leave.

Indar put his hand on Yvette's thigh. When she turned to him he said gently, "I'll see what I can find out about Raymond's book. But you know those people in the capital. If they don't reply to your letters, it's because they don't want to reply. They're not going to say yes or no. They're going to say nothing. But I'll see."

Their embrace, just before we got off, was no more than formal. Ferdinand was cool. No handshake, no words of farewell. He simply said, "Salim." And to Yvette he gave a nod rather than a bow.

We stood on the dock and watched. After some maneuvering the steamer was clear of the dock wall. Then the barge was attached; and steamer and barge did a slow, wide turn in the river, the barge revealing at its stern tiers, slices, of a caged backyard life, a mixture of kitchens and animal pens.

A departure can feel like a desertion, a judgment on the place and people left behind. That was what I had been accustoming myself to since the previous day, when I thought I had said goodbye to Indar. For all my concern for him, I had thought of him—as I had thought of Ferdinand—as the lucky man, the man moving on to richer experience, leaving me to my little life in a place once again of no account.

But I didn't think so now, standing with Yvette on the exposed dock, after the accident and luck of that second goodbye, watching the steamer and barge straighten in the brown river, against the emptiness of the far bank, which was pale in the heat and like part of the white sky. The place where it was all going on after all was where we were, in the town on the riverbank. Indar was the man who had been sent away. The hard journey was his.

11 It was past two, a time when, on sunny days, it hurt to be in the open. We had neither of us had anything to eat—we had only had that bloating beer—and Yvette didn't reject the idea of a snack in a cool place.

The asphalt surfacing of the dock area was soft underfoot. Hard black shadows had pulled back to the very edges of buildings, buildings which here on the dock were of the colonial time and substantial—ochre-washed stone walls, green shutters, tall, iron-barred windows, green-painted corrugated-iron roofs. A scratched blackboard outside the closed steamer office still gave the time of the steamer sailing. But the officials had gone; the crowd outside the dock gates had gone. The market around the granite wall of the ruined monument was being dismantled. The feathery leaves of the flamboyant trees made no shade; the sun struck right through. The ground, hummocked around tufts of grass, scuffed to dust elsewhere, was littered with rubbish and animal droppings and patches of wet which, coated and bound on the underside with fine dust, seemed to be curling back on themselves, peeling off the ground.

We didn't go to Mahesh's Bigburger bar. I wanted to avoid the complications—Shoba hadn't approved of Yvette's connection with Indar. We went instead to the Tivoli. It wasn't far away, and I hoped that Mahesh's boy Ildephonse wouldn't report. But that was unlikely; it was the time of day when Ildephonse was normally vacant.

The Tivoli was a new or newish place, part of our continuing boom, and was owned by a family who had run a restaurant in the capital before independence. Now, after some years in Europe, they had come back to try again here. It was a big investment for them—they had skimped on nothing—and I thought they were taking a chance. But I didn't know about Europeans and their restaurant habits. And the Tivoli was meant for our Europeans. It was a family restaurant, and it served the short-contract men who were working on various government projects in our region—the Domain, the airport, the water supply system, the hydroelectric station. The atmosphere was European; Africans kept away. There were no officials with gold watches and gold pen-and-pencil sets, as at Mahesh's. While you were at the Tivoli you could live without that tension.

But you couldn't forget where you were. The photograph of the President was about three feet high. The official portraits of the President in African garb were getting bigger and bigger, the quality of the prints finer (they were said to be done in Europe). And once you knew about the meaning of the leopard skin and the symbolsim of what was carved on the stick, you were affected; you couldn't help it. We had all become his people; even here at the Tivoli we were reminded that we all in various ways depended on him.

Normally the boys—or citizen waiters—were friendly and welcoming and brisk. But the lunch period was more or less over; the tall, fat son of the family, who stood behind the counter

by the coffee machine, superintending things, was probably having his siesta; no other member of the family was present; and
the waiters stood about idly, like aliens in their blue waiters'
jackets. They weren't rude; they were simply abstracted, like
people who had lost a role.

The air conditioning was welcome, though, and the absence of
glare, and the dryness after the humidity outside. Yvette looked
less harassed; energy returned to her. We got the attention of a
waiter. He brought us a jug of red Portuguese wine, chilled down
and then allowed to lose its chill; and two wooden platters with
Scottish smoked salmon on toast. Everything was imported;
everything was expensive; smoked salmon on toast was in fact
the Tivoli's plainest offering.

I said to Yvette, "Indar's a bit of an actor. Were things really
as bad as he said?"

"They were much worse. He left out cashing the traveller's
cheques."

She was sitting with her back to the wall. She made a small
arresting gesture—like Raymond's—with the palm of her hand
against the edge of the table, and gave a slight tilt of her head to
her right.

Two tables away a family of five were finishing lunch and
talking loudly. Ordinary people, the kind of family group I had
been used to seeing at the Tivoli. But Yvette seemed to disapprove, and more than disapprove; a little rage visited her.

She said, "You can't tell about them. I can."

And yet that face, of rage, still seemed close to a smile; and
those slanting eyes, half closed above the small cup of coffee
which she was holding at the level of her mouth, were quite
demure. What had irritated her about the family group? The
district she had judged them to come from? The job the man did,
the language, the loud talk, the manners? What would she have
said about the people in our nightclubs?

I said, "Did you know Indar before?"

"I met him here." She put the cup down. Her slanting eyes
considered it and then, as though she had decided on something,
she looked at me. "You live your life. A stranger appears. He is

an encumbrance. You don't need him. But the encumbrance can become a habit."

My experience of women outside my family was special, limited. I had had no experience of dealing with a woman like this, no experience of language like this, no experience of a woman with such irritations and convictions. And in what she had just said I saw an honesty, a daringness which, to a man of my background, was slightly frightening and, for that reason, bewitching.

I was unwilling for us to have Indar in common, as Indar and she seemed to have had Raymond in common. I said, "I can't tell you how much I liked being in your house that evening. I've never forgotten the blouse you wore. I've always been hoping to see you in it again. Black silk, beautifully cut and embroidered."

I couldn't have touched a better subject. She said, "There hasn't been the occasion. But I assure you it's still there."

"I don't think it was Indian. The cut and the work were European."

"It's from Copenhagen. Margit Brandt. Raymond went there for a conference."

And at the door of the Tivoli, before we went out again into the heat and the light, during that moment of pause which in the tropics is like the pause we make before we finally go out into the rain, she said to me, as though it were an afterthought, "Would you like to come to lunch at the house tomorrow? We have to have one of the lecturers, and Raymond finds that kind of occasion very trying these days."

The steamer would have been about fifteen miles downriver. It would have been travelling through bush; it would have passed the first bush settlement. There, though the town was so close, they would have been waiting for the steamer since morning, and there would have been the atmosphere of a fair until the steamer passed. Boys would have dived off dugouts and swum towards the moving steamer and barge, trying to get the attention of passengers. Trading dugouts, poling out from their stations on the bank with their little cargoes of pineapples and roughly made chairs and stools (disposable furniture for the river journey, a specialty of the area), would have been attached in clusters to the sides of the steamer; and these dugouts would be taken—

were being taken—miles downriver, to paddle back for hours, after that brief excitement, through the fading afternoon, dusk and night, in silence.

Yvette had cancelled the lunch. But she hadn't let me know. The white-jacketed servant led me to a room which obviously awaited no visitors and was not at all like the room I remembered. The African mats were on the floor, but some of the upholstered chairs that had been taken away for that evening (and, as I remembered Yvette saying, stored in a bedroom) had been brought out again—fringed imitation velvet, in the "old bronze" colour that was everywhere in the Domain.

The buildings of the Domain had been run up fast, and the flaws that lamplight had hidden were noticeable in the midday brightness. The plaster on the walls had cracked in many places, and in one place the crack followed the stepped pattern of the hollow clay bricks below. The windows and doorways, without architraves or wooden facings, were like holes unevenly cut out of the masonry. The ceiling panels, compressed cardboard of some sort, bellied here and there. One of the two air conditioners in the room had leaked down the wall; they were not on. The windows were open; and with no projecting roof, no trees outside, just the levelled land, the room was full of light and glare and there was no feeling of shelter. What fantasies I had built around this room, around the music that had come out of the record player—there, against the wall next to the bookcase, with its smoked Perspex cover showing dust in the bright light!

To see the room like this, as Yvette lived in it every day, to add my knowledge of Raymond's position in the country, was to catch her unawares and get some idea of her housewifely ordinariness, some idea of the tensions and dissatisfactions of her life at the Domain, which had until then seemed so glamorous to me. It was to fear to be entangled with her and this life of hers; and it was to be surprised and relieved at the disappearance of my fantasies. But relief and fear lasted only until she came in. The surprise then, as always for me, was herself.

She was more amused than apologetic. She had forgotten, but she knew there was something she had had to remember about that lunch. There had been so many changes of plan about the lunch—which was in fact taking place in the staff room of the polytechnic. She went away to make us some scrambled South African eggs. The servant came in to clear some receipts from the oval table, which was dark and highly polished, and to lay the table. "You live your life. A stranger appears. He is an encumbrance."

On the upper shelf of the bookcase I saw the book Indar had shown me that evening in which there was a mention of Raymond and Yvette as generous hosts at one time in the capital—a mention which had mattered to Yvette. The bright light and the altered room seemed to make it a different book. Colour had faded from the backs of books. One book I took out carried Raymond's signature and the date 1937—a note of ownership, but also perhaps at that date a statement of intent, Raymond's expression of faith in his own future. That book felt very tarnished now, with the paper brown at the edges, the red letters on the paper spine almost bleached away—something dead, a relic. Another, newer book carried Yvette's signature with her unmarried name: very stylish, that Continental handwriting, with a fancy *y*, and speaking in much the same way as Raymond's signature of twenty-three years before.

I said to Yvette while we were eating the scrambled eggs, "I would like to read something by Raymond. Indar says he knows more about the country than any man living. Has he published any books?"

"He's working on this book, and has been for some years now. The government were going to publish it, but now apparently there are difficulties."

"So there are no books."

"There's his thesis. That's been published as a book. But I can't recommend it. I couldn't bear to read it. When I told Raymond that, he said he could scarcely bear to write it. There are a few articles in various journals. He hasn't had time for many of those. He's spent all his time on that big book about the history of the country."

"Is it true that the President has read parts of that book?"

"That used to be said."

But she couldn't tell me what the difficulties now were. All I learned was that Raymond had temporarily put aside his history to work on a selection of the President's speeches. Our lunch began to feel sad. Understanding Yvette's position in the Domain now, knowing that the stories I had heard about Raymond would have been heard by others, I began to feel that the house must have been like a prison to her. And that evening when she gave a party and wore her Margit Brandt blouse began to appear like an aberration.

I said, as I was getting ready to leave, "You must come with me to the Hellenic Club one afternoon. You must come tomorrow. The people there are people who have been here a long time. They've seen it all. The last thing they want to talk about is the situation of the country."

She agreed. But then she said, "You mustn't forget them."

I had no idea what she was talking about. She left the room, going through the door that Raymond had gone through after he had made his exit speech that evening; and she came back with a number of magazines, *Cahiers* of this and that, some of them printed by the government printery in the capital. They were magazines with articles by Raymond. Already, then, we had Raymond in common; it was like a beginning.

The rough-bladed grass of the lawns or open areas of this part of the Domain was high; it almost buried the low-level lights housed in mushroom-like aluminum structures that lined the asphalted avenues. A number of those lights had been smashed, some a long time ago; but there seemed to be no one to mend them. On the other side of the Domain the land for the model farm had become overgrown; all that remained of the project was the Chinese gateway that the now absent Taiwanese or Chinese had built, and the six tractors standing in a line and rotting. But the area where the public walked on Sundays, following a fixed one-way route—watched now by the Youth Guard and not the army—was maintained. New statues were still added from time to time to this public walk. The most recent, at the end of the main avenue, was a bulky sculpture in stone, unfinished-looking, of a mother and child.

Nazruddin's old words came to me. "This is nothing. This is

just bush." But my alarm wasn't like Nazruddin's. It had nothing to do with my business prospects. I saw the empty spaces of the Domain, and the squatters from the villages camping just outside; and my thoughts were of Yvette and her life on the Domain. Not Europe in Africa, as it had seemed to me when Indar was there. Only a life in the bush. And my fear was at once the fear of failing with her, being left with nothing, and the fear of the consequences of success.

But that alarm vanished the next afternoon when she came to the flat. She had been there before with Indar; in that setting, my own, she had for me a good deal of her old glamour. She had seen the Ping-Pong table with my household junk and with one corner left clear for Metty's ironing. She had seen the paintings of European ports that the Belgian lady had bequeathed me with the white studio–sitting room.

It was against this white wall that, after some talk about the paintings and the Hellenic Club, both of us standing, she showed me her profile, turning away when I drew close, not rejecting me or encouraging me, just seeming weary, accepting a new encumbrance. That moment—as I read it—was the key to all that followed. The challenge that I saw then was what I always saw; it was the challenge to which I never failed to respond.

Until then my fantasies were brothel fantasies of conquest and degradation, with the woman as the willing victim, the accomplice in her own degradation. It was all that I knew. It was all that I had learned from the brothels and nightclubs of our town. It had been no hardship to me to give these places up while Indar was around. I had grown to find those occasions of vice enervating. For some time, in fact, though it still excited me to see these women in groups in a bar or a brothel front room, I had shrunk from true sex with bought women, and restricted myself to subsidiary sexual satisfactions. Familiarity of this kind with so many women had bred something like contempt for what they offered; and at the same time, like many men who use brothels alone, I had grown to think of myself as feeble, critically disadvantaged. My obsession with Yvette had taken me by surprise; and the adventure with her (unbought but willing) that began in the white sitting room was for me quite new.

What I have called my brothel fantasies hurried me through the initial awkwardness. But in the bedroom with the very large bed with the foam mattress—at last serving the purpose for which I was certain the Belgian painter had intended it—in the bedroom those fantasies altered. The self-regard of those fantasies dropped away.

Women make up half the world; and I thought I had reached the stage where there was nothing in a woman's nakedness to surprise me. But I felt now as if I was experiencing anew, and seeing a woman for the first time. I was amazed that, obsessed with Yvette as I had been, I had taken so much for granted. The body on the bed was to me like the revelation of woman's form. I wondered that clothes, even the apparently revealing tropical clothes I had seen on Yvette, should have concealed so much, should have broken the body up, as it were, into separate parts and not really hinted at the splendour of the whole.

To write about the occasion in the manner of my pornographic magazines would be more than false. It would be like trying to take photographs of myself, to be the voyeur of my own actions, to reconvert the occasion into the brothel fantasy that, in the bedroom, it ceased to be.

I was overwhelmed, but alert. I did not wish to lose myself in the self-regard and self-absorption of that fantasy, the blindness of that fantasy. The wish that came to me—consuming the anxiety about letting myself down—was the wish to win the possessor of that body, the body which, because I wished to win its possessor, I saw as perfect, and wanted continuously, during the act itself, to see, holding myself in ways that enabled me to do so, avoiding crushing the body with my own, avoiding that obliteration of sight and touch. All my energy and mind were devoted to that new end of winning the person. All my satisfactions lay in that direction; and the sexual act became for me an extraordinary novelty, a new kind of fulfilment, continuously new.

How often before, at such moments, moments allegedly of triumph, boredom had fallen on me! But as a means of winning, rather than the triumph in itself, the present act required constant alertness, a constant looking outward from myself. It wasn't tender, though it expressed a great need for tenderness. It became a brute physical act, an act almost of labour; and as it developed it became full of deliberate brutality. This surprised me. But I was altogether surprised by my new self, which was as far from the brothel man I had taken myself to be, with all his impulses to feebleness, as this act was from the brothel act of surrender, which was all I had so far known.

Yvette said, "This hasn't happened to me for years." That statement, if it was true, would have been a sufficient reward; my own climax was not important to me. If what she said was true! But I had no means of gauging her response. She was the experienced one, I was the beginner.

And there was a further surprise. No fatigue, no drowsiness overcame me at the end. On the contrary. In that room with the window panes painted white, a white that now glowed with the late afternoon light, in that heated room, at the end of one of our heavy, hot days, sweating as I was, with a body slippery with sweat, I was full of energy. I could have gone and played squash at the Hellenic Club. I felt refreshed, revitalized; my skin felt new. I was full of the wonder of what had befallen me. And awakening from minute to minute to the depth of my satisfactions, I began to be aware of my immense previous deprivation. It was like discovering a great, unappeasable hunger in myself.

Yvette, naked, wet, unembarrassed, her hair lank, but already herself again, her flush gone, her eyes calm, sat with crossed legs on the edge of the bed and telephoned. She spoke in patois. It was to her house servant: she was coming home right away: he was to tell Raymond. She dressed and made up the bed. This housewifely attention reminded me—painfully, already—of attentions like this that she gave elsewhere.

Just before she left the bedroom she stopped and kissed me briefly on the front of my trousers. And then it was over—the corridor, Metty's dreadful kitchen, the landing, the yellowing afternoon light, the trees of back yards, the dust in the air, the cooking smoke, the active world, and the sound of Yvette's feet pattering down the external staircase. That gesture, of kissing my trousers, which elsewhere I would have dismissed as a brothel courtesy, the gesture of an overtipped whore, now moved me to sadness and doubt. Was it meant? Was it true?

I thought of going to the Hellenic Club, to use up the energy that had come to me, and to sweat a little more. But I didn't go. I wandered about the flat, letting the time pass. The light began to fade; and a stillness fell over me. I felt blessed and remade; I wanted to be alone for a while with that sensation.

Later, thinking of dinner, I drove out to the nightclub near the dam. It was doing better than ever now, with the boom and the expatriates. But the structure hadn't been added to and still had a temporary look, the look of a place that could be surrendered without too much loss—just four brick walls, more or less, around a cleared space in the bush.

I sat outside at one of the tables under the trees on the cliff and looked at the floodlit dam; and until someone noticed me and turned on the coloured bulbs strung about the trees, I sat in the darkness, feeling the newness of my skin. Cars came and parked. There were the French accents of Europe and Africa. African women, in twos and threes, came up in taxis from the town. Turbanned, lazy, erect, talking loudly, they dragged their slippers over the bare ground. It was the other side of the expatriate family scene that had offended Yvette at the Tivoli. To me it all felt far away—the nightclub, the town, the squatters, the expatriates, "the situation of the country"; everything had just become background.

The town, when I drove back, had settled down to its own night life. At night now, in the increasingly crowded main streets, there was the atmosphere of the village, with unsteady groups around the little drinking stalls in the shanty areas, the cooking fires on the pavements, the barring off of sleeping places, the lunatic or drunken old men in rags, ready to snarl like dogs, taking their food to dark corners, to eat out of the sight of others. The windows of some shops—especially clothing shops, with their expensive imported goods—were brightly lit, as a precaution against theft.

In the square not far from the flat a young woman was bawling—a real African bawl. She was being hustled along the pavement by two men, each one twisting an arm. But no one in the square did anything. The men were of our Youth Guard. The officers got a small stipend from the Big Man, and they had been given a couple of government jeeps. But, like the officials at the docks, they really had to look for things to do. This was their new "Morals Patrol." It was the opposite of what it said. The girl would have been picked up from some bar; she had probably answered back or refused to pay.

In the flat I saw that Metty's light was on. I said, "Metty?" He said through the door, "*Patron.*" He had stopped calling me Salim; we had seen little of one another outside the shop for some time. I thought there was sadness in his voice; and going on to my own room, considering my own luck, I thought: Poor Metty. How will it end for him? So friendly, and yet in the end always without friends. He should have stayed on the coast. He had his place there. He had people like himself. Here he is lost.

Yvette telephoned me at the shop late the next morning. It was our first telephone call, but she didn't speak my name or give her own. She said, "Will you be at the flat for lunch?" I seldom had lunch at the flat during the week, but I said, "Yes." She said, "I'll see you there." And that was all.

She had allowed no pause, no silence, had given me no time for surprise. And indeed, waiting for her in the white sitting room just after twelve, standing at the Ping-Pong table, turning over a magazine, I felt no surprise. I felt the occasion—for all its unusualness, the oddity of the hour, the killing brightness of the light—to be only a continuation of something I had long been living with.

I heard her hurry up the steps she had pattered down the previous afternoon. Out of every kind of nervousness I didn't move. The landing door was open, the sitting room door was open—her steps were brisk and didn't falter. I was utterly delighted to see her; that was an immense relief. There was still briskness in her manner; but though her face seemed set for it, she wore no smile. Her eyes were serious, with a disturbing, challenging hint of greed.

She said, "I've been thinking of you all morning. I haven't

been able to get you out of my head." And as though she had entered the sitting room only to leave it, as though her arrival at the flat was a continuation of the directness of her telephone call, and she wanted to give neither of us time for words, she went into the bedroom and began to undress.

It was as before with me. Confronted with her, I shed old fantasies. My body obeyed its new impulses, discovered in itself resources that answered my new need. New—it was the word. It was always new, familiar though the body and its responses became, and as physical as the act was, requiring such roughness, control and subtlety. At the end (which I willed, as I had willed all that had gone before), energized, revivified, I felt I had been taken far beyond the wonder of the previous afternoon.

I had closed the shop at twelve. I got back just after three. I hadn't had any lunch. That would have delayed me further, and Friday was a big day for trade. I found the shop closed. Metty hadn't opened up at one, as I had expected him to. Barely an hour of trade remained, and many of the retailers from the outlying villages would have done their shopping and started back on the long journey home by dugout or truck. The last pickup vans in the square, which left when they had a load, were more or less loaded.

I had my first alarm about myself, the beginning of the decay of the man I had known myself to be. I had visions of beggary and decrepitude: the man not of Africa lost in Africa, no longer with the strength or purpose to hold his own, and with less claim to anything than the ragged, half-starved old drunks from the villages who wandered about the square, eyeing the food stalls, cadging mouthfuls of beer, and the young trouble-makers from the shanty towns, a new breed, who wore shirts stamped with the Big Man's picture and talked about foreigners and profit and, wanting only money (like Ferdinand and his friends at the lycée in the old days), came into shops and bargained aggressively for goods they didn't want, insisting on the cost price.

From this alarm about myself—exaggerated, because it was the first—I moved to a feeling of rage against Metty, for whom the previous night I had felt such compassion. Then I remembered. It wasn't Metty's fault. He was at the customs, clearing the goods that had arrived by the steamer that had taken Indar and Ferdinand away, the steamer that was still one day's sailing from the capital.

For two days, since my scrambled-eggs lunch with Yvette at her house in the Domain, the magazines with Raymond's articles had lain in the drawer of my desk. I hadn't looked at them. I did so now, reminded of them by thoughts of the steamer.

When I had asked Yvette to see something Raymond had written, it was only as a means of approaching her. Now there was no longer that need; and it was just as well. The articles by Raymond in the local magazines looked particularly difficult. One was a review of an American book about African inheritance laws. The other, quite long, with footnotes and tables, seemed to be a ward-by-ward analysis of tribal voting patterns in the local council elections in the big mining town in the south just before independence; some of the names of the smaller tribes I hadn't even heard of.

The earlier articles, in the foreign magazines, seemed easier. "Riot at a Football Match," in an American magazine, was about a race riot in the capital in the 1930s that had led to the formation of the first African political club. "Lost Liberties," in a Belgian magazine, was about the failure of a missionary scheme, in the late nineteenth century, to buy picked slaves from the Arab slave caravans and resettle them in "liberty villages."

These articles were a little more in my line—I was especially interested in the missionaries and the slaves. But the bright opening paragraphs were deceptive; the articles weren't exactly shop-time, afternoon reading. I put them aside for later. And that evening, as I read in the large bed which Yvette a few hours earlier had made up, and where her smell still lingered, I was appalled.

The article about the race riot—after that bright opening paragraph which I had read in the shop—turned out to be a compilation of government decrees and quotations from news-papers. There was a lot from the newspapers; Raymond seemed to have taken them very seriously. I couldn't get over that, be-cause from my experience on the coast I knew that newspapers in small colonial places told a special kind of truth. They didn't lie, but they were formal. They handled big people—business-men, high officials, members of our legislative and executive councils—with respect. They left out a lot of important things—often essential things—that local people would know and gossip about.

I didn't think that the papers here in the 1930s would have been much different from ours on the coast; and I was always hoping that Raymond was going to go behind the newspaper stories and editorials and try to get at the real events. A race riot in the capital in the 1930s—that ought to have been a strong story: gun talk in the European cafés and clubs, hysteria and terror in the African *cités*. But Raymond wasn't interested in that side. He didn't give the impression that he had talked to any of the people involved, though many would have been alive when he wrote. He stuck with the newspapers; he seemed to want to show that he had read them all and had worked out the precise political shade of each. His subject was an event in Africa, but he might have been writing about Europe or a place he had never been.

The article about the missionaries and the ransomed slaves was also full of quotations, not from newspapers, but from the mission's archives in Europe. The subject wasn't new to me. At school on the coast we were taught about European expansion in our area as though it had been no more than a defeat of the Arabs and their slave-trading ways. We thought of that as Eng-lish-school stuff; we didn't mind. History was something dead and gone, part of the world of our grandfathers, and we didn't pay too much attention to it; even though, among trading fam-ilies like ours, there were still vague stories—so vague that they didn't feel real—of European priests buying slaves cheap from the caravans before they got to the depots on the coast. The Africans (and this was the point of the stories) had been scared out of their skins: they thought the missionaries were buying them in order to eat them.

I had no idea, until I read Raymond's article, that the venture had been so big and serious. Raymond gave the names of all the liberty villages that had been established. Then, quoting and quoting from letters and reports in the archives, he tried to fix the date of the disappearance of each. He gave no reasons and looked for none; he just quoted from the missionary reports. He didn't seem to have gone to any of the places he wrote about; he hadn't tried to talk to anybody. Yet five minutes' talk with someone like Metty—who, in spite of his coast experience, had travelled in terror across the strangeness of the continent—would have told Raymond that the whole pious scheme was cruel and very ignorant, that to set a few unprotected people down in strange territory was to expose them to attack and kidnap and worse. But Raymond didn't seem to know.

He knew so much, had researched so much. He must have spent weeks on each article. But he had less true knowledge of Africa, less feel for it, than Indar or Nazruddin or even Mahesh; he had nothing like Father Huismans's instinct for the strangeness and wonder of the place. Yet he had made Africa his subject. He had devoted years to those boxes of documents in his study that I had heard about from Indar. Perhaps he had made Africa his subject because he had come to Africa and because he was a scholar, used to working with papers, and had found this place full of new papers.

He had been a teacher in the capital. Chance—in early middle age—had brought him in touch with the mother of the future President. Chance—and something of the teacher's sympathy for the despairing African boy, a sympathy probably mixed with a little bitterness about the more successful of his own kind, the man perhaps seeing himself in the boy: that advice he had given the boy about joining the Defence Force appeared to have in it something of a personal bitterness—chance had given him that extraordinary relationship with the man who became President and had raised him, after independence, to a glory he had never dreamed of.

To Yvette, inexperienced, from Europe, and with her own ambitions, he must have glittered. She would have been misled by her ambitions, much as I had been by her setting, in which I had seen such glamour. Really, then, we did have Raymond in common, from the start.

THREE

The Big Man

---

12 I often thought about the chance that had shown me
Yvette for the first time that evening in her house, in that
atmosphere of Europe in Africa, when she had worn her black
Margit Brandt blouse and had been lighted by the reading lamps
placed on the floor, and every kind of yearning had been stirred
in me by the voice of Joan Baez.

Perhaps in another setting and at another time she would not
have made such an impression on me. And perhaps if I had read
Raymond's articles on the day Yvette had given them to me,
nothing would have happened the following afternoon when she
came to the flat. I wouldn't have given her cause to show me her
profile against the white wall of the studio–sitting room; we
might instead have simply gone to the Hellenic Club. Seeing her
house in the light of midday had already given me a little alarm.
To have understood more about Raymond immediately after
might have made me see her more clearly—her ambition, her
bad judgment, her failure.

And failure like that wasn't what I would have chosen to be
entangled with. My wish for an adventure with Yvette was a wish
to be taken up to the skies, to be removed from the life I had—
the dullness, the pointless tension, "the situation of the country."
It wasn't a wish to be involved with people as trapped as myself.

But that was what I had now. And it wasn't open to me to
withdraw. After that first afternoon, my first discovery of her, I
was possessed by Yvette, possessed by that person I never
stopped wanting to win. Satisfaction solved nothing; it only
opened up a new void, a fresh need.

The town changed for me. It had new associations. Different
memories and moods attached to places, to times of day,

weather. In the drawer of my desk in the shop, where Raymond's magazines had once lain forgotten for two days, there were now photographs of Yvette. Some of them were quite old and must have been precious to her. These photographs were her gifts to me, made at various times, as favours, rewards, gestures of tenderness; since, just as we never embraced when we met, never wasted the sense of touch (and in fact seldom kissed), so, as if by unspoken agreement, we continued as we had begun and never exchanged words of tenderness. In spite of the corrupt physical ways our passion had begun to take, the photographs of Yvette that I preferred were the chastest. I was especially interested in those of her as a girl in Belgium, to whom the future was still a mystery.

With these photographs in my drawer, the view from my shop had a different feel: the square with the bedraggled trees, the market stalls, the wandering villagers, the unpaved roads dusty in the sun or running red in the rain. The broken-down town, in which I had felt neutered, became the place where it had all come to me.

With that I developed a new kind of political concern, almost a political anxiety. I could have done without that, but it couldn't be helped. Through Yvette I was bound to Raymond, and through Raymond I was bound more closely than ever to the fact or the knowledge of the President's power. Seeing the President's photograph everywhere had already made me feel that, whether African or not, we had all become his people. To that was now added, because of Raymond, the feeling that we were all dependent on the President and that—whatever job we did and however much we thought we were working for ourselves—we all were serving him.

For that brief moment when I had believed Raymond to be as Indar had described him—the Big Man's white man—I had been thrilled to feel so close to the highest power in the land. I felt I had been taken far above the country I knew and its everyday worries—the mountainous rubbish dumps, bad roads, tricky officials, shanty towns, the people coming in every day from the bush and finding nothing to do and little to eat, the drunkenness, the quick murders, my own shop. Power, and the life around the

President in the capital, had seemed to be what was real and essential about the country.

When I understood what Raymond's position was, the President had once again appeared to zoom away and to be high above us. But now there remained a link with him: the sense of his power as a personal thing, to which we were all attached as with strings, which he might pull or let dangle. That was something I had never felt before. Like other expatriates in the town, I had done what was expected of me. We hung up the official photographs in our shops and offices; we subscribed to the various Presidential funds. But we tried to keep all that as background, separate from our private lives. At the Hellenic Club, for instance, though there was no rule about it, we never talked of local politics.

But now, taken deep into the politics through Raymond and Yvette, and understanding the intent behind each new official photograph, each new statue of the African madonna with child, I could no longer consider statues and photographs as background. I might be told that thousands were owed in Europe to the printers of those photographs; but to understand the President's purpose was to be affected by it. The visitor might snigger about the African madonna; I couldn't.

The news about Raymond's book, the history, was bad: there was no news. Indar, in spite of his promise to find out about the book (and that farewell hand on Yvette's thigh on the steamer), hadn't written. It didn't console Yvette to hear that he hadn't written me either, that he was a man with big problems of his own. It wasn't Indar she was worried about; she wanted news, and long after Indar had left the country she continued to wait for some word from the capital.

Raymond in the meantime had finished his work on the President's speeches and had gone back to his history. He was good at hiding his disappointments and strains. But they were reflected in Yvette. Sometimes when she came to the flat she looked years older than she was, with her young skin looking bleached, the flesh below her chin sagging into the beginning of a double chin, the little wrinkles about her eyes more noticeable.

Poor girl! It wasn't at all what she had expected from a life with Raymond. She was a student in Europe when they had met. He had gone there with an official delegation. His role as the adviser of the man who had recently made himself President was supposed to be secret, but his eminence was generally known and he had been invited to lecture at the university where Yvette was. She had asked a question—she was writing a thesis about the theme of slavery in French African writing. They had met afterwards; she had been overwhelmed by his attentions. Raymond had been married before; but there had been a divorce some years before independence, while he was still a teacher, and his wife and daughter had gone back to Europe.

"They say that men should look at the mother of the girl they intend to marry," Yvette said. "Girls who do what I did should consider the wife a man has discarded or worn out, and know they are not going to do much better. But can you imagine? This handsome and distinguished man—when Raymond took me out to dinner for the first time he took me to one of the most expensive places. He did it all in a very absent-minded way. But he knew the kind of family I came from and he knew exactly what he was doing. He spent more on that dinner than my father earned in a week. I knew it was delegation money, but it didn't matter. Women are stupid. But if women weren't stupid the world wouldn't go round.

"It was wonderful when we came out, I must say that. The President invited us to dinner regularly and for the first two or three times I sat on his right. He said he could do no less for the wife of his old *professeur*—but that wasn't true: Raymond never taught him: that was just for the European press. He was extraordinarily charming, the President, and there was never any hint of nonsense, I should add. The first time we talked about the table, literally. It was made of local wood and carved with African motifs at the edge. Rather horribly, if you want to know. He said the Africans had prodigious skills as wood-carvers and that the country could supply the whole world with high-quality furniture. It was like the recent talk about an industrial park along the river—it was just an idea to talk about. But I was new then and I wanted to believe everything I was told.

"Always there were the cameras. Always the cameras, even in those early days. He was always posing for them; you knew that, and it made conversation difficult. He never relaxed. He always led the conversation. He never let you start a new topic; he simply turned away. The etiquette of royalty—he had learned it from somebody, and I learned it from him, the hard way. He had this very abrupt way of turning away from you; it was like a piece of personal style. And he seemed to enjoy the stylishness of turning and walking straight out of a room at the appointed time.

"We used to go out on tours with him. We appeared in the background in a few of the old official pictures—white people in the background. I noticed that his clothes were changing, but I thought it was only his way of wearing more comfortable clothes, African-style country clothes. Everywhere we went there used to be these welcoming *séances d'animation*, tribal dancing. He was very keen on that. He said he wanted to give dignity to those dances that Hollywood and the West had maligned. He intended to build modern theatres for them. And it was during one of those animations that I got into trouble. He had put his stick on the ground. I didn't know that had a meaning. I didn't know I had to shut up, that in the old days of the chiefs, to talk when that stick was down was something you could be beaten to death for. I was close to him and I said something perfectly banal about the skill of the dancers. He just curled his lips in anger and looked away, lifting up his head. There wasn't any stylishness in that. All the Africans were horrified at what I had done. And I felt that the make-believe had turned horrible and that I had come to a horrible place.

"After that I couldn't appear with him in public. But of course that wasn't why he broke with Raymond. In fact, he was friendlier than ever with Raymond afterwards. He broke with Raymond when he decided that he didn't need him, that in the new direction he was taking the white man was an embarrassment to him in the capital. As for me, he never spoke to me. But he always made a point of sending me his regards, of having some official come to ask how I was getting on. He needs a model in everything, and I believe he heard that de Gaulle used to send personal regards to the wives of his political enemies.

"That was why I thought that if Indar made some inquiries about Raymond's book in the capital, it would get back to him. Everything gets back to the President here. The place is a one-man show, as you know. And I was expecting to get some indirect word. But in all these months he hasn't even sent me his regards."

She suffered more than Raymond appeared to. She was in a country that was still strange to her and she was dangling, doubly dependent. Raymond was in a place that had become his home. He was in a situation that he had perhaps lived through before, when he was a neglected teacher in the colonial capital. Perhaps he had returned to his older personality, the self-containedness he had arrived at as a teacher, the man with the quiet but defiant knowledge of his own worth. But I felt there was something else. I felt that Raymond was consciously following a code he had prescribed for himself, and the fact that he was following this code gave him his serenity.

This code forbade him expressing disappointment or envy. In this he was different from the young men who continued to come to the Domain and called on him and listened to him. Raymond still had his big job; he still had those boxes of papers that many people wanted to look through; and after all his years as the Big Man's white man, all those years as the man who knew more about the country than any man living, Raymond still had a reputation.

When one of these visitors spoke critically about somebody's book or a conference that somebody had organized somewhere (Raymond wasn't invited to conferences these days), Raymond would say nothing, unless he had something good to say about the book or the conference. He would look steadily at the eyes of the visitor, as though only waiting for him to finish. I saw him do this many times; he gave the impression then of hearing out an interruption. Yvette's face would register the surprise or the hurt.

As it did on the evening when I understood, from something one of our visitors said, that Raymond had applied for a job in the United States and had been rejected. The visitor, a bearded man with mean and unreliable eyes, was speaking like a man on Raymond's side. He was even trying to be a little bitter on Raymond's behalf, and this made me feel that he might be one of those visiting scholars Yvette told me about, who, while they were going through Raymond's papers, also took the opportunity of making a pass at her.

Times had changed since the early 1960s, the bearded man said. Africanists were not so rare now, and people who had given their life to the continent were being passed over. The great powers had agreed for the time being not to wrangle over Africa, and as a result attitudes to Africa had changed. The very people who had said that the decade was the decade of Africa, and had scrambled after its great men, were now giving up on Africa.

Yvette lifted her wrist and looked carefully at her watch. It was like a deliberate interruption. She said, "The decade of Africa finished ten seconds ago."

She had done that once before, when someone had spoken of the decade of Africa. And the trick worked again. She smiled; Raymond and I laughed. The bearded man took the hint, and the subject of Raymond's rejected application was left alone.

But I was dismayed by what I had heard, and when Yvette next came to the flat I said, "But you didn't tell me you were thinking of leaving."

"Aren't you thinking of leaving?"

"Eventually, yes."

"Eventually we all have to leave. Your life is settled. You're practically engaged to that man's daughter, you've told me. Everything is just waiting for you. My life is still fluid. I must do something. I just can't stay here."

"But why didn't you tell me?"

"Why talk of something you know isn't going to come off? And it wouldn't do us any good if it got around. You know that. Raymond doesn't stand a chance abroad now anyway."

"Why did he apply, then?"

"I made him. I thought there was a possibility. Raymond wouldn't do a thing like that by himself. He's loyal."

The closeness to the President that had given Raymond his reputation, and had made people call him out to conferences in different parts of the world, now disqualified him from serious consideration abroad. Unless something extraordinary happened, he would have to stay where he was, dependent on the power of the President.

His position in the Domain required him to display authority. But at any moment he might be stripped of this authority, reduced to nothing, with nothing to fall back on. In his place I don't think I would have been able to pretend to have any authority—that would have been the hardest thing for me. I would have just given up, understanding the truth of what Mahesh had told me years before: "Remember, Salim, the people here are *malins*."

But Raymond showed no uncertainty. And he was loyal—to the President, to himself, his ideas and his work, his past. My admiration for him grew. I studied the President's speeches—the daily newspapers were flown up from the capital—for signs that Raymond might be called back to favour. And if I became Raymond's encourager, after Yvette, if I became his champion and promoted him even at the Hellenic Club as the man who hadn't published much but really *knew*, the man every intelligent visitor ought to see, it wasn't only because I didn't want to see him go away, and Yvette with him. I didn't want to see him humiliated. I admired his code and wished that when my own time came I might be able to stick to something like it.

Life in our town was arbitrary enough. Yvette, seeing my life as settled, with everything waiting for me somewhere, had seen her own life as fluid. She felt she wasn't as prepared as the rest of us; she had to look out for herself. That was how we all felt, though: we saw our own lives as fluid, we saw the other man or person as solider. But in the town, where all was arbitrary and the law was what it was, all our lives were fluid. We none of us had certainties of any kind. Without always knowing what we were doing, we were constantly adjusting to the arbitrariness by which we were surrounded. In the end we couldn't say where we stood.

We stood for ourselves. We all had to survive. But because we felt our lives to be fluid we all felt isolated, and we no longer felt accountable to anyone or anything. That was what had happened to Mahesh. "It isn't that there's no right and wrong here. There's no right." That was what had happened to me.

It was the opposite of the life of our family and community on the coast. That life was full of rules. Too many rules; it was a pre-packed kind of life. Here I had stripped myself of all the rules. During the rebellion—such a long time ago—I had also discovered that I had stripped myself of the support the rules gave. To think of it like that was to feel myself floating and lost. And I preferred not to think about it: it was too much like the panic you could at any time make yourself feel if you thought hard enough about the physical position of the town in the continent, and your own place in that town.

To see Raymond answering arbitrariness with a code like the one he had worked out for himself seemed to me extraordinary.

When I said so to Yvette she said, "Do you think I would have married someone who was not extraordinary?"

Strange, after all the criticism, or what I had seen as criticism! But everything that was strange in my relationship with Yvette quickly stopped being strange. Everything about the relationship was new to me; I took everything as it came.

With Yvette—and with Yvette and Raymond together—I had acquired a kind of domestic life: the passion in the flat, the quiet family evening in the house in the Domain. The idea that it was my domestic life came to me when the life itself was disturbed. While it went on I simply lived it. And it was only when the life was disturbed that amazement came to me at the coolness with which I had accepted a way of living which, if it had been re-ported to me about someone else when I was younger, would have seemed awful. Adultery was horrible to me. I continued to think of it in the setting of family and community on the coast, and saw it as sly and dishonourable and weak-willed.

It was Yvette who had suggested, after an afternoon in the flat, that I should have dinner with them that evening in the house. She had done so out of affection, and a concern for my lonely evening; and she seemed not to see any problems. I was nervous; I didn't think I would be able to face Raymond in his house so soon afterwards. But Raymond was in his study when I arrived, and remained there until it was time to eat; and my nervousness disappeared in the novel excitement I felt at seeing Yvette, so recently naked, corrupt with pleasure, in the role of wife.

I sat in the sitting room. She came and went. Those moments were utterly delicious to me. I was stirred by every housewifely gesture; I loved the ordinariness of her clothes. Her movements in her house were brisker, more assertive, her French speech (with Raymond now at the table) more precise. Even while (all anxiety gone) I was listening to Raymond, it was a thrill to me to distance myself from Yvette, to try to see her as a stranger, and then to look through that stranger to the other woman I knew.

On the second or third occasion like this I made her drive back with me to the flat. No subterfuge was necessary: immediately after eating, Raymond had gone back to his study.

Yvette had thought I had only wanted to go for a drive. When she understood what I had in mind she made an exclamation, and her face—so mask-like and housewifely at the dinner table —was transformed with pleasure. All the way to the flat she was close to laughter. I was surprised by her reaction; I had never seen her so easy, so delighted, so relaxed.

She knew she was attractive to men—those visiting scholars drove home that message. But to be desired and needed again after all that had happened during our long afternoon seemed to touch her in a way she hadn't been touched before. She was pleased with me, absurdly pleased with herself, and so companionable that I might have been an old school friend rather than a lover. I tried to put myself in her place, and just for a while I had the illusion of entering her woman's body and mind and understanding her delight. And I thought then, knowing what I did of her life, that I had been given an idea of her own needs and deprivations.

Metty was in. In the old days, following old manners, I had

taken care to keep this side of my life secret from him, or at any rate to appear to be trying to do so. But now secrecy wasn't possible and didn't seem to matter. And we never worried about Metty in the flat again.

What was extraordinary that evening became part of the pattern of many of the days we were together. The dinner with Raymond in the house, or the after-dinner gathering with Raymond, occurred in a kind of parenthesis, between the afternoon in the flat and the late evening in the flat. So that in the house, when Raymond appeared, I was able to listen with a clear mind and real concern to whatever he had to say.

His routine didn't change. He tended to be working in his study when I—and visitors, if there were visitors—arrived. He took his time to appear, and in spite of his absent-minded air his hair was always freshly damped, nicely combed backwards, and he was neatly dressed. His exits, when they were preceded by a little speech, could be dramatic; but his entrances were usually modest.

He liked, especially at after-dinner gatherings, to begin by pretending to be a shy guest in his own house. But it didn't take much to draw him out. Many people wanted to hear about his position in the country and his relations with the President; but Raymond no longer talked about that. He talked instead about his work, and from that he moved on to general intellectual topics. The genius of Theodor Mommsen, the man Raymond said had rewritten the history of Rome, was a favourite theme. I grew to recognize the way Raymond built up to it.

He never avoided making a political comment, but he never raised the subject of politics himself and never became involved in political argument. However critical our guests were of the country, Raymond allowed them to have their say, in that way he had of hearing out an interruption.

Our visitors were becoming increasingly critical. They had a lot to say about the cult of the African madonna. Shrines had been set up—and were being set up—in various places connected with the President's mother, and pilgrimages to these places had been decreed for certain days. We knew about the cult, but in our region we hadn't seen too much of it. The President's mother came from one of the small downriver tribes, far away, and in our town we had only had a few statues in semi-African style, and photographs of shrines and processions. But visitors who had been to the capital had a lot to report, and it was easy enough for them as outsiders to be satirical.

More and more they included us—Raymond and Yvette and people like myself—in their satire. It began to appear that in their eyes we were people not of Africa who had allowed ourselves to be turned into Africans, accepting whatever was decreed for us. Satire like this from people who were just passing through, people we weren't going to see again but did our best for, people who were safe in their own countries, satire like this was sometimes wounding. But Raymond never allowed himself to be provoked.

To one crass man he said, "What you are failing to understand is that this parody of Christianity you talk so warmly about can only make sense to people who are Christians. In fact, that is why, from the President's point of view, it may not be such a good idea. The point of the message may be lost in the parody. Because at the heart of this extraordinary cult is an immense idea about the redemption of the woman of Africa. But this cult, presented as it has been, may antagonize people for different reasons. Its message may be misinterpreted, and the great idea it enshrines may be set back for two or three generations."

That was Raymond—still loyal, trying hard to make sense of events which must have bewildered him. It did him no good; all the labour that went into those thoughts was wasted. No word came from the capital. He and Yvette continued to dangle.

But then, for a month or so, their spirits appeared to lift. Yvette told me that Raymond had reason to believe that his selections from the President's speeches had found favour. I was delighted. It was quite ridiculous; I found myself looking in a different way at the President's pictures. And though no direct word came, Raymond, after being on the defensive for so long, and after all the talking he had had to do about the madonna cult, began to be more argumentative with visitors and to hint, with something of his old verve, that the President had something up his sleeve that would give a new direction to the country. Once or twice he even spoke about the possible publication of a book of the President's speeches, and its effect on the people.

The book was published. But it wasn't the book Raymond had worked on, not the book of longish extracts with a linking commentary. It was a very small, thin book of thoughts, *Maximes*, two or three thoughts to a page, each thought about four or five lines long.

Stacks of the book came to our town. They appeared in every bar and shop and office. My shop got a hundred; Mahesh got a hundred and fifty at Bigburger; the Tivoli got a hundred and fifty. Every pavement huckster got a little stock—five or ten: it depended on the commissioner. The books weren't free; we had to buy them at twenty francs a copy in multiples of five. The commissioner had to send the money for his entire consignment back to the capital, and for a fortnight or so, big man as he was, he ran around everywhere with his Land-Rover full of *Maximes*, trying to place them.

The Youth Guard used up a lot of its stock on one of its Saturday-afternoon children's marches. These marches were hurried, ragged affairs—blue shirts, hundreds of busy little legs, white canvas shoes, some of the smaller children frantic, close to tears, regularly breaking into a run to keep up with their district group, everybody anxious to get to the end and then to get back home, which could be many miles away.

The march with the President's booklet was raggeder than usual. The afternoon was overcast and heavy, after early morning rain; and the mud in the streets, drying out, had reached the nasty stage where bicycles and even footsteps caused it to fly about in sticky lumps and pellets. Mud stained the children's canvas shoes red and looked like wounds on their black legs.

The children were meant to hold up the President's book as they marched and to shout the long African name the President had given himself. But the children hadn't been properly drilled;

the shouts were irregular; and since the clouds had rolled over black, and it looked as though it was going to rain again soon, the marchers were in a greater hurry than usual. They just held the little book and scampered in the gloom, spattering one another with mud, shouting only when the Youth Guard shouted at them.

The marches were already something of a joke to our people, and this didn't help. Most people, even people from the deep bush, understood what the madonna cult was about. But I don't think anyone in the squares or the market had any idea what the *Maximes* march was about. I don't think, to tell the truth, that even Mahesh knew what it referred to or was modelled on, until he was told.

So *Maximes* failed with us. And it must have been so in other parts of the country as well, because shortly after reporting the great demand for the book, the newspapers dropped the subject.

Raymond, speaking of the President, said: "He knows when to pull back. That has always been one of his great virtues. No one understands better than he the cruel humour of his people. And he may finally decide that he is being badly advised."

Raymond was still waiting, then. In what I had seen as his code I began to recognize a stubbornness and something like vanity. But Yvette now didn't even bother to conceal her impatience. She was bored with the subject of the President. Raymond might have nowhere else to go. But Yvette was restless. And that was a bad sign for me.

13 Mahesh was my friend. But I thought of him as a man who had been stunted by his relationship with Shoba. That had been achievement enough for him. Shoba admired him and needed him, and he was therefore content with himself, content with the person she admired. His only wish seemed to be to take

care of this person. He dressed for her, preserved his looks for her. I used to think that when Mahesh considered himself physically he didn't compare himself with other men, or judge himself according to some masculine ideal, but saw only the body that pleased Shoba. He saw himself as his woman saw him; and that was why, though he was my friend, I thought that his devotion to Shoba had made him half a man, and ignoble.

I had longed myself for an adventure, for passion and physical fulfilment, but I never thought that it would take me in that way, that all my idea of my own worth would be bound up with the way a woman responded to me. But that was how it was. All my self-esteem came from being Yvette's lover, from serving her and pleasing her in the physical way I did.

That was my pride. It was also my shame, to have reduced my manhood just to that. There were times, especially during slack periods in the shop, when I sat at my desk (Yvette's photographs in the drawer) and found myself mourning. Mourning, in the midst of a physical fulfilment which could not have been more complete! There was a time when I wouldn't have thought it possible.

And so much had come to me through Yvette. I had got to know so much more. I had lost the expatriate businessman's way of not appearing to take too much notice of things, which could end up in genuine backwardness. I had been given so many ideas about history, political power, other continents. But with all my new knowledge, my world was narrower than it had ever been. In events around me—like the publication of the President's book, and the book march—I looked only to see whether the life I had with Yvette was threatened or was going to go on. And the narrower my world became, the more obsessively I lived in it.

Even so, it was a shock when I heard that Noimon had sold up and left, to go to Australia. Noimon was our biggest businessman, the Greek with a finger in every pie. He had come out to the country as a very young man at the end of the war to work on one of the Greek coffee plantations in the deep bush. Though speaking only Greek when he came, he had done very well very quickly, acquiring plantations of his own and then a furniture business in the town. Independence had appeared to wipe him out; but he had stayed put. At the Hellenic Club—which he treated like his private charity, and ruled, having kept it going through very bad times—he used to say that the country was his home.

All during the boom Noimon had been reinvesting and expanding; at one time he had offered Mahesh a lot of money for the Bigburger property. He had a way with officials and was good at getting government contracts (he had furnished the houses in the Domain). And now he had sold up secretly to some of the newfangled state trading agencies in the capital. We could only guess at the foreign-exchange ins and outs, and the hidden beneficiaries, of that deal; the newspaper in the capital announced it as a kind of nationalization, with fair compensation.

His departure left us all feeling a little betrayed. We also felt foolish, caught out. Anybody can be decisive during a panic; it takes a strong man to act during a boom. And Nazruddin had warned me. I remembered his little lecture about the difference between the businessman and the man who was really only a mathematician. The businessman bought at ten and was happy to get out at twelve; the mathematician saw his ten rise to eighteen, but didn't sell because he wanted to double his ten to twenty.

I had done better than that. What (using Nazruddin's scale) I had bought at two I had taken over the years to twenty. But now, with Noimon's departure, it had dropped to fifteen.

Noimon's departure marked the end of our boom, the end of confidence. We all knew that. But at the Hellenic Club—where only a fortnight before, throwing dust in our eyes, Noimon had been talking in his usual practical way about improving the swimming pool—we put a brave face on things.

I heard it said that Noimon had sold up only for the sake of his children's education; it was also said that he had been pressured by his wife (Noimon was rumoured to have a second, half-African family). And then it began to be said that Noimon would regret his decision. Copper was copper, the boom was going to go on, and while the Big Man was in charge, everything would keep on running smoothly. Besides, though Australia and Europe and North America were nice places to visit, life there wasn't as rosy as some people thought—and Noimon, after a lifetime in Africa, was going to find that out pretty soon. We lived better where we were, with servants and swimming pools, luxuries that only millionaires had in those other places.

It was a lot of nonsense. But they had to say what they said, though that point about the swimming pools was especially stupid, because in spite of the foreign technicians our water supply system had broken down. The town had grown too fast, and too many people were still coming in; in the shanty towns the emergency standpipes used to run all day long; and water was now rationed everywhere. Some of the swimming pools—and we didn't have so many—had been drained. In some the filtering machinery had simply been turned off—economy or inexperience—and those pools had become choked with brilliant green algae and wilder growths, and looked like poisonous forest ponds. But the swimming pools existed, whatever their condition, and people could talk about them as they did because here we liked the idea of the swimming pool better than the thing itself. Even when the pools worked they hadn't been used much; it was as if we hadn't yet learned to fit this bothersome luxury into our day-to-day life.

I reported the Hellenic Club chatter back to Mahesh, expecting him to share my attitude or at least to see the joke, bad as the joke was for us.

But Mahesh didn't see the joke. He, too, made the point about the superior quality of our life in the town.

He said, "I'm glad Noimon has gone. Let him get a taste of the good life out there. I hope he relishes it. Shoba has some Ismaili friends in London. They're having a *very* nice taste of the life over there. It isn't all Harrods. They've written to Shoba. Ask her. She will tell you about her London friends. What they call a big house over there would be like a joke to us here. You've seen the salesmen at the van der Weyden. That's expenses. Ask them how they live back home. None of them live as well as I live here."

I thought later that it was the "I" in Mahesh's last sentence that offended me. Mahesh could have put it better. That "I" gave me a glimpse of what had enraged Indar about his lunch with Mahesh and Shoba. Indar had said: "They don't know who I am or what I've done. They don't even know where I've been." He had seen what I hadn't seen: it was news to me that Mahesh thought he was living "well," in the way he meant.

I hadn't noticed any great change in his style. He and Shoba still lived in their concrete flat with the sitting room full of shiny things. But Mahesh wasn't joking. Standing in his nice clothes by his imported coffee machine in his franchise-given shop, he really thought he was something, successful and complete, really thought he had made it and had nowhere higher to go. Bigburger and the boom—and Shoba, always there—had destroyed his sense of humour. And I used to think of him as a fellow survivor!

But it wasn't for me to condemn him or the others. I was like them. I, too, wanted to stay with what I had; I, too, hated the idea that I might have been caught. I couldn't say, as they did, that all was still for the best. But that, in effect, was my attitude. The very fact that the boom had passed its peak, that confidence had been shaken, became for me a good enough reason for doing nothing. That was how I explained the position to Nazruddin when he wrote from Uganda.

Nazruddin hardly wrote. But he was still gathering experience, his mind was still ticking over; and though his letters made me nervous before I opened them, I always read them with pleasure, because over and above his personal news there was always some new general point that Nazruddin wanted to make. We were still so close to our shock about Noimon that I thought, when Metty brought the letter from the post office, that the letter was going to be about Noimon or about the prospects for copper. But it was about Uganda. They were having their problems there too.

Things were bad in Uganda, Nazruddin wrote. The army people who had taken over had appeared to be all right at first, but now there were clear signs of tribal and racial troubles. And these troubles weren't just going to blow over. Uganda was beautiful, fertile, easy, without poverty, and with high African traditions. It ought to have had a future, but the problem with Uganda was that it wasn't big enough. The country was now too small for its tribal hatreds. The motorcar and modern roads had made the country too small; there would always be trouble. Every tribe felt more threatened in its territory now than in the days when everybody, including traders from the coast like our grandfathers, went about on foot, and a single trading venture could take up to a year. Africa, going back to its old ways with modern tools, was going to be a difficult place for some time. It was better to read the signs right than to hope that things would work out.

So for the third time in his life Nazruddin was thinking of moving and making a fresh start, this time out of Africa, in Canada. "But my luck is running out. I can see it in my hand."

The letter, in spite of its disturbing news, was in Nazruddin's old, calm style. It offered no direct advice and made no direct requests. But it was a reminder—as it was intended to be, especially at this time of upheaval for him—of my bargain with Nazruddin, my duty to his family and mine. It deepened my panic. At the same time it strengthened my resolve to stay and do nothing.

I replied in the way I have said, outlining our new difficulties in the town. I took some time to reply, and when I did I found myself writing passionately, offering Nazruddin the picture of myself as someone incompetent and helpless, one of his "mathematicians." And nothing that I wrote wasn't true. I was as helpless as I presented myself. I didn't know where I could go on to. I didn't think—after what I had seen of Indar and other people in the Domain—that I had the talent or the skills to survive in another country.

And it was as if I had been caught out by my own letter. My panic grew, and my guilt, and my feeling that I was provoking my own destruction. And out of this, out of a life which I felt to be shrinking and which became more obsessed as it shrank, I began to question myself. Was I possessed by Yvette? Or was I—like Mahesh with his new idea of what he was—possessed by myself, the man I thought I was with Yvette? To serve her in the way I did, it was necessary to look outward from myself. Yet it was in this selflessness that my own fulfilment lay; I doubted, after my brothel life, whether I could be a man in that way with any other woman. She gave me the idea of my manliness I had grown to need. Wasn't my attachment to her an attachment to that idea?

And oddly involved with this idea of myself, and myself and Yvette, was the town itself—the flat, the house in the Domain, the way both our lives were arranged, the absence of a community, the isolation in which we both lived. In no other place would it be just like this; and perhaps in no other place would our relationship be possible. The question of continuing it in another place never arose. That whole question of another place was something I preferred not to think about.

The first time she had come back to the flat after dinner at the house I felt I had been given some idea of her own needs, the needs of an ambitious woman who had married young and come out to the wrong country, cutting herself off. I had never felt I could meet those needs. I had grown to accept, and be excited by, the idea that I was an encumbrance that had become a habit. Perhaps she was for me too. But I had no means of finding out and didn't particularly want to. The isolation that kept me obsessed had become something I saw as necessary.

In time it would all go; we would both return to our interrupted lives. That was no tragedy. That certainty of the end—even while the boom slackened and my fifteen dropped to fourteen, and Nazruddin and his uprooted family tried to establish themselves in Canada—was my security.

Quite suddenly, Shoba left us to go and visit her family in the east. Her father had died. She had gone for the cremation.

I was surprised when Mahesh told me. Not by the death, but by the fact that Shoba could go back to her family. That wasn't at all what I had been led to believe. Shoba had presented herself as a runaway, someone who had gone against the rules of her community by marrying Mahesh, and was living in this remote place to hide from her family's vengeance.

When she had first told me her story—it had been at lunch on a still, silent day during the rebellion—she had said that she had to be cautious with strangers. It had occurred to her that her family might hire someone, of any race, to do what they had threatened: to disfigure her or to kill Mahesh. Acid on the face of the woman, the killing of the man—they were the standard family threats on these occasions, and Shoba, conventional in so many ways, wasn't too displeased to let me know that the threats had been made in her case. Usually these threats were meaningless, and made only to satisfy convention; but sometimes they could be carried out to the letter. However, as time passed, and Shoba appeared to be forgetting some of the details of her first story, I stopped believing in that drama of the hired stranger. But I took it as settled that Shoba had been disowned by her family.

In my own predicament I had always been conscious of Shoba's example, and it was a letdown to discover that she had kept her lines of communication open. As for Mahesh, he began to behave like the mourning son-in-law. It might have been his way of making a public drama out of the business, taking expensive orders for coffee and beer and Bigburgers (the prices these days!) with an air of tenderness and sorrow. It might have been his way of showing sympathy for Shoba and respect for the dead. But it was also a little bit like the behaviour of a man who felt he had at last earned his place. Well!

But then the joke turned sour. Shoba was to have been away for two months. She returned after three weeks, and then she seemed to go into hiding. There were no invitations to me to lunch; that arrangement—almost that tradition now—at last came to an end. She had hated the political situation in the east, Mahesh said. She had never liked Africans and had come back raging about thieving and boastful politicians, the incessant lies and hate on the radio and in the newspapers, the bag-snatchings in daylight, the nightly violence. She was appalled by the position of her family, whom she had grown up thinking of as solid and secure. All this, combined with her grief for her father, had made her strange. It was better for the time being, Mahesh said, for me to stay away.

But that hardly seemed explanation enough. Was there something more than political and racial rage, and grief for the father whom at one time she had shamed? Was there perhaps a new vision of the man she had chosen and the life she had been living? Some regret for the family life she now saw she had missed, some greater grief for the things she had betrayed?

The air of mourning that Mahesh, in Shoba's absence, had been so glad to put on became a deep and real gloom after Shoba's return; and then this gloom became shot through with irritations. He began to show his age. The confidence, which had irritated me, left him. I grieved for it, grieved that he should have enjoyed it for so short a time. And he, who had spoken so sharply about Noimon, and spoken with such pride about the way he lived here, now said, "It's junk, Salim. It's all turning to junk again."

No longer able to lunch with them or visit their flat, I took to dropping in at Bigburger on some evenings to exchange a few words with Mahesh. One evening I saw Shoba there.

She was sitting at the counter, against the wall, and Mahesh was sitting on the stool next to hers. They were like customers in their own place.

I greeted Shoba, but there was no warmth in her acknowledgment. I might have been a stranger or someone she barely knew. And even when I sat down next to Mahesh she continued to be distant. She seemed not to be seeing me. And Mahesh appeared not to notice. Was she rebuking me for those things she had grown to condemn in herself?

I had known them both for so long. They were part of my life, however much my feelings about them shifted about. I could see the tightness and pain and something like illness in Shoba's eyes. I could also see she was acting a little. Still, I was hurt. And when I left them—no cry of "Stay!" from either of them—I felt cast out and slightly dazed. And every familiar detail of street life at night—the cooking fires gilding the thin, exhausted-looking faces of the people who sat around them, the groups in the shadows below the shop awnings, the sleepers and their boundary markers, the ragged lost lunatics, the lights of a bar fanning out over a wooden walkway—everything had a different quality.

A radio was on in the flat. It was unusually loud, and as I went up the external staircase I had the impression that Metty was listening to a football match commentary from the capital. An echoing voice was varying its pace and pitch, and there was the roar of a crowd. Metty's door was open and he was sitting in pants and undershirt on the edge of his cot. The light from the central hanging bulb in his room was yellow and dim; the radio was deafening.

Looking up at me, then looking down again, concentrating, Metty said, "The President."

That was clear, now that I had begun to follow the words. It explained why Metty felt he didn't have to turn the radio down. The speech had been announced; I had forgotten.

The President was talking in the African language that most people who lived along the river understood. At one time the President's speeches were in French. But in this speech the only French words were *citoyens* and *citoyennes*, and they were used again and again, for musical effect, now run together into a rippling phrase, now called out separately, every syllable spaced, to create the effect of a solemn drumbeat.

The African language the President had chosen for his speeches was a mixed and simple language, and he simplified it further, making it the language of the drinking booth and the street brawl, converting himself, while he spoke, this man who kept everybody dangling and imitated the etiquette of royalty and the graces of de Gaulle, into the lowest of the low. And that was the attraction of the African language in the President's mouth. That regal and musical use of the lowest language and the coarsest expressions was what was holding Metty.

Metty was absorbed. His eyes, below the yellow highlights on his forehead, were steady, small, intent. His lips were compressed and in his concentration he kept working them. When the coarse expressions or the obscenities occurred, and the crowd roared, Metty laughed without opening his mouth.

The speech, so far, was like many others the President had made. The themes were not new: sacrifice and the bright future; the dignity of the woman of Africa; the need to strengthen the revolution, unpopular though it was with those black men in the towns who dreamed of waking up one day as white men; the need for Africans to be African, to go back without shame to their democratic and socialist ways, to rediscover the virtues of the diet and medicines of their grandfathers and not to go running like children after things in imported tins and bottles; the need for vigilance, work and, above all, discipline.

This was how, while appearing just to restate old principles, the President also acknowledged and ridiculed new criticism, whether it was of the madonna cult or of the shortage of food and medicines. He always acknowledged criticism, and he often anticipated it. He made everything fit; he could suggest he knew everything. He could make it appear that everything that was happening in the country, good or bad or ordinary, was part of a bigger plan.

People liked to listen to the President's speeches because so much was familiar; like Metty now, they waited for the old jokes. But every speech was also a new performance, with its own dramatic devices; and every speech had a purpose. This speech was of particular concern to our town and region. That was what the President said, and it became one of the dramatic devices of the later part of the speech: he broke off again and again to say that he had something to say to the people of our town and region, but we had to wait for it. The crowd in the capital, recognizing the device as a device, a new piece of style, began to roar when they saw it coming.

We in the region liked our beer, the President said. He liked it better; he could outdrink anyone of us any day. But we mustn't get pissed too soon; he had something to say to us. And it was known that the statement the President was going to make was about our Youth Guard. For a fortnight or more we had been waiting for this statement; for a fortnight he had kept the whole town dangling.

The Youth Guard had never recovered their prestige after the failure of the book march. Their children's marches on Saturday afternoons had gown raggeder and thinner, and the officers had found that they had no means of compelling children to take part. They had kept on with the Morals Patrol. But the nighttime crowds were now more hostile; and one evening an officer of the Guard had been killed.

It had begun as a squabble with some pavement sleepers who had barred off a stretch of pavement in a semi-permanent way with concrete blocks looted from a building site. And it could easily have ended as a shouting match, no more. But the officer had stumbled and fallen. By that fall, that momentary appearance of helplessness, he had invited the first blow with one of the concrete blocks; and the sight of blood then had encouraged a sudden, frenzied act of murder by dozens of small hands.

No one had been arrested. The police were nervous; the Youth Guard were nervous; the people of the streets were nervous. There was talk a few days later that the army was going to be sent in to beat up some of the shanty towns. That had caused a little scuttle back to the villages; the dugouts had been busy. But nothing had happened. Everyone had been waiting to see what the President would do. But for more than a fortnight the President had said and done nothing.

And what the President said now was staggering. The Youth Guard in our region was to be disbanded. They had forgotten their duty to the people; they had broken faith with him, the President; they had talked too much. The officers would lose their stipend; there would be no government jobs for any of them; they would be banished from the town and sent back to the bush, to do constructive work there. In the bush they would learn the wisdom of the monkey.

"*Citoyens-citoyennes*, monkey smart. Monkey smart like shit. Monkey can talk. You didn't know that? Well, I tell you now. Monkey can talk, but he keep it quiet. Monkey know that if he talk in front of man, man going to catch him and beat him and make him work. Make him carry load in hot sun. Make him paddle boat. *Citoyens! Citoyennes!* We will teach these people to be like monkey. We will send them to the bush and let them work their arse off.''

14 It was the Big Man's way. He chose his time, and what looked like a challenge to his authority served in the end to underline his authority. He showed himself again as the friend of the people, the *petit peuple*, as he liked to call them, and he punished their oppressors.

But the Big Man hadn't visited our town. Perhaps, as Raymond said, the reports he had been receiving were inaccurate or incomplete. And this time something went wrong. We had all thought of the Youth Guard as a menace, and everybody was happy to see them go. But it was after the disbanding of the Youth Guard that things began to get bad in our town.

The police and other officials became difficult. They took to tormenting Metty whenever he took the car out, even on the short run to the customs. He was stopped again and again, sometimes by people he knew, sometimes by people who had stopped him before, and the car's documents were checked, and his own papers. Sometimes he had to leave the car where it was and walk back to the shop to get some certificate or paper he didn't have. And it didn't help if he had all the papers.

Once, for no reason at all, he was taken to police headquarters, fingerprinted and—in the company of other dispirited people who had been picked up—made to spend a whole afternoon with blackened hands in a room with backless wooden benches, a broken concrete floor and blue distempered walls grimy and shining from the heads and shoulders that had rubbed against them.

The room, from which I rescued him late in the afternoon, having spent a lot of time tracking him down, was in a rough concrete and corrugated-iron shed at the back of the main colonial building. The floor was just a few inches above the ground; the door was open, and chickens were scratching about in the bare yard. But rough and homely and full of afternoon light as it was, the room hinted at the jail. The one table and chair belonged to the officer in charge, and these scrappy pieces of furniture emphasized the deprivation of everybody else.

The officer was sweating under the arms in his over-starched uniform, and he was writing very slowly in a ledger, shaping one letter at a time, apparently entering details from the blotched fingerprint sheets. He had a revolver. There was a photograph of the President showing his chief's stick; and above it on the blue wall, high up, where the uneven surface was dusty rather than grimy, was painted *Discipline Avant Tout*—"Discipline Above All."

I didn't like that room, and I thought it would be better after that for Metty not to use the car and for me to be my own customs clerk and broker. But then the officials turned their attention to me.

They dug up old customs declaration forms, things that had been sealed and settled in the standard way long ago, and brought them to the shop and waved them in my face like unredeemed IOUs. They said they were under pressure from their superiors and wanted to go through certain details with me again. At first they were shy, like wicked schoolboys; then they were conspiratorial, like friends wanting to do me a secret good turn; then they were aggressive, like wicked officials. Others wanted to check my stock against my customs declarations and my sales receipts; others said they wanted to investigate my prices.

It was harassment, and the purpose was money, and money fast, before everything changed. These men had sniffed some change coming; in the disbanding of the Youth Guard they had seen signs of the President's weakness rather than strength. And in this situation there was no one I could appeal to. Every official was willing, for a consideration, to give assurances about his own conduct. But no official was high enough or secure enough to guarantee the conduct of any other official.

Everything in the town was as it had been—the army was in

its barracks, the photographs of the President were everywhere, the steamer came up regularly from the capital. But men had lost or rejected the idea of an overseeing authority, and everything was again as fluid as it had been at the beginning. Only this time, after all the years of peace and goods in all the shops, everyone was greedier.

What was happening to me was happening to every other foreign businessman. Even Noimon, if he had still been around, would have suffered. Mahesh was gloomier than ever. He said, "I always say: You can hire them, but you can't buy them." It was one of his sayings; it meant that stable relationships were not possible here, that there could only be day-to-day contracts between men, that in a crisis peace was something you had to buy afresh every day. His advice was to stick it out. And there was nothing else we could do.

My own feeling—my secret comfort during this time—was that the officials had misread the situation and that their frenzy was self-induced. Like Raymond, I had grown to believe in the power wisdom of the President, and was confident he would do something to reassert his authority. So I prevaricated and didn't pay, seeing no end to paying if I should start.

But the patience of the officials was greater than mine. It is no exaggeration to say that not a day passed now without some official calling. I began to wait for their calls. It was bad for my nerves. In the middle of the afternoon, if no one had yet called, I could find myself sweating. I grew to hate, and fear, those smiling *malin* faces pushed up close to mine in mock familiarity and helpfulness.

And then the pressure eased. Not because the President acted, as I had been hoping. But because violence had come to our town. Not the evening drama of street brawls and murders, but a steady, nightly assault in different areas on policemen and police stations and officials and official buildings.

It was this, no doubt, that the officials had seen coming, and I hadn't. This was what had made them greedy to grab as much as they could while they could. One night the statue of the African madonna and child in the Domain was knocked off its pedestal and smashed, as the colonial statues had once been smashed, and the monument outside the dock gates. After this the officials began to make themselves scarce. They stayed away from the shop; they had too many other things to do. And though I couldn't say things were better, yet the violence came as a relief and for a while, to me as well as to the people I saw in the streets and squares, was even exhilarating, the way a big fire or a storm can be exhilarating.

In our overgrown, overpopulated, unregulated town we had had any number of violent outbursts. There had been riots about water, and on many occasions in the shanty towns there had been riots when someone had been killed by a car. In what was happening now there was still that element of popular frenzy; but it was also clear that it was more organized, or that at least it had some deeper principle. Some prophecy, perhaps, had been making the rounds of the *cités* and shanty towns and had found confirmation in the dreams of various people. It was the kind of thing the officials would have got wind of.

One morning, when he brought me coffee, Metty, looking serious, gave me a piece of newsprint, folded small and carefully, and dirty along the outer creases. It was a printed leaflet and had obviously been folded and unfolded many times. It was headlined "The Ancestors Shriek," and was issued by something called the Liberation Army.

The ANCESTORS shriek. Many false gods have come to this land, but none have been as false as the gods of today. The cult of the woman of Africa kills all our mothers, and since war is an extension of politics we have decided to face the ENEMY with armed confrontation. Otherwise we all die forever. The ancestors are shrieking. If we are not deaf we can hear them. By ENEMY we mean the powers of imperialism, the multi-nationals and the puppet powers that be, the false gods, the capitalists, the priests and teachers who give false interpretations. The law encourages crime. The schools teach ignorance and people practise ignorance in preference to their true culture. Our soldiers and guardians have been given false desires and false greeds and the foreigners now qualify us everywhere as thieves. We are ignorant of ourselves and mislead ourselves. We are marching to death. We have forgotten the TRUTHFUL LAWS. We of the LIBERATION ARMY have received no education. We do not print books and make speeches. We only know the TRUTH, and we acknowledge this land as the land of the people whose ancestors now shriek over it. OUR PEOPLE must understand the struggle. They must learn to die with us.

Metty said he didn't know where the leaflet came from. Somebody had just given it to him the night before. I thought he knew more than he said, but I didn't press him.

We didn't have many printeries in the town, and it was clear to me that the leaflet—very badly printed, the type broken and mixed—came from the printing shop that used to do the weekly newspaper of the Youth Guard. That, while it lasted, had been our only local paper, and it was a nonsense sheet—like the wall newspaper of a school, with meaningless advertisements from traders and businessmen and even stall holders in the market, and a few items of so-called news (more like open blackmail) about people breaking traffic rules or using government vehicles as night taxis or building shacks where they shouldn't.

Still, it was very strange. The officers of the Youth Guard, while they had been serving the President, had been hateful to the people they tried to police. Now, humiliated by the President in that "monkey" speech, stripped of power and jobs, they offered themselves to the people as humiliated and anguished men of the region, as defenders of the people of the region. And the people were responding.

It was like the time before the rebellion. But there had been no leaflets then, no leaders as young and educated as these. And there was something else. At the time of the rebellion the town was just beginning to be re-established, and the first disturbances took place far away, in the villages. Now everything was happening in the town itself. There was a lot more blood as a result; and the violence, which at first seemed directed against the authorities alone, became more general. African stalls and shops in the outer areas were attacked and looted. People began to be killed in horrible ways, by rioters and police and shanty town criminals.

Africans and the outer areas first, foreigners and the centre later—that was the way I saw things happening here. So that, having just been freed from a kind of official blackmail against which there was no appeal, I once again had to think of myself as exposed, with nothing to hold on to. I took this fear with me into the familiar streets, this feeling that I was now physically vulnerable. The streets had always been dangerous. But not for me. As an outsider I had so far been allowed to be separate from the violence I observed.

The strain was great. It corrupted everything, and for the first time I considered the idea of flight. If there had been a safe house waiting for me in some far city which would have allowed me in, I believe I might have left during this time. Once there was such a house; once there were several such houses. But there was no such house now. The news from Nazruddin was disheartening. His year in Canada had been bad, and he was uprooting his family yet again, and going to England. The outside world no longer offered refuge; it had remained for me the great unknown and was, increasingly, perilous. What I had once falsely written to Nazruddin had come true. I was in no position to act. I had to stay where I was.

And, forgetting goals, I kept on, living my life: I had learned that years ago from Mahesh. And more and more it happened, in my dealings with people I knew well, that I forgot to study their faces, forgot my fear. In this way fear, the feeling that everything could at any moment go, became background, a condition of life, something you had to accept. And I was made almost calm by something a German from the capital, a man in his late fifties, said to me at the Hellenic Club one afternoon.

He said, "In a situation like this you can't spend all your time being frightened. Something may happen, but you must make yourself think of it as a bad road accident. Something outside your control, that can happen anywhere."

Time passed. No explosion came, no cataclysm such as I had been expecting at the beginning. Fires didn't burn in the centre; the rebels' means were limited. The assaults and killings continued; the police made their retaliatory raids; and something like a balance was achieved. Two or three people were killed every night. But, strangely, it all began to seem far away. The very size and unregulated sprawl of the town muffled all but the most extraordinary events; people in the streets and squares no longer waited for news. News, in fact, was scarce. The President made no statement, and nothing was reported on the radio or in the newspapers from the capital.

In the centre of the town life went on as before. The businessman who came in from the capital by air or by the steamer and put up at the van der Weyden, and went to the better-known restaurants and nightclubs and asked no questions, would not have guessed that the town was in a state of insurrection, that the insurrection had its leaders and—though their names were known only in their own districts—its martyrs.

For some time Raymond had been like a stunned man. At some moment he seemed to have decided that he wasn't going to be called back to the President's favour, and he had stopped waiting, stopped reading the signs. At dinner in the house he no longer analyzed or explained events; he no longer tried to make the pieces fit together.

He didn't talk about history or about Theodor Mommsen. I didn't know what he was doing in his study, and Yvette couldn't tell me; she wasn't too interested. At one time I got the impression that he was reading old things he had written. He mentioned a diary he had kept when he had first come out to the country. He had forgotten so many things, he said; so many things were doomed to be forgotten. That used to be one of his dinner-table themes; he seemed to recognize that, and broke off. Later he said, "Strange, reading those diaries. In those days you used to scratch yourself to see whether you bled."

The insurrection added to his confusion; and after the madonna statue in the Domain had been smashed he became very nervous. It wasn't the President's habit to appear to support those of his men who had been attacked; he tended to dismiss them. And Raymond now lived in fear of dismissal. This was what it had come down to for him—a job, a house, his livelihood, simple security. He was a defeated man, and the house in the Domain was like a house of death.

The loss was mine as well. That house was important to me; and much, as I now saw, depended on the health and optimism of both the people who lived in it. A defeated Raymond made nonsense of my evenings there. Those evenings in the house were part of my relationship with Yvette; they couldn't simply be transferred to another site. That would have meant a new geography, another kind of town, another kind of relationship, not the one I had.

My life with Yvette depended on the health and optimism of all three of us. I was astonished by this discovery. I had discovered it first about myself, when I was under pressure from the officials. I wanted to hide from her then. I felt I could go to her, and be with her in the way I wanted, only in strength, as I had always gone to her. I couldn't present myself to her as a man tormented and weakened by other men. She had her own cause for restlessness; I knew that, and I couldn't bear the idea of the lost coming together for comfort.

It was at this time—as though we understood one another—that we began to space out our meetings. The first days without Yvette, the first days of solitude, subsiding excitement and clear vision, were always a relief. I could even pretend that I was a free man and that it was possible to do without her.

Then she would telephone. The knowledge that I was still needed would be like satisfaction enough, and would be converted, while I waited for her in the flat, into irritation and self-disgust, which would continue right up to the moment when, after pattering up the external staircase, she came into the sitting room, all the strain of Raymond and the intervening days showing on her face. Then very soon, in my own mind, the intervening days would drop away; time would telescope. Physically now I knew her so well; one occasion would very soon seem linked to the last.

But that idea of continuity, however overpowering at those intimate, narrow moments, was an illusion, as I knew. There were the hours and days in her house, with Raymond; there was her own privacy, and her own search. She had less and less news. There were events now we didn't share, and there were fewer things that could be told me without some gloss or explanation.

She telephoned me now every ten days. Ten days seemed to be the limit beyond which she couldn't go. It occurred to me on one of these days—when, the big foam bed already straightened, she was making up her face and considering parts of herself in the dressing table mirror, before going back to the Domain—it occurred to me then that there was something bloodless about our relationship just at that moment. I might have been a complaisant father or husband, or even a woman friend, watching her prepare herself for a lover.

An idea like that is like a vivid dream, fixing a fear we don't want to acknowledge, and having the effect of a revelation. I suppose that, thinking of my own harassment and Raymond's defeat, I had begun to consider Yvette a defeated person as well, trapped in the town, as sick of herself and the wasting asset of her body as I was sick of myself and my anxieties. Now, looking at Yvette in front of the dressing table mirror, seeing her bright with more than I had just given her, I saw how wrong I had been. Those blank days when she was away from me, those days about which I didn't inquire, would have been full of possibilities for her. I began to wait for confirmation. And then, two meetings later, I thought I found it.

I knew her so well. With her, even now, I had never ceased to look outward from myself. No other way would have had meaning, no other way would have been possible. What she drew out of me remained extraordinary to me. Her responses were part of the gift, and I had grown used to them as they had developed; I had learned to gauge them finely. On each occasion I was aware of her sensual memory of me beginning to work, linking the present to the past. But now, on the occasion I speak of, her responses were confused. Something had intervened; some new habit had begun to form, breaking up the delicate membrane of older memory. It was what I had been expecting. It had to be, one day. But the moment was like poison.

Afterwards came that bloodless interlude. The big foam bed had been made up—that housewifely service still, after what used to be passion. I was standing. She was standing too, considering her lips in the mirror.

She said, "You make me look so good. What will I do without you?" That was a standard courtesy. But then she said, "Raymond will want to make love to me when he sees me looking like this." And that was unusual, not like her at all.

I said, "Does it excite you?"

"Older men are not as repulsive as you seem to think. And I am a woman, after all. If a man does certain things to me, I react."

She didn't mean to wound me, but she did. And then I thought: But she's probably right. Raymond's like a whipped boy. It's all he can turn to now.

I said, "I suppose we've made him suffer."

"Raymond? I don't know. I don't think so. He's never given any sign. Of course, he may tell himself something different now."

I walked with her to the landing: the shadow of the house over the yard, the trees above the houses and the wooden outbuildings, the golden afternoon light, the dust in the air, the flamboyant blooms, the cooking smoke. She hurried down the wooden steps to where the sunlight, slanting between the houses, struck full on her. Then, above the noises of the surrounding yards, I heard her drive off.

And it was only some days later that I thought how strange it was for us to have talked of Raymond at that moment. I had talked of Raymond's pain when I was thinking of my own, and Yvette had talked of Raymond's needs when she was thinking of her own. We had begun to talk, if not in opposites, at least indirectly, lying and not lying, making those signals at the truth which people in certain situations find it necessary to make.

I was in bed one evening, about a week later, reading in one of my encyclopaedia magazines about the "big bang" origin of the universe. It was a familiar topic; I liked reading in my encyclopaedias about things I had read in other encyclopaedias. This kind of reading wasn't for knowledge; I read to remind myself in an easy and enjoyable way of all the things I didn't know. It was a form of drug; it set me dreaming of some impossible future time when, in the middle of every kind of peace, I would start at the beginning of all subjects and devote my days and nights to study.

I heard a car door slam. And I knew, before I heard the footsteps on the staircase, that it was Yvette, wonderfully arrived at this late hour, without warning. She hurried up the steps; her shoes and clothes made an extraordinary amount of noise in the passage; and she pushed the bedroom door open.

She was carefully dressed, and her face was flushed. There must have been some function she had been at. Dressed as she was, she threw herself on the bed and embraced me.

She said, "I took a chance. All through dinner I was thinking about you, and as soon as I could I slipped away. I had to. I wasn't sure you would be here, but I took the chance."

I could smell the dinner and the drink on her breath. It had all been so quick—from the sound of the car door to this: Yvette on the bed, the empty room transformed, Yvette in that exclamatory, delighted mood which was like the mood that had overtaken her the first time we had come back to the flat after dinner at the Domain. I found myself in tears.

She said, "I can't stay. I'll just give the god a kiss and go."

Afterwards she remembered the clothes of which so far she had been quite careless. Standing before the mirror, she raised her skirt to pull down her blouse. I, at her insistence, stayed in the bed.

Holding her head to one side, looking at the mirror, she said, "I thought you might have been in your old haunts."

She seemed to be talking more mechanically now. The mood she had brought to the room had left her. At last she was ready. When she looked from the mirror to me she seemed once again, though, to be genuinely pleased with herself and with me, pleased at her little adventure.

She said, "I'm sorry. But I have to go." When she was almost at the door she turned and smiled and said, "You don't have a woman hidden in the cupboard, do you?"

It was so out of character. It was so much the kind of thing I had heard from whores who thought they should pretend to be jealous in order to please. It blasted the moment. Opposites: again this communication by opposites. That woman in the cupboard: that other person outside. That journey out from the Domain: that other journey back. Affection, just before betrayal. And I had been in tears.

It exploded then, all that had been building up in me since she had begun to straighten her clothes. And I was out of the bed, and between her and the door.

"Do you think I'm Raymond?"

She was startled.

"Do you think I'm Raymond?"

This time she was given no chance to reply. She was hit so hard and so often about the face, even through raised, protecting arms, that she staggered back and allowed herself to fall on the floor. I used my foot on her then, doing that for the sake of the beauty of her shoes, her ankles, the skirt I had watched her raise, the hump of her hip. She turned her face to the floor and remained still for a while; then with a deep breath such as a child draws before it screams, she began to cry, and that wail after a time broke into real, shocking sobs. And it was like that in the room for many minutes.

I was sitting, among the clothes I had taken off before going to bed, in the round-backed Windsor chair against the wall. The palm of my hand was stiff, swollen. The back of my hand, from little finger to wrist, was aching; bone had struck bone. Yvette raised herself up. Her eyes were slits between eyelids red and swollen with real tears. She sat on the edge of the foam mattress, at the corner of the bed, and looked at the floor, her hands resting palm outwards on her knees. I was wretched.

She said after a time, "I came to see you. It seemed such a good thing to do. I was wrong."

Then we said nothing.

I said, "Your dinner?"

She shook her head slowly. Her evening was ruined; she had given it up—but how easily! And that head-shaking gesture made me enter into her earlier joy, now gone. My error: I was too ready to see her as someone lost.

She prised her shoes off, using one foot against the other. She stood up, undid her skirt and took it off. Then, just as she was, with her hair done up, her blouse on, she got into the bed, pulled the top cotton sheet over herself and moved to the far side of the bed, always hers. She settled her fluffed-out head on the pillow, turned her back to me; and the encyclopaedia magazine, which had remained on that side of the bed, fell to the floor with its own little noise. And that was how, at this time of farewell, in this parody of domestic life, we stayed for a while, oddly reposed.

She said after some time, "Aren't you coming?"

I was too nervous to move or talk.

A while later, turning to me, she said, "You can't keep sitting on that chair."

I went and sat on the bed beside her. Her body had a softness, a pliability, and a great warmth. Only once or twice before had I known her like that. At this moment! I held her legs apart. She raised them slightly—smooth concavities of flesh on either side of the inner ridge—and then I spat on her between the legs until I had no more spit. All her softness vanished in outrage. She shouted, "You can't do that!" Bone struck against bone again; my hand ached at every blow; until she rolled across the bed to the other side and, sitting up, began to dial the telephone. Who was she telephoning at this hour? Who could she turn to, who was she so sure of?

She said, "Raymond. Oh, Raymond. No, no. I'm all right. I'm sorry. I'm coming right away."

She put on her skirt and shoes, and through the door that she left open she swung out into the passage. No pause, no hesitation: I heard her pattering down the staircase—what a sound now! The bed, where nothing had occurred, was in a mess—for the first time, after she had been: I had had the last of that housewifely service. There were the marks of her head on the pillow, the gathers in the sheet from her movements: things now rare, indescribably precious to me, those relics in cloth that would go so soon. I lay down where she had lain, to get her smell.

Outside the door Metty said, "Salim?" He called again, "Salim." And he came in, in his underpants.

I said, "Oh, Ali, Ali. Terrible things happened tonight. I spat on her. She made me spit on her."

"People quarrel. After three years a thing doesn't just end like this."

"Ali, it isn't that. I couldn't do anything with her. I didn't want her, I didn't want her. That is what I can't bear. It's all gone."

"You mustn't stay inside. Come outside. I will put on my pants and shirt and I will walk with you. We will walk together. We will walk to the river. Come, I will walk with you."

The river, the river at night. No, no.

"I know more things about your family than you, Salim. It is better for you to walk it off. It is the best way."

"I'll stay here."

He stood about for a little, then he went to his room. But I knew that he was waiting and watching. All the back of my swollen hand was aching; my little finger felt dead. The skin was blue-black in parts—that too now a relic.

I was ready when the telephone rang.

"Salim, I didn't want to leave. How are you?"

"Dreadful. And you?"

"When I left I drove slowly. Then after the bridge I drove very fast, to get back here to telephone you."

"I knew that you would. I was waiting for it."

"Do you want me to come back? The road is quite empty. I can be back in twenty minutes. Oh, Salim. I look dreadful. My face is in an awful state. I will have to hide for days."

"You will always look wonderful to me. You know that."

"I should have given you some Valium when I saw how you were. But I thought about that only when I was in the car. You must try to sleep. Make some hot milk and try to sleep. It helps to have a hot drink. Let Metty make some hot milk for you."

Never closer, never more like a wife, than at this moment. It was easier to talk on the telephone. And when that was over, I began to watch through the night, waiting for daylight and another telephone call. Metty was sleeping. He had left the door of his room open, and I heard his breathing.

There came a moment, with the coming of the light, when

suddenly the night became part of the past. The brush strokes on the white-painted window panes began to show, and at that time, out of my great pain, I had an illumination. It didn't come in words; the words I attempted to fit to it were confused and caused the illumination itself to vanish. It seemed to me that men were born only to grow old, to live out their span, to acquire experience. Men lived to acquire experience; the quality of the experience was immaterial; pleasure and pain—and above all, pain—had no meaning; to possess pain was as meaningless as to chase pleasure. And even when the illumination vanished, became as thin and half nonsensical as a dream, I remembered that I had had it, that knowledge about the illusion of pain.

The light brightened through the white-painted windows. The disturbed room changed its character. It seemed to have become stale. The only true relic was now my aching hand, though if I had looked I would have found a hair or two from her head. I dressed, went downstairs and, giving up the idea of a morning walk, began to drive about the awakening town. I felt refreshed by the colours; I thought this early morning drive was something I should have done more often.

Just before seven I went to the centre, to Bigburger. Sacks and boxes of uncollected rubbish were on the pavement. Ildephonse was there, the jacket of his uniform now as worn as the décor. Even at this early hour Ildephonse had been drinking; as with most Africans, he needed just a little of the weak local beer to top up and get high. He had known me for years; I was the first customer of the day; yet he hardly acknowledged me. His beer-glazed eyes stared past me at the street. In one of the lines or furrows of his lower lip he had fitted a toothpick, very precisely, very snugly, so he could talk or let his lower lip fall without the toothpick being disturbed; it was like a trick.

I called him back from wherever he was, and he gave me a cup of coffee and a slice of processed cheese in a roll. That was two hundred francs, nearly six dollars; prices were ridiculous these days.

A few minutes before eight, Mahesh came. He had been letting himself go. He had always been proud of his smallness and spareness. But he wasn't as spare as he had been; I could just begin to see him as a simpler kind of small fat man.

The effect of his arrival on Ildephonse was electric. The glazed look left Ildephonse's eyes, the toothpick disappeared, and he began to jump about, smiling and welcoming the early morning customers, mainly guests from the van der Weyden.

I was hoping that Mahesh would notice my condition. But he made no reference to it; he didn't even seem surprised to see me.

He said, "Shoba wants to see you, Salim."

"How is she?"

"She is better. I think she is better. She wants to see you. You must come to the flat. Come for a meal. Come for lunch. Come for lunch tomorrow."

Zabeth helped me to get through the morning. It was her shopping day. Her business had gone down since the insurrection, and her news these days was of trouble in the villages. Young men were being kidnapped here and there by the police and the army: it was the new government tactic. Though nothing appeared in the newspapers, the bush was now again at war. Zabeth seemed to be on the side of the rebels, but I couldn't be sure; and I tried to be as neutral as I could.

I asked about Ferdinand. His time in the capital as an administrative cadet was over. He was due for some big post soon, and the last I had heard from Zabeth was that he was being considered as a successor to our local commissioner, who had been sacked shortly after the insurrection had broken out. Ferdinand's mixed tribal ancestry made him a good choice for the difficult post.

Zabeth, speaking the big title quite calmly (I thought of the old subscription book for the lycée gymnasium, and of the days when the governor of the province signed by himself on a whole page, like royalty), Zabeth said, "I suppose Fer'nand will be commissioner, Salim. If they let him live."

"If he lives, Beth?"

"If they don't kill him. I don't know whether I would like him to take that job, Salim. Both sides would want to kill him. And the President will want to kill him first, as a sacrifice. He is a jealous man, Salim. He will allow nobody to get big in this place. It is only his photo everywhere. And look at the papers. His photo is bigger than everybody else's, every day. Look."

The previous day's paper from the capital was on my desk, and the photograph Zabeth pointed to was of the President addressing government officials in the southern province.

"Look, Salim. He is very big. The others are so small you can scarcely see them. You can't tell who is who."

The officials were in the regulation dress devised by the President—short-sleeved jackets, cravats, in place of shirts and ties. They sat in neat packed rows and in the photograph they did look alike. But Zabeth was pointing out something else to me. She didn't see the photograph as a photograph; she didn't interpret distance and perspective. She was concerned with the actual space occupied in the printed picture by different figures. She was, in fact, pointing out something I had never noticed: in pictures in the newspapers only visiting foreigners were given equal space with the President. With local people the President was always presented as a towering figure. Even if pictures were of the same size, the President's picture would be of his face alone, while the other man would be shown full length. So now, in the photograph of the President addressing the southern officials, a photograph taken from over the President's shoulder, the President's shoulders, head and cap occupied most of the space, and the officials were dots close together, similarly dressed.

"He is killing those men, Salim. They are screaming inside, and he knows they're screaming. And you know, Salim, that isn't a fetish he's got there. It's nothing."

She was looking at the big photograph in the shop, which showed the President holding up his chief's stick, carved with various emblems. In the distended belly of the squat human figure halfway down the stick the special fetish was thought to be lodged.

She said, "That's *nothing*. I'll tell you about the President. He's got a man, and this man goes ahead of him wherever he goes. This man jumps out of the car before the car stops, and everything that is bad for the President follows this man and leaves the President free. I saw it, Salim. And I will tell you something. The man who jumps out and gets lost in the crowd is white."

"But the President hasn't been here, Beth."

"I saw it, Salim. I saw the man. And you mustn't tell me that you don't know."

Metty was good all that day. Without referring to what had happened, he handled me with awe (awe for me as a violent, wounded man) and tenderness. I recalled moments like this from our own compound life on the coast, after some bad family quarrel. I suppose he recalled such moments too, and fell into old ways. I began in the end to act for him, and that was a help.

I allowed him to send me home to the flat in the middle of the afternoon; he said he would close up. He didn't go to his family afterwards, as was his custom. He came to the flat and discreetly let me know that he was there, and staying. I heard him tiptoeing about. There was no need for that, but the attention comforted me; and on that bed, where from time to time I caught some faint scent from the day before (no, that day itself), I began to sleep.

Time moved in jerks. Whenever I awakened I was confused. Neither the afternoon light nor the noisy darkness seemed right. So the second night passed. And the telephone didn't ring and I didn't telephone. In the morning Metty brought me coffee.

I went to Mahesh and Shoba's for lunch: it seemed to me that I had been to Bigburger and received that invitation a long time ago.

The flat, with its curtains drawn to keep out the glare, with its nice Persian carpets and brass, and all its other fussy little pieces, was as I remembered it. It was a silent lunch, not especially a lunch of reunion or reconciliation. We didn't talk about recent events. The topic of property values—at one time Mahesh's favourite topic, but now depressing to everybody—didn't come up. When we did talk, it was about what we were eating.

Towards the end Shoba asked about Yvette. It was the first

time she had done so. I gave her some idea of how things were. She said, "I'm sorry. Something like that may not happen to you again for twenty years." And after all that I had thought about Shoba, her conventional ways and her malice, I was amazed by her sympathy and wisdom.

Mahesh cleared the table and prepared the Nescafé—so far I had seen no servant. Shoba pulled one set of curtains apart a little, to let in more light. She sat, in the extra light, on the modern settee—shiny tubular metal frame, chunky padded armrests—and asked me to sit beside her. "Here, Salim."

She looked carefully at me while I sat down. Then, lifting her head a little, she showed me her profile and said, "Do you see anything on my face?"

I didn't understand the question.

She said, "Salim!" and turned her face full to me, keeping it lifted, fixing her eyes on mine. "Am I still badly disfigured? Look around my eyes and my left cheek. Especially the left cheek. What do you see?"

Mahesh had set down the cups of coffee on the low table and was standing beside me, looking with me. He said, "Salim can't see anything."

Shoba said, "Let him speak for himself. Look at my left eye. Look at the skin below the eye, and on the cheekbone." And she held her face up, as though posing for a head on a coin.

Looking hard, looking for what she wanted me to find, I saw that what I had thought of as the colour of fatigue or illness below her eye was also in parts a very slight staining of the skin, a faint lividness on her pale skin, just noticeable on the left cheekbone. And having seen it, after having not seen it, I couldn't help seeing it; and I saw it as the disfigurement she took it to be. She saw that I saw. She went sad, resigned.

Mahesh said, "It isn't so bad now. You *made* him see it."

Shoba said, "When I told my family that I was going to live with Mahesh, my brothers threatened to throw acid on my face. You could say that has come to pass. When my father died they sent me a cable. I took that as a sign that they wanted me to go back home for the ceremonies. It was a terrible way to go back

—my father dead, the country in such a state, the Africans being so awful. I saw everybody on the edge of a precipice. But I couldn't tell them that. When you asked them what they were going to do, they would pretend that it was all all right, there was nothing to worry about. And you would have to pretend with them. Why are we like that?

"One morning I don't know what possessed me. There was this Sindhi girl who had studied in England—as she said—and had set up a hairdresser's shop. The sun is very bright in the highlands there, and I had done a lot of driving about, visiting old friends and just driving about, getting out of the house. Every place I used to like, and went to see, I began to hate, and I had to stop. I suppose it was that driving about that had darkened and blotched my skin. I asked the Sindhi girl whether there wasn't some cream or something I could use. She said she had something. She used this something. I cried out to her to stop. She had used peroxide. I ran home with my face scorched. And that house of death became for me truly a house of grief.

"I couldn't stay after that. I had to hide my face from everybody. And then I ran back here, to hide as before. Now I can go nowhere. I only go out at night sometimes. It has got better. But I still have to be careful. Don't tell me anything, Salim. I saw the truth in your eyes. I can't go abroad now. I so much wanted to go, to get away. And we had the money. New York, London, Paris. Do you know Paris? There is a skin specialist there. They say he peels your skin better than anybody else. That would be nice, if I could get there. And then I could go anywhere. Suisse, now—how do you say it in English?"

"Switzerland."

"You see. Living in this flat, I'm even forgetting my English. That would be a nice place, I always think, if you could get a permit."

All the while Mahesh looked at her face, half encouraging her, half irritated with her. His elegant red cotton shirt with the stiff, nicely shaped collar was open at the neck—it was part of the stylishness he had learned from her.

I was glad to get away from them, from the obsession they had forced on me in their sitting room. Peeling, skin—the words made me uneasy long after I had left them.

Their obsession was with more than a skin blemish. They had cut themselves off. Once they were supported by their idea of their high traditions (kept going somewhere else, by other people); now they were empty in Africa, and unprotected, with nothing to fall back on. They had begun to rot. I was like them. Unless I acted now, my fate would be like theirs. That constant questioning of mirrors and eyes; compelling others to look for the blemish that kept you in hiding; lunacy in a small room.

I decided to rejoin the world, to break out of the narrow geography of the town, to do my duty by those who depended on me. I wrote to Nazruddin that I was coming to London for a visit, leaving him to interpret that simple message. What a decision, though! When no other choice was left to me, when family and community hardly existed, when duty hardly had a meaning, and there were no safe houses.

I left eventually on a plane which travelled on to the east of the continent before it turned north. This plane stopped at our airport. I didn't have to go to the capital to take it. So even now the capital remained unknown to me.

I fell asleep on the night flight to Europe. A woman in the window seat, going out to the aisle, rubbed against my legs and awakened me. I thought: But that's Yvette. She's with me, then. I'll wait for her to come back. And wide awake, for ten or fifteen seconds I waited. Then I understood that it had been a waking dream. That was pain, to understand that I was alone, and flying to quite a different destiny.

15 I had never travelled on an airplane before. I half remembered what Indar had said about airplane travel; he had said, more or less, that the airplane had helped him to adjust to his homelessness. I began to understand what he meant.

I was in Africa one day; I was in Europe the next morning. It was more than travelling fast. It was like being in two places at once. I woke up in London with little bits of Africa on me—like the airport tax ticket, given me by an official I knew, in the middle of another kind of crowd, in another kind of building, in another climate. Both places were real; both places were unreal. You could play off one against the other; and you had no feeling of having made a final decision, a great last journey. Which, in a way, was what this was for me, though I only had an excursion ticket, a visitor's visa, and I had to go back within six weeks.

The Europe the airplane brought me to was not the Europe I had known all my life. When I was a child Europe ruled my world. It had defeated the Arabs in Africa and controlled the interior of the continent. It ruled the coast and all the countries of the Indian Ocean with which we traded; it supplied our goods. We knew who we were and where we had come from. But it was Europe that gave us the descriptive postage stamps that gave us our ideas of what was picturesque about ourselves. It also gave us a new language.

Europe no longer ruled. But it still fed us in a hundred ways with its language and sent us its increasingly wonderful goods, things which, in the bush of Africa, added year by year to our idea of who we were, gave us that idea of our modernity and development, and made us aware of another Europe—the Europe of great cities, great stores, great buildings, great universities. To that Europe only the privileged or the gifted among us journeyed. That was the Europe Indar had gone to when he had left for his famous university. That was the Europe that someone like Shoba had in mind when she spoke of travelling.

But the Europe I had come to—and knew from the outset I was coming to—was neither the old Europe nor the new. It was something shrunken and mean and forbidding. It was the Europe where Indar, after his time at the famous university, had suffered and tried to come to some resolution about his place in the world; where Nazruddin and his family had taken refuge; where hundreds of thousands of people like myself, from parts of the world like mine, had forced themselves in, to work and live.

Of this Europe I could form no mental picture. But it was there in London; it couldn't be missed; and there was no mystery. The effect of those little stalls, booths, kiosks and choked grocery shops—run by people like myself—was indeed of people who had squashed themselves in. They traded in the middle of London as they had traded in the middle of Africa. The goods travelled a shorter distance, but the relationship of the trader to his goods remained the same. In the streets of London I saw these people, who were like myself, as from a distance. I saw the young girls selling packets of cigarettes at midnight, seemingly imprisoned in their kiosks, like puppets in a puppet theatre. They were cut off from the life of the great city where they had come to live, and I wondered about the pointlessness of their own hard life, the pointlessness of their difficult journey.

What illusions Africa gave to people who came from outside! In Africa I had thought of our instinct and capacity for work, even in extreme conditions, as heroic and creative. I had contrasted it with the indifference and withdrawal of village Africa. But now in London, against a background of busyness, I saw this instinct purely as instinct, pointless, serving only itself. And a feeling of rebellion possessed me, stronger than any I had known in my childhood. To this was added a new sympathy for the rebellion Indar had spoken of to me, the rebellion he had discovered when he had walked beside the river of London and had decided to reject the ideas of home and ancestral piety, the unthinking worship of his great men, the self-suppression that went with that worship and those ideas, and to throw himself consciously into the bigger, harder world. It was the only way I could live here, if I had to live here.

Yet I had had my life of rebellion, in Africa. I had taken it as far as I could take it. And I had come to London for relief and rescue, clinging to what remained of our organized life.

Nazruddin wasn't surprised by my engagement to his daughter Kareisha. He had always, as I realised with dismay, held fast to that idea of my faithfulness which years before he had seen in my hand. Kareisha herself wasn't surprised. In fact, the only person who seemed to examine the event with some astonishment was myself, who marvelled that such a turn in my life could occur so easily.

The engagement came almost at the end of my time in London. But it had been taken as settled from the start. And, really, it was comforting, in the strange big city, after that fast journey, to be taken over by Kareisha, to have her call me by my name all the time, to have her lead me about London, she the knowing one (Uganda and Canada behind her), I the primitive (acting up a little).

She was a pharmacist. That was partly Nazruddin's doing. With his experience of change and sudden upheaval, he had long ago lost faith in the power of property and business to protect people; and he had pushed his children into acquiring skills that could be turned to account anywhere. It might have been her job that gave Kareisha her serenity, extraordinary for an unmarried woman of thirty from our community; or it might have been her full family life, and the example of Nazruddin, still relishing his experiences and looking for new sights. But I felt more and more that at some stage in Kareisha's wanderings there must have been a romance. At one time the idea would have outraged me. I didn't mind now. And the man must have been nice. Because he had left Kareisha with an affection for men. This was new to me; my experience of women was so limited. I luxuriated in this affection of Kareisha's, and acted out my man's role a little. It was wonderfully soothing.

Acted—there was a lot of that about me at this time. Because always I had to go back to my hotel (not far from their flat) and there I had to face my solitude, the other man that I also was. I hated that hotel room. It made me feel I was nowhere. It forced old anxieties on me and added new ones, about London, about this bigger world where I would have to make my way. Where would I start? When I turned the television on, it wasn't to marvel. It was to become aware of the great strangeness outside, and to wonder how those men on the screen had had themselves picked out from the crowd. And always in my mind then was the comfort of "going back," of taking another airplane, of perhaps not having, after all, to be here. The decisions and the pleasures of the day and early evening were regularly cancelled out by me at night.

Indar had said about people like me that when we came to a great city we closed our eyes; we were concerned only to show that we were not amazed. I was a little like that, even with Kareisha to guide me around. I could say that I was in London, but I didn't really know where I was. I had no means of grasping the city. I knew only that I was in the Gloucester Road. My hotel was there; Nazruddin's flat was there. I travelled everywhere by underground train, popping down into the earth at one place, popping up at another, not able to relate one place to the other, and sometimes making complicated interchanges to travel short distances.

The only street I knew well was the Gloucester Road. If I walked in one direction I came to more buildings and avenues and got lost. If I walked in the other direction I went past a lot of tourist eating places, a couple of Arab restaurants, and came to the park. There was a wide, sloping avenue in the park with boys skate-boarding. At the top of the slope there was a big pond with a paved rim. It looked artificial, but it was full of real birds, swans and different kinds of ducks; and that always struck me as strange, that the birds didn't mind being there. Artificial birds, like the lovely celluloid things of my childhood, wouldn't have been out of place. Far away, all around, beyond the trees, were the buildings. There you really did have an idea of the city as something made by man, and not as something that had just grown by itself and was simply there. Indar had spoken of that too; and he was right. It was so easy for people like us to think of great cities as natural growths. It reconciled us to our own shanty cities. We slipped into thinking that one place was one thing, and another place another thing.

In the park on fine afternoons people flew kites, and sometimes Arabs from the embassies played football below the trees. There were always a lot of Arabs about, fair-skinned people, real Arabs, not the half-African Arabs of our coast; one of the newsstands outside the Gloucester Road station was full of Arabic papers and magazines. Not all of the Arabs were rich or clean.

Sometimes I saw little groups of poor Arabs in dingy clothes squatting on the grass in the park or on the pavements of the streets nearby. I thought they were servants, and that seemed to me shameful enough. But then one day I saw an Arab lady with her slave.

I spotted the fellow at once. He had his little white cap on and his plain white gown, proclaiming his status to everybody, and he was carrying two shopping bags of groceries from the Waitrose supermarket on the Gloucester Road. He was walking the regulation ten paces ahead of his mistress, who was fat in the way Arab women like to be, with blue markings on her pale face below her gauzy black veil. She was pleased with herself; you could see that being in London and doing this modern shopping with other housewives at the Waitrose supermarket had excited her. For a moment she thought I was an Arab and she gave me a look, through her gauzy veil, which was meant to get back a look of approval and admiration from me.

As for the fellow carrying the groceries, he was a thin, fair-skinned young man, and I would have said that he had been born in the house. He had the vacant, dog-like expressions that house-born slaves, as I remembered, liked to put on when they were in public with their masters and performing some simple task. This fellow was pretending that the Waitrose groceries were a great burden, but this was just an act, to draw attention to himself and the lady he served. He, too, had mistaken me for an Arab, and when we crossed he had dropped the burdened-down expression and given me a look of wistful inquisitiveness, like a puppy that wanted to play but had just been made to understand that it wasn't playtime.

I was going to the Waitrose place to get a gift of wine for Nazruddin. He hadn't lost his taste for wine and good food. He was happy to be my guide in these matters; and indeed, after years of that Portuguese stuff in Africa, white and meaningless or red and acrid, the range of wines in London was a small daily excitement for me. At dinner in the flat (and before television: he watched for a couple of hours every night) I told Nazruddin about the slave in white. He said he wasn't surprised; it was a new feature of life in the Gloucester Road; for a couple of weeks he had been noticing a grubby fellow in brown.

Nazruddin said: "In the old days they made a lot of fuss if they caught you sending a couple of fellows to Arabia in a dhow. Today they have their passports and visas like everybody else, and walk past immigration like everybody else, and nobody gives a damn.

"I'm superstitious about the Arabs. They gave us and half the world our religion, but I can't help feeling that when they leave Arabia terrible things are about to happen in the world. You just have to think of where we come from. Persia, India, Africa. Think of what happened there. Now Europe. They're pumping the oil in and sucking the money out. Pumping the oil in to keep the system going, sucking the money out to send it crashing down. They need Europe. They want the goods and the properties and at the same time they need a safe place for their money. Their own countries are so dreadful. But they're destroying money. They're killing the goose that lays the golden egg.

"And they aren't the only ones. All over the world money is in flight. People have scraped the world clean, as clean as an African scrapes his-yard, and now they want to run from the dreadful places where they've made their money and find some nice safe country. I was one of the crowd. Koreans, Filipinos, people from Hong Kong and Taiwan, South Africans, Italians, Greeks, South Americans, Argentines, Colombians, Venezuelans, Bolivians, a lot of black people who've cleaned out places you've never heard of, Chinese from everywhere. All of them are on the run. They are frightened of the fire. You mustn't think it's only Africa people are running from.

"Mostly nowadays, since Switzerland closed down, they are going to the United States and Canada. And they are waiting for them there, to take them to the cleaners. There they meet the experts. The South Americans are waiting for the South Americans, the Asians for the Asians, the Greeks for the Greeks. And they take them to the cleaners. In Toronto, Vancouver, California. As for Miami, that is one big cleaning establishment.

"I knew about this before I went to Canada. I didn't let anybody sell me a million-dollar villa in California or an orange grove in Central America or a piece of swamp in Florida. You know what I bought instead? You wouldn't believe it. I bought an oil well, part of one. The man was a geologist. Advani introduced him to me. They said they wanted ten of us to form a little private oil company. They wanted to raise a hundred thousand dollars, everybody putting up ten. The authorized capital, though, was to be more than that, and the arrangement was that if we struck oil the geologist was to buy the rest of the shares at nominal rates. That was fair. It was his stake, his work.

"The stake was in order, the land was there. In Canada you can just go and do your own drilling. You can hire the equipment, and it doesn't cost all that much. Thirty thousand for a trial well, depending on where you want to drill. And they don't have the fruits-of-the-earth legislation you have where you are. I checked it all out. It was a risk, but I thought it was only a geological risk. I put up my ten. And guess what. We struck oil. Overnight, then, my ten was worth two hundred—well, say a hundred. But since we were a private company the profit was only a paper profit. We could only sell to one another, and none of us had that kind of money.

"The geologist exercised his options and bought up the remaining shares of the company for virtually nothing. So he acquired control of our company—but all that was in the agreement. Then he bought a semi-bankrupt mining company. We wondered about this, but we didn't question the wisdom of our man now. Then he disappeared to one of the black islands. He had linked the two companies in some way, borrowed a million dollars for our company on the strength of our oil, and transferred the money on some pretext to his own company. He left us with the debt. The oldest trick in the book, and the nine of us stood and watched while it was happening as though we were watching a man dig a hole in the road. To add insult to injury, we found out that he hadn't put up his ten. He had done it all with our money. Now I suppose he is moving heaven and earth to transfer his million to some safe place. Anyway, that was how I achieved the impossible, converting ten into a debt of a hundred.

"In time the debt will settle itself. The oil is there. I might even get my ten back. The trouble with people like us, running about the world with money to hide, is that we are good about business only in our own places. Still. The oil was only a sideline. What I was trying to do was to run a movie theatre, an ethnic theatre. You know the word? It means all the foreign groups in a place. It was very ethnic where I was, but I suppose I got the idea only because there was a theatre for sale, and it seemed a nice downtown property to get.

"Everything was working when I looked at the place, but when I took over I found we couldn't get a clear picture on the screen. At first I thought it just had to do with the lenses. Then I realised that the man who had sold me the place had changed the equipment. I went to him and said, 'You can't do this.' He said, 'Who are you? I don't know you.' So. Well, we straightened out the projectors in the end, we improved the seating and so on. Business wasn't too good. An ethnic theatre downtown wasn't such a good idea. The thing about some of those ethnic groups over there is that they don't like moving around too much. They just want to go home as fast as they can and stay there. The pictures that did well were the Indian pictures. We got a lot of Greeks then. The Greeks love Indian pictures. Did you know that? Anyway. We struggled through the summer. The cold weather came. I threw some switches for the heating. Nothing came on. There was no heating system. Or what was there had been taken away.

"I went to the man again. I said, 'You sold me the theatre as a going concern.' He said, 'Who are you?' I said, 'My family have been traders and merchants in the Indian Ocean for centuries, under every kind of government. There is a reason why we have lasted so long. We bargain hard, but we stick to our bargain. All our contracts are oral, but we deliver what we promise. It isn't because we are saints. It is because the whole thing breaks down otherwise.' He said, 'You should go back to the Indian Ocean.'

"When I left him I walked very fast. I stumbled on an unevenness in the pavement and turned my ankle. I took that as a sign. My luck had run out; I knew that it had to. I didn't feel I could stay in that country. I felt the place was a hoax. They thought they were part of the West, but really they had become like the rest of us who had run to them for safety. They were like people far away, living on other people's land and off other people's brains, and that was all they thought they should do. That was why they were so bored and dull. I thought I would die if I stayed among them.

"When I came to England all my instincts were to go into light engineering. A small country, good roads and railways, power, every kind of industrial facility. I thought that if you identified some area, got in good equipment, and employed Asians, you couldn't lose. Europeans are bored with machines and factories. Asian people love them; they secretly prefer factories to their family life. But after Canada I had lost my nerve. I thought I would play safe. I thought I would go into property. That was how I came to the Gloucester Road.

"It is one of the centres of the tourist trade in London, as you see. London is destroying itself for its tourist trade—you can see that here. Hundreds of houses, thousands of flats, have been emptied to provide hotels, hostels and restaurants for the tourists. Private accommodation is getting scarcer. I thought I couldn't lose. I bought six flats in a block. I bought at the height of the boom. Prices have now dropped twenty-five percent, and interest rates have risen from twelve percent to twenty and even twenty-four percent. Do you remember the scandal on the coast when it came out that Indar's people were lending money at ten and twelve percent? I feel I no longer understand money. And the Arabs are in the streets outside.

"I have to charge ridiculous rents to break even. And when you charge ridiculous rents you attract strange people. This is one of my souvenirs. It is a betting slip from one of the betting shops in the Gloucester Road. I keep it to remind myself of a simple girl who came down from the north. She got her Arabs mixed up. The Arab she became involved with was one of the poor ones, from Algeria. She used to dump her rubbish outside her flat door. The Algerian used to gamble on the horses. That was how they were going to make the big time.

"They won, and then they lost. They couldn't pay the rent. I reduced it. They still couldn't pay. There were complaints about the rubbish and the quarrels, and the Algerian was in the habit of pissing in the lift when he was locked out. I asked them to leave. They refused, and the law was on their side. I had a new lock put in one day when they were out. When they came back they simply called the police, and the police opened up for them. To prevent me getting in again, they put in another lock. By this time, on that door, keyholes and their metal surrounds were like buttons down a shirt front. I gave up.

"Every kind of bill was unpaid. I went up one morning and knocked. The flat was full of whispers, but no one opened. The lift was close to the flat door. I opened the door of the lift and closed it. They thought I had gone down, and sure enough they opened up to check. I put my foot in the door and went in. The little flat was full of poor Arabs in undershirts and horribly coloured pants. There was bedding all over the floor. The girl wasn't with them. They had sent her away, or she had left. So for two months, while I had been paying twenty percent interest and other charges, I had been giving free shelter to a whole tentful of poor Arabs. They are a strange people racially. One of them had bright red hair. What were they doing in London? What were they expecting to do? How are they going to survive? What place is there in the world for people like that? There are so many of them.

"Here is another girl who ran out on me. Seven hundred pounds went with her. She came from Eastern Europe. Refugee? But she was a woman. She must have spent quite a bit of money to get these photographic cards printed. Here she is, up to her neck in water; I don't know why she thought she should put that on her card. And here she is, pretending to thumb a lift, in a kind of button-up overall open at the top, and showing a little breast. Here she is wearing a big black bowler hat and black leather trousers and sticking out her little bottom. 'Erika. Model-Actress-Singer-Dancer. Hair: Red. Eyes: Grey-Green. Specialties: Fashion-Cosmetic-Footwear-Hands-Legs-Teeth-Hair. 5'9". 32-25-33.' All that, and nobody wants to buy. All that happened to her was that she became pregnant, ran up a telephone bill of

£1200—twelve hundred pounds!—and ran away one night, leaving these picture cards of herself. A big pile. I couldn't bear to throw them all away. I felt I should keep one, for her sake.

"What happens to these people? Where do they go? How do they live? Do they go back home? Do they have homes to go back to? You've talked a lot, Salim, about those girls from East Africa in the tobacco kiosks, selling cigarettes at all hours of the night. They've depressed you. You say they don't have a future and that they don't even know where they are. I wonder whether that isn't their luck. They expect to be bored, to do what they do. The people I've been talking about have expectations and they know they're lost in London. I suppose it must be dreadful for them when they have to go back. This area is full of them, coming to the centre because it is all they know about and because they think it's smart, and trying to make something out of nothing. You can't blame them. They're doing what they see the big people doing.

"This place is so big and busy you take some time to see that very little is happening. It's just keeping itself going. A lot of people have been quietly wiped out. There's no new money, no real money, and this makes everybody more desperate. We've come here at the wrong time. But never mind. It's the wrong time everywhere else too. When we were in Africa in the old days, consulting our catalogues and ordering our goods and watching the ships unload in the harbour, I don't suppose we thought it would be like this in Europe, or that the British passports we took out as protection against the Africans would actually bring us here, and that the Arabs would be in the streets outside."

That was Nazruddin. Kareisha said, "I hope you know you've been listening to the story of a happy man." She didn't have to tell me.

Nazruddin was all right. He had made himself at home in the Gloucester Road. The London setting was strange, but Nazruddin appeared to be as he had always been. He had moved on from fifty to sixty, but he didn't look particularly older. He still wore his old-style suits; and the broad lapels (with the curling tips) which I associated with him were back in fashion. I didn't think he doubted that his property venture would eventually right itself. What oppressed him (and made him talk about his luck running out) was his inactivity. But he had found in the half mile or so of the Gloucester Road, between the underground railway station and the park, the perfect retirement resort.

He bought his newspaper in one shop, read it with morning coffee in a tiny café that also offered old watercolour paintings for sale; took a turn in the park; shopped for delicacies in the various food shops. Sometimes he gave himself the luxury of tea or a drink in the big, old-fashioned lounge of the red-brick hotel near the station. Sometimes he went to the Arab or Persian "Dancing Room." And there was the nightly excitement of television in the flat. The population of the Gloucester Road was cosmopolitan, always shifting, with people of all ages. It was a friendly, holiday place, and Nazruddin's days were full of encounters and new observations. He said it was the best street in the world; he intended to stay there as long as he was allowed to.

He had chosen well once again. That had always been his gift, to suggest that he had chosen well. At one time it had made me anxious to find the world he had found. Nazruddin's example, or the way in which I had secretly interpreted his experience, had after all helped to determine my life. Now in London, glad though I was to find him in good spirits, that gift of his depressed me. It made me feel that after all these years I had never caught up with him, and never would; that my life would always be unsatisfactory. It could send me back to my hotel room in an agony of solitude and dread.

Sometimes as I was falling asleep I was kicked awake by some picture that came to me of my African town—absolutely real (and the airplane could take me there tomorrow), but its associations made it dream-like. Then I remembered my illumination, about the need of men only to live, about the illusion of pain. I played off London against Africa until both became unreal, and I could fall asleep. After a time I didn't have to call up the illumination, the mood of that African morning. It was there, beside me, that remote vision of the planet, of men lost in space and time, but dreadfully, pointlessly busy.

It was in this state of indifference and irresponsibility—like the lost Gloucester Road people Nazruddin had spoken about—that I became engaged to Kareisha.

One day, near the end of my time in London, Kareisha said, "Have you been to see Indar? Are you going to see him?"

Indar! His name had come up often in our talk, but I didn't know that he was in London.

Kareisha said, "That's just as well. I wouldn't recommend a visit or trying to get in touch or anything like that. He can be difficult and aggressive when he's in the mood, and it isn't funny. He's been like that ever since his outfit folded."

"His outfit folded?"

"About two years ago."

"But he knew it was going to fold. He talked as though he expected it to fold. Lecturers, universities, African interchange —he knew the excitement couldn't last, that no local government really cared one way or the other. But I thought he had his plans. He said he could exploit himself in lots of other ways."

Kareisha said: "It was different when the time came. He cared more about his outfit than he pretended. Of course, there are many things he can do. But he's determined not to do them. He can get a job in a university, certainly in America. He has the contacts. He can write for the papers. We don't talk about it now when we see him. Naz' says Indar's become help-resistant. The trouble is he invested too much in that outfit of his. And after it folded he had that bad experience in America. A bad experience for him anyway.

"You know Indar. You know that when he was young the most important thing to him was that his family was rich. You remember the house they lived in. When you live in a house like that, I suppose you think ten or twelve or twenty times a day that you are very rich or that you are richer than nearly everybody else. And you remember how he used to get on. Not talking about money, but it was always there. You would say that he felt that money had made him holy. All rich people are like that, I suppose. And that was one idea about himself that Indar never lost. His outfit didn't give him back his money, but it made him holy again. It raised him again above everybody else and made him equal with the big boys of Africa, being a guest of the government in this place and that place, meeting foreign ministers and presidents. So it was a blow when the outfit folded, when the Americans decided there was nothing in it for them.

"Indar went to America, to New York. Being Indar, he stayed in an expensive hotel. He saw his American people. They were all very nice. But he didn't like the direction in which they were pushing him. He felt they were pushing him towards smaller things and he pretended not to notice. I don't know what Indar was expecting from these people. No, I know. He was hoping to be made one of them, to keep on at the old level. He thought that was his due. He was spending a lot of money, and the money was running out. One day, much against his will, he even looked at cheaper hotels. He didn't want to do that because he thought that even to start looking for cheaper hotels was to admit that it soon might be over for him. He was appalled by the cheaper hotels. In New York you drop fast, he said.

"There was one man in particular he used to deal with. He had met this man in London right at the beginning, and they had become friends. It wasn't always like that. In the beginning he had thought the man foolish and had been aggressive with him. That used to embarrass Indar, because it was this man who had brought him out of the mess he was in the first time in London. This man had given Indar back his confidence then, had made him think positively about Africa and himself. It was this man who had drawn the good ideas out of Indar. Indar had grown to depend on this man. He thought of him as his equal, and you will know what I mean by that.

"They used to meet in New York. Lunch, drinks, meetings in the office. But nothing seemed to be happening. It was always just back to the hotel, and waiting. Indar was getting lower. The man invited Indar to dinner one evening at his apartment. It was an expensive-looking building. Indar gave his name downstairs and took the elevator up. The elevator man waited and watched until the apartment door was opened and Indar was let in. When Indar went inside he was stunned.

"He had thought of the man as his equal, his friend. He had opened himself to the man. He found now that the man was immensely rich. He had never been in a richer room. You or I would have found it interesting, the money. Indar was shattered. It was only there, in the rich apartment with the costly objects and pictures, that Indar understood that while he had opened himself to the man, and talked of all the little things that made him anxious, he had received very little of that in return. This man was much, much holier. It was more than Indar could bear. He felt he had been cheated and fooled. He had grown to depend on this man. He tested his ideas on him; he looked to him for moral support. He thought of this man as someone like himself. He felt he had been led on all these years, and exploited in the worst way. All that optimism dragged out of him, after he had lost so much. All those constructive ideas! Africa! There was nothing of Africa in that apartment, or in the dinner party. No danger, no loss. The private life, the life with friends, was quite different from the life outside. I don't know what Indar expected.

"During the dinner he focussed all his resentment on a young woman. She was the wife of a very old journalist who had written books that had made a lot of money at one time. Indar hated her. Why had she married the old man? What was the joke? Because apparently the dinner had been arranged around her and the man she was having an affair with. They didn't keep it too secret, and the old man pretended not to notice. He just kept babbling on about French politics in the 1930s, still keeping himself in the centre of things, though, telling about the important people he had met and what they had told him personally. No one paid him the slightest attention, but he didn't mind.

"Still, he had been a famous man. Indar thought a lot about that. He was trying to put himself on the old man's side, to hate the others better. Then the old man noticed who Indar was, and he began to talk about India in the old days and his meeting with

Gandhi in some famous mud hut. As you know, Gandhi and Nehru aren't Indar's favourite subjects. He decided he wasn't doing any social work that night, and he was very rough with the old man, much rougher than anybody else had been.

"So at the end of the dinner Indar was in a state. He thought about the cheap hotels he had looked at, and as he was going down in the elevator he had a wild panic. He thought he was going to pass out. But he got outside all right, and there he calmed down. He had got a simple idea. The idea was that it was time for him to go home, to get away.

"And that's how it has been with him. From time to time that is all he knows, that it is time for him to go home. There is some dream village in his head. In between he does the lowest kind of job. He knows he is equipped for better things, but he doesn't want to do them. I believe he enjoys being told he can do better. We've given up now. He doesn't want to risk anything again. The idea of sacrifice is safer, and he likes the act. But you will see for yourself, when you come back."

Kareisha, talking about Indar, touched me more than she knew. That idea of going home, of leaving, the idea of the other place—I had lived with it in various forms for many years. In Africa it had always been with me. In London, in my hotel room, I had allowed it on some nights to take me over. It was a deception. I saw now that it comforted only to weaken and destroy.

That illumination I held on to, about the unity of experience and the illusion of pain, was part of the same way of feeling. We fell into it—people like Indar and myself—because it was the basis of our old way of life. But I had rejected that way of life—and just in time. In spite of the girls in the cigarette kiosks, that way of life no longer existed, in London or Africa. There could be no going back; there was nothing to go back to. We had become what the world outside had made us; we had to live in the world as it existed. The younger Indar was wiser. Use the airplane; trample on the past, as Indar had said he had trampled on the past. Get rid of that idea of the past; make the dream-like scenes of loss ordinary.

That was the mood in which I left London and Kareisha, to go back to Africa, to wind up there, realise as much as I could of what I had. And make a fresh start somewhere else.

I got to Brussels in the late afternoon. The plane for Africa was leaving from there at midnight. I felt afresh the drama of airplane travel: London vanished, Africa to come, Brussels now. I gave myself dinner and went to a bar afterwards, a place with women. All the excitement lay in the idea of the place rather than the place itself. What followed, some time later, was brief and meaningless and reassuring. It didn't lessen the value of what I had had in Africa: that was no delusion; that remained true. And it removed the special doubt I felt about my engagement to Kareisha, whom I had not yet even kissed.

The woman, naked, unruffled, stood in front of a long mirror and looked at herself. Fat legs, roundish belly, chunky breasts. She said, "I've begun to do yoga with a group of friends. We have a teacher. Do you do yoga?"

"I play a lot of squash."

She paid no attention. "Our teacher says that a man's psychic fluids can overpower a woman. Our teacher says that after a dangerous encounter a woman can become herself again by clapping her hands hard or by taking a deep breath. Which method do you recommend?"

"Clap your hands."

She faced me as she might have faced her yoga teacher, drew herself up, half closed her eyes, pulled her outstretched arms back, and brought her hands violently together. At the sound, startling in the over-furnished little room, she opened her eyes, looked surprised, smiled as though she had been joking all along, and said, "*Go!*" When I was out in the street I took a deep breath, and went straight to the airport to catch the midnight plane.

FOUR

Battle

---

16 The dawn came suddenly, in the west pale blue, in the east red with thick horizontal bars of black cloud. And for many minutes it was like that. The scale, the splendour—six miles above the earth! We came down slowly, leaving the upper light. Below the heavy cloud Africa showed as a dark-green, wet-looking land. You could see that it was barely dawn down there; in the forests and creeks it would still be quite dark. The forested land went on and on. The sun struck the bottom of the clouds; it was light when we touched down.

So at last I had come to the capital. It was a strange way to come to it, after such a roundabout journey. If I had come to it fresh from my upriver town it would have seemed immense, rich, a capital. But after Europe, and with London still close to me, it seemed flimsy in spite of its size, an echo of Europe, and like make-believe, at the end of all that forest.

The more experienced among the European passengers, paying no attention to the big photograph of the President with his chief's stick, made a rush at the immigration and customs officials and appeared to force their way through. I wondered at their confidence, but they were mainly people with protection—embassy people, people working on government projects, people working for big companies. My own passage was slower. When I was through, the terminal building was almost empty. The airline posters and the photograph of the President had no one to look at them. Most of the officials had disappeared. And it was fully morning.

It was a long drive into the town. It was like the drive, in my own town, from the Domain to the town centre. But the land was hillier here and everything was on a larger scale. The shanty towns and *cités* (with the maize plantings between houses) were bigger; there were buses, even a railway train with old-fashioned open coaches; there were factories. All along the road were big boards about ten feet high, uniformly painted, each with a separate saying or maxim of the President. Some of the painted portraits of the President were literally as big as a house. We had had nothing like that in our town. Everything in our town, as I realized, was on a smaller scale.

Portraits, maxims, occasional statues of the African madonna —they continued all the way to the hotel. If I had come to the capital fresh from our town I would have felt choked. But after Europe, and after what I had seen of the country from the air, and still with my sense of the flimsiness of the capital, my attitude was different, and I was surprised by it. There was to me an element of pathos in those maxims, portraits and statues, in this wish of a man of the bush to make himself big, and setting about it in such a crude way. I even felt a little sympathy for the man who was making such a display of himself.

I understood now why so many of our later visitors at the Domain found our country, and our awe of the President, comic. What I saw on the road from the airport didn't seem comic, though. I felt it more as a shriek. I had just come from Europe; I had seen the real competition.

Overnight I had changed one continent for another, and this odd sympathy for the President, this vision of the impossibility of what I thought he was trying to do, came just at the moment of arrival. The sympathy wore off as the town became more familiar and I began to see it as a larger version of my own town. The sympathy, in fact, began to wear off when I got to the new big hotel (air-conditioned, shops in the lobby, a swimming pool no one was using) and found it full of secret police. I can't imagine that they had much to do there. They were there to show themselves to visitors. And also because they liked being in the smart new hotel; they wanted to show themselves to visitors in that modern setting. It was pathetic; or you could make a joke of it. But those men weren't always funny. Already, then, the tensions of Africa were returning to me.

This was the President's city. This was where he had grown up and where his mother had worked as a hotel maid. This was where, in colonial days, he had got his idea of Europe. The colonial city, more extensive than ours, with many residential areas rich with decorative, sheltering trees now fully grown, was still to be seen. It was with this Europe that, in his own buildings, the President wished to compete. The city, while decaying in the centre, with dirt roads and rubbish mounds just at the back of the great colonial boulevards, was yet full of new public works. Large areas near the river had been turned into Presidential reserves—palaces with great walls, gardens, state houses of various sorts.

In the Presidential gardens near the rapids (the rapids here matching ours, a thousand miles upriver), the statue of the European explorer who had charted the river and used the first steamer had been replaced by a gigantic statue of an African tribesman with spear and shield, done in the modern African style; Father Huismans would have had no time for it. Beside this statue was a smaller one of an African madonna with a bowed, veiled head. Nearby were the graves of the earliest Europeans: a little dead settlement, out of which it had all grown, out of which our town had been seeded. Simple people, with simple trades and simple goods, but agents of Europe. Like the people who came now, like the people on the airplane.

The rapids made a constant, unchanging noise. The water hyacinths, "the new thing in the river," beginning so far away, in the centre of the continent, bucked past in clumps and tangles and single vines, here almost at the end of their journey.

The next morning I went back to the airport, to take the upcountry plane. By now I was more in tune with the place, and the spread of the capital made a greater impression on me. Always, beside the airport road, there was some new settlement. How did all these people live? The hilly land had been scraped clean, cut up, eroded, exposed. Had there been forest here? The posts that supported the President's maxim boards were often set in bare clay. And the boards themselves, spattered with mud from the road and dust-blown at the bottom, not as fresh as they had seemed to me the previous morning, were like part of the desolation.

At the airport, in the section for internal flights, the departures board announced my flight and one other. The board was electrically operated and, according to a sign it carried, made in Italy. It was a modern piece of equipment; it was like the boards I had seen in the airports of London and Brussels. But below it, around the checking-in desks and weighing machines, was the usual scramble; and what was being checked in, with a lot of shouting, was like the cargo of a market jitney: metal trunks, cardboard boxes, cloth bundles, sacks of this and that, big enamel basins tied up in cloth.

I had my ticket and it was in order, but my name wasn't on the passenger list. Some francs had to pass first. And then, just as I was going out to the plane, a security man in plain clothes who was eating something asked for my papers and decided that they had to be examined more closely. He looked very offended and sent me to wait in an empty little inner room. This was standard procedure. The offended, sideways look, the little private room —this was how middle-rank officials let you know they were going to take some money off you.

But this fellow didn't get anything, because he played the fool and kept me waiting in that little room so long, without coming to collect, that he delayed the flight and was bawled out by an airline man, who, clearly knowing where I was to be found, burst into the little room, shouted to me to get out at once, and sent me running across the asphalt to the plane, last man in, but lucky.

In the front row was one of the airline's European pilots, a small, middle-aged family man; beside him was a little African boy, but it was hard to tell whether there was any connection. Some rows behind there was a group of six or eight Africans, men in their thirties, with old jackets and shirts buttoned right up, who were talking loudly. They were drinking whisky, straight from the bottle—and it was nine in the morning. Whisky was expensive here, and these men wanted everybody to know that they were drinking whisky. The bottle was passed to strangers; it was even passed to me. These men were not like the men of my region. They were bigger, with different complexions and features. I couldn't understand their faces; I saw only their arrogance and drunkenness. Their talk was boastful; they wanted the rest of us to know that they were men who owned plantations. They were like people who had just come into money, and the whole thing struck me as odd.

It was a simple flight, two hours, with a halfway stop. And it seemed to me, with my experience of intercontinental travel, that we had just begun to cruise above the white clouds when we began coming down for that stop. We saw then that we had been following the river—brown, rippled and wrinkled and streaked from this height, with many channels between long, thin islands of green. The airplane shadow moved over the forest top. That top became less even and tight as the airplane shadow grew bigger; the forest we came down to was quite ragged.

After we landed we were told to leave the airplane. We went to the small building at the edge of the airfield, and while we were there we saw the airplane turn, taxi, and fly away. It was needed for some Presidential service; it would come back when it had done that service. We had to wait. It was only about ten. Until about noon, while the heat built up, we were restless. Then we settled down—all of us, even the whisky drinkers—to wait.

We were in the middle of bush. Bush surrounded the cleared area of the airfield. Far away, a special density about the trees marked the course of the river. The airplane had shown how complex it was, how easy it would be to get lost, to waste hours paddling up channels that took you away from the main river. Not many miles from the river, people would be living in villages more or less as they had lived for centuries. Less than forty-eight hours before, I had been in the overtrampled Gloucester Road, where the world met. Now, for hours, I had been staring at bush. How many miles separated me from the capital, from my own town? How long would it take to do the distance by land or by water? How many weeks, how many months, and against what dangers?

It clouded over. The clouds grew dark and the bush grew

dark. The sky began to jump with lightning and thunder; and then the rain and the wind came, driving us in from the verandah of the little building. It rained and stormed. The bush vanished in the rain. It was rain like this that fed these forests, that caused the grass and bright green weeds around the airfield building to grow so high. The rain slackened, the clouds lifted a little. The bush revealed itself again, one line of trees behind another, the nearer trees darker, the further trees fading line by line into the grey colour of the sky.

Empty beer bottles covered the metal tables. Not many people were moving about; nearly everyone had found the place where he was going to stay. No one was talking much. The middle-aged Belgian woman whom we had found in the building waiting to join our flight was still absorbed in the French paperback of *Peyton Place*. You could see that she had shut the bush and weather out and was living somewhere else.

The sun came out and glittered on the tall, wet grass. The asphalt steamed, and for a while I watched that. Later in the afternoon one half of the sky went black, while the other half stayed light. The storm that began with vivid lightning in the black half then spread to us and it became dark and chill and very damp. The forest had become a place of gloom. There was no excitement in this second storm.

One of the African passengers, an elderly man, appeared with a grey felt hat and a blue bathrobe of towelling material over his suit. No one paid him too much attention. I just noted his oddity, and thought: He's using a foreign thing in his own way. And something like that went through my head when a barefooted man turned up wearing a fireman's helmet with the transparent plastic visor pulled down. He was an old man with a shrunken face; his brown shorts and grey check shirt were ragged and soaked through. I thought: He's found a ready-made dancing mask. He went from table to table, checking the beer bottles. When he decided that a bottle was worth emptying he raised the visor of his mask and drank.

It stopped raining, but it remained dark, the darkness of late afternoon. The airplane, at first only a brown smoke trail in the sky, appeared. When we went out to the wet field to board it I saw the man with the fireman's helmet—and a companion, also helmeted—standing unsteadily beside the gangway. He was, after all, a fireman.

As we rose we saw the river, catching the last of the light. It was gold-red, then red. We followed it for many miles and minutes, until it became a mere sheen, a smoothness, something extra-black between the black forests. Then it was all black. Through this blackness we flew to our destination. The journey, which had seemed so simple in the morning, had acquired another quality. Distance and time had been restored to it. I felt I had been travelling for days, and when we began to go down again, I knew that I had travelled far, and I wondered how I had had the courage to live for so long in a place so far away.

And then, suddenly, it was easy. A familiar building; officials I knew and could palaver with; people whose faces I understood; one of our old disinfected taxis; the well-known lumpy road to the town, at first through bush which had distinguishing features, then past the squatters' settlements. After the strangeness of the day, it was like organized life again.

We passed a burnt-out building, a new ruin. It had been a primary school, never much of a place, more like a low shed, and I might have missed it in the dark if the driver hadn't pointed it out to me; it excited him. The insurrection, the Liberation Army —that was still going on. It didn't lessen my relief at being in the town, seeing the nighttime pavement groups, and finding myself, so quickly after arrival, something of the forest gloom still on me, in my own street—all there, and as real and as ordinary as ever.

It was a shock, a puncturing, to find Metty cold. I had made such a journey. I wanted him to know; from him I had been expecting the warmest welcome. He must have heard the slam of the taxi door and my palaver with the driver. But Metty didn't come down. And all that he said when I went up the external staircase, and found him standing in the doorway of his room, was: "I didn't expect to see you back, *patron*." The whole journey seemed to turn sour then.

Everything was in order in the flat. But about the sitting room and especially the bedroom there was something—perhaps an extra order, an absence of staleness—that made me feel that Metty had been spreading himself in the flat in my absence. The telegram that I had sent him from London must have caused him to retreat. Did he resent that? Metty? But he had grown up in our family; he knew no other life. He had always been with the family or with me. He had never been on his own, except on his journey up from the coast, and now.

He brought me coffee in the morning.

He said, "I suppose you know why you come back, *patron*."

"You said this last night."

"Because you have nothing to come back to. You don't know? Nobody told you in London? You don't read the papers? You don't have anything. They take away your shop. They give it to Citizen Théotime. The President made a speech a fortnight back. He said he was radicalizing and taking away everything from everybody. All foreigners. The next day they put a padlock on the door. And a few other doors as well. You didn't read that in London? You don't have anything, I don't have anything. I don't know why you come back. I don't think it was for my sake."

Metty was in a bad way. He had been alone. He must have been beside himself waiting for me to come back. He was trying to provoke some angry response from me. He was trying to get me to make some protective gesture. But I was as lost as he was.

Radicalization: two days before, in the capital, I had seen the word in a newspaper headline, but I hadn't paid attention. I had thought of it as just another word; we had so many. Now I understood that radicalization was the big new event.

And it was as Metty had said. The President had sprung another of his surprises, and this surprise concerned us. I—and others like me—had been nationalized. Our businesses had ceased to be ours, by decree, and were being given out by the President to new owners. These new owners were called "state trustees." Citizen Théotime had been made the state trustee of my business; and Metty said that for the last week the man had actually been spending his days in the shop.

"What does he do?"

"Do? He's waiting for you. He'll make you the manager. That is what you have come back for, *patron*. But you will see. Don't hurry yourself. Théo doesn't come to work too early."

When I went to the shop I saw that the stock, which had gone down in six weeks, was displayed in the old way. Théo hadn't touched that. But my desk had been moved from its place next to the pillar in the front of the shop to the storeroom at the back. Metty said that had happened on the first day. Citizen Théo had decided that the storeroom was to be his office; he liked the privacy.

In the top drawer of the desk (where I used to keep Yvette's photographs, which had once transformed the view of the market square for me) there were many tattered French-African photo-novels and comic books: Africans shown living very modern lives, and in the comic books they were drawn almost like Europeans—in the last two or three years there had been a lot of this French-produced rubbish around. My own things—magazines, and shop documents I had thought Metty would need—were in the two bottom drawers. They had been handled with care; Théo had had that grace. Nationalization: it had been a word. It was shocking to face it in this concrete way.

I waited for Théo.

And when the man came I could see that he was embarrassed and his first impulse, when he saw me through the glass, was to walk past the door. I had known him years before as a mechanic; he used to look after the vehicles in the health department. Then, because he had certain tribal connections, he had risen politically, but not very high. He would have had trouble signing his name. He was about forty, undistinguished in appearance, with a broad, dark-brown face beaten up and spongy with drink. He was drunk now. But only on beer; he hadn't yet moved on to whisky. Nor had he moved on to the regulation official dress of short-sleeved jacket and cravat. He stuck to trousers and shirt. He was, really, a modest man.

I was standing where my desk used to be. And it occurred to me, noticing how sweated and grimy Théo's white shirt was, that it was like the time when the schoolboys, treating me like prey, used to come to the shop to try to get money out of me in simple ways. Théo was sweating through the pores on his nose. I don't believe he had washed his face that morning. He looked like a man who had added fresh drink, and nothing else, to a bad hangover.

He said, "Mis' Salim. Salim. Citizen. You mustn't take this personally. It has not come about through any wish of mine. You know that I have the highest regard for you. But you know what the situation was like. The revolution had become"—he fumbled for the word— "*un pé pourrie*. A little rotten. Our young people were becoming impatient. It was necessary"—trying to find the right word, he looked confused, clenched his fist and made a clumsy cuffing gesture—"it was necessary to radicalize. We had absolutely to radicalize. We were expecting too much of the President. No one was willing to take responsibility. Now responsibility has been forced on the people. But you will suffer in no way. Adequate compensation will be paid. You will prepare your own inventory. And you will continue as manager. The business will run as before. The President insists on that. No one is to suffer. Your salary will be fair. As soon as the commissioner arrives, the papers will come through."

After his hesitant start, he had spoken formally, as though he had prepared his words. At the end he became embarrassed again. He was waiting for me to say something. But then he changed his mind and went to the storeroom, his office. And I left, to go and look for Mahesh at Bigburger.

There it was business as usual. Mahesh, a little plumper, was pulling coffees, and Ildephonse was jumping about and serving late breakfasts. I was surprised.

Mahesh said, "But this has been an African company for years. It can't be radicalized any more. I just manage Bigburger for 'Phonse and a few others. They formed this African company and they gave me a little part in it, as manager, and then they bought a lease from me. That was during the boom. They owe the bank a lot. You wouldn't believe it when you look at 'Phonse. But it's true. That happened in a lot of places after Noimon sold out to the government. That gave us an idea which way the wind was blowing, and some of us decided to compensate ourselves in advance. It was easy enough then. The banks were flush with money."

"Nobody told me."

"It wasn't the kind of thing people would talk a lot about. And your thoughts were elsewhere."

That was true. There had been a coolness between us at that time; we had both been scratchy after Noimon's departure.

I said, "What about the Tivoli? All that new kitchen equipment. They invested so much."

"That's crippled with debt. No African in his right mind would want to be the trustee of that. They queued up for yours, though. That was when I knew you hadn't done anything. Théotime and another man actually came to blows, right here in Bigburger. There were a lot of fights like that. It was like a carnival after the President announced the measures. So many people just going into places, not saying anything to the people inside, just making marks on doors or dropping pieces of cloth on the floor, as though they were claiming a piece of meat in the market. It was very bad for a few days. One Greek burnt down his coffee plantation. They've calmed down now. The President issued a statement, just to let everybody know that what the Big Man gives the Big Man can take away. That's how the Big Man gets them. He gives and he takes back."

I spent the rest of the morning at Bigburger. It was strange for me, wasting the working day in chat, giving news, asking for news, watching the coming and going in Bigburger and the van der Weyden across the road, and all the time feeling myself separated from the life of the town.

Mahesh had little to tell me about Shoba. There was no change there. She still hid with her disfigurement in the flat. But Mahesh no longer fought against that situation or seemed irritated by it. It didn't make him unhappy—as I had feared it might—to hear about London and my travels. Other people travelled; other people got away; he didn't. For Mahesh it had become as simple as that.

I became Théotime's manager. He seemed relieved and happy, and agreed to the salary I suggested for myself. I bought a table and chair and set them next to the pillar, so that it was almost like old times. I spent many days assembling old invoices, checking stock and preparing the inventory. It was a complicated document, and of course it was padded. But Théotime approved it so readily (sending me out of the storeroom while he struggled to sign Cit:Theot:) that I felt that Mahesh was right, that no compensation was going to be paid, that the most I could expect, if anybody remembered, were government bonds.

The inventory only reminded me of what I had lost. What remained? In a bank in Europe I had about eight thousand dollars, proceeds from my gold dealings in the old days; that money had just stayed and rotted, losing value. There was the flat in the town, for which there would be no buyer; but the car would fetch a few thousand dollars. And I had about half a million local francs in various banks—about fourteen thousand dollars at the official rate of exchange, and half that on the free market. That was all; it wasn't a great deal. I had to make more, as fast as I could; and the little I had, I had to get out of the country.

As manager in the shop I had opportunities; but they were not extraordinary. And so I began to live dangerously. I began to deal in gold and ivory. I bought, stored and sold; or, acting for bigger operators (who paid directly to my bank in Europe), I stored and shipped on, for a percentage. My suppliers, and sometimes the poachers, were officials or army people, and these people were always dangerous to deal with. The rewards were not great. Gold only sounds expensive; you have to handle kilos before your percentage amounts to anything. Ivory was better, but ivory was more difficult to store (I continued to use the hole at the bottom of the staircase in my yard) and trickier to ship. For shipping I used one of the ordinary market vans or jitneys, sending the stuff (larger tusks in mattress consignments, smaller pieces in sacks of cassava) with other goods, always doing so now in the name of Citizen Théotime, and sometimes getting Théotime himself to pull a little political rank and give the driver a good talking to in public.

Money could be made. But to get it out of the country was another matter. Money can be got out of countries like these only if you deal in very large sums and can get high officials or ministers to take an interest; or if there is a certain amount of business activity. There was little activity now, and I had to depend on visitors who for various reasons needed local currency. There was no other way. And I had to trust these people to pay up when they got back to Europe or the United States.

It was a slow, tout-like, humiliating business. I wish I could say that I discovered certain rules about human behaviour. I wish I could say that people of a certain class or country were to be trusted and people of another class and country not trusted. That would have made it much simpler. It was a gamble each time. I lost two-thirds of my money in this way; I gave it away to strangers.

I was in and out of the Domain on this money business; it was there that I made many of my contacts. At first it made me uneasy to be there. But then I proved Indar's point about trampling on the past: the Domain quickly ceased to be what it had been for me. It became a place where honourable people—many of them first-time lawbreakers, who were later to use their respect for the law to cheat me with a clear mind—tried to get better rates than the ones we had agreed on. What was common to these people was their nervousness and contempt—contempt for me, contempt for the country. I was half on their side; I envied them the contempt that it was so easy for them to feel.

One afternoon I saw that Raymond and Yvette's house had a new tenant, an African. The house had been closed since I had come back. Raymond and Yvette had gone away; no one, not even Mahesh, could tell me where or in what circumstances. The doors and windows of the house were wide open now, and that emphasized the shoddiness of the construction.

The new man, barebacked, was forking up the ground just in front of the house, and I stopped to have a chat. He was from somewhere downriver, and friendly. He told me he was going to grow maize and cassava. Africans didn't understand large-scale agriculture; but they were passionate planters in this smaller way, growing food for the house and liking to grow it very close to the house. He noted my car; he remembered his bare back. He told me he worked for the government corporation that ran the steamer service. And to give me some idea of his standing, he said that whenever he travelled on the steamer he travelled first class and free. That big government job, this big government house in the famous Domain—he was a happy man, pleased with what he had been granted, and asking for nothing else.

There were more households like his in the Domain now. The polytechnic was still there, but the Domain had lost its modern, "showplace" character. It was scruffier; every week it was becoming more of an African housing settlement. Maize, which in that climate and soil sprouted in three days, grew in many places; and the purple-green leaves of the cassava, which grew from a simple cutting even if you planted it upside down, created the effect of garden shrubs. This piece of earth—how many changes had come to it! Forest at a bend in the river, a meeting place, an Arab settlement, a European outpost, a European suburb, a ruin like the ruin of a dead civilization, the glittering Domain of new Africa, and now this.

While we were speaking, children began to appear from the back of the house—country children still, bending a knee at the sight of the adult, before coming up shyly to listen and watch. And then a large Doberman came bounding out at me.

The man with the fork said, "Don't worry. He'll miss you. He can't see very well. A foreigner's dog. He gave it to me when he went away."

It was as he said. The Doberman missed me by about a foot, ran on a little way, stopped, raced back, and then was all over me, wagging his docked tail, beside himself with joy at my foreigner's smell, momentarily mistaking me for somebody else.

I was glad for Raymond's sake that he had gone away. He wouldn't have been safe in the Domain or the town now. The curious reputation that had come to him in the end—of being the white man who went ahead of the President, and drew on himself the bad things that should have fallen on the President—that reputation might have encouraged the Liberation Army to kill him, especially now, when the President was said to be planning to visit the town, and the town was being made ready for that visit.

The rubbish hills in the centre were being carted away. The corrugated streets were being levelled and graded. And paint! It was everywhere in the centre, slapped onto concrete and plaster and timber, dripping on the pavements. Someone had unloaded his stock—pink and lime and red and mauve and blue. The bush was at war; the town was in a state of insurrection, with nightly incidents. But suddenly in the centre it seemed like carnival time.

17 Citizen Théotime would come in in the mornings, red-eyed and tormented-looking, high on his breakfast beer, with a couple of comic books or photo-novels to see him through office hours. There was an informal system of magazine exchange in the town; Théo always had something new to look at. And oddly, his comic books or photo-novels, tightly rolled up, gave him a busy, businesslike air when he came into the shop. He went straight to the storeroom, and could stay there without coming out for the whole morning. At first I thought it was because he wanted to be out of the way and not to be any trouble. But then I understood that it was no hardship for him. He liked being in the dark storeroom with nothing in particular to do, just looking at his magazines when the mood took him, and drinking his beer.

Later, when he became easier and less shy with me, his storeroom life became fuller. He began to be visited by women. He liked them to see him as a real *directeur*, with a staff and an office; and it pleased the women too. A visit could take up a whole afternoon, with Théotime and the woman chatting in the way people chat when they are sheltering from the rain—with long pauses and long hypnotized stares in different directions.

It was an easy enough life for Théotime, easier than anything he could have imagined when he was a mechanic in the health department. But as he gained confidence, and lost his fear that the shop might be taken away from him by the President, he became difficult.

It began to worry him that as a *directeur* he didn't have a car.

Some woman had perhaps given him the idea, or it might have been the example of other state trustees, or it might have been something he had got from his comic books. I had a car; he began to ask for lifts, and then he required me to drive him to and from his house. I could have said no. But I told myself it was a small thing to do to keep him quiet. The first few times he sat in the front; then he sat in the back. This was a four-times-a-day duty.

He didn't stay quiet for long. It might have been my easiness, my wish to appear unhumiliated: Théotime was soon looking for new ways of asserting himself. The trouble now was that he didn't know what to do. He would have liked to live out his role in fact—to take over the running of the shop, or to feel (while enjoying his storeroom life) that he was running the shop. He knew, though, that he knew nothing; he knew that I knew he knew nothing; and he was like a man enraged by his own helplessness. He made constant scenes. He was drunken, aggrieved and threatening, and as deliberately irrational as an official who had decided to be *malin*.

It was strange. He wanted me to acknowledge him as the boss. At the same time he wanted me to make allowances for him as an uneducated man and an African. He wanted both my respect and my tolerance, even my compassion. He wanted me, almost, to act out my subordinate role as a favour to him. Yet if, responding to his plea, I did so, if I took some simple shop document to him, the authority he put on then was very real. He added it to his idea of his role; and he would use that authority later to extort some new concession. As he had done with the car.

It was worse than dealing with a *malin* official. The official who pretended to be offended—and bawled you out, for instance, for resting your hand on his desk—was only asking for money. Théotime, moving quickly from a simple confidence in his role to an understanding of his helplessness, wanted you to pretend that he was another kind of man. It wasn't funny. I had resolved to be calm about my dispossession, to keep my mind on the goal I had given myself. But it wasn't easy to be calm. The shop became a hateful place to me.

It was worse for Metty. The little services that he had done for Théotime in the beginning became things that he was required to do, and they multiplied. Théotime began sending Metty out on quite pointless errands.

Late one evening, when he returned to the flat after being with his family, Metty came into my room and said, "I can't take it, *patron*. I will do something terrible one of these days. If Théo doesn't stop it, I'll kill him. I'd rather hoe in the fields than be his servant."

I said, "It won't last long."

Metty's face twisted with exasperation, and he did a silent stamp with one foot. He was close to tears. He said, "What do you mean? What do you mean?" and went out of the room.

In the morning I went to collect Théotime to drive him to the shop. As a well-to-do and influential local man, Théotime had three or four families in different parts of the town. But since becoming a state trustee he had (like other trustees) picked up a number of new women, and he lived with one of them in one of the little back houses in a *cité* yard—bare red ground intersected with shallow black drains all down one side, scraped-up earth and rubbish pushed to the edge, mango and other trees scattered about, cassava and maize and clumps of banana between the houses.

When I blew the horn, children and women from the various houses came out and watched while Théotime walked to the car, with his comic book rolled up. He pretended to ignore the watchers and spat casually on the ground once or twice. His eyes were reddened with beer and he tried to look offended.

We drove out of the bumpy *cité* lane to the levelled red main road, where the buildings were freshly painted for the President's visit—each building done in one colour (walls, window frames, doors), and each building a different colour from its neighbour.

I said, "I want to talk to you about Citizen Metty's duties in our establishment, citizen. Citizen Metty is the manager's assistant. He is not a general servant."

Théotime had been waiting for this. He had a speech prepared. He said, "You astonish me, citizen. I am the state trustee,

appointed by the President. Citizen Metty is an employee of a
state establishment. It is for me to decide how the half-caste is to
be used." He used the word *métis*, to play on the adopted name
of which Metty had once been so proud.

The vivid colours of the buildings became even more unreal to
me. They became the colours of my rage and anguish.

I had been growing smaller and smaller in Metty's eyes, and
now I failed him altogether. I could no longer offer him the
simple protection he had asked for—Théotime made that plain
during the course of the day. So the old contract between Metty
and myself, which was the contract between his family and mine,
came to an end. Even if I had been able to place him in another
establishment in the town—which I might have been able to do
in the old days—it would have meant that our special contract
was over. He seemed to understand this, and it made him un-
balanced.

He began to say, "I am going to do something terrible, Salim.
You must give me money. Give me money and let me go away. I
feel I'm going to do something terrible."

I felt his pain as an extra pressure. I mentally added his pain
to mine, made it part of my own. I should have thought more of
him. I should have made him stay away from the shop, and given
him an allowance from my own salary, while that lasted. It was,
really, what he wanted. But he didn't put it like that. He involved
it in that wild idea of going away, which only frightened me and
made me think: Where is he going to go?

So he continued to go to the shop and Théotime, and became
more and more tormented. When he said to me one evening,
"Give me some money and I will go away," I said, thinking of
the situation in the shop, and trying to find comforting words, "It
isn't going to last forever, Metty." This made him scream,
"*Salim!*" And the next morning, for the first time, he didn't bring
me coffee.

That happened at the beginning of the week. On Friday afternoon, after closing up the shop and driving Théotime to his yard,
I came back to the flat. It was a place of desolation for me now. I
no longer thought of it as my own. Since that morning in the

car with Théotime I had felt nausea for the bright new colours of the town. They were the colours of a place that had become strange and felt far away from everywhere else. That feeling of strangeness extended to everything in the flat. I was thinking of going to the Hellenic Club—or what remained of it—when I heard car doors slam.

I went out to the landing and saw police in the yard. There was an officer—his name was Prosper: I knew him. One of the men with him had a fork, another a shovel. They knew what they had come for, and they knew exactly where they had to dig— below the external staircase. I had four tusks there.

My mind raced, made links. Metty! I thought: Oh, Ali! What have you done to me? I knew it was important to let someone know. Mahesh—there was no one else. He would be at his flat now. I went to the bedroom and telephoned. Mahesh answered, and I only had time to say, "Things are bad here," before I heard footsteps coming up. I put the phone down, went to the bathroom, pulled the lavatory chain, and went out to see the round-faced Prosper coming up alone, smiling.

The face came up, smiling, and I retreated before it, and this was how, not saying anything, we moved down the passage before I turned and led Prosper into the white sitting room. He couldn't hide his pleasure. His eyes glittered. He hadn't yet decided how to behave. He hadn't yet decided how much to ask for.

He said, "The President is coming next week. Did you know that? The President is interested in conservation. This is why this is very serious for you. Anything might happen to you if I send in my report. This is certainly going to cost you a couple of thousand."

This seemed to me very modest.

He noticed my relief. He said, "I don't mean francs. I mean dollars. Yes, this is going to cost you three or four thousand dollars."

This was outrageous. Prosper knew it was outrageous. In the old days five dollars was considered pretty good; and even during the boom you could get many things done for twenty-five dollars.

Things had changed since the insurrection, of course, and had become very bad with the radicalization. Everyone had become more greedy and desperate. There was this feeling of everything running down very fast, of a great chaos coming; and some people could behave as though money had already lost its value. But even so, officials like Prosper had only recently begun to talk in hundreds.

I said, "I don't have that kind of money."

"I thought you would say that. The President is coming next week. We are taking a number of people into preventive detention. That is how you will go in. We will forget the tusks for the time being. You will stay in until the President leaves. You might decide then that you have the money."

I packed a few things into a canvas holdall and Prosper drove me in the back of his Land-Rover through the brightly coloured town to police headquarters. There I learned to wait. There I decided that I had to shut out thoughts of the town and stop thinking about time, that I had as far as possible to empty my mind.

There were many stages in my progress through the building, and I began to look upon Prosper as my guide to this particular hell. He left me for long periods sitting or standing in rooms and corridors, which gleamed with new oil paint. It was almost a relief to see him coming back to me with his chunky cheeks and his stylish briefcase.

It was near sunset when he led me to the annex in the yard at the back, where I had once gone to rescue Metty, and where I now had to be fingerprinted myself, before being taken to the town jail. The walls had been a dusty blue, I remembered. Now they were a brilliant yellow, and *Discipline Avant Tout*—"Discipline Above All"—had been freshly painted in big black letters. I lost myself contemplating the bad, uneven lettering, the graining of the photograph of the President, the uneven surface of the yellow wall, the dried yellow spattering on the broken floor.

The room was full of young men who had been picked up. It was a long time before I was fingerprinted. The man at the table behaved like an overworked man. He didn't seem to look at the faces of the people he fingerprinted.

I asked whether I couldn't get the ink off my hands. It wasn't a wish to be clean, I decided after I had asked. It was more a wish to appear calm, unhumiliated, to feel that the events were normal. The man at the table said yes, and from a drawer brought out a pink plastic soap dish with a slender-waisted wafer of soap streaked with black lines. The soap was quite dry. He told me I could go outside and use the standpipe.

I went out into the yard. It was now dark. Around me were trees, lights, cooking smoke, evening sounds. The standpipe was near the open garage shed. The ink, surprisingly, washed out easily. A rage began to possess me when I went back and gave the man his soap and saw the others who were waiting with me in that yellow room.

If there was a plan, these events had meaning. If there was law, these events had meaning. But there was no plan; there was no law; this was only make-believe, play, a waste of men's time in the world. And how often here, even in the days of bush, it must have happened before, this game of warders and prisoners in which men could be destroyed for nothing. I remembered what Raymond used to say—about events being forgotten, lost, swallowed up.

The jail was on the road to the Domain. It was set a good way back, and in the space in front there had grown up a market and a settlement. This was what registered—the market and the settlement—when you drove by. The concrete jail wall, no more than seven or eight feet high, was a white background. It had never seemed like a real jail. There was something artificial and even quaint about it: this new jail in this new settlement, all so rough and temporary-looking, in a clearing in the bush. You felt that the people who had built it—village people, establishing themselves in a town for the first time—were playing at having a community and rules. They had put up a wall just taller than a man and put some people behind it; and because they were village people, that was jail enough for them. In another place a jail would have been a more elaborate thing. This was so simple: you felt that what went on behind the low wall matched the petty market life in front.

Now, at the end of the lane, after the lights and radios of the little huts and shacks and stalls and drinking booths, that jail opened to let me in. A wall taller than a man is a high wall. Below electric lights the outside wall gleamed with new white paint; and again, but in large black letters about two feet high, was *Discipline Avant Tout*. I felt damned and mocked by the words. But that was how I was expected to feel. What a complicated lie those words had become! How long would it take to work back from that, through all the accumulated lies, to what was simple and true?

Inside, behind the jail gates, there was silence and space: a large, bare, dusty yard with rough low buildings of concrete and corrugated iron arranged in squares.

The barred window of my cell looked out on a bare courtyard, lit by electric lamps high up on poles. There was no ceiling to my cell; there was only the corrugated-iron roof. Everything was rough, but everything held. It was Friday night. And of course Friday was the day to pick people up: nothing would happen over the weekend. I had to learn to wait, in a jail that was suddenly real, and frightening now because of its very simpleness.

In a cell like mine you very quickly become aware of your body. You can grow to hate your body. And your body is all you have: this was the curious thought that kept floating up through my rage.

The jail was full. I found that out in the morning. Quite a time before, I had heard from Zabeth and others about the kidnapping operations in the villages. But I had never suspected that so many young men and boys had been picked up. Worse, it had never occurred to me that they were being kept in the jail past which I drove so often. In the newspapers there was nothing about the insurrection and the Liberation Army. But this was all that the jail—or the part of it I was in—was about. And it was awful.

It had sounded, bright and early in the morning, like a class of some sort: people being taught poems by many instructors. The instructors were warders with big boots and sticks; the poems were hymns of praise to the President and the African madonna; the people being compelled to repeat the lines were those young men and boys from the villages, many of whom had been trussed up and dumped in the courtyard and were being maltreated in ways I don't want to describe.

These were the dreadful sounds of the early morning. Those poor people had also been trapped and damned by the words on the white jail wall. But you could tell, from their faces, that in their minds and hearts and souls they had retreated far. The frenzied warders, Africans themselves, seemed to understand this, seemed to know that their victims were unreachable.

Those faces of Africa! Those masks of child-like calm that had brought down the blows of the world, and of Africans as well, as now in the jail. I felt I had never seen them so clearly before. Indifferent to notice, indifferent to compassion or contempt, those faces were yet not vacant or passive or resigned. There was, with the prisoners as well as with their active tormentors, a frenzy. But the frenzy of the prisoners was internal; it had taken them far beyond their cause or even knowledge of their cause, far beyond thought. They had prepared themselves for death not because they were martyrs; but because what they were and what they knew they were was all they had. They were people crazed with the idea of who they were. I never felt closer to them, or more far away.

All day, through the mounting and then lessening heat of the sun, those sounds continued. Beyond the white wall was the market, the outside world. Every image that I had of that world outside was poisoned for me by what was going on around me. And the jail had seemed quaint. I had thought that the life of the jail would match the market life outside. Yvette and I had stopped at a stall one afternoon to buy sweet potatoes. At the next stall a man was selling hairy orange-coloured caterpillars— he had a big white basinful. Yvette had made a face of horror. He, the vendor, laughing, had lifted his basin and pushed it into the window of the car, offering it all as a gift; later, he had held a squirming caterpillar over his mouth and pretended to chew.

All that life was going on outside. While here the young men and boys were learning discipline and hymns to the President. There was a reason for the frenzy of the warders, the instructors. I heard that an important execution was to take place; that the President himself was going to attend it when he came to the town; and that he would listen then to the hymns sung by his enemies. For that visit the town had burst into bright colour.

I felt that almost nothing separated me from those men in the courtyard, that there was no reason why I shouldn't be treated like them. I resolved to maintain and assert my position as a man apart, a man waiting to be ransomed. The idea came to me that it was important for me not to be touched physically by a warder. To be touched in one way might lead to more terrible things. I determined to do nothing to provoke any physical contact, however slight. I became cooperative. I obeyed orders almost before they were given. So at the end of my weekend, with my rage and obedience, my exposure to the sights and sounds of the courtyard, I was a hardened jailbird.

Prosper came for me on Monday morning. I was expecting someone to come. But I wasn't expecting Prosper, and he didn't look too happy. The loot-glitter had gone from his eyes. I sat beside him in his Land-Rover and he said, almost companionably, as we drove through the jail gates, "This business could have been settled on Friday. But you've made it much worse for yourself. The commissioner has decided to take a particular interest in your case. All I can say is that I hope it goes well for you."

I didn't know whether this was good news or bad news. The commissioner might have been Ferdinand. His appointment had been announced some time before, but so far he had not appeared in the town; and it was possible that the appointment had been rescinded. If it was Ferdinand, however, this wasn't the best way for me to meet him.

Ferdinand, progressing through the world, had, as I remembered, accepted all his roles, and lived them out: lycée boy, polytechnic student, new man of Africa, first-class passenger on the steamer. After four years, after his time as an administrative cadet in that capital so dominated by the President, where would he be? What would he have learned? What idea would he have about himself as one of the President's officials? In his own eyes he would have risen; I would have got smaller. It had always unsettled me a little—the knowledge that the gap between us would get bigger as he grew older. I had often thought how ready-made and easy the world was for him, the village boy, starting from nothing.

Prosper delivered me to the people in the front office of the secretariat. There was a wide verandah all around the inner courtyard, and on three sides the verandah was screened from the sun by big reed blinds. It gave an odd feeling, walking through the thin stripes of light and shadow, watching them appear to move over you as you moved. The orderly let me into a room where, after the shifting verandah dazzle, spots of light momentarily danced before my eyes; and then I was let into the inner office.

It was Ferdinand, strange in his polka-dotted cravat and short-sleeved jacket, and unexpectedly ordinary. I would have expected style, a certain heartiness, a little arrogance, a little showing off. But Ferdinand looked withdrawn and ill, like a man recovering from fever. He wasn't interested in impressing me.

On the newly painted white wall was a larger-than-life photograph of the President, just the face—that was a face full of life. Below that face, Ferdinand seemed shrunken, and characterless in the regulation uniform that made him look like all those officials who appeared in group photographs in the newspapers. He was, after all, like other high officials. I wondered why I thought he would be different. These men, who depended on the President's favour for everything, were bundles of nerves. The great power they exercised went with a constant fear of being destroyed. And they were unstable, half dead.

Ferdinand said, "My mother told me you had gone away. I was surprised to hear that you were still here."

"I went to London for six weeks. I haven't seen your mother since I've come back."

"She's given up the business. And you must do that too. You

must go. You must go right away. There's nothing here for you. They've taken you into jail now. They haven't done that before. Do you know what it means? It means they'll take you in again. And I won't always be here to get you out. I don't know how much Prosper and the others wanted from you. But next time it will be more. That's all that it is about now. You know that. They haven't done anything to you in jail. That's only because it hasn't occurred to them. They still think you are not that kind of man. You are a foreigner; they are not interested in you in that way; they just beat up bush people. But one day they will rough you up and then they will discover that you are like everybody else, and then very bad things will happen to you. You must go. Forget everything and go. There are no airplanes. All the seats have been reserved for officials coming up for the President's visit. That's standard security for these visits. But there's a steamer on Tuesday. That's tomorrow. Take it. It may be the last. The place will be full of officials. Don't draw attention to yourself. Don't take too much luggage. Don't tell anyone. I will keep Prosper busy at the airport."

"I will do what you say. And how are you, Ferdinand?"

"You don't have to ask. You mustn't think it's bad just for you. It's bad for everybody. That's the terrible thing. It's bad for Prosper, bad for the man they gave your shop to, bad for everybody. Nobody's going anywhere. We're all going to hell, and every man knows this in his bones. We're being killed. Nothing has any meaning. That is why everyone is so frantic. Everyone wants to make his money and run away. But where? That is what is driving people mad. They feel they're losing the place they can run back to. I began to feel the same thing when I was a cadet in the capital. I felt I had been used. I felt I had given myself an education for nothing. I felt I had been fooled. Everything that was given to me was given to me to destroy me. I began to think I wanted to be a child again, to forget books and everything connected with books. The bush runs itself. But there is no place to go to. I've been on tour in the villages. It's a nightmare. All these airfields the man has built, the foreign companies have built—nowhere is safe now."

His face had been like a mask at the beginning. Now he was showing his frenzy.

I said, "What are you going to do?"

"I don't know. I will do what I have to do."

That had always been his way.

On his desk there was a glass paperweight—small flowers set in a half-sphere of crystal. He put the paperweight on the flat palm of his left hand and looked at it.

He said, "And you must go and get your steamer ticket. That was where we last met. I've often thought about that day. There were four of us on the steamer. It was midday. We drank beer in the bar. There was the director's wife—you left with her. There was the lecturer who was your friend. He travelled down with me. That was the best time. The last day, the day of leaving. It was a good journey. It became different at the other end. I've had a dream, Salim. I've had a terrible dream."

He took the paperweight off his palm and rested it on the desk again.

He said, "An execution is to take place at seven in the morning. That is what we are meeting for. We are going to witness the execution. It is one of us who is going to be executed, but the man doesn't know. He thinks he is going to watch. We are meeting in a place I can't describe. It may be a family place—I feel the presence of my mother. I am in a panic. I have soiled something in a shameful way and I am trying hard to clean it or to hide it, because I have to be at the execution at seven. We wait for the man. We greet him in the usual way. Now, here is the problem in the dream. Are we going to leave the man alone, to be driven alone to the place of his execution? Will we have the courage to be with him, to talk in a friendly way to the last? Should we take one car, or should we go in two cars?"

"You must go in one car. If you go in two, it means you are halfway to changing your mind."

"Go and get your steamer ticket."

The steamer office was famous for its erratic hours. I sat on the wooden bench outside the door until the man came and opened up. The *cabine de luxe* was free; I booked it. This took most of the morning. The market outside the dock gates had built up: the steamer was due that afternoon. I thought of going to see Mahesh at Bigburger, but decided against it. The place was too open and central, and there were too many officials there at lunchtime. It was strange, having to think of the city in this way.

I had a snack at the Tivoli. It looked a little demoralized these days, as though awaiting radicalization. But it had kept its European atmosphere, and there were European artisans and their families at the tables and men drinking beer at the bar. I thought: What is going to happen to these people? But they were protected. I bought some bread and cheese and a few expensive tins—my last shopping in the town—and decided to spend the rest of the time at the flat. I wanted to do nothing else. I had no wish to go anywhere or look at anything or talk to anyone. Even the thought of having to telephone Mahesh was like a burden.

Late in the afternoon there were footsteps on the external staircase. Metty. I was surprised. Normally at this time he was with his family.

He came into the sitting room and said, "I heard they let you out, Salim."

He looked wretched and confused. He must have spent some bad days after reporting me to Prosper. That was what he wanted me to talk about. But I didn't want to talk about it. The shock of that moment of three days before had vanished. My head was full of other things.

We didn't talk. And soon it was as though we had nothing to talk about. There had never been a silence like this between us before. He stood around for a little, went to his room, then came back.

He said, "You must take me with you, Salim."

"I'm not going anywhere."

"You can't leave me here."

"What about your family? And how can I take you with me, Metty? The world isn't like that nowadays. There are visas and passports. I can hardly arrange these things for myself. I don't know where I'm going or what I'll do. I hardly have any money. I'm scarcely able to look after myself."

"It's going to be bad here, Salim. You don't know what they're talking about outside. It's going to be very bad when the President comes. At first they were only going to kill government people. Now the Liberation Army say that isn't enough. They say they have to do what they did the last time, but they have to do it better this time. At first they were going to have people's courts and shoot people in the squares. Now they say they have to do a lot more killing, and everybody will have to dip their hands in the blood. They're going to kill everybody who can read and write, everybody who ever put on a jacket and tie, everybody who put on a *jacket de boy*. They're going to kill all the masters and all the servants. When they're finished nobody will know there was a place like this here. They're going to kill and kill. They say it is the only way, to go back to the beginning before it's too late. The killing will last for days. They say it is better to kill for days than to die forever. It is going to be terrible when the President comes."

I tried to calm him down. "They always talk like this. Ever since the insurrection they've been talking of the morning when the whole thing is going to go up in flames. They talk like that because that is what they would like to happen. But nobody knows what is going to happen. And the President is smart. You know that. He must know they're preparing something for him here. So he'll get them excited, and then he may not come. You know the President. You know how he plays on the people."

"The Liberation Army isn't just those boys in the bush, Salim. Everybody's in it. Everybody you see. How am I going to make out alone?"

"You have to take your chance. That's what we've always done. Everybody has done that here. And I don't think they'll trouble you—you don't frighten them. Hide the car, though. Don't tempt them with it. Whatever they say about going back to the beginning, they'll be interested in the car. If they remember and ask you about it, tell them to ask Prosper. And always remember that the place is going to start up again."

"How am I going to live then? When there is no shop, and I have no money? You gave me no money. You gave it away to other people, even when I was asking you."

I said, "Ali! I gave it away. You're right. I don't know why I did that. I could have given some of it to you. I don't know why I didn't. I never thought of it. I never thought of you in that way. You've just made me think of it. It must have driven you crazy. Why didn't you tell me?"

"I thought you knew what you were doing, Salim."

"I didn't. I don't know now. But after this is over you'll have the car and you'll have the flat. The car will be worth quite a lot, if you keep it. And I'll send you money through Mahesh. That will be very easy to arrange."

He wasn't comforted. But it was all I could do now. He recognized that and didn't press me any further. Then he left to go to his family.

In the end I didn't telephone Mahesh; I thought I would write him later. Security at the docks the next morning wasn't extraordinary. But the officials were tense. They were like people with a job to do; and that was to my advantage. They were less interested in a foreigner who was leaving than in the African strangers in the market encampment around the monument and the dock gates. Still, I was constantly stopped.

A woman official said, when she gave me back my papers, "Why are you leaving today? The President is coming this afternoon. Wouldn't you like to see him?" She was a local woman. Was there irony in her voice? I was careful to take all irony out of mine. I said, "I would like to, citizen. But I have to go." She smiled and waved me on.

At last I went aboard the steamer. It was hot in my *cabine de luxe*. The door faced the river, which dazzled; and the sun fell on the deck. I went around to the shaded side, which overlooked the quay. That wasn't a good idea.

A soldier on the quay began to gesture at me. Our eyes met, and he began to scramble up the gangway. I thought: I mustn't be alone with him. I must have witnesses.

I went down to the bar. The barman was standing in front of his empty shelves. A fat man with big, smooth arms, a steamer official of some sort, was drinking at a table.

I sat at a table in the centre, and the soldier soon appeared in the doorway. He remained there for a while, nervous of the fat man. But then, overcoming his nervousness, he came to my table, leaned over and whispered, *"C'est moi qui a réglé votre affaire.* I fixed it for you."

It was a smiling request for money, from a man who might soon have to fight a battle. I did nothing; the fat man stared. The soldier felt the fat man's stare and began to back away, smiling, saying with his gestures that I was to forget his request. But I took care after that not to show myself.

We left at about midday. The passenger barge was not towed behind these days—that was now considered a colonial practice. Instead, the barge was lashed to the forward part of the steamer. The town was soon past. But for some miles that bank, though overgrown, still showed where in colonial days people had laid out estates and built great houses.

After the morning heat it had turned stormy, and in the silver storm light the overgrown, bushy bank was brilliant green against the black sky. Below this brilliant green the earth was bright red. The wind blew, and ruffled away reflections from the river surface near the bank. But the rain that followed didn't last long; we sailed out of it. Soon we were moving through real forest. Every now and then we passed a village, and market dugouts poled out to meet us. It was like that all through the heavy afternoon.

The sky hazed over, and the sinking sun showed orange and was reflected in a broken golden line in the muddy water. Then we sailed into a golden glow. There was a village ahead—you could tell from the dugouts in the distance. In this light the silhouettes of the dugouts and the people in them were blurred, not sharp. But these dugouts, when we came to them, had no produce to sell. They were desperate only to be tied up to the steamer. They were in flight from the riverbanks. They jammed and jostled against the sides of the steamer and the barge, and many were swamped. Water hyacinths pushed up in the narrow space between the steamer and the barge. We went on. Darkness fell.

It was in this darkness that abruptly, with many loud noises, we stopped. There were shouts from the barge, the dugouts with us, and from many parts of the steamer. Young men with guns had boarded the steamer and tried to take her over. But they had failed; one young man was bleeding on the bridge above us. The fat man, the captain, remained in charge of his vessel. We learned that later.

At the time what we saw was the steamer searchlight, playing on the riverbank, playing on the passenger barge, which had snapped loose and was drifting at an angle through the water hyacinths at the edge of the river. The searchlight lit up the barge passengers, who, behind bars and wire guards, as yet scarcely seemed to understand that they were adrift. Then there were gunshots. The searchlight was turned off; the barge was no longer to be seen. The steamer started up again and moved without lights down the river, away from the area of battle. The air would have been full of moths and flying insects. The searchlight, while it was on, had shown thousands, white in the white light.

July 1977–August 1978

.62-19

A NOTE ON THE TYPE

This book was set on the Linotype in Electra, a typeface
designed by W. A. Dwiggins. The Electra face is a simple
and readable type suitable for printing books by present-day
processes. It is not based on any historical model, and hence
does not echo any particular time or fashion.

Composed by Maryland Linotype, Inc.,
Baltimore, Maryland
Printed and bound by The Haddon Craftsmen, Inc.,
Scranton, Pennsylvania

Typography and binding design by Judith Henry